Secrets
on the
Wind

Books by
Stephanie Grace Whitson

A Garden in Paris
A Hilltop in Tuscny
Jacob's List
Unbridled Dreams

PINE RIDGE PORTRAITS
Secrets on the Wind
Watchers on the Hill
Footprints on the Horizon

PRAIRIE WINDS
Walks the Fire
Soaring Eagle
Red Bird

KEEPSAKE LEGACIES
Sarah's Patchwork
Karyn's Memory Box
Nora's Ribbon of Memories

DAKOTA MOONS
Valley of the Shadow
Edge of the Wilderness
Heart of the Sandhills

NONFICTION
How to Help a Grieving Friend

STEPHANIE GRACE WHITSON

Secrets
on the
Wind

9/2009

Three Captivating Novels

SECRETS ON THE WIND
WATCHERS ON THE HILL
FOOTPRINTS ON THE HORIZON

MINNEAPOLIS, MINNESOTA
BETHANY HOUSE

Published by Bethany House Publishers
11400 Hampshire Avenue South
Bloomington, Minnesota 55438

Bethany House Publishers is a division of
Baker Publishing Group, Grand Rapids, Michigan.

Printed in the United States of America

Library of Congress Cataloging-in-Publication Data is available for this title.

Whitson, Stphanie Grace.
   Secrets on the wind : three captivating novels / Stephanie Grace Whitson.
      p.   cm.
   ISBN 978-0-7642-0652-8 (alk. paper)
   1. Nebraska—Fiction. I. Title. II. Title: Watchers on the Hill. III. Title: Footprints on the Horizon.

   PS3573.H555S435   2008
   813'.54—dc22

                                                                                    2008028772

STEPHANIE GRACE WHITSON, bestselling author and two-time Christy Award finalist, pursues a full-time writing and speaking career from her home studio in Lincoln, Nebraska. Her husband and blended family, her church, quilting, and Kitty—her motorcycle—all rank high on her list of "favorite things."

Secrets
on the
Wind

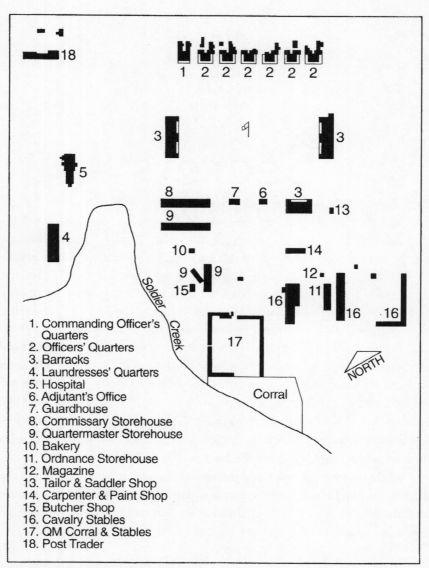

1. Commanding Officer's
   Quarters
2. Officers' Quarters
3. Barracks
4. Laundresses' Quarters
5. Hospital
6. Adjutant's Office
7. Guardhouse
8. Commissary Storehouse
9. Quartermaster Storehouse
10. Bakery
11. Ordnance Storehouse
12. Magazine
13. Tailor & Saddler Shop
14. Carpenter & Paint Shop
15. Butcher Shop
16. Cavalry Stables
17. QM Corral & Stables
18. Post Trader

Fort Robinson, September 1879

Chapter One

Whither shall I flee from thy presence? . . .
If I make my bed in hell, behold, thou art there.
PSALM 139:7-8

THE ACRID SCENT of burned grass and scorched earth clung to the still air. Fire had blackened the hillside above the half-ruined dugout. He felt his stomach clench. Arrows clung to the dugout's sod face like quills from a porcupine. Dismounting, he pulled one from between the earthen bricks. He could feel the hair stand up on the back of his neck as he touched the tip of the arrow, envisioning what it must have been like in this place only hours ago—the wild rush of painted ponies, the unearthly yelps and cries, the raised war lances, all synchronized into a horrible beauty.

It was so quiet now he could hear the buzzing of a horsefly as it streaked past him and landed on the crosspiece of the broken window. He took his hat off and slapped it against his dusty thigh. Swiping the sweat off his forehead with the back of his hand, he clamped the hat back on, then handed the arrow up to the grizzled soldier still astride his horse a few feet away. He walked back to peer through the doorway. The carcass of a massive white dog lay toward the back wall.

While his partner examined the arrow, the young sergeant circled the dugout on foot, examining the earth, squatting by a pile of horse manure and prodding it with a stalk of dried grass. Returning to stand beside his horse he said, "Cheyenne arrow. Here about six hours ago, I'd say."

The older man dismounted with a grunt and traced the officer's steps, still holding the arrow in his left hand. He looked at the tracks, grimacing when he squatted down to examine the manure. Grunting again, he stood up and headed back to where his sergeant waited, watching the horizon. He sent a stream of tobacco from between his pursed lips toward the horsefly still crawling along the window frame a few feet away. The fly buzzed off. "Right. About six hours ago. Good tracking, sir."

"I told you not to 'sir' me when we're out on patrol, Dorsey," the sergeant said.

Dorsey shrugged. "You earned your stripes, sonny. Guess you deserve the 'sirs' that go along with 'em." He sent another stream of tobacco into the dust.

First Sergeant Nathan Boone looked away from the deserted soddy and squinted at the wiry man next to him. "Is it true you can hit a rattlesnake in the eye doing that?"

Dorsey grinned, revealing almost brown teeth. "You better hope you never have to find out."

"I'll head up the hill in back. Check things out."

Dorsey offered, "I'll do it."

Boone pretended not to hear the old soldier grunt as his arthritic knee crackled. "No need," he said. "You climbed your share of these Sandhills last summer with General Crook."

The older man swore, "I may be older'n you, Sergeant Boone, but I ain't used up yet. Not by a long shot. I'll see you in your grave and still climb a thousand more hills. And don't you think I can't."

Nathan shrugged. "Go on up, then." He turned back toward the door. "I just thought you could check inside and see what you think. It'd help to know if this was a lone squatter or a family." He took a deep breath. "I'm thinking just a lone squatter, but if there's women and children involved. . . ."

Mollified, Dorsey shrugged. "All right, then." He took the reins of Nathan's horse. "Don't get your head shot off up there. We think they're gone, but—"

"I know, I know," Nathan nodded. " 'Just where you don't see any Indians, that's where the most of 'em are.' "

"And where'd you learn that?" Dorsey asked, nodding.

"From some old coot named Emmet Dorsey. Stubborn old guy. Earned a commission in the 'recent unpleasantness' a few years back. Then stepped back into the ranks so he could stay in the army and fight another war out here."

"The man's a darned fool," Dorsey said, grinning.

"You got that right." Nathan headed around the side of the dugout and scrambled up the blackened hillside. Near the top, the smell of scorched earth was overpowered by another stench. Sweat broke out across his forehead. *No women. No children. Please.* He pulled his red kerchief up over his nose and crept forward, willing himself to keep going. He swallowed the knot in his throat and sent it down to his gut where it wreaked havoc with his innards. He tasted bile.

Breathe. Steady . . . breathe . . . steady . . . breathe . . . Beneath the kerchief, he opened his mouth. It helped a little, but now it seemed he could even taste the putrid smell. He reached the crest of the hill and peered over the ridge.

Thankful breakfast had been little enough and long enough ago that there wasn't much to give up, he gazed at the still form only a foot or so away. A man. That helped some. Unless Dorsey found evidence he'd missed inside the dugout. Before they could chase after a captive, they would have to go for help. He started to slide back down the hill, then stopped himself. *Do your job. Look around. Use what Dorsey taught you.*

His dark eyes scanned the horizon carefully. When he was certain he and Dorsey were the lone living humans in the area, he headed back down the hill. Toward the bottom, he lost his footing and finished the slide in a crazy tumble. Just as he scrambled to his feet, Dorsey stuck his head outside.

"Squatter's dead," Nathan said, jerking his chin toward the top of the hill. He swallowed again to keep from gagging. "You find anything?"

Dorsey shook his head. "You can relax, sonny. Far as I can tell there's no call to go tearing off after 'em. Leastways not without first going back to camp and telling the cap'n what we found. No captive woman to save." He spit. "Most of that stuff is just fodder for dime novels." He grinned. "Guess you'll have to wait to be a hero."

Boone took a deep breath. "I was just thinking how stupid I was going to look back at camp. Glad to know I didn't cost some poor kid's life because I didn't have a company of men ready to move out."

"I been out here ten years and I had no idea of any whites setting up stakes. Whoever this was just made a bad decision, that's all. Probably thought that dog inside could defend him." The man held up a piece of beaded leather. "He tried, though. Got a piece of whoever killed him. My inspection got momentarily distracted." He held up a rattle. "Fell out of the ceiling. Wasn't in a good mood."

"I didn't hear your gun go off," Nathan said, examining the rattle.

"Didn't need a gun." Dorsey spit. "Held him down with my foot and . . ." He made slicing motions with his hand. Sticking the rattle in his pocket, he motioned toward the side of the dugout. "There's a pile of junk around there. I'll look for a shovel." He pointed at the well. "Get yourself a drink. Clear the smell out of your innards."

While Dorsey retrieved a shovel, Nathan led their two horses toward the well. When he hoisted the first bucketful of water up, a giant bullfrog came along for the ride. Nathan scooped the frog out and offered the water to the horses. The next bucketful was cleaner. After taking a long drink, he doused his face before tying the horses to the windlass and heading to the side of the dugout where Dorsey had found his shovel. A broken rake was the only other tool in sight. But in the pile of rubble he saw pieces of a broken-up trunk. One piece of wood still had a remnant of paper glued to it featuring an idyllic country scene. He closed his eyes. *Just like Lily's.* Rummaging through the woodpile, he found a few more pieces of what he was convinced had been a woman's trunk.

He headed to where Dorsey had started to dig on the other side of the dugout. "There's no more shovels, but I found this." He held up a piece of wood.

Dorsey took it and stared down at the paper.

"You know what that is?" Boone asked.

"Reckon I do," Dorsey said. He spit and thought for a moment. Shrugging, he handed the wood back to his sergeant. "Could mean anything." He stabbed the earth with his shovel. "Suppose you take your giant self inside the dugout and drag that dog's carcass out here. We might as well bury him with his master. While you're inside, look around some. Maybe I missed something."

Nathan headed for the soddy, pausing just inside the door to let his eyes adjust to the dim light. Three crates piled atop one another against the wall to his left must have served as a pantry. The crates were empty now, except for one can lying on its side. To the left of the crates stood a small potbellied stove. Behind the stove Nathan found the base of an oil lamp. There was a wick and a small amount of oil, but no chimney. He set it on the stove. A broad shelf protruding from the base of the right wall must have served as a bed, but no blankets or pillows were in sight. There was no other furniture. The remains of the rattlesnake Dorsey had killed had been tossed in a corner. Nathan shuddered. The thing must have been three feet long before it was beheaded and de-rattled.

Dorsey was right. It was all typical of some lone bachelor's claim. Except for the massive white carcass stretched across the back wall. Nathan would have thought the animal asleep if it were not for the broad red gash that ran the length of its belly.

"So, old fella," he said, stroking the soft white fur. "Dorsey was right. You died defending your master. Good boy." Maybe the white dog was the only friend this settler had. Or maybe he didn't have any friends at all. Maybe he was a heartless thief who deserved what happened to him. *And maybe you think too much. Maybe you should just do your job. Get the burial done and hightail it back to camp. File your report, get a fresh mount, get after the Cheyenne.* He bent down, grabbed the dog's front legs, and started to drag the carcass outside.

"What in—?!" Nathan dropped the dog's front legs and stared at the dirt floor. His outstretched hand swept away a thin layer of dust to reveal a wood plank. Standing up slowly, he backed to the doorway. "Dorsey," he said quietly, motioning for the other man.

Dorsey looked at his sergeant's face, dropped the shovel, and came to his side.

"There's a trapdoor under that dog." Nathan kept his voice low. The two men drew their revolvers and went back inside.

Nathan pulled the canine carcass off the door.

Dorsey knelt. He pointed down and carefully brushed the dirt away so Nathan could see the iron loop attached to the trapdoor. Signaling for Nathan to be ready, he slipped his index finger through the iron ring. Nathan backed away, positioning himself between the bed and the door so the most light possible illuminated the dugout's interior. He cocked his revolver and nodded. Dorsey grunted and lifted the trapdoor.

An unearthly scream pierced the air. A blur of yellow and brown emerged and flung itself at Nathan, screeching and clawing with such ferocity it was all he could do to keep his balance. Dorsey dropped the door, cursing loudly when it fell back and banged against his knees. He wrestled with it for a moment before finally getting it closed and taking aim at the creature attacking Nathan. What he saw made him hesitate. It sounded animal, it smelled animal, but not only did it appear human, it was wearing yellow calico, meaning it was a human of the female variety. Dorsey dared not fire on a woman. Confused, he holstered his gun and waited for Nathan to subdue the woman-beast.

Nathan would always remember the savagery of the woman's attack as a blurred image of feral eyes and bared teeth made even more repulsive by the terrible smell of a body unfamiliar with soap and water. When she lashed out and raked a swath of flesh off his jaw with her filthy, jagged fingernails, he mustered all the strength in his six-foot-five-inch frame to subdue her. Only when he had finally forced her onto her back and had straddled her and pinned her arms to the ground did he get a good enough look to convince himself that underneath all the filth there was, indeed, a woman. Or at least what had once been a woman.

"Can you pin her legs down?" Nathan looked across the room at Dorsey.

Dorsey howled in agony when she landed a well-placed kick below his beltline.

"Listen," Nathan said to the writhing female. "Do you understand English? We won't hurt you. We won't hurt—" He stopped abruptly when the woman sent a shower of spittle directly into his eyes. "Hey!" he roared and slammed her hard against the earth. She quieted momentarily and stared up at him, defiant, wild-eyed, breathing hard. "That's better," Nathan said. "We aren't going to hurt you."

She stared up at him, then looked past him and concentrated on the ceiling.

"Do you speak English?" Nathan repeated. "Are you . . . ?" The woman eyed Dorsey. "Say something in Cheyenne, Dorsey. She's got dark skin. Maybe she's Cheyenne."

Dorsey complied, but the woman didn't respond. When her breathing slowed, Nathan loosened his hold. The second he did, she launched a new series of savage kicks. She was quick and so surprisingly strong that she managed to turn sideways beneath him. And then, suddenly, she uttered an unearthly, keening, cry.

"Is that your dog?" Nathan asked.

The woman narrowed her eyes to two slits and stared up at him with undisguised hatred.

"We didn't hurt him," Nathan said. "He was dead when we got here." He nodded toward the trapdoor. "We found him sprawled over the door." He looked down at the creature. When a tear trickled out of the corner of her eyes, leaving a smeared trail through the dirt on her temple, he felt the first glimmer of something besides revulsion. She lay quietly, looking at the lifeless white form stretched across the doorway. "He must have been protecting you," Nathan said. "He must have died standing over that trapdoor."

"I'll be," Dorsey said. "You really think that's what happened?"

"It's the only explanation for why they didn't find her. He was so big, they didn't notice the trapdoor. And he took a good chunk out of one of them. They got their revenge by killing him. But they never knew about the hiding place."

"How long you think she's been down there?" Dorsey asked.

Nathan looked down at the woman, who was still staring at the dog. "If I let you up, will you behave?" When she didn't look at him, he shifted his weight. Pinning her arm down with his knee, he reached for her face. The minute he touched her jaw to make her look at him, she bared her teeth and bit down. Hard.

"Hey!" Nathan yelped and slapped her cheek. She let go, and Nathan felt his cheeks blush with shame for hitting a woman—albeit a savage one. "I told you we aren't going to hurt you," he repeated. "But if you're going to fight, I'm going to have Corporal Dorsey bring in some rope, and we'll tie you up so you can't move."

"No!" The woman squealed and began to struggle again. "No!"

"So," Nathan looked down at her. "You do understand what I'm saying?" He could feel her beginning to tremble. Her breath came in short gasps. More tears spilled out. A clap of thunder sounded.

Dorsey moaned. "Now I know why my knees have been giving me such fits. All right with you, Sergeant, if I go back out and try to get the digging done before we got to mess with a mudhole?"

Nathan nodded. "I'll be out directly."

Dorsey chuckled, "Don't count on it, Sergeant, sir," and hobbled outside.

Nathan looked down at the woman. "Your husband didn't make it, ma'am. I assume he's your husband?" The woman snorted and snatched her head to the side again.

"Children," Nathan said. "Did you have children? Did the Indians take them?"

She shook her head from side to side. Nathan relaxed a little. She seemed young, he thought, although it was hard to tell through the layers of dirt. He wondered what creatures had taken up residence in the nasty snarl of her hair. He couldn't even tell what color it was. She was thin. More than thin. Half-starved, really. He wondered how such a scrawny little thing could contain the staying power to struggle against him. Looking down, he noticed bruises encircling both her arms. His eyes traveled up to her face. He should have known she wasn't Cheyenne. Her eyes weren't brown. It was hard to tell in the dim light inside the soddy, but they were some light shade of something.

Nathan swallowed hard. He looked back down at the purple splotches on her arms. "Listen," he said firmly, "I'm going to get up in a minute. There's a storm coming in, and we've got to get your husband—or whoever that is up on the hill behind the soddy—buried. We'll bury the dog too. And then we're heading to Camp Robinson. You ever been there? It's about a day's ride from here." He didn't expect a response, but he kept talking, hoping that something in his voice would calm her down. He didn't want to have to tie her up. "We'll take you with us. If you've got family anywhere, we can send word. You'll be safe." He looked at the dog again.

Stephanie Grace Whitson

When he glanced back down at the woman she lifted her chin. A shudder passed through her entire body.

"I'm sorry about your dog," Nathan said, and as quickly as he had pinned her to the ground, he stood up, ready to pounce again should the need arise.

This time she didn't fight. Instead, she rolled onto her side and scrabbled across the floor to the still, white form of the gigantic dog. She bent low, caressing the massive head, crooning softly.

"I'm going to help Corporal Dorsey finish digging the grave," Nathan said. Stepping over the dog, he went outside.

The sky was an ugly yellow-gray. Far in the distance, lightning flashed, an occasional bolt of it stretching toward the earth. Before he headed up the hill Nathan looked back through the doorway. The woman had pulled the dog's massive head into her lap and was sitting stroking the broad place between the floppy ears, rocking back and forth with her eyes closed, tears streaming down her face.

"I'll bring him down," he said to Dorsey, who was standing in a waist-high trench digging furiously. Pulling the red kerchief up over his nose again, Nathan headed up the embankment.

———

The woman was quiet when Nathan approached later. He cleared his throat. "I'll take him now, ma'am," he said, and bent down to grab the dog's front legs.

"No!" she screeched, batting his hand away. "Mine!" She stood up and began to drag the carcass toward the dugout door, panting and staggering with the effort.

"Please, ma'am," Nathan said, still reaching for the dog. "Let me help."

But she would have none of it. She screamed *no* again and flailed so wildly at him with her thin arms that he backed away. "All right. All right. You do it, then. But hurry up. That storm's headed this way."

Nathan retreated to stand beside Dorsey and watch as the frantic little woman pulled her dog across the earth, leaving a broad place swept clean in the dust. She paused at the grave and looked over the edge at the scalped, arrow-ridden body. She got down on her hands and knees.

Nathan had just opened his mouth to express sympathy when the woman leaned forward and spat on the body. She picked up a clod of dirt and hurled it at the scalped skull, smiling when it hit its mark. Dusting her hands off, she pushed the dog over the edge of the grave where he landed with a thud atop the man. Then she sat back and hid her face against her bent knees.

Nathan stepped forward and put his hand on her shoulder. She spun away from him, grabbed the shovel that lay beside the grave, and wielding it like a weapon, backed away from the two soldiers.

"I need that shovel to finish this," Nathan said quietly, pointing to the grave.

"All due respect, sir," Dorsey said in a low voice, "I think the two of us can take her."

The woman looked at Dorsey and backed away again. She lifted her upper lip in derision. "Try it," she said, and raised the shovel higher.

Nathan took his hat off and ran his hand through his long dark hair. "Now listen here, ma'am," he said. "We don't mean you any harm." He nodded toward the grave. "I understand why you might think different, but we're just two soldiers hoping to get back to Camp Robinson as soon as possible. We've spent nearly a week tracking the Cheyenne that visited you. I'm sorry we didn't get here in time to stop what happened, but the fact is, we didn't have any idea there was a white settler within two days' ride of here. So we're just as confused about all this as you are. And we need to get back to camp and file our report so the captain can decide what to do next."

The woman lowered the shovel slightly, but she didn't budge.

They stood for what seemed like a quarter of an hour, taking measure of one another. Finally, Nathan broke the silence. "I'll tell you what," he said. "You take the shovel and head for the dugout. Go on inside."

"We need that shovel," Dorsey protested.

Nathan ignored him and continued talking to the woman. "We'll fill in the grave by hand. Maybe by then you'll see your way to trusting us enough to let us take you back to Camp Robinson with us."

The woman seemed to be wavering. At least she was lowering the shovel a little more. "There's other women at Camp Robinson. You can stay with Granny Max. She has her own quarters on Soapsuds Row. She'll see to it you get a good meal. Granny took care of me last winter when I was sick. You'll like her. You can stay with her until you decide what to do next."

Another clap of thunder sounded. Dorsey nodded his head toward the approaching storm clouds. "You got to let us get this grave filled in, ma'am."

Cautiously, the woman backed away. She sidled around the edge of the grave, her bare feet soundless in the dust. Clutching the shovel to herself, she ran for the dugout and disappeared inside.

Corporal Emmett Dorsey and Sergeant Nathan Boone knelt in the dirt and filled in the grave as best they could, using a half-rotten plank to scrape the earth atop the bodies. They worked feverishly, but the downpour began before they could get to the dugout, and by the time they stepped across the threshold and out of the rain, their blue wool pants were smeared with filth. Just inside they saw the woman perched on the bed. At the sight of them, she plastered her back against the wall and brandished the shovel at them.

A clap of thunder and a bolt of lightning made them all jump. Rivulets of water began to run through the door.

"I'm gonna bring the horses closer," Dorsey said. "Maybe we can rig up our India rubber to keep some of the rain away from the door and the window."

"Good idea," Nathan said. He nodded toward the makeshift cupboard. "I'll pull those crates apart. Maybe we can get a fire going in the stove."

Dorsey's stomach rumbled. "I'll cook." He nodded toward the rattle-snake before stepping into the downpour.

Both men busied themselves with their self-assigned duties. Before long, the horses were unsaddled and huddled against the front wall of the soddy, their rumps hunched against the furious storm. Nathan took matches from his bedroll and lighted the oil lamp he'd found on the floor, then started breaking up the empty crates. In a few minutes he had a fire going in the stove.

Dorsey found a way to hang their rubber ground cloths across the door and the window by cramming rocks along the top and sides, forcing the edges of the rubber into the cracks between the sod bricks and then holding them in place with more rocks.

Finally Dorsey began to dig out their rations. He skinned the rattle-snake and chopped it up, then set about frying the pieces in the small tin skillet from his field kit. While Dorsey cooked, Nathan pondered the cellar beneath the soddy. He looked at the woman. "If I come over there to check the cache down below, are you going to brain me with that shovel?"

She shrugged and shuttled to the opposite end of the bed as he reached for the oil lamp, and watched him descend into the hole.

Nathan whistled in surprise as he ran the lamp along the cellar walls. He studied the impressive assortment of traps hung above tall piles of cured hides. *Whoever we buried was a trapper. A good one.*

Then he saw a moth-eaten tick and a tattered quilt tucked back in a corner. When he picked up the quilt, half a dozen field mice scurried across the floor and disappeared beneath the furs. The putrid contents of a rusty bucket told the rest of the story. Nathan looked up at the opening. She'd had to live in this hole. At least part of the time. No wonder she'd spat into that grave.

"You all right?" Dorsey called.

Nathan climbed up the ladder. He avoided the woman's gaze.

Dorsey was chewing on a piece of fried snake. "What about you?" he asked, offering Nathan a piece.

Nathan glanced back at the hole and then at the woman. "I'm not hungry," he said. He grabbed a piece of fried rattler and held it up. Looking at the woman, he said gently, "You must be hungry, though. I'll just set this beside you. I won't touch you. I promise." Gingerly, he stepped toward the bed and tossed the meat so it landed next to her. Resting the shovel across her lap, and still gripping it firmly with her right hand as she watched Nathan, she snatched up the food and popped it into her mouth. Nathan retrieved his canteen. "Think I'll fill this up. Check on the horses."

"In this storm?" Dorsey's mouth was so full, Nathan could hardly tell what he said.

"A little spring rain never did a man any harm." Nathan worked the rubber sheet loose along one side and stepped outside. The first blast of rain shocked his system, but he resisted the urge to hustle back inside. Instead, he clomped through the mud to the well. He pulled up a bucket of water and wasn't surprised when he set it down and a small snake slithered out. As the storm raged, he took off his hat and lifted his face to the skies.

———

"She's gonna' fall over," Dorsey whispered.

Sitting next to him on the damp dirt floor, Nathan nodded agreement. Opposite them, still perched on the wooden ledge that had once been the trapper's bed, the woman was beginning to fade. Weariness showed in her slumped shoulders. Her eyelids drooped and her chin dipped slightly. Just when Nathan thought she might give in to sleep, a clump of mud crashed to the floor right beside him. The woman started awake and clutched the shovel with renewed determination, suspicion burning in her pale eyes. Rain began to fall in through the hole in the roof. A similar leak had sprung near the wooden ledge.

Dorsey took his turn inspecting the cache beneath the trapdoor. When he came back up the ladder into the pale lamplight, he settled next to Nathan to wait the woman out. He didn't mention overpowering her again.

As time wore on and she gave no sign of relaxing, Dorsey spoke up. "I don't blame you for not wanting to trust us, ma'am. But you got to be mighty tired. Now I'm just gonna spread my bedroll out over here." While he talked he was moving slowly, reaching for his saddle, untying his pack.

As she watched Dorsey's movements, the woman's knuckles grew white around the shovel handle. A leak had sprung above her head. Water was seeping down the sod wall, wetting the earth behind her. She inched forward to get away from it.

"You got to be mighty tired, ma'am." Slowly, he was stretching himself out on his blanket. "We've got a long ride ahead of us tomorrow."

Finally, Nathan decided to follow Dorsey's lead. The leaking roof was quickly turning their shelter to mud. With nowhere dry to unroll his blanket, Nathan tipped his campaign hat forward and leaned against the wall. He had just nodded off when a soft thud sounded across the room. The woman was slumped over on her side, finally asleep, one hand still holding on to the shovel handle.

The India-rubber ground cloth Dorsey had put over the door had blown down. Nathan looked up at the sky. The clouds were beginning to roll off to the east. Without bothering to pick up the sheet of rubber, he grabbed his army blanket and crossed the room toward the bed. When he tried to position her more comfortably, the woman stiffened and cried out, but she never fully awakened. Nathan took the shovel out of her hand and covered her with his blanket before setting the shovel outside the door. He put a couple more pieces of the crates on the fire in the stove before dragging the damp rubber sheet away from the door and, using his saddle for a pillow, stretched out and fell asleep to the sound of mud sliding down the walls around them.

———

What woke him, he didn't really know. But in the manner of soldiers, one minute Nathan was fast asleep and the next he was sitting bolt upright, the hair on the back of his neck standing up while he held his breath and listened. It had stopped raining and the moon was out. He saw a shadow fall across the threshold.

Crouching down, he moved to the window. *Breathe. Steady. Breathe. Think. Cheyenne? After the horses?* He listened to the footsteps just outside.

Only one set. *Please only one*. He chastised himself for sending the rest of Company G back to camp. And for lingering. They should have subdued the woman and headed back to Camp Robinson in the rain. He rubbed his forehead. His childhood penchant for trying to gentle wild things had made him the butt of jokes in school and had caused no end of trouble with his parents as he brought home a steady stream of wounded things. Now it just might get him and Dorsey killed.

He reached for his gun. The holster was empty. So was the wooden ledge. Inhaling sharply, he inched his way to the door. The grass still clinging to the sod bricks brushed against his cheek as he peeked outside.

She was there, her back to the dugout, standing in the moonlight alongside the freshly dug grave, swaying from side to side. *Singing*. Nathan could barely hear it. Almost didn't. He turned his head to listen more carefully and relaxed a little. *She's saying farewell to the dog*. As he watched, she raised her hand. He saw his gun. She pointed it at her temple.

Nathan launched himself out the door and was nearly at her side when she pulled the trigger.

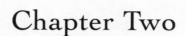

Chapter Two

As we have therefore opportunity,
let us do good unto all men.
GALATIANS 6:10

NATHAN SOARED THROUGH the night air, strangely removed from everything, blinded by the flash of light and dazed by the roar of a gun going off next to his ear. His left shoulder slammed hard into the mud atop the freshly dug grave and his neck snapped to one side, sending a hot burst of pain across his shoulder and down into his arm. He yelped and reached for his shoulder, but instantly forgot about it at the sight of the crumpled form beside him. In the moonlight he could see the hair on the left side of the woman's head smoking. Pushing himself to his knees, Nathan brushed his hand across the place where the hair was singed, grunting in dismay when a handful of it came away from her head. He brushed his hand clean against his thigh and turned her over. Nauseated by the sight before him, Nathan closed his eyes against the blood. He inhaled sharply at the scent of burned flesh and hair.

"What in—?" Dorsey was limping toward him.

Nathan put his palm against his left ear in a vain attempt to still the roar. "Shot herself," he muttered.

"Shot herself? How?" Dorsey leaned over to get a better look.

"My gun." Nathan winced, newly aware of the burning pain in his left shoulder.

Dorsey grunted softly. Nathan sat staring at the soiled yellow dress blazing bright in the full moonlight.

"Probably for the best," Dorsey finally said. "Wasn't much woman left anyway." He paused, then said, "We'll need another grave. I'll get the shovel and get to the digging."

She moaned. At first, Nathan thought it was some animal far off across the prairie. Maybe up on the bluffs in the distance. He leaned over her

face. He could feel her breath against his cheek. Oblivious to the pain in
his neck and shoulder, he gathered her in his arms and leaped up. "Dorsey!
She's alive," he called hoarsely, running for the dugout. "Get that lamp!"
He rushed inside, stretched her out on the shelf-bed and turned her head
to one side, his heart pounding.

Dorsey brought the lamp and held it close. What the golden light
revealed sickened both men.

"Better off if she had died," Dorsey whispered hoarsely.

"Don't say that," Nathan snapped. He reached for the lamp. "Get
water."

Dorsey protested. "What for? Nothing can fix that. Even if we had her
back at camp, Doc Valentine himself wouldn't know what to do. You can't
even see her face under all that blood, son. Maybe she don't even *have* a
face anymore."

Nathan set the lamp down to keep Dorsey from seeing how his hands
were shaking. "We've got to try."

Muttering to himself, Dorsey headed outside. "All the water in the
world can't fix that."

Staring down at the unconscious woman, Nathan was tempted to pray.
If Granny Max were here, she'd pray. But the last time he'd been desperate
enough to pray about something, it hadn't done any good. He looked
around the soddy trying to figure what Granny Max might do with such a
fearful wound. *She'd pray first.* Swearing under his breath, Nathan descended
into the cache and dragged the feather tick up the ladder behind him.
Dorsey came in with a bucket of water.

"How can a person bleed like this and still be alive?" Nathan asked. He
ripped a strip of cloth off the end of the feather tick.

"Look up," Dorsey said.

"I'm not a praying man anymore," Nathan said.

"And I never was," Dorsey said. "Look up at the crossbeam. See all
those cobwebs? My mama used to say there's something in cobwebs that
makes the blood flow stop. It's worth a try."

Nathan stepped up on the bed. Positioning one foot on either side of
the unconscious woman, he swiped at the ceiling, collecting a gray mass
of sticky cobwebs around his hand. Shuddering at the feel of the silk collecting on his fingers, he climbed down.

While Dorsey tore off more strips of fabric and soaked them in the
bucket, Nathan lifted the woman's singed hair away from the wound. He
dipped the tin cup from his field kit in the bucket and used it to flood the
wound with water. Finally he spread the cobwebs on another strip of fabric

and lay it atop the wound, pressing down. The woman groaned, but she didn't resist. For a while, the only sound in the dugout was ripping cloth as Dorsey tore the old feather tick apart.

"All right," Dorsey finally said. "Let's see it now."

Nathan pulled his hand away and lifted the bandage. At sight of the woman's skull showing inside the wide gash running the entire breadth of her head, he almost gagged. He looked at Dorsey. "More water?"

Dorsey shook his head. "There's nothing else we can do but wrap her up and head for camp."

Nathan nodded. He felt dizzy, and his hearing still wasn't right. His shoulder and neck burned with a tingling kind of pain he'd never felt before. He wondered if the flash of light from the gun had impaired his vision too. Surely no one could live through something like this. *God, help her*. Maybe God would listen if he wasn't asking for himself.

Dorsey brought in another bucket of fresh water before hoisting a saddle over his shoulder and heading outside to ready the horses for the ride back to camp. With a trembling hand, Nathan lifted the bandage one last time. Maybe the cobwebs were working. There wasn't so much blood now. Rinsing another strip of cloth in the bucket of fresh water, he wiped her face and realized she was quite young. Considering the life she'd led, she might not even be as old as she looked. It was hard to tell. He unbuttoned the cuffs of her tattered dress and rolled them up, then swiped at her arms with another damp strip of cloth. Her hands were crusted with dried mud. He couldn't do anything about the dried blood and filth beneath her broken nails.

"Horses are saddled. I gave 'em the last of the grain." Dorsey's voice sounded from the door. "It's near sunrise."

Nathan stood up.

"Get yerself a piece of hardtack once we get outside," Dorsey said. "It's a natural thing to feel it in your gut when you seen something like that, son. Nothin' to be ashamed of. It'll ease a bit if you chew on something."

Nathan nodded, wishing he could get a long-ago ill-fated ride with an injured woman in his arms out of his mind. "The ride will probably kill her long before we get back to camp."

"Likely," Dorsey said. He shrugged. "But you were right. We got to try."

Together they wrapped strip after strip of cloth around the woman's head. Her breathing was shallow, but regular. Nathan cradled her in his arms and together the men headed outside.

Dorsey mounted his horse. "Hand her up," he said. "Give your shoulder a while to loosen up. Besides, there's no need for you to put up with that stink all the way back to camp."

Nathan lifted the woman up, and Dorsey positioned her across his lap, her head resting against his chest. "Not much to her, is there?" Without waiting for a response, Dorsey urged his dun gelding forward.

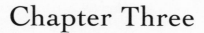

Chapter Three

If a man have an hundred sheep, and one of them be gone astray, doth he not leave the
ninety and nine, and goeth into the mountains, and seeketh that which is gone astray? . . .
Even so it is not the will of your Father which is in heaven,
that one of these little ones should perish.

MATTHEW 18:12, 14

BY THE TIME Nathan and Corporal Dorsey descended the steep pine-covered ridges looming over Camp Robinson and headed down into the broad valley below, Nathan was convinced God had once again ignored him. Not that he and God were exactly on speaking terms. But over the past few hours he *had* taken the opportunity to fling a word or two heavenward on behalf of the woman. Without any discernible result.

He and Dorsey had passed her back and forth several times during the daylong ride, and she'd never stirred. For a creature who had fought so savagely to stay as far away as possible from a man's touch, Nathan thought that was a bad sign. Something inside him felt sick. He scolded himself. *She's not Lily with a rattlesnake bite. She's a crazy woman. Don't forget she nearly blew your head off, too. And you're not some mountain boy saving wounded birds and orphaned calves anymore. You're a sergeant in the United States Army. So just do your duty, and don't get involved personally.*

"All due respect, sir," Dorsey said, riding closer to Nathan. "I'm thinking you might ride west around camp and just take her on down to your Granny Max." He reached inside his shirt and withdrew a leather pouch, inserting a wad of tobacco between his cheek and gum before adding, "No reason to make a spectacle of her to the whole camp."

Nathan turned his head to look at the weather-beaten old man. "You'd better watch it, Dorsey. I'll be thinking there's a gentleman hiding somewhere under that scruffy beard."

In response, Dorsey snorted and spat a long stream of tobacco between the ears of his horse.

"Duly noted, Corporal," Nathan said. "Good idea, though. I'll take her straight over."

"And I'll get Doc Valentine." Dorsey kicked his horse into a lope, heading south in a line that would take him between the now-deserted Red Cloud Agency to the east and Camp Robinson about a mile and a half to the west.

Taps was being played as Nathan rode along the back side of the row of adobe officers' quarters bordering one side of the square military parade ground. In the still night air he could hear someone strumming a guitar. Charlotte Valentine's strident soprano voice pierced the night air. Hoping he hadn't been seen, Nathan continued around the back of the post trader's log store and the hospital and headed south toward the long line of attached two-room apartments everyone called Soapsuds Row.

———

Granny Max had just lit her oil lamp and settled into her rocking chair when Nathan's characteristic *rap-rap-kick* sounded at her back door. Laying her Bible aside, Granny hefted her ample frame out of the rocker and hurried through the doorway separating the living area and kitchen from her bedroom.

"Hey, boy, what you doin' scarin' ol' Granny thataway?" she teased as she undid the latch and threw open the back door. Her boy was there all right, and an unconscious woman with her head swathed in bandages lay limp in his arms.

"Dorsey's bringing Doc Valentine," Nathan said, sweeping past Granny into the room. "We were on patrol up on Hat Creek," he explained. "Stumbled on a dugout. Thought it was deserted—"

Granny held up her hand as she peered down at the unconscious woman Nathan had just dumped on her bed. "I need water. Lots of clean water. That downpour last night likely filled the rain barrel out back. I left a bucket by the stove. And stir up the fire." While Granny examined the unconscious woman, Nathan hurried to collect firewood from the stack beside her back door.

By the time Doctor Valentine arrived, Nathan had water heating on the stove and two buckets of fresh water beside the bed. Granny had torn two clean muslin dishcloths into strips. She held the kerosene lamp high while the doctor unwrapped the bandages and examined the wound. Glancing over the doctor's shoulder, Granny caught her breath. When she looked at Nathan, he answered the unspoken question in her amber-colored eyes.

"A bullet deflected off her skull. At least I think it deflected."

Doctor Valentine nodded. "There's no bullet. It's a clean wound."

"We did what we could."

"You did well, Sergeant," the doctor said while he worked. "The bleeding's controlled, too. That's good."

Nathan shrugged. "Dorsey thought I was crazy pouring water everywhere."

"And they thought I was crazy after Bull Run when I insisted on washing my hands between amputations." He finished examining the wound and reached for something in his bag before adding, "But at the end of the day fewer of my patients got gangrene. You can't tell me cleanliness doesn't have anything to do with patient recovery. I can't prove a connection between washing and infection. But I'm convinced somebody will someday."

"Do you think she'll live?" Nathan asked.

The doctor sighed. "It's hard to say. The gunpowder burned the edges of the wound. I doubt stitches will hold, but I'm going to try. She'll have less of a scar if I can just get it held together a little." Talking more to himself than to Nathan or Granny, he murmured. "It isn't going to be pretty, though. At least she's got plenty of hair. Maybe she'll be able to hide most of it." He looked over his shoulder at Granny Max. "You sure you want to take this on?"

"I never turn away a lamb the Lord brings to my door," Granny said.

The doctor nodded. For the next half hour he worked, doing his best to minimize the damage to the woman's head. As he left he said, "There's nothing more I can do. I'll be back after sick call in the morning. If anything changes before then, you send for me."

As soon as he was gone, Granny sprang to action. "Poor thing. Look at those tattered clothes." She wrinkled her nose. "Whew. She sure needs a bath." She waved toward the front of the little apartment. "Warm me up some more water, Nathan. There's a piece of fried chicken beneath the towel covering that blue crock if you're hungry. Corn bread, too."

"Don't worry about me, Granny. You've got enough to do."

"I'm not worried."

Nathan rubbed his growling stomach. "All right. As soon as I get Whiskey bedded down I'll head back this way." He hesitated at the door and called back over his shoulder, "I'll . . . um . . . get something out of Lily's trunk for her."

Granny's voice was gentle. "That would be kind of you, Nathan."

The woman on the bed moaned softly. Granny laid a huge brown hand across her forehead. No fever. At least infection hadn't set in.

Granny heard Nathan whistle, followed by a soft nicker and the creak of leather as Whiskey came to his master. She smiled. The boy always had been good with animals. She remembered Lily retelling the story she'd heard from Nathan's mother about him carrying a one-legged rooster to school every day for a week, insisting it would learn to get along, just like the three-legged dog on a neighboring farm. He'd cried when the rooster died and conducted quite a funeral behind his father's barn.

Granny looked down at the unconscious woman. Nathan hadn't let his gentle side show in a long time. It was good to see he hadn't lost it.

"My name is Clara Maxwell," Granny said, as if the woman could hear. "Everyone calls me Granny Max. I'm going to take good care of you, you hear me? So you rest easy, little gal. Now we are going to get you cleaned up. Nathan's going to bring you some of poor Lily's things. Lily was Nathan's wife. She's gone now. Been gone two years, Lord rest her soul. Nathan hasn't touched her things in all that time. It's bothered me, him not seeming to be able to let go of Lily's things. Guess now I know why. At least part of it. The good Lord knew we'd be needing them for *you*."

Granny wrung a cloth out and began to clean the woman's face. She lifted her head from the pillow and in one motion swept her long hair up off her neck and across the pillow. "I'm going to need daylight to deal with all that hair of yours." Granny paused. "No, I won't cut it. Not unless I have to. The Good Book says that a woman's hair is her adorning beauty. You've sure got a mess of it, lamb. I'll do my best with it."

Nathan came in with a bowl and the coffeepot. He set the bowl on the bedside table and filled it with water, then set the warm pot on the floor. "You're going to need more than one bowl of water," he said. "I don't think I'll eat just now, Granny. But I'll be back directly. You'll be all right?" He was already heading for the door.

"I'll be fine."

He paused at the door to look back. "Lily wouldn't mind my bringing you some of her things. Would she?"

"Of course not," Granny said. "Lily had a generous heart."

"Well"—he tugged on the brim of his campaign hat—"I'm going to report in now. I'll be back as soon as I can." He cleared his throat. "And I'll make myself some coffee if I need anything. Don't worry about me. Just take care of her."

Granny nodded and turned her attention to her patient. She made short work of removing the yellow calico, cutting it away with a few snips of her scissors. "Now, I know the good doctor would think I am an old fool, to be talking to you this way. But the fact is, those doctors don't know everything. And I am thinking that somewhere past your mind is your soul, and what the mind don't hear, maybe the soul does. So I'll just be talking to you while we are getting you cleaned up. I don't know where you've been or what all happened, but—" Granny paused when she pulled a sleeve away. Even in the dim lamplight she could see bruises. On closer inspection, she saw the scars encircling the woman's wrists. She blinked away tears and laid her hand on the woman's shoulder as she whispered, "Lord bless you, child. What you been through?"

Gently, she washed the woman's body, turning her first to one side, then the other, occasionally laying her broad hands over a bruise or a scar and pausing to pray. By the time she had finished washing the woman and covered her with a soft quilt, Granny was trembling with emotion. She perched on the edge of the bed and stared down at the pale face, the dark shadows beneath the eyes. *Poor little lamb. You can't be even twenty years old. Where you been?*

The lamp burned low. Granny got up. She gathered the woman's tattered clothes in a ball and hurled them out the back door. For a few moments, she let the warm night air blow in, grateful when it cleared out the last traces of the stench of unwashed body and dried blood.

———

Nathan sat on the edge of his bed in the dark, facing the corner where his dead wife's trunk had sat for the better part of two years. His hand trembled as he reached up, took a chain from around his neck, and ran his index finger along the contours of the key he'd worn since the day he'd returned from Lily's graveside and stowed all her belongings in the depths of the trunk.

Stoic before the men of Camp Robinson at Lily's funeral, he'd wept freely once inside the two-room apartment they had occupied together. He'd fallen to his knees beside that trunk and buried his face in the folds of Lily's blue silk ball gown and soaked it with his tears. Remembering, he inhaled sharply. The pain was still there. Two years, and the pain was still there, sharp enough at times to literally take his breath away.

The last thing he wanted to do was open that trunk and face the memories stored inside. He looked at the wall opposite his bed and envisioned the still form of the wounded woman lying next door in Granny Max's bed. Granny was right. Lily had a kind heart. She would want him to do this.

He could almost hear her gentle voice. *"Sweetheart. Remember that linen nightgown Granny edged with lace? That's just the thing. A lady likes to feel pretty, even when she is slumbering. Why, I bet that poor darling has never had a lace-trimmed nightgown in her life. You give her whatever she needs."*

While he listened to Lily's imaginary urgings in his head, Nathan slid to the floor and half crawled across to the trunk. He put the key in the lock and turned it. Opening the lid with trembling hands, he pulled the top tray out and set it on the floor, grunting aloud in an attempt to control his emotions at the sight of the blue ball gown. Memories swirled through his mind of balls and receptions where Miss Lily Bainbridge was the most sought after dance partner. And then the best memory of all came, sweet in spite of the pain it induced, of the evening Lily crossed a Nashville ballroom to lay her small white hand on his arm and tell a lie.

"I believe you are next on my dance card, Private."

He'd wanted to put his name on her card. Oh, how he'd wanted to. But he'd hesitated, telling himself that the belle of Nashville could not possibly have any interest in a greenhorn private from the backwoods of Missouri. He'd proven the adage about hesitating and being lost, for Lily Bainbridge's dance card always filled quickly, and by the time Private Boone summoned courage to add his name, the opportunity was lost. Except it really wasn't. Lily lied and got her dance. Eventually, she got an adoring husband with a promising military career.

Kneeling, Nathan reached for the blue ball gown. He had memorized the contents of the trunk. He knew the red one lay next, followed by three calico everyday dresses, first gray, then pink, then a green one that made Lily's skin look even paler unless she softened it with a lace collar. He knew every fold, every ruffle, every button of each garment stored here. His heart pounding, he lifted the blue ball gown to his face and inhaled. Tears sprung to his eyes. It didn't smell like Lily anymore. Only two years, and the essence of Lily Bainbridge had vanished.

Gripping the edge of the trunk, Nathan reminded himself, *Breathe. Steady. Breathe.* Feeling calmer, he sorted the trunk's contents, setting aside two nightgowns, the gray calico dress, and a pair of slippers. These he stacked on his bed, then returned to the trunk and blushed as he collected a sampling of undergarments.

Satisfied that he had enough, even if the woman survived a week, which he doubted she would, he returned the top tray to the trunk. Lily's Bible caught his eye. He picked it up, remembering the many Sundays she had lamented the lack of proper church services here at Camp Robinson. In the absence of a regular army chaplain, she and Granny Max had conducted their own makeshift service. But Lily's deep faith longed for more. He opened the Bible and leafed through it briefly before tossing it back into the tray.

The Bible had no more than landed in the tray than he heard Lily's voice. *"Don't let your sorrows come between you and the Lord, darlin'."* She hadn't lived long enough to say much. She'd been in so much pain. But she'd known exactly how he would react to losing her.

"Oh, Lily." Nathan groaned aloud.

A few minutes later, when he finally closed the lid and locked the trunk, Nathan had managed to regain his composure.

———

By the time she heard Nathan's approaching footsteps, Granny had emptied two bowls of filthy water and rinsed out her washcloths.

"Lord bless you, Nathan," she whispered as she accepted the pile of clean clothing and set them on the stand beside her bed. It was almost midnight and she was weary, but Granny knew that after going through Lily's trunk, Nathan might need some comforting. "Why don't you make us some good strong coffee while I get her into a fresh nightgown."

When Granny finished dressing her patient, Nathan was already sitting out on the front porch, coffee cup in hand. A second cup of coffee sat on a chair. Granny cupped her massive hands around its warmth and sighed with pleasure as she sipped the strong, dark liquid.

"I'm sorry to burden you, Granny," Nathan said. "I didn't know what else to do. I know Doctor Valentine's authorized to take female patients up at the hospital, but . . . well . . . Mrs. Valentine is prone to gossip and I—"

"There is no need to apologize, Nathan," Granny replied. "As I told Dr. Valentine, I would never turn away one of God's lambs from my door."

Nathan leaned forward and let the front legs of the chair drop to the porch. "When I was a boy, there was a woman we called Crazy Jane. Folks in the hills didn't lock that kind of person up the way the city folks do now. Jane's family did their best, but they just couldn't keep her home. They tried just about everything short of tying her down. She always got away. It got to where people set out food on their porches, and Crazy Jane came in the night and ate. Just like a possum.

"I caught a glimpse of her once. She was staring at me from a perch high up in a pine tree. Scared me half to death. Her eyes glittered in the moonlight. When she started laughing I hightailed it home, and it was a week before I would go past the edge of our farmyard." He took another swallow of coffee. "I was just a boy, but I knew then no one should have to live like that."

"That would be a terrible thing," Granny agreed.

"Crazy Jane's family said she was a real bright little girl until she got scratched by some animal and came down with a sickness and a high fever."

"Well, the little gal inside doesn't have a fever," Granny Max said. "And we have Doctor Valentine. I don't think it will be like it was for Crazy Jane."

Nathan stood up. "I hope you're right. I'm going to rouse the quartermaster and get you a cot. I'll be back before long. And don't worry about the company laundry. I'll send someone over to help you."

"Becky O'Malley will help," Granny offered.

"I've got at least a half dozen men complaining about how boring their lives are. They can help, too." He stepped off the porch. "If it will help, I can sit up with her so you can maybe get some rest."

"There's no need for you to do that," Granny said.

"I'd like to," Nathan said. "I feel sort of . . . responsible."

"Well, you aren't responsible for what happens to her now, Nathan. You leave that to God and Granny Max—like the good doctor said."

"God doesn't have a very reliable record with me and mine," Nathan replied. He turned to go and was swallowed by the darkness before he had taken five steps.

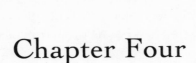

Chapter Four

Behold, He taketh away, who can hinder Him?
Who will say unto him, What doest thou?
JOB 9:12

"I HAD A CASE something like this during the war." Doctor Valentine talked while he rewrapped the woman's head. It was so early in the morning that they needed lamplight. "I don't mean to worry you, but we must be realistic. She's been unconscious for two days. Her fever has stayed down. That's good. But . . ." He grunted as he finished the bandaging and stood upright. "Everything seemed to be going well with the other case, too. The wound was healing up clean as could be. Then the soldier went unconscious. His fever came up. Next came delirium." The doctor picked up his medical bag and headed toward the front room of Granny's apartment. "That patient was dead in a few hours."

He set his medical bag on the table and sat down, accepting Granny's proffered cup of coffee. "I don't mean to frighten you, Granny. But the night Sergeant Boone brought her in, I remember him saying *'Nothing that comes to Granny Max ever dies.'* I don't want you to be hard on yourself if this doesn't work out as we all hope."

He sipped his coffee. "When that soldier died it haunted me. There was absolutely no sign of infection. I just couldn't understand it." He set his mug down. "So I did an autopsy. I've never seen anything like it, and I never hope to again. All the infection had gone inside. The poor man's brain was half mush." He swallowed and stared up at the ceiling for a minute before looking back at Granny. "The point of all this isn't to frighten you. It's just to say we never know. And that's the truth. So don't you be blaming yourself if this doesn't work out."

"Nathan was wrong to say that about me—about nothing dying that comes to me. The dear Lord has let me help with many of His lambs. But not every one I care for survives."

The doctor nodded. "Yes. I heard about Mrs. Boone. Unfortunate. Very unfortunate. You do know, Granny, there was nothing anyone could have done to save her. From what I heard, she wasn't able to get to help for quite some time. The outcome would have been no different with or without a doctor here at the post. I understand the post surgeon had been called away?"

Granny nodded. "He was out on a detail, and they got caught up in a skirmish between some miners and Indians. And I know what you are saying is true. No one on this earth could have helped by the time we found her. It was too late for humans. I knew that the minute I saw her leg." Granny cleared her throat. "Of course, I was still hoping the Lord might look kindly upon the situation and cast a miracle toward Pine Ridge. Rattlesnakes got nothing over the good Lord. He could have healed Miss Lily."

The doctor nodded agreement. "From what I have heard, Mrs. Boone was a delightful young woman. A real lady." He grabbed his black leather bag and stood up, bowing to Granny. "And this young lady's in good hands, too, Granny Max." He saluted her before leaving.

After the doctor had gone, Granny ate a piece of corn bread before rinsing out the coffee cups and returning them to the shelf that served as her combination china cupboard and pantry. Across Soldier Creek, trumpets sounded guard mount. Nathan would be assigning fatigue details. He'd promised her two soldiers to help with laundry this afternoon and said he would sit with the patient while she showed the men what to do. She pulled the laundry basket closer to the table and set aside three light blue shirts that needed mending. She'd have to hold them out of today's laundry if she didn't get them done.

Heading back into the other room, she touched the woman's forehead. She frowned, then dampened a cloth in the bucket Nathan had left by the bed. Folding the cloth, she bathed the woman's face. The woman began to mutter in her sleep. Her hands twitched. Once she tossed her head sideways, bumping her head against the wall. With a yelp that sounded half animal, she jerked away from the wall, then fell silent.

Granny carried her rocker in from the other room and positioned it beneath a small window where daylight would illuminate her mending.

We need a miracle, Lord. Doctor doesn't think this little gal has much chance of living. And if you are in the mind of doing miracles, could I just remind you, Lord, my boy Nathan is still drowning in an ocean of bitterness. I been prayin' 'bout him for two years now, Lord. And I will keep praying. Not trying to tell you how to do your job. Just reminding you like that widow woman that kept beating on the judge's door in the Good Book. You remember her, Lord. That's me, I guess.

Old Granny Max beating on the Lord's door asking Him to open up and give her what she wants. It ain't for me so much Lord as it is for Lily. I just don't think she can rest easy knowing that man she loved is so miserable.

Pondering miracles made Granny think of her own past. She was, in many ways, something of a miracle herself. She had lived all her life on one plantation. While others were bought and sold, Granny had remained at Lily Bainbridge's side. When Lily married her soldier and headed west, Granny rode alongside her, marveling at the beauty of the vast wilderness sky, even while she dried her own and Lily's tears of homesickness.

Granny Max was confident she could make a home anywhere. She had encouraged Lily. *"Where two or three are gathered the Lord is there in the midst of them. He's right here with us. With you and me and your young man, too. We'll be all right."*

And they had been. For a while. Back then, Camp Robinson was nothing more than a collection of canvas tents on the windswept flats a mile north of the confluence of the White River and Soldier Creek. Lily was only the second white woman to live at the camp, and it was obvious early on that she didn't belong. She just didn't have the toughness for army life. Granny had suspected it. But she'd hoped that between her and Nathan and God, Lily would get healthier and tougher, and things would be all right. Certainly if love for a man could have brought it about, it would have happened. Lily Boone had loved her man. There was never any doubt about that. Even that morning they had had the fight and she stormed off toward Pine Ridge alone, Granny knew her anger was only because deep inside she was afraid she was disappointing Nathan.

Granny rocked and remembered, brought back to the moment by the realization that her patient's breathing had eased a bit. She dipped the cloth back into the cool water and laid it across the pale forehead. At her touch, the woman seemed to take a deep breath and settle a little. Granny sat back down. Soon the room was again filled with the rhythmic creaking of her rocking chair.

Chapter Five

Do justice and righteousness,
and deliver the one who has been robbed
from the power of his oppressor. . . .
JEREMIAH 22:3 NASB

WHAT HAS HE done to me this time? She lay quietly, trying not to move. Sometimes, if she didn't move for a while, he didn't notice she was awake. Sometimes it helped. He left her alone. She had made it a game, lying still, breathing shallow, drawing in on herself until she almost willed herself invisible.

He must have hit her again. Only harder than usual. There was a constant roar between her and the wall, like a wind blowing past her ear and drowning out all the other sounds in the dugout. Her head pounded so hard she could feel tears seeping from beneath her eyelids. It wasn't the worst of the pain she had felt since belonging to him, but it was bad enough.

What has he done to me this time? She wasn't down in the hole. She could tell that just by inhaling. Usually, whenever he had been near her, the stench of him lingered. But all she could smell now was fresh straw. Still, she didn't dare open her eyes because she could sense a presence in the room. She kept her hand from rising to her head just in time, reminding herself not to move. For a moment or two she played the game, concentrating on breathing in time with the pounding inside her head. Inhaling, she envisioned herself placing her fingers on the keyboard at Miss Hart's Academy for Young Ladies and pressing down in perfect rhythm with her own clear, soprano voice. Here, in this place in the wilderness, she could still hear the music of her own breathing, let out in perfect rhythm with the pounding inside her head. She gave herself to the music of her pain and slipped back into unconsciousness.

———

The next time she woke, she went through the same ritual of shallow breathing and deliberate quiet. The roaring in her ears was less now, and she could hear a soft hissing. There must be green wood in the stove. That meant he wasn't far away. Her head still pounded, but now she was aware of a wide path of searing pain above her ear. Wondering what time of day it was, she relaxed her eyelids a little to let in just enough light to see the doorway beyond the foot of the bed. If it was dark outside, she would have to remain motionless for a long time, for he would be asleep someplace nearby. If daylight shown through the door, he might have gone out. She could try to do something about her head before he got back.

But the doorway beyond the foot of the bed led . . . into another room? And a small window. With . . . curtains? Her eyes flew open. Above her several strong crossbeams supported a roof. There were no cobwebs, no threatening bulges sagging down into the room from the layers of sod above. The scent of new hay and the softness beneath her raised new questions. If she was in a cabin with a window, lying on a mattress stuffed with fresh hay, then where was *he*?

Her mind raced back to the dugout. Slowly, in still-life frames, she began to remember. Cheyenne surrounding the dugout, her retreat to the cellar, the great white dog above her growling, and then . . . the awful sound as he yelped, the thump when he collapsed above her. Then silence and waiting, thirst and hunger, pushing her terror back, willing herself to wait. And then someone dragging the dog away, opening the trapdoor . . . making it impossible for her to do anything but attempt to defend herself.

She clamped her eyes shut and took inventory of her body. She could move her legs. One time he had knocked her into the cellar, and she'd sprained her ankle so badly she hadn't been able to do much more than hobble through the entire winter. Her muscles were sore, but she didn't think anything was really damaged. Without trying to give away her return to consciousness, she thought her way through each joint and each body part, taking stock. Her entire body hurt. Not until she tried to lift her head did she locate the reason she couldn't remember much. Raising her hand instinctively to the place that hurt most, she realized her head was swathed in strips of cloth.

They must have done this to her. Those men who dragged her out. Two soldiers. She thought hard. *Surely not only two.* There must have been more. Didn't they always travel in—companies? That was it. They called them companies, and there were always several dozen of them. She'd seen them from a distance sometimes and wondered what they would have done if she'd run to them and begged them to help her get away. But she'd always been too afraid.

What else had they done . . . what else . . . ? Even in the dim light she could see that the door in the next room was barred shut. A barred door meant only one thing. He was here. Even if she could not smell him. If not him, those other two. They had her trapped again. They would be waiting for her to wake up.

Something moved across the room from where she lay. Instinctively, she drew her legs up and curled onto her right side. She tried to position her arm to protect her head, but she could not bear pressure above her ear. She lay in a ball, tense, eyes tightly closed, awaiting the first blow.

When a hand closed over her shoulder, she flinched and grunted in anticipation. He was going to use his bare hands. That meant the attack would end more quickly but that he planned to hurt her in a more personal way. She probably wouldn't have any more broken bones tonight. That was something. She could usually block the other out by going back to Miss Hart's in her mind. Or to the riverboat. Already she was halfway there, standing on the stage in a beautiful gown, smiling at the crowd of men and preparing to sing.

"You awake, child?" The voice was deep, but soft, almost feminine. The hand moved from her shoulder to her forearm, gently pressuring her to let down her guard.

She tensed and, in spite of herself, let out a word that sounded too much like a refusal. It was always worse for her when she did that. Her heart began to race.

"Don't be afraid, child. You are going to be all right. Granny Max is going to take good care of you."

Over the last few months, she had conjured up all kinds of memories to help her maintain some level of sanity. But she had never conjured a voice like this. Instinct made her draw away even as she opened her eyes to see what form the voice might take. The hand withdrew from her shoulder even as the voice repeated, "You are going to be all right, child. No one is going to hurt you."

She touched the spot above her ear.

"Yes. I know it must hurt. You were shot. But it only made a path through your beautiful hair. You'll have a scar, of course. But it didn't hurt anything important. Do you understand, child? You don't have to be afraid anymore."

She pulled her fist down from above her ear and let it rest alongside her jaw so she could squint at the woman looming above her. Were it not for the thick braid dangling across one shoulder and the simple gray dress, she could have been a man. She had broad shoulders and a square jaw. In the dim light of the cabin, it was impossible to discern the features of her dark face. But her large amber eyes were warm with kindness.

"I'm going to get you some of my tea. It'll help with your headache. Make you sleepy, too. You'll heal better if you can rest. Right now that's what you need most. Sleep."

While she talked, the woman headed into the next room toward a small stove where a coffeepot sat, sending a faint trail of steam into the air. A small table beside the stove and a rocking chair in the corner were all the furnishings she could see in the other room. But then a man came into view. Her heart lurched. He was conversing with the Granny-woman in a voice so quiet she couldn't discern the words. While they talked, the old woman took a towel off a hook to use as a hot pad and poured a stream of steaming liquid into a tin mug. She set the mug down on the table momentarily. The man handed her a pillow, then went to the opposite side of the room and out of her sight.

When the large woman came back into the bedroom she was alone. The pillow was meant to help her sit up. She lifted her up and tucked the pillow beneath her shoulders. "I know. Makes you dizzy to sit up. You just take some tea. You've been unconscious for three days. You drink some tea, then go back to sleep. Rest is what you need."

It was drink or have the liquid poured down her front. She drank. As she had feared, the concoction made her even more dizzy. The woman's dark face blurred. She pushed the tea away. With a groan, she lay back down. Before the woman had crossed the cabin to set the half-empty mug of tea on the stove, she slipped away.

———

Sometime in the middle of the night, she woke again. Moonlight streamed in the window casting a four-paned shadow on the rough board floor. With a soft grunt, she managed to push herself upright. Slowly, she dropped her legs over the edge of the bed and sat up. A savage bolt of pain shot through her skull, and for a moment she thought she might pass out. She waited, concentrating on her breathing until it mellowed a little, then she stood up, weaving back and forth unsteadily.

Grateful when the woman sleeping on the cot against the opposite wall showed no signs of stirring, she crept across the few feet between her and the barred back door. Once she tripped on the hem of the muslin gown.

She could feel sweat trickle between her shoulder blades with the exertion of walking. At the door, she leaned her forehead against the frame, grateful for the cool feel of the wood against her skin.

It took nearly all her strength to soundlessly wrestle the bar across the door, up and out of the iron cradle holding it in place. When she had it in her arms, she almost fell over, but she managed to lean it against the wall. Her hand closed over the rope pull. Trembling with weakness and fear, she pulled.

At the first sound of the creaking door, the woman on the cot snorted in her sleep. Her heart pounding, she yanked the door open and flung herself into the darkness beyond the cabin. She willed herself to run even as she realized she was too weak to go far. And then, just as the Granny-woman was calling out from the cabin door, someone grabbed her from behind and wrapped her up inside his arms so tightly she could feel the buttons on his jacket pressing into her through the thin cotton nightgown.

Everything was forgotten in the panic of being trapped in a man's arms. She began to shriek. Kicking and writhing, she spit at his face. She would have bit him, but her efforts to bite through the wool uniform were worthless. She had found a well of unbelievable determination somewhere inside, past the physical pain and the weariness, but it was being drained quickly, and the man holding her wasn't going to let go. He clamped a hand over her mouth.

"Stop," he said calmly. "You're going to wake up the whole camp. Or hurt yourself."

She twitched again and moaned softly, then bit down hard on her lower lip to keep from making another sound. It never went well when she let a man know how much he was hurting her, how much she hated it. She inhaled sharply and began to retreat from the moment, back to Miss Hart's and the music that somehow always got her through.

His grip didn't loosen one bit, even as she felt herself go limp in his arms, even as he picked her up, headed back inside the cabin and to the mattress where she had been sleeping. She wanted to turn her head away, but the wound above her ear was hurting again, so she closed her eyes and willed herself to listen to her own breathing while she waited.

"I can't believe she had the strength to try to run," he said while he reached to the foot of the bed and pulled a quilt over her tense form. She felt his hand brush across her hairline. He smelled faintly of pipe smoke. He must have been outside smoking when she tried to escape.

"I wish you would believe we aren't going to hurt you," he said as he tucked the quilt beneath her chin.

She opened her eyes. It was hard to tell details in the dim light of the lamp the Granny-woman had lit. She had the impression of a handsome face, but when he turned to look at the big woman, the lamplight revealed four scratch marks along his jaw. That made her even more suspicious. He didn't smile. His eyes were little more than dark pools in the dim light.

"Whoever was keeping you at that dugout is dead. Do you remember that, miss?" He touched the back of one of her fingers just where she gripped the top of the quilt.

She snatched her hand away.

He took a step away from the bed. "My name is Boone. Sergeant Nathan Boone of Camp Robinson, Nebraska. Corporal Dorsey and I were on patrol when we found the dugout. We've brought you to Camp Robinson. Granny Max is going to take good care of you. Maybe you'll tell her your name."

The pounding in her head returned. She raised her hand to her head and squeezed her eyes shut to prevent tears from spilling over.

The man leaned down and put his hand across her forehead.

She flinched.

"She's got a fever." He sighed, then sat down.

She heard a rocker creak and opened her eyes. He had taken his hat off and was sitting in a rocking chair beside her. The lamplight he sat beneath proved her earlier impressions correct. Dark eyes, dark hair. Square jaw. Thick moustache. Handsome.

"We want to help you, miss. Do you understand that?" He leaned forward, resting his elbows on his knees, still holding his hat in his hands. "The man who hurt you is dead. It's over now. All you have to do is rest and get well. You can stay here with Granny Max. Doctor Valentine has been checking on you. When you're better, you can tell us how to let your family know you are all right. There's a telegraph."

She closed her eyes, wearied by his persistent kindness. She might be sick, but she wasn't stupid. She'd memorized her share of little sayings, just like the other girls at Miss Hart's. Things like "Do unto others as you would have them do unto you" and "Love one another." And then she had learned the truth. People did what they did to get what they wanted. And you could never trust a handsome man. Especially not one with fingernail tracks on his face.

The Granny-woman came in with another cup of tea. She didn't need it. Exhaustion closed her eyes once more.

———

"Yes. He told me the same thing this mornin'." Motioning for Nathan to follow suit, Granny Max picked up a kitchen chair, moved quietly through the back room, past the sleeping woman, and out the back door where she settled within earshot of her patient and within plain view of a glorious sunset. She sighed, and without turning to look at Nathan, said, "If she goes another couple days without a fever, she'll likely make it. I expect she won't even remember trying to run off."

Nathan sat down and leaned back, balancing against the wall, the front two legs of his chair up off the ground. When Granny opened her mouth to scold him, he dropped the chair back to the earth. "Yes, ma'am. 'Don't tip your chair.' " He turned the chair around and, straddling it, crossed his arms across the back and rested his chin on his forearms. "You're still worried about her."

"She has nightmares," Granny said.

"I don't wonder at that," Nathan said quietly. "Has she said anything? Anything at all?"

Granny sighed and shook her head. "She's stopped fighting me. She drinks my tea when I tell her to. She even ate a couple bites of grits this morning. But she's not talking. I almost wonder if she *can* talk. A whole lot more healing needs to go on inside that little gal than what Doctor Valentine can see on the outside of her head. But if she can't talk about it—"

"She can talk," Nathan said. He rubbed the back of his neck and murmured, "She's been hurt—other ways besides just . . . what we can see."

"I know," Granny said quietly.

Taking the broad-brimmed campaign hat off his head, Nathan swiped his hand through his hair. He began to shape the crown of his hat while he talked. "It was just the usual patrol—wandering around in the hills and not finding much of anything. We'd already headed back for camp when Dorsey thought maybe he'd picked up a fresh trail. At first we didn't think it was much. Only a couple of horses. I sent the rest of the men back and told them we'd catch up. Didn't expect to find anything. We planned on heading back here to camp before noon. Then suddenly the trail that was only two horses joins up with one that looks like it's a huge war party. And just as we decide we'd better come back to camp for reinforcements, we come up over a hill and there's this dugout." Nathan paused. "In three years of patrolling those hills, I never came across anything like it. Arrows everywhere. A man's body at the top of the hill behind the dugout." He shook his head. "There's been talk of closing down Camp Robinson and sending us all up to Camp Sheridan. That won't be happening now."

Nathan spared Granny Max the details of what had been done to the man and went on to describe finding the dead dog and then the woman's emergence from the cache. "We thought we had her calmed down, and so we decided to get some sleep. I don't know what woke me, but I went to the door and there she was standing beside the grave with my gun to her head." He stopped fiddling with his hat.

Granny's hand clamped over her mouth. She spoke through her fingers. "She did that . . . to *herself?*"

He nodded, then looked sideways at Granny. "I don't think Doc Valentine needs to know. But if she's going to live, and with the nightmares and all . . ." He shrugged. "You should know." When Granny was quiet, he said, "I am truly sorry, Granny. I had no right to put this burden on you. There's no way to know if she'll heal up and be all right, or—"

"—or if you've brought me another Crazy Jane." Granny patted his hand. "The Lord gave you a tender heart, Nathan, and now He has used it to rescue one of His lost lambs and bring her to old Granny for some loving. You stop apologizing. Your tender heart is one of the things I love most about you."

Nathan shrugged. "There was no trace of a tender heart when I went down in the cellar beneath that trapdoor. It's a good thing the Cheyenne took care of the—" He swallowed the word. "It's a good thing he was already dead. Or I'd likely be in the guardhouse waiting trial for the cold-blooded murder of a civilian." He was quiet for a moment, watching the sunset. Finally, he asked, "You ever know anyone to be treated like her and be able to be . . . normal . . . again?"

Granny lifted her chin and closed her eyes. Finally, she said carefully, "I've known dozens of women been treated like that." Her eyes glowed with emotion. "Most learned to be normal well enough. Once they were free."

Nathan shifted uncomfortably. He looked down at the earth. "If we'd gone a few rods east or west, I'd never have known that dugout was there. And if it hadn't been for that dog having a piece of some warrior's leggings or moccasin in his mouth, we'd likely have just left his carcass to rot. She would have starved down in that . . ." He gulped. "In that hole." He changed the subject abruptly and nodded toward the sunset. "Beautiful."

Granny nodded. "Mm-hmm. The good Lord is a wonderful artist." She paused before asking, "What do you suppose that looks like from the *other* side?" When Nathan didn't answer, she went on. "I like to imagine Lily just the other side watching like we are. Only her view is unclouded by sinful sight."

Nathan snorted. "I'd like it a far-sight better if God had just stayed out of my affairs and left my wife *this* side of His sunsets."

"I know that, dear Nathan. I know it." Granny laid one great dark hand on his tensed shoulder. "The Lord's ways certainly are not ours, are they? He had other plans for Lily. And now He's brought another of His children into our lives. We can't see His plan, but I know one thing: I'm willing to do whatever He wants. And if she's addled, that don't change a thing. She still needs love and a place to live, and with God's help, we'll give her both."

"I may not agree with you about God's role in it all, Granny. But I do agree with you about this woman. It doesn't matter if she's crazy or not. We'll do our best by her."

Movement out of the corner of his eye made Nathan look around. The woman was standing at the doorway. The setting sun made Lily's lace-trimmed nightgown glow with golden light. It illuminated the woman's waist-length auburn hair, turning it flaming red. For a moment, she stood looking from Nathan to Granny and back to Nathan again. Her green eyes shone so bright Nathan thought she might be sleepwalking.

Finally, she looked away from him and toward Granny. "Laina," she said clearly. "My name is Laina Gray." She looked back at Nathan. "And I'm not addled."

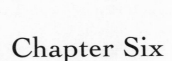

Chapter Six

For God hath not given us the spirit of fear;
but of power, and of love, and of a sound mind.
2 TIMOTHY 1:7

WELL, SHE HAD done the unthinkable. She had tried to take her own life. Standing at the back door and listening while Sergeant Boone told Granny about her had been the catalyst that spurred Laina's memories. She had remembered it all. And according to the preacher who used to visit Miss Hart's on Sundays, those who did such things would never see the Kingdom. They would spend eternity in everlasting fire for having struck at the very image of God himself. Laina only had to close her eyes to see Reverend Fitzpatrick shaking his bony fist to illustrate his rantings.

As the days passed and she considered her fate, the idea of a life such as hers being the image of God filled Laina with doubt. Surely God had no interest in the likes of her. Surely He put His image into things greater than dance hall girls and gamblers. She didn't really think God had much concern over whether she lived or died or how her life or her death were accomplished. And if He was concerned, then He would just have to understand that she didn't mean anything against Him personally when she took that sergeant's gun and pointed it at her head. She was just taking the only way she knew to make the hurting stop. That night back at the soddy, had someone asked about the idea of fearing hell if she took her own life, she was fairly certain she would have said she had already been there—and would have pulled the trigger anyway.

Now, nearly a month after her supposed rescue, she was trapped again. Not by circumstances like those on the riverboat. Not by ropes that tied her down. Not by a trapdoor too heavy to lift. Now Laina was trapped by her own body. She was too weak to stand up for more than a few minutes. Almost too weak to care what happened.

Here she was, at a place called Camp Robinson, being cared for by a woman who assured her she was God's little lamb and things would be all right. When Granny talked about God, it was like nothing Laina had ever heard before. Granny seemed to have some kind of special friendship with "the good Lord." She talked to Him as naturally as if He were sitting at the breakfast table eating her flapjacks, waiting to hear her news. Considering Granny's close relationship with God, Laina expected Granny to preach. But even after Laina was feeling better and had begun to go to the table for her meals, Granny did not preach.

Maybe she meant to and just forgot. Or got distracted. Granny Max did a prodigious amount of work. Sergeant Boone's Company G of the Third Cavalry included nearly fifty men. Granny had explained that each company usually had three laundresses, but when the Sioux were moved to their new agency up on the Missouri in '77, the army transferred most of the troops away from Camp Robinson. And with the troops went their wives—the company laundresses. The row of twelve apartments where she lived—called Soapsuds Row—now housed only a few families, and keeping up with the laundry wasn't easy.

Granny had already told her a lot about Camp Robinson. She seemed to think information would help Laina overcome her fear. The long row of attached apartments where she was staying was called Soapsuds Row because the women living here did laundry for the soldiers. The log building to the north was the hospital, and beyond it was the post trader's store. "The Grubers are the only civilians allowed to live on the military camp," Granny Max had explained. "The rest of us are army, through and through."

The first evening Granny Max managed to get Laina outside, they sat on the front porch. From there, they could see the whole of Camp Robinson just across a well-defined trail that ran between their building and the rest of the camp. Laina gripped the edge of her seat with whitened knuckles, trying to control what she knew was unreasonable fear.

"That's Soldier Creek," Granny said, waving her hand toward the winding stream looping between the Row and the rest of camp. "You can see how everything is arranged around the parade ground—that's the big square with the flagpole in the middle. Over on the north, there's the commanding officer's place. And the long row of adobe duplexes is for the officers. We know it as Officers Row. Doctor Valentine and his family live in that one," Granny pointed. "You can just barely see the edge of the front porch." She motioned toward a long building across the trail from the hospital. "That's the back of one of the infantry barracks. There's another one just like it on the opposite side of the parade ground. These buildings right there across the trail are the commissary storehouse and the quartermaster's stores. All the camp supplies come through the quartermaster. Makes him a powerful man. That other building is the guardhouse," Granny said. "Crazy Horse himself was brought there." She sighed before going on. "Past the guardhouse is the adjutant's office and the cavalry barracks. As first sergeant, Nathan has use of a room attached to the front of the barracks." Granny stopped her running commentary on the layout of Camp Robinson and explained how after Lily Boone's death, she had been given her own apartment on Soapsuds Row.

Laina soon learned that while, officially, Sergeant Boone slept and ate over at the cavalry barracks with his men, he'd also been allowed to keep the apartment next to Granny's that he had shared with his wife. Sometimes in the night, when Laina woke from her own bad dreams, she could hear Sergeant Boone pacing on the opposite side of the wall. Sometimes she heard his voice. She couldn't discern the words, but she didn't need words to recognize anguish.

It was apparent that while she had come to Camp Robinson because she was a servant of the sergeant's wife, Granny loved Sergeant Boone as if he were her son. She spent nearly half an hour ironing just one of his dress parade shirts. She creased his pants and insisted on custom tailoring his uniforms. One morning when the sergeant protested what he thought was the unreasonable amount of time Granny spent on his appearance, she argued, "A man has got to look his best. And you know Lily would be very unhappy to see the way that coat hangs on you. *'My Nathan surely cuts a fine figure, Granny,'* she used to say. Now, I don't want Lily scolding me up in glory for letting you go downhill. So you just get over here and let me mark this coat." Nathan acquiesced.

Granny's salary as a laundress was handled by the paymaster and deducted from the soldier's pay. She earned extra for mending shirts and darning socks. But soldiers got more than clean laundry and darned socks from Granny, who had a reputation for baking some of the best corn bread west of the Mississippi. Laina soon learned that it was the corn bread that afforded Granny the opportunity to do what she considered her real work, which was being a creative combination of drill sergeant and confidante for the men of Company G. While "the boys" sat at her kitchen table waiting for a fresh batch of corn bread to emerge from Granny's tiny oven, they inevitably ended up talking about home. Or about the bully in the company bent on picking a fight. Or their plans for life after the army.

Laina never went into the front room when men were present. Sergeant Boone had mounted two brackets on either side of the door, and Granny had hung two thick quilts across the doorway to give Laina privacy. But she heard nearly every word that was spoken across Granny Max's kitchen table. Occasionally she would hear a man's voice quaver as he fought back homesick tears. Once a recruit, known as the Professor, broke down and cried over a letter from a girl back home. Granny prayed out loud for him.

Laina found herself wondering about Granny's history. She was old enough to have gray hair. Her skin was the same shade of brown as some of the leather hides Josiah Paine had stacked in the cache beneath his dugout. Even when she was scolding Laina, saying that it was high time she went outside for some fresh air, her eyes shone with kindness.

And her hands. How, Laina wondered, was it possible for hands so roughened with calluses to be so gentle? Granny's hands were always clean, with neatly filed nails and not a speck of dirt beneath them. Laina still couldn't seem to get the grime of that soddy out from beneath hers. Granny's hands patted her shoulder to calm her, stroked her arms to help her awaken from a nightmare, and sometimes combed out the tangles in Laina's hair in the long hours of night when she could not go back to sleep.

And even better than Granny's hands was her voice. It was almost as deep as a man's but was so warm and comforting. Laina could not remember very much of her first days and nights at Camp Robinson, but she did remember Granny singing. Hymns, mostly. Some Laina remembered from Miss Hart's. But there were others she had never heard, with haunting melodies and lyrics about sweet chariots and crossing Jordan and sweet Jesus.

Granny had a prodigious appetite. When she made flapjacks for breakfast, she ate eight. Eight flapjacks and exactly two cups of coffee. If breakfast was grits, Granny smothered hers with blackstrap molasses and so much butter, the grits were barely visible. Although not nearly as tall as Sergeant Boone, Granny towered over most of the soldiers. Once when Laina stumbled and almost fell, Granny picked her up and carried her to bed as effortlessly as a man might have.

As the weeks went by and Laina's waking hours lengthened and her strength returned, Granny seemed to feel a need to fill the silence between them. When some noise from the camp across the creek startled her, Granny would say, "That's just Company G headed out for drill. They got to be sharp so those new recruits that came in yesterday can see what's expected of them. Some of those new boys never even sat a horse. Can you imagine that?"

"You'll get used to the bugles," Granny had said another morning.

She counted the various calls that organized the soldiers' days. "Reveille, assembly, morning stables call, breakfast call, sick call, fatigue call. From reveille to taps, a soldier never has to wonder what time it is. Lily's mantle clock quit running a few months ago, and I didn't even notice. You'll learn the tunes soon enough."

One morning, when reveille was sounding, Granny chuckled and sang, "I can't get 'em up, I can't get 'em up, I can't get 'em up at all. The corp'ral is worse than the private, the sergeant's worse than the corp'ral, the lieutenant's worse than the sergeant, and the captain is worse than them all."

On the day Laina first offered to help Granny with her mending, the older woman said, "Now that you're feeling better, maybe we'll have some of the women in for tea. They are all eager to meet you." She smiled encouragement. "Now don't you be worrying over meeting a few old hens. Or young ones, neither. They're nice women. Mostly. Mrs. Doctor can be a little high-minded, but I guess she has a right. She's a real lady from some highfalutin' family back East. Underneath her fancy airs there's a good heart. You'll see."

———

She was dancing. She was one of many, but she was the best—kicking her knees a little higher, bending over a little farther, encouraging the men to holler and clap and howl and hoot. Sometimes she even let her hair down. They loved it when she let her hair down.

Wearing his signature stovepipe hat, Rooster pounded on the out-of-tune piano, increasing the tempo until . . . he jumped up on stage—and turned into a monster.

She looked off into the wings for Eustis. But her father was playing cards. Poker. At a table she hadn't noticed before. Odd, that it would be set up right here on the stage. She called for him. "Father." He glanced her way. His black eyes glittered with greed. He waved and grinned, nodding his approval as the monstrous man—with yellow eyes and skin, with rotting teeth and vermin crawling through his beard—grabbed her and—

"NNNOOOOOOO!!!"

She gasped, lingering between her dream and the reality of Granny Max's room. She tried to sit up.

"Shh. Shh." A gentle hand on her shoulder. A familiar voice spoke her name. "It was a dream, honey-lamb. Only a dream. Remember? You are here with Granny Max. You are safe. Shh."

She opened her eyes. *One, two, in, out. One, two, in, out.* Counting helped her even out her breathing. Helped her escape the dream and come back.

Granny was humming softly. The woman's kindness had become its own kind of tyranny. Laina squeezed her eyes shut, blinking the tears away. Night after night, Granny Max comforted her, never complaining about the lost sleep. How long had it been now? Over a month, and here Granny sat again, stroking her patient's hair, holding her hand, talking of safety and healing and God's love.

"When I was a child," she said, "I had nightmares, too. I'd just sit up and start screaming. Mama would come and I'd know she was there, but somehow I couldn't get out of the dreamworld and back to her." She paused. "Mama said if I could ever put the dreams into words, they'd go away. And you know, Laina, Mama was right. I had three dreams over and over and over again. And one by one, as I was able to put them into words, they went away." She patted Laina's hand. "There's nobody here in this room but God and old Granny Max. And they both care about you. Can't you give words to the dream? Make it go away?"

The little girl attending Miss Hart's Academy for Young Ladies in St. Louis would have tried. She might even have believed that bad dreams could be willed away. But the grown woman couldn't bring herself to do it. She turned her face to the wall and whispered, "I can't." She couldn't keep the tears from spilling down her cheeks.

"Fear does some strange things to a body," Granny said. "I remember one boy come back from the war and his mama almost didn't recognize him. That boy had snow-white hair." She leaned closer. "He'd been hurt worse than some of the men who'd lost a leg."

Granny smoothed over her own head with the palm of her hand. She leaned back in her rocker, adding its creaking rhythm to the cadence of her voice. "I started to go gray in the winter of eighteen-and-thirty-seven. December. I was fifteen years old. I will never forget that winter. A woman doesn't forget. But sometimes, with the Lord's help and the kindness of others, she can decide to get on with life." She asked, "Do you hear what I am saying to you, child?"

"I hear," Laina whispered.

"I wanted to take a gun and go after him. And I could have, too. He wasn't like some varmints that do their evil and slither away. He stayed right near where I lived for a time."

Laina shuddered. "How'd you ever—"

"My mama got the missus—Miss Lily's grandmother—to take me into the house. That's when I started taking care of Miss Lily's mother. She was just a baby. It helped a little, but I was still afraid.

"One day, I saw some man coming up to the house, and it scared me so that I ran and hid in a closet. I thought it was him. I was shaking and crying and mad all at the same time. Because there I was in that closet when where I really wanted to be was downstairs in the kitchen where Birdie, the cook, was making raspberry pie. I knew she'd give me a taste, if I could just make it down to that kitchen. All of a sudden, it seemed like I could see the hideous face of the very person I feared laughing at me hiding in that closet and missing my favorite food in all the world.

"It was when I got mad—I like to think it was a righteous anger, that the Lord showed me something. He helped me understand that if I didn't get out of that closet, those ugly faces were going to be looming over me all the rest of my days. I realized right then, there was nothing I could do about what had been done. Someone evil owned my past. I was just a girl, and I didn't have control. But I could keep him from taking my future. And I could sure do something about that raspberry pie."

Laina took in a sharp breath. She lifted her hands and hid her face. "You were just a girl, a slave. I'm a grown woman and free. I should have found a way. I'd seen soldiers in the distance before. I should have—"

"You were afraid."

"But I could have—"

"Stop it, child. Just stop it. Don't go back there and punish yourself and relive it. The good Lord sent them Indians—and Nathan. The *Lord* stopped it. He has given you a new home—if you want it. But there's that battle in here," Granny patted the place over her heart. "The Lord loves you, Laina Gray, and so do I. And we both want you to win the battle going on inside you." She reached up and tucked a strand of auburn hair behind Laina's ear. "You got to come out of that closet in your mind, child. Come out and have some raspberry pie."

Laina turned on her side where she could look up at Granny Max.

"Tell me his name," Granny said abruptly.

Laina frowned. "What?"

"His name. When I was in that closet, I was seeing Spinner's face. Whose face do you see?"

Laina whispered, "Josiah. Josiah Paine."

"Josiah Paine is dead, Laina Gray. Don't bring him back out of his grave. Don't let him rummage around in your life anymore."

"That day you went down to the kitchen and had pie," Laina asked. "Was that . . . was that the end of it? Were you ever afraid again?"

"Oh, plenty of times."

"What did you do?"

"I just kept eating raspberry pie, honey. Or playing with Lily's mama—and later, Lily. Or whatever the next thing was to do. I just did the next thing. And one day I realized I hadn't thought about old Spinner Barnes for a while."

Laina was quiet for a few moments. Presently she asked, "You ever wonder where God was when you were in those dark places?" Laina asked.

Granny nodded. "Everybody that's ever lived has wondered about that."

"Did He answer you? Did He tell you where He was?"

" 'Whither shall I flee from thy presence? . . . If I make my bed in hell, behold, thou art there.' He was there. With me. Whether I knew it or not."

"Then why didn't He make it stop?"

"*Where* He was, I can answer, child. *Why* is a different question. He doesn't always answer *why*." Granny smiled at her. "Maybe it was because some day I'd be taking care of a girl named Laina Gray, and where I was back then would help me understand where she is today."

"You really think that?"

"I really think that *nothing* is for *nothing*. The good Lord doesn't waste things, Miss Laina. I'd be lying if I didn't say I do a lot of wondering. His ways are not mine."

"Do you wonder about Mrs. Boone? About why she had to die?"

Granny nodded.

"But you don't seem bitter—like Sergeant Boone."

"Well, I have lived a lot longer than Nathan. And I have learned to trust the Lord."

"Even when you wonder?"

"*Especially* when I wonder," Granny said. "That is what faith is, child. Learning to live in peace in the very center of all the things that don't seem to make sense."

Laina frowned as she pondered what Granny had said. "I don't think I could ever do that."

"Neither did I, honey-lamb, neither did I. I had to take baby steps toward it. Just like I had to practice not thinking about Spinner. And when I took those baby steps, the Lord gave me what I needed to run the rest of the way to His peace."

Granny smiled. "You think that's all just talking in circles, don't you, child. That's all right. You just let it all circle around in your head. Maybe if God's ways circle around in there, those nightmares won't have room."

Leaning back in her rocker, Granny began to hum. From across the creek, reveille sounded. Still humming, Granny rose and got dressed. She went into the front room and started up the fire. A dog barked. Hoofbeats and marching, bugles and yelling all combined into the familiar rhythm of morning at Camp Robinson. Finally, the noise of routine and the swirling thoughts about God and baby steps drowned out the nightmares, and Laina slept.

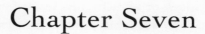

Chapter Seven

*For the lips of a strange woman drop as an honeycomb, and her mouth is smoother than oil:
but her end is bitter as wormwood, sharp as a two-edged sword.*

PROVERBS 5:3-4

BEAUREGARD PRESTON TRUDGED along beside the supply wagon, doing his best not to limp. He'd planned to pull the infernal, ill-fitting army-issue boots off when they stopped to make camp at noon. But now he figured he'd better not. His feet were so raw with blisters, he'd never get the boots back on. If they'd told him that cavalry recruits had to walk the hundred or so miles between the railroad station at Sidney, Nebraska, and Camp Robinson to the north, he—well, he still would have enlisted. But he'd have done something about the boots.

He'd had it with making two dollars a week as a dry-goods store clerk. He'd had it with the uppity wives of the St. Louis rich and their whining daughters, who mooned over choosing between six bolts of fabric—all the same basic color—while they made eyes at him and then pretended shock if he showed any sign of interest. He'd had it with Mr. Cruikshank, the store owner, who made snide remarks about Rebels every chance he got, as if Beau didn't know Cruikshank was a southern sympathizer. During the war, the man had had to get bars put over the windows of his house for fear of what his neighbors might do. Now he acted like he was doing his young southern charge a favor by letting him work eighteen-hour days and providing him a corner in the warehouse across the alley as sleeping quarters.

Yankee customers had annoyed Beau for over two years. As he plodded along, he pondered the other reasons he'd enlisted. He'd been sinking fast and he knew it. It had all begun when he decided the riverboats were a much more entertaining way to fill the long evenings and weekends than pious hymn-sings and church socials. He didn't think there could be any harm in a few drinks and a hand or two of cards. At first there wasn't.

Until, little by little, Beau found himself drinking more and more. With the drinking came losing at the tables. To make himself feel better about drinking and losing, he stayed for the entertainment.

Beauregard Preston couldn't remember the first time he'd realized he had a peculiar power over women. Even his mama, ordinarily a strict woman, could be made to forget herself under the gaze of her youngest son's clear-blue eyes. Once, she had literally dropped the switch right out of her hand and rumpled his tawny hair while she laughed, "I declare, Beauregard, you are going to do some damage to more than one girl's heart with looks like that! Go on, now! And please don't call the cook that name again."

The girls on the river were no different than any other girl he had ever charmed. He had his choice of them all, and he was one of the few Riverboat Annie favored with her attentions. She singled him out and looked straight at him when she danced on stage. And later, she backed up her flirtation, which was more than he could say for the rich girls who shopped at Cruikshank's store.

By the time Beau admitted to himself that he should do something about being more than a little in debt and more than a little enslaved to whiskey and women, something happened that solved all his problems at once. He came into the store early one morning to unload some dress goods and found himself looking down the barrel of Mr. Cruikshank's rifle. It seemed, Mr. Cruikshank said, that Miss Mavis Cruikshank had been found to be in a family way, and since Beauregard Preston was, in Mr. Cruikshank's mind, the only possible culprit, he was informed that he was engaged. The experience went a long way toward awakening Beau to the dangers of residing in St. Louis.

About ten minutes after Mr. Cruikshank lowered his rifle and sent Beau back to his room in the warehouse to "think about his duty," Beauregard Preston of Mecklenburg County, Virginia, was so thoroughly impressed with his need to reform that he had exited Cruikshank's warehouse empty-handed and headed south to Jefferson Barracks to volunteer for the army. The ten-mile walk effected such a complete reform that, upon his arrival, Beauregard Preston had not only sworn off wine and women, he had become Caleb Jackson.

Thinking back over the recent past, Private Jackson realized that, in spite of the unpleasant aspects, army life had its advantages. Yes, he thought, given the alternative of becoming Mr. Mavis Cruikshank, he'd still have enlisted and marched wherever he was told without complaining. But he would have spent his last twenty cents on an extra pair of socks, if he had it to do over again.

The greenhorn next to him wasn't much better off. He was limping, too. The sleeve of his blue army jacket was tinged with sweat and dust where the kid had swiped his forehead as they marched. At least he'd finally shut up. Jackson had done everything possible to stay clear of the kid at the recruit depot in Jefferson Barracks.

Harlan Yates was round-faced and freckled, and he looked to be about twelve years old. He had a crop of the reddest hair Jackson had ever seen, two huge ears that stuck out from his head like flags in a gale, and a bodacious nasal Yankee twang. And he talked. And talked. And talked. Worse yet, he'd picked up on Jackson's southern accent right away and called him "Reb". Well, he'd tried it, anyway. Once. The fist Jackson had planted on the kid's chin had stopped that. You would have thought he'd have backed off after getting knocked to the ground. But, no. Instead of making him stay away, the blow seemed to have somehow galvanized Yates's intentions to make a friend. He'd come up off the ground rubbing his chin and grinning.

"Good punch, Private. So . . ." He grinned sheepishly. "Should I just call you Jackson?" He lowered his voice then and leaned in to say, "Truth is, the accent's almost gone anyway. I'd never have guessed except we got kin south of the Mason-Dixon Line ourselves." Then he said, "You know horseflesh? I seen you ride the other day, and you sit a horse like you know what you're doin'." When Jackson didn't answer, Yates continued, "The reason I'm askin' is . . . well, I signed up for cavalry. But . . . I don't . . ." He blushed furiously. "Of course we had plow horses and all that on the farm. But I never had such a thing as a real horse to ride. And I was thinkin' that maybe you could . . . well, maybe you could help me pick out a good one. Once we get to Camp Robinson, that is." Harlan grinned, and Jackson noticed he had a chipped tooth. And blast it if that chipped tooth didn't remind Jackson of his older brother.

Jackson glowered at the kid. "Why should I care whether or not you get a good horse?"

The kid scrunched up his face like it hurt to think. He peered up at the sky, formulating an answer, then grinned again and said, "Well, it's like this. Say we're out on patrol and we get surrounded." He crouched down and held his arms out to dramatize the imaginary situation. "There's warrin' Sioux on all sides. Somebody has to go for help." He dropped his arms to his sides and straightened up. "If that somebody's me, don't you think it'd work out better for all concerned if I'm on a horse I can *ride* instead of one that's gonna toss me in the nearest dry creek bed and hightail it for Deadwood?"

Jackson stifled his laughter. He shrugged and jabbed his forefinger in Yates's chest. "Listen up, greenhorn. I've had enough jokes about Johnny Reb spoken in my hearing to last the rest of my life. So I'll make you a deal. You forget about which side I was on in 'the late unpleasantness,' and I'll look the herd over when we get to camp and tell you what I think."

Harlan grinned at him. "You do know horseflesh, then?"

"My daddy had about the best stable of thoroughbreds in Mecklenburg County."

That had been over a week ago. The kid had stuck to him like glue ever since. Of course it could be worse. He could have been paired off with the German who barely spoke English and had breath bad enough to kill a buffalo at fifty feet. At least this kid could take a hint and was learning to keep his mouth shut. He still liked to tease and had played more than his share of practical jokes. But to his credit, he hadn't said another word about the South. Or Jackson's knowledge of horses. Jackson had come to the grudging conclusion that when they got to Camp Robinson, he'd probably even be able to tolerate Harlan Yates as his bunky.

———

"Whoa!" Corporal Emmet Dorsey pulled his six-mule team to a halt. He stood up slowly, appearing to survey the land around their noon campsite, hoping none of the recruits caught on to what he was really doing, which was giving his knees and back a chance to loosen up a little before he tried to climb off the wagon seat. Gritting his teeth, he worked his way down.

Their time at Jefferson Barracks near St. Louis had taught the recruits exactly what was expected of them, and they made camp quickly. Dorsey made a mental note to tell Sergeant Boone to make sure he got the private called Frenchy attached to Company G. The man could do amazing things with army-issue rations.

After unharnessing his team and filling a nose bag with grain for each mule, Dorsey made his way to the campfire, where Frenchy sat on his haunches tending a skillet. He saw a few bits of something unrecognizable sizzling in the pan, but it smelled so good the corporal's mouth started to water. With a grunt, he sat down by the fire. Before he'd even settled, Frenchy thrust a mug of hot coffee in his hand. "You drink this—you'll feel better, eh?"

"Feel better about what?"

Frenchy rubbed his hand over his knees but didn't say anything.

"What's your real name, anyway?"

"Dubois," the man said, puckering up his lips when he said the *u*. "Charles Dubois."

"Well, *Sharl Doo-bwa*," Dorsey said, doing his best to mimic the Frenchman's pronunciation, "Where'd you learn to cook? I never saw a man who could make something out of nothing like you."

"My family have been chef back to Charlemagne." He stirred what was in the skillet with his fork and pulled it off the fire. "Cooking is in the Dubois blood." He held the pan out to Dorsey, who took a chunk of meat between forefinger and thumb and popped it into his mouth. It was hot, and for a few minutes the corporal alternately sucked in air and tried to chew without burning his tongue. Finally, he swallowed. "You assigned to a company yet?"

Dubois shrugged. "I don sink so."

"We need a cook in Company G. I raised a respectable garden last year, but the men ate the same old same old."

"Garden? You haf a garden?"

Dorsey nodded. "Planted it myself. Lettuce. Beans. Beets. Tomatoes. Onions."

Dubois's brown eyes crinkled at the corners. Dorsey couldn't see the mouth, as it was hidden by a brown moustache that covered even the Frenchman's bottom lip. It was a wonder he could get food past the hairy mess, but as Dorsey watched, Dubois took a bite from the skillet and sat back in the dust, savoring his lunch.

"Between the post trader, the quartermaster, my garden, and your cooking, Company G would do all right."

The greenhorn Yates sidled up. "Couldn't help hearing, sir." He saluted smartly for the corporal. "Any way you could get me and Jackson into your outfit with Frenchy, sir?"

Dorsey frowned and took a sip of coffee. "And why would I care to do that?"

"Well, Jackson's a good rider. Real good. Told me his family had one of the best stables in the county. I figure he's one of them rich boys who's been riding since before they could walk."

"So much for Jackson. Why do we want you?"

Yates worked his eyebrows up and down and made a face. "I, good sir, have the gift of laughter. I know enough jokes to last you all winter. Laughing at me will give you something to do besides playin' checkers when the snow's blowing outside . . . and the wolves are howlin' and. . . ."

you're hankerin' for a little entertainment like they got in that there *Paree*." He winked at Dubois.

"What do you know about *Paree*?" Dorsey asked.

Yates looked at Dubois and worked his eyebrows again. "That's for me to know and him to find out, right *Sharl*?" He jumped up and did a perfect imitation of a dancing girl high kicking and tossing her ruffled petticoats around as he circled the campfire. He wiggled his hips and then, with a loud "whoo-whoo", circled Frenchy's head with one pointed toe while he hopped up and down on the other.

Dorsey snorted, spraying coffee in all directions. Yates added to his routine until the men were howling with laughter. Finally, when Yates dropped to the earth beside the two men, Dorsey wiped the tears away from his eyes and said, "All right, Yates. All right. I'll put in a word with Sergeant Boone. But I make no guarantees."

He got up slowly and stretched his lower back, wincing. "Get Jackson and tell him I need help harnessing up my mules."

When Yates jumped up to obey, Dorsey leaned over and said, "I saw you boys limping pretty bad before we stopped. We'll be crossing a creek in about an hour. When we do, see that you wade in it long enough to get that leather soaking wet. I mean soaking. Then don't take those boots off until they are dry. As they dry, they'll mold to your feet. You'll have the best-fitting boots you can get until you muster out and go to a fancy cobbler in Denver."

"Thanks, Corporal." Yates saluted smartly. "I owe you."

Dorsey nodded. "You got that right. Now get Jackson over here. We're supposed to be in camp by tattoo—that's 'lights-out' to you, green-horn."

———

For the twentieth time in an hour, Miss Charlotte Valentine laid her needlework aside and peered out the front window toward the log barracks to the southwest. Seeing nothing but an empty parade ground and a group of men returning from target practice, Charlotte sighed. It had been a long day of waiting, and she was beginning to think Sergeant Boone might not be coming for dinner after all. There was no sign of the new recruits her father had said would arrive today from Sidney. And Nathan had to meet them, get them inspected, and give them orders before he could think of socializing. "Nathan." Charlotte whispered the name to herself. Not *Sergeant Boone*. He was *Nathan* to her. Of course he didn't know that. Yet.

Charlotte got up and went to the window. Shoving her mother's heavy brocade drapes aside, she leaned against the window frame and let out another sigh. Less than a year ago Camp Robinson had been bustling with activity, with hundreds of Indian camps less than a mile away near Red Cloud Agency, and nearly a thousand men stationed both at Camp Robinson, and a number of makeshift camps scattered around the Pine Ridge area. Now it was almost a ghost fort. With the Indian Wars all but over, and the Sioux moved to their new agency, most of the troops had left Camp Robinson.

There was only the Friday-night hop to attend these days. And the same soldiers to dance with. Not that Charlotte cared for any of *them*. But it was her duty as an army officer's daughter to do what she could to keep morale high. Dancing every dance with a different soldier was something she could do. There just weren't enough women to go around at those things. Even old Granny Max from over on Soapsuds Row got asked to dance every dance, and soldiers still had to tie a white scarf around their arms to designate themselves "ladies" so everyone could have a partner.

Thinking of Soapsuds Row made Charlotte frown. She'd never given the women living there much thought. First, because they were all married. And second, because there wasn't a lady among them. Even when Meara O'Malley's husband got himself killed, thereby providing a single woman for all the soldiers to court, Charlotte didn't worry. Only the lower classes of soldiers would give a laundress any thought at all.

But something had happened a few weeks ago that worried Charlotte. Nathan and Corporal Dorsey had ridden in late one night with a woman they'd found in the wilds. Charlotte's father had been summoned to tend a gunshot wound. He feared the "poor woman" would die. But she had surprised everyone and lived. Which was, of course, a good thing. Miss Charlotte Valentine was not one to wish evil upon anyone, least of all some poor creature drug in from the hills. But with the arrival of that woman, whom her father eventually described as "about twenty and quite pretty, in spite of a terrible head wound," Sergeant Boone had begun dining with his old Granny Max more often than he joined the Valentine family.

Charlotte was only seventeen years old and, therefore, was not privy to her parents' private conversations about the various members of the infantry and cavalry troops stationed at Camp Robinson. But she was not averse to passing beneath the dining room window on her way to gather eggs from the chicken coop out back. And was it her fault if, pausing to inspect a spot old Granny Max had failed to remove from her new apron, she just happened to hear what her parents discussed?

Sergeant Boone had grieved deeply the death of his wife. He had almost resigned his commission. He still visited her grave in the post cemetery across the river several times a week. Rumor had it the Boones' quarters over on Soapsuds Row remained exactly the same as the day Mrs. Boone died, although Nathan rarely slept there. He spent most of his time in the barracks with his men. At least he *had,* Charlotte thought with a frown. *Until he found that woman.*

She had overheard more than one parental discussion about Sergeant Boone's grief. Her father was concerned about the young sergeant, although he never knowingly let Charlotte hear him say it. Mrs. Doctor, however, was not so careful. She let Charlotte know all about her concerns that such a "fine young man" was allowing "an unfortunate first marriage" to impact his military career.

While both of Charlotte's parents were concerned about Sergeant Boone, it was her mother who took action and began extending frequent invitations for him to join the Valentines for dinner. After a few of those dinners, Mrs. Valentine tactfully shared news of a dear friend of hers in the East who had nearly gone mad with grief after losing her beloved husband. She had left everything untouched. Created a shrine to the man. And then one day she had risen from her grief and realized she was destroying herself. She had donated her dead husband's suits to charity and was remarried within a month. "And she's so *happy* now," Mrs. Valentine had said. "I'm just so pleased for her."

When Sergeant Boone did not learn from the example of Mrs. Valentine's friend, when he left things unmoved over on Soapsuds Row and continued to visit his late wife's grave, Mrs. Valentine confided to Charlotte that she was beginning to suspect Granny Max was an obstacle to the sergeant's recovery, and perhaps it would be in his best interest if his wife's servant left Camp Robinson.

"Just think of it, dear," Emmy-Lou had said one evening as she helped Charlotte set the table for dinner. "The poor man doesn't have a chance to get on with his life while Granny Max is there, reminding him daily of poor Mrs. Boone's absence. They were very close, you know." She sighed. "Sometimes it's best just to put the past behind us and not talk about it anymore. But of course Sergeant Boone can't do that. Not with Granny Max living right next door. If he no longer has her to reminisce with," Emmy-Lou continued, "he will be better able to move on." Charlotte thought her mother's reasoning made sense.

But later that evening, when the subject of Granny Max came up at dinner, Sergeant Boone had launched into a litany of praise for the old woman that squashed Mrs. Doctor's plans.

"I assumed Granny would want to head back East after—"

"Yes," Mrs. Doctor echoed. "I've been telling Avery the old dear should be reunited with her own people. Being a laundress is far too grueling for a woman her age."

Nathan chuckled. "Well, I only brought it up once. Granny was stirring soap into a batch of laundry. She put her hands on her hips and just glared at me. 'Are you ordering me to leave Camp Robinson, Sergeant Boone?' she asked. She was mad." Nathan leaned back in his chair. " 'Why, no, Granny,' I said. 'I just thought—'

" 'Good.' That big voice of hers was booming so loud I bet every woman on the row heard her. 'Because I been taking orders from white boys for most of my life. And as I recall, there was a war fought so I would no longer be obliged to do so.' She grabbed up her stick and began to stir that laundry so hard the water sloshed over the side and almost put the fire out.

"I started to apologize, but Granny didn't let me say another word. She said, 'You say I am free to go, and that means I am just as free to stay, and I would kindly appreciate it if you would allow me to decide my own future.' Then she stopped stirring and marched right up to me. She looks up at me and shakes her finger not an inch from my nose. I've never seen her so angry. 'You may not realize it, Sergeant Boone, but the fact is you need me. I don't intend to stand before the Lord God and Lily someday and have them asking me just exactly why I deserted my post. Now I'm going to mend your shirts and keep liniment ready for when you get the quinsy and bake your favorite chokecherry pie come July. So don't you be bringing up my leaving Camp Robinson again!' "

Nathan shook his head and laughed. He looked around the table. "The truth is I'm grateful she's stayed. She makes me feel . . . connected. Keeps me grounded. I'm thankful Granny Max was smart enough to know I need her. It took me a while, but I've finally realized it for myself. And since she does the work of two women, there's no argument about her value to the army, either."

For a moment, the conversation around the Valentine's dinner table had ceased. Then the doctor cleared his throat and offered, "Sometimes I think she's the unofficial camp chaplain too. The men seem drawn to her."

"Unless they've been in the guardhouse," Nathan said. "Then they avoid her like the plague. Granny doesn't put up with mischief."

Charlotte admired how her mother had deftly guided the conversation to other things, how she was sensitive to Nathan's wishes, dispensing with any more talk of Granny Max leaving Camp Robinson. Mama also stopped hinting that Mrs. Boone's things should be removed from Soapsuds Row. But not long after that dinner, she had taught Charlotte how to make Sergeant Boone's favorite chokecherry pie.

Chokecherry pie. Watching out the front window, Charlotte now smiled to herself. She was becoming a very good cook. Mama said she had heard that Lily Boone couldn't cook worth anything. In fact, Mama said Mrs. Boone hadn't been much use as a soldier's wife at all. "She just wasn't cut out for military life, Charlotte. Mrs.Gruber said so. Sergeant Boone's next wife should be from military stock. If he has any sense at all, he realizes that."

Sighing with impatience, Charlotte went back to her needlework. She was piecing a nine-patch quilt with squares so tiny it would likely take the rest of her natural life to get enough squares to make a quilt. But Mama said that a good military wife realized the importance of letting nothing go to waste. Charlotte picked up two squares of cloth about the size of her thumbnail and began to stitch them together with a neat running stitch.

Charlotte sewed. And thought. She reviewed her many assets, not the least of which was her abundant straw-colored hair and light blue eyes. She was the best dancer at Camp Robinson. She was learning to play the guitar and sing. And she was a good shot, as well prepared as any military wife could be to protect herself against savages. Nathan's career would benefit if he married into an officer's family. All in all, Charlotte could not think of a single thing to keep Sergeant Nathan Boone from falling to one knee and proposing.

The sound of marching brought Charlotte back into the present. She hopped up and ran to the window just in time to see the new recruits marching into camp.

"Dinah! Dinah Valentine! You come here!" Charlotte ran for her parasol and bonnet. When there was no sight of her eight-year-old sister, she hurried to the back door. "Dinah! Dinah, where are you?!"

"I'm here, Charlott-ah," Dinah said, sticking her head out the door of the shed. "I think Maizy's calf is on the way."

"Oh, who cares about old Maizy and a calf! You come here! The recruits have arrived. You come and walk with me."

Dinah frowned. "I don't care about a bunch more soldiers," she protested.

"Well, I can't exactly go strolling up and down the picket fence gawking at the soldiers by myself," Charlotte said. "Mama would have a fit."

"Get Mama to go with you," Dinah said. She didn't budge from the shed door.

"I can't. Mama's over at Mrs. Gruber's seeing if the freighter brought a new supply of canned meat." She hesitated, then blurted out, "I'll give you the rest of my candy from Christmas."

Dinah considered. "You got any horehound left?"

"Three pieces," Charlotte said.

Within five minutes, the Misses Charlotte and Dinah Valentine were promenading up the picket fence bordering along the adobe duplexes.

They giggled about one soldier's fiery red hair. "Won't *he* be a fine target for the Indians." Another seemed so old Charlotte couldn't imagine he'd be much use. Others were declared to be too short, too skinny, or too dirty. Besides the one with the red hair, Charlotte found nothing of interest among the new recruits. Save one.

———

Standing toe-to-toe with the recruit who called himself Caleb Jackson, Nathan spoke with authority, "Jackson?"

"Yes, sir." The recruit snapped his reply and saluted smartly, shifting his gaze so that he was staring just past Nathan's left earlobe.

Nathan frowned as he looked down at the footsore recruit. "I see you've met Corporal Dorsey."

"Sir?"

"Your boots. Feel better, don't they?"

"Yes, sir."

Nathan folded his arms across his chest. "Civilian experience?"

"I worked in a variety store in St. Louis, sir. Behind the counter."

"Seems to me you should be assigned to the quartermaster, then."

"No, sir!" Jackson barked. He shifted his gaze back so he was peering into Nathan's eyes, pleading. "I joined up to see action, sir."

"Didn't like working in a store?"

"Hated it, sir."

Nathan nodded and let his eyes run down the row of Jackson's shirt buttons. "Can you sit a horse?"

"Yes, sir."

"Really?" Nathan asked. "Seems to me a St. Louis store clerk wouldn't have much call to ride."

"My family owned horses, sir. I grew up riding."

"If your family owned horses, what landed you behind the counter of a store in St. Louis?"

The recruit narrowed his gaze. He swallowed. "We lost it. Everything." His thin lips sneered. "Apparently my father's stables threatened some great moment of military bravery." The slightest southern accent flavored his last sentence. "As did the house, the servant's houses, and the cotton fields. Yankees burned it all."

Nathan cleared his throat. "Camp Robinson is not the place for settling old scores with the Yankees, Private Jackson."

"I'm not here to settle old scores, sir." He stared straight ahead.

Nathan touched the brim of his hat with his index finger and took a step back. "Well, then, maybe you can help some of the boys when we turn them loose with their new mounts."

"I'll do that, sir."

Nathan moved to the next recruit and the next, moving down the line until he had sized up the men to be integrated into Company G of the Third Cavalry. They'd gained a cobbler and a tailor, along with a few farm boys; two railroad workers, who would likely be the first men to discover that Sergeant Nathan Boone would back up his orders with his fists; and a couple of Irishmen whom Nathan expected to desert the first time they ventured north into gold country. But Private Caleb Jackson, though not the only galvanized Yankee in the bunch, was certainly the most intriguing.

Nathan wasn't likely to have forgotten the night he and a fourteen-year-old Confederate drummer boy named Beauregard Preston met. It had been nearly fifteen years ago, but they'd spent the night picking their way through a battlefield so strewn with dead bodies that they could scarcely find a place to step without landing on some body part. They'd seen each other once after the war. Nathan didn't remember Beau talking much about his home or family. But then, Nathan had been so enamored with Lily at the time, he was hardly in his right mind. After that chance encounter in Nashville, he'd never seen Beau again, but he would have known him anywhere.

Jackson. You've got to remember to call him Jackson.

Nathan dismissed his men with orders to report to the quartermaster before afternoon roll call. "If any of you other men have an eye for horse-flesh, you can look over the new mounts with Private Jackson here." Nathan nodded toward his old friend. "Mounted drill starts tomorrow."

Jackson hoisted his bedroll and hurried off across the parade ground toward the cavalry barracks on the southeast corner of the post. Watching him go, Nathan wondered what could have happened to make Beau

Preston change his name and lose his accent. He had almost decided to say something when Jackson turned and looked back at him. He hesitated a minute, then touched the bill of his cap with one finger and nodded.

Nathan returned the salute. "I'd like to talk to you after you look over those horses, Private," he called out. "Alone."

"Yes, sir," Jackson called back. "I'll be glad to answer your questions, sir."

"Meet me at the corral in half an hour," Nathan called out and turned to go. Reporting in to the captain required Nathan to go by the row of officer's duplexes.

"I see you have some new men to break in, Sergeant Boone," Charlotte called out in her most grown-up voice as Nathan approached the Valentine residence.

Nathan smiled and touched the brim of his hat in a brief salute. "Yes, ma'am."

"The ladies will be even more outnumbered at the next hop," Charlotte observed.

"But there is a bright side to the dilemma," Nathan said, grinning. "At least two of the new men actually know how to dance."

"Oh?" Charlotte opened her fan with a flick of her wrist. "Let me guess. The flaming redhead."

Nathan laughed. "No. I don't think Yates is much for the quadrille. But keep an eye on the one with the beard."

"Which one?" Charlotte made a show of peering over her fan toward the retreating backs of the recruits.

"The one you were eyeing so carefully as they marched by."

Charlotte's cheeks burned. "Why, Sergeant Boone, I don't know what on earth you are talking about."

"Jackson."

"I beg your pardon?"

"His name. It's Private Caleb Jackson. I'll introduce you at the next hop." He bowed and backed away, hoping Charlotte's flirtation would distract her from wondering just how it was a company sergeant could tell which of his new men knew how to dance.

———

"Buckskin mare's a looker," Nathan said. He draped his arms over the top bar of the quartermaster's corral and waited for Jackson, who stood next to him, to comment.

"Cow-hocked," was all the man said.

The mare wheeled around on her hind legs and set off for the opposite side of the corral. Nathan watched her movement and nodded. "You do have an eye for horseflesh." He looked at Jackson. "Yates said you were going to help him pick out a mount."

"Yates has a big mouth," Jackson said, pulling the brim of his hat down on his forehead.

"He's all right. Green as they come. But he'll do. If he survives tomorrow."

"He will." Jackson pointed at the buckskin mare, who had crowded up against a scrawny-looking dun gelding and was nibbling playfully at his withers. "She's cow-hocked, but she's got a sweet temperament. I figure she'll put up with Yates."

"How do you figure that?"

Jackson whistled. The mare's ears went up, and she trotted over to the fence and thrust her nose between the boards.

Nathan nodded, smiling. "You always had a way with the ladies. Even when you were only fourteen. I remember how you sweet-talked those Sanitary Commission ladies into letting you have an extra pair of socks."

"*Two* extra pair," Jackson said, still rubbing the mare's forehead. He kept his head down as he murmured, "I couldn't believe my eyes when I looked up and saw who my new sergeant was. Thanks for not letting on that you know me."

Nathan cleared his throat. "Look, Beau . . . er . . . Caleb. I've learned not to ask many questions about the men under me. Fact is, I don't even *know* some of their given names. I suspect there's more than just you using a name their own mama wouldn't recognize. That's their business. As long as they obey orders and do the job."

"You won't have any trouble from me." Jackson said quickly. "I won't be expecting any special treatment just because we knew each other in another life. Fact is, I'd appreciate it if nobody ever knew about that."

"You running from the law?" Nathan asked.

Jackson shook his head. "The only crime I ever committed was not marrying a certain young lady back in St. Louis when her papa thought I should."

"Meaning?"

"Meaning I didn't have anything to do with the baby on the way, and I wasn't about to pay for somebody else's mistakes. Even if the papa in question was my employer at the time." Caleb tugged on the mare's forelock and began to scratch behind her ears. "St. Louis was bad for me, that's all.

I'd seen enough of soldiers coming up to the city from Jefferson Barracks to know accents and origins don't matter so much in the army."

"You pretty much got rid of the accent. Last time I saw you I could hardly believe you were from the some country as me."

"In some ways Mecklenburg County *isn't* the same country." Jackson nodded toward the horizon. "I never been any place like this—where you can see so far you'd swear you can see tomorrow coming at you."

Nathan chuckled. "It sure isn't anything like home."

"I like it," Jackson said quickly. "A man can breathe out here."

"Or get lost," Nathan added.

Jackson shrugged. He pushed the buckskin mare away and swatted her on the rump. "Go on, now." The little mare trotted off.

Sergeants' assembly sounded. Nathan turned to go. "Well, I guess we're straight then, Private Jackson."

"Yes, sir," he saluted. "Thank you, sir."

Nathan returned his friend's salute and headed off toward the adjutant's office where he'd receive the next day's orders from his commander.

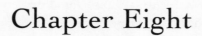

Chapter Eight

My heart is sore pained within me:
and the terrors of death are fallen upon me.
Fearfulness and trembling are come upon me,
and horror hath overwhelmed me.

PSALM 55:4-5

THE INTERNAL MUSIC Laina usually summoned to calm herself wouldn't play. Instead, drums pounded against her temples. She felt dizzy. Her heart began to race and beads of sweat broke out across her forehead. She braced herself against the doorway, fighting a wave of nausea.

Across the road on the parade ground, a company of men marched in cadence to the bawled orders of their drill sergeant. Here and there, small groups of soldiers stood or sat in clusters near the bakery and the quartermaster's stores. Over by the stables, a few men had tethered their horses in the morning sun and were making halfhearted attempts to comb out manes and tails.

Nothing to be afraid of. Just soldiers going about their normal day. More than usual because of the recruits who arrived a couple weeks ago. But nothing to be afraid of.

Still, her heart raced.

Sergeant Boone seems nice enough. He's a gentleman. Harmless. Focus on him. Don't think about the others. Nothing to be afraid of.

It didn't help. The drums still pounded inside her head, her stomach still roiled. Pulling away from Granny Max, Laina propelled herself backward away from the door, and fled to the back room, where she wretched into the basin perched on a washstand beside the back door. Wiping her mouth with a trembling hand, she looked up at Granny's reflection in the clouded mirror hanging above the washstand.

"Maybe tomorrow," she said, swiping the kerchief off her head. Making her way back into the front room, she sat down in Granny's rocker and retrieved a shirt from the always overflowing mending pile.

Granny followed Laina's gaze across Soldier Creek to where perhaps a hundred or so men were engaged in their morning routine. "We'll go the back way," she said. "Mrs. O'Malley and the other girls are already in the washhouse working. We can go in the trading post by the back door. Mrs. Gruber won't mind. You'll like her, Laina. She's a good woman. When Lily died, it was Mrs. Gruber who cut up one of her own quilts to line the casket. She spent the night helping me work on it." Granny added, "She'll make you tea, and you can rest while I do some shopping. The freighter was supposed to be bringing in some bolts of calico. I was hoping you'd pick out one for a new dress of your own."

Laina picked at the sleeve of Lily Boone's gray calico work dress. "I've no way to pay for a new dress," she said.

"Mrs. Gruber says when you're better, you can help her out at the store a few days."

"There's nothing wrong with this dress," Laina argued. "Unless . . . unless maybe Sergeant Boone doesn't like me wearing *her* things?"

"Of course he doesn't mind," Granny said. "That's not the reason I want you to go with me. You need some fresh air and sunshine. It's time you got out a little."

Laina sighed. "Later." She put her hand to her stomach. "I just don't feel good enough right now."

"There is nothing to be afraid of," Granny said gently.

Laina hung her head. Pressing the back of her hand to her forehead she said, "I know that in my head." She looked up at Granny. "But my heart pounds." She spread her fingers across the front of her dress. "It feels like it's coming right out of me."

Granny closed the door and sat down at the table. Taking one of Laina's hands in hers, she murmured, "Like I said the other night, you've got a choice to make. You *can* keep Josiah Paine from taking your future."

Laina pulled her hand away and took up the shirt atop the mending pile, checking for loose buttons. "I can't. It keeps coming back to me." She ran her hands across the layer of buttons in Granny's button box. Selecting a small white button, she compared it to the ones already sewn onto the shirt in her lap. Laying it aside, she looked for another.

Granny reached into the button box and handed Laina a button.

"Everyone will stare," Laina said. "They'll be wondering . . . imagining . . ."

"Imagining what, child? All anyone here at Camp Robinson knows is that you survived an Indian attack."

"*They* know. Sergeant Boone and that corporal. They know all of it." Laina looked up at Granny. "*Where* I was—*what* I was."

"You stop that." Granny's voice was stern. Almost angry. "That was not your fault. And they both know it." Granny sighed. "What is it that has you so determined to let go of life, child?"

Laina folded her arms across the edge of the table and rested her forehead atop them. "I was so stupid. So stupid." She began to talk. The past spilled out of her, details flooding the room like waves of the Mississippi in a storm, crashing against its banks, leaving empty bottles and rusted cans in its wake.

"The earliest thing I remember is my father—Eustis Gray—sitting at a table playing cards. He was frowning at me. Then he whispered something to the woman who'd brought me to him, and I was taken away. I guess my mama must have died. I don't really know. But I think I must have got my auburn hair from her. My father had black hair. As black as coal. I remember how it used to glisten in the sunlight when he went up on deck." She paused, picking up a large button and circling it nervously with one finger. "I was taken off the riverboat to a place that turned out to be a school—mostly for wealthy girls whose parents did not want to be bothered with them. At least that's how it seemed to me. I don't remember seeing anyone's parents very often.

"When I was about seven years old, a girl named Nellie Pierce got mad at me one day and sneered, '*Don't you think you can order me around, Laina Gray. Everybody knows your father is a no-good gambler. The only reason Miss Hart even let you come to our school is because he pays twice what everybody else does.*' That was the first time I knew why Miss Hart never treated me quite like the other girls.

"When I was about fourteen—that's a guess; I'm not certain how old I am—my father came and took me away from Miss Hart's. He'd begun losing at the tables. Miss Hart had told him what a fine musician I was. He asked me to play the piano and sing for him. When I did, he smiled and said I would do just fine on the riverboat and not to be afraid. But I was afraid. Nellie and the other girls told stories late at night about all the bad people who lived down on the riverfront. I was terrified to go, but when I told my father, he got mad. Told me I could walk the streets by myself if I wanted to, but he had given Miss Hart his last dollar.

"Life on the river wasn't all bad. The women who sang and danced in the saloon were kind to me. One of them named Rose talked my father into letting me room with her. I soon learned that Rose did more than sing and dance to earn her keep, and when my father hinted that I would soon be doing the same, I made plans to run away.

"I was creeping along the deck of the riverboat late one night when suddenly my father stepped in front of me and wanted to know where I was going. He grabbed my arm and dragged me to his room. He told me Rose had filled my head with uppity ideas and that if I tried to get away again, he'd see to it that Rose was punished. I hid the bruises on my arms and did what he said.

"Performing with Rose and the girls wasn't all bad. The men cheered and waved at us and most of the time they didn't bother me. One night a wealthy man from New Orleans came to the show, and afterward he sent a note to me that he would like to have me join him at a private party up on Locust Avenue. My father had lost a lot of money to this man at the gambling tables that night.

"Rose said this was my chance to get away. She said I would be off the riverboat and that once I was at the private party, I could get away. She helped me stash all the money I had saved inside my corset. So I went to the party with the man from New Orleans. He called himself Pierre Dupre, but I don't know if that was his real name."

Laina paused. She swiped a trembling hand over her eyes. "I woke up the next morning in the back of a covered wagon. My hands and feet were tied. There was a foul-smelling rag stuffed in my mouth. Josiah Paine said he'd won me from Dupre. I couldn't remember anything after Dupre lured me into a back room of his mansion. He gave me something to drink and I passed out." She sobbed. "I actually thought my father might come after me. Might rescue me. So I waited. Until we were so far out in the wilderness, there was no one to run to." She tried to laugh. "Stupid, stupid girl. I should have tried to get away."

Granny snorted. "To where? To some Indian camp? If you're like most women, whatever you heard about Indians was depradation and damnification. No one can blame you for not running." She touched the scars on Laina's wrists. This time Laina endured the touch. "No one blames you, child."

Laina laid her free arm on the edge of the table and hid her face against it. Granny let go of her hand and patted her shoulder while Laina hid her face in her folded arms and sobbed. "Why couldn't Sergeant Boone have been just a second later? Why didn't God just let me *go*."

Granny sat down next to her. "Come here, honey-lamb. Come to Granny Max." Gently, she pulled Laina into her arms. She slid to her knees on the floor and buried her face in Granny's apron, sobbing and shuddering while Granny stroked her back and whispered words of love.

Granny patted her shoulder. "Even now, Josiah Paine reaches out from the grave and harms you. He makes you a prisoner in my house, a prisoner afraid to take a step outside, afraid to hope for better things." Granny's hand covered the back of Laina's bowed head. "You got a choice to make. Maybe the hardest one you will ever make. You can let him keep you a prisoner or you can tell him *no*. You can't change the past. And Josiah Paine owns a big, awful piece of yours. But you do *not* have to give him your *future*."

Laina looked up into the older woman's lined face. Granny's eyes burned with the conviction of what she had just said. "Do you . . . do you think I could really just . . . *leave it*? Stop being so afraid all the time?"

"Yes. Yes." Granny squeezed her hand.

Laina closed her eyes, imagining what life might be like without the nightmares and the day fears. "I . . . I want to try, Granny. I do." She clutched her stomach. "But . . ."

"Baby steps, child. Baby steps." Granny bent down and kissed the top of her head. Instead of urging her out the door, Granny asked, "Where did you learn to sew?"

"Rose taught me."

Granny stood, pulling Laina up off the floor and guiding her back into her chair. "All right, then. That's someone in your memories that did something *good* for you."

She studied Laina's tear-stained face. "You know, Laina, if I could just walk into your head right now and clean up all those evil memories, I would do it. Fact is, I can't. But there is something in my Bible that has helped me." Granny reached for her Bible, still lying open on the kitchen table from her morning reading. Thumbing through the pages, she found the place and read, " 'Finally brethren, whatsoever things are true, whatsoever things are honest, whatsoever things are just, whatsoever things are pure, whatsoever things are lovely, whatsoever things are of good report; if there be any virtue, and if there be any praise, think on these things.' "

Granny closed the book and laid it back on the table. "Now I am not one of those people who thinks you just open that book and read a verse and that makes everything all better. I know the battle is raging inside your pretty head, and I know it is a terrible one. You got people like Rose and you got Josiah Paine—and maybe more than just him. I don't know." She leaned down and hugged Laina fiercely. "But you got a quick mind to help you fight this battle. And the battle for you right now is this: Which one you gonna think on? Josiah Paine or Rose?"

Laina nodded.

"Everybody has sad memories. Some worse than others. Yours are among the worst I've ever heard. But you got good things you can think on too. Rose. Sergeant Boone. Shelter. Food. A new dress—"

"—you," Laina interrupted her. Tears welled up in her eyes. "And you, Granny Max."

Granny smiled down at Laina. "Thank you, honey. I am pleased to be one of your *good things*. You got any others that come to mind?"

"Music," Laina whispered. "I always liked singing."

Granny reached over to the table and handed her button box to Laina. "Maybe you will have a song ready for old Granny when I get back from Mrs. Gruber's."

Laina nodded and returned to the seat beside the kitchen table. She bent to the work of sewing buttons on Sergeant Boone's shirt.

Granny slung the market basket back over her forearm and went to the door. "You are going to be all right, Laina Gray. It may take some time. But if you are willing to work at *thinking on these things,* you will be all right." She turned to go, then stopped and turned back, calling Laina's name again.

Laina looked up at her.

"Don't you be worrying about what Nathan and Corporal Dorsey might be thinking when they see you. They are men," Granny said, smiling. "When they see you, all they see is pretty."

Laina touched the side of her head where the gunpowder had burned away her hair. She could feel a blush rising up the back of her neck and spreading to her cheeks. She shook her head and concentrated on moving the button beneath her thumb into position as Granny closed the door. In the quiet, she was drawn back into the past, and just as Granny had predicted, the specter of Josiah Paine returned. Looking up from her work, Laina tried what Granny had said. Instead of retreating into the dugout in her mind, she went to Miss Hart's, to music class. She began to hum to herself, surprised when the words to a song came to mind.

Presently, singing softly to herself, Laina went to the back door, opened it, and peeked out. There was no one in sight. The sensation of the spring breeze against her face felt good. If she angled the rocker just right, she could enjoy the fresh air and a view of the broad valley stretching off toward pine-covered ridges in the distance and still be almost completely shielded behind the open door. She took a few minutes to arrange things before settling into the rocker and taking up a shirt. The same creek that looped between Soapsuds Row and Camp Robinson's main buildings meandered toward the south. Its banks were hidden by low growing brush and scrubby looking trees covered with white blossoms. Laina bent to her task, but not before judging the distance to the nearest clump of trees and thinking that perhaps she and Granny could walk down there this afternoon.

———

Raucous laughter. *That only sounds close. Those men are over at the stables. Sergeant Boone said the recruits would be riding again today. And at least a few were still saddlesore. That's what they are laughing about. Think on these things.*

Pounding hooves. *The cavalry is drilling. Think on these things.*

Marching. *The infantry. They drill every day. Think on these things.*

More hoofbeats. *Sergeant Boone and Company G are going out for target practice. Today is Monday. They do target practice every Monday. Think on these things.*

Laina had done well at remembering some good things from Miss Hart's. She even had a funny story to tell Granny Max when she got back from the trading post. She willed herself to stay seated in her rocker while the sounds of the military camp assaulted her good intentions with new fears. She recited what she knew about life at Camp Robinson to herself. There was a very good explanation for nearly every noise. She even recognized water call when the bugler sounded.

But in spite of her attempts to replace fears with good thoughts, the empty room began to get on her nerves. She began to feel queasy again. Thinking she heard footsteps coming toward Soapsuds Row, she began to tremble with fear. She reminded herself to notice the beautiful spring day. There was nothing to be afraid of. She knew all these things. She even half believed them. But suddenly all she wanted to do was stop the mental battle and crawl beneath the quilt on her bed and go to sleep.

Someone slammed a door up at the opposite end of Soapsuds Row. Jumping up, Laina quickly closed the back door and lifted the bar into place. She stood with her back to the door. *There. Safe.* She sat on the edge of her bed in the muted light, nervously tugging at one gray cuff.

She could hear muffled laughter. That would be Katie and Becky—the O'Malley girls, likely headed toward the washhouse to help their mother. Granny said Meara O'Malley and her girls had arrived not long after the Boones and had caused quite a stir when they banged on the captain's front door demanding to see Paddy O'Malley of Company I, Fourth Infantry. Due to O'Malley's being out on patrol, it had been a few days before the family was reunited.

Meara O'Malley had ignored the camp gossip that placed Paddy O'Malley in a Sioux tepee over at the agency instead of out on patrol.

"My Paddy? Takin' up with the savages? The dear Lord preserve me," she'd said, and crossed herself. "I won't believe that until Paddy tells me himself."

Paddy had not told her. He'd come home smiling and seemed completely delighted to have the life nearly squeezed out of him by the overzealous greeting of his overweight wife and the enthusiastic hugs from his two daughters, the youngest of whom did not even remember her father.

When Paddy O'Malley died in a freak accident out on maneuvers, Meara dressed in black and grieved her husband. But it wasn't long before Meara, wide-of-body and sharp-of-tongue, succumbed to the flattery of all the attention she received from a long line of soldiers. Women were scarce on the frontier. None stayed single for long, Granny said. Meara's girls had a new father within three months of Paddy's death. He was gone now, too—a victim of his own affinity for whiskey. He'd been shot in a drunken brawl at one of the hog ranches off the military reservation. But he'd left a lasting memory of himself. Meara was pregnant.

Laina found herself wondering what the O'Malley girls were like. She wondered if they minded living at Camp Robinson. How they felt about losing *two* fathers. If they missed anyone back home.

"Home." There was a word. She whispered, *Chez moi. Ma maison,* pronouncing the French words carefully, strangely satisfied that she remembered them from her French lessons at Miss Hart's. All Miss Hart's students went home for the holidays. It had caused Laina a few sleepless nights the first time she faced the awful possibility of Nellie Pierce sneering goodbye as she walked down the broad front steps of Miss Hart's Academy for Young Ladies, leaving Laina behind.

To avoid the disgrace, Laina had created an alternative scenario. By forging her father's signature on a note asking that she be taken to the train station, Laina succeeded in creating the illusion of *going home* for herself. No one ever guessed that while the girls from Miss Hart's were at *home,* one from among their number was living on the streets of St. Louis. After that first Christmas, when she'd broken out in a cold sweat from the fear of being discovered, Laina had developed a routine of sorts that amounted to her own holiday traditions. She always attended Christmas Eve mass in the Cathedral down on the waterfront. The year she managed to hide in an alcove and get locked in was one of her better Christmases. *A good memory.* Granny would be pleased.

Up the row the same door slammed again. "Kathleen Eileen O'Malley!"

Mrs. O'Malley shouted. Laina closed her eyes. "Get that creature *out* of here right this minute! Look at that! He's ruined the handle on my best knife. I declare, Katie, if he chews on one more thing of mine . . . !"

Laina thought of the night Eustis Gray had caught her trying to run away again and cut her with the tip of his knife, just beneath her jawline. Not so the scar would show, but so she would remember. That knife and the realization her father would make good on his threat to hurt Rose ended any plan Laina had to leave. Eventually, when she made a name for herself as "Riverboat Annie," she learned how to keep the real Laina separate from the dancing and drinking and everything else that went on in the narrow hallways and darkened rooms below deck. Not until Josiah Paine came along did anyone manage to pierce the veil between Riverboat Annie's performances and Laina Gray's life. Eventually, his depravity plunged her into a darkness so complete that Laina Gray was nearly snuffed out.

Nearly. But Laina Gray was still alive. She was more than a little crazy at times. She panicked at the thought of going outside. She hid from the soldiers. But she was learning not to hide when Sergeant Boone came for dinner. Two nights ago she had even sat at the table with him and Granny Max. She hadn't said much. But it was a start.

She could remember some of the French from Miss Hart's. She could still sing. And she could, at least part of the time, do what Granny Max said. She could choose to push the bad memories away and replace them with good things. Laina pondered Granny Max's words. *"He has your past. You do not have to give him your future."*

She looked around her, at the evidence of Clara Maxwell having done exactly what she said Laina must do. The two rooms were tangible evidence of Granny's making things better. Instead of leaving the windows bare, Granny Max had made curtains. She had picked some spring flowers and put them in a tin can on the table. She'd monogrammed the linen towel hanging on the hook above the washbasin. And instead of using plain army-issue blankets on the beds, Granny had made quilts.

Perched on the edge of her narrow bed, Laina looked down at the quilt. It must have a thousand pieces, tiny brown and pink triangles joined to make squares, the squares joined to make bigger squares. The quilt represented hundreds of hours of stitching and a strong determination to make something beautiful. In the long-ago past, Clara "Granny Max" Maxwell had stopped hiding in a closet and started eating raspberry pie. In the present, she had taken two bare rooms and made them a home.

Looking at the door she had just barred, Laina thought, *And I've taken these same two rooms and locked myself inside and made a prison. I might as well still be in the dugout.*

Slowly, Laina stood up. Going to the window above Granny's bed, she pushed the curtains aside and let the morning light stream in the window. It highlighted a worn spot on Granny's quilt. Leaning down to inspect it, Laina decided that once she was finished sewing buttons on Sergeant Boone's dress parade shirt, she should patch Granny's quilt.

Walking into the next room, she stirred up the fire and set the coffeepot on the stove. It was getting near lunchtime. She'd never learned to cook much, but maybe she could manage flapjacks. Granny liked flapjacks.

While the water heated, Laina took up the straw broom propped in the corner behind the front door and swept the floor. Guiding the dust toward the back room, she swept all the way to the barred door. And then she unbarred the door and swept the dust outside.

———

Anyone passing by would have had no idea of the battle being waged inside the mound of quilts in Granny Max's rocker. Only a fringe of auburn hair gave witness to the humanity inside the quilt. But having finally opened the front door to the outside world at Camp Robinson, Laina had determined not to close it until Granny came back. She had made flapjacks and they were being kept warm in the oven. She had finished sewing the buttons on Sergeant Boone's dress shirt. She had swept a floor. She had opened a door. And she had made a choice. She was exhausted, but as she huddled inside her pink-and-brown quilt, listening to the sounds of Camp Robinson, Laina was deliciously conscious of a newly arrived inner quiet. She had nearly dozed off when she heard the shuffle of childish footsteps approaching from up the row of apartments.

She had wondered what Kathleen O'Malley looked like, how old she might be. About eight, Laina now guessed as she returned the startled gaze of two brilliant blue eyes. Just as their eyes met, the fat white puppy clutched in Kathleen's arms wriggled nearly out of her grasp. Her tangle of blond hair completely obscured her face as she leaned down to deposit the squirming puppy on the ground. Wagging its entire rear end, the pup snuffled along the dirt before padding confidently to where Laina sat.

"No, Wilber, no," the child called. "Come back here!"

To Wilber's credit, he did at least hesitate. He even yapped an answer. And kept going. Straight for where Laina sat. She slipped her feet to the floor. Wilber's tail wagged even more furiously. She held her hand out. Joyously, he kissed her fingers, then wriggled away just far enough so that when he squatted to relieve himself the puddle didn't land on Laina's feet.

"Wilber, *no.*" Kathleen rushed for him and gathered him up in her arms. "I'm sorry," she gasped. "I'll clean it up. I'm sorry. Oh, *please* don't tell Ma. Please don't."

"Don't worry. I like puppies."

The child drew away, still clutching her puppy. She nodded and struggled to keep from dropping the impatient dog.

"Puppies can't help it sometimes." Laina let the quilt fall away from her.

Kathleen blurted out, "Why aren't you mad? Ma gets terrible mad when Wilber forgets he's in the house. She said if he does it one more time, he's a goner."

Laina smiled. "You have to watch a puppy every minute for a while."

"How come you know about dogs?"

Laina had gone to the kitchen and was returning with a bucket and a rag. As she bent to wipe up the puddle, she said, "I had a dog. He looked a lot like Wilber." She reached out and scratched under the puppy's chin.

"What happened to your dog?"

Laina put the used rag in the bucket and set it outside the back door. "He died," she said.

"Wilber came from the Indians. Pa—my *new* pa—gave him to me." She added, "I got to teach him to stay home so he don't get et. He's fat and they like the fat ones. At least that's what Pa said."

Laina touched the soft black nose. Her eyes misted over. "Make certain when he comes to you he always gets something good. He'll be staying close by soon enough."

Kathleen looked doubtful. "Wilber's awful stubborn." The puppy struggled and managed to wriggle out of her grasp. With a delighted yelp, he tore off toward a clump of trees down on the creek. Kathleen shrieked his name and set off after him.

Laina followed.

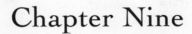

Chapter Nine

*But when thou makest a feast,
call the poor, the maimed, the lame, the blind:
And thou shalt be blessed; for they cannot recompense thee:
for thou shalt be recompensed at the resurrection of the just.*
LUKE 14:13-14

"MY MAMA SAYS you're crazy," the girl said as she plunked herself down beside Laina. "I think you're nice. You can call me Katie. Everybody does. Except Ma, when she's angry about something."

"Thank you," Laina choked out. Discouraged to learn only a short walk made her feel faint, she leaned back against a fallen log and waited to catch her breath. Wilber, who had been exploring the creek bank just a few feet away, bounded over and invited himself into Laina's lap. His muddy paws dotted her skirt with filth.

"Wil-*brrrrrrr,*" Katie scolded, reaching for him.

Laina waved her away. She swallowed and took a deep breath. Wilber snuggled into the gray calico folds of her skirt and fell asleep. "It's all right," she said, smiling. "Crazy women don't care about mud on their dresses."

"But you're *not* crazy," Katie said. She brushed her blond curls out of her eyes and looked sideways up at Laina. "I hear you at night sometimes. When you have a bad dream." She nodded. "I have bad dreams, too. You ever hear *me?*"

Laina shook her head.

"Well, I don't always yell. Becky—that's my sister—Becky makes fun of me if I yell." She reached over and touched the top of Wilber's head. "That's why Pa brought me a puppy. He said I could have Wilber sleep with me, and if I woke up scared, Wilber would help. Ma didn't want me to have a dog. Said they are dirty and good for nothing but fleas. But I quit waking her up at night, so she lets Wilber stay. Now that Pa's died, Ma don't mind having a dog so much." She ducked her head and then, leaning over, looked up into Laina's face. "Is that why *you* had a dog? To help with bad dreams?"

Laina looked up at the blue sky. She shook her head.

The young girl kept talking. "They got whole *herds* of dogs over by the Agency. Just running loose all over the place since the Indians left. Pa said there's so many the soldiers use 'em for target practice sometimes. Some of 'em are half wild. Not Wilber, though. Wilber's nice. Are you going to stay with Granny Max?" She didn't wait for an answer. "Because if you are going to stay, maybe you could help me teach Wilber so Ma wouldn't yell at him so much."

"Kathleen! Kathleen Eileen O'Malley!"

"Oh no. Now she's really going to be mad. I was supposed to put Wilber in his cage and sweep the floor." Katie scrambled to her feet. "Here, Ma!" She jumped up and yelled at the top of her lungs. "I'm here!" She turned back around. "I better go," she said, and scooped the puppy up in her arms. "You want to meet my Ma?"

Laina shook her head.

"Come on," Katie pleaded. "She won't be so mad if you come with me. Please." She held out her hand and Laina took it.

———

"This is . . ." Katie frowned. "What's your name?"

"Laina," Laina said and extended her hand to Katie's mother. "Laina Gray."

"Laina helped me with Wilber," Katie said, completely oblivious to her mother's openmouthed stare. "She can show me how to make Wilber behave, Ma. And he won't make any more puddles inside, and he'll come when I call him. Isn't that so, Laina?" Katie nudged her.

Laina dropped the offered hand, which had been ignored, and looked down at the ground. She could feel her face burning as her cheeks turned red beneath the woman's careful inspection.

"We'll have to see, Katie," Mrs. O'Malley said.

"But, Ma . . . you said if—"

"I said we will see, Kathleen. Now come inside and do the sweeping you were told to do an hour ago." The woman pulled her daughter inside and closed the door without so much as another glance in Laina's direction.

Once back inside, Laina shoved Granny's rocker over and barred the front door before crawling beneath her quilt and falling into a dreamless sleep.

———

Pounding on the front door roused Laina, but before she could get up, Granny Max burst in the back door.

Laina sat up, still groggy.

Granny put her hand on her forehead. "You all right, honey-lamb? Why'd you bar the door?"

"I was . . . the noises . . . the marching . . ."

Granny clucked and made her way into the front room where she lifted the bar from the door and admitted a soldier, who dumped packages on the table as Granny bustled about the kitchen. "Now you just sit yourself down for a minute, Private," Granny was saying as she opened the oven door. "I'll pop this in and warm—" Granny stopped abruptly and set the pan of cold corn bread down on top of the stove. She withdrew the plate of warm flapjacks.

"They . . . they probably aren't even edible. But I tried." Laina had pulled the quilt-curtain aside and was standing in the doorway.

Granny didn't answer. Instead, she looked at the soldier who was blushing furiously even as he removed his hat and bobbed his head to greet Laina. "Well, Private Yates, I guess you can eat flapjacks instead of corn bread. This is Miss Laina Gray. Sit down."

The soldier did as he was told.

Laina ducked into the back room, presently returning with a stack of folded shirts in her arms. She placed the shirts on the edge of the table opposite the soldier and retreated to the doorway. Resisting the instinct to disappear into the back room, she stood still, her hands clasped behind her.

Private Yates stammered a thank-you. Blushing furiously, he stood up. "I got fatigue duty to finish up, ma'am," he said, backing to the door.

"I'm not finished with you yet, young man," Granny said. "How much do you owe the canteen?"

"I ain't been drunk again, Granny," Yates said, sidling for the door. "Honest. I told Jackson no more drinking for me."

"You didn't answer my question, Private."

"Now, Granny," the young man looked longingly out the door. For a moment, Laina thought he might make a run for it.

"So how much do you owe?"

"Two dollars." He hung his head.

"Mrs. Gruber said it's two-fifty," Granny said. "And by the time the quartermaster deducts for your laundry bill, are you gonna have anything left to send your mama? You said you stopped drinking with Private Jackson. But are you still playing cards with him?"

Yates pressed his lips together stubbornly. "I will have some money to send home, ma'am."

"It is a nice thing for you to be buying little Katie O'Malley hair ribbons, Private Yates."

"Yes, ma'am," Yates nodded his head.

"But your own mama has got to come first."

"Yes, ma'am. You are right."

"And you need to remember your mama's lessons and keep away from the poker table," Granny said. "Now I may be an old woman, and you may think I don't have much sense—"

"Oh no, ma'am!" Yates interrupted her. "I know better than that, Granny."

Granny put her hands on her hips and nodded. "Good. Then you listen when I say you need to stay out of the canteen and away from card games. Those men know you are a greenhorn, and they beat you every time you play. Gambling is foolishness, Private Yates. But since your mama is a good Christian woman, I reckon you already know that."

"Yes, ma'am, I do. I just forget sometimes. You know how lonely it is here, ma'am. There's not much to do once fatigue duty is done."

Granny's voice gentled. "Yes, I do know that. Most of you boys come out here to the West with some fool dime novel in your heads, thinking you're going to be Indian-fighting heroes. And then you come to Camp Robinson and end up doing the same thing every day, with lots of free time to fill and not much to fill it with." She smiled. "The next time you are longing for home and your ma, you come sit on my front porch and play me a tune on that mouth harp I hear you bragging about playing so pretty."

With a glance in Laina's direction, Yates pulled on the brim of his hat. "I'll do that, Granny. Truly I will."

"From what I've heard about Private Jackson, he won't be forgiving you any gambling debts. And Mr. Gruber will be there with his hand out the minute the paymaster puts that thirteen dollars in your hand. Now, I don't want to be the cause of your mama not being able to pay her rent. I'll credit you your laundry bill for this month."

"You don't have to do that, Granny."

"I know I don't," Granny snapped. "And it's not a gift. I need some things done around here. You think you could come by after roll call a couple of evenings next week and do a few chores?"

Yates nodded. "Yes, ma'am."

"Don't you be telling any of those other soldiers Granny Max is a pushover about paying the laundry bill now, you hear?"

"Oh no, ma'am. I won't." Yates shook his head from side to side.

"And don't be expecting me to cancel any more debts after this month, either."

"I won't."

"Now git. Sergeant Boone will have your hide for being late for assembly again. And if you're in the guardhouse you won't be any use to me."

———

Private Yates took his leave of Granny Max and headed for the stables. Once inside, he walked down the broad center aisle to the last stall on the left. Tying a lead onto the halter of a buckskin mare, he led her out of her stall. He brushed her black mane and tail, remembering to spend an extra minute or two scratching her favorite spot just below her withers.

"I saw her, Babe. I saw the woman Sergeant Boone brought in. And Dorsey didn't tell the half of it. She's more'n pretty, Babe. She's an outright angel."

Babe stomped her foot and snorted.

"Oh, I know, I know. A pretty little thing like that isn't going to be interested in me. But she might give me a dance or two at the hop, mightn't she? Even that snooty surgeon's daughter dances with me at the hops. 'Course she acts like she's doing me a favor, but it's better'n bein' stepped on a thousand times by old Corporal Dorsey. That man may be a good soldier, but he's got no music sense at all."

Babe tossed her head and turned it sideways so she could eyeball Yates.

"Oh, go on, Babe. I know what you're thinking. But I got to go on over there at least a couple times. I got to work off the laundry bill. And Granny asked me to play harmonica sometime. There's no harm in that, is there? Who knows, maybe Miss Gray *likes* music."

———

As it turned out, Miss Gray *did* like music. But Private Yates didn't learn that for a couple of weeks. First, he learned that Miss Gray was shy and awkward around men. He assumed it was because she was self-conscious about the bandage on her head. She wore a kerchief to keep it covered, but she always seemed to reach up and touch the left side of her head whenever one of the soldiers came to collect his laundry. She had stopped hiding in the back room of Granny Max's as much, but Harlan could tell she was still nervous around strangers. It made him feel protective.

Another thing Harlan learned was that Granny Max didn't really need all that much done. He felt bad about it at first, letting her credit his laundry bill for so little work. He scavenged some lumber and put three more shelves on the wall beside the stove. He begged some whitewash from the quartermaster and whitewashed the kitchen walls. He repaired a kitchen chair leg. Finally, when he realized Granny was trying to find work for him, he insisted that she let him do some of the company laundry.

The first time one of the boys from Company G saw him hanging drawers out to dry, he thought he would die of embarrassment. But that very day Miss Gray brought him a piece of pie, and while she didn't exactly sit down and talk to him while he ate, she didn't run away, either. And when he said "Thank you," she said "You are welcome, Private Yates" before she went back inside. Harlan didn't mind the teasing that night in the barracks. He let the men poke fun at him while he lay on his cot with his hands behind his head smiling.

When it became common knowledge that Private Yates had actually seen "the crazy woman Sergeant Boone had rescued," Harlan acquired new status among the men. In the tradition of soldiers lonely for female attention, they pumped Yates for details and wondered when the woman might come to a Friday-night hop.

It took only two weeks for Harlan to work off his debt to Granny Max, but by the end of the two weeks Miss Gray had stopped acting so nervous around him. He had even told her some of his better jokes and been rewarded with smiles. Once, she laughed out loud when he did a perfect imitation of a rooster and strutted around the kitchen table to illustrate a story.

The Sunday morning at the end of his stint with Granny Max, Harlan was taking special care to make certain his cowlick was plastered down, when Private Jackson nudged him out of the way, teasing, "Give it up, Yates. It's no use. And what are you primping for, anyway?"

"Nothing special," Yates lied. He tucked his mouth harp into his pocket.

"Well 'nothing special' sure has you flustered. You gonna play that harmonica for the horses?"

"I'm just going over to the Row to play some music for Granny, that's all."

"For Granny and who else?" Jackson teased.

"Granny Max and the O'Malley girls and maybe Miss Gray."

"Whoa," Jackson said, holding up his hands. "Harlan Yates and all those females?" He reached for his hat. "You need some help, boy. I'd better come along."

"Y-You're not invited!" Yates stammered.

"Bet you two bits I can *get* invited," Jackson said. He grabbed Yates's arm. "Let's go."

Yates pulled away. "Now wait a minute, you can't just show up."

"Sure I can," Jackson said. "Everybody knows Granny Max has a soft spot. I bet I can find it just as good as you. I'll have her eating out of my hand."

"L-Listen, Jackson. You just can't show up. Miss Gray . . . well, she gets nervous around men."

Caleb arched one eyebrow and peered at Yates. "Aren't *you* a man?"

"She knows me. That's different."

"And she'll know me as soon as you introduce us," Jackson said again.

"You can't go!" Yates blurted out. "You just can't."

Jackson scowled. "You telling me I'm not good enough to be around your precious ladies, Private?"

"No. That's not—"

"Good. I didn't think you meant that." Jackson dragged Yates outside.

"But you still can't go."

"How you gonna stop me?" Jackson said.

Yates gulped. "Look, Jackson, you been a good bunky, but I—"

"You got that right," Jackson said. "Who got you a good horse?"

"You did."

"And who kept you from blowing your own foot off at target practice the other day?"

"You did."

"So now you can pay me back. Introduce me to the ladies. Come on, Yates. It's time to put up or shut up." Jackson headed off toward Soapsuds Row.

"Don't make me stop you," Yates croaked.

Jackson turned around, his head cocked to one side. "What did you say?"

"I said," Yates repeated, doubling up his hands into fists. "Don't make me stop you."

Jackson snorted. "Very funny. As if you could, you ugly carrot-topped jerk."

"No need to call names," Yates said. "It's just that Miss Gray isn't ready to meet new people yet."

"What's her problem, anyway? I heard she's crazy. Do they have to keep her on a leash or something?"

Yates lowered his head and plowed into Jackson, who was caught off-balance and went down flat on his back in the dust just outside the barracks. Instantly there was a crowd around the two men. A minute later, Sergeant Boone and Corporal Dorsey were pulling the two men apart.

"He insulted a lady!" Yates screeched, struggling to pull away from Dorsey while at the same time putting a hand up to his bloodied nose.

Jackson didn't say anything at first, other than to quietly tell Sergeant Boone that Private Yates had started the fight by tackling him without provocation.

"Without . . . what?" Yates protested. "What's that mean, anyway?"

"It means," Boone explained, "that you started it."

"I did," Yates agreed. When Sergeant Boone looked surprised, he explained. "Well, I couldn't get him to listen."

Boone looked at Jackson. "Tell me something that's news," he said.

"He's going to have a little social with the ladies over on the Row. When I said I wanted to come, he went crazy," Jackson said.

"That's because Miss Gray—" Yates stopped. Looking around him at the crowd of soldiers who had suddenly grown quiet at mention of the mystery woman over on Soapsuds Row, Yates pressed his lips together. He thought for half a second and then said to Nathan, "You know what I mean, sir."

Nathan nodded. He bent down and picked up Yates's hat, which still lay in the dust at his feet. "Is your nose going to be all right?" he asked, handing the private his hat.

Yates put the hat on. "Yes, sir. Nothing to worry about."

Nathan turned to Jackson. "You in the habit of inviting yourself into the company of ladies who haven't requested your presence?"

Jackson thrust his chest out and boasted, "I am in the habit, Sergeant Boone, of having whatever female company I choose. Even the ones who don't initially request my presence are eventually glad they got to experience it—at least by the next morning."

A number of hoots and whistles went up.

"Well, that sort of female company doesn't exist at Camp Robinson, Private," Nathan snapped. "And you'll remember that, or you'll become very familiar with the interior of our newly appointed guardhouse." He thought for a moment. "Suppose you make use of this fine spring afternoon by mucking out all the cavalry stalls, Private Jackson."

"*All* of them, sir?"

Nathan nodded. "You seem to desire female company. There's plenty of fillies over in the stable who will appreciate your attentions to their feed troughs and water buckets. Braid a few manes if you get really bored," Nathan said sarcastically. His voice grew more serious, "But remember that Soapsuds Row is strictly off limits to you until further notice."

"What about clean laundry, sir?"

"Have someone pick it up for you," Nathan said. "Someone who has sense enough to mind their own business and time enough to mind yours."

"Yes, sir."

Turning his back on Jackson, Nathan smiled at Yates. "Private Yates."

"Sir?"

"It's never good to keep Granny Max waiting when she has her mind set on something."

"Thank you, sir," Yates said. Trying not to gloat, he gave Jackson a wide berth and walked away.

————

Private Yates almost expected Granny to hear his heart pounding before his knuckles rapped on her door. When Granny opened the door and Miss Gray was right there in the kitchen, his face flushed bright red. Years of being the butt of jokes—about his long neck or huge ears or his red hair—had provided Yates with enough internal voices to render him almost speechless around most females. Private Jackson's name-calling a few minutes ago didn't help, either. *I must look like a chicken, bobbing my neck at her that way. I'm gonna scare her if I keep staring.* Harlan turned his attention to Granny. "You said to come and play for you sometime. I was hoping—"

Granny motioned for him to come in. "We're just packing a lunch."

Harlan could see that Miss Gray was wrapping something in a cloth and settling it into Granny's market basket. Was it his imagination or had she turned just a little bit so her back was to him? He noticed her reach up and touch her head. She didn't have the kerchief on. In fact, her auburn hair had been braided into a thick rope that hung down her back all the way down to her waist. Why, Harlan thought, if she didn't have it tied into that braid, she just might be able to sit on her hair. He glanced at Granny, who was smiling knowingly at him.

"Why don't you join us, Private?" Granny asked. "We're just heading down to the creek for a little picnic."

"Oh, no," Harlan stammered. "I couldn't. I mean, I wouldn't want to be a bother."

"You'd be welcome company. Wouldn't he be, Miss Gray?"

Laina glanced over her shoulder at him. Her hand went to the left side of her head. She didn't say anything, but neither did she frown or disagree with Granny.

"Just get that dried-apple pie down off the shelf for me, Laina. We'll have plenty."

Harlan watched, his mouth watering at sight of the pie Miss Gray was just then taking down and settling into the basket. "You like apple pie, don't you, Private Yates?" Granny asked.

Yates bobbed his head up and down. "Sure do, ma'am."

"Well, then," Granny said, "that's settled. You just wait around back for a few minutes while we finish, and we'll be out directly. The O'Malley girls will be joining us. Mrs. O'Malley isn't feeling well, and I told her we'd love to have the girls go along. We're going to have a little hymn sing by way of a church service, and you can play your mouth harp for us. How does that suit you?"

Harlan smiled and nodded and made agreeable sounds as he scooted out the door, drawing it closed behind him. Once on the front porch, he allowed himself a huge smile and a glance toward the stables where he pictured Private Jackson mucking out stalls while he, the "ugly carrot-topped jerk," accompanied Miss Laina Gray on a picnic.

———

While Yates rejoiced outside, Laina was battling the inner demons launching a full-scale attack on her newly acquired determination to follow Granny's lead down the path of normalcy and into an as yet uncharted future. "Just do the next thing, honey-lamb," Granny had urged when Laina felt panic rise inside her at the prospect of facing the world. Granny always knew how to help her face something new. Only Granny appreciated what it had taken for Laina not to crawl beneath her quilts and plead illness at the prospect of a long walk and a picnic with a soldier—even if the soldier *was* Private Yates.

Laina reminded herself that Yates was so shy he could barely form a complete sentence in her presence. Had she ever had a brother, Laina could imagine someone funny and endearing, just like him. He was oversized, clumsy, and amusing—in fact, Laina thought as she wound her long braid around her head, Private Yates shared some of Wilber's finer qualities. And he was housebroken. She smiled at her own joke.

Sergeant Boone appeared at the door. He was talking almost before he stepped inside, "He's just so stubborn," he was saying to Granny, "I can't get him to go to Doc Valentine, but he can barely walk, and I was wondering—" He stopped short and stared at Laina, who was just finishing pinning her hair up.

Laina's hand went to the left side of her head. She smoothed her hair back and reached for her bonnet.

"Good morning," Boone said. "It's good to see you're feeling better."

Granny interrupted. "We are taking a picnic down to the creek. The O'Malley girls are coming. And Private Yates. Why don't you come?"

Laina reached for a stack of blue napkins, counting to make certain there were enough, hoping Sergeant Boone didn't notice her hands were shaking.

"When we get back, I'll mix up some liniment for Corporal Dorsey's knees."

There was a clatter at the door, and Katie and Becky O'Malley tumbled into the room with Wilber yapping at their heels. The dog ran to Laina and, standing on his hind legs, planted his paws on her knees and looked up at her adoringly, yapping and wagging his tail. Grateful for the sudden distraction, Laina smiled down at the puppy and bent to scratch his ears. She buried her face in his soft fur and kissed the top of his head. "Sit," she said.

Wilber sat, staring up at her adoringly.

"Oh my goodness!" Katie exclaimed. "Look at that! I can't believe it! He *did* it! Did you see him Becky? Wilber *sat*!"

"I told you he'd learn," Laina said. She kissed the top of the puppy's head again. "Good boy. Good boy." She lifted him into her arms and stood up, glancing in Sergeant Boone's direction and feeling the color rise in her cheeks when she realized he was watching her intently. She didn't remember noticing the cleft in his chin before. She looked away quickly and handed Wilber to Katie.

"Will you come on our picnic, Sergeant Boone? Please?" Becky O'Malley was staring up at the sergeant, her gray eyes pleading.

Laina glanced sideways at Becky. If ever a girl had had a crush on a man, Becky O'Malley was mad for Sergeant Nathan Boone. She smiled to herself and reached for the picnic basket, but Sergeant Boone was offering his arm to her.

"I've been hornswoggled into guarding you ladies from wild beasts," he said.

Laina picked up the picnic basket and looped it over the sergeant's outstretched arm. "If you brought that piece of rope," she said to Katie, "We could work on teaching Wilber to walk on a lead." Katie held out the rope, and Laina quickly fashioned both leash and lead.

"You have bait in your pocket?" Laina asked.

Katie nodded and produced a small dark chunk of meat, which immediately got Wilber's attention.

"All right then," Laina said. She concentrated on Katie and Wilber so hard she barely noticed Sergeant Boone take the picnic basket off his arm. Or Becky O'Malley tuck her hand under the sergeant's elbow.

Laina joined everyone as they made their way out the door and around the side of the apartment to the back where Private Yates waited, hat in hand. At the sight of his sergeant, the private snapped to attention and saluted smartly.

"At ease, Private," Sergeant Boone said gruffly.

"Uh-um." Granny cleared her throat. "Didn't your mama teach you manners, Private?"

Blushing again, Yates offered Granny his arm. Laina walked beside Katie O'Malley, helping her teach Wilber not to fight being on a leash.

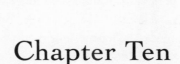

Chapter Ten

*A wise man will hear, and will increase learning;
and a man of understanding shall attain unto wise counsels.*

PROVERBS 1:5

"WELL, WHAT DID you expect, sonny?" Emmet Dorsey spat tobacco and swiped his mouth with the back of his hand. "Don't you appreciate the fine scenery out here on the plains?" He took off his hand and swept it through the air, outlining the high ridge in the distance.

With a glance in Sergeant Boone's direction, Jackson shot back, "Well, I sure didn't expect to be bored. I had enough of that standing behind the counter in that dry goods store in St. Louis."

Nathan walked up. "There's worse things than being bored, Private," he said.

"Got that right," Dorsey agreed. "When we made dinner out of the hindquarters of a starving mule back in '77, I would have welcomed a little boredom." He laughed. "Now I wonder what Frenchy would have done with *mule* on his menu."

Jackson said, "I was expecting to see some Indians by now. Not be assigned to some half-deserted army outpost where the biggest action is chasing after some rancher's cattle."

"Well, cheer up, sonny," Dorsey interrupted, slapping him on the back. "There's trouble down in Indian Territory. Dull Knife and Little Wolf been makin' noise about coming back up this way. Maybe you'll get some action after all. In the meantime, you better do what you can to make sure you don't end up getting shot at by Cheyenne who aim better than you. Now let 'er rip." He handed Jackson his rifle and stepped away.

Jackson winced as he settled the rifle butt against his shoulder. "Got some bruises yesterday," he said.

"That's what you get for trying so hard to impress those ladies out for their Sunday afternoon drive," Dorsey teased.

"Small price to pay for seeing the look on Miss Valentine's face when I hit that target dead center." Jackson winked at Nathan. "I just bet I'm first on her dance card at the next hop. She likes me. I can tell."

"Well, it isn't ladies' day at the firing range today, Private," Dorsey snapped. He stepped closer, pulled something out of his pocket, and nudged Jackson's arm. "Stick this inside your shirt. Extra cushion." He looked from side to side. "And don't be telling anybody I done this. I don't want the fellers thinkin' I've gone soft." He stepped back and exchanged a smile with Nathan.

Jackson stuck the sock he'd been given beneath his shirt. He raised the rifle to his shoulder.

"Settle it in there good," Dorsey admonished. "It's a Springfield. You're still gonna get recoil. You want that sharpshooter medal, you'll have to put up with a sore shoulder."

Squinting, Jackson took aim and squeezed the trigger. Seconds later he was lying flat on his back in a daze while the seasoned veterans in Company G were pounding Dorsey on the back and laughing.

Nathan did his best to suppress a smile as Jackson, all cockiness at least momentarily gone, staggered to his feet and cupped his hands over his ringing ears.

"Corporal Dorsey," Nathan scolded, "You know we use fifty-five-grain cartridges in the Springfield. It's the Long Tom's that get the seventy-grain shells. Did you switch 'em again?"

Dorsey shook his head and scratched his goatee. "Looks like I did, Sergeant. I must be gettin' old." He looked at Jackson. "What was that you called me, sonny? Old-timer? Guess you were right. I'm old and forgetful."

Shouting a stream of curses, Jackson plowed into Dorsey. Nathan heard a sick popping sound as the old soldier went down, howling with a mixture of pain and rage. Dorsey's hands went up instinctively as Jackson leaped on top of him and began pummeling his face. Nathan grabbed Jackson by his collar and jerked him off the corporal. While three recruits held the enraged private down, Nathan knelt beside the veteran.

"Let me up!" Dorsey yelled. "Let me at 'im!"

"Hold on, Corporal," Nathan said, checking Dorsey's knee.

Dorsey ignored Nathan and tried to get up. His face went white and he sank back to earth. "You idiot!" he screamed at Jackson. "You broke my leg!"

If Jackson had cursed back at the older man, Nathan would have felt better about what happened next. But Jackson's voice was calm and free of emotion when he said, "Be glad I didn't kill you, you washed-up old—"

"That's enough, Private," Nathan said, cutting him off. He looked at the three recruits standing around Jackson. "Professor. Frenchy. Escort Private Jackson to the guardhouse. Yates. Splint Corporal Dorsey's leg."

"S-Sir?" Yates stammered.

"You heard me. If it's broken he shouldn't be moved without stabilizing that leg."

"But . . . but, sir . . . what do I use for a splint?"

"Your imagination, Private," Nathan snapped. "You think you'll never be out in the field without a surgeon waiting to take care of the wounded? Figure out a way to splint the leg. I'm going for Doc Valentine and the ambulance."

"I don't need no ambulance!" Dorsey roared angrily, struggling to get up.

Nathan planted one foot on Dorsey's shoulder and gently forced the man back to the earth. He looked at Yates. "It'll take about half an hour to get back to camp and get an ambulance headed this way. If he tries to get up again, knock him out." He mounted Whiskey and set out for Camp Robinson. On the way, he passed the soldiers escorting Private Jackson to the guardhouse.

———

Later that evening, after filing reports and visiting Dorsey in the hospital—where he learned the corporal's knee was only badly twisted—Nathan sat in the doorway of the first sergeant's room at the barracks thinking over the incident. He'd been uneasy about Caleb Jackson since the day the man arrived in camp. It was more than just the name change. Plenty of men in the army were serving under assumed names. As long as they did their job and obeyed orders, no one begrudged a man a second chance at life, but as he thought back over the past weeks, Nathan realized Jackson's fight with Dorsey was only one symptom of more disturbing troubles lying just beneath a thin veneer of mostly good behavior.

Jackson had an obvious weakness for gambling. Nathan had watched him play at the canteen, and when he took a seat at a poker table, Jackson had a gleam in his eye as intense as a hunter about to kill a trophy antelope. The man relished emptying another soldier's pockets, and he had no mercy when it came to collecting debts. He'd even taken advantage of his bunky, Harlan Yates. Happily, Yates was refusing to play poker anymore.

Liquor was another problem. The post trader could sell it, but he had to keep a record of his customers and was only allowed to sell them three drinks a day, and those had to be at least an hour apart. Civilians were always trying to find a way to get contraband liquor onto the post. The summer before, one enterprising gardener had sold the men watermelons at a dollar apiece—ten times the usual price because the melons contained bottles of liquor. Just last week Nathan had discovered several barrels of contraband brew buried a few rods south of the cavalry stables. He couldn't prove Jackson was involved in the attempted smuggling, but he also couldn't explain Jackson's seemingly intimate friendship with the freighters who regularly passed through the area, nor the sudden increase in his available cash for the poker table.

And Jackson was too familiar with the ladies. It was more than just a soldier's good-natured teasing when in female company—more than the usual loneliness and desire for a companion. Jackson played with the ladies like he played poker, with veiled eyes and secretive smiles. Today's comment about Charlotte Valentine especially rankled Nathan. A gentleman didn't brag about a lady being interested in him that way. Not to a bunch of soldiers. It wasn't right to put a young innocent like Charlotte Valentine on display like that. Like she was a trophy to be won.

Nathan blamed himself for that incident. If he hadn't changed his usual Sunday ritual of visiting Lily's grave and then dining with the Valentine's, Charlotte wouldn't have been out driving. She never would have witnessed Jackson's impromptu showing off. And she would be less vulnerable to the soldier's attentions. But he'd gone on that picnic with Granny Max and set himself back at least two hours. By the time he got back from the cemetery the Valentines had already dined and were off on a Sunday drive. He'd been relieved. Now he felt guilty. Miss Charlotte Valentine had no idea what kind of attention she might be inviting by flirting with Caleb Jackson.

And then there was Jackson's temper. No one could begrudge a bored, lonely soldier throwing a punch or two out of frustration. Such fights were actually fairly commonplace at Camp Robinson. But things usually flashed up like a brush fire and were doused quickly with no hard feelings lingering to cause trouble. Jackson's murderous rage at being the butt of a relatively harmless joke was something else again.

The man seemed to be harboring a whole library full of hard feelings against the world in general and several of the men in Company G in particular. Today's attack on Corporal Dorsey was not going to set well with anyone. Nathan had seen it happen at least a dozen times. Raw recruits often quickly sized up the old man and relegated him to a category of "washed up and useless." Then they got to know him. They heard his stories. Saw his grit. Respect flickered and grew into an intense loyalty for the veteran that only a soldier could understand. One by one, recruits inevitably came to a place where they realized that when Corporal Emmet Dorsey played a practical joke on you, he was exercising his right to test you. And when you passed, and Dorsey pounded you on the back and said you were "all right, although a little wet behind the ears," you felt honored.

Nathan thought back to his own initiation into the regular army. It happened at the hands of an Emmet Dorsey twin, who had inked his belt buckle and impressed it into the skin on his thigh so that it looked exactly like a tattoo. When he displayed it and informed Nathan that he'd better report to the surgeon's office for company tattooing, Nathan obeyed orders.

The surgeon played his part in the prank perfectly. Nathan's bare posterior was hanging over a hospital cot ready to accept the "company tattoo" when the surgeon pulled back a curtain around the cubicle and Nathan was backside-to-face with half the company. Scrambling to pull up his pants, he had flushed with embarrassment, but he had the good sense to realize not one of the men laughing at him meant it as a personal attack. It was just a good joke. When he went to buckle his belt and recognized the source of the "company tattoo," Nathan didn't have to pretend to join the men in laughing. It *was* funny.

Thinking back to that event, Nathan puzzled over why Jackson wouldn't just accept his share of hazing in a good-natured way and let it be. If anyone had a right to tease the younger recruits, it was Emmet Dorsey. Jackson had spent enough evenings in barracks listening to the man's war stories to know that. No one could blame Emmet Dorsey for having a little harmless fun at the expense of the greenhorns. It was part of army life. Jackson should know that every recruit just had to accept his turn at being the butt of pranks with grace, knowing his turn would come to be on the other side of the joke—*if* he proved himself to his company and won his own place in the ranks. Either Jackson just didn't understand the unspoken rules of army camaraderie, or he was purposely ignoring them. Either way, the men didn't like him. That would be a problem the next time Company G engaged the enemy.

There was no arguing the point that life at Camp Robinson wasn't what recruits usually expected. With the departure of the natives to their reservations and the future of Camp Robinson uncertain, filling the long hours and days of routine probably had led to a little more practical joking than even Nathan would have liked. Still, if Jackson couldn't find a sense of humor, he was going to be a problem. He'd have to talk to him. But not until the private spent a couple of days cooling off in the guardhouse.

"Sergeant Boone?" Dinah approached from across the parade ground, trotting along with her hands raised to hold imaginary reins.

Nathan jumped up. "I'm late for dinner."

Dinah nodded.

Nathan looked down at his mud-encrusted boots. "You know what, Dinah, by the time I get cleaned up that roast your mother promised me is going to be cold. Maybe you'd better just give her my regrets."

"Papa wants to talk to you about something," Dinah said. "And Charlott-ah will be mad if you don't come. She's been primping all afternoon."

He grinned. "Is that right?"

Dinah nodded. She tilted her head and looked up at him. She sniffed. "You've been around the horses too long, Sergeant."

Nathan burst out laughing. "Duly noted, Miss Valentine."

Dinah turned to go. "Put on some of that fancy cologne you wear. Charlotte likes that."

"She does?"

"Oh, yeah," Dinah said, rolling her eyes. "She goes *on* and *on* about it. You should hear her—"

Nathan held up his hand. "I get the general idea, Miss Dinah. If you're sure they don't mind waiting—what does your papa want to talk to me about?"

Dinah shrugged. "I don't know. I just heard him promise Mama he would. They both got real quiet after I came into the room. So it must be important." Slapping her skirt with the flat of her hand, she shook her imaginary reins. "I hope you hurry up. I'm real hungry," she said, and trotted off.

———

After dinner Doctor Valentine invited Nathan to play chess while the ladies did dishes. The two men proceeded into the parlor, where the doctor's chessboard waited atop a small table in front of the window facing the parade ground. After a few moments wherein Nathan barely managed to stand off a checkmate, Dr. Valentine took a moment to pack and light his pipe. After a couple of satisfied puffs, he asked, "Happy with the new recruits?"

Nathan shrugged. "The usual complement of greenhorns, crooks, and star-struck do-gooders."

Valentine contemplated the chessboard. "I wanted to apologize for Emmy-Lou's prying questions at dinner tonight, Sergeant. I hope you can appreciate that it's just natural curiosity. All the ladies at Camp Robinson are anxious to make Miss Gray's acquaintance."

"Only natural. As you said," Nathan replied.

Moving his bishop, the doctor said, "Check." While Nathan studied the board, he continued, "That head trauma was one of the worst I've ever seen a person survive. Her physical recovery appears to be almost complete. I am, however, somewhat concerned about what appears to be a tendency to reclusiveness. She's been at Camp Robinson for almost two months now, and as far as I know she hasn't taken more than a few steps outside that apartment." He puffed on the pipe. "Do you know if that manifested itself before the incident? Or is it something new?"

Nathan didn't look up when he said, "She's getting better. She went on a picnic Sunday."

"Really? With whom?"

"Granny Max. The O'Malley girls. Private Yates." Nathan shrugged. "At the last minute I went along."

"Well, now. That's fine. How did she seem to you?"

"Nervous. On edge. But I don't think she's a recluse." He looked up at the doctor. "Granny thinks she's going to be all right."

The doctor puffed on his pipe. "If I were a betting man I'd put my money on God and Granny Max to bring Miss Gray around."

"I hope you're right," Nathan said earnestly. "She deserves a chance at some kind of life."

"A word to the wise, Sergeant Boone," the doctor said. "Do not let your men see this side of you."

Nathan grinned and held out his right hand for the doctor to see his skinned knuckles. "The only side of me most of them are likely to see in the near future is the one that barks orders and doesn't back down from a fight."

"Good," Valentine nodded. He picked up his rook and slid it along the board, murmuring as he did so, "A couple of those new men worry me."

"How so?" Nathan asked.

"McElroy is going to bolt," the doctor said.

Nathan agreed. "And likely take O'Brien with him when he does. They're far too interested in the subject of Black Hills gold. First time we're on patrol they'll probably hightail it for Deadwood. Or at least try. I'll be watching." He leaned back and stretched his long legs out before him. "Who else concerns you?"

"Jackson."

"He's in the guardhouse for what he did to Dorsey today."

The doctor puffed on his pipe thoughtfully, "That young man is disturbed."

Nathan forced a laugh. "Doesn't a man have to be disturbed to volunteer for the United States Army?"

Valentine pulled his pipe out of his mouth and lifted it as if toasting his guest. "*Touché*, Sergeant. Unfortunately I suspect there's more to Jackson's problems than just that."

"What makes you say that?"

"Instinct. Something in his eyes." He shook his head. "I hope I'm wrong." The doctor puffed on his pipe. "My family took a little drive on Sunday. Watched the men at target practice."

"I'm sorry about Sunday, sir. I've been ignoring Granny's urgings to socialize for so long, that when she invited me on her picnic, I felt obligated."

The doctor gestured, "I wasn't fishing for an apology, Sergeant. There was never a formal invitation issued, and if you find other distractions you are certainly at liberty to enjoy them." He cleared his throat. "That wasn't the purpose for my bringing this up at all. As I said, we watched some of the men at target practice Sunday afternoon." He drew on his pipe before continuing. "I don't mind telling you I don't like the way Private Jackson looks at my daughter." He gazed evenly at Nathan. "Nor should you."

Nathan shifted in his chair. "If any of my men are guilty of ungentlemanly conduct—"

"Private Jackson never crossed the line of propriety. But he does like to dance along its edge. I've known men like that before. I've just never had one select my daughter as an audience."

"I'll speak to him."

"Oh, I don't think that's necessary," the doctor said. "That's not my point. And besides, Charlotte encourages a certain amount of harmless flirtation. She is no different than any other young woman her age, Sergeant. And being one of the few ladies at a military camp does result in a great deal of attention." He sighed. "I'm afraid it's gone to her head a little." The doctor puffed on his pipe while he peered at Nathan. "Of course, Charlotte also has serious intentions of becoming an officer's wife some day."

Suddenly uncomfortable, Nathan dropped his gaze and began to study the chessboard with new intensity.

Dr. Valentine cleared his throat. "When soldiers behave in a way that makes me suspect they might be contemplating desertion, it is my duty to call that to their commanding officer's attention. I consider I've done that this evening by telling you I suspect McElroy and O'Brien.

"When a man like Jackson shows signs of instability, it is my duty to be concerned. I have expressed that concern. And I've also let you know that Jackson is of special interest to me because I have a daughter who may be vulnerable to his attentions—which I am not convinced are strictly honorable. And that leads me to you, Sergeant Boone."

"Sir?" Nathan frowned. He sat up so quickly he bumped the table and sent several chess pieces tumbling to the floor.

The doctor sighed. He bent his head and with index finger and thumb, pressed the narrow bridge of his nose where his glasses usually perched. "You would have to be blind, Sergeant Boone, not to have noticed that my daughter thinks she is in love with you."

Nathan stared at him, dumbfounded. He frowned. "Sir, I can assure you, I haven't meant to in any way—"

"Oh, calm down, Sergeant. I'm merely trying to ascertain as a father whether it's an unrequited crush or a possibility. I'd like to know what I'm dealing with."

Nathan bent down to pick up the chess pieces. One by one, he set them on the board. "Charlotte is a lovely young woman, Doctor Valentine."

"I'm not asking for an independent review of Charlotte's assets, Sergeant. Are you or are you not interested in courting my daughter?"

Nathan ran his hand along the edge of the chessboard. He moistened his lips. "Sir, I'm not interested in courting anyone." He looked at Doctor Valentine. "And I don't honestly think I ever will have such an interest."

"I see," the doctor said. He looked up at Nathan. For a moment, he held his gaze. "Thank you for your honesty, Sergeant Boone. Now, may I be just as honest with you?"

"Of course, sir."

"For a while, after we lose someone we love, our first thought in the morning is of them. That thought is quickly followed by the pain of their absence. But time passes, and in the normal way of healing, there comes a morning when, perhaps, just for a second, we do not think of our loss. Or if we do, it is a happy memory. In a healthy person, these seconds multiply, until one day we realize that when we think of our loved one, there is more joy than pain. This is as it should be, Sergeant Boone." He paused before saying, "I don't know why, but you seem determined to prevent this from happening in your own life."

Nathan sat forward in his chair. "With all due respect, Dr. Valentine," he said stiffly. "This is not really any of your business."

"Everything that affects the ability of the men of Camp Robinson to perform their duty is my business, Sergeant Boone."

Nathan stood up. "I strenuously object, sir, to your intimation that I am somehow not doing my duty." He bowed. "And if you'll excuse me, sir, that duty requires me to leave now."

"Sit back down, Sergeant." The doctor waved Nathan back to his seat. "We've plenty of time before the day's final assembly. And we *are* going to have this conversation. Whether it takes place here or over at the captain's office is up to you."

"The captain has no interest in my private life, sir."

"Well, now. That's where you are wrong, son. Because the captain needs to know when a sergeant's men are beginning to have questions about a man's leadership because of behavior they consider unusual."

Nathan sat down, his mind racing as he wondered where this nonsense originated. *Dorsey.* Locked away in the hospital with nothing better to do than imagine problems. He had never thought Dorsey was the type to be given to gossip.

"It does not escape notice when you spend several hours a week in the cemetery, Sergeant Boone. And it does not escape notice that things over on the Row remain exactly as they were the day Mrs. Boone died two years ago. That you are maintaining something of a shrine has been mentioned." The doctor looked at Nathan. "Or are the rumors mistaken?"

"Corporal Dorsey is the only man at Camp Robinson who could have let you know about these things, Doc. I've served with him long enough to appreciate that he probably thinks he's acting in my best interest to bring this up to you. But—"

Dr. Valentine interrupted him. "What you are doing, Sergeant—or not doing, as the case may be—guarantees that every single morning of your life you pick at the wound of your wife's death and prevent it from healing. As your physician, I can tell you this is unhealthy behavior. It is unhealthy emotionally for you, and it may be ultimately unhealthy for your men, who deserve better. They are within their rights to wonder if their sergeant may unnecessarily put their lives at risk at some critical moment in a battle because he does not value his own life."

"That's absurd," Nathan said. "Ridiculous. If anything, I'm more motivated to protect my men because I don't want anyone else to ever feel like I do. And what can you or Dorsey possibly know about it, anyway. Especially you, the good doctor with his wife and two daughters in the next room."

The doctor stared across the chessboard at Nathan. His glare softened.

He nodded. "That's a fair question. It deserves an answer." He got up. "Shall we take a walk, Sergeant Boone."

They headed outside, slowly making their way down the picket fence toward the hospital. "Emmy-Lou is not the wife of my youth, Nathan. Nor is Charlotte my firstborn. My first wife died in childbirth. It was a boy. I named him Avery. We would have called him Junior, of course."

Nathan's anger abated. "I didn't know that, sir. I'm sorry. Truly, I am."

Dr. Valentine shrugged. "I never speak of it. It is part of a past that seems to upset Mrs. Valentine for reasons I won't go into. But when I speak of managing a great loss, Sergeant Boone, I speak from experience." He cleared his throat. "Just because our great love dies, does not mean we cannot go on to have a happy life. Some men were just not meant to live alone, Nathan. And friendship is as good a basis for marriage as passion. Friendship is a comforting thing long after passions burn out. I've over-stepped the privilege of my rank this evening, Sergeant Boone. But I don't apologize for it. It pains me to see you using the past as an excuse to stop living. I have been where you are. And I don't recommend any man remain in hell when he has a chance to climb out."

"It was my fault," Nathan choked out. "It would be different if she'd died of cholera. Or in childbirth. Or something else I couldn't control."

"You can control the rattlesnakes of Pine Ridge?"

"We'd had an argument. I could have controlled my temper. And she would never have been out there alone."

The doctor sighed. "What's done is done, Sergeant. There is no profit in lingering over our mistakes. We must accept God's forgiveness, forgive ourselves, and move on. That's all we can do."

"Just like that," Nathan said. He let the bitterness sound in his voice.

"Of course not 'just like that'. But you've had two years to absorb the shock."

"Where is it written that after two years a man should be done with grieving?" Nathan said.

"My dear boy, you'll never be done with grieving. You just learn to contain it. I guess what I'm trying to do is encourage you to start the process of containment so your personal pain doesn't overflow into your daily routine to the point it destroys you."

Doctor Valentine looked toward the opposite end of Officer's Row. "Mrs. Valentine has just come out on the front porch. I've got to get back home."

He put his hand on Nathan's shoulder. "Look, Nathan. Whether you are serious about my daughter or not isn't my greatest concern. It merely provided the excuse for me to start this conversation. I've been watching you, and I've been concerned for a long time. You should be grateful for Corporal Dorsey. If he hadn't landed in my hospital and brought up his concerns for you, I may never have acted on my own. He's a good friend. You can't control what happened in the past. But you can keep it from ruining your future. I have been down that road and it is not a place you want to travel for long. I trust you'll consider what I've said and take appropriate action." He took a step away, then stopped short. "One more thing, Sergeant," the doctor said.

"Sir?"

"I would appreciate it very much if you would decline the next invitation to dinner with my family."

"Sir?"

"And should you attend Friday evening's dance, perhaps you'll neglect to dance with Charlotte. She's clearly misinterpreted your attentions for something a great deal more serious than they are."

"Yes, sir. I understand, sir."

"Thank you. God bless you, son." He headed back up the Row where his wife was waiting.

Crossing the parade ground in the dark, Nathan paused and looked up at the sky. *"God bless you." It always comes back to Him.* The moon was rising, looking twice its usual size behind a shroud of feathery clouds. Just the kind of night Lily would have loved. She would have whispered in his ear and led him outside. They would have walked arm in arm down to the creek, where the water would look silver in the moonlight. He would have swept her up in his arms and kissed her. Memories flooded in, sweet and so savagely painful they brought tears to his eyes.

———

"Well?" Emmy-Lou Valentine spoke as soon as her husband was within earshot. "What did he say about Miss Gray?"

"About Miss Gray?" The doctor stepped up on the front porch.

"Yes. Miss Gray!" Emmy-Lou sounded annoyed. She waved her hand in the air. "Come inside. I declare the mosquitoes in this place are as big as horseflies." Once they were in the parlor, she sat down in the green brocade chair recently vacated by Sergeant Boone. "I asked you to ask Sergeant Boone about Miss Gray. What did he say? Could you tell? Is he . . . does he find her attractive? Charlotte is practically in tears. He scarcely looked at her the entire evening."

Avery sighed inwardly. He knew that tone. Emmy-Lou had latched on to something, and she would hold on until she had shaken a reaction out of him. If he resisted, she would make his life miserable. Feeling not unlike a master trying to get his bulldog to let go of his favorite shoe, Avery packed his pipe with fresh tobacco. He moved deliberately, first lighting the pipe and taking a puff before sitting down, leaning his head back and looking up at the ceiling. "I was thinking, Emmy-Lou. Maybe the quartermaster *could* order that drapery fabric you've been hankering after."

"Avery Valentine," Emmy-Lou glowered at him. "I will not be treated like those hounds of yours. You can't distract me by tossing me scraps."

The doctor drew on his pipe. He smiled at his wife. "According to Sergeant Boone, Miss Gray is shy. She is recovering. And Sergeant Boone really didn't seem too interested in talking about her."

"Well, you talked about *something* half the night," Emmy-Lou wheedled. "I had coffee ready but you never called. The girls finally went to bed. And then I saw you'd gone outside, which I assume was so you couldn't be overheard."

Doctor Valentine was silent.

"You really aren't going to tell me anything, are you?"

"My dear, I have already told you everything I know about Miss Gray. She is recovering from a grave wound. She is able to be up and about, but she is weak with very little energy and certainly not enough energy to accept any callers. Sergeant Boone seems to agree."

"What do you mean he agrees? What exactly is his interest in Miss Gray? That's what I wanted you to find out!"

Inwardly scolding himself for taking pleasure in annoying his annoying wife, Valentine said, "He went on a picnic with her this past Sunday."

"He . . . he . . . *what*?!"

"He went on a picnic with Granny Max and the O'Malley girls and Sergeant Yates. And Miss Gray. Obviously Miss Gray is beginning to gain some strength. She'll probably attend a hop one of these Fridays before long, and then you and all the other ladies can form your own opinions of the elusive Miss Laina Gray."

"What about Charlotte? Did he say anything about Charlotte?"

"Yes. That she is lovely. And that he has no desire to court anyone and does not expect to ever have such a desire." He looked at his wife.

"A handsome young man like him? That's ridiculous. It isn't healthy. I hope you told him so. Charlotte's beside herself," Emmy-Lou fussed.

Why does she have to see everything that happens at Camp Robinson only as it relates to our family? To Charlotte? Can't she be concerned for Miss Gray and Sergeant Boone for their own sakes? The doctor's voice was tinged with impatience when he next spoke. "No, it isn't particularly healthy, Emmy-Lou. But then there isn't anything healthy about death and dying. We all have to manage it our own way. Sergeant Boone has chosen his method." He paused and nibbled on his moustache, a gesture intended to send the message to his wife that what he was about to say was worthy of note and would not be subject to wifely influence. "Just because you may not approve of Sergeant Boone's way of handling grief does not mean it is faulty. Nor does it mean it has to change."

The doctor's words surprised even the doctor. He didn't even agree with what he was saying. He had, in fact, just challenged Sergeant Boone with exactly the opposite advice. He most definitely did think Sergeant Boone needed to make some changes. But in the face of Emmy-Lou's self-serving "concern," Doctor Valentine felt compelled to put a wall of defense up around the wounded soldier. "Give the man some peace, Emmy-Lou. In fact, I think it would be very wise if you would *not* invite him to dinner again for a while."

"Avery! How can you suggest such a thing? How can you be so blind to your own daughter's charms?"

He felt his temper rising. "It's got nothing to do with being blind to Charlotte's charms, Mrs. Doctor, which, I agree, are many. But they are wasted on Sergeant Boone, and the sooner you and Charlotte realize that, the sooner I will have peace in my house!"

"It is obvious that you are hiding something from me." Emmy-Lou straightened her shoulders and lifted her chin. "You and the sergeant spoke for a long time. It had to be more than just 'Miss Gray is healing nicely'. I demand to know what else he said about my daughter."

The doctor groaned audibly. "You may not be able to comprehend this, Emmy-Lou, but everything at Camp Robinson does not have direct bearing on Charlotte. To be quite honest, Sergeant Boone and I really didn't discuss Charlotte at length. We talked about him. I offered some unwanted advice, and he was gracious enough not to deck me for giving it."

"If not about Charlotte or Miss Gray, what on earth did you advise him about?"

"About life, Emmy-Lou. About grieving loss."

Emmy-Lou pressed her lips together in disgust. Her nostrils flared. She inhaled sharply. Her tone was accusing. "You *told* him!"

"Yes. I told him." The doctor studied the chessboard. "And I pray to God it helps him."

"I thought we agreed. It won't help Charlotte's chances if people know—"

"If people know what, Emmy-Lou? Why would anybody care one bit to know that my first wife was a cook's daughter? What difference does it make? It doesn't have anything at all to do with Charlotte."

"Well, maybe it doesn't make a difference to *your* people, Avery, but it certainly gave my *father* pause to think someone of your position in society would stoop to—"

Doctor Valentine jumped up. Red-faced, he barely kept himself from shouting. "Oh, for goodness' sake, Emmy-Lou. Stop it. This isn't even about Charlotte anymore. It's degenerated into another battle for control of this marriage. You wanted me to pump Sergeant Boone for information about Miss Gray. I didn't. You don't want me to share my past with people. I did. You wanted me to dangle my daughter beneath Sergeant Boone's nose like I bait the dogs. I didn't."

"Avery," Emmy-Lou sniffed, "there's no need to be crude."

Valentine nodded. "You are right. There isn't." Grabbing his hat, he headed for the front door. Before going back outside he turned around. "Why don't you just take Charlotte East to your mother's for a few weeks, Emmy-Lou. Troll for a husband at the lake house. Give Sergeant Boone a rest. Give us all a rest."

Chapter Eleven

He that is slow to anger is better than the mighty;
And he that ruleth his spirit than he that taketh a city.

PROVERBS 16:32

THE MORNING AFTER Private Jackson put Corporal Dorsey in the hospital, Nathan ordered him to march double time around the perimeter of the parade ground shouldering a log. After lunch, he had the recruit put the log down and wait for him at the stables. While Jackson waited, Boone saddled Whiskey. He filled two canteens with water and then ordered Jackson to shoulder his forty-pound saddle and field equipment and head south, while he followed at a distance, leading Jackson's horse and watching the soldier's shirt grow dark with sweat.

When the private finally stumbled and fell to the earth, Nathan rode up to him and offered him a drink. Neither man spoke as Jackson sucked in half a canteen of water, then gathered up his equipment and headed off again.

"A little to the east, Private," Nathan corrected him. "There's a spring just over that hill. That's where we're headed."

Jackson gritted his teeth and regained the double-time pace. Watching him, Nathan couldn't help but admire the determination on the man's face. He would make it to the spring or die trying. Nathan offered to let him slow to regular marching pace, but Jackson ignored him and kept going.

When they finally arrived at the spring, Jackson didn't wait for permission before he threw down his saddle and dipped his entire head in the bubbling cold water, far enough to soak his collar and the front of his shirt. Nathan rode a short distance downstream and dismounted to water the horses. Hobbling both horses and turning them out to graze, he walked back and sat down on the boulder overshadowing the spring while Jackson sopped a kerchief in cool water and tied it around his neck.

"Didn't think you'd have a Sandhills version of the bull ring," Caleb said, panting.

"Bull ring?"

"Big corral at Jefferson Barracks. When we were ornery they had us run around it double time carrying logs." He gave a wry laugh. "How far do you suppose it is from the stables to here?" He nodded toward where Camp Robinson sat inside its fence of cordwood, far enough away the men going about their various duties were little more than insects crawling around a model made of wood building blocks.

"Only a couple of miles," Nathan said.

Caleb bent and picked up the saddle. "Where to now?"

One thing a man had to admire about Private Jackson, Nathan thought. He never shirked hard work. Even in the form of punishment. At times he seemed to enjoy it.

"I brought you out here so we could talk without all the 'sirs' and salutes," Nathan said. He settled his back against the boulder in the shade of a small pine tree growing in a cleft of the rock. "So have a seat."

Jackson took another drink from his canteen, then poured a stream of water over his head. He sputtered and shook his head like a wet dog before walking over and, using a boulder as a seat, positioning himself opposite Nathan.

"Doc Valentine says Dorsey's going to be all right," Nathan began. "So as far as I'm concerned, you've served your sentence with the march out here—as long as we can get some things straight between us." He leaned forward. "You've got to get control of your temper, Caleb," Nathan said. "I don't want to have to be part of court-martial proceedings against a friend. But if you keep getting yourself into scrapes, I'm not going to have much choice."

"I know it," Jackson said abruptly. He shrugged. "I've got a short fuse."

"You didn't have a short fuse when we first met," Nathan said. He drew his legs up and leaned forward, resting his elbows on his knees. "Whatever it is that's wound tight inside you, you got to learn to hold it together."

Caleb shot back, "I'm not the only one in Company G with something wound tight inside him."

"That may be," Nathan said, "but the things inside me aren't going to get me court-martialed." He leaned back. "Some of the men already think I'm too soft on you. Think you should have been hazed out a couple of weeks ago after the incident at Gruber's."

"Over *that*?" Jackson snorted. "That wasn't anything."

"'Tell Gruber that. You nearly destroyed his store with that stunt. And you could have broken a perfectly good horse's leg.'"

"I knew that mare could clear the billiard table or I'd have never ridden her in there in the first place."

Nathan laughed in spite of himself. "All right, Beau—"

"Call me Caleb."

"Right," Nathan said. "Caleb. The thing is, this deal with Dorsey isn't just your everyday troublemaking. You could have ended the man's career. Emmet Dorsey has given his heart and soul and body to the United States Army. All he's got to look forward to is a pension, and if any man deserves it, he does. I won't have you ruining a good man just because you can't control your temper."

"Then drum me out," Caleb snapped. "Quit being such a good Christian and be done with it."

Nathan took his hat off and slapped it against his knee. He swore mildly. "I'm not trying to be any kind of Christian. I am trying to be your friend." He paused, then said, "If you don't make it in the army, what's next? You say you hated working in that store. Your family's gone. So what's next for you? Panning for gold?"

The recruit snorted. "There's nothing up in Black Hills for me. I'd head south. That rancher—Bronson, is it?—he could probably use a man who's good with horses."

Nathan agreed. "Until you picked a fight with his best cowhand and broke his leg."

"Dorsey's leg isn't broken." Caleb shrugged. "But I get your point."

"What is it with you, anyway? You can take the orneriest nag in the herd and sweet-talk her until she performs like some harmless circus horse. I've seen you get kicked and bit so many times I've lost count. But not once have I ever seen you lose your temper with a horse. But let a man dare say something that riles you, and you dive in with both fists."

"Horses don't mean any harm. If you watch 'em and get to know 'em, you understand. They are just being horses."

"Well, Corporal Dorsey didn't mean any real harm, either. He was just acting like the old buzzard he is and giving a greenhorn a proper welcome into the army. It happens with every new recruit," Nathan said. He told Caleb about his own experience with company tattoos.

Jackson would not be convinced. "You may put up with that kind of thing, but I won't be made the laughingstock of Company G. I can outshoot and outride every one of 'em, and they'll remember that or they'll pay."

"You're going to kill somebody someday if you don't get control of that temper of yours," Nathan snapped. "And then it won't matter what the men remember. And it won't matter if we were friends or not. I'll have to do my duty. And that means court-martial and time at Leavenworth. Maybe even hanging." Nathan stared off into the distance. "What's eating you up inside, anyway?"

Jackson snorted and jerked the kerchief off his neck. He bent to dip it in the spring again and wiped his face. "You want me to tell you my troubles so you can fix it all up?"

Nathan's voice showed the frustration he felt as he said, "I want you to convince me there's hope of making a soldier out of you." He paused. "Look, Caleb. Since the day I picked up that snare drum and walked into battle with my Uncle Billy's regiment, I've known this is the life for me. I've never wanted anything else." His voice wavered, and he tugged on his hat brim. "Even when I knew in my gut Lily wasn't cut out for the army, I still didn't give it up. When she—" He swallowed. "After she was gone, I didn't have anywhere else to turn but to the army. Reveille to tattoo, I live by the bugle, and I expect I'll die by it. The fact is, I'm married to the army now. And there's worse things than that. If you came into the army looking to put some kind of order and discipline in your life, the army can do that. But it won't cure any of the demons you're running from."

Caleb's blue eyes narrowed. He stared at his friend. "You know that from experience, do you?"

"Everybody's got demons," Nathan said. "Soon as you learn that, you'll be a long way toward managing yours." He paused. "You spend enough time around company campfires, and you'll learn you're not even close to being the only man in the army who's spent a night walking a battlefield looking for his brother's head so he could write home and tell his mama he buried her son proper. Some of these old-timers out here have stories that'll curdle even your blood. And that's the truth."

Caleb peered off into the distance as he spoke. "You went home from the war to your little cabin in the Missouri hills and saw your mama and family. And then you headed off to Nashville and fell in love and your uncle got you into officer's school."

"That's right," Nathan said, his voice bitter. "I've had a perfect life. Who am I to tell you to get over your troubles?"

"That's not what I mean. I know you've got troubles. I know you don't want anything to do with the fair Charlotte Valentine and that old hen of a mother's plans to get you two hitched. You're tied to Lily as strong as the day she died. It's eating you up inside trying to live without her, but you're doing it. And you are likely bound for a commission and a command. For all I know, I'll be calling you General someday. You've got what it takes."

Caleb took his hat off and, rolling the brim while he talked, continued. "But, Nathan, I didn't have an Uncle Billy. I never met a Lily Bainbridge. And there wasn't any officer's school taking in Confederate drummer boys. I went home to a burned-out plantation, courtesy of the United States government. When I looked at the ruination of everything my pa had worked for all his life, it lit something inside of me. You want to know what's wound up inside me so tight? It's the memory of coming over the hill at home and seeing nothing but charred ruins where the stable once stood. It's finding my mother and father's graves in the family burial ground and seeing they'd been dug into by somebody looking for gold." He paused and wet his lips. When he turned to look at Nathan, Caleb's eyes were red with unspilled tears. He stood up and began to pace.

"I finally figured out that if Beauregard Preston was going to have any kind of life at all, it was going to be up to him to make it. There wasn't anything left for me but ashes and desecrated graves in Mecklenburg County. Most of my friends were dead.

"So I talked Abel Griffin from the next place over into leaving with me. We worked our way to St. Louis, and along the way I learned to talk like you Yankees. By the time I started work at that dry-goods store in St. Louis, you wouldn't have known me for a Rebel unless I wanted you to know." He paused. "So I thought that was it. I was doing good work, and I figured if I just kept at it, someday I'd own my own store and make something of myself." He shook his head. "And then I discovered the riverboats and gambling." He put his hat back on. "I liked the feeling I got sitting at a poker table holding a good hand. It was the first time in my life I felt like I had control over something. Before I knew it, I was playing regular. And winning some."

He laughed. "And then I discovered the ladies. Have you ever seen the women on some of those riverboats? They are something to behold. And they don't play games with a man, either. Those highfalutin daughters of Mr. Cruikshank's customers would flirt and fawn and then act shocked if I took them up on what they were offering. I got to hating them.

"The girls on the river aren't like that. They flirt and fawn and then they make good on what they been promising. There was one called herself Riverboat Annie. She was something else. Better than all the others. Had fine manners and a voice like an angel. In some ways, she didn't seem like she really belonged. Kind of . . . innocent. You know?"

"None of those women are innocent," Nathan said.

"Yeah, well, even if she was sort of innocent when I knew her, I don't expect it lasted, because she disappeared not long after I got to know her. Went off to some rich party. Private entertainment. Never heard of again."

He swiped a hand over his eyes and sat back down. "Somebody told me her papa started off as a big-time gambler. But after she left, he started going downhill. And the last I heard, he was a bum begging for low stakes games across the river." Caleb shrugged. "That's what got me to thinking maybe I ought to change my ways. A girl just drops off the face of the earth and nobody knows—or cares—what happened. And her pa goes from being a high roller to a bum. Just like that.

"About that time Mr. Cruikshank's daughter was making eyes at me. And more. I thought maybe things were looking up. Until Cruikshank points his rifle at me and tells me how I'll be marrying sweet Mavis come Saturday." He shuddered. "I felt like I was drowning."

"And that's when you headed for Jefferson Barracks."

Caleb nodded. "You know it." His voice lowered. He cleared his throat. "But it was more than just Cruikshank's threats that gave me that feeling I was drowning. I'd started having too many mornings with a hangover and no memory of what happened the night before. When I really made myself think about it, I knew I wasn't the one in control at those poker tables. The gambling and the drinking and the women were beginning to own me—not the other way around.

"But what finally got my attention was that after Mr. Cruikshank lowered his rifle and sent me back to my room to 'think about what I had done,' I thought about how easy it would be to kill him and make it look like an accident. That rifle of his was from the war. He never cleaned it. Who would know the difference if it misfired?"

Caleb shuddered again. He swiped his hand across his eyes. "When I realized I was thinking about doing murder, my blood ran cold. And I had to face something about myself I'd kept inside for a long time. Something that started the night you and I met on that battlefield." He finally looked directly at Nathan. "There's something inside me. Something dark. Something that really could kill a man." He started pacing again. "The army has kept that part of me under control. I hate the bugles and getting up before dawn. I hate it. And I love it all at the same time. I know I drink too much. And I gamble. But there's the guardhouse to keep it under control." He added, "And there's no riverboat women. These ladies here, they expect a man to treat them with respect. And they give respect right back. I know I got a little too familiar with Miss Valentine a couple of times. But I didn't mean anything by it."

He stopped pacing, stopped fiddling with his hat. "You can't drum me out, Nathan. This is all I've got now. I know I've got a temper. I know I've got to control it. And I'll do it. I need the army. I need it."

Slowly, Nathan stood up. He dusted his backside off and went to get the horses. When he came back to where Caleb was waiting, he said, "You say you need discipline. I guess you know by now the army can give you that. What you don't seem to know yet is that these men will be your family and your home if you get them to respect you, and then it won't matter if Company G ends up riding to hell and back in the next few years, you'll have friends who'll risk their lives for you. But you've got to earn their respect and their trust. They all know you can outride and outshoot them. The question you've got to answer for them is, will you ride and shoot for *them*? Will you do it when your own life is at risk?

"Lighting in to one of the best soldiers this army ever had just because he plays a little joke on you is not the way to convince these men you want to be part of their family. But I think you already know that." Nathan pulled his hat on and tugged the brim down. "It's up to you, Caleb. You can either put the past in the past and get control of your demons, or you can let them rip you apart and destroy you. I can't help you with that. What I can do is give you a fresh start with Company G." He handed Caleb the reins to his horse. "So that's what you've got. But if you start any more fights, I won't be able to save your hide. In fact, I won't even try. Are we straight on that?"

"We're straight," Caleb said.

"All right, then. Let's get back to camp."

Caleb saddled up and the two men mounted their horses. As they rode along, Caleb said, "All due respect, sir, I did have one thing to say. If we're still talking as friends. Without the 'sergeants' and 'sirs', as you put it."

Nathan nodded. "Say it."

"You said every man has his demons. The thing is how we deal with 'em. I raise hell against mine. Or *with* 'em on occasion. But at least I recognize mine and take them on. You're right that I let my feelings drive me too much. But at least I still *feel* 'em. I think my way might turn out better than yours."

"What do you mean, better than mine?" Nathan asked.

"Your way seems to be *not* feeling. Or pretending you don't. Miss Valentine falls all over herself to get your attention. But you mostly look right through her. I noticed that right away, and at first I couldn't understand it. Until I realized that you mostly look right through everybody, Nathan. You said we've all got our demons. I'm trying to get a handle on mine. And with a little help from the army, I think I just might do it. But what about you? Are you trying to get a handle on yours? Or are you just ignoring them and waiting for them to leave you alone? Because if that's what you're doing, Nathan my friend, you can take it from me—they don't leave you alone. They take control. I just told you how they did that to me, one shot glass at a time, one hand of poker at a time, one Riverboat Annie at a time. Until I had to do something to stop 'em."

He pulled his hat down farther over his eyes and sat back in his saddle. "What about you, Nathan? What are you doing to get the demons off *your* back? You're tending the shrine over on the Row, coming out to bugles, doing what they say. You're getting through the day. But you aren't alive. Not really. I know about your little rituals. I see you go across the river every Sunday. You don't just take flowers over to Lily's grave, Nathan. You practically spend the afternoon over there. You see what I am trying to say?"

"I see it's time we got back to Camp Robinson, Private Jackson," Nathan said. He spurred Whiskey and took off toward camp.

Chapter Twelve

A foolish woman is clamorous:
she is simple, and knoweth nothing.
PROVERBS 9:13

Camp Robinson, Nebraska
June 16, 1878
Dearest Mama,

Life for the ladies of Camp Robinson in the year of our Lord 1878 is not at all what you are imagining. While it is true that when Avery first brought us here, things were undeveloped, all has changed a great deal in the past two years. The men have been busy building, and now there is a neat row of adobe officers' quarters on the north side of the parade ground. We have ample room in our little apartment. There is a wide hall down the center of the building, and opposite us is an apartment identical to ours. That apartment is empty now, and so the girls have their own rooms—something I am certain you did not envision when you wrote your last letter.

We have a chicken coop and a cow, and last summer we raised a great amount of vegetables in the garden. Avery has seen to it that we usually have a striker staying in the lean-to at the back beside the kitchen. A striker, dearest Mama, is a soldier who is assigned to help the officers and their families with domestic duties. Most of the men are rough and uneducated, and we have not had a striker for a few weeks, but Avery has introduced us to a new private who hails from France. He is apparently an excellent cook, and I am determined to have him become a permanent part of our household before the captain's wife learns of him.

We have developed a lovely relationship with the sergeant of Company G (cavalry), who will be accompanying our family on a Sabbath day drive. I intend to use all my womanly charms to convince him to give me Frenchy. Just think, Mama, your two granddaughters might learn French right here in the wilds of Nebraska. You need not fret that I am raising ignorant country bumpkins.

The ladies of Camp Robinson maintain all social decorum. In the mornings we make calls on one another. Many hours each day must be relegated to sewing, but that is no different than if we were living with you. Since she finished her linen sampler, Charlotte has begun piecing a patchwork quilt. The scarf you sent us from the Centennial celebration in Philadelphia will be at the center, with tiny squares all around.

Dinah is working on her sampler now, although it is more of a struggle for her, as she is much more prone to want to spend time in the cavalry stables with the animals than in my parlor stitching.

All of the ladies are encouraged to participate in target practice twice weekly. This is perhaps the only part of our week that is much different than yours, Mama. We must be able to defend ourselves—although against what I cannot imagine, as all the Indians have been shipped to their respective reservations, and things here at camp are almost boring. You really must stop believing every news article you read about depradations and danger, Mama. Crazy Horse is dead and with him went the hopes of the Sioux nation. It is perhaps a tragedy, but it was an inevitable one, and now one hopes the natives will adopt a more progressive view and realize that only in giving up their wild ways can they expect to survive into the next century.

In addition to target practice, we ride or take a drive every day, always escorted by one or two soldiers. Avery tells me that one of the new cavalry recruits is an accomplished horseman. Riding lessons for the ladies of Camp Robinson may be in our future.

In the evenings we often play euchre or chess, and on Friday nights the enlisted men usually hold a hop (that's a dance, Mama) that everyone enjoys. On these evenings, social divisions are set aside for the good of all. Even the laundresses and the enlisted men's wives attend, and you would not know there was any difference between us. We ladies are always quick to compliment our dear friends' attempts at finery, and no one cares whether a lady is dressed in silk or gingham. All dance as many dances as possible. Even the old servant of one of the officers finds many dance partners. She is fondly loved by all, and if you could meet dear Granny Max, you would agree that she is as fine an example of her race as ever lived.

Granny has taken in a poor woman recently rescued from abject squalor and conditions too horrible to describe, and according to Avery, her tender care literally rescued the poor creature from the brink of insanity. All the ladies of Camp Robinson are anticipating the opportunity to meet this new resident and assure her of our sincere good wishes. If anything can be said about military ladies, it is that we support one another.

I intend to encourage Avery that perhaps this poor woman would benefit from a position in our household. Certainly I could use help with the housekeeping. The constant wind has a way of dusting furniture and flora with successive layers of grit and grime. It is a challenge to keep a proper home in the West.

From your letter, it seems you think that we are in the wilds, with our lives hanging by a thread. Nothing could be further from the truth. In fact, I must hasten to close this epistle as Charlotte is calling for me to come and join her and her young Sergeant Boone for a Sunday drive.

Sergeant Boone is the subject for another letter, but rest assured that he is one of whom you would approve. His dear wife passed on just before we arrived on the frontier. His recovery from the loss has been quite slow, but we are heartened to see the flicker of life begin to return to his handsome face. He seems to have taken to Charlotte, and nothing would please Avery and me more than to see our eldest make such a fine match.

Your invitation to spend the summer with you at the lake house is tempting, Mama. I have discussed it with Avery, and in his unselfish way he has said I must do what is best for the girls. At the moment, I do not think it advisable for us to leave. Should you want to experience the West for yourself, we would be overjoyed to welcome you to Camp Robinson, where the night air carries the song of coyotes and the star-filled sky is unobscured by the light of gas street lamps.

Your affectionate daughter,

Emmy-Lou

"Come *on*, Mother!" Charlotte pleaded from the doorway. "He's waiting. And Private Dubois came, too."

Emmy-Lou looked up from the small writing desk positioned beside the parlor window. "Where's your father?"

"Driving the carriage, silly. Dinah's already out there, too."

"Calm yourself, Charlotte," Emmy-Lou ordered. "Your blush will make it appear you are too eager. Men do not like for their ladies to wear their feelings on their sleeve."

Charlotte rolled her eyes. "As if Nathan doesn't *know* I care."

While her daughter emoted, Emmy-Lou Valentine was tying her bonnet beneath her chin and making her way back to the kitchen for the picnic basket. "Get the dining cloth from the sideboard, dear," she called. Back in the living room, she reached out to adjust Charlotte's lace collar. She tapped Charlotte's pointed chin. "Now breathe evenly, dear. Calm yourself. Be a lady." While she waited for the blush to recede from her daughter's cheeks, Emmy-Lou lectured. "And don't forget to inquire about Miss Gray. There isn't a man alive whose heart doesn't soften when he sees a woman truly touched with concern for the fate of another. When it comes to permanent attachments like marriage, compassion is a much more endearing—and enduring—emotion than the passions elicited by physical beauty."

Charlotte frowned slightly. "I don't have to *pretend* to care about Miss Gray, Mama."

"Well, of course not, dear," Emmy-Lou said quickly. Taking Charlotte's elbow she headed for the door. "But it never hurts to let the gentlemen *see* evidence of one's tender heart."

———

Riding along on the opposite side of the carriage from Miss Charlotte, Nathan conversed with Miss Dinah and her father, pointing out flora and fauna to the younger Valentine daughter, while Mrs. Doctor Valentine tried to convince Private Charles Dubois to become a striker for the Valentine family.

"And if you'd agree to instruct my daughters in French, Private Dubois, that would be even more delightful. Of course your remuneration would be increased to make the French instruction worthwhile for you."

"Frenchy eez not a teacher, Meez Valentine," Nathan interjected. He spoke in a terrible imitation of Frenchy's accent, "His family have been chef, all ze way back to Charlemagne."

"Zat is true," Frenchy said, smiling. "But only on ze side of *ma mere, Monsieur Sergeant.* On ze side of my father were many *professeurs.*" Dubois bowed toward Charlotte. "If *mon sergeant* says I may come, I would be delighted to instruct *les jeunes filles.*"

"Oh, Avery," Mrs. Valentine sang to her husband's back as they drove along. "Just think how far it would go with Mama if the girls spoke *French* the next time they went East for a visit!" She glanced at Dubois. "Mama seems to think we are hopelessly lost to civilization."

Doctor Valentine nodded toward Nathan. "Sergeant Boone would have to approve of the situation. After all, he's the one giving up a soldier."

Nathan looked over at Frenchy, who was smiling at Miss Charlotte. "It appears that Private Dubois could be convinced." He raised his voice. "Is that right, Frenchy? Would you care to apply for the position as cook and French tutor for the Doctor Valentine family?"

"French?" Dinah protested. "What use is it to learn French?" She frowned. "I want to learn to *ride.* That's something a girl can *use* out here."

Nathan smiled at her. "We have a Private Jackson who's an expert horseman. You may remember him from your drive that day when the men were having target practice. Tall, with a reddish beard and blue eyes."

Dr. Valentine frowned. "Isn't he the one who tore up Corporal Dorsey's knee?"

"The same," Nathan said. "He's repented of that particular sin. And he really is a fine horseman. Private Yates could go along, too. Perhaps some of the other ladies would want to join in."

"Do it, Papa," Charlotte interjected. "Someone needs to teach her to ride like a lady." She turned toward Nathan. "Dinah wants to go tearing over the prairie like a maniac, bareback, skirts flying, legs exposed!"

"Charlotte!" Mrs. Doctor glared at her daughter.

Dinah tossed her head. "Why does everybody want me to ride like a *lady*?" She pronounced the word as if it were cussing.

"I could drag that old sidesaddle out of the shed and polish it up for you, Dinah," Doctor Valentine said. "It's the very one Charlotte used when she was a girl."

"I'm fairly certain Private Jackson would welcome the diversion," Nathan said. "I'll talk to him before the day is out. It won't hurt him to miss target practice. He's already qualified for his sharpshooter medal."

Before they had gone far, it was arranged that Frenchy would take up domestic duties as the Valentine family striker. He would be paid extra for cooking and other odd jobs with a bonus for French lessons. And on Monday morning, any ladies interested in riding lessons with Private Caleb Jackson would report to the cavalry stables.

"Here I was languishing without domestic help, and it's all been solved on one lovely Sunday afternoon drive," Mrs. Valentine enthused. "Thank you, Sergeant Boone, for being so agreeable." She sighed. "A lady needs all the help she can get to keep a proper home on the frontier."

The group rode along in silence for a few moments. Then Mrs. Valentine said, "You know, Sergeant Boone, I will admit to a secret hope that you might somehow arrange for us to make Miss Gray's acquaintance before any of the other ladies on Officer's Row can hire her."

"Hire her?" Nathan asked.

"Well, I just assumed she would be looking for employment. Once she has recovered completely."

With a slight frown at her mother, Charlotte interrupted. She smiled up at Nathan. "We are all anxious to welcome Miss Gray to Camp Robinson. We've been quite concerned about her. We hoped she would be up and about long before now. It's been weeks since she arrived, poor thing."

"Mama," Dinah piped up. "Maybe Miss Gray doesn't *want* to be a maid.

Maybe she's a *princess*, and she got lost from her kingdom, and that's when Private Boone found her."

Nathan smiled at Dinah. Something in the child's innocent imaginings was at the heart of his discomfort with Mrs. Valentine's prodding. What was it in human nature, he wondered, that led people like her to automatically assign social position to others. And why did they always assign *inferior* positions? Mrs. Valentine assumed Laina was a servant. Dinah thought she might be a princess. He liked Dinah's way of thinking much better.

Mrs. Valentine spoke up. "Oh, Dinah. Forever dreaming fairy tales. Princesses do not reside in sod dugouts."

"Maybe not," Nathan said, "but dukes and royalty surely visit. Who's to say?" He winked at Dinah. "Maybe one of the princesses did get lost. Just like Dinah said."

"Well," Mrs. Valentine said, "Perhaps the princess will honor us with her presence at supper some evening. You'll ask her for us, won't you, Sergeant Boone? As soon as she is able. I hear she is young."

"I don't really know how old she is."

"But she is able now to be up and about? Private Yates said she is helping Granny with the mending."

"Yes. As her strength permits." Nathan pulled his horse up, let the carriage pass, and then moved alongside Charlotte. "Perhaps Miss Valentine would want to recruit interest from the other ladies on Officer's Row for the riding lessons? I'll send Private Yates over this evening to check with you on how many ladies might participate."

Just as they rounded a low ridge that created a sheltered spot along Soldier Creek—and, hence, a favored picnic site—they saw Private Yates of the flaming red hair stand up and stretch. Granny Max was walking along the creek bank with a child in tow. A white puppy tore ahead of them, yapping and darting into the shallow water. Nathan saw Laina glance in their direction before jumping up and hurrying toward Granny Max.

"Sergeant Boone." Mrs. Doctor said, looking up at him with an expression he couldn't quite decipher. "Would you help Charlotte down from the carriage, please? We've brought enough food to feed all of Company G. We shall invite Granny to join us. And I assume that is the elusive Miss Gray? No one ever mentioned just how lovely she is. How nice to see her so well recovered."

———

When the carriage bearing the Valentine family approached, Laina had been reaching into the picnic basket to get a piece of Granny's pie for Private Yates. Becky O'Malley had attached herself to the private as completely as was socially acceptable, and he seemed grateful for the female attention.

With Private Yates's attention expended elsewhere, Laina had been able to relax, coming as near to enjoying the outing as was possible for her, given her still-jittery nerves. She and Katie had had another session of training with the puppy, and Wilber had performed almost flawlessly— sitting on command and following along obediently without pulling on his lead. Laina realized she had been away from the protecting walls of Granny Max's quarters for over an hour, and not once had she been overwhelmed by unreasonable fear or panic.

And now the peace of the outing was shattered by the arrival of unwelcome guests. She heard rather than saw the approach of the carriage and horses. She felt her heart begin to pound and her hands to shake. Private Yates must have noticed. Laina inwardly blessed him for moving so that he was positioned between her and the oncoming carriage.

While the people clamored down from the carriage and the soldiers dismounted, Laina jumped up and headed off along the edge of the creek to where Granny Max and Katie O'Malley were inspecting the tiny white blossoms of some wildflower just peeking above the landscape. The clatter and strange voices behind her sent a chill down her spine. She gazed toward Soapsuds Row.

Granny took her hand. Squinting at the arriving party, she said, "It's only Nathan with Doctor Valentine and his family. Looks like he's brought along someone else from the barracks. That's just one private and two grown women you don't know. And Dinah Valentine. She's about Katie's age." She caught Laina's gaze and held it. "No dark closets, right?"

Laina stared into Granny's loving face. She nodded and forced a faint smile. "No dark closets. Raspberry pie instead."

Granny squeezed her hand and held it close. "That's my girl." She led her along the creek bank toward the group of newcomers.

————

Not since the moment his wife had seen Camp Robinson for the first time had Sergeant Nathan Boone seen such abject terror reflected in a woman's eyes. Laina only proffered him a fleeting glance, but he registered the emotions roiling inside her as easily as he could interpret the mood of a wounded animal. She was pale, and the knuckles of the hand that clutched Granny Max's arm were white. He didn't need to see her trembling to sense it.

"Miss Gray," he said, bowing low. "It's good to see you've regained some strength." He did his best to communicate peace and encouragement in a lingering glance before turning aside to introduce Frenchy.

Frenchy stepped forward and bowed. With a flourish, he bent over Granny's hand and kissed it. He murmured a greeting and turned to Laina.

"*Enchanté, mademoiselle,*" he said. In one sweeping gesture he removed his hat and bent low over her hand, lifting it to his lips and barely brushing it with his moustache.

Encouraged by Katie's giggle, Laina said softly, "*Enchantée, monsieur.*"

Frenchy stood up abruptly. His blue eyes twinkled. "*Vous parlez français, mademoiselle? Mais, c'est incroyable!*"

"*Un tout petit peu,*" Laina said. "Only a little."

"*C'est merveilleux!*" Frenchy exclaimed with delight. "You must tell me how you learned such good accent. Is beautiful, *mademoiselle.*"

Aware of being the center of attention, Laina blushed and leaned into Granny, who had slipped an arm about her waist.

Dr. Valentine introduced his wife, who extended her hand. "How good it is to finally meet you, my dear." The kindness dripping from her elicited little more than a murmur from Laina.

Mrs. Doctor enthused. "May we impose on you and share this lovely spot and our meal?"

Miss Charlotte Valentine pretended Nathan had offered his arm to her. She tucked her hand beneath his elbow as she nodded at Miss Gray. "Yes," she said. "Please do join us. We've been wanting to welcome you to Camp Robinson." She smiled up at Nathan. "But Sergeant Boone insisted you weren't able to receive callers." She looked at Laina. "What a pleasant surprise it is to see that he was mistaken."

Private Yates trilled a scale on his mouth harp. "Granny invited us out here for a Sunday service. We haven't even started the hymn sing yet, have we, Granny?"

"Well, we got to serve up some raspberry pie first, Private." She shook her head. "Did I say raspberry? I mean *apple*." She grinned at Laina.

"And we've brought Sergeant Boone's favorite. Chokecherry," Charlotte offered quickly.

Wilber nearly ended things when he tore across the picnic cloth in hot pursuit of some imaginary prey. While Charlotte screeched, Laina caught the erring pup by the scruff of his neck, flipped him on his back and, holding his face in her hands, scolded him. "Now sit!" she said sternly. She released the pup, and he immediately planted his posterior upon the earth and stared up at her adoringly.

"What magic do you have hidden up your sleeve, Miss Gray?" Mrs. Doctor asked.

"Oh, Laina knows about dogs," Katie O'Malley offered. "She had one just like Wilber. She's been teaching me how to train him. And Ma don't mind him near so much now." Katie beamed at Laina. "He hasn't peed on the carpet in a long time, Laina."

Laina nodded while she sat down to pet Wilber, who slowly slumped against her, finally tumbling into a white ball at her side and falling asleep.

After lunch, Charlotte asked, "Do you know 'Amazing Grace,' Private Yates?"

Harlan began to play, and Charlotte's reedy soprano joined quickly, albeit slightly off key. Becky and Katie O'Malley's strong duet corrected Charlotte's wavering notes, and on the second verse even the elder Valentines sang. Granny's rich contralto supported them all. And then, Laina joined them. Her clear soprano was pure and sweet and so clear it made all the other voices meld into a garble of background noise.

One by one, the other singers dropped out. Laina was unaware. She sang, "When we've been there ten thousand years, bright shining as the sun, we've no less days to sing God's praise, than when we'd first begun." As the last note rang across the clearing, she opened her eyes. Suddenly aware that she was giving a solo performance, she stopped abruptly.

Doctor Valentine said, "I do not think I have ever heard a more lovely voice in all my life."

Blushing furiously, Laina touched the left side of her bonnet and thanked him.

"Please, Miss Gray. Honor us with another song," the doctor asked.

"You know this one?" Harlan began to play a spiritual.

Laina shook her head.

"Go on, honey," Granny said, nudging her. She whispered, "Best piece of raspberry pie old Granny has tasted in years."

Laina smiled at her. She caressed Wilber's sleeping form. As the music floated out of her, every ounce of fear and stress melted away. Her shoulders relaxed and the line between her finely arched eyebrows disappeared. She opened her eyes and saw Sergeant Boone staring at her. Their eyes met. She looked away quickly, giving Wilber her full attention.

When the song ended, Sergeant Boone got up and retreated from the gathering to check on the horses. Laina saw him take something out of his pocket and look at it.

Charlotte Valentine was watching, too. She rose and followed Sergeant Boone. Laina saw him tuck whatever he was looking at back in his pocket. He said something to Miss Valentine while he undid the knot tethering his bay gelding to the Valentines' carriage. Then, turning around to glance back toward Laina, he tipped his hat before mounting and heading off toward the east.

Charlotte made her way back up the path to join the small group just beginning to enjoy Mrs. Doctor's picnic lunch.

"Sergeant Boone offers his apologies," Charlotte said. "He has some things to attend to back at camp."

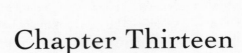

Chapter Thirteen

As for me, I will call upon God;
and the Lord shall save me.
PSALM 55:16

HE HAD COME here every Sunday for two years now. Unless he was out on patrol. Most of the time he came with a bouquet of wildflowers. Whatever was in season. It didn't matter. Lily had loved flowers. And color. Especially bright blue and red and yellow. But she had always oohed and aahed over whatever Nathan brought and put them in that fancy vase she'd received from her mother. The one her mother called a *vahz*. So he brought her flowers on Sunday afternoons and pretended he could hear her exclaiming over them.

Now that he didn't talk to God anymore, he tended to stay longer at Lily's grave. He could talk to her. Of course, she didn't answer him. Not so he could hear. But then neither did God, so all things being equal, he'd just as soon talk to Lily. At least he could imagine an answer from her. He'd given up trying to imagine what God thought or said about things over a year ago.

For the first year after Lily died, Nathan had tried to reason things through. He kept Granny Max up until all hours of the night with his questions. She listened and nodded and tried her best to give him counsel. She always had Bible verses that spoke to his doubts. But every conversation seemed to end with the same answer, which was that either he had faith to live with unanswered questions—like why God let his wife die—or he didn't. As it turned out, Nathan didn't.

Granny said he could ask God for faith. She seemed pretty confident God would answer that request with a *yes*. But Nathan didn't really want to have faith in a God who might say *no* when His very own children asked Him for important things. There wasn't anything comforting about that. And besides, when it came right down to it, Nathan could think of only one thing he really wanted. Well, one thing he wanted that he couldn't get on his own, that is. He also wanted a commission. But he could handle that one. He was a good soldier, and all the right people had their eye on him. He wouldn't disappoint them. As Nathan saw it, becoming an officer would not require any assistance from the Almighty. What he really wanted was a face-to-face talk with the woman he loved—and he knew the Almighty wouldn't be helping him with that.

As he dismounted at Lily's grave in the tiny Camp Robinson cemetery, Nathan Boone had new problems to talk over with his wife. He wanted to tell her about Doctor Valentine saying the men might be a little nervous about him. He was worried about Caleb Jackson. Did she remember meeting him? Beauregard Preston back then. Beau had so much anger and hate and bitterness bottled up inside him, Nathan didn't know if he'd make it in the army. Doctor Valentine was what really bothered him, though. He was telling Nathan to move on. Forget Lily. Well, not really to forget her. Just to put her things away.

Nathan laughed bitterly. "He actually said I should give myself a chance to *heal,* Lily. Like I cut myself or broke a leg. He knows it isn't as simple as that. He's been there himself." Nathan swallowed the lump in his throat. "Lily, if he'd loved that other woman half as much as I love you, he'd never tell me to give myself a chance to heal. Not if healing means forgetting you. I'll never do that." He bowed his head and let the tears come.

For the first half hour or so that Nathan sat beside Lily's grave, his mind ran in circles. He would try to talk, then get choked up and stop. He took her picture out of his pocket. He'd never felt uncomfortable about Lily when he was around Charlotte Valentine. But today he'd felt a need to look at Lily's photo. To remind himself. It was, Nathan realized, because of Miss Gray. When she sang, Nathan thought how good it was to see her finally free of all the fear and pain she carried locked up inside her. And he'd noticed she was pretty. Not in the way of Lily's delicate beauty. Laina Gray was small but there was an intensity about her, a raw power that would surprise a man. He knew about that because of what had happened at the soddy. There hadn't been much sign of it when she was sick and afraid to go outside. But today, when she'd made herself greet everyone at the picnic, he thought he'd seen a new kind of strength smoldering behind her green eyes. She'd looked at him, and he'd felt guilty.

"I don't know, Lily," he said to the tombstone. "I just felt like I had to get away and come talk to you about it."

He couldn't find any more words. He'd come here every Sunday and poured out his heart, and now, as he sat by Lily's grave, Nathan had nothing left to say. Life stretched out before him, empty and meaningless. He was alone, and he would be alone for the next . . . What would it be, he wondered? How many years before he rested beside Lily?

And then what?

The thought brought him up short. He'd given up God. What *would* happen when he died? What exactly had happened to Lily? Where was she right this instant?

Whiskey whickered softly. Nathan turned in time to see the horse raise his head and look toward the west, his ears pricked, with liquid brown eyes fixed on a lone figure walking toward the cemetery. It wasn't any use to run away from Granny Max. If she had something to say, it would get said, whether now or next month. He might as well hear it.

Granny didn't waste any time getting to her point. "Why'd you come running off up here? That was rude, Nathan, leaving us the way you did."

"I just had to get away."

Granny studied him carefully. "I saw you take Lily's picture out of your pocket."

Nathan looked at the tombstone. "I'm forgetting her." He looked at Granny, his eyes brimming with unspilled tears. "How can that be? How could I forget?" He took his hat off and held it, staring off toward Soapsuds Row.

"Time moves us forward, Nathan. It's part of God's plan for us to move away from the past. And we do some forgetting of what is back there so we can go into the future and the Lord's will for us." Granny patted his hand. "A little forgetting is good for us. Sometimes we try to remember so hard we stand still. That's not what this life is for. When God's ready for us to stop changing, He takes us to the next life." She sat on a thick patch of grass and patted a spot beside her. "Sit down here, Nathan. I wasn't thinking of saying this at Lily's grave, but maybe it will mean even more to you if I say it here." Granny waited for Nathan to sit and then shifted her entire body so she could look straight at him. "You'll never forget Lily, Nathan. And you will always love her. But maybe you felt a little guilty today when Miss Valentine—"

"Charlotte Valentine doesn't mean anything to me."

"I know that," Granny said. "All the times you've danced or dined with Miss Valentine, I bet you haven't felt you had to take out Lily's photo once. It wasn't Miss Valentine today, either. It was Laina's singing. I saw your face. Just for an instant today, while Laina was singing, you weren't thinking of Lily. That's what's bothering you."

Nathan looked away. He reached over and touched one of the blossoms in the bouquet he'd brought Lily. "People were so smug at her funeral. The way they said 'You're young. You'll find someone else.' I never wanted to smash faces so bad in my life as I did that day." With his forearm, he brushed some tears off his face.

Granny patted his arm. "Tell me your brother's name. The older one."

"James."

"Did your mama love you, Nathan?"

"Of course she did."

"But how? How could she love you? Didn't she love James? And what about your sister? Did she love your sister?"

"Of course."

"But not as much as you."

Nathan frowned. "She loved us all."

"That can't be, Nathan. There's not enough love. She must have loved some less, some more."

"Well, if she did, I never knew it."

Granny nodded. "When a woman has a child, Nathan, her love pours into that child to the extent she thinks her heart will break. She gives it everything. Then the good Lord smiles on her again and she is expecting another child. And not a mother or a father on the earth doesn't worry, thinking, 'I love this baby I already have so much. . . . How will I ever love another child? There's not that much love in me.' They worry. That second baby comes. And you know what happens? God just pours more love into their hearts, and suddenly they are loving that new baby with love they didn't know they had."

Granny reached out to trace Lily's name on the tombstone. "You are acting like you used up all the love you will ever have in this world on Lily Bainbridge. But, Nathan, God doesn't give us just a certain amount of love for all our lives to be parceled out. Your mama didn't have to take some love away from your brother to be able to love you. God is the Author of love. He gives and He gives and He gives. More love. There's never an end to it. It's like He is at the other end of a telegraph line. *His* lines don't ever get cut. They run all day, every day, all year for eternity. Just sending love for us to spread around."

She put her wrinkled hand alongside Nathan's cheek. "You gave so much love to Lily. And since she died you haven't ever asked for more. But He has more. If you will only ask for it. It won't diminish or change what you had with Miss Lily. God would never expect you to give anyone the part of your heart you gave to Lily. But, Nathan, He can give you a *new* heart full of *new* love." She patted his cheek. "There is no shame in whatever it was that happened for that instant today. I've been praying for over two years that the Lord would heal your broken heart, Nathan. You have done everything you can manage to keep that from happening. You've kept things as they were to remind you. From the minute you wake up until the minute you lie down, you have reminders everywhere. They keep you from healing. From moving on. Let it happen, Nathan. Let the Lord heal the crack in your heart. He can heal it and still keep what you had with Lily safe."

"The only thing I want from God is an answer to *why?*" Nathan said.

Granny sighed. She patted his arm. "Don't I know that, child." She shook her head. "I got that question on my list, too. And I've lived long enough to have a lot more *whys* in this old gray head of mine than you have in yours. We all have a list of 'whys'. You. Me. Miss Gray."

Nathan said. "What's *she* think of a God who doesn't answer *why?*"

Granny thought for a moment before saying, "Why don't you ask her?"

"Maybe I will."

———

Perched on a rock ledge overlooking the valley below, Laina lifted her face to the sun. She smiled. *If you really are there, then thank you for today. I think I did well, don't you?* She inhaled deeply and settled back against a rock, humming to herself.

Happiness was such a new sensation she didn't quite know how to deal with it. She was tired, but it was a delicious weariness—the result of battling and defeating some of her most persistent demons. Being in the company of Harlan Yates, Becky and Katie, Granny, and to some extent even Sergeant Boone, today had helped her claim a small victory over herself, over the past, and perhaps even over Josiah Paine.

A few yards away, Katie was wading in the creek. On the opposite bank, Wilber was on the trail of something. The others had left long ago, but she and Katie had lingered, wanting to work a little more on Wilber's training. Now as she sat thinking back over the afternoon, Laina almost laughed aloud at the idea of Riverboat Annie at a hymn sing with Mrs. Doctor Valentine and her uppity daughter. They had a way about them that Laina recognized immediately. It was the same attitude Nellie Pierce and the other girls at Miss Hart's expressed toward the gambler's daughter.

It was amusing watching them adjust their opinions when Laina spoke French with Private Dubois.

She smiled to herself. God surely had a sense of humor. Sundays in her former life meant sleeping late and less business. And here she was going on a picnic and singing hymns. It felt good. It felt almost right. She'd been to hell, and she'd brought some demons back with her, but she was also beginning to sense that a new life might be possible here at Camp Robinson.

Mrs. Valentine had hinted at wanting a housekeeper. She also seemed to have an interest in Laina's helping Dubois teach the girls French, although Laina doubted the little one—Dinah?—would have much interest in it. Still, Laina smiled. She had handled uppity women before. They didn't scare her. That was the best part of all, Laina realized. Terror had challenged her today. She had met it head on and defeated it. Like Clara Maxwell, she had forced herself out of the closet and had eaten a piece of raspberry pie. And here she was thinking of getting a respectable position with a respectable family. If that wasn't a change for the better, Laina didn't know what was. Maybe Granny's God *was* going to work out something, after all.

"Wilber. No, Wilber. Come!" Katie shouted.

Four men were riding toward them. Wilber had forgotten every bit of training and was yowling and tearing out in pursuit, ignoring Katie's pleas.

Laina stood up. The dog's howls had unsettled one of the horses, who began to crow-hop and buck and finally dumped its rider in a bush. Swearing followed, and then one of the riders pulled a pistol and aimed for Wilber.

Laina screamed. "No! Stop! Wilber! Come, Wilber!" She kept yelling at the top of her lungs, pumping her legs hard and running toward the men.

The man who'd been thrown was drawing his pistol too. He fired and missed. Laina grabbed for his gun just as he cocked the pistol and took aim again. "Stop!" she pleaded. "It's a puppy. Only a puppy."

Wilber was barking and yapping at the horses, chasing hooves and having a grand time, oblivious to the danger at hand. One of the horses finally landed a well-placed kick, and Wilber went rolling. He landed in a semiconscious pile, which Katie immediately scooped up. She ran to Laina's side.

Laina put her hand on Katie's shoulder. She noticed the men weren't soldiers. Maybe cowboys, she thought. She didn't like the way they had circled around her and Katie.

"That cur of yours is a menace."

It was the one who'd been thrown by his horse. He was standing behind her. She turned around. He'd caught his horse, but he hadn't gotten back in the saddle. His dirty blond hair hung to his shoulders from beneath a stained, wide-brimmed gray hat.

"He's mine," Katie said. She thrust her chin out and glared at him. "And you're not supposed to be on the military reservation."

The cowboy arched one eyebrow. "That so, little lady. And who's gonna make me get off? That killer dog of yours?" He laughed, showing brown crooked teeth.

Say something, Laina urged herself. She should speak up. But she was trembling so hard, it was all she could do to hold herself upright.

Katie flinched and pulled away from Laina's terrified grasp on her shoulder.

"Let's go home now, Laina." Katie took her hand.

"Not so fast," the cowboy said. He took a step toward them.

Laina grabbed Wilber from Katie's arms. Together, they began to walk toward Camp Robinson. They'd come too far, Laina realized. Too far for anyone to hear if they called for help. *Oh, God. Katie.*

She could hear the men behind her talking.

"Never thought I'd see a speck of a woman get the best of you."

"You can't handle a couple little gals, what's gonna happen if the Cheyenne head back up this way?"

"The gang's gonna love hearin' how Charlie Bates was throwed by his own horse."

She heard the creaking of leather as the man climbed into the saddle, and then hoofbeats as he came up behind them.

"Hey, you." From behind, he snatched Laina's bonnet off. The ribbons caught beneath her chin. He tugged on her bonnet a couple of times, then let go, leaving it dangling down her back.

"Keep walking," Laina whispered to Katie. "Don't say anything. Just walk."

"I'm talkin' to you." The man said. He rode up alongside them. "It ain't polite to ignore a man when he's talkin' to you."

God. Katie. Please.

He moved his horse in front of them, blocking the way back to camp.

Laina stopped. She put her hand on Katie's shoulder. Wilber had begun to struggle to be put down. Laina gripped harder, and Wilber struggled more until finally he succeeded in wriggling free. He dropped to the earth with a thud, jumped up, and tore off like a shot for Camp Robinson. Watching him go, Laina could only be thankful he had lost interest in barking at horses.

Laina found her voice. "They'll be expecting us back." Surprised at how confident she sounded, she forced herself to look into the cowboy's eyes. The face was handsome in spite of the cruelty etched in the lines around his mouth. She had seen men like him before. They were the ones her father especially watched when he played them at cards. The ones who would play all night and lose with seeming grace—but then return later to hide behind a grain barrel up on deck and take a shot at the winner. You could see evil in their eyes, and when this man looked at Laina, her midsection tightened. She had thwarted his cruelty to Wilber. His buddies were making fun of him. He was going to have to show them some proof of his manhood. Her throat constricted with fear.

God. Katie. Please.

"Run, Katie. Run!" Laina grabbed Katie's hand. Together, they took off. As Laina expected, she got about three steps before the cowboy grabbed her from behind. He tried to drag her up behind him, but his half-wild horse wouldn't cooperate.

"Run, Katie! RUN!" Laina screamed. She saw Katie hesitate, then head out. The men seemed content to hold on to Laina and let Katie get away. She wanted to fight. She wanted to kick and scream and spit. But maybe, just maybe if she didn't—maybe they would let Katie be.

There was the sound of hoofbeats. A horse breathing hard. A rifle being cocked.

"Put the lady down."

Laina landed in the dirt. She sprung up and almost cried with relief at the sight of Nathan Boone.

"Now hold on, Sergeant." One of the cowboys was talking. "We didn't mean no harm. Charlie here gets a little crazy sometimes. That's all. We was just chasing some strays."

"And you strayed onto the military reservation, and into more trouble than you bargained for. Get down off your horses." He spoke to her without taking his eyes off the men. "Miss Gray. Come over by me."

Laina went to Nathan while the cowboys considered their options. When Nathan fired his rifle in the air, Charlie's horse threw him again. Swearing, the man got up.

"He's the one you want, Sergeant," one of the men was saying. "He caused all the trouble."

"And you're the ones who didn't do much to stop it." Nathan said. "Get off your horses."

The cowboys complied. The one they had called Charlie got up and dusted himself off.

"Drop your guns and step away from them."

Laina had come up next to Whiskey. Still watching the cowboys, Nathan said to her, "Can you climb up behind me? I'm sort of preoccupied at the moment."

While Laina scrambled up behind him, Nathan kept his rifle trained on the cowboys.

"All right, boys. Now we're going for a nice Sunday afternoon stroll. You'll find the guardhouse at Camp Robinson to your liking. Much better than camping out under the stars. And we have a French cook. Let's go."

With the cowboys walking ahead of him, Nathan followed astride Whiskey.

"Do you know how to shoot a pistol?" he asked Laina. When she said no, he urged her, "Pull it out of my holster and pretend like you do. Just don't shoot me. And maybe you should attend target practice tomorrow."

———

"I know you know what you are doing, Lord," Granny said as she waited for Nathan to bring Laina back. "But . . . are you sure about this? She's done little more than hide inside for nearly two months now. Today was such a victory, Lord. She wanted to run and hide when the Valentines drove up. You know she did. But she stayed. She even enjoyed herself a little. And now . . . this. Like I said, Lord, I know you know what you are doing, but . . . are you sure about this?"

She shouldn't have left Laina and Katie back there at the creek. She should have stayed, too. She should have made Harlan stay. They all should have left earlier. Or later. She should be up helping Meara O'Malley calm little Katie, who had come tearing up to the Row screaming for help.

The fact was, Granny didn't know what to do. A dozen mounted soldiers were flying to the rescue even as Granny worried. All she could do right now was wait for Laina to get back. While she waited, she made herb tea. She got Laina's bed ready. She prayed. *Oh Lord, is she going to just crawl back under these quilts and be done trying?*

It was more excitement than Camp Robinson had seen in weeks, and when the four offenders straggled into camp and were locked up in the guardhouse, it provided fodder for a week's worth of campfires and checker games. Rumor had it the cowboys weren't really cowboys at all. Rumor had it Nathan Boone had captured four members of Doc Middleton's gang of horse thieves. Rumor had Sergeant Boone and Miss Gray courting.

Rumor was wrong.

Laina Gray sat wrapped in a quilt at Granny Max's table drinking coffee. She'd asked for coffee instead of Granny's calming tea. "I . . . I need to think, Granny. I don't want to sleep. Not yet."

Harlan had come, red-faced and stammering concern.

Doctor Valentine had checked in.

Sergeant Boone had come, too—after seeing to the arrest, caring for Whiskey, and filing his report.

Laina had greeted them all with an almost unearthly calm. She'd reassured them. She'd even insisted on going up to the O'Malleys' and seeing Katie. And Wilber. As it turned out, it was Wilber who had saved them. Sergeant Boone said he had seen the pup charging toward the Row and for some reason decided to make sure nothing else had been left at the picnic site. Were it not for Wilber, rescue would have been delayed long enough for . . . Well, Granny just wasn't going to think about that.

Granny watched her carefully, but as evening wore on, Laina just didn't seem to need calming. So Granny made coffee. Stirred up some corn bread. Sewed on a button. Watched. Waited.

Laina finally spoke. "Granny, He did it." Her hand trembled when she set down her coffee cup.

"Who did what, honey-lamb?" Granny answered, internally gathering all the forces of heaven to help her handle whatever challenge might be coming.

"God," Laina said. "He answered me." She looked up at Granny. "A prayer, I mean. At least I think He did. I didn't think He'd ever answer one of my prayers. But today I just kept thinking *God. Katie. Please.* I didn't even know I was praying. But I was." She smiled at Granny. "And He *answered* me, Granny. *God said yes.*" Laina looked down at the table. "Wilber took off and Sergeant Boone came. And no one got hurt. God said *yes,* Granny. He heard me." She started to cry.

Granny nodded and smiled.

"You thought I was going to come in here and go back to hiding under those quilts in the back room again."

"The thought occurred to me."

"That's why you made your tea. To help with the nightmares."

Granny nodded again.

"Well, I'm not hiding anymore," Laina said. "I don't know Him like you do. But something in here," she touched the place over her heart, "Just feels—better, somehow. Peaceful."

Granny hugged her. They talked long into the night, Laina asking questions, Granny giving answers when she had them. As they talked, Laina moved past *why* into *how*. How could she know God the way Granny did? How could God possibly forgive her all those past sins? How could Jesus love her enough to die for her? And then, with Granny holding her hand, Laina Gray, who had for the first time in her life felt God say *yes* to her, said *yes* to Him.

———

On Monday afternoon, when the ladies of Camp Robinson gathered for target practice, they were joined by Miss Laina Gray.

Miss Charlotte Valentine thought Private Yates made a fool of himself over her.

On Tuesday, Miss Gray accompanied Granny Max to Gruber's trading post and selected a madder-print calico for a new dress.

Miss Charlotte Valentine thought any woman with *that* color of hair should know better than to wear anything with orange in it.

On Wednesday, Miss Gray could be seen helping Private Yates hang shirts to dry just outside the washing shed where Granny Max and Mrs. O'Malley did Company G's laundry.

Miss Charlotte Valentine was pleased to see that Miss Gray at least recognized her status at Camp Robinson was that of domestic servant.

On Thursday, Miss Gray made arrangements with Mrs. Doctor Valentine to begin working for her the following Monday.

And on Friday. Well, all day on Friday, it was rumored there would be another lady at the hop.

Miss Charlotte Valentine applied a bit of rouge to her cheeks. And her mother, who had *words* for young ladies who painted themselves to gain masculine attention, pretended not to notice.

Chapter Fourteen

Be not far from me, for trouble is near;
for there is none to help.
PSALM 22:11

THE SPRING AND early summer of 1878 in the Sandhills of Nebraska had been nothing special. As they had for years and years, endless lines of birds streamed across the sky, honking and whooping and settling overnight along the banks of spring-fed lakes before rising at dawn to continue their trek north.

The men of Camp Robinson followed their rigid daily schedule, obeying the almost hourly bugles and almost always owly drill sergeants, while they complained about having nothing much to do and wished the army would decide whether or not they were going to close the place down and move everyone over to Camp Sheridan.

Private Frenchy Dubois planted a huge garden and boasted that Company G would raise the best crop of fresh vegetables the army ever had.

Private Harlan Yates became Camp Robinson's all-around handyman. He was always in demand by someone for carpentry or repairs, and thanks to Granny Max's influence in keeping him away from the less virtuous elements of the camp—and Miss Gray's presence, which encouraged his affinity for Sunday afternoons over on the Row—he was able to make a real financial difference for his mother and younger sister back home.

Over on Soapsuds Row laundresses laundered and children played. Meara O'Malley grew great with child. She was miserable most of the time, and her two daughters took on more of her duties. Soon she was spending most of her time in bed, and Katie and Becky were spending most of their time in the company of Granny Max and Laina Gray.

———

Beginning in mid-June, Laina Gray spent the first three days of every week at the Valentines'. On Mondays she did the family laundry. On Tuesday she ironed and mended what she had washed on Monday. On Wednesday she cleaned. But when asked to prepare a meal, she had to admit she did not cook.

"I'm sorry, Mrs. Valentine," Laina said the first Wednesday. "But you don't want me trying to help in the kitchen. I can't cook worth anything."

"Nonsense," Mrs. Valentine said. "I don't expect anything fancy. Just roast a hen and throw in some potatoes."

"You have to kill and clean a hen to roast it," Laina said. "I've seen Granny do it. But I don't know how."

"That's ridiculous," Mrs. Valentine said. "Even *I* know how to do that. Girls learn this sort of thing when they're in grammar school. Where *did* you grow up, Miss Gray?"

A "Riverboat Annie" retort rose to Laina's lips. Barely managing not to utter it, Laina grabbed the flat iron off the stove behind her and slammed it onto the linen tablecloth she was pressing. "I *didn't* grow up. I was hatched and raised by loons."

"There's no need to be impertinent, Miss Gray," Mrs. Valentine snipped.

Just when Mrs. Valentine had opened her mouth—Laina would never know if she intended to apologize or fire her—Private Charles Dubois knocked at the back door and stepped into the silence looming between the two women. He was bearing a handful of green onions and some herbs from the company garden.

Thank God. Laina smiled to herself. *Yes. Really. Thank you, God.* And she hadn't even prayed about the cooking. At least not consciously. And here was Private Dubois, smiling instead of criticizing, teaching her how to kill, clean, and cook the hen.

"*Mais non!*" he exclaimed, when Laina tried to stretch the chicken's neck beneath a broom handle. "What are you doing?!"

"Isn't that how you do it?" Laina asked.

"You have seen zis done—with a *broom?*"

Laina nodded. "That's how the cook on the riverboat did it."

"Well, zat is not how to kill a shik-en," Frenchy said, muttering to himself in French. He grabbed an ax. "*Tenez . . . la*" he ordered, pointing at the feet. "*Et la tête, mademoiselle.*" When Laina obeyed, he brought down the ax. "*Comme ça.*" He explained, "She never know what happen. Ze broomstick is torture. Barbarism." He walked away shaking his head.

Later, when the hen was plucked clean, Frenchy instructed Laina to add potatoes, green onions, and parsley to the cooking pot. Pulling a leather pouch from his pocket, he sprinkled some of its contents over the bubbling liquid. Winking at Laina, he raised his finger to his lips and whispered. "This, I cannot tell you, *mademoiselle. C'est magique.*"

Whatever magic Charles Dubois carried in the leather pouch, it elicited adoration from the Valentine family when they sat down to dinner that evening. Laina had gone back over to the Row long before that happened, but she heard about it Friday evening at the hop where Mrs. Valentine's snagging a French cook was subject of many whispered conversations and enough associated envy that Emmy-Lou's face fairly beamed with joy.

As time went by, daily life took on a monotony Laina adored. For the first time in many years, she felt safe. Her biggest challenge in life was not laughing aloud at Charlotte Valentine's ability to make a tragedy out of something so unimportant as whether or not her father would let her have the money to buy a certain lace for a new dress.

Physically, Laina was almost back to normal. While she bore permanent scars, she'd learned to cover the one on her head and on some days she didn't even think about the others. She felt tired most of the time, and her stomach still rebelled on occasion. But all in all, Laina Gray was content with taking baby steps toward the unknown future and baby steps toward the God she was learning to trust.

Sergeant Nathan Boone came around Soapsuds Row more often for dinner. He found time to teach Katie O'Malley to play chess. He treated Becky much like a younger sister, keeping an eye on her at the hops and steering her clear of the Caleb Jacksons, both in Company G and the infantry. The sergeant occasionally favored Wilber, who it seemed would grow taller than any of Dr. Valentine's greyhounds, with a bone fished out of Frenchy's stew pot. And he spent more than one Sunday afternoon listening to Harlan Yates play his mouth harp while Laina Gray sang.

Anyone inspecting Camp Robinson would have detected nothing out of the ordinary. Unless, of course, they talked to Granny Max, who often looked beyond what she could see and caught glimpses of what was really happening.

———

What is it about her? Nathan Boone wondered. He was standing with his back to the wall, his arms folded, watching Laina Gray dance with Corporal Dorsey. It was the usual Friday night hop. The enlisted men had planned it and invited the officers and their wives. They'd cleared out the barracks to create a dance floor. The company band was providing music. A table along one wall was groaning beneath the weight of Frenchy's now famous delectables. The air was filled with the mingled scents of dust and sweat, and occasionally a fragrance of lavender or lemon verbena as a woman swept by. Laughter rang out above the stomping of boots on the board floor as first one, then another of the men tied a handkerchief on his upper arm to designate himself as a lady.

And in the middle of the foot stomping and laughter, Miss Laina Gray soared around the dance floor like a bird gliding over the smooth surface of a lake.

Nathan had been sure Laina would withdraw after the outlaw incident. When he went to help her down off Whiskey, Miss Gray had run to Granny Max without looking back. She hadn't even thanked him—which didn't really bother him, because he expected her hasty retreat. He was sure she would disappear inside Granny Max's apartment and never come out again. He'd felt bad for Granny Max and the sleep she was going to lose again. That night, he had even slept in his old apartment next to Granny's, expecting to hear screams from another of Miss Gray's nightmares. He'd been ready to help. And then he hadn't been needed.

In fact, the next day Private Yates had reported that Miss Gray, who had accompanied Miss Valentine and the other ladies to target practice, was a good shot. And then when he himself stopped by Granny's, Nathan had been surprised to find Miss Gray down on all fours, cutting up a length of fabric spread out on the floor. "A new dress," she had said by way of explanation. He'd felt a little guilty, realizing that Lily's gray calico was showing some wear. He should have noticed. He had decided to take her another of Lily's dresses weeks ago. But time had gone by and he hadn't done it. Watching her dance, he decided Lily's pink dress wouldn't really look good with Miss Gray's auburn hair. He'd give her the green one. No. He'd take them both. What good were they doing in Lily's trunk, anyway?

His conversation with Granny beside Lily's grave came back. *"Why don't you ask her?"* Granny had said when Nathan wondered aloud what Miss Gray thought of a God who was silent when asked *why*. *"Maybe I will,"* had been his reply. But he hadn't done that, either. Maybe tonight he would.

Movement along the opposite wall of the barracks reminded Nathan he wasn't the only man keeping an eye on Miss Laina Gray. He spotted Jackson, who lately seemed to have found a way to avoid the temptations of gambling and drinking at Camp Robinson by volunteering for every escort detail and patrol that came up. He was rarely in camp for longer than a day, and when he was, he requested and was assigned stable fatigue. He spent hours longeing horses around the corral. Corporal Dorsey said Jackson knew the personalities of the Company G horses better than the captain knew the men. He'd even helped Dorsey cure a new mount of a nasty biting habit. With Jackson making peace with Dorsey, Nathan had hoped the recruit's personal troubles had been laid to rest. He had congratulated himself on the success of his own attempts to mold Jackson into a good soldier.

But now, watching Jackson eyeball Miss Gray, Nathan wondered if a new problem was in the making. He had shrugged off Dr. Valentine's comments about the way Jackson looked at Charlotte. Now, seeing the soldier almost leering at Miss Gray from a shadowy corner of the barracks, Nathan understood what the doctor meant. He was glad he'd ordered Jackson to stay away from Soapsuds Row.

He cross-examined himself. Why should it matter to him if Private Caleb Jackson took an interest in Laina Gray? She was a grown woman. He was going to have to get beyond this proprietary attitude he had toward her. She wasn't some injured puppy he had rescued and needed to find a good home for. And she wasn't his personal possession. It was foolish for him to be so overprotective.

He'd talk to her tonight. Watching her dance and smile made him feel good about his role in her recovery. Tonight he would find out how she was really doing. Maybe ask her that question about the God who doesn't answer *why*. If she was truly doing all right, then maybe he could relax a little about her having to deal with the Private Jacksons at Camp Robinson.

The reasonable Sergeant Nathan Boone had almost won his internal argument, had almost decided maybe he should back off and let Miss Gray handle her own affairs, when Private Jackson took a step in Laina's direction. Even as he scolded himself for doing it, Nathan reasoned that Miss Gray had had more than her share of poor treatment from men. If he had anything to say about it, Miss Laina Gray would never be hurt again. He moved quickly to intercept Jackson.

"May I have this dance?" Nathan bowed low and held out his hand.

Corporal Dorsey winked at him. He swiped his forehead with a kerchief. "Thank goodness," he said, grinning. "This lady is too polite to complain, but I do believe I've trounced on enough of her toes for one evening." He turned to Laina. "Thank you, ma'am." He spun about and immediately asked Charlotte Valentine to dance.

Nathan saw Miss Valentine shoot an icy glare in Laina's direction. He assumed Laina didn't see it, but he was taken aback when, with a quick nod and a smile, Miss Gray guided his hand to her waist. He felt her hand linger over his longer than what he thought necessary before she slid it up his arm to his shoulder. She laced the fingers of her left hand through his. The music began. Not what he expected. A waltz. A slow waltz. The musicians were letting the dancers catch their breath. Why, then, Nathan wondered, was he having trouble catching his?

"Private Yates tells me you're a good shot, Miss Gray."

"Private Yates is a good liar," Laina said.

"You . . . um . . . you finished your dress." *Confound it.* Why'd he say that? Much too personal. But the green fabric *did* bring out the color in her eyes. Sort of made her auburn hair look prettier, too, now that he thought about it. She'd pinned a bunch of wildflowers to the bun at the nape of her neck. They smelled good. She was talking. He should be listening.

" . . . thankful you took the notion to check what Wilber was barking about."

Did he imagine it, or had she squeezed his hand just then? What had happened to her? She was acting like . . . well . . . she was acting like a normal lady at a dance. How had she come to *normal,* anyway?

Had she asked him a question? "I'm sorry. What did you say?"

"I was wondering," Laina repeated, "just what's going to happen to those men in the guardhouse?"

Obviously, Nathan thought, she still needed protecting. "We're holding them until the sheriff from Deadwood arrives. Found out they're wanted up there for horse thieving." He smiled encouragement. "You don't worry about them. The sheriff will be down soon to take them off our hands." He spun her around the dance floor, sensing her relief, feeling a surge of emotion inside him when she smiled and the light came back into her eyes.

He would offer to walk her home after they talked. Just as a precaution, in case Jackson was lingering outside.

————

"Hey, Jackson!" The recruit everyone called "Professor" was walking toward him from the direction of the barracks. "We're gettin' up a game of poker at Grubers. Low stakes. Why don'cha come?"

Jackson shook his head. "Thanks. I've got to check on a mare that went lame today." He started off in the direction of the stable while the group of men headed toward the trading post. As soon as they were out of sight, Jackson doubled back. Sidling along the barracks's log wall, he pulled his hat down over his forehead and turned his collar up. Then he peered around the window frame, watching the dancers.

———

"You're a good dancer." Nathan leaned down so Laina could hear him above the music while he waltzed her around the room.

"I had a good teacher," she said. "In another life."

"Your teacher . . . she taught you French, too?"

She shook her head. "No. That was another part of the other life. And the French teacher wasn't a lady." She laughed lightly, "But he wasn't really a gentleman, either."

He looked down at her. Was she teasing him?

"You are staring, Sergeant."

"I'm sorry. It's just . . . well . . . I can't quite . . ." She probably thought he was flirting with her. Lord, keep him from *that* misunderstanding. All he wanted to do was to have that conversation Granny Max had suggested that day at Lily's grave. "You seem different."

Nathan sensed rather than saw her tense up, but he could tell she was distancing herself from him just slightly. She lowered her voice. "Different as in *no longer a raging animal* or different as in *not what I expected* or different as in *get me out of here—why did I ever ask this creature to dance with me in the first place?*"

Nathan leaned down again so the other dancers couldn't hear him. "Would you mind taking a walk with me?" He felt her hair brush his cheek as she turned her head to look up into his eyes. She arched one eyebrow. He hadn't seen that expression before. She took his arm.

Weaving through the other dancers, they headed outside where the moonlight shone bright enough to cast shadows around them. Here and there, small groups of soldiers stood around, telling tales, wagering on a coming horse race, complaining about army food or their recent fatigue duty. Nathan scanned the shadows. No Private Jackson as far as he could tell. They turned left—Nathan made certain they didn't head toward the cavalry barracks or the guardhouse—and began to walk slowly around the perimeter of the parade ground.

———

Private Jackson watched Sergeant Boone and Miss Gray promenade along one side of the parade ground. He'd seen them head for the door and ducked around the corner of the barracks just in time to escape Sergeant

Boone's notice. Now, as they walked away, he watched, wondering how it could be that the woman he'd known as Riverboat Annie could have found her way to Camp Robinson, Nebraska.

He'd had his doubts when he first saw her. He'd never really seen Annie in daylight. He'd never seen her with her hair up, either. He'd thought maybe he was wrong. Maybe this woman only looked like Annie. But watching her dance with Sergeant Boone convinced him. The way she smiled up at him. The way she slid her hand up his arm right before the music started. The way she laced her fingers through Boone's. Jackson remembered every gesture as if it had been only yesterday she had danced with him as Riverboat Annie. She'd done a skillful job of covering up what looked to be a pretty awful scar. The part that showed on her temple wasn't too bad, but it must be worse above her ear because she'd twisted her hair in a way Jackson couldn't ever remember seeing before. Leave it to Annie to think of a way to cover up.

He smiled to himself, wondering what Rose and the other girls from the riverboat would think if they knew the little gal they'd worried about so much after she disappeared, was out west dancing it up with a bunch of soldiers and romancing a sergeant. At least it sure looked like she had him on the hook and was ready to reel him in.

Watching her walk away with Sergeant Boone, Jackson shook his head. She was up to something—that was certain. Even Dr. Valentine's daughter Charlotte thought so. He hadn't missed the look on her face when Boone asked Annie to dance. Private Jackson had played enough games in his life and caused enough jealousy to recognize it for what it was.

Charlotte Valentine was a pretty little thing though. With a high opinion of herself. It would be a challenge to turn that little lady's head. A challenge that would relieve the boredom of tending horses and riding patrol. And flirting didn't have the addictive risks of whiskey and gambling. Jackson smiled to himself, wondering if he'd be able to overcome the girl's parents' reluctance to let their precious daughter be romanced by a lowly enlisted man.

But I'm not just any enlisted man. I've always been able to turn their heads. I need a little beard trimming and a barber to tame my hair. Or maybe not. Maybe a little of the mountain-man look would give these ladies something different from all the spit-and-polished Sergeant Boones they see. Maybe he'd let just a glimmer of his southern accent back into his speech. He could hint at a tragic past. That always got to the girls' mothers. And he wouldn't have to pretend about that part. With a glance over his shoulder, Jackson removed his hat and slicked his hair back with both hands. Then he pulled a lock of it down over his forehead. Hat in hand, he ducked inside. The band was only halfway through their introduction to "Annie Laurie" when Private Caleb Jackson had his hand on Charlotte Valentine's tiny, corseted waist.

"I'm honored you'd see fit to dance with me, ma'am," he drawled. "Some of the other women on the post don't seem to think a galvanized Yankee has much use. Makes it mighty lonely for a poor boy from North Care-lina." He made sure his face was a picture of regret and sadness.

Charlotte looked up at him. When he squeezed her hand, her cheeks blushed pink. "Well, I'm not those women. And I'm happy to dance with you, Private."

"Thank you, ma'am," Jackson said. "It . . . it helps to have a pretty face to block out the . . ." He shook his head.

"To block out what, Private?"

"Never mind, ma'am. The past is past." He forced a smile and pretended to blink away tears. It worked. The girl was almost crying herself. He moved his hand to her back and applied just enough pressure to bring her closer—but not enough so as to raise a red flag in the mind of the old biddy watching them from near the punch bowl. *The mother.* His next challenge.

————

"I wanted to tell you how glad I am . . . after those outlaws . . . well . . . I wondered if it would somehow set you back." Nathan slowed his pace, trying to match his long stride with Laina's as they walked along in the moonlight.

She reached up and touched the left side of her head. "I'm just as surprised as you that it didn't." Her voice lowered. "As strange as this may sound, I think it helped me somehow."

"Helped you?" Now he really wanted to hear what she had to say.

They had come to the picket fence that created front lawns for the row of officer's duplexes. Laina paused there. They stood together in the moonlight while she explained, "When those . . . men . . . confronted Katie and me, I was so terrified I could hardly stay standing. I couldn't say anything. All I could do was hang on to Katie. My mind kept going blank. Except for three words. *God. Katie. Please.*" She looked up at him. "And you arrived. Later when I was thinking about it all, the possibility dawned on me that God had used you to answer a prayer." She leaned against the fence. Nathan could see her profile in the moonlight. "Thinking God might actually care about someone like me was . . . profound. Moving."

"Someone like you?" Looking down at her in the moonlight, he wished he could see her eyes, but they were hidden in shadow.

She touched the left side of her head again and smoothed her hair. "You don't need to be gallant, Sergeant. You were there in that soddy." Her hands went to the scars around her wrists. "You know what went on there." Her voice trembled. "I always thought God was for good people. Not people like me."

He touched her wrist. "That wasn't your fault."

She pulled away. "But I made the choices that led up to that—that place." She looked down at her wrists. "To these."

"You're not that woman anymore."

"Well, I'm not so certain that *woman,* as you so kindly call her, isn't still in here somewhere." She raised one hand and patted her chest. "Sometimes fear just sort of sneaks up on me." She looked back over her shoulder toward the barracks. She shook her head and laughed. "But amazingly enough, *that woman* has had an encounter with God. And it's making a difference. In a lot of ways."

"That's good. That's really good," Nathan said. "I'm glad for you. Everyone is."

"Oh, not everyone at Camp Robinson is as caring as you, Sergeant. But that's another discussion. We should be getting back. You have a reputation to uphold."

He moved a little so that he could look down into her eyes. "There's nothing wrong with your reputation at Camp Robinson."

"Now you really are being gallant," she said. "If Katie O'Malley has heard rumors, so have you." She held up her fingers as she talked. "One: I'm crazy. Two: I was formerly a lady of the night in Deadwood. Three: I was formerly the lover of Doc Middleton or Little Bat Garnier—take your pick—and those men were after a bag of gold I stole from Doc or Bat. Four: I am the long-lost daughter of the Grand Duke of somewhere. I was captured by Indians when he was on a hunting trip and languished until rescued by"—she pointed at him—"you."

"Rumors die after a while. You'll live them down." He looked up and saw that people were beginning to leave the barracks. "Looks like the dance is almost over. How about if I walk you back to Granny's. There's something I've been wanting to ask you."

"Ask away," Laina said, tucking her hand beneath his arm, allowing herself to be led along the picket fence.

"Just now you said God answered a prayer of yours. You said that helped you. What I wondered was"—he paused just opposite the Valentine's quarters—"did you ever wonder why . . . why God didn't hear you sooner? Why He didn't spare you some of those bad choices? Or where He was when you were in that dugout?"

"Only a thousand times a thousand," she said. "I don't expect I will ever know."

He looked down at her. "And you're okay with that?"

She shrugged. "I'm okay with letting God be God and just trying to get through tonight and tomorrow out here in the middle of nowhere. Just trying to become an honorable woman—God help me. And I really mean that. If God is going to start working on Laina Gray, there's a lot of cleanup to do."

"Stop that," Nathan said.

"Stop what?"

"Stop dragging yourself back into the past. Like I said before, you aren't that woman any more."

Voices at the far end of Officer's Row caught Nathan's attention. He looked up. *Oh no.* Here came Charlotte. On the arm of . . . Private Jackson? He forced his mind back to the conversation with Miss Gray. "No one else knows about that woman in the soddy, and I don't think about her—except maybe to be amazed at how much she's changed."

"Sergeant Boone, Miss Gray," Charlotte nodded, obviously intent on sweeping by them with her escort. The escort swept his hat off his head and gave an exaggerated bow as the couple passed.

Nathan heard Laina take in a deep breath. He could almost sense her counting—*one, two, three, breathe.* Just the way he did when something awful had happened and he needed to regain control. He felt her grip on his arm tighten. She moved closer to him. As they walked in silence toward Soapsuds Row, Laina crowded even closer to him, clutching his arm with both hands.

"What's wrong? Are you feeling ill?" he asked.

She shook her head. "I'm just tired. Could we . . . talk . . . some other time?"

"Of course." He frowned, trying to understand what had just happened.

The minute they were inside the door of Granny's apartment, Miss Gray mumbled a thank-you and disappeared behind the quilt curtain into the back room.

Nathan sat in the amber glow of a kerosene lamp, looking down into the top tray of Lily Boone's trunk. *"Stop dragging yourself into the past."* He'd said that to Laina Gray less than an hour ago. And here he was, plunging back into the past. Reaching into his pants pocket, he grasped the rattle-snake rattle he had carried for the past two years. He ran his finger along it, counting the rattles. *Eighteen.* He tossed it into the tray alongside Lily's personal things: her silver mirror and comb, a cameo brooch, letters from home tied with a faded silk ribbon. The small leather *Book of Common Prayer*. And Lily's Bible.

He picked up the Bible, opening it at random and reading. She'd under-lined some of her favorite passages. Lily Bainbridge had been a devout woman with a faith so strong she had faced death with amazing calm.

"Don't blame God, Nate. Promise me you won't blame God."

Sitting here remembering how she'd clutched his hand when she said those words, Nathan realized he hadn't fooled Lily. She'd known his faith was more form than substance. That's why she'd worried about him more than herself. He didn't have anything against going to church. It was some-thing civilized people did. In time he even grew to like the ritual. But he didn't get personally involved, and Lily had known that.

Thumbing through her Bible, Nathan realized that if things had gone the other way, if he had died, there wouldn't be any Bible with underlined passages for Lily to keep. His mother had given him a Bible when he left home, but he didn't even know what had happened to it.

Nathan sat back, remembering how he'd held Lily's small hand between his own and, sobbing, blurted out a promise. "I won't, darling, I won't." He would have said anything she wanted to hear, just to make her passing more peaceful.

He'd lied. He did blame God. Who else was there to blame? After all, God was the One who supposedly had the power to reach down and heal Lily Boone, who believed in Him with all her heart and prayed to Him every day.

At first Nathan only *blamed* God, but as time went on, blame fermented and grew into a full-scale resentment that colored everything to do with faith. He stopped talking to God. He locked Lily's Bible up with the rest of her things. Thankfully there wasn't any church at Camp Robinson, but if there had been, he'd have stopped going. Eventually, he decided to give up on God altogether. He would have been happy to never hear the name of God again. He probably would have succeeded in making that happen—if it weren't for Granny Max.

Nathan liked being around Granny. She provided a tangible connection to Lily. But it was more than that. In the years since he had met her, Nathan had grown to love Granny Max for herself. Military life was hard enough without a man deliberately turning his back on things like fresh-baked pie and a listening ear. Granny Max made Camp Robinson feel like home. He liked eating at her table. He liked spending Sunday afternoons with her and whatever gaggle of Camp Robinson misfits she collected for the day. And Nathan knew that if he was going to continue to be around Granny, he was going to have to put up with a certain amount of God-talk, because God slipped into Granny's conversations just as naturally as if she were talking about the weather. God-talk was just part of who Granny Max was. Nathan would never expect her to change just for him. Now it seemed that Laina Gray was becoming accustomed to God-talk, too. She didn't seem to be angry at God about what had happened to her. That—more than anything else about her—amazed him. How could she not be angry at God?

Hearing about God from people like Granny Max and Miss Gray was only one thing that prevented Nathan's putting God out of his mind. The other was something Nathan wouldn't have admitted to anyone. But sitting in the lamplight looking down at his dead wife's Bible, he admitted it to himself. He just couldn't bring himself to deny God existed. Everywhere he looked he saw evidence of something bigger than himself. Might as well call it God. He remembered a Bible verse that said something like *the heavens declare the glory of God*. And if the heavens weren't enough to convince a man there was a God, Nathan Boone thought the Nebraska Sandhills surely were.

But seeing evidence of God in the ridges, the valleys, and the sky brought Nathan back around in the circle of reasoning where he had been trapped for over two years. Someone big enough to create the universe had to be powerful enough to keep bad things from happening to good people. But Lily died. And Laina Gray was tied up and abused. So Nathan was caught. He couldn't deny God existed, but he couldn't reconcile what happened to Lily and Laina with a loving God. It was asking too much to expect a man to accept both. And so as long as he couldn't reconcile those things, he *would* refuse to call God *Father* and worship him.

Nathan took a deep breath and let it out again. He was tired. Tired of not having answers. Tired of being alone. Tired of being confused. Tired of coming back to these empty rooms. Tired of looking at Lily's trunk.

Nathan's hand trembled as he began to sort the things in the tray. He had decided to give Miss Gray those other two calico dresses weeks ago. It was time he did it. Maybe it was time he took the advice he'd given Miss Gray earlier—*"Stop dragging yourself into the past."* Maybe it was time he took Dr. Valentine's advice, too. Maybe the doctor had a point. Granny Max believed God could heal the crack in his heart and still keep his love for Lily safe. Nathan wasn't ready to trust God for anything, but Granny was a wise woman. Dr. Valentine seemed to agree with her. And his own way of handling things *wasn't* working very well.

He took his hat off and rumpled his hand through his hair, thinking. He'd keep Lily's Bible and those garnet earbobs. He set them aside and opened a velvet ring box, touching the oval stone of a brooch that had been Lily's grandmother's. He would send it back to the Bainbridges along with the letters Lily had read so many times and then tied into a bundle with a lavender silk ribbon. Sending it all back East would necessitate a letter from him. He would worry over that later.

In only a few moments, Nathan had sorted through the tray and was looking down at the blue silk ball gown. As Granny Max had said, Lily was a giving person. The thought brought him a momentary flash of pleasure. He tried to concentrate on the sense of rightness. *Lily would approve of this.* And Miss Gray's eyes would probably look blue instead of green if she wore this dress.

Thinking about Miss Gray brought a new sensation of guilt. His hand went to his breast pocket and he withdrew Lily's picture. He sat staring at it for a long time. "I miss you," he whispered, touching the face in the photograph. "Sometimes it feels like a thousand years ago you were here. Sometimes I still expect to hear your voice when I come in the door. What's happening, Lily?"

He closed his eyes and let the tears come. After a moment, he put the tray back in place and closed the trunk. When he locked it, instead of putting the chain back over his head and tucking it inside his shirt, he left the key in the lock.

———

Friday night flowed into Saturday. Nothing of consequence happened over the weekend until on Sunday afternoon, with much stammering, Sergeant Boone appeared at Granny Max's door and asked if Miss Gray might be able to make use of a trunk full of ladies' things, and without waiting for a reply, hauled Lily Boone's trunk in the door. Handing Laina the key, he quickly excused himself, leaving her to sort through the contents while Granny Max praised God out loud for working in her boy's heart.

Monday melded into Tuesday, and still Laina pondered and tried to convince herself she was imagining things. After all, she'd only seen that soldier in the moonlight. Maybe his exaggerated greeting was just evidence of one too many mugs of punch at the hop. He hadn't made any effort to talk to her since that night. She hadn't even seen him from a distance. When she'd gotten up enough courage to ask Charlotte about the handsome young man who walked her home from the dance, Charlotte had called him Caleb Jackson.

But when Private Caleb Jackson arrived to collect the Misses Valentine for a Wednesday morning riding lesson, he didn't realize he was being watched as he helped Dinah saddle her pony with the despised sidesaddle. But from where Laina stood ironing in the kitchen, she had a good view. He had a full beard now. The wind and sun had weathered his face considerably. He wasn't a fresh-faced boy anymore. He didn't swagger quite as much. He might have changed his name, but there was no question that Caleb Jackson was the man Laina had known in St. Louis as Beauregard Preston—one of Riverboat Annie's best customers after she'd been forced to start earning money to pay her father's gambling debts with more than just dancing and flirting.

Dear God, Laina prayed, *what am I going to do?*

Maybe he wouldn't cause any trouble. He'd changed his name. Maybe he wanted a fresh start, too. If that were true, then he might be just as worried about her knowledge of his past as she was about his knowledge of hers. Still, Laina worried. People forgave men their "little weaknesses," but those same weaknesses could ruin a woman's reputation, and with it, her life.

She wondered what Sergeant Nathan Boone would think. He had said *"You aren't that woman anymore."* Of course, he thought he knew everything about her past. When he'd said *"Stop dragging yourself back into the past"* he had only been thinking about the woman he'd found in the cellar. He didn't know anything about Riverboat Annie. What if he knew what her life had been like before the dugout?

"Miss Gray," Charlotte said, rushing into the kitchen. She plopped an elaborately trimmed bonnet on her head and begged, "Help me with this bonnet. Please. I'm all thumbs." She peered out the window. "Oh . . . he's here. Isn't he . . . handsome?"

Laina tied a bow beneath Charlotte's chin, and the girl hurried outside.

Jackson greeted her with a smile. He made a joke, and they laughed.

Laina knew that laugh. And knowing what lay behind it, she cringed.

Lord. Dear Lord. What should I do? Please. Tell me what to do.

FIFTEEN

*O my God, I trust in thee; let me not be ashamed,
let not mine enemies triumph over me.*
PSALM 25:2

LAINA LAY ON her back looking up at the rough board ceiling of the Camp Robinson hospital. "Take it out," she said, looking straight at Dr. Valentine.

"What?" He cocked his head to one side, a puzzled expression on his face.

"Take it out. Now. I know you can do it. You can just blame my fainting on the heat. Tell Mrs. Valentine you ordered me to rest here in the hospital for the afternoon. Granny Max doesn't expect me back until suppertime. No one ever has to know." She clutched her midsection. "I'll find a way to pay you. I'll work it off. I promise."

The doctor went to a table near the door and poured some fresh water in a basin. He washed his hands and reached for a clean towel. Only then did he turn around and face Laina. "What you are asking is impossible, Miss Gray."

"It isn't," she snapped. She sat up. "I knew a girl who had it done."

"That may be, Miss Gray," the doctor said, hanging the towel back up, "but it is impossible here at Camp Robinson because I am the only doctor. And I won't do it." He crossed the room and put his hand over Laina's. "When you have had time to think about this, my dear, you will change your mind."

Laina snatched her hand away. "Don't tell me what I'll think."

"I know this is a shock," the doctor said.

Was it her imagination, or was he forcing a fatherly tone into his voice? He was getting very annoying. *God, where are you in this?* "I'll hate it."

"You won't," the doctor said. "No mother hates her own child. You won't be alone in this, Miss Gray. Arrangements can be made. I know of a place." He seemed to gain confidence as he spoke. "Really. We can work things out. Everything will be fine."

"Fine? Everything will be *fine*?" Laina laughed, barely managing to stop before the laugh began to sound like hysteria. She was trembling with the effort to keep herself under control.

"We'll work it out. Trust me."

Laina forced a laugh. "That's very kind of you, Doctor Valentine. I suppose Mrs. Valentine will feel the same way and let me keep my job. And of course Mrs. O'Malley won't mind if her girls spend time with me. And the men here at Camp Robinson." She thought about Private Jackson. "Why, the men will all just accept that Miss Gray has had an immaculate conception. They'll all show me the same respect they always have." She hid her face in her hands.

"No one has to know for a while. Although I would advise you to trust Granny Max so she can help you make some plans." He continued trying to reassure her. "Mrs. Valentine shouldn't have had you moving that heavy furniture in this heat. It scared her when you just keeled over like that. I can promise you she'll not be expecting such things of you in the future. And neither she nor anyone else is going to question my ordering you to rest this afternoon. Let me walk you back to the Row. I'll talk to Granny Max. I'll take care of everything. And I won't tell anyone what we've discussed here, so you have time to think."

"Tell anyone you like," Laina snapped. "It'll be camp gossip soon enough. Secrets like this have a way of traveling on the wind, you know." She sat up and straightened her shoulders. "I don't care."

"Well, I do care," Dr. Valentine said. "About you *and* about the life growing inside you. And I won't be the one sending any of your secrets out on the wind, as you put it. I am here to help you—whether you believe it or not." He rolled down his shirt sleeves and buttoned the cuffs. "You know, Miss Gray, you might consider this: it isn't all that unusual for women who've been . . . ahh . . . treated as you have . . . to be unable to conceive. For you to be in such good health in that respect is something of a miracle."

Laina laughed harshly. "Aren't you glad it's *my* miracle to deal with and not Charlotte's?"

Dr. Valentine took a deep breath. "It may not make you feel better right now. But it is something for you to think about while you decide what to do. God's hand is at work, Miss Gray. We must believe that. Even when we don't understand what He's doing, He is at work. That's all I meant to say."

"God certainly gets blamed for a lot of messes, doesn't He? A flood comes along and it's an *act of God*. Someone dies and *it's God's will*. A woman gets pregnant out of wedlock and *God has a plan*. That may make you feel better about things, Dr. Valentine, but it doesn't help me one bit." She swung her legs over the side of the examining table and hopped down. "Can I go now?"

Retrieving his medical bag, Doctor Valentine said, "I'll walk you."

"No, thank you." Laina said. She adjusted her bonnet and headed for the door.

"I need to check in on Mrs. O'Malley anyway," the doctor insisted as he took her arm. Laina relented and they made their way south to Soapsuds Row. When they came to the Row the doctor said, "I'll do my best to keep Granny Max busy with Mrs. O'Malley, Miss Gray. I know you'll be wanting some time to yourself."

Back at Granny Max's, Laina curled up into a ball upon her bed. She wanted to pull the quilt up over her head and completely close herself off from the world. But it was too hot. She felt like she couldn't breathe. Sitting up, she unbuttoned the top five buttons running down the front of Lily Boone's gray calico dress, then went to the washbasin and soaked a cloth in water and pressed it to the back of her neck. She closed her eyes.

It had taken weeks, but she had finally clawed her way from the brink of insanity. She hadn't had a nightmare in several nights. She almost enjoyed working at the Valentines'. Mrs. Doctor, while a bit of a snob, made few demands beyond basic housekeeping. Dinah's energy and sense of humor more than made up for Charlotte's whining, and Laina enjoyed Frenchy's cooking lessons very much.

She peered at herself in the clouded mirror hanging above the washstand. "You idiot," she said aloud. "Little Laina Gray, making a new life for herself. Brave soldiers to rescue her, Granny Max to love her, God to make everything better." She tapped the image in the glass. "Happily ever after only happens in fairy tales, little girl. And yours just ended."

Turning sideways, she inspected her midsection. How long would it be before everyone would be able to tell? She shook her head. It didn't matter. Granny had said she didn't have to let the past control her. But Granny Max's past wasn't out at the corral right now giving the Misses Valentine riding lessons. And Granny Max's future didn't include her attacker's child.

To make matters worse, Laina had a feeling Caleb Jackson didn't plan on making life easy for her. As time had passed she'd reasoned herself into believing he might be relieved if they just acknowledged one another and agreed to forget the past. But earlier that day, after lunch, she had been kneading dough in the kitchen when someone knocked on the door.

Thinking it was Frenchy coming to help her, Laina had gone to the door all smiles. And there, hat in hand, was Private Caleb Jackson.

"So," he'd said. "I wasn't dreaming. It is you." He motioned for her to step outside and asked, "You ever let your pa know what happened to you? He thinks you're dead, Annie." He drawled the name, looking down at her with a sly little smile.

She touched the left side of her head, wondering if the scar was showing. "Annie *is* dead." She inhaled sharply, trying to organize her thoughts.

But then Charlotte had called out a greeting, her voice warm with pleasure.

Looking past Laina, Jackson smiled. "I was hoping you could accompany me on a walk, Miss Valentine." Charlotte was so quick about getting her bonnet, Jackson only had time to tell Laina he wanted to talk with her before Charlotte was at his side, taking his arm, blushing and chattering something in abominable French.

Laina had thought the day couldn't have gotten any worse. But it had. That afternoon Mrs. Valentine had suggested a thorough cleaning of a bedroom. Trying to move a wardrobe the size of Nebraska, Laina had fainted. And now Caleb Jackson's presence and intentions were only a very small part of an overwhelming, impossible, unbearable reality.

I'm going to have to leave Camp Robinson, Laina thought, turning sideways to look at herself in the mirror. Whether Jackson revealed her past or not, her body eventually would.

She smoothed her skirt over her abdomen and tilted her head as she inspected her profile. *I wonder what Dr. Valentine meant when he said he knew of a place I could go. I wonder how long I have to decide what to do.*

She went into the front room. Standing at the open front door, she looked out on Camp Robinson. Just across the road half a dozen soldiers were standing outside the commissary talking. A shout went up and one of the soldiers shoved another. The rest of the men laughed. It hadn't been all that long ago that roughhousing like that would have sent her scurrying back to her room. She'd come a long way.

All those talks with Granny. All that believing that things could change. All that praying. For what? So *she* could be the one those soldiers over at the commissary joked about? She could just hear them now. Oh, they'd bow and smile at the Friday night dances. For a while. But that, too, would end once the truth about her came out. Mrs. Valentine surely wouldn't want a pregnant housekeeper defiling her daughters. Even Meara O'Malley might have something to say about Katie spending time alone with a scarlet woman. Laina began to tremble. Private Caleb Jackson was the least of her problems.

Get a grip on yourself, girl. You didn't really think you could escape the past, did you? Remember? That only happens in fairy tales. White knights can't always rescue damsels in distress.

Turning away from the door, she thought of Granny's bottle of medicinal liquor high on a shelf above the cookstove. A drink might calm her down. Help her think. Moving a chair to the shelf, she climbed up to get it. But she stepped on the hem of her dress and stumbled. She caught herself just in time to keep from falling, but then she bumped into the table and sent a vase of flowers crashing to the floor. At the sound of breaking glass, anger and fear broke through the thin veil of self-control she'd been clinging to all afternoon. She grabbed the edge of the small table and overturned it. That wasn't enough. Next, she flung one of Granny's rickety kitchen chairs across the room.

As quickly as it had come, the violent rage departed. She staggered toward the doorway to the bedroom, oblivious to the broken glass and water on the floor. Her feet went out from under her, and she landed on her backside on the floor amidst broken glass and scattered flowers. Her anger spent, she rolled onto her side, hugged her knees to her chest, and began to cry.

She was still crying when Nathan Boone appeared at the door. He crouched down beside her and put his hand on her shoulder. "What's wrong, Miss Gray? Are you hurt?"

Drawing her knees even closer to her chest, Laina hid her face in her arms and began to sob. *Oh, God.* She hadn't thought she could feel any worse. She was wrong. Without looking at him, she waved her hand toward the door. "Go away."

He touched the back of her hand. "You're bleeding. Let me help you up."

She jerked her hand away and put the cut to her mouth. "Leave it alone." She inhaled, embarrassed to hear the shuddering sound, like her midsection was shaking and wouldn't let the air come. She sat up, hiding her face with her hands.

"I saw you and Dr. Valentine coming from the hospital. Private Jackson said you fainted."

Laina swiped at her hair, trying to brush it back out of her face. "I just got overheated."

"No wonder," Nathan said. "Jackson and I finished moving that wardrobe. I don't know what Mrs. Valentine could have been thinking expecting a little thing like you to move *furniture*. It's not as if there aren't a hundred men available. You shouldn't have even tried to do that."

She resented the mild scolding. "And you should mind your own business, Sergeant Boone."

"Hey," he said gently, putting his hand on her shoulder. "My friends *are* my business. Let me help you up."

She shrugged his hand off and got up. "Point made. Point taken. Don't make such a huge thing of it. I'm all right." She bent to pick up a chair.

"No," he said, "You aren't." He took her hand off the back of the chair.

"Don't," she whispered and tried to pull away.

When he put his free hand behind her back and pulled her toward him, circling her with his arms, she began to sob. Tears streamed down her face, dampening his shirt.

He pulled away and looked at her with concern written all over his face. "I'll get Granny."

"No!" She clutched his shirt. "Please. Mrs. O'Malley has been feeling so terrible. She really needs Granny Max right now." She closed her eyes, leaning against him and drawing strength from his presence and his arms around her. Finally, she pushed herself away and looked up at him, forcing a half smile. "I'm feeling better. Really. Just an attack of nerves."

He looked around him at the chaos. He picked up the other chair, righted the table. "What brought it on?"

"Oh, well. You know me. Crazy." She bent down to collect the broken pieces of the vase.

"You're not crazy," he said. He touched her again, this time covering her hand with his so she would stop collecting the pieces of broken glass. Lifting her chin, he peered into her eyes. "And you're not telling me the truth. Sit down for a minute."

When Laina obeyed, Boone took both her hands in his and squeezed them. "This may not be any of my business. And maybe I should just let it be. But I'd rather you trust me with whatever is bothering you so much."

"You can't fix it," Laina said, looking down at her hands in his. "What's the point?"

"The point is, sometimes it just helps to talk things over." He ducked his head and made her look at him. "And how do you know I can't help if you don't give me a chance?"

Part of her longed to tell him. Everything. But just then she noticed a corner of Lily Boone's picture barely showing above the rim of his shirt pocket. She pulled her hand away. "You really do need to get a handle on this knight-in-shining-armor complex you have," she said. "Don't you ever tire of role-playing, Sir Nathan?"

He leaned back in his chair. "I'll make you a promise, Lady Gray." He smiled. "You'll be the first one to know when I want to resign."

Well, you'll be resigning soon, Sir Nathan. As soon as you hear the latest about this damsel in distress. She laughed nervously and looked away from him. She swiped tears away with the back of her hand and forced the tension out of her voice. "If I make you coffee, will you drink it and then go home?"

"I don't want coffee. But I'll make *you* something to drink," he said. "Something cold. Wait here." He took her by the shoulders and urged her out of the kitchen chair and into Granny's rocker. "Close your eyes and try to relax. I'll be back in a minute." She leaned her head back and closed her eyes.

Some of the girls at Miss Hart's had had secrets like this. No one there ever spoke of it. The girls went to class, grew large, gave birth, and left. None of the other girls ever saw a baby at Miss Hart's. Once, when they were whispering after hours, the subject came up.

"I know where they go," Nellie Pierce had said, her mouth turning upwards in the smug little smile Laina hated. "One night I heard a scream, and I woke up and looked outside. I saw a carriage waiting down by the door, and Miss Hart came outside with a bundle in her arms. She looked this way and that, and then she went down the stairs and handed the bundle up into the carriage."

"That doesn't tell us anything," one of the girls whined. "We still don't know where they go. What do they do with them?"

"Oh, who cares?" Nellie said abruptly. She looked pointedly at Laina. "No one cares about orphans or bastards. They are a pox on society. My papa says so."

Laina looked down at her abdomen. "You hear that? You're aren't born yet, but you're a pox on society."

She held out her unadorned left hand. What was it, she wondered, that made it all right for an entire world of people to determine an unborn child's worth based on the presence or absence of a piece of metal around its mother's finger—something the child couldn't control. It made Laina angry. Why should a baby be punished for the circumstances of its birth? It wasn't fair.

Right, Laina. It isn't fair. So why did you want Dr. Valentine to kill it? She answered herself. *I was desperate. I know how this is going to work. What people are going to think. Especially if the good Private Jackson starts telling Riverboat*

Annie stories in the barracks. Neither Sergeant Boone's friendship nor Granny Max's faith are going to be able to change what people are going to think and say about me . . . and how they are going to treat this child. "My child."

She bowed her head and looked down at her still-flat abdomen. *But I can change it. If I leave Camp Robinson and go where no one knows me, I can create any reality I want. Any past I need.*

Her mind racing, Laina got up and began to straighten the mess she'd made. She worked mechanically, and by the time Sergeant Boone reappeared at the door, she had the nucleus of a plan. She looked up at the tall glass in his hand. "Is that what I think it is?" she asked in disbelief.

"Fresh squeezed," Nathan said, rattling the ice cubes in the glass. "Courtesy of Frenchy. I told him about Mrs. Valentine's idea of 'light housework'. And the aftereffects. He mixed this up special just for you. It's lemonade—mostly."

"I thought all the ice from last winter's cutting was long since gone."

"The men are hoarding a last chunk of it for the Fourth. They won't miss three little pieces." He plunked the glass upon the table and sat down. "Besides, if rank can't get a man a little ice on a hot day, what good is it?"

Laina draped the wet rag she'd used to scrub the floor over the back of the stove and returned to sit down at the table and sip the cool drink. Raising the glass she said, "Tell Frenchy his 'lemonade—mostly' is delicious." Pressing the side of the glass against her cheek, she closed her eyes, relishing the rare sensation of something really cool.

"You might as well tell me the whole story," Nathan said. He crossed his arms across his chest. "Because I'm not leaving until you do."

His jaw was set and he had a stubborn little smile on his face. Laina wondered if this was the look he gave recalcitrant recruits. She shifted in her chair while her mind raced for something to satisfy his curiosity. She pulled her hands into her lap and looked down at the table. "All right. You win."

She took another sip of lemonade while she mentally organized the story she hoped he would believe. "You remember when you asked me where I learned to dance and I said something about another life?"

He nodded. "That other life doesn't matter anymore, Laina. When are you going to finally realize that?"

She shrugged. "I *was* starting to believe it." She took a swallow of lemonade and set the glass back on the table. "But then the *past* escorted Miss Valentine home from last Friday's hop. And then it came by the Valentines' this afternoon to take Miss Valentine for a walk after lunch."

"You're talking about Private Jackson," Nathan said. When Laina nodded, he continued, "I don't know exactly what it is you're talking about, but I can promise you Private Caleb Jackson won't give you any trouble. He and I go way back, and he has enough skeletons in his own closet to worry over without threatening to bring out anyone else's." He added, "And why would he threaten you, anyway?"

Yes, Laina thought. *Why, indeed.* This story wasn't sounding very convincing. "Maybe I *am* overreacting."

"Has he threatened you?" Laina could see the muscles working in Nathan's jaw. "Because if he has, I—"

"No," Laina said. "No. He only stopped by the Valentines' to see Charlotte while I was over there this morning." She shivered and rubbed her arms. "I'm probably reading things into it. But I knew him. In that other life." *Yes, this is sounding more believable.*

"Whatever he knows about you can't hurt you now," Nathan insisted.

Laina took a sip of lemonade. *Tell him the truth. Not all of it. Just enough to convince him that fear of Private Jackson is the only reason you're upset.* She took a deep breath and swallowed a little more lemonade. If she said this just right, he might believe the only reason she fainted, the only reason she was so upset, was because of Jackson. She focused on the top button of Nathan's uniform as she recited. "Once upon a time, there was a riverboat called the Missouri Princess. On the riverboat lived a gambler. And the gambler had a daughter named Laina." She hesitated. She moistened her lips and glanced up at Nathan, who was staring at her with such sincere concern it sent a pang of guilt through her. She looked back at the button and continued, telling him about being sent to Miss Hart's, about her father's gambling debts and having to leave the school to live on a riverboat, and about being known as Riverboat Annie.

"I still don't see what any of this has to do with what happened today," Nathan said, "unless you aren't telling me everything. Is that it?" He leaned forward. "Did Jackson say something to upset you?"

Laina shook her head. She cleared her throat. "He didn't have to say anything." She shifted in her seat before reaching out to slide her hand up and down the cool glass. "He doesn't have to say a word, Nathan. Because he knows exactly how Riverboat Annie helped her father pay his gambling debts." She looked him in the eyes. "He knows because when he was still calling himself Beauregard Preston, he was one of her best customers." She could feel the blush rising up the back of her neck. Her cheeks began to burn.

Nathan nodded, and Laina thought his face looked redder, too. "That's an interesting story, Miss Gray. But the fact still remains that no one named Riverboat Annie lives at Camp Robinson. And if Private Jackson has an interest in Miss Valentine, he'll realize that your knowledge of his past gives you a certain amount of power over his future, too." He paused. "Dr. and Mrs. Valentine wouldn't want a man like that anywhere near their daughter. And I'll remind him of that. You can be assured he won't be bringing up anything from the past here at Camp Robinson. We were friends once, but you and I are friends *now*. If he dares cause you any trouble, he'll answer to me."

Laina sighed. She rubbed the back of her neck and forced a smile. "Thank you, but I'd really rather you not get involved. I've had my grand self-pity party. I've thrown my fit. What you said earlier is probably right. I just overreacted. It isn't really fair of me to assume he means to cause trouble. And I certainly don't want to be responsible for coming between old friends." She paused. "I need some time to think. Then I'll talk to him. Perhaps he just needs reassurance that I'm not going to ruin things between him and Miss Valentine." She forced a smile. "Everything will probably work out."

Boone nodded. "Look, Miss Gray. I know a few things about Jackson, too. And I've been keeping my eye on him ever since he arrived at camp. We've had a couple of . . . talks. I think he's sincere about wanting to stay out of trouble here. He hasn't always managed it, but I'd like to see him succeed."

"Well, I don't have anything against him, and I don't plan to stand in the way of anything he wants to accomplish. I'll tell him just that. And if what you're saying about him is true, then there aren't going to be any more problems."

"Or fainting spells?"

"Right."

"I'll bring him over whenever you say."

"I appreciate your concern, but I don't think Private Jackson and I will need a referee."

"I'd feel better if you'd let me come with him," Boone said.

Laina closed her eyes. She took a deep breath. "Don't take this wrong, Sergeant, but I'd appreciate it very much if you would climb down off your white horse and just let me be a grown-up. It may be hard for you to believe, but I am clothed and in my right mind most of the time these days." She stood up. "In spite of what you saw earlier."

After a silence that felt to Laina like it lasted for five minutes, Sergeant

Boone got up and reached for his hat. "You get some rest," he said, and let himself out.

Laina took another deep breath. It had been one of her better performances, she thought. She was exhausted. Dr. Valentine would have told Granny Max he wanted her to rest. How glad she was of that as she crept to her bed. She undressed slowly, dropping Lily Boone's worn gray calico dress and petticoats on the floor. She removed her shoes and stockings. Letting down her hair, she dampened another cloth for the back of her neck and slipped beneath a sheet where she lay still, enjoying the sensation as she ran the last fragment of ice from her drink over her parched skin. *God bless Frenchy Dubois.* She didn't know when she fell asleep, but sometime after sundown she heard Granny Max come in. She could sense Granny looking down at her, but she feigned sleep.

"You all right, lamb?"

When Laina didn't answer, Granny went back into the front room. Her rocker creaked as she sat down. Laina could picture the old woman opening her Bible. Granny always read her Bible before she went to bed. The rhythm of her rocking was soon joined with the comforting sound of humming.

Full circle. Here I am hiding again, while Granny rocks and prays.

Her thoughts swirled from Granny to God, from Doctor Valentine to Sergeant Boone to Private Jackson, around and around and back again. Both with Dr. Valentine and with Sergeant Boone, she had performed well. She'd almost convinced herself that she was capable of handling things. But she still had to face her past in the form of Private Caleb Jackson. And now, in the darkness, fear returned. *God. Oh, God. Why are you doing this to me?* She smothered her tears with her pillow.

"Granny Max?" Laina whispered, half hoping Granny wouldn't hear her.

The rocker creaked as Granny got up and came to the door. "Yes, honey-lamb. What is it?"

"Do you remember what you told me about Josiah Paine? About the past and the future?"

"I said he may have your past, but you don't have to give him your future."

Tears welled up in her eyes as Laina struggled to reply. She swiped them away with the back of her hand and clutched her pillow as she looked toward Granny's silhouette in the doorway. "I'm afraid you were mistaken."

"Why do you say that?"

"I'm going to have a baby, Granny. J-Josiah Paine's baby." The fragments of her bravery were washed away when she said that name aloud. In the time it took Granny to cross the room to her, Laina had curled up into a ball and begun to sob.

"Oh, darlin'," Granny said, rubbing her back. "Oh, honey-lamb. Are you sure?"

She told Granny Max about Private Jackson, about fainting, and about Dr. Valentine. "At least Sergeant Boone believed me when I told him the only thing wrong was Private Jackson's showing up here at Camp Robinson."

"So no one knows about the baby but Dr. Valentine?"

Laina nodded. "But everyone *will* know. You can't exactly keep a secret like this for long, can you?" She began to cry again. "Oh, Granny. What am I going to do?"

She had grown so accustomed to Granny Max having an answer for her questions, Laina was taken aback when Granny didn't respond. Moments went by, with her own sobs quieting, and Granny just sitting on the edge of the bed rubbing Laina's back in the dark.

"Lord," Granny finally said. "This is hard news. Hard." Granny's voice wavered. "It seems, Lord, like this little gal has had enough troubles. She didn't need this. I got to tell you, Lord, I am wondering exactly what you are up to. I know you have a plan. I know you work in mysterious ways. But this is one of the most mysterious yet. She is asking me what to do, and I don't know what to say. Show me how to help her. Show us what to do."

Granny Max stopped for more than a few minutes. Laina waited for her to finally come up with something helpful. Some wisdom. Some answers. She didn't.

"Most of all, Lord, show Laina that your love is just as strong as it ever has been. That Josiah Paine might have meant what he did for evil, Lord, but you can work it out for good. Help me believe that and live it so that Laina can believe it and live it, too. Help us both believe in spite of the way things look. Amen."

After a few more minutes had gone by, Granny said, "I don't expect that was what you were hoping to hear me say, was it, honey-lamb?"

"I don't really know what I expected," Laina said. "I'm sorry I've had to burden you with this, Granny. I really am."

"Don't you be sorry for that. Ever. I love you, child," Granny said. "And love bears all things, believes all things, hopes all things, endures all things. So you and I will bear and believe and hope and endure . . . *together*. I promise."

Laina turned onto her back. She clutched a pillow to her midsection. "I asked Dr. Valentine to end it. Does that . . . shock you?"

Granny answered, "It takes a lot more than that to shock old Granny Max, child." She felt for Laina's hand in the dark. "But that's not an answer you want to live with."

"No. It isn't. Not really."

Granny Max squeezed her hand. "Right. So we will wait on the good Lord to give us an answer we can live with."

"And what do we do while we wait?" Laina wanted to know.

"We just do the next thing, honey-lamb. Just like always."

Laina fell asleep holding Granny Max's hand.

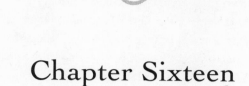

Chapter Sixteen

The words of a talebearer are as wounds,
and they go down into the innermost parts of the belly.
PROVERBS 18:8

"ANNIE?" SOMEONE CALLED.

Laina jumped and turned her head just in time to see Wilber tear across Soldier Creek toward Private Jackson. The dog wasn't barking, which Laina soon realized meant he might be a threat, because with a low growl he chomped on to Jackson's pant leg and began to throw all his weight into keeping the soldier from getting any closer to the woman seated beside the creek.

"Wilber," Laina said firmly. "No." The dog let go. "Come," Laina said, laying her comb on the grass and letting her hair fall down her back. Wilber went to her and sat down beside her, ears alert, muscles tense as he watched Jackson.

Jackson didn't come any farther. Instead, he took his hat off and stood, twirling it in his hands. "I . . . uh . . . I wanted to apologize." He motioned to her wet hair. "But I shouldn't be bothering you now."

"It's not like you haven't seen me with my hair down before," Laina said. She stood up. "But aren't you supposed to be doing some kind of fatigue duty this time of day?" She looked toward Soapsuds Row, wondering if anyone had seen the soldier pushing his way through the stand of bushes that afforded her a measure of privacy, both for drying her hair and for thinking.

Jackson nodded. "Sergeant Boone gave me permission to come over to the Row. I talked Granny Max into telling me where you were"—he grinned—"and into letting me come down here alone." He nodded at Wilber. "She doesn't need to worry about you, anyway. Not with that pup around. He seems to think he's a guard dog."

Laina reached up to smooth her hair back off her forehead. "How did you get Sergeant Boone to give you leave from duty?"

"I told him the truth," Caleb said. "Part of it, anyway." He rushed to add, "Not any part that would cause you trouble, though."

"Sergeant Boone knows all about me," Laina said. She lifted her chin. "You can't hurt me by telling him about St. Louis."

"Hey," Jackson protested. "I don't want to hurt you. You were always good to me. I've got no reason to bring up the past. That's what I wanted to tell you yesterday, but then Miss Valentine came out, and I didn't dare say any more. The next thing I knew you'd fainted." He scowled. "Are you all right?"

Laina bent over and picked up her comb. With studied calm, she pulled a hank of wet hair over her shoulder and went back to combing it. "I'm fine, Private."

"I'm glad to see you are safe," he said, sounding sincere. "And I'm hoping you'll agree that there's no reason for the past to have any part in our lives here at Camp Robinson."

Laina peered up at him. He met her gaze straight on and didn't waver. She let go of her hair and tucked the comb into her apron pocket. "You've worked hard on your accent. I don't hear any southern at all. Except when you let it out on purpose to impress Miss Valentine."

He cleared his throat. "Yeah, well . . . old habits die hard." He took a deep breath. "You remember how it is, playing the game. Smiling, flirting, making them want . . ." He shrugged, then shook his head. "I was just playing when I first asked her to dance. But there are things to like about her. She's not perfect, but she can be really sweet." He grinned. "I haven't been with a girl who was honestly *sweet* and truly naïve since . . ." He looked at her apologetically. "Ever."

"It's all right," Laina said. "I don't take that personally. It's the truth."

He smiled at her. "I'm working to change. You could have made things hard for me—could have told Dr. Valentine some colorful stories. I'm grateful you didn't."

Laina said, "I'll admit to being more than a little worried that night you walked Charlotte home from the hop." She paused. "Of course, some of that was on my own account. You could have made things hard for me, too. And I'm grateful you didn't. I guess we both can agree that everybody deserves a second chance. As far as I'm concerned, we can consider both Riverboat Annie and Beauregard Preston dead." She held out her hand. "Care to shake on it?"

Caleb took her hand. "Long live Private Caleb Jackson and Miss Laina Gray."

When Laina saw him looking down at her scarred wrist, she pulled her hand away.

"What happened to you, anyway? It was like you just disappeared."

"I thought I found a way off the river," Laina said.

"It looks like you did," Jackson said. "I'm glad for you. Eustis treated you bad. You deserve something good."

Laina reached up to the left side of her head. She lifted the hair away to expose the scar. "See that?" she said.

Jackson touched her temple. "It barely shows."

"That's what Granny says." Laina shrugged. "It doesn't matter, I guess. It's not like I'm competing for male attention anymore. I've had more than my share of that." Impulsively, she pulled her cuffs back so Jackson could see both her wrists. "There's worse things than living on the river. I learned that."

Jackson swore violently. "Who did this to you? Somebody ought to teach him a lesson he won't forget."

"Someone did," Laina said softly. "He's buried up in the Sandhills." She told him about Josiah Paine's sod dugout. "Sergeant Boone and Corporal Dorsey found me. Brought me here." She nodded toward Soapsuds Row. "Granny Max brought me back from the darkness. With some help from God. At least I like to think God was in there somewhere. Although I never was one to think much about God before." She looked up at him. "Never figured God thought much about me."

Jackson's voice was almost gentle. "You were always one of the nicer girls. It doesn't surprise me that God would pick you out to see what He could do with you." He nodded. "And it looks like He's doing all right by you. You even got your own personal guardian angel."

Laina nodded. "Yes. Granny Max would fit that title."

"Oh, I don't mean Granny Max," Jackson said. "I mean the one in the blue uniform." He grinned. "He takes his duties real serious, too. In fact," he said, looking past Laina, "here he comes now."

Wilber tore off again, yapping and chasing after Whiskey's feet.

"That dog's gonna get himself killed one of these days chasing after horses that way," Jackson said.

"I know he shouldn't do that," Laina said. "But I don't know how to break him of it."

Just then Whiskey landed a kick to Wilber's midsection. The dog yelped and went rolling, then got up, shook himself, and slunk off.

"Maybe Whiskey will do the job for you," Jackson said, offering his hand and helping Laina up. They stood together, waiting for Sergeant Boone to dismount.

"It looks like I've just missed a real serious powwow," he said, looking in Laina's direction.

Laina didn't respond to Sergeant Boone's comment. "I've got to get back to help Granny with the afternoon chores. Thank you for letting Private Jackson spend some time with me." She smiled at Jackson. "I'll likely see you at the hop Friday night, Private."

"Save me a dance," he said, bowing and waving his hat across his body in an exaggerated flourish.

Laina laughed in spite of herself. "You, sir, are an incorrigible flirt."

"I am," Jackson said. "But I'm harmless. At least to you."

———

Doctor Valentine had said that time would change Laina's feelings. Whether the doctor was right and time changed them, or Granny Max's prayers changed them, or God himself did it, the reality was that Laina's feelings about the new life growing inside her did change. She thought about how the doctor said her getting pregnant was nothing short of a miracle. The idea of Josiah Paine being part of a miracle repulsed her. But after a few more late-night talks with Granny Max, Laina began to think that maybe it was possible for God to take the evil men did and turn it for good.

One Sunday afternoon Granny Max read her an Old Testament story about a man named Joseph, whose brothers were so jealous they made their father believe Joseph had been killed and then sold him as a slave. Even when things changed, and it looked like Joseph was going to build a new life, he was accused of rape and sent back to prison. Laina could relate to the idea of feeling like the worst was over only to learn the worst was still to come. What astounded her was that when Joseph had the chance to take his revenge on his good-for-nothing brothers, he *forgave* them. Joseph's story was where Granny Max had gotten that phrase *"You meant it for evil, but God meant it for good."*

Laina couldn't quite see her pregnancy as a *good* thing. But Joseph's story did help her not be mad at God. She decided she really didn't want to kick God out of her life. With a baby and no husband, she wasn't going to be able to count on getting a lot of sympathy from most people. If God wanted to work something out, she would be all for it.

Granny said a person's faith could only grow if it was tested. Laina couldn't help thinking that, if this was a test, it sure was a big one for someone with her amount of faith. Granny Max told her she should talk to God about the things that worried her. "Don't wait for me to pray for you, child. Talk to Him yourself. Now that you're in His family, you got the same telegraph line to the Lord God I do."

"What do you mean *now that* I'm in God's family?" Laina asked.

They were standing over a tub of laundry in the washhouse. Granny Max looked around her. "You think everybody's in God's family?" she asked.

"Of course not," Laina said. "Josiah Paine certainly wasn't."

"So how does a person get from outside to inside the family?" Without waiting for Laina to answer, Granny Max grabbed up a pile of filthy shirts. "A person has to say yes to God—like you did after them rustlers bothered you. The Bible says all the good things we can do are just like dirty laundry." Then she put the shirts into the washtub. She took up a piece of lye soap. "Only the blood of Jesus can wash us white as snow. We can scrub and scrub and scrub ourselves, and we never get clean enough to please God." She scrubbed at the collar in her hands. "Just like Harlan Yates's shirt collars. I declare there is no soap in the *world* that will get this boy's collars as clean as they were when they were new. And as soon as I get 'em 'Granny-Max clean,' he dirties 'em up all over again—and worse."

"Just like me," Laina said. "I get my life cleaned up a little, and then something happens to get it all messed up all over again—and worse."

"So the whole point, honey-lamb, is we stop trying to get ourselves cleaned up. We just let the good Lord Jesus take all the dirt. That's what He was doing on that cross. And we say 'thank you, Jesus, I'm gonna trust you to take care of all this dirt in my life.' " Granny wrung Harlan's shirt out and plopped it into the rinse tub for Laina. "And that's it. It's gone."

"Without me *doing* anything to clean it up myself?"

Granny nodded. "He already took care of that for you, honey-lamb—just because you said yes. We can't make a soap strong enough to clean up our dirt, child. Only God can do that. And He did it. Only He didn't use lye soap. He used blood."

Laina grabbed Harlan Yates's shirt and rinsed it as clean as she could. While she was wringing it out, she asked, "Granny, do you think Sergeant Boone is in God's family?" She finished pressing the excess water out of Harlan's shirt and added it to the pile of laundry waiting to be hung outside.

Granny sighed. "I don't know, child. I hope so."

"He seems pretty intent on cleaning up his own dirt. I mean, he likes to manage things for himself. It seems like it might be harder for someone like that to just humble down and let God have at their problems."

Granny nodded. "You've got Nathan figured pretty well, child. That is his struggle, as near as I know. He just doesn't want to humble down."

Laina nodded and stooped to lift the laundry basket. Outside in the sunshine, she went to work filling the clothesline with clean shirts. When she finished and headed back to the washhouse, she looked back toward the row of clean shirts flapping in the breeze.

For Laina, understanding her new faith came in fragments, at places like Granny Max's table or the washhouse. Bit by bit she began to put the pieces together. She finally believed God truly loved her. He would listen to her. He would help her. She was, as Granny Max said, one of God's lambs. Imperfect, sinful, pregnant, scared, unworthy. And loved.

She grew more confident in her conversations with God. She asked Him to help her and her little girl—she was fairly certain the baby would be a girl. She just could not think that God would expect her to mother a miniature version of Josiah Paine. She was still afraid, but underneath the fear was a sense that things might work out. So, while nothing changed in Laina's circumstances, it was as if everything had changed, because she was doing her best to look at everything in a different way: *You meant it for evil, but God meant it for good.*

———

It was on a blistering Sunday afternoon picnic late in July when Laina first felt the baby move. Sergeant Boone had taken Katie down to the creek to fish. Harlan and Becky were playing euchre. Granny and Laina, with Wilber stretched out at Laina's side sound asleep, were sitting stitching away at some quilt blocks, when suddenly Laina thought she felt something different deep inside her. She lay her needlework aside and stroked Wilber's soft white fur while she concentrated and waited. It wasn't long before the sensation came again. *Quickening.* She couldn't resist the impulse to place her hand over her abdomen while she sent a message to the baby. *Hello. I'm your mama. I am going to take good care of you.*

In recent weeks, Laina had grown less resentful of her predicament and more determined to see that her baby have at least a chance at a decent life. Whatever it took, she would make it happen. *Her* child was *not* going to grow up an outcast. *Her* child was never going to be the one the Nellie Pierces of the world looked down upon—not if Laina Gray had anything to say about it.

Mrs. Gruber had asked if Laina could help out at the trading post a couple of days a week. When another laundress left the camp, Laina took on her job. It kept her working from early morning until late at night, and it took every ounce of her strength, but one coin at a time, her savings account grew. She kept her money tied up in a square of calico in the bottom of her workbasket.

She still didn't have a complete plan, but by fall she hoped to have enough saved to leave Camp Robinson and start a new life elsewhere. She could wear a wedding ring and talk about Army life. People would make assumptions, and if she kept her mouth shut, she could become the 'Widow Someone.' And the baby would have a chance. Maybe Dr. Valentine was right. Maybe no one would have to know.

———

"Stop!" Charlotte gasped. She clutched Caleb's hand. "We mustn't. Mother and Papa will be back soon from their ride. And I'm supposed to be sick with a headache. I'm supposed to be home taking a nap."

Caleb lowered his head and nuzzled her neck. He kissed her ear. "Good idea. Let's take a nap. Right here." His hands encircled her waist for a minute, then he traced her jaw with his fingertip. "I care for you, Miss Valentine," he whispered, bringing a slight southern drawl back into his voice even as he was backing her into an empty stall.

"I love you, too, Caleb. But—stop it!" She slapped his hand away and reached for the button he had just undone.

"You don't love me. You're just saying that." Jackson slumped down onto the clean straw. He removed his cap and swiped his forehead. He held his head in his hands for a minute. When he looked up at Charlotte, his face was streaked with tears. "I'll make Sergeant someday, Charlotte. I promise I will." His voice was dejected, "But by that time you'll be out of my life. You'll be married to someone else."

"I won't," Charlotte protested. She stroked his bowed head with her gloved hand. "Don't say that, Caleb. Please. I do love you. And I'll wait. For as long as it takes. I'll wait forever."

Jackson snorted. "Forever?" He leaned back on the straw. Without looking up at her he said, "Or just until Sergeant Boone stops mooning over his dead wife?"

"I don't care about Nathan Boone anymore," Charlotte said. She sat down next to him on the hay. "And he doesn't care for me, either. He's much too caught up with rescuing people over on the Row to even think about love. First there was Laina Gray with all her troubles. And now it's those O'Malley girls. And just because their mama is sick. You'd think Nathan Boone was personally responsible for Becky and Katie, the way he pampers them." She pouted, ducking her head and peering at Caleb from beneath the brim of her straw bonnet. She smiled at him. "And besides, the *crush* I had on Sergeant Boone wasn't *anything* like what I feel for you."

Charlotte only meant to comfort Caleb when she kissed his cheek and leaned over to put her head on his shoulder. She didn't expect what happened when he kissed her back, in a way that wasn't anything like the kisses he had sneaked before. There was nothing prim or shy about it. Before she quite knew what had happened, they were lying close together in the hay. She tried to tell herself she should be shocked. She tried not to like it. But he kept kissing her, and in a matter of minutes Charlotte had quite forgotten to care about her virtue.

She would never be able to recall exactly what it was being shouted that brought everything between her and Caleb to an abrupt halt. She would only remember an unbelievable roar and the rage behind it. And she would remember being afraid of her own father for the first time in her life as he shook Caleb Jackson by the neck and shouted at him. "What do you think you are *doing* with my *daughter*?!"

He followed the question with expletives so vile, Charlotte would never be able to repeat it to anyone. She had no idea her father even *knew* such words. They didn't frighten her, because she didn't know what they meant, but her father's rage most certainly did frighten her. For a moment, she feared for Caleb's life. But then her father turned his white-hot anger on her.

"Get yourself put back together, young lady," Doctor Valentine snapped.

It seemed to take an eternity for Charlotte's trembling hands to button the dozen small buttons Caleb had managed so easily. Finally, she fastened the last one. She pulled her hat back on and caught the elastic strap beneath the loose bun at the back of her head. Then she stood up, slapping at her dress to rid it of the last vestiges of hay.

Dr. Valentine was calmer by the time she had reassembled herself. But calmer was even more frightening, because with deliberate intent, he lifted his left leg and planted the bottom of his foot against Caleb's midsection with such force the private fell backward on the hay, arms and legs flung out in all directions. He gasped and clutched his stomach, rolling onto his side.

"Papa!" Charlotte pleaded. "Papa, please. Don't hurt him!"

"Avery."

For the first time, Charlotte saw her mother. She must have been waiting outside by the carriage. Or had she retreated there after seeing into the stall for herself?

"Avery, we need to handle this in private."

Without looking at his wife, Dr. Valentine pointed at Charlotte. "You," he said, lowering his voice with great effort. "You get yourself home before I take a notion to rattle your teeth! *One* unwed mother at Camp Robinson is quite enough! God forbid that *my daughter* join the ranks! Do you want to live out your life over on Soapsuds Row, too?!" Grasping Charlotte by the shoulders, the doctor spun her around and shoved her none too gently toward her mother. "Go home. And you'd better be waiting in your room when I get there."

When her mother slipped an arm about her shoulders, Charlotte leaned against her and allowed herself to be led away.

As the two women scurried across the parade ground toward home, Dr. Valentine took a deep breath and turned to face the stall where Caleb Jackson still lay on his side, afraid to move.

"If you know what is good for you, Private Jackson, you will still be in this stall when I get back."

"Sir," Caleb stammered. "Sir, please. I . . . I've done some stupid things in my life. This is one of the worst. But, Doctor Valentine, I . . . I do care about your daughter."

Valentine glared at the soldier, who had scooted to sit up and was staring up at him clutching his side. "How dare you. *Caring* does not drag a young girl into a barn and treat her like a common harlot. *Caring* doesn't sully an innocent girl's reputation. Do you have any idea the price Charlotte could pay for your kind of *caring*, Private?"

"Look, I was wrong. It won't happen again, sir. Please." He hung his head and murmured, "You've got to believe me."

"No, Private. That is where you are wrong. I do *not* have to believe you." Doctor Valentine closed the bottom half of the stall door. He peered down at Jackson. "If I can figure out a way to see you drummed out of the army without dragging my daughter's name through the mud, I'll do it, Private. And *you* can believe *me* about that!"

Dr. Valentine kicked the stall door and stormed off to find Sergeant Boone. His rage made him want to skip talking with the sergeant and take the matter directly to the lieutenant. But it had long been the tradition in the army for officers to trust most of the company discipline to their sergeants. And as he walked along the trail curving behind the log ordnance storehouse, around the quartermaster's corral and toward Soapsuds Row, a doubt that had been flickering beneath the doctor's rage finally took form.

What if, he wondered, his flirtatious daughter had done something to *invite* the private's attentions. What if—and he didn't want to believe it, but he had to think it was a possibility—what if Charlotte was a willing partner to what was going on in that stall? The handsome Private Jackson had certainly gotten more than his share of dances at last Friday's hop. He'd been invited to dinner more than once. And Charlotte hadn't mentioned Sergeant Boone in a while. Could there possibly be some truth to the young man's stammered protests just now? And, Dr. Valentine wondered with a growing knot in his stomach, what if what he discovered today had happened before? What if, as he had shouted at his daughter, there was already a second unwed mother-to-be residing at Camp Robinson?

Emmy-Lou was right, of course. The whole thing must be handled in private. What was left of Charlotte's reputation had to be protected. She didn't deserve to have her life ruined because of one mistake. As he walked toward the barracks in search of Sergeant Boone, Dr. Valentine decided two things. First, he would inform Sergeant Boone of the situation, but he would insist on no public punishment of Private Jackson. He would leave Private Jackson to stew for an hour or so and then go back and tell him to resume his regular duties until Sergeant Boone decided what to do. Second, it was high time Dinah and Charlotte paid a visit to their grandmother. August had to be cooler—in more ways than one—on the shores of Lake Michigan, where Emmy-Lou's mother summered, than it was here in the West.

————

He'd had his share of run-ins with military authority since enlisting, but if there was one thing Private Caleb Jackson understood about the frontier army, it was that guard duty was not to be taken lightly. He'd recently been present when another recruit was sentenced to six months in the guardhouse after the officer of the day discovered the young private asleep at his post. Jackson had determined that while he might be on metaphorically "thin ice" because of other infractions, he would never be caught for anything so stupid as falling asleep while on guard duty.

Other men might grumble about the long, lonely hours spent guarding a post where nothing happened, but Jackson never felt alone at his post near the cavalry stables. After all the hours he'd spent handling the Company G horses, being around the stables was like being with some of his best friends. He recognized Whiskey's unique, trumpeting whinny and Renegade's rumbling complaints against the horse in the next stall. And he knew just when to expect Dinah Valentine to slip into the stables to feed her pony dried apples or peppermint candies. Private Jackson almost enjoyed guard duty.

But tonight, Jackson found no joy in his assignment. He was, in fact, as close to becoming a nervous wreck as he had ever been. Even when he'd lost two weeks' pay at the poker tables in St. Louis, he had not felt this bad. As he paced back and forth, his mind reeled between the past and the future.

About an hour after he and Charlotte were discovered, Dr. Valentine had returned as promised. He'd grasped the top of the stall door in both hands and said without emotion, "Sergeant Boone has been informed of the situation. He will deal with you later. In the meantime, you are to resume your duties." His usually kind eyes became hateful slits as he added, "And *stay away from my daughter*. Do not discuss this with anyone. Is that clear, Private?"

It had taken every ounce of courage Caleb Jackson had to look Doctor Valentine in the eye, but he'd done it. "Yes, sir. Perfectly clear, sir." He held the doctor's gaze until the man nodded and left. Then he had clamped his hat back on his head, brushed the straw off his uniform, and answered the day's second water call with the rest of Company G. He'd gone to the mess hall with everyone else and waited through one of the longest evenings of his life until his turn came to relieve the sentry posted near the stables. And now, here he was, pacing back and forth, cursing himself—for his stupidity, for not controlling himself with Charlotte, for taking advantage of her inexperience, for losing what little self-control he had—and feeling terrified by the very real possibility that tomorrow he would no longer be in the United States Army. He didn't think Dr. Valentine could do that without a formal inquiry, which he wouldn't call to protect Charlotte, but then Jackson hadn't thought he'd get so carried away with Charlotte, either.

Sergeant Boone had once asked him what he would do if he couldn't be in the army. He'd displayed bravado and a self-assured attitude when he said he'd get a job on a ranch. But the truth was, he wanted to make the army his life. While other men complained about the endless rolling Sandhills, Jackson reveled in the open country and the canopy of sky above him. He wouldn't have admitted it to anyone, but he had come to admire men like Corporal Dorsey, soldiers who had given themselves to a cause and made good on the gift. Men who would throw themselves into a battle with all they had and win. Private Caleb Jackson hadn't ever made good on anything, unless you counted his keeping that promise to Annie about not yapping about her past. Protecting Annie had been pretty well cancelled out by what he'd almost done with Charlotte today.

The only winnings he'd experienced in life had been at a poker table when he cheated better than anyone else in the game. It wasn't much to be proud of. He had begun to wish that when he looked in the mirror, the man who looked back at him would be someone who had a sense of honor, and the self-respect that went along with it.

Being in the army had helped him begin to control some of the demons inside him. He wasn't drinking as much and he hadn't been in a fight in a long time. He even had some of last month's pay left. He hadn't gambled it all away. As a result of forced military discipline, he was beginning to see signs of a developing self-discipline.

A wolf howled, and Jackson shivered. Boone would be coming any minute now, and he had to have a defense ready. Charlotte Valentine had gotten under his skin, and now, having almost conquered his worst vices, he was about to lose everything because of her. He shook his head and cursed himself. *You really can pick 'em, you idiot. Why'd you have to go and pick an officer's daughter? And the very same girl a sergeant's been squiring around. And not just any sergeant. Sergeant Nathan Boone, the unofficial guardian of all that's good in Camp Robinson.*

He wondered what Boone would think if he knew Miss Valentine had been a more than willing participant in their romance. At the thought, he could almost hear his own father saying *"It isn't honorable for a man to hide behind a woman's skirts."* To his surprise, Caleb realized that he wanted to at least try to do the honorable thing when it came to Charlotte Valentine. The truth was, she didn't deserve to have her life ruined because of one mistake. And if the doctor hadn't interrupted them, it could have happened. Maybe he hadn't exactly planned things, but once he and Charlotte were in that stall together, Beauregard Preston had taken over, and Beauregard Preston never stopped with the undoing of a few buttons.

By the time Whiskey gave his signature welcoming whinny to his master, and Boone's voice boomed for the sentry, Jackson had decided to take the blame for the incident. He hoped he wouldn't have to beg for his career, but he was almost ready to do that, too. He answered Boone's call and braced himself for the worst.

"I know you've probably been practicing your explanation for the situation with Miss Valentine," Boone said.

"There's no reason you or the doctor should believe me, but it won't happen again. I swear it. I'll give the same assurance to Dr. Valentine, if he'll only give me the chance." He could feel the sweat trickling down his back as he spoke.

"Unfortunately, Private Jackson, your assurances are not something people around here can depend on."

"But I mean it this time, sir," Jackson said. "I make no excuses. I behaved badly. Dr. Valentine was right. If I cared for Charlotte, I'd never have led her into that situation. It won't happen again. I mean it."

"Dr. Valentine has already seen to that," the sergeant said. "When he told me about this situation he informed me he's sending Charlotte back East to visit her grandmother."

"He doesn't have to do that," Caleb said. "I'll . . . I'll stay away." He swallowed. "Come on, Sergeant—Nathan. You know how it's been with me. I've never had much experience with a girl like Charlotte. The rules are different with girls like her. You can't treat them like—"

"Like you treated Riverboat Annie?" Boone folded his arms and looked down at Jackson, rocking back on his heels as he spoke.

"What . . . what's *she* got to do with anything?" Caleb frowned. He glanced in the direction of Soapsuds Row. Why would Nathan even mention Riverboat Annie? He'd kept his promise and kept his mouth shut about all of that. It didn't make any sense for that to be brought up now. Unless . . . Caleb's mind raced to rewind the confrontation in the stable. A light went on when he remembered Dr. Valentine shouting *"One unwed mother at Camp Robinson is quite enough. God forbid that my daughter join the ranks! Is it your ambition to end up on Soapsuds Row, too?"* Is it possible? . . . *Annie's pregnant? . . . and they're looking for someone to blame?* It was as if Caleb were looking down the barrel of Cruikshank's rifle again. Only this time, he couldn't run off and join the army to get away.

"Listen, Nathan. I don't know what Annie's told you about me, but I've had nothing to do with her since I got to Camp Robinson, beyond a couple conversations and a dance or two at the last hop. I promised her I'd keep my mouth shut, and I have. I told you I came out here to get myself a new life. I messed up a few times at the beginning, and I paid for it. But I haven't had anything to do with Annie since those times in St. Louis. I swear it. If she wants to call herself Laina Gray, that's fine with me. I told her that. And I haven't touched her." He grabbed Boone's arm. "That's the truth. I'd swear on a stack of Bibles I haven't touched her. I don't care what she says."

The sergeant jerked his arm away and smoothed his sleeve. "What makes you think Laina has said anything at all about you, Private?"

Desperation took over. All of Caleb's best intentions faded. "Look," he said hoarsely, "I know what's going on here. Valentine is just mad enough to do it, too. He's just like all the other high-class jerks who enjoy putting the screws to any lowly private who dares to touch his precious daughter. He won't drag Charlotte's name through the mud to get me drummed out, but Riverboat Annie is another story. She doesn't have a reputation to protect in the first place."

"What are you talking about?" Boone asked.

"Come on. As if you and I don't both know Annie's 'in the family way'. Lord knows *somebody* has to take the blame." Caleb laughed harshly and shook his head. "I walked right into this one, didn't I?"

Boone grabbed him by the front of his shirt and nearly lifted him off the ground. "You watch your mouth, Private."

Caleb jerked away. He thrust his chin out and stepped toward his sergeant. "All due respect, sir, I'll grovel all you want. I'll serve time in the guardhouse. I'll tote a log from here to Sidney and back. But I am *not* taking the fall for a riverboat whore." One second he was on his feet, the next he was on the ground looking up at an entirely new galaxy in the night sky.

Boone crouched down next to him and grabbed him by the throat, nearly closing off his windpipe as he growled, "You listen to me, you good-for-nothing—I came out here tonight for two reasons. One was to tell you Doctor Valentine isn't going to make a public spectacle of his daughter just to teach you a lesson. The other was to hear your promise that you won't bring up Laina's past. In light of the *first* item, which grants you yet another chance to make a career of the army, I thought you'd be able to agree to the *second,* thereby giving Miss Gray the same chance you've been given. It appears," he growled, closing his hand around Caleb's throat, "that I've overrated your worth as a human being. You've sunk to an all-time low, Private, bringing an innocent woman into your own troubles—in the worst way possible."

Caleb struggled and gagged. He clamped his hands around his sergeant's wrist. Just when he was about to pass out, Boone let go. Coughing and sputtering, Caleb choked out, "You didn't know?" He sat up, rubbing his neck. "You didn't know."

Boone spat out, "You don't have to be spreading lies about Laina Gray just to make yourself look good."

Caleb rubbed his jaw. "Okay. Okay. I earned that. But, Nathan, I swear . . . Dr. Valentine *said* it. I didn't make it up. He was yelling at Charlotte, and he said something about Camp Robinson not needing *two* unwed mothers—about her ending up being a laundress over on Soapsuds Row, too." Caleb held his hands out, palm up. "He didn't name Annie. But it didn't take any imagination for me to figure out who he was talking about." He rubbed the back of his neck. "Look, if you want to know, I felt kind of bad for her when I figured this out. We had that talk, and I thought we had things all settled. Then you come down here talking about Annie and honor and . . ." He shrugged. "You can't blame me for jumping to conclusions. Like I said, if somebody's going to take the fall for anything with the ladies around here, I've pretty well opened up myself to be the one."

"Get up," Boone ordered. When Caleb obeyed, he said, "I've got to do some thinking. When you get off guard duty, I want you to report to my quarters over on the Row."

"What are you going to do?"

"I'm going to take a walk," Boone said. He spun on his heels and headed off toward the river.

Caleb shouldered his rifle and marched along the southern perimeter of the camp. He wasn't sure, but he thought the worst was over for him. Boone was now distracted by a bigger problem—Annie. So Valentine was sending Charlotte away. He'd miss her, but if he had to choose between Charlotte and his career, he'd choose the army. Why, then, he thought as he marched along, didn't he feel relieved? He felt something, but it wasn't relief. It took Jackson a few minutes to recognize the emotion clenching at his gut when he thought about Laina Gray. *Guilt.*

Chapter Seventeen

For what is your life? It is even a vapour,
that appeareth for a little time, and then vanisheth away.
JAMES 4:14

EVEN AS A SMALL BOY, Nathan had been drawn to cemeteries. If that
was weird, so be it. In cemeteries people left you alone. If you cried, they
didn't interrupt you. If you sat with your head down, thinking, no one
asked what the matter was. A cemetery was a good place to just be alone
with your thoughts. And sometimes the thoughts had nothing to do with
death and dying.

The cemetery at Camp Robinson was nothing like the one back home
in Missouri. It wasn't very well tended, and there were only a few graves.
Lily's grave was the only one with a stone marker, and he'd had to spend
nearly two months' pay to have it shipped from Grand Island into Sidney. The freighter who had brought it to Camp Robinson clearly thought
Nathan Boone was crazy. Nathan didn't care. Leaning against the tombstone
tonight, Nathan was glad he had done his best to do right by Lily Boone.
She'd certainly done her best to do right by him, following him out here
when the whole idea of Indians and the Wild West terrified her.

He had spent a lot of time at Lily's grave in the past two and a half years.
But he'd never come up here to think about another woman. Somehow, it
seemed to Nathan that Lily wouldn't mind. She knew his heart, and like
Granny had said, he would never give the part of his heart that belonged
to Lily Bainbridge Boone to anyone else. So, Nathan reasoned, it was all
right to come out here to think about Laina Gray. If Lily was aware of
what was going on here below, she also would know that Laina Gray had
no chance of usurping Lily's place in his heart. What the two of them had
shared was part of a past that he'd always be able to revisit. Nothing could
change it or tarnish it.

People certainly did crazy things for love. Well, Nathan thought, people just did crazy things. *Crazy.* Miss Gray used that excuse a lot when she did things he didn't understand. She'd used it as the excuse for him finding her in tears last month when she'd broken that vase. She'd babbled on about Caleb Jackson and her past as some riverboat girl as if that mattered to anyone now. Nathan looked up at the sky and shook his head. He'd sensed that wasn't the whole story. But he'd let it go. Thinking back, he realized he'd maybe even been relieved that she didn't seem to *need* to tell him the rest. It was easier to be someone's friend when the problems were simpler.

She couldn't be pregnant. Could she? It just had to be some sort of misunderstanding. Something Jackson *thought* he heard. He'd said himself that Valentine was raving mad. In that situation, people could easily misunderstand what was being said. *Shoot,* Nathan thought, *ask fighting men to describe a skirmish with the Sioux, and you'll get as many versions as men you asked.* It wasn't that they lied intentionally. They just saw things through fear, and that wasn't exactly an objective view. That was probably what happened in the stable. Jackson was listening to Valentine through his own fear. He didn't hear exactly right.

She couldn't be pregnant. He counted back on his fingers. *God, wasn't it enough to let that monster get hold of her in the first place? Did you have to get her pregnant, too?*

He thought back over recent weeks. She wasn't hiding at Granny's anymore. She spent time with Katie and Wilber, who was being transformed from a bumbling puppy into a well-behaved dog. She helped Charlotte and Dinah Valentine with their French lessons. She cleaned for the Valentines. She had even started working at the trading post for Mrs. Gruber a couple of days a week and had taken on Mrs. O'Malley's share of infantry laundry. She picnicked on Sunday afternoons and sang hymns. She went to the hops. She danced. But in some ways, Nathan suddenly realized, Laina did seem different.

He hadn't seen her wear any of the things from Lily's trunk. Of course, he couldn't exactly ask Granny Max if Miss Gray was using Lily's unmentionables. But now he wondered if the reason Miss Gray wasn't wearing Lily's dresses was because they wouldn't fit. He didn't *think* she looked pregnant, but . . . He counted on his fingers again. When could you tell just by looking?

He remembered more changes. More than one evening, when he stopped in after taps for a chat with Granny Max, Laina had already gone to bed. And just today, when they had taken the picnic lunch out to the White River, when Miss Gray was singing hymns with Private Yates, she cried. It didn't affect her singing voice much, but by the time she finished the song, tears were running freely down her cheeks. His mother had cried a lot when she was expecting Nathan's little sister. Nathan wondered if Miss Gray was crying a lot more than anyone knew.

"Why didn't she tell me? Why doesn't she ask for my help?"

And exactly what are you going to do to help her, Sergeant Boone?

Nathan's head came up. *I could marry her.* He dismissed the idea as quickly as it came. Stupid idea. Ridiculous. But was it? A man could do worse than Laina Gray for a wife. A lot worse. They got along. They were friends. Plenty of people built good marriages on friendship. Look at the Valentines. You didn't have to be in love to get married. He'd already married once for love. Maybe he *could* marry again. For friendship. It would solve all of Laina's problems. And some of his. He'd have a home again. Single women would stop batting their eyelashes at him. Even the idea of the child didn't seem all that much of a problem. He'd be a good father. He felt sure of it.

He laid his open hand on the earth beside Lily's tombstone. "Well, sweetheart, if you can hear me and if you have any wisdom to share, I am open to anything you can send my way. I've been thinking some pretty crazy things tonight." His voice wavered. "I love you, Lily. Always will." He rubbed his face with his hands, trying to scrub the tears away. "I'm lonely," he whispered. "The fact is, Lily, I'm a mess. And I wish you could tell me what to do."

He got up and stretched his legs. He kissed the inside of his fingertips and laid them on the top ridge of the tombstone.

———

Nathan was in his quarters on Soapsuds Row waiting for Caleb Jackson to show up when he heard someone pounding on Granny Max's back door. He recognized Katie O'Malley's voice calling for Laina.

He opened his own back door just in time to see Laina kneel down and pull Katie into her arms. She closed her eyes and rocked back and forth.

Katie pushed away and looked up at her. "He just wouldn't breathe. Doctor tried and tried, and then Granny tried while Doctor helped Mama, and then she d—" Katie threw herself onto Laina's shoulder sobbing.

"Where's Becky?" Laina asked.

"With M-Mama," Katie sobbed. "They said I should come up here."

"Come inside," Laina said, taking Katie's hand.

Nathan walked over to them. "What can I do?" he asked.

Laina sat down in Granny's rocker and invited Katie into her lap. "I guess you could warm up some milk." She motioned toward the shelf on the wall. "From the blue crock."

Nathan stoked the fire. Before long Katie's sobs were fading, and Laina was coaxing her to drink some warm milk.

"Wilber," Katie said drowsily. "Mama's gonna get mad again if Wilber—" She opened her eyes wide and looked up at Laina. "I g-guess Mama don't have to worry over Wilber anymore." She burst into fresh tears.

"Shh." Laina looked up at Nathan. Her eyes pleaded with him as she said, "Sergeant Boone will find Wilber. He can come sleep with you here tonight. In my bed."

Nathan smiled at her and headed off to find Wilber. When he returned with the dog, he paused beside Granny Max's kitchen window to look in. Katie O'Malley was asleep in Laina's lap, her body occasionally wracked by a sob or a shudder. Laina held the child close. Her head was leaning back against the rocker's high back. Her eyes were closed and she was singing.

Nathan stood still and watched. *That's beautiful. She's beautiful.*

Nathan listened through an entire chorus before heading inside. When Laina rose and led a groggy Katie into the back room, Wilber followed, wagging his tail. While he waited for Laina to return, Nathan put on the coffeepot. When Laina came back into the room, he said, "Thought I'd just get it going. It's probably going to be a long night." He reached for Katie's cup.

"Here," Laina said. "Let me."

When her hand brushed his, he pulled away. He could feel color rising up the back of his neck. "I'll go see about things up at the O'Malleys'," he said. But he didn't move. Instead, he asked, "Have I . . . have I done something to offend you?"

Laina frowned. "Why would you think that?"

"Something's different. With you. Is something wrong?"

"There's nothing wrong with me, Sergeant Boone."

"Dang it, you are a stubborn woman."

"Don't swear, Sergeant Boone," she said. "I'll go see if Granny Max and Becky need any help."

"Then I'll rouse Yates and get him to making a coffin." He looked toward the back room. "What about Katie?"

"Oh, don't worry about Katie. She has Wilber. He's a good listener. And I won't be gone that long."

"All right, then," Nathan said. He followed her outside and stood watching as she made her way up the Row toward the O'Malley quarters.

Chapter Eighteen

How long, ye simple ones, will ye love simplicity?
And the scorners delight in their scorning,
and fools hate knowledge?
Turn you at my reproof: behold,
I will pour out my spirit unto you,
I will make known my words unto you.
PROVERBS 1:22-23

RELIEVED OF GUARD DUTY, Caleb headed for Sergeant Boone's quarters. He had just stepped up on the board porch running the length of Soapsuds Row when Boone opened the door, not to his own quarters, but to those of Granny Max. *Lord help me, he's been talking to Annie.* Caleb took a deep breath and steeled himself for whatever might be coming his way.

"I need you to head over to the barracks and rouse Yates." The sergeant stepped outside and closed the door behind him before saying, "There's need for a coffin. Meara O'Malley's died in childbirth. Come with me. We'll take some measurements." Motioning for Caleb to follow, Boone headed around back and up the Row toward an oblique splotch of light being cast outside the O'Malleys' back door. Caleb followed with a sense of dread.

Sergeant Boone stepped inside Mrs. O'Malley's back door. Caleb lingered just outside, his heart pounding. He'd picked his way across battlefields strewn with bodies and body parts and thought that was what made death awful. But the orderly scene inside that apartment was just as awful in its own way. Mrs. O'Malley and the baby were dressed and laid out, their bodies surrounded by quart jars filled with ice water. Candles and lamps lighted the room where mourners would spend the rest of the night sitting with the remains, both as a ritual of respect and as protection against insects and rodents. The thought sent shivers up Caleb's spine.

Laina Gray came to the door. "Sixty inches," she said to Boone. "A little extra width." She swallowed hard. Her voice wavered. "We thought she'd want to be holding . . . the baby." The sergeant put his hand on her shoulder. She glanced at Caleb, then back up at Boone.

"I'm sending Jackson over to get Yates," Boone said. "He can get started right away on the coffin."

Granny Max came to the door. "Dr. Valentine said to plan for noon tomorrow." She lowered her voice. "The girls can have the morning with their mama and the baby. Doctor says the heat just won't allow them any more time than that. Thank you for getting the ice, Nathan."

It was well past midnight when Caleb roused Private Yates, who in turn roused the quartermaster to help scrounge up enough good lumber to build a coffin. They ended up tearing the sides off a freighter's broken-down wagon. Yates lamented not having time to smooth the lumber and build a properly shaped coffin. He told Caleb the best he could do quickly would be a long rectangular box.

It didn't cool off much overnight, and at dawn, when Private Dubois and Corporal Dorsey shouldered shovels with Jackson and headed across the river to dig a grave in the camp cemetery, the heat was oppressive. The parched earth made the digging go slowly, and it wasn't long before all three men were drenched with sweat.

Caleb welcomed the hard labor, relieved to be granted at least a momentary reprieve from disciplinary action over the incident with Miss Valentine. But he was still struggling with guilt over having brought Laina Gray into the mess he'd created. He didn't look at her once through the forty-five-minute service.

After Mrs. O'Malley's funeral, Caleb volunteered to stay behind and fill in the grave. He figured it couldn't hurt his cause if he volunteered, and shoveling dirt alone down here by the river was better than toting a log around the parade ground in full view of the entire garrison. He hoped it might buy him a little more time to think over his situation and come up with a plan before the inevitable boom was lowered.

Looking off toward where the mourners were filing over the bridge, he saw Laina Gray stop. She said something to Granny Max. The old woman looked back at Caleb and patted Laina on the shoulder. Then, putting one arm around each of the O'Malley girls, Granny continued on her way while Laina turned back toward the cemetery.

Caleb's heart began to thump. His mouth went dry. He bent to the work, still keeping an eye on the doings at the bridge. Sergeant Boone seemed inclined to accompany Laina, but she put her hand on his arm and said something. He glanced toward Jackson, then headed off in the direction of the Row. Caleb gave a little sigh of relief, until he saw Boone hurry to catch up with Dr. Valentine.

Charlotte had been conspicuously absent from Mrs. O'Malley's funeral. Caleb had overhead the doctor tell Mrs. Gruber his daughter had a terrible headache and needed to rest before her departure the next day for the East. His heart pounding, Caleb resumed shoveling as Laina Gray approached. He tried to steel himself for what was coming. He thought of a few excuses he could give for his behavior. None of them were very good, but he'd never let that keep him from trying to avoid taking blame before.

"I'm not certain this is a good idea," Laina said as soon as she was within earshot.

Caleb stopped shoveling. He removed his cap and mopped his forehead with a dirty kerchief. Looking at her, he hesitated. She really had changed. Riverboat Annie would have charged up here with her hands on her hips, and let go with a stream of profanity that would wither a man faster than the Sandhills' heat could kill a fresh daisy. But this woman seemed almost shy. There was a gentleness about her that made him uncomfortable. She wasn't angry. He was surprised at his own words when he motioned to the grave and blurted out, "I wouldn't blame you if you pushed me in and started shoveling." He felt like a boxer warily circling his opponent. Except that she didn't seem inclined to fight.

"Now, why would I want to do that?" she asked. "I just walked up here to invite you to join us. Mrs. Gruber is going to set out a supper for everyone. I thought you might want to come."

Is it possible Boone hasn't talked to her yet? Maybe he's waiting until later. He felt a brief surge of relief, but it lasted only a second or two before his conscience broke in.

You've got to tell her.

I can't. She'll want revenge. She'll tell Doc all about my past. And that'll be the end of me. He won't believe I'm trying to change. He'll see me drummed out or die trying.

So just go on being a coward. Slink around and wait while everybody else decides things for you. Run off and change your name again. How many times you going to do that? You're disgusting. You're not even man enough to own up to this. What did she ever do to you? She didn't have to come back and invite you to supper. She didn't have to promise not to say anything about your past. You could at least warn her that Boone knows about the baby.

While Miss Gray waited for his answer, he argued with himself. Finally, he cleared his throat. "Thank you. Sure. That'd be nice."

"Dr. Valentine will be there. And maybe Charlotte." She smiled as she turned to go. "We'll see you this evening, then."

Jackson tipped his hat and let her go, all the while arguing with himself. Finally, he threw down his shovel and ran after her, catching up at the bridge. "Wait, Miss Gray. Wait." She turned around. He took his hat off and began rolling the brim nervously while the internal argument continued.

Finally, he spoke up. "There's something you've got to know." He tugged on his beard nervously. "Look, you're never going to want to hear the name Caleb Jackson again after this, but . . ." He began to pace back and forth. Her calm was worse than any anger she could have rained down. Seeing her just standing there waiting drove him crazy. Finally, he said, "Look. I've made a lot of mistakes in my life. Most of them from pure meanness. But the truth is, I really have been trying for a fresh start out here. But it's hard to change. You may not have seen him lately, but Beauregard Preston is still in here." He tapped his chest.

"I know what you mean," Laina said. She smiled. "Riverboat Annie is still inside of me, too. It's not that easy to get away from the past we've had."

Caleb blurted out, "Well, Riverboat Annie wasn't caught in the stables yesterday in a . . . uh . . . compromising situation with a member of the opposite sex."

Laina closed her eyes. Her voice was miserable, but sympathetic. "Oh, Private Jackson. Charlotte?"

He nodded. "Old Beauregard Preston stuffed a sock in Caleb Jackson's conscience and did some serious . . . you know."

"So *that's* why Charlotte didn't come to the funeral." She nodded. "And that explains the sudden trip East." She looked puzzled. "But why are you telling me this?"

"It gets worse," Jackson said. "Dr. Valentine and his wife caught us."

Laina studied his face. "Maybe that was good. I bet it put Private Jackson back in control of Mr. Preston in a hurry."

He shrugged. "Maybe. Maybe not." He looked away. "The thing is, Dr. Valentine was raving mad. He hollered. A lot. He was so mad, he didn't trust himself to even be around me just then. I think he could have just as soon killed me as look at me. He ended up just telling me to get on with the day. Said he would handle it later. That he and Sergeant Boone would discuss 'the situation.' He wanted it kept quiet for Charlotte's sake. He let me stew all the rest of the day and into the night.

"I was on guard duty last night when Sergeant Boone finally came to lower the boom." He paused and moistened his lips. "You know how it's been for me here. I've had just about every discipline there is. I've probably spent more time in the guardhouse than I have in the barracks. But I've been trying. I kept volunteering for patrol. Worked with the horses. And I've been changing. At first with Miss Valentine, I was just playing. But then I started to think maybe I had a *reason* to make it all work out." He put his hands to his waist and stood looking off into the distance as he talked. "But I messed that up, too. And I thought Sergeant Boone was getting ready to tell me my army career was over. I was feeling pretty desperate, and I blurted out something." He swatted at a fly buzzing around his face. His voice was miserable when he finally looked back at Laina and said, "All I was thinking about was me. As usual. I wanted to shift the attention away from myself. I thought maybe I could at least save my career."

"What are you talking about?"

"It's about you. About the baby."

"What?" She sounded like he'd knocked the air out of her. She clasped her hands against her midsection and her face paled.

He reached for her arm. "Let's go down to the river where there's some shade. You're going to faint."

"Tell me what you said," she said, pulling away from him.

"You're going to have a baby. Right?"

"Who . . . who said such a thing?"

"Look, he didn't come right out and say it. Not like that."

"He?"

"Dr. Valentine. He was raging mad. He was yelling at Charlotte about his daughter not ending up as the second unwed mother on Soapsuds Row. Something like that." He paused again. "It wasn't until later I realized exactly what he said, and that he must have been talking about you." He mumbled, "Something Sarge said made me think they were going to make me take the blame for your situation, so they could discipline me without mentioning Charlotte." He took off his hat and swiped his forehead. "So now Sergeant Boone knows about the baby."

"Charlotte . . . and Mrs. Valentine . . . heard this?" Laina's voice was almost a whisper.

"No!" Jackson shook his head. "No. Not what I said to Nathan."

"But they heard . . . they heard what the doctor said?"

Caleb shrugged. "Well, they were there. But they probably didn't *hear* it. Not so as to connect it to *you*. Not the way I did." He slapped the side of his thigh with his hat. "I'm really sorry."

"Tell me what you said to Sergeant Boone." She barely croaked out the words.

He'd expected rage. Swearing. Defensiveness. Maybe even a physical response. He'd seen her go after an especially lascivious customer once with a kitchen knife. But this . . . hurt . . . the fright in her eyes, the lostness. Facing Laina's despair, Jackson didn't know what to do.

Feeling sorrow for others was a new sensation for him, and now he'd felt it three times in rapid succession. At first he'd only been sorry he got *caught* in a compromising situation with Charlotte Valentine. But then he'd realized he really could have destroyed her future, and he'd felt truly sorry for taking advantage of her.

He was sorry for the O'Malley girls losing their mother and baby brother. He had even wondered what would happen to them and felt sorry about that.

And now, standing before Laina Gray, he was sorry again. She really did seem to be doing her best to escape the past and get herself a new life. And, from what he could tell, she was doing a respectable job of it. She didn't deserve the trouble he was causing her. Being pregnant was trouble enough.

For the first time since he'd been a Confederate drummer boy, the desire to do *right* conquered Jackson's overactive instincts for self-preservation. As accurately as he could, he told Laina about his encounter with Sergeant Boone. He didn't make excuses for himself. "All I cared about was getting myself out of this mess. I didn't think. I didn't *care* what it might mean for you. And after you've kept quiet about *my* past." He hung his head. "I'm sorry. Please believe me."

Laina let out a huge breath. "Get back to work, Private."

Her response was so abrupt Caleb hesitated until she repeated herself.

"I need to think. Please. Just let me be alone for a while."

Caleb watched her walk away along the riverbank. When she came to a depression in the shore, she sank down in the shade, drew her knees up to her chest, and bowed her head. Caleb did as he was told. *Where you gonna run to now, boy? Where you gonna run?*

Can it get much worse, Lord? How can things possibly get much worse? Laina crossed her arms over her knees and let the tears flow. Maybe she should just give up altogether. What was the use of trying to build a new life when things like this could blindside you at any minute.

I don't even know how to pray about this. I'm tired, Lord. I'm tired of being the Tragedy of Camp Robinson. The Crazy Woman. Granny's Patient. Nathan Boone's Latest Stray. And now it seems I get to be the Scarlet Woman of Camp Robinson, after all. I was going to leave and start again somewhere else where no one knew me. I only needed a few more weeks' income before I could do that. Granny even thought it might work, just letting people think I was a military widow. But now Meara is dead. And with the girls needing us, and Granny not getting any younger . . . I think she really needs me to help with the girls. They don't have family anywhere else. There's nothing for them to do but stay. But how can I stay? How can I stay here and let this baby become the Bastard Child of Camp Robinson? She won't have a chance in life. You can't mean for that to happen, Lord. You just can't.

The longer Laina thought, the more confused she became. Nothing made any sense.

You said if anyone lacks wisdom they should ask you. Granny just read me that verse a couple of days ago. You said your plans for me include a future and a hope. Or was that just for Jeremiah? Isn't that for me? Maybe that promise isn't for the Riverboat Annies of the world. If you love me, Lord, why are you letting this happen?

Her body was wracked by sobs as she looked up at the blue sky and shouted, "WHAT AM I SUPPOSED TO DO?!"

————

"Miss Gray. Laina." Caleb Jackson had walked down to the river. "That was stable call a minute ago. They'll be bringing the horses down here to water them before too long. What do you want me to do, ma'am?"

"I don't know." She made no attempt to hide the misery from her voice. She swiped the tears off her face and started to get up.

"I wish I could take it all back."

Laina shrugged. "It doesn't matter. I was going to go away, but Meara's death complicates things. I can't just leave Granny Max with two girls to raise. So people were going to find out anyway. Sergeant Boone would likely have been one of the first we told. Doctor Valentine's outburst just started things sooner, that's all."

"But I'm the one who made him mad enough to say those things in the first place."

She sighed. "It's not as if you meant to hurt me personally." She forced a smile. "I believe you about that. I know you didn't mean to cause me trouble."

"Maybe not," Jackson said, "but I usually do whatever it takes to cover for myself, and I don't usually care what happens to anybody else." He shook his head. "In fact, I'm surprised this bothers me at all. But it does."

Laina smiled at him. "Listen to yourself, Private Jackson. Those words were a foreign language to Beauregard Preston. As I recall, he was all about blaming someone else for everything bad that ever happened to him."

"Yeah," Caleb nodded. "First it was the Yankees. Then it was the Yankees again. Then it was a storekeeper named Cruikshank and his Yankee customers. Then . . ." he shrugged. "What I was missing my whole life was the idea that my biggest problem is me. And *me* has sunk to an all-time low—and dragged you down with him."

"Granny says you can't sink lower than God can reach," Laina said. "Just look at me."

"You were never all that bad," Caleb said.

Laina touched the scar at her left temple. "You've forgotten about this and what it represents. There's nothing attractive about *me* to make God pick me out."

"That scar's nothing," Jackson said. "It barely shows. You're still a beautiful woman. To hear Yates talk, you're as good as they come."

"Granny said all the good deeds we do are just like filthy laundry, anyway." She smiled. "So don't think you're out of God's reach. And besides that, you've been trying. You joined the army."

"There's plenty of booze and gambling—even women—in the army, if a man knows where to look. And Caleb Jackson, God help him, knows where to look." He shook his head. He was quiet for a minute, then he asked, "What are you going to do?"

"I don't know," Laina said. "Keep hollering at God, I guess. Ask Him to show me what to do."

"Wasn't that you shouting at God a minute ago? It sounded like maybe He wasn't answering."

Laina nodded. "Sometimes it does feel that way."

"What's your Granny Max say about that?" Caleb asked.

"To just keep pounding on the door," Laina said. She cocked her head and looked up at him. "Want to do some pounding with me?"

Jackson frowned. "What?"

"Well, I believe you're sorry about all of this. And I believe Miss Valentine brought out something good in you. Maybe something you didn't even know you had. Maybe we could ask God about all that together."

"You mean . . . pray? Me?" He laughed.

"Sure. Why not?"

He shook his head. "Hey. This is me. You really think God wants to hear from me?"

"Granny Max says—"

"Yeah, yeah. We can't sink lower than God can reach." He snorted. "Wanna bet?"

"All right, Private," Laina said. "You don't have to say anything. You can just listen." She bowed her head. "God, I'm worried about the baby. I had a plan that would give her at least a chance at a good life. But now Meara is dead, and how can I leave Granny Max to take care of those girls all by herself? Private Jackson doesn't have much hope for things getting better for him, either. We both have reason to believe you might not care to answer us." She tried to swallow the knot in her throat. Tears were welling up, and she was embarrassed, but she let them spill out and went on. "So I don't even know what to ask for because I don't see any clear way for this mess we have gotten ourselves into to get fixed. Thank you for listening. Amen."

They both looked up just in time to see a small herd of horses headed down to the water on the opposite side of the bridge.

"I've got to go," Caleb said. He stood up and held out his hand to Laina. She took it and let him help her up. Together they walked toward the bridge. "Wait a minute," Caleb said, and he ran to the graveside to get his shovel. When he came back, he shouldered the shovel and offered Laina his arm. As they walked along, Laina said, "I don't know what Sergeant Boone has in mind for you, but it will be fair, and I'm thinking you'll be able to handle it. I'm not so sure you've ruined your life. Not yet, anyway. Maybe you don't want to come to dinner up at the trading post. But you can always write to Charlotte."

"Oh, I'm certain her father will allow *that!*" Jackson exclaimed.

"You might be surprised what Dr. Valentine will allow," Laina said. They started across the bridge. "Give it a couple of weeks and then go to him. Ask him what he would do if you brought him a letter for Charlotte. Ask him if he would consider reading it and then maybe sending it on to her." She patted his arm. "If you really care for her, don't give up. And don't give up on Caleb Jackson, either. For whatever it's worth, his old friend thinks he has promise."

Jackson looked down at her. "Maybe you *are* crazy. At least a little. I spread that news about you, and now you're *praying* for me, for heaven's sake."

"No," Laina chuckled. "The praying is for *your* sake, Private Jackson."

"So," he said. "You know what *you're* going to do?"

Laina shook her head. "Maybe you could tell Sergeant Boone we've had this talk and that things are all right between us. Maybe he'll respect my privacy. In fact, please tell him that's what I'd like. If the Valentine women are leaving tomorrow, maybe that will keep them from talking behind my back and give me more time to think things through."

"Like I said earlier, they might not have even understood what the doctor was talking about. As for Sergeant Boone not saying anything to you, I wouldn't count on that. He's not going to want me telling him what to do when it comes to you. Especially if I'm telling him to leave you be. He's been fixing everything for everybody around him since I first met him. And that was a lot of years ago." He shook his head. "Too bad he can't fix himself as well as he fixes everybody else."

"Yes," Laina agreed. "It is." She patted his arm. "Well, don't give up on Charlotte. Love hopes all things, you know."

"Is that a little Sandhills wisdom?"

"It could be, I suppose. But I think it's from the Bible." She smiled up at him.

He touched the brim of his cap, saluting her. "People have told me to go to a lot of places in my day, Miss Gray—mostly to regions below the earth. You're the first one who's ever suggested I go to God with my troubles. I don't know exactly what just happened, but I do feel better. And I'm grateful to you. I'll do what I can to convince Sergeant Boone you'd like some time to yourself before the two of you talk this over."

———

Caleb headed off toward the stables. Halfway there, he turned around to watch Laina. Ever since that night he'd first recognized her, he'd been watching, waiting for her act to slip, expecting to catch a glimpse of the real reason behind her playacting at respectability. But the woman walking away from him toward Soapsuds Row was no actress. He was convinced of that. Laina Gray was the genuine article. He'd hurt her. Misused knowledge against her. Caused her the worst kind of trouble. And she'd prayed for him. *Prayed,* for heaven's sake. He smiled, hearing her voice when she said *"No. The praying was for your sake, Private Jackson."*

She seemed to want to see things go well for him. She thought he still had a chance with Charlotte Valentine. She even gave him good advice on how to make that happen. Jackson turned back around and headed for the stables. *Maybe she is crazy, but it's a good kind of crazy.*

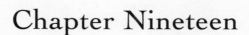

Chapter Nineteen

Lo, children are an heritage of the Lord:
and the fruit of the womb is his reward.
PSALM 127:3

"GOOD-BYE, PAPA." Charlotte kissed her father on the cheek and climbed up into the stage beside Dinah. Once seated, she leaned over and looked out the window, dabbing her eyes with a handkerchief.

"What's the matter with *you*?" Dinah teased. "Disappointed because there isn't an honor guard of former beaus waiting to announce the queen's departure?"

"You hush," Charlotte snapped. She dabbed at her eyes again and looked mournfully out the window.

"Don't be sad, Charlott-ah. We're going to *like* it at Grandmother's. Remember what Mama said about it? Big porches and cool night breezes and lots of trees and a lake and a beach and swimming! We're gonna learn to swim and . . ."

While Dinah babbled, Charlotte stared toward the cavalry barracks off across the parade ground. If wishing could conjure it, there would be a blue uniform or two emerging from the doorway any minute and coming toward the trading post. Surely Sergeant Boone would say good-bye to her. If not Private Jackson, then certainly Sergeant Boone. *Please.*

———

Outside the stagecoach, Doctor Valentine bent to kiss Emmy-Lou on the cheek. "Give my best to your mother," he said. His embrace communicated what he did not say—*We are doing the right thing.*

Emmy-Lou echoed her husband's unspoken sentiment. "I know we are doing the right thing, Avery. I just feel like a fool when I've been writing letters singing the praises of Camp Robinson and giving Mother a hundred reasons why we can't possibly come back East." She looked toward the cavalry barracks. "It seems that Sergeant Boone could have at least come to say good-bye," she muttered.

"I expressly asked him not to," the doctor said. "He's busy finally moving the last things out of his old quarters over on the Row so the O'Malley girls can live next door to Granny Max."

Emmy-Lou's eyes brightened. "Then there's hope. He's moving on."

Dr. Valentine took his wife by the shoulders and peered down at her. "What you hope for is impossible, Emmy-Lou. It never has and never will enter Sergeant Boone's mind." He shook her gently. "Move on, Emmy-Lou. Move on. Have a *wonderful* visit. I'll write you every day." He hugged her. "And I will miss you." He helped her step up into the stagecoach and, closing the door, peered through the window at his daughters.

He pointed to Dinah. "Don't go near the water until your mother has hired a swimming instructor."

He patted Charlotte's hand. "Don't go near any young men your mother doesn't approve."

He blew a kiss at his wife. "Don't forget I love you."

The stage driver laced the reins through his hands and, in a flurry of colorful language and slapping of reins, urged his team off. Dr. Valentine watched the stage until it was out of sight. On his way to the hospital to make his rounds, he was intercepted by Sergeant Boone.

"I wanted to talk to you about a . . . uh . . . delicate matter." The two men paused in the shadow of the hospital. "It's about Miss Gray. I know about the baby."

"She's told you?" Dr. Valentine made no attempt to hide his surprise.

"Not her," Nathan said. "Private Jackson told me."

"How on earth would Private Jackson know about this?"

"He deduced it from something you said day before yesterday in the stables." Nathan repeated the doctor's angry words back to him.

Dr. Valentine closed his eyes. *Thank God Charlotte and Emmy-Lou didn't make that connection. And thank God they are gone.* He looked at Nathan. "Is Jackson making trouble for Miss Gray now?"

"I would have handled that without bothering you," Nathan said, frowning. "Actually, it's strange. Apparently they've made peace."

"Really," Dr. Valentine said. "Well, I hope you are right, for Miss Gray's sake. But I don't have quite the faith you do in Private Jackson. He has a self-serving talent for explaining things so that he comes out looking like an innocent—or almost innocent—victim of even the most suspicious situation."

"I really wanted to talk about Miss Gray," Nathan said. He shifted his weight and tugged nervously on the brim of his hat. "Is everything all right with her? Her health, I mean."

"She's in excellent health," Dr. Valentine replied.

"It's a shame," Nathan said. "I'm just wondering what she's going to do now."

"You should be discussing this with her, Sergeant. I've made a few suggestions. I've offered to help. But it's up to her to decide."

"Just when she gets a start at a better life. It isn't fair."

"Life isn't fair, Sergeant. You of all people know that. But once again, I have faith that, between God and Granny Max, Miss Gray is going to be all right."

Nathan snorted. His voice dripped with sarcasm. "How could I forget? Granny can explain just what God is doing, and that will make everything turn out just fine."

"Or perhaps Miss Gray will follow another example she's had lived out before her," Dr. Valentine said abruptly. "Perhaps she'll curse God and spend the rest of her life reminding Him about the horrible mistake He allowed that ruined her life." He gave Nathan a pointed look and turned to go. "I hope you are right about Private Jackson and Miss Gray making peace. I deeply regret that my personal anger caused Miss Gray further troubles. I'll speak to her later today and offer my apologies." He walked away.

Feeling like a child just scolded by a parent, Nathan walked down to the Row and finished moving out of the apartment he and his wife had shared. He swept a few things—including Lily's Bible and garnet earbobs, the packet of letters, and the heirloom ring—into a pillowcase. Back at the barracks, he asked Emmet Dorsey to help him take over an empty trunk, which he then filled with the rest of his things.

While Boone and Dorsey were moving Nathan's things *out,* Private Harlan Yates was helping the women move the O'Malley girls *in.*

"I've taken what I need, Granny," Nathan said as he and Dorsey lugged his trunk out the front door. "Do what's best for the girls. I don't want anything else from here." He didn't stay to witness the change.

———

Unbeknownst to Katie O'Malley, during the week after her mother's death, there was much discussion about the future of the O'Malley sisters, who had no family this side of the Atlantic Ocean. Granny Max ended the discussion, at least for the time being, by presenting herself at the post commander's quarters and making a very convincing argument for how fifteen-year-old Becky O'Malley was more than capable of taking up her mother's duties as laundress and that, between Becky and Granny Max and Miss Gray, the O'Malley girls would be all right.

"Mrs. O'Malley was quite ill for some weeks. Those girls have become like family for both Miss Gray and me," Granny Max said. "They love us and we love them. There's no need to send those girls away. I've been mammy to a whole flock of children since I was not much more than a child myself. There's plenty of love left in this old heart for Becky and Katie O'Malley."

"I don't doubt that, Granny," the commander said. "But the fact remains that a child should have an education, and Katie especially is of an age to take advantage of schooling if we can find a good placement for her. Dr. Valentine has mentioned a possible position with his mother-in-law. He said he and his wife are thinking of Dinah's remaining with her grandmother to attend a school in Michigan. The doctor has offered to investigate the possibilities for Katie. The girls are the same age. They might get along."

"Miss Gray attended a fine school in St. Louis until her fourteenth year," Granny replied. "She can teach Becky and Katie all they need to know. You can ask Dr. Valentine about Miss Gray's teaching. She was helping Dinah and Miss Charlotte learn French before they left on their trip."

When the commander wanted to know if Miss Gray might be willing to teach a morning school for any children at the camp whose parents might be interested, Granny Max was noncommittal. Once again, Josiah Paine was reaching into the future and taking things away from Laina Gray. Once it was known Laina was expecting a baby, no one would be sending their children to a school where she was the teacher. But Granny couldn't tell the commander about that. She could only promise to ask Miss Gray about the idea of a small school.

Granny Max's meeting with the camp commander didn't solve much. In fact, Granny thought later, it complicated matters. It was going to be hard to explain why Miss Gray couldn't teach a few children some basic skills. And it was going to be even harder to talk Dr. Valentine out of putting pressure on everyone to let Katie go back East to attend school with Dinah.

It just seems to me like things are getting harder, not easier, Lord. When are you going to let up on Laina Gray?

———

"You invited *who*?!" Granny Max exclaimed as they packed their Sunday picnic.

"Private Jackson," Laina replied, smiling at Granny's reaction.

"He's handsome," Becky O'Malley added.

"I don't like him," Katie said. "He kicked Wilber once."

"Well, he won't be kicking Wilber today," Laina said. "Wilber's big enough to bite his foot off if he tried it. Isn't that right, Wilber?" Hearing his name, the dog stood up and wagged his tail. He walked to Laina and thrust his nose into her hand and nudged it. "See how ferocious you are," Laina laughed, grabbing the big dog's snout in her hands and kissing him on the head.

Granny Max peered at Laina with a question in her eyes. She lowered her voice so the O'Malley sisters couldn't hear her. "This wouldn't have anything to do with that little prayer meeting you told me about up at the cemetery would it?"

"It might," Laina said. "I just thought it wouldn't hurt to give him something to do besides playing cards. He said he'd come."

Granny nodded. "What's Private Yates going to think? They don't exactly get along, as I recall."

"He said he owes Jackson. Credits him for keeping him from breaking his neck that week they were all learning to ride. Harlan says Jackson hasn't had a fistfight in a long time."

"All right," Granny Max said. "He's not the first black sheep I've tried to get into the Lord's fold. And Lord willing he won't be the last. Does he like chokecherry pie?"

"No," Yates answered from the doorway. He nudged Private Jackson, who was standing next to him. "He hates it. Said I could have his share."

Wilber's ears went up at the sight of Jackson. He approached the uneasy soldier tentatively. Jackson backed away, his hands in his pockets.

Wilber stalked forward, a low growl sounding deep in his throat.

"Don't kick him," Katie warned.

"I've got no intention of kicking him," Jackson said. He swallowed. "But it looks like he's planning to have me for lunch." He looked at Katie. "You won't let him do that, will you?"

Katie shook her head. "Of course not." She walked to Wilber's side and put her hand on the dog's head. "It's all right, Wilber." She went to Jackson and held out her hand. "Shake. Show him you're friendly."

Pulling his fist out of his pocket, Jackson shook Katie's hand. Wilber stopped growling. "Come here, Wilber," Katie said. The dog marched forward slowly. Holding Jackson's hand, Katie encouraged the dog to sniff.

"Friend," Katie said. Wilber sniffed. His tail moved slowly from side to side.

"Pet him under his neck first," Katie instructed.

Jackson obeyed and Wilber stretched out his neck and leaned against him. When Jackson's hand went from the dog's neck to his ears, and then down his broad back, all tension between man and dog relaxed.

"Whew," Jackson said. "That's the scariest introduction I've ever survived," he said. "Except for maybe the time I met my first Yankee."

"Your first Yankee?" Katie asked. "Why'd you be afraid of a Yankee?"

Jackson grinned at her. "Cause they spoke a foreign language," he said. In his thickest Southern drawl, he added, "Y'all jus' don' know how hahd it is fer a southern chile tuh unnerstan' y'all."

Katie eyed him for a moment. "Can you teach me to talk like that?" she asked. "Laina knows French. I'd rather talk Southern. It's prettier." She added, "I was worried about you. You kicked Wilber once."

"I'm sorry," Jackson said.

Katie shrugged. "It's okay. He was barking at the horses. He shouldn't do that." She put her hand on Wilber's head. "Private Yates says you know about horses. Could you maybe help Laina and me teach Wilber to behave around horses?"

Jackson was quiet for a moment. "I could try."

Watching Jackson and Katie talk, Laina was reminded of Katie's helping her come out of her shell. It was good of the Lord to put children in people's lives, she thought. They were so much more open and honest about their thoughts. They could often break down barriers no one else could. *Thank you, God, for Katie O'Malley.* Her own baby moved. Yes, Laina thought. Children could be a blessing. She had to believe that. Even about her own. Even when it looked like an impossible situation.

Chapter Twenty

Wait on the Lord: be of good courage,
and he shall strengthen thine heart:
wait, I say, on the Lord.
PSALM 27:14

THE STENCH OF SWEAT and body odor rising from the pile of filthy uniforms and drawers on the floor opposite the washpot nearly knocked Laina backward. It was only four in the morning, but the air was still, and the August night was so hot Laina had given up on sleep and decided to tackle the day's laundry before the sun rose and the temperatures climbed even higher. Now, just inside the washhouse, she was having second thoughts.

She'd spent most of the night trying to soothe Katie to sleep. The freighters still hadn't delivered the mosquito netting Mrs. Gruber had ordered from Omaha, and the steaming summer nights on Soapsuds Row had become a long battle against the swarms of mosquitoes that seemed to find young Katie especially delicious. Granny had concocted a salve to ease the itching of some of the welts that covered her arms and legs, but Katie was still miserable.

Laina didn't have the heart to wake her to come help with the laundry. Even Granny Max had complained of feeling "frazzled and plumb wore out" yesterday. So here Laina stood, facing hours over pots of boiling water, when she already felt like she herself was boiling. The smells in the washhouse overwhelmed her good intentions. Inhaling sharply, Laina staggered back to the door and sat down abruptly, trying to catch her breath.

"What you think you're doing, child?"

Granny Max was headed toward the washhouse.

Laina sucked in a breath of stinking air. "Just trying to get a start on the day," she panted. "Before it gets too hot."

Granny sat down beside her. "It's already too hot for *you* to be doing this, honey-lamb." She patted Laina's shoulder. "I don't want you passing out and falling into a lye bath."

"And I don't want *you* wearing out, either," Laina protested. "You seemed so exhausted yesterday. *You* even complained about the heat, and that's not like you."

"Don't you worry 'bout me," Granny said. "I'll be all right." She looked behind her at the waiting uniforms. "I do wonder sometimes, though, at the great minds that dictated these men wear *wool* on hundred-degree days. Seems there ought to be a way to get around that." She sighed. "But I guess that's not a decision the army will be putting on its list of things to worry over in the near future."

Laina stretched and reached up to rub her neck. She felt a seam give way.

Granny heard the rip, too. She chuckled. "You can get to adjusting that other dress while I get to the laundry. Sounds to me like you need a little extra room."

"I didn't think it would happen this soon."

"Every woman's different, honey," Granny said. "It seems you are one that blooms early." She added, "And one whose nose gives her trouble."

Laina shuddered. "It's a wonder the soldiers didn't faint dead away when they were fighting that prairie fire. We'll never get those things clean. The way the wind blows all the time, it drives grit into every seam and crease. And now there's smoke, too." She raised her hand to her cheek. "I haven't felt really clean in a long time." She paused. Her voice lowered. "I'm sorry, Granny. I'm turning into a grumbler. Something you said the Lord just doesn't abide."

"Nathan says the men are in a state, too." Granny sighed. "That baseball game yesterday was supposed to get some of the grumbles out of them. And then they couldn't even play."

Laina shook her head. "I never would have believed anyone telling me a ball game had to be cancelled because the ball kept blowing away." She laughed. "All those fine ladies' parasols getting turned inside out."

Wilber came ambling up. He submitted to one pat on the head before slumping into the dusty pit he'd dug for himself just beside the washhouse door. He sighed deeply, looking up at Laina.

Granny laughed. "Even God's creatures are praying for a break in this heat." She put her hands to her knees and pushed herself upright. "Well, I guess there is no putting it off." When Laina started to follow her inside,

Granny stopped her. "I meant what I said, child. I won't be responsible for your fainting, or Lord forbid, falling into the fire. You can't help what your nose can't stand." She smiled. "But you can rouse Becky and Katie and send them out here. Maybe we can get a load or two done before daylight."

As Laina walked the path back to the Row, she paused and looked up at the dark sky. She closed her eyes, imagining she could almost hear the heat waves rising from the earth around her. There was just no way to describe August at Camp Robinson other than miserable.

———

"Maybe you'll see some action after all, sonny," Emmet Dorsey said. He was sitting on a hay bale watching Caleb Jackson curry a horse. The men had been discussing the latest round of rumors from the Indian agency down south. Rumors that Dull Knife's band of Cheyenne—and maybe more than just Dull Knife's band—might soon defy the United States government and head north toward their home in the Powder River country.

Jackson nodded. "I'm ready." He peered over the horse's withers at Dorsey. "Just hope I can remember to load the right size shells in the Springfield."

Dorsey raised his eyebrows. Was the young troublemaker actually making a joke about their altercation? He rubbed the knee Jackson had injured.

Jackson didn't look up. He seemed to be concentrating on a snarl in his horse's tail. But when Dorsey went to get up and the knee popped, the young private said, "Granny Max has a good liniment for that. I could bring you some."

"I don't need no nursemaid, sonny," Dorsey snapped. "And even iffen I did, it wouldn't be you."

"Suit yourself," Jackson said and untied the horse's halter to lead him into his stall.

Dorsey's grunt filled the air. "What's in it, anyhow?"

"I think she said something about grumble weed and graybeard," Jackson said. "Sounds like it was made just for you."

"Don't go to any trouble," Dorsey said and limped off.

That night Corporal Dorsey found a blue jar of vile-smelling grease on his cot. While he was rubbing it on his knee, Private Jackson walked by.

"Don't get any ideas about us being friends just because I'm trying this," Dorsey said.

"Who said anything about being your friend?" Jackson retorted. "I'm just sick of hearing you grunt, that's all." He tossed Dorsey a small muslin bag tied with a piece of string. "Granny said you should make strong tea with that. Between the tea and the liniment, she claims you'll be winning footraces in no time."

"Well, that would be something," Dorsey said, tucking the bag in his shirt pocket. "Seeing as how I never could run worth a darn."

———

Laina turned onto her back and stared up at the ceiling of the room that used to house the Boones. She prayed for Katie, who lay at her side, her childish body wracked by an occasional shudder in her sleep, the remains of a long cry she had had in Laina's arms that evening. Wilber lay curled up by the back door, but the minute Laina lifted her head, he raised his. His tail thumped the floor. His ears came up.

Laina sat up, careful not to disturb Katie's sleep. She headed for the back door. It was the third time tonight she'd had to make this trip. Along with what Granny called "early blooming" and Laina's inability to abide certain smells, she was now "enjoying" frequent trips to the outhouse in the dead of night. She was thankful Granny Max was here to explain what was going on and to assure Laina "it's just part of growing a new life, child." Wilber followed her outside and then back into the kitchen.

In the kitchen, Laina pulled out a chair, grateful for the rug that muffled the sound. She looked down. *Lily Boone made that rug. Granny said they gathered rags for weeks and spent most of their first winter working on it.*

Being surrounded by Lily Boone's things made her uncomfortable, almost as if when she touched them she sensed Nathan's despair. It hadn't really bothered her to wear Lily's calico dresses. Laina wondered what was different now. Maybe it was being in the apartment the Boones had shared. It made her more aware of what Nathan had lost. And how lost he was.

She went to the front door and opened it, then stepped outside in her nightgown, looking off toward the cavalry barracks.

Granny's door opened. "Is Katie all right, honey-lamb?"

The familiar voice seemed unusually weary. "She's asleep," Laina said. "Get yourself some rest. It'll be dawn soon."

Instead of going back inside, Granny Max stepped out on the porch. "It *is* a hot one tonight."

"I thought maybe there would be a cool breeze. But it's as still as can be," Laina said, settling down on the steps. Granny came to sit beside her, grunting a little as she lowered herself and leaned against one of the posts that supported the roof and created a porch across the front of the Row.

"Granny, I still don't know what to do. Time's running out. I have to decide whether to go or stay before this baby grows too much more." She took a deep breath. "I remember you reading something about how we should ask in faith believing. Maybe my faith just isn't strong enough for me to see God's answer. Sometimes I think maybe it's right in front of me, and I just can't see it." She sighed. "I think I'm beginning to understand a little bit of how Sergeant Boone feels. All questions and no answers."

"But what dear Nathan doesn't understand, Laina, is that sometimes it takes more faith to stay put and wait than it does to act out and demand answers." Granny reached over and took her hand. "If you don't have peace yet, wait on the Lord."

"Do *you* know what I should be doing?" Laina said. "Do you know and you just aren't saying?"

"If I thought I knew what you should do, honey-lamb, I wouldn't hold it back." Granny Max took Laina's hand. "But the fact is, you can't always depend on me to tell you what to do. You've got your own faith. I've seen it growing."

"Well, it needs to grow faster," Laina said. "So I can be more like you. You're a rock, Granny."

Granny chuckled. "I been called a lot of things in my life. Never a rock. But I will take that as a compliment and tell you the only thing I know to do is what we've been doing. Keep praying and asking the Lord to show us what to do. He trusted this baby to you. I think you can be trusted to make the right decision."

"My head tells me a thousand reasons why it's better for the baby if I start over somewhere else. I could keep house for someone. Thanks to Frenchy Dubois, I can even *cook*. Or I could go to that place Dr. Valentine knows about. Either way, no one would have to know any details. They could assume I'm a widow, and that would change everything. It seems like a perfect solution. But when I think about actually doing those things, the old feeling of panic tears through me. The only thing I want is to stay here with you and Becky and Katie. But that doesn't make any sense. If I stay here, where everyone knows, what happens to *her*?" Laina looked down at her stomach.

"We funnel love to her. Love straight from heaven. So much love she can't keep it all in her," Granny Max said.

Laina leaned over and put her head on Granny's shoulder. "I don't *want* to go anywhere, Granny." She started to cry. "I can't imagine being anywhere without you and the girls."

"Then I have something to say to you," Granny said.

"What?" Laina asked, stifling a sob.

Granny wrapped her long arms around Laina. "Welcome home, honey-lamb. Welcome home."

Chapter Twenty-One

For as the heavens are higher than the earth,
so are my ways higher than your ways,
and my thoughts than your thoughts.
ISAIAH 55:9

THE WEATHER BROKE the first week of September with a ferocious hailstorm that shredded trees down by the river and destroyed Frenchy Dubois's fall garden. The hail damaged buildings and broke windows over on Officer's Row. Private Yates needed an apprentice to help him manage all the repairs, and Caleb Jackson volunteered.

"What do you know about carpentry, Jackson?" Sergeant Boone asked when the private requested special duty to assist Yates.

"About as much as he knew about horses when he signed up for the cavalry, sir," was the answer.

"Is this agreeable to you, Yates?" Nathan asked.

Yates bobbed his head and grinned. "It is, sir."

"I thought you were sick of this greenhorn," Nathan asked Jackson.

Jackson shrugged. "I'm getting used to him."

"That doesn't mean you're going to want to take orders from him," Boone said. "We both know you sometimes have problems following orders."

Jackson nodded. "But we've settled our differences. And you'll notice I've stayed clear of the guardhouse, too."

"You telling me all your troubles are behind you?"

Jackson shrugged. "I'm just saying, sir, I'm doing my best to be a good soldier. And I'd like to learn a trade. Harlan and I get along. Carpentry makes sense. And there's a lot of work to be done." He looked at Nathan. "I need to keep busy, sir."

"Then get out of here and get to work," Nathan said abruptly. "I'll have to clear it with the lieutenant, of course, but as far as I'm concerned you can both consider yourselves excused from regular fatigue duty in favor of making repairs around the camp."

Between the cooler temperatures, which seemed to have a positive effect on everyone's temper, and the time he spent with Harlan Yates, which kept him out of the canteen and away from the card tables and liquor, Caleb was keeping his promise to stay out of trouble. Dr. Valentine noticed and said he would consider forwarding a letter to Charlotte if Jackson kept it up for a while longer. Yates's increasing interest in religion didn't bother Caleb. In fact, as the days went by and the two men spent more time together, Jackson was surprised to realize he actually enjoyed Yates's company.

Granny Max seemed to have a special interest in Harlan Yates. Jackson didn't get it. The private was ugly as could be, and no one would ever accuse him of being intelligent. Yet Granny's face crinkled into a wreath of smiles every time Harlan Yates showed up. Jackson suspected it was no coincidence that Granny Max's roof got fixed first. Nor was he surprised when the first precious glass panes that arrived at Camp Robinson via a freighter from Ogallala found their way into Granny's windows instead of one of the officer's duplexes. And it wasn't long before Caleb realized that Harlan Yates had a deep and abiding crush on Miss Laina Gray. He was tempted to make merciless fun of Yates. But something held him back. The something was Miss Gray.

The more he observed her, the more Caleb was amazed by the ongoing transformation of the woman he had known as Riverboat Annie. When Laina confided in him her decision to stay at Camp Robinson and brave the inevitable judgment and gossip, Caleb's respect for her blossomed into admiration. One evening after a hop, he asked permission to walk Laina home.

"You've changed so much, no one back on the river would even recognize you, Miss Gray," he said. "They'd think maybe Annie had a twin or something. I've got to tell you I admire you for staying here. Putting myself in your shoes, I'd be worried to death. Shoot, I'd be choosing a new name and the next place to run to. You just seem to be calmly going about your life."

Laina objected, "Don't give me too much credit. I may be different from the girl you knew, but I'm still very human."

"So what's happened?"

"If you really want to know, this is going to be a fairly religious talk and a longer one than we had that day at the cemetery. Are you sure you want to hear it?" When Caleb insisted he did, Laina did her best to tell him.

"I believe you," he said when she was finished. "But I still have questions."

Laina nodded. "So do I. I just try to keep learning."

"So how do you learn about these things?" Jackson asked. "We don't have a chaplain and there's no church services."

"Granny and the girls and I read the Bible together," Laina said.

"That's it?"

"That's it," Laina said. "We read and pray. Want to join us sometime?"

Caleb shook his head. "I don't think so."

"You ever change your mind, you're welcome. Does being on special fatigue duty mean you have more say about how you spend your time?"

"It means we have something to keep us busy," he said. "Something besides poker and trying to smuggle whiskey into camp." He hurried to add, "Of course, Yates was never involved in any of that. He's been a good guy since I met him."

They stepped up on the porch together. "Thank you for walking me home, Private," Laina said. "And thank you for the roof repairs and the new window panes." She teased, "I suspect there's a wife or two among the officers who doesn't think too highly of you at the moment."

Jackson shrugged. "From what I've been hearing, there's not a person here at Camp Robinson that hasn't benefited one way or another from knowing Granny Max. I don't think anyone is going to holler too loud when they find out just who we gave those first pieces of glass to. And besides, if they do, they can take it up with Sergeant Boone. He authorized it."

Laina nodded. "He would. He's always been loyal to Granny."

"Oh, it wasn't Granny he was thinking about when it came right down to it."

Laina frowned. "I beg your pardon?"

"All due respect, ma'am, you *can't* have forgotten everything Riverboat Annie knew about men. Don't you see him glaring at me every time I ask you to dance?" When she shook her head, Jackson said, "Good. Because you're a good dancer. And with my reputation, you're about the only woman left in camp that'll trust me—even for a dance."

Laina smiled. "You're fairly harmless from what I can see."

He leaned his head back and looked down at her from half-closed eyes. "I'm not sure I like you thinking I'm harmless," he said. "I may be trying to be honorable, but don't take it to the point of stupidity. You're a beautiful woman, Laina Gray. A man would be a fool not to take notice."

"I'm a pregnant woman, Private Jackson. A man would be a fool not to take notice of *that*." She spread her hands over her waist.

Jackson took her hands. "I don't have a right to say this, Laina. Not with my history. But some man, some day, is going to be very fortunate to have you as his wife. I don't mean me. You'll do lots better than me. I've got a feeling that God of yours is going to come through for you in a big way." He leaned down to kiss her on the cheek. That was when someone tackled him from behind and sent him spinning off the porch, face first into the dirt.

"You get your filthy hands off her!" Nathan Boone roared. He stood over Jackson, his fists clenched.

"What do you think you are doing?!" Laina charged him and hit him full force in the chest, knocking him backward and nearly putting him off balance.

"Defending you," Nathan said.

"When I need defending, I'll let you know!" Laina said, barely controlling her anger. "Were you *following* us?"

Nathan glanced away.

"You were! You were following us." Laina turned around and offered her hand to Jackson. "Are you all right?" she asked as he picked himself up off the ground.

"I'm fine," he said, dusting off his backside and bending down to get his hat.

"Get yourself back to barracks," Nathan ordered.

"This is absurd," Laina said.

"Well, it's going to get even more absurd if he doesn't obey orders."

"It's all right, Miss Gray," Jackson said when Laina opened her mouth to defend him again. "Sergeant Boone is right. You probably shouldn't be seen with me this time of night. At least not without Granny Max or one of the girls in tow." He put his hat on and nodded. "Thank you for letting me walk you home. I enjoyed our talk."

Saluting smartly, he spun on his heels and headed for the cavalry barracks.

———

Nathan reached for Laina's shawl, which had fallen to the ground when she charged at him. She bent down and snatched it up. "Thank you, Sergeant, but you've helped me quite enough this evening."

"Are you . . . are you *interested* in him? Please tell me you aren't."

"I beg your pardon?"

"He was kissing you."

"He was kissing me on the cheek to say good-night. As a friend. Not that it's any of your business. And why do you care anyway?"

"Because I—"

Laina stepped closer. Her eyes blazing, she lit into him. "You listen to me, Sergeant Boone. I will never be able to repay you for what you did for me. Never. I know that. If I could think of a way, I would. But I can't. What you don't seem to realize is I'm better. You can go off duty now, Sergeant. I'm not crazy, and I don't need to be your project anymore."

"I know that," Nathan said. "I don't think of you that way."

"You *do*. You watch me at the hops like some brooding father-figure in the corner. You're always trying to make everything better. You can't *make* it all better, Sergeant Boone. Some things are just out of your reach. And I don't expect you to solve my problems. So, please, give yourself a break. Give *me* a break."

"I think I can solve your biggest problem. That's why I was coming over here. I didn't follow you. I was up at the trading post playing cards."

"You don't play cards."

"Well, that's something else you don't know about me," Nathan said. "As a matter of fact, I do. From time to time. And tonight, when we were finished, I realized I don't even like playing cards. I just do it to fill time. And I've been thinking maybe there's a way to help us both. And so I came down here, and I saw Private Jackson, and I made an assumption—"

"A *wrong* assumption," Laina interrupted.

"All right. A wrong assumption. I'm wrong, and Private Jackson's turned into the precious golden boy of Camp Robinson. The demon turned arch-angel."

"You don't have to be sarcastic, Sergeant. Private Jackson's just like you. He's searching."

"And I suppose you're just the woman to satisfy the search," Nathan said.

Laina slapped him.

"I'm sorry. Oh, Laina. I'm—" He pulled her into his arms and kissed her.

She pushed him away and they stood, both of them breathing hard, staring at each other in the moonlight.

"Marry me," Nathan said.

"*What* did you just say?"

"I said marry me," he repeated. His voice was calmer, his breathing steadier.

"*That's* your solution to my problem?"

"Well, think about it. If you're married, then all your problems with the baby coming are solved. The baby has a family. You have a husband. And a home."

"I already have a home, Sergeant Boone. Right here with Granny Max and Becky and Katie."

"Are you telling me no?" Nathan asked.

He seemed so amazed, Laina felt her anger boiling up again. "Is that so unbelievable?"

"It doesn't make any sense," Nathan said. "I mean, it solves everything."

"For whom?" Laina wasn't letting him off the hook. "Tell me something, Sergeant Boone, just what does it solve for you?"

"I . . . I'm not sure I know what you mean."

"What do you get out of the arrangement?" She watched his expression. "I see. And how is that different from what I did for a living before the honorable Josiah Paine came into my life?"

"Surely you aren't suggesting—"

"No. But you are. You don't love me. You've never loved anyone in your entire life but Lily Bainbridge. And to this day, you are still tied to her."

"My feelings for Lily are none of your business," he barked.

"Get away from me," Laina said.

He reached for her. "No. Wait. We can . . . we can make this work."

"Did you think I'm so helpless and so desperate that I'd just fall to your feet and bless you for saving this poor hopeless wretched woman?"

"Of course not. It's not like that."

"Well, then, how about you tell me what it is like? What were you thinking?"

"All kinds of people have good marriages based on friendship."

"Really? Name one."

"Doctor and Mrs. Valentine."

"Is that what you want? You want a life like Doctor Valentine's?"

"A person could make it work. If they wanted to."

"Well, I don't want to."

"Look," Nathan pleaded. "This isn't the way I meant for this to happen. You think I just blurted that out. All right. I did. But I've been thinking about it ever since I found out about the baby. I've respected your wishes, and I haven't said anything. But—" When he spoke again, his voice was calmer. "It would work. We could make it work. I like you, Laina. Really, I do."

"And I like you. Which is exactly why it would never work. You may be content with half a life. Half a love. But I'm not."

"Well, maybe you should be," Nathan said abruptly. "Maybe you should be grateful for what God's put in front of you, and stop daydreaming about the impossible."

Laina nodded. "Thank you for the advice, Sergeant."

"Hey. I didn't mean that the way it sounded." He reached out to her.

She waved her hand in the air and backed away from him. Hot tears were stinging her eyes, but she didn't want him to see how deeply his remarks had cut. "Actually, I think you did. And that's exactly the reason I have to say no. I'll never be anything to you, Nathan, but a rehabilitated version of that creature who came at you from beneath the trapdoor in Josiah Paine's dugout."

"That's not true. You . . . you've turned into someone amazing."

Laina smiled and shook her head. "Look, I've done all right. With a lot of help from my friends. And you are one of those friends. Goodness, Nathan, you've gone so far as to offer to mortgage the rest of your life just to help me out."

"We'll learn to love each other," Nathan said again.

Laina nodded. "We could. We already have in some ways. But I repeat: part of you—most of you, I fear—will go to your grave as Mr. Lily Boone. I don't know if you can help that or not. But the fact is, I don't see any evidence of you being willing to even try to love someone else. I'm not willing to live with a man who married me just to be the savior of the downtrodden. If that sounds harsh, I'm sorry. But it's the truth. That's why you'd be doing it, Sergeant Boone. And when you cool off, you'll know it."

"You really are turning me down, aren't you?"

"Yes, Sergeant Boone, I am. And with—as Corporal Dorsey would say—all due respect."

"Well, then," he tipped his hat, "I guess that's it."

"Can we still be friends?" Laina asked.

He laughed. "You're the only woman I know who would turn down being my fiancée and ask to still be my friend."

"Well, maybe that's why God put me in your life," Laina said. "Maybe you need a woman with the guts to say no to you once in a while."

He nodded slowly. "I'll think on that one. You think on the proposal. The offer stands if you change your mind."

"You sound like you're making a deal to buy a horse," Laina said.

He closed his eyes and shook his head. "I think I'm going to quit before I make you mad again," he said, rubbing his cheek as if it still stung. "Good night, Miss Gray."

"Good night, Sergeant Boone."

———

Are you out of your mind? How could you say no?

He doesn't love me.

Look at him. Are you blind? Half the women at Camp Robinson practically swoon when he walks by!

He doesn't love me.

So he learns to love you. Later. Or even if he doesn't, he'll provide for the baby. He was right, you know. Marrying him would solve all your problems.

But he doesn't love me.

He'd be a great father. I bet he'd dote on a little girl.

He doesn't love me.

And who ever promised a man would love you? Look at yourself. Look at that scar. The minute you tell them about your past, they'll all run screaming the other way. Nathan knows about all that and he still proposed. He's willing to give you a home. You've been praying about this for weeks. God sends you the perfect answer, and you turn him down. You know what I think? I think you are crazy.

God didn't send this answer.

Right. How can you say that? Because Nathan doesn't love you?

Because he doesn't love God.

———

Laina Gray second-guessed her refusal of Sergeant Nathan Boone on an hourly basis the day after their encounter. But as she thought and prayed over the next few days, she grew more confident. Gradually, she stopped questioning her refusal and began to really believe she had done the right thing. It would have been logical to marry him, but it wouldn't have been right. Somehow, Laina knew. One of the things that confirmed the rightness of her decision lay in the fact she didn't feel the need for Granny's approval. From somewhere deep inside came faith to trust in things not seen—without first discussing it with Granny Max. God had a plan. He had a purpose. Laina clung to the truth in spite of logic. *"Faith isn't always logical, honey-lamb,"* Granny Max had once said. Laina had gained a new appreciation for just how right Granny was.

Chapter Twenty-Two

Precious in the sight of the Lord is the death of his saints.
PSALM 116:15

THE FIRST TIME Doctor Valentine had warned Granny to be careful was about a year after Lily Boone died. Granny hadn't exactly gone to the doctor for attention. He'd discovered her plopped down in a corner in the washhouse clutching her chest and insisted she let him check her over. "Clara Maxwell, I don't like the sound of your heart. It seems to skip a beat every now and then, and it isn't as strong as it should be. You need to slow down."

"When the Lord wants me to slow down, I expect He will let me know," Granny Max had said.

"Maybe He is letting you know through me," the doctor replied as he took the stethoscope from around his neck.

"I don't think so, Doctor Valentine," Granny said. "I think His voice on this subject is much more definite than that."

"Oh, really?" Doctor Valentine said.

Granny nodded. "When He wants me to slow down and stop feeding His lambs, I expect He'll just swing down with one of His chariots and carry me home." She hadn't mentioned feeling poorly to anyone again. She'd tried to rest a little more and had asked for help hauling water and washtubs more often than in her younger days. But she hadn't had any more "attacks" of pain worthy of mention. She'd just continued working and fulfilling her calling to feed God's lambs.

On the night of September 9, 1878, a chariot was sent from heaven to collect Granny Max. She was sitting in her rocking chair reading her Bible by lamplight when she was overwhelmed by the urge to just lean her head back and close her eyes for a minute. And that is where Laina Gray found her, well before dawn the next morning.

Laina assumed Granny was sleeping. "Oh, Granny," she scolded, "let's get you to bed." The hand Laina touched was cool. Laina leaned her head down to listen for Granny's heartbeat, but her own heart was racing so hard she couldn't be sure if she heard it or not. She tore out the door, across the trail, past the infantry barracks, and down Officer's Row to the Valentine quarters. She pounded on Doctor Valentine's door and begged him to come to Granny's apartment.

Together, they ran back. Together, they moved Granny to her bed. Together, they sat at her table for a long time before either of them said a word.

"You said it was her heart," Laina said.

"She was having some early signs of trouble. I advised her to slow down over a year ago."

"She never said anything," Laina choked out. "All those nights I kept her up—and she never said a word." She bowed her head and let the tears spill down her cheeks.

Doctor Valentine patted her hand. "If you hadn't been here, it would have been someone else. Granny Max had an inherent need to nurture others. That was her gift. And *slow down* was not in her vocabulary. It was just her time. There's no need for anyone to go blaming themselves." He paused. "There really is no better way to die than to wear yourself out loving and serving other people. Granny Max died a happy woman."

Laina nodded. After a moment she said, "Poor Private Yates is going to wish he'd never shown a talent for carpentry. It's going to break his heart to make this coffin." She sighed and looked around her. "This is impossible. It *can't* be true. How am I going to tell Becky and Katie? And Sergeant Boone." She swallowed hard. "He's going to be devastated."

Doctor Valentine nodded. "I'll come with you. Becky and Katie are young. And they have each other. Grief is a lighter load when shared." He smiled warmly at Laina. "I know your head is swimming with questions. I just want you to know you won't have to find the answers alone. I hope you'll allow me to be of service in the coming days."

Laina sighed. "I'm numb. I can't even think. This changes . . . everything." She spread her hand over her abdomen. "Everything." She shook her head. *What now, Lord? What next?*

The doctor patted her shoulder. "This must feel overwhelming. But take one thing at a time. Right now, that's Katie and Becky. And Sergeant Boone."

Laina nodded. She inhaled sharply. "All right." She got up. *Lord. Help. Katie. Becky. Nathan. Help. Help me. Please. Help me.*

Laina opened Lily Boone's trunk. Reaching for the blue silk ball gown, she hesitated. From behind her, Nathan said, "It's the best use possible. Do it. Use them both. I'll get Mrs. Gruber to come down and help you."

Laina rose and carried the ball gown into the kitchen. She had Granny's sewing scissors in her hand, but something made her hide them behind her back. *Wait until he's gone.*

Nathan was kneeling beside Katie, who was sitting on the floor crying. Wilber had come inside to lay beside her and was giving mute comfort, his massive white head in her lap. Nathan put his hand on Katie's head and rumpled her hair gently. "Things are going to be all right, Katie. I promise. Don't you be afraid. You hear?" Katie looked up at him. She sniffed and nodded.

He rose and turned around to nod at Becky, who was just coming into the kitchen with Lily's red ball gown in her arms. He repeated the same promise. "Things will be all right, Becky. We'll work it out. I don't want you to worry about anything."

Out of the corner of her eye, Laina saw him pause at the doorway. She tucked the scissors beneath her apron.

"We'll need to talk," he said. "Later."

Laina nodded.

He seemed to have more to say and stood for a long time just staring at her. Finally he cleared his throat. "After I talk to Mrs. Gruber, I'll get Yates started on the coffin."

"You might ask Private Jackson if he'd want to help," Laina said.

"I'll be helping Harlan," Nathan said. His voice was strained. "We won't need anyone else."

"It's not a question of you needing the help," Laina said quietly. "It's a question of Private Jackson needing to do it." She looked down at the dresses for a moment before adding. "He and Granny have had some good talks lately. I think he might feel better if he helped."

Nathan seemed to be about to protest.

"Please," Laina said. "Just ask him."

"Whatever you want," he said, and he turned to go.

Becky and Mrs. Gruber and Laina worked in silence, cutting the skirt of the blue gown away from the bodice, snipping seams, undoing the work of some long-ago dressmaker to create straight panels of the exquisite Prussian blue silk. Katie rose from the floor. Sniffing, she demanded to help. Laina paused, thought, and then handed her the red gown. "Mrs. Gruber and I are going to do Granny's hair." Her voice wavered. "You and Becky work together and make a pillow cover." She handed Katie her needle and thread.

Privates Yates and Jackson, along with Sergeant Boone, arrived with the casket. Laina suggested to Nathan that Doctor Valentine direct Granny's graveside service. Nathan thought that would be fitting and went to ask him. Laina heard assembly and roll call sound while she and the others worked on the casket lining. By morning fatigue call, the casket was lined, the body was ready, and the women led the funeral procession as it wound its way down to the bridge, across the White River, and into the Camp Robinson cemetery.

———

"She fought the good fight. She kept the faith."
"She loved me when no one else did."
"She made the best corn bread I ever ate."
"She held me when I cried."
"She gave me a home when my mother died."
"She sang."
"She always read the Bible before starting her day."
"She didn't put up with gambling or drinking."
"She made sure I sent money home."
"Because of her, I know how to love."
"Because of her, I know how to make a home."
"Because of her, I pray about everything."
"Because of her, I value the Bible."
"Because of her, I've stayed out of trouble."
"Because of her, I know Christ."

The good about Clara "Granny" Maxwell would long be spoken of and long be carried in the hearts of those who knew her and in the lives of those who listened when she gave advice.

———

When the doctor opened Granny Max's Bible as they stood at the graveside, two envelopes fluttered to the ground. Katie picked them up and handed them to Laina, whose eyes filled with tears when she saw Granny's tiny handwriting on them. One was addressed to her, the other to Nathan. From where he was standing behind her, Sergeant Boone must have seen the names. He put his hand on her shoulder and stepped closer. She tucked the envelopes into her apron pocket, gleaning comfort from Nathan's closeness.

"Granny Max had a prodigious knowledge of the book in my hands," the doctor said. "I wish there were some way to know what she would say to us today if God allowed her the opportunity. But as He has not, I have chosen for her. Granny Max was, above all, a gifted comforter of souls. Every single person standing here has, at some time in their stay at Camp Robinson, benefited from Granny Max's gift of mercy. She would want us to be comforted. She would share something from God's Word, not as some potion where the reciting of the words would fix everything, but as something that had become a part of her life. We saw God's Word become flesh in Clara Maxwell's life. May we continue her legacy by taking this message to our hearts."

Then Dr. Valentine began to read, " 'But I would not have you to be ignorant, brethren, concerning them which are asleep, that ye sorrow not, even as others which have no hope. For if we believe that Jesus died and rose again, even so them also which sleep in Jesus will God bring with him. For this we say unto you by the word of the Lord, that we which are alive and remain unto the coming of the Lord shall not prevent them which are asleep. For the Lord himself shall descend from heaven with a shout, with the voice of the archangel, and with the trump of God: and the dead in Christ shall rise first: Then we which are alive and remain shall be caught up together with them in the clouds, to meet the Lord in the air: and so shall we ever be with the Lord.'

"If Granny Max were able today, I feel certain she would tell us not to sorrow for her. She would remind us to have hope, and she'd likely be angry with us if we made a big show of grief over her home-going."

Laina reached down and took Katie's hand.

Dr. Valentine continued. "This passage of Scripture promises us that we can see Granny Max—indeed, all of our loved ones—again. The promise is for all who believe that Jesus died and rose again."

Looking up at Dr. Valentine, Laina met his gaze and nodded. She could almost hear Granny Max saying *"Amen, brother."* She wondered if the man standing behind her was listening.

"So the best way for those of us who respected and loved Clara Maxwell to honor her life, is to ask ourselves if we believe. If we believe, then we must not sorrow as others who have no hope. If we do not believe, certainly hopelessness is an appropriate response to this loss, for there is no hope apart from Christ. Let us ponder that reality in honor of Granny Max and the Christ she served.

"The passage of Scripture I have read provides the best conclusion possible for our memorial of Clara Maxwell. It says—because if we believe Jesus died and rose again, we shall also rise again, because Christ is coming back for us, because the dead in Christ *shall* rise, because one day we shall be with the Lord *forever,* never again to be separated from those we love—'comfort one another with these words.' "

Doctor Valentine paused and looked at the crowd gathered around Granny Max's grave. "Let us pray," he said, and began to lead the group in the Lord's Prayer.

At some point during the prayer, Sergeant Boone stepped to Laina's side and took her hand. When the prayer was finished and people opened their eyes, they seemed to take Nathan's holding Laina's hand as a kind of signal, and in a moment or two everyone was holding hands. Laina began to sing. Others joined in. "I looked over Jordan and what did I see, comin' for to carry me home. A band of angels comin' after me, comin' for to carry me home."

When the song was done, everyone hesitated. Laina closed her eyes and swallowed, choking back the sobs of mingled joy for Granny Max and the sadness for herself that threatened to conquer her self-control. Finally, after Dr. Valentine handed Granny Max's Bible to Laina and took his leave, the small group began to break up and head back toward the bridge. Only Privates Yates and Jackson lingered behind, waiting to fill in yet another grave.

Sergeant Boone kept hold of Laina's hand. She held out Granny's Bible. "You should have this."

"You keep it," he said, stepping forward and crushing the book between them as he wrapped his arms around her. "I'm so sorry about this, Laina. I . . . I hope you know . . . I loved her, too." His body shook as he gave way to his own tears. For a moment they stood together crying.

A soldier came running from across the river. "You're wanted at the commander's office, sir. Big news from down South."

Nathan smiled sadly and left.

Laina looked across to where Yates and Jackson waited, clearly feeling awkward about the scene they'd just witnessed. "I hope you'll both come by this evening," she said to them.

"Mrs. Gruber took Katie and Becky back over to the Row. Said there was some things needed cleaning up," Yates said.

Laina nodded. "Yes. The fabric from . . ." Her voice wavered. She shook her head, swiped away a tear, and forced a smile. Looking from Yates to Jackson, she said, "Thank you for all you've done."

Yates bobbed his head. "Granny was a good woman."

"As good as they come," Jackson added. He looked at Laina. "I'll walk you back to the Row if you'd like." When Yates looked at him in surprise he said, "I mean, if you don't want to be alone, that is."

"Thank you," Laina said. "I'd like that. Very much."

Stabbing the loose earth with his shovel, Jackson offered his arm. He looked at Yates. "I'll be back to help. Don't kill yourself shoveling."

Yates nodded.

Together Caleb and Laina walked toward the bridge.

"I never heard a service quite like that before," Jackson said as they walked along. "I mean, preachers always read the Bible and all, but Dr. Valentine sounded pretty convinced he was reading something special." He cleared his throat. "I never thought about things like that as much more than just 'pie in the sky'. You really think you're going to see her again?"

"I really do," Laina said.

"You think that Book is more than just some wise sayings?"

"It's not a great leap of faith to go from believing there is a God to believing He could write a book and protect its message for a couple thousand years or so. What's a thousand years to the God of the universe?"

Caleb was quiet for a while. They were almost at Granny's front door when Wilber came bounding up out of the brush beside the creek to greet them. Jackson patted his head. "Well, you take care."

"You come for coffee tonight, all right?" Laina said.

"As long as Sergeant Boone allows it, Yates and I will be here." He headed back toward the cemetery.

Katie and Becky and Mrs. Gruber had finished straightening Granny's apartment. There was no sign of blue or red silk, and Mrs. Gruber was urging them all to come to the trading post. "We'll make a lunch and find out what the commander told Sergeant Boone." Mrs. Gruber smiled down at Katie. "I might even be convinced to give that pony you call a dog a special treat," she said. "And at least we'll be together." She blinked back tears. "I just can't quite grasp it."

Laina looked around the room. "I keep waiting for Granny's voice to say something wise and wonderful, to tell me what to do next." The minute the words were out, she smiled. Through her tears, she said, "But I know what she'd say. She'd just say 'Do the next thing, honey-lamb. Just do the next thing.' "

"And what would that be, Miss Gray?" Mrs. Gruber asked.

"Making lunch," Laina said. Laying Granny's Bible down on the table, she led the way to the trading post.

Chapter Twenty-Three

Behold, thou desirest truth in the inward parts.
PSALM 51:6

KATIE AND BECKY had gone to bed and Laina was sitting up drinking tea with Nathan Boone when she opened Granny's Bible and took out two small envelopes. She placed the envelopes side by side on the tabletop so Nathan could see the cramped handwritten names on each one. *Laina. Nathan.*

"Dr. Valentine said he'd warned her to slow down over a year ago," Laina said.

Nathan nodded. Laina saw his jaw clench as he reached for the letter. "I'll read it later," he said. "Have you read yours?"

Laina shook her head. "As long as I don't read it, there's still a way to hear her voice. Something to look forward to." She ran her index finger across the letter penned by Granny Max's hand.

Nathan nodded. He tucked Granny's letter inside his jacket. "You going to be all right?"

"I think so," Laina croaked. She covered her mouth with her hand and closed her eyes, fighting for control of her emotions. "Just when I think I've cried all I can, it washes over me again."

"Maybe you and the girls should have stayed next door," he said, looking around him. "It can be terrible looking at all the things your loved one touched and held. The cup she drank out of. The quilt she made."

"I wondered what that would be like," Laina said. "So far for me, it's comforting being surrounded by Granny's things. Becky and Katie said that, too. They wanted Granny's quilt on their bed." She sighed. "I don't know how to explain it. It's like she's still here, in a way." She could feel tears gathering again beneath her closed eyes. She swiped them away. "I thought we might read the letters together," she said. "Kind of our own private memorial."

"I don't have to read my letter to know what it says," Nathan said. He pulled it out of his pocket and held it up. "It says I shouldn't be bitter. It says I should trust God." He looked over the top of the envelope at Laina. "It probably says I should think about marrying again. And although I doubt she actually wrote your name, you're the one she'd have been thinking about when she wrote the letter." He tapped the corner of the envelope on the table. "If you want to read yours, you go ahead. I'll wait."

Laina shook her head. "It's all right." She got up. "You'll be wanting to get back to the barracks. Is it true what I heard? That there's a band of Cheyenne headed this way?"

Nathan nodded. "Dull Knife and some others. They never really settled in down South. Couldn't seem to get along with the tribes already there. Doctor Valentine said the doctor at that agency is one of his old war buddies. He's written Doc about it. He's supposed to take care of five thousand Indians, and he'd had nothing but delayed supplies and other troubles. The northern tribes, especially, aren't doing very well. They've never had to handle the heat and humidity. They've had malaria, measles, ague." He shook his head. "Can't blame them for wanting to come home. I can imagine the Powder River country sounds like heaven to a warrior boiling under an Oklahoma sun."

"But it's cooler down there now," Laina said. "Won't that make a difference?"

Nathan shrugged. "It could. Or it could just make them more desperate to get up north before snow falls. Captain says there are a lot of other problems besides the sickness. I guess they're starving half to death. Like I said, I can't blame them for wanting to come back North."

"Why can't that be allowed?" Laina asked.

"Probably because the people making the decisions aren't making decisions based on *people*. They just see a *problem* to contain. Not people to care about."

"How do you see it?" Laina asked softly. "As a problem or people?"

"All I know is we're being put on alert. Captain doesn't seem to think we'll have to get involved at all. It's expected they'll all be rounded up and returned to the agency before long. They're crossing the plains, in unfamiliar territory. No place to hide. And they can't travel very fast with their women and children and old folks along." He smiled at Laina. "Nothing to worry about." He scooted his chair back and stood up. "You get some rest," he said.

She nodded. "I'm fine. You take care." As he turned to go, she said, "We should still do the Sunday picnic. It's getting cooler. There won't be many more Sundays when we can." She shrugged. "I don't feel like it, but . . ."

She looked behind her toward the back room where Katie and Becky were sleeping. "It's reassuring if some things stay the same." She looked up at him with a question in her eyes. "Do you think?" She felt the baby moving, and with that quivering deep inside, she began to tremble.

"Hey," he said. "Hey. Come here." He pulled her into his arms.

Laina relaxed against him and let another wave of grief wash over her.

When she was quiet, he released his grip and, looking down at her, said, "I'll ask Frenchy to make something for a picnic lunch. You try sleeping a little later than usual." He lifted her chin. "You hear?"

She nodded.

He touched the tip of her nose lightly and smiled down at her. "We'll be all right."

After Nathan left, Laina reached for her envelope. There was no good reason to wait. She needed to hear Granny's voice—now.

Dear Laina,

I can imagine Dr. Valentine saying he was right—I should have slowed down. And I imagine you wondering what to do now. When I thought about writing these letters just in case something happened, I imagined putting all kinds of advice in them. Things I've wanted to say but didn't. But the fact is I've no right to try to take the Lord's place in your life and guide your future. These past weeks I have wondered just as much as you what the Lord was doing. And I will tell you that I was none too happy with Him expecting you to raise a child by yourself. Maybe it won't be by yourself. But you've got to be prepared to do that. In the end, we all just have to rest ourselves in the everlasting arms of the Good Lord and do the next thing, all the time believing. You have been one of the sweetest lambs the Lord has brought me, Miss Laina, and He's brought me a good flock of lambs in my day.

You talk to the commander about staying on at Camp Robinson. He's a good man, and you and Becky are hard workers. He won't send you off without a place to go to. If you want to go to that place Dr. Valentine knows, I hope you will take Katie and Becky with you. But in my heart I hope you stay and watch over Nathan for me. Give him time, Laina. I think he will finally come to healing and some kind of peace, if he only has someone around him living the love. You could be that person for him. I have prayed it might be so.

The best advice I can give you for life, Laina, is written inside my Bible cover.

Never forget, honey-lamb, YOU ARE LOVED.

I will be waiting to welcome you. Give your little darling extra hugs and kisses from her Granny Max. Maybe you will tell her about me.

On Sunday morning, in spite of Sergeant Boone's advice that she try to sleep later than usual, Laina woke with a sense of urgency. She sent Wilber outside. Quickly, she made a batch of flapjacks for Becky and Katie while she downed a cup of coffee. Leaving the flapjacks wrapped in a towel on the stove, she dressed and headed off toward Officer's Row, where she let herself in at the Valentines' back door and set to making breakfast for the doctor.

He appeared in the kitchen, slightly rumpled and not a little surprised. "Miss Gray? I didn't expect you this morning. I can fix my own breakfast, you know. You shouldn't feel obligated to—"

"I don't feel obligated, Dr. Valentine. I've got to get some things settled, and I've come to ask your help."

"Give me a moment to wash up," the doctor said. "I'll be right back." He smiled at her. "That coffee smells good."

When Dr. Valentine was settled at the table enjoying scrambled eggs and biscuits, Laina sat across from him. "I need to talk to the commander, and I'm hoping you'll go with me," she said. She outlined her plan, and as soon as the doctor was finished with breakfast, they rose to go.

"I apologize for interrupting your Sunday morning, sir," Laina said as she sat down. She felt nervous, sitting across the massive desk from the uniformed stranger. Of course, everyone at Camp Robinson *knew* the commander, but officers and enlisted men led completely separate lives in the military. Laina had only Granny's encouragement that the commander was "a kind man" to still her pounding heart.

"I . . . I've asked Dr. Valentine to come with me as a sort of character witness," she began. She stopped and swallowed. "Look, sir. I know it isn't considered very polite to really say what a person means. People tend to talk *around* situations more than they talk *about* them." She glanced from the commander to Dr. Valentine. "At least, that's been my experience." She clasped her hands together. "But I'm going to beg your forgiveness this morning and . . . Well, I'm going to be as honest and open about some things as I can be." She stared into the commander's gray eyes, looking for some encouragement, some inkling of a smile. When none appeared, she launched a one-word prayer. *Help.* Taking a deep breath, she told her story. She told the commander everything. About her past, about the dugout, about her changed life.

When Laina paused, the commander leaned forward. "Why are you telling me these things, Miss Gray?"

"Because with Granny Max's and Mrs. O'Malley's deaths, Katie and Becky and I no longer have any association with the military that would officially allow us to stay here. But we all want to stay." She glanced at Dr. Valentine, who nodded encouragement. "It's the only life these girls know," she said. "And it's the only life I *want* to know. I'm hoping you'll let us stay on as laundresses."

"And Mrs. Valentine will certainly want Miss Gray's domestic help when she returns to Camp Robinson in the spring," Dr. Valentine added.

"I see no reason why you can't continue on here," the commander said. "Even if it is determined that you cannot continue as military employees, it would be unthinkable to send three women off toward Sidney until Dull Knife and the Cheyenne who left their agency are rounded up and sent back where they belong." He started to get up. "So, for at least the time being, you and the Misses O'Malley are quite secure in your positions here at Camp Robinson. Now, if you'll excuse me—"

"You need to know something else, sir. Rumors are going to be circling. I'll feel better if you know everything."

"Everything, Miss Gray?"

"I'm going to have a baby," Laina said.

The commander plopped back into his chair. He listened to her explanation and then looked at Dr. Valentine, who nodded yes when asked to confirm what had just been said.

"All I'm asking for is a new start. A chance to earn an honest living," Laina concluded.

The commander twirled the tip of his mustache thoughtfully. He looked from Laina to Dr. Valentine and back again. Finally, he spoke up. "You were quite right, Miss Gray, when you mentioned it isn't fashionable for people to be so candid about themselves." He chewed on his lower lip. "More's the pity," he said, and held out his hand. "I do appreciate your honesty. It took no small amount of courage to walk in here this morning. Even with the good Dr. Valentine as your champion." As Laina shook his hand, the commander said, "I won't be interfering with things over on Soapsuds Row." He stood up. "Now if you'll excuse me, I've got to see to the latest dispatches from General Crook." He nodded and showed them to the door.

———

"You're early, Private Yates," Laina said as she greeted Harlan. She waved him inside. "Becky and Katie have gone up to the Grubers' to see if they'd like to join us for today's picnic." She smiled at him. "I'm glad to see Sergeant Boone told you we want to keep up the tradition." She looked past him. "Is Private Jackson coming?"

Harlan bobbed his head. "Yes'm. He'll be along directly. Said maybe this afternoon you could work some more with Wilber. With the horses, I mean. To teach him to behave hisself."

Laina nodded. "That's a wonderful idea." She pushed her hair back out of her face. "It'll give Katie something new to keep her mind off . . ." She sighed and shook her head. Handing him a knife and a loaf of bread, she said, "Thick slices, Private. And don't cut yourself. Granny just sharp—" Laina swallowed hard and blinked away the tears.

"Now, Miss Laina," Harlan said, laying down the knife and patting her awkwardly on the shoulder. "Don't you cry. Everything's going to be all right."

Laina put her hand over his and patted it. "Thank you, Harlan. I know. It's just so . . . fresh." She sighed. "It doesn't seem real. I keep expecting her to come in the back door."

Harlan nodded. "I expect that will be so for a long time to come." He cleared his throat. "The reason I come over early was . . ." He looked up at the ceiling, then down at the floor.

"The reason you came over early was . . ." Laina repeated.

He dropped to one knee. "With Granny gone, Miss Gray, I know you must be wondering what to do. And I was thinking that if—" His voice cracked. He ducked his head. "Well, if you was married, that would solve everything. And we get along good." His face glowed red as he blushed and croaked, "Will you marry me, Miss Gray?"

Dumbfounded, Laina could only slide into the chair next to where Harlan was kneeling. He waited, awkwardly balanced on one knee, watching her. She leaned one arm on the table and, closing her eyes, rested her forehead on her open hand. She shook her head. "Oh, Harlan . . ."

He hopped up. "I know." His voice was miserable. "I was stupid to think you'd want to—"

"Harlan. You're a kind and generous and good man." Looking up, she took his hand. "A woman could do a lot worse than to be Mrs. Yates."

He shrugged. "A woman could do a lot better, too. I reckon."

"You don't love me, Harlan," Laina said quietly. She squeezed his hand.

"I do," he protested.

"And I love you. If I had a brother, I'd want him to be just like you."
She picked up the knife. "Now slice the bread. Here come the girls."

"It's no, then?"

"It's no. But thank you." Laina said.

With a sigh, Harlan picked up the knife and got to work.

———

It was as if Granny Max's death had opened the floodgates. Within the
week after Granny's funeral service, Laina had received proposals from
four soldiers. Becky O'Malley thought it was hilarious. "Don't get mad,
Laina. When Papa died, Mama had someone propose to her *at the funeral*.
You can't blame the men. They're lonely. The only reason you haven't had
this happen before is Granny guarded you like a bear protecting her cub.
Now that she's gone, the men just naturally assume you need a husband."
She giggled. "The funniest one was that Corporal Dorsey." She grimaced.
"Can you imagine cleaning up after a man who spits tobacco every twenty
seconds?"

"Can you imagine *kissing* him?" Katie chimed in. She made a face.
"Yuck."

"But he assured me he can hit the spittoon from clear across the room,"
Laina said, laughing. "What do you suppose those men would have said if
I told them the rest of my story?" She patted her stomach.

"Harlan knows," Becky said. She blushed. "He told me after you turned
him down."

Laina studied her expression. "Rebecca O'Malley! Harlan discussed
proposing to me? With *you*? He talked about my baby? With *you*?"

Becky shrugged. "I told him it was all right to ask you."

"You did?"

"Well," she ducked her head. "Harlan and me . . . we sort of . . ."

"Yes?"

She grinned. "I knew you'd say no. He just needed to feel like he did
the manly thing."

"But how does he know about the baby? Who told him that?"

"Nobody had to tell him," Becky said. "Harlan's got a gentle heart. He
notices things. He figured it out. He said he wondered for a long time, but
when you started letting out your dresses, that's when he was sure."

Laina took a deep breath. What a relief it was to have talked this over
with the commander. What a blessing not to have to wonder what was

going to happen when he found out. *Thank you, God.* It wouldn't be long before everyone would know. It was going to be an interesting winter.

———

"Laina!" Katie came tearing around the edge of the Row and skidded to a stop beside Laina, who was hanging laundry out to dry. "Laina! The Cheyenne. They're coming!"

"Calm down, Katie," Laina said. "Those rumors have been flying around camp for nearly a month now."

"Well, this time it's true!" Katie said. "Private Jackson was helping me introduce Wilber to some of the horses over in the corral—Wilber's getting real good about not chasing them—and Corporal Dorsey came up and said the Cheyenne had crossed the Kansas Pacific Railroad. And they escaped the troops again. And they been raiding and killing white people all over Kansas. And there's cavalry coming to Camp Robinson!" She paused, gasping for breath.

"Sergeant Boone said Camp Robinson wasn't going to be involved. There's no reason for the Cheyenne to come here now that their agency's been moved," Laina said. "In fact, he was mighty upset about not getting in on the action."

"Well, he's not upset anymore," Katie insisted. "The lieutenant's ordered drills and inspections, and everything has to be perfect for Major . . . Major . . . oh . . ." Katie stomped her foot. "I *knew* I wouldn't remember his name."

"Calm down, Katie," Laina said. "Nothing you've said changes our jobs. We still have to keep the laundry done."

"But it's *exciting*!" Katie said, and tore off toward Gruber's trading post.

"What'll happen to Harlan?" Becky said from the washhouse doorway.

Laina looked over. Becky's face was flushed. Her eyes brimmed with unspilled tears. Laina closed her eyes. *What do I say?* She thought of Sergeant Boone and Corporal Dorsey, of Privates Yates and Jackson, all in the same tangle of fear.

"Get back inside and tend your washpot," she said to Becky.

"But, *Laina* . . ."

"You can't help Private Yates by worrying," Laina said. "But you can help by praying while you do the laundry." Becky nodded and went back inside. Laina was grateful the girl couldn't see how her own hands trembled as she went to hang up one of Private Jackson's shirts.

Chapter Twenty-Four

Therefore if any man be in Christ, he is a new creature:
old things are passed away; behold, all things are become new.
II CORINTHIANS 5:17

KATIE O'MALLEY LEANED on the lower rung of the corral and watched as Private Jackson and some other soldiers drove a herd of decrepit Indian ponies across the snow-covered ground and into the Camp Robinson corral. There were too many horses to all be corralled, but even Katie could tell from the condition of these animals that there would be no danger of them stampeding off somewhere. She ran to the stables and scooped a handful of grain. Running back to the corral, she made the same clicking sound she had heard Private Jackson make when he wanted to get a horse's attention. A pony's head went up. The little mare came over and practically inhaled the grain, then began whickering plaintively and bumping Katie's gloved hand.

"I'm sorry," Katie whispered. "I can't give you any more."

When Private Jackson dismounted nearby, Katie ran to him. "Wilber doesn't chase the horses anymore, see?" She pointed to where the giant white dog sat watching the horses mill around. "Laina and me been working with him the whole month you been gone."

"That's good, Katie," Jackson said. He headed for the stables.

Katie followed. "Did you see the Indians? Are they coming?"

"I saw 'em," Jackson muttered. "They'll be coming soon, I suppose. They don't have much choice." He pulled the saddle off his horse. Steam rose from the animal's back.

"How's Private Yates?" Katie asked. "Becky's been awful worried about him. You've all been gone so long."

"I haven't seen much of Private Yates," Jackson said. He grabbed a brush and began rubbing his horse down. "His battalion went one way, mine went another, most of the time."

"You think he'll be coming back soon?"

"Can't say. They're still trying to negotiate something."

"What's nego-shate?" Katie asked.

"That's when you try to get someone to do something they don't want to do," Jackson said. "The Cheyenne don't want to come to Camp Robinson. They want to go home—up north."

"So how do you nego-shate them to come here, anyway?"

Jackson closed his eyes and shook his head.

Corporal Dorsey rode up. "Orders are to ride back to Chadron Creek," he said. "Looks like there's gonna be a fight. And there's a storm brewing. Temperatures are dropping. Could be a big snow this time. We got to be ready to leave in ten minutes with fresh mounts." He climbed down.

"Hey there, little miss," Dorsey said. He unsaddled his horse and turned it loose in the corral. The half-starved Indian ponies ignored the unfamiliar horse and stood with their heads down. "Most pitiful lot of critters I ever saw," Dorsey said. A stream of tobacco stained the snow.

"We had to shoot over a dozen on the way here," Jackson said. He swore softly. "This isn't the kind of war I signed on to fight—I can tell you that. Women and children—" Glancing at Katie he stopped talking. He nodded at her. "You tell Becky I'll look out for Private Yates for her," he said. "And don't tell Miss Gray you heard me swear."

"And Sergeant Boone?" Katie asked. "Will you look after Sergeant Boone, too? 'Cause she don't say it, but I know Laina worries over him."

Jackson nodded. "Sure."

Calling Wilber to her, Katie trotted off toward Soapsuds Row.

———

Sergeant Boone dismounted and hurried toward the wagon filled with Cheyenne women and children. When a woman stumbled getting down and almost dropped her baby, he went to help her. She jerked away from him, muttering something under her breath and glaring at him with unbridled hatred. She joined the other women and children. The little girl he'd gotten to know as Lame Deer was among them. She smiled at him as she walked by.

With a twinge of sadness, he remembered the evening he'd met Lame Deer. He'd offered half his rations to a rail-thin Cheyenne child about Katie O'Malley's age and had been surprised when she thanked him in English and told him her name. When he saw her break the biscuit in pieces and share it with about four other children, he'd had to walk away to keep his emotions under control.

Looking at them, it was hard to believe they had crossed hundreds of miles of unfamiliar flatland and eluded the military for nearly two months. One of the troopers, who'd gotten involved in the chase earlier than Nathan had, told him that at least once the Cheyenne had traveled nonstop for three days. "Can you believe it?" the trooper had said, reciting statistics. "Ninety men, a hundred-and-twenty women, and even more children. And it took us all this time to catch up to them."

"The only reason we caught them when we did," Nathan said, "was because Dull Knife probably didn't realize Red Cloud Agency was moved after they left for Indian territory."

The other trooper had nodded agreement. "And we still don't have 'em all. Captain says they found signs that Little Wolf's band separated from Dull Knife down on Whitetail Creek. We'll be going after 'em." He had shivered. "I'm not looking forward to *that* ride."

Nathan felt a sense of relief that Company G was finally back at Camp Robinson with Dull Knife's band. They'd caught up with them in a driving snowstorm. If it was going to practically blizzard in October, he was glad he wasn't among the soldiers chasing farther north after Little Wolf. It made him shiver just to think about the cold days and nights in the saddle. He was glad they had brought a wagon out from Camp Robinson so the women and children hadn't had to walk in the snow.

Nathan felt ashamed. He'd heard more than one of these prisoners echo Dull Knife's sentiment, that it was better to die than to go back South. Some of them already looked half dead. He blocked it out. He'd gotten orders to round up two enlisted men to cook for the captives. If he had anything to say about it, Lame Deer and her young friends were about to be treated to some French-American cooking. As the last of the captives filed into the barracks, Nathan headed off to look for Frenchy Dubois.

———

I want to master this Book, so the Master of this Book can master me.
Sitting in Granny Max's rocking chair, Laina reread the now-familiar quotation written on the inside cover of Granny's Bible. In her letter, Granny had said the best advice she could give Laina was written inside her Bible. This was it. Laina ran her finger along the neat row of printing. *I am trying, Granny Max. I am really trying.*

The baby prodded her back. Laina reached behind her to knead the aching away. She shivered and moved closer to the stove, wondering if the Cheyenne captives she'd seen coming in earlier that day were warm inside their barracks. She wondered about Sergeant Boone and Private Yates, Corporal Dorsey and Private Jackson. She'd taken to praying for them more often since they had left Camp Robinson. Now she longed to see them, to see for herself that they were all right.

Becky and Katie came in from the washhouse. Laina could hear them stomping snow off their shoes just inside the back door.

"Brrrrr!"

At first Laina didn't recognize the voice. When Private Jackson came in with the girls, she smiled and started to get up.

"Stay put," he ordered. "You look comfortable wrapped up inside that quilt. Kind of like a sausage."

"Very funny," Laina said.

"A very cute sausage," he added, winking at Katie.

Laina shivered. "How cold is it, anyway?"

"You don't want to know," Jackson said. "Nobody in Jefferson Barracks told us about the mercury dropping like a stone in *October* out here."

"I don't think this is exactly normal," Laina said.

Jackson nodded toward the back door. "Your woodpile is shrinking. I'll get Yates to help me haul some more up to the back door for you. Sergeant Boone will let that be our morning fatigue duty if I ask."

"When did you all get back in camp?" Laina asked. "Can you eat with us? Can you ask Sergeant Boone and Harlan?" She smiled at Becky.

"We all rode in this afternoon with the wagon. Thanks, but I don't think Yates and I can eat with you. I can't speak for Sergeant Boone, but I'll tell him you asked. They're running things very close to the book these days," he said. "No regulation ignored." He slapped his hands together and held them up to the stove.

"What do you think is going to happen?" Laina asked.

"I don't have any idea. Last I heard, Washington was still saying they have to go back South. And Dull Knife was still saying they'll die before they do that." He paused. "But two good things will happen for the Cheyenne while they are working it all out. Regular rations—which I understand wasn't very common down at Darlington Agency. And a little freedom. Captain says they don't have to be locked up." He smiled. "Sergeant Boone introduced me to a little girl about Katie's age a little while ago—name of Lame Deer." He motioned toward Granny Max's Bible, still lying in Laina's lap. "You spending a lot of time listening to Granny Max's advice?"

Laina smiled. "Morning and evening. Or most mornings and evenings, anyway."

"How you feeling?"

"Good," Laina said. "Really good." She unconsciously reached behind her and rubbed her back.

"Good, except for your back is killing you?"

Laina shrugged. "Part of the territory, I guess. Mrs. Gruber says so, anyway."

"Lean forward," Jackson said.

"What?"

"Hey, Katie," he said. "Would you get Miss Gray a pillow to lean on? I guess she isn't quite as bendable as before." He chuckled.

Katie tossed a pillow at Laina, who took it and put it on the edge of the table. She crossed her arms and leaned forward onto the pillow while Jackson took off his buffalo coat. When Laina was settled, Jackson reached down inside the quilt and began to knead her lower back. "My mama used to make me and my brother rub her back when she was carrying our little sister."

It was the first time Jackson had ever mentioned his family. Laina wanted to ask about that brother and little sister. Instead, she said, "You're hired," as she closed her eyes and concentrated on the release of tension in her aching muscles.

"I already have a job," Jackson replied. "Hauling wood, cleaning stalls, hauling more wood. I expect I'll get the astoundingly fascinating job as sentry inside the barracks with the Cheyenne, too."

"Won't you be afraid?" Katie asked.

Jackson shook his head. "Dorsey did some guard duty up in Minnesota back in '62. He said to expect the men to play cards and smoke while the women do beadwork and make moccasins. Which reminds me," he said, nodding at Katie. "If you'll check the pockets of my coat, there's a couple of packages for you ladies."

Squealing with delight, Katie pounced on the coat and withdrew two packages wrapped in brown paper. She ripped one open and found a pair of moccasins for herself and one for Becky.

"I traded with Lame Deer's mother. I gave her blankets for those," Jackson said. "There's a pair for you, Miss Gray, in the other package." He began to massage her shoulders with both hands.

"You don't have to—"

"Be quiet," Jackson snapped. "I haven't been this close to a warm stove in a long time. This is entirely a self-serving exercise," he said. "So just hush and suffer while I get my backside warm."

Katie giggled. Becky blushed.

"Sorry. I shouldn't have said that," he apologized.

"Do they need more blankets?" Laina asked. "Because we could send a couple. From Lily Boone's trunk."

"That'd be kind of you," Jackson murmured. "They don't have much in the way of blankets. It's always the women and children who suffer most, huh." After a couple minutes of quiet he said, "Well, I best be getting back up to camp. Sergeant Boone only gave me about three minutes to come over here and check on his women." He pulled on his coat.

"You look like a bear with that coat and that scruffy beard," Katie said. "We didn't even know you at first!"

Jackson tugged on his beard. He turned his head so the girls could see his profile. "I let it grow while we were out on patrol. Personally, I think I look rather like Lincoln. Wouldn't you agree?"

"Oh, not at all," Becky said. "President Lincoln wasn't nearly as handsome as you, Private Jackson."

Jackson grinned at her. His brown eyes twinkled. "And now, having finally garnered the compliment for which I was waiting, I shall depart." He bowed stiffly and headed for the door, calling back over his shoulder, "Firewood. Tomorrow."

"Thank you," Laina said.

"What's happened to *him*?" Becky said as soon as he was gone.

Laina shook her head. "I haven't any idea. But whatever it is, I think I like it."

———

Katie stood on tiptoe and pulled the last wooden clothespin off the line above her, pulling a pair of freeze-dried men's drawers down with it. They were so stiff they wouldn't bend, so she just laid them atop the stack of laundry in the basket at her feet. Wilber, who had been dozing in the sun, suddenly rolled over and raised his head. Ears alert, he thrust his nose into the air. He sat up, thumping his tail as he looked toward the creek. He started to get up, then held back, looking up at Katie and whining.

"What's there, fella?" Katie said, putting her hand on the dog's back and peering toward the creek. But Wilber wasn't looking toward the creek, after all. Katie smiled. "Why, hello there."

A Cheyenne girl about her age stepped out from where she had been hiding around the corner of the Row. She raised her hand in greeting. "Hel-lo," she said carefully.

Wilber stood up. The girl took a step back and pulled the blanket across her shoulders tighter. "Big dog," she said.

Katie glanced down at Wilber. "Yes. He's big. But he won't hurt you." She motioned to the girl. "His name is Wilber. You can pet him."

The girl looked doubtful.

"Come on," Katie said, motioning for the girl to step closer.

She shook her head so hard her long dark braids waved back and forth.

"You have pretty ribbons in your hair," Katie said, pointing to the blue-and-red bows adorning each braid.

"Soldier Jack-Son give," the girl said.

Katie nodded. "That's nice." She took Wilber's collar. "I'll hold onto him. Come say hello."

The girl took a step forward. Wilber wagged his tail. Finally, she extended one hand out of the blanket toward the dog. When Wilber thrust his snout into her hand she screeched with fear and snatched it away. But when Wilber nosed at the opening of the blanket and began to lick her arm, she giggled. Wilber kept licking, literally washing her arm until the girl began to pet him, smiling and cooing.

"My name's Katie." Katie pointed to the back door of Laina's apartment. "I live there." She pointed down at the basket of laundry. "We do laundry for the soldiers."

"Lame Deer," the girl said, pointing to herself. She pointed toward the pine-covered bluffs in the distance. "I live there." Then she gestured toward the barracks across the creek to the east. "Soldiers keep us there."

Katie nodded. "Maybe you'll get to go home soon."

The girl shook her head. "Great Father says no. Says we must go back to Dar-ling-ton." She said the word syllable by syllable.

"You don't like it there?" Katie asked.

"We die there," the girl said. She looked at Katie. "My father die there. My brother, too. Lame Deer and Brave Hand alone now."

"Brave Hand," Katie murmured. "Is that your mother?"

The girl nodded. Her stomach rumbled.

Katie smiled. "You hungry? I have to take this laundry inside." She motioned toward the door. "Laina's making lunch. You could eat with us." When the girl hesitated, Katie said, "You'll like Laina." Katie added, "My papa died, too."

"Soldiers kill white people, too?" Lame Deer asked.

Katie frowned. She shook her head. "Of course not. Soldiers didn't kill my papa. Indians killed him."

"Cheyenne?"

Katie shook her head. "No. Sioux."

Lame Deer made a fist and raised it to her chest. "Killing makes hurt here."

"Yes," Katie said, surprised when tears sprung to her eyes. She blinked them away.

Laina came to the back door.

"That your mother?" Lame Deer asked.

Katie shook her head. "No. My mama died, too. My sister, Becky, and I stay with Laina now." She called out to Laina. "This is Lame Deer. Can she have lunch with us?"

Laina smiled. "Of course."

"Jack-Son say you give us blankets," she said, smiling. "Thank you."

Laina nodded. "You are very welcome, Lame Deer." She motioned the girls inside. "Come in. I have flapjacks on the griddle."

Chapter Twenty-Five

But be ye doers of the word, and not hearers only, deceiving your own selves. For if any be a hearer of the word, and not a doer, he is like unto a man beholding his natural face in a glass: For he beholdeth himself, and goeth his way, and straightway forgetteth what manner of man he was. But whoso looketh into the perfect law of liberty, and continueth therein, he being not a forgetful hearer, but a doer of the work, this man shall be blessed in his deed.

JAMES 1:22-25

"YOU SHOULDN'T BE making friends with them," Nathan said one November Sunday evening when he and Yates and Jackson had come over to the Row for dinner. "It's only going to make things harder when we have to move them. And they are going to have to go back South. Orders are orders."

Harlan Yates shifted his weight in his chair. "All due respect, Sergeant," he said, "I realize they can't stay here at Camp Robinson. But why do they have to go south? They're perfectly willing to go anywhere but there. It seems a reasonable request not to want to return to where you just sit and watch each other get sick and die."

"I was there when Dull Knife said 'You may kill us. But you cannot make us go back'," Jackson said. "And I don't blame him for standing his ground."

"I don't blame him, either," Nathan said. "But I'm a soldier, and I'll do what I'm told. I'll try to do it in a way nobody gets hurt. But a soldier who won't obey orders isn't worth anything to his country."

"A soldier who harms women and children isn't worth anything to anybody," Jackson said abruptly.

"Nobody said anything about intentionally harming women and children," Nathan snapped. "But that doesn't mean we ought to be buying them hair ribbons, either." He glowered at Jackson.

Laina broke in. "Why can't the people giving those orders understand? If those generals had seen them when they arrived—compared to now.

Lame Deer was little more than a reed of grass blowing in the wind when I first saw her. And look at her now." She smiled at Nathan. "The results of a few weeks of Frenchy Dubois' cooking are obvious."

Nathan got up and went to the window. He looked out toward the barracks where the Cheyenne were being housed. "Well, you can see those provisions being stockpiled over by the barracks. There's a change coming, that's certain."

"The army can't possibly move them in *this* weather!" Laina said. She rubbed her own numb hands together. "They don't have proper clothing. They'll freeze."

Nathan looked at Laina. "No one's going to deliberately *harm* them."

"No," Jackson interrupted, "we're going to do it more slowly. By sending them back to an unfit climate where measles and malaria can do it for us."

"Well," Nathan said gruffly, "army life isn't all training horses and giving riding lessons to the ladies, Private. Sometimes it means doing things you don't personally approve."

"Who in any name under heaven could ever approve of what's being done to those Cheyenne?" Jackson blurted out. His face flushed with anger. "We call ourselves a Christian nation. How can any Christian do this to people?"

Nathan glared at Jackson. "May I remind you, Private Jackson, that these wonderful so-called defenseless people you want to give a home murdered over three dozen people in Kansas on their way back up here? Or do you think we should be good Christians about that and turn the other cheek? Or is that not the verse of the week?"

As the conversation got more and more heated, Laina Gray grew more ill at ease. These were not the same three men who had left Camp Robinson to help round up the Cheyenne. They were not the same men who'd been guarding the barracks, either. Yates seemed more sure of himself. Less apologetic about himself in general. She was happy for him.

Jackson was different, too. He seemed more at peace with himself. Apparently he was the one who had given Lame Deer the hair ribbons. Nathan disapproved, but Laina was touched by Jackson's kindness to a child—especially a child whose contact with white people in general and soldiers in particular had undoubtedly created some horrific memories. Laina couldn't see why Granny Max's image of a "funnel of love" from heaven shouldn't operate for Cheyenne children, too.

What did Nathan mean by that *verse of the week* comment? As the men argued over the Cheyenne's fate, Laina watched Caleb, amazed at his self-control. He obviously had intense feelings about the situation, but he was nothing like his old self. His old self would have likely disregarded the fact that he was arguing with an officer and made a point or two with his fists by now. His old self would have probably landed in the guardhouse before the night was over.

But instead of using his fists, Caleb was maintaining control, even while he defended Dull Knife's position. Finally, he raised his hands, palms up. "Hey, Sarge, I've got no intention of refusing to obey orders. I'm just saying it's not right making them go back. And I don't think they will. We're sitting on powder keg, sir."

Nathan walked back toward the table. He snatched his coffee mug up and drained it. "Well, I agree with you about that, soldier. And God help us all when it blows up. Which, thanks to the blind guides back in Washington, it is most certainly going to do."

While an awkward silence reigned in the room, Laina got up from the table and reached for the coffeepot. She bumped the table when she came back, hard enough to slosh Katie's milk out of her mug. "Sorry," she said, blushing. "I don't have a sense of where I begin and end anymore." She smoothed her dress over her bulging abdomen and moved to pour Nathan more coffee. The men exchanged embarrassed glances. "Sorry," Laina apologized again. "I didn't mean to embarrass anyone." *But I did mean to stop the arguing. And between Caleb and me we did it.*

Harlan Yates spoke up. "The men aren't going to let Christmas go by without a hop," he said, looking pointedly at Becky. "You ladies will come, won't you?"

"As long as there isn't a blizzard," Becky said, blushing. "Maybe if we get everyone into one room we'll finally thaw out." She shivered. "I don't remember ever seeing the mercury in a thermometer freeze before. How cold does it have to be for that to happen?"

"Forty below," Nathan said. "And it froze in the thermometer at the adjutant's office just last night."

Laina looked across the room at Caleb. "Many thanks for the firewood, Private."

He nodded back and smiled at her. "A small price to pay for that lined wool shirt you made me. Dorsey wants to know what you charge."

"Mrs. Gruber said the ones she gets from Omaha are a dollar and a half," Laina said. "But tell Corporal Dorsey the girls and I would rather barter if it's all the same to him. If he'll dig us a garden come spring, I'll be happy to make him *two* shirts."

They finished their meal and the men got up to go. Katie and Becky said good-night.

Nathan lingered. "You keep warm, girls," Nathan said as they slipped behind the quilt curtain he'd helped Granny hang the previous spring.

"You don't have to worry about us," Katie said, with her hand holding up a corner of the quilt. "Wilber keeps us warm. He lies across our feet. It's like having a stove right there on the bed."

Nathan smiled. "I knew that dog would be worth something someday if you could keep him from getting kicked in the head by a horse."

"Oh, he doesn't chase horses anymore."

"Really?" Nathan said.

"Nope," Katie shook her head. "Laina and me and Private Jackson taught him not to."

Nathan looked at Laina as Katie disappeared behind the quilt curtain. "When was that?"

"Before the snow," Laina said. "While you were out on that first patrol. Caleb showed us how to teach him before his battalion left camp. Then we kept working at it while you were all gone."

Nathan nodded. "Well, good for Private Jackson. Glad to see he made some use of himself besides providing work for the men assigned guard-house duty."

"I think those days are probably over for Private Jackson," Laina said.

"Yes," Nathan agreed. "Amazing what a dose of self-righteousness can do for a man."

"What?"

"Hasn't he told you? Our old friend Beauregard Preston has gotten religion."

"I thought something was different. I didn't know what."

"Don't ask him about it until you have time for a sermon. He's got a good one all ready for anyone who asks him about it."

"You sound like you've heard it."

He nodded. "It's as good a sermon as Granny Max ever preached."

"I don't recall Granny Max preaching very much," Laina said carefully. "At least not with words. She spoke pretty loud with how she *lived*, though."

"With Jackson, it's more like what he *doesn't* do that preaches the sermon."

"What doesn't he do?"

"Swear. Gamble. Refuse to obey orders. Start fights."

"You sound disappointed. I thought that's exactly what you hoped would happen for him."

Nathan shrugged. "If he's going to start preaching brotherly love and kindness toward the Cheyenne over in the barracks, it's just going to make more trouble for him. He'll be right back where he started. In the guard-house, serving time for dereliction of duty."

"What he was saying tonight didn't sound too unreasonable to me," Laina said.

"You aren't down in Kansas visiting the graves of half your family."

Laina sat down in a chair. "Did you stay behind to argue with me about the Cheyenne?"

"Of course not," Nathan said. "I just wanted a chance to talk to you without anyone around." He leaned down and put his hand on her shoulder. "I think about you and the girls a lot. I worry about you."

"You don't need to worry about us," Laina said. "The girls and I are doing fine. I'm feeling fine. We have plenty of firewood and plenty to eat and shelter over our heads. What more could a girl ask for?"

"Well," he said, taking his hand away and walking over to stare out the small square window beside the front door. "Most girls ask for a husband at some point in their lives."

"I'm not most girls," Laina said. "And we've already had this conversa-tion. I appreciate what you've offered to do for me. But it just wouldn't be right."

"How can it not be right? Becky and Katie love me."

"They love Harlan Yates and Caleb Jackson, too. But I'm not marrying either of them."

"Maybe you should let them hear you say that," Nathan said.

"What?" She looked at him. He was still staring out the window, but she could see the muscles in his jaw working. "Oh, you mean Harlan." She laughed. "As a matter of fact, I did tell Harlan exactly that. And he was mightily relieved when I turned him down. You and I both know he's going to ask Becky. If he ever gets up the nerve. She's got her acceptance all ready. If he can manage to get his proposal said, I'll be making a wedding dress come spring. She's young, but I think it'll be a good match."

"I wasn't talking about Harlan Yates," Nathan said.

The baby pounded against her bladder, and with a little "Oh," Laina winced and shifted in her chair.

"Hey," Nathan said, stepping away from the window and touching her hand.

"I'm all right," Laina said, standing up. "But I have to . . . um . . ." She felt her face turning red. "I have to go."

Nathan nodded and reached for his coat and hat and gloves.

"You know," Laina said, watching him pull everything on. "The soldiers all look alike now. Except you. You stand out because you're so tall. Add that hat, and Katie says you look like a giant. I'm inclined to agree with her."

"It's good to be back in camp," Nathan said, "even if we're here because of them." He nodded toward the barracks.

"We're all glad to have you back," Laina said, as she moved toward the doorway to the back room. "Becky was so worried about Harlan I was tempted a few times to use some of Granny's sedating tea on her."

"You ever worry about anyone out on patrol?" Nathan asked bluntly.

She paused. "I pray for you every day, Sergeant Boone. I expect I always will."

"What do you pray?"

"Things that would likely make you really mad," Laina said. She winced again as the baby kicked her bladder. "I'm sorry, Nathan, I really do have to *go*." She slipped behind the curtain. When she heard the front door close, she sighed with relief and pulled the chamber pot out from under the bed.

Chapter Twenty-Six

A mighty man is not delivered by much strength.
PSALM 33:16

"THE ONLY THING I could disguise myself as these days is a whale," Laina joked. "And besides that, I don't think the ladies of Camp Robinson would appreciate me flaunting my condition. Especially on Christmas. I don't think I could dance, even if I wanted to. My idea of a good evening these days is propping my swollen ankles up and enjoying a warm cup of tea as close to the stove as possible." She sipped her tea. "Just like this."

"I still don't feel right leaving you all alone," Becky had protested, even as she dusted her hair with flour to whiten it. She was going to the Christmas Eve masked ball as a shepherdess, thanks to some creative sewing of lace trim to an old dress, a staff made from a cane wired to a stick, and a crocheted mobcap Mrs. Gruber had dug out of an old trunk.

"You *haven't* left me alone," Laina said. "We've had oyster stew with the Grubers and sung Christmas carols. It's been the best Christmas Eve I've ever had," Laina said.

"Are you sure?" asked Katie, who had braided her hair into two long braids and donned a small pair of overalls and a red flannel shirt to transform herself into what she called a country bumpkin.

"I'm sure." Laina smiled. "Except for maybe the night I got locked in the cathedral in St. Louis and had to sleep in a pew."

Katie stared at her. "You did?"

"I did," Laina nodded. "It was beautiful. All golden candlelight and stained glass."

A knock at the door announced Sergeant Boone's arrival. She nodded at the girls. "Be sure you thank Sergeant Boone for escorting you. You both look wonderful." She asked Becky, "Do you know what Harlan's going to be?"

Becky blushed. "He wouldn't tell me. But he said I'd recognize him as soon as I see him." She giggled. " 'Course, unless he dyes his hair, he'll be easy to spot." She opened the door and admitted Sergeant Boone.

"You're not in costume," Laina scolded.

He smiled. "But I am. I'm going as a sergeant in the United States Army."

"Very creative," Laina said. She pulled the quilt up around her shoulders.

"You look comfortable," Boone said.

"I am. And I'm not freezing myself silly walking across the trail and up to the barracks, either, like the rest of you." She smiled at the girls. "You two pay very close attention to everything that happens, because I want to hear all about it when you get back." She waved them out the door. "Dance 'til your feet drop off."

Nathan helped the girls pile on coats and scarves. "They won't be too late," he promised.

"I'm not worried," Laina said, opening Granny's Bible as they left. She closed her eyes and relaxed, her feet propped up on a pillow atop another chair, listening to the sound of Wilber's rhythmic breathing. His paws twitched as he chased imaginary rabbits in his sleep. She closed her eyes, relishing the quiet. But another knock at the door prevented her dozing off. *What now?* She groaned and hoisted herself out of the chair and went to the door. "Who's there?"

"It's me. Jackson. And Corporal Dorsey. We brought you a Christmas present." He stepped inside. "Look out the window."

Scratching the frost off the window, Laina peered outside. Someone waved back from the driver's seat of a sleigh and motioned for her to come out.

"Corporal Dorsey and I thought you might enjoy a moonlight ride."

"He must be frozen solid!"

Jackson grinned. "He's had just enough 'holiday cheer' to warm himself up. And we've put warm bricks on the floor for his feet. And there's some for yours—and mine. But you need to hurry. It won't stay warm for long."

Laina was doubtful.

"Come on. It'll be fun. We won't be gone long. You'd be doing me a favor."

"I can't see how," Laina said, but she was already pulling on her coat and reaching for a scarf hanging on a hook behind the door.

"No one wants to believe Private Jackson doesn't want to drink himself into a stupor tonight." He smiled and shrugged. "This way I won't be around for them to hound me about it. And besides that, we just thought it would be fun to do something nice for you."

"How could I say no to that, after all the work you've done hitching that sleigh up? Where on earth did you find a sleigh, anyway?"

"Oh, Dr. Valentine had it in that shed out back. He had it sent here last winter for his girls. I remembered it from when I was giving them riding lessons. Dinah and I used to saddle her pony out there." He grinned. "Remember the despised sidesaddle?" He produced another scarf and a fur muff. "Mrs. Gruber sent these."

"Mrs. Gruber?" Laina asked as he opened the door.

"She thought you might say yes, as long as we had a chaperone." When Wilber jumped up in the back of the sleigh, Jackson laughed. "And now we have two." He helped her up into the backseat and climbed up beside her, shoving Wilber over against the far side of the seat. "You can be a chaperone, you big oaf, but *I* sit beside the lady." Sitting down, he covered their laps with two more buffalo robes. "You feel the heat from the bricks?" he asked. When she nodded, Dorsey slapped the reins and they took off gliding across the snow.

Laina looked up at the starlit sky. The moon shone just above the ridge in the distance, a sliver of light barely illuminating the white landscape with blue light. As they headed west across the valley, the music from the masked ball receded into the distance, and soon there was only the sound of the horse's hooves swishing through the snow.

"I hope you agree I'm at least better company than Wilber," Jackson said after a few minutes.

Laina nodded. "You both went to a lot of trouble." She raised her voice so Corporal Dorsey could hear. "Thank you."

The warm bricks at her feet and the mountains of buffalo robes around them both soon had their effect on her. Laina closed her eyes. When she woke, her head was on Jackson's shoulder, and beneath the buffalo robes he was holding her hand. She could feel his beard against her forehead. He smelled of bay rum cologne and tobacco. When she started to lift her head, he nuzzled the top of her head and whispered, "Thanks for coming."

"Hmm," Laina said, and, relaxing against him, dozed off again.

"Hey, sleeping beauty." Someone was whispering, tickling her cheek.

She opened her eyes and realized with a start the sleigh had stopped outside her apartment on Soapsuds Row. Wilber had jumped down and was waiting beside the front door. Before she could maneuver her belly up off the bench, Jackson slipped his arms around her and lifted her out of the sleigh. She thought maybe she should protest, but she didn't. It was delightful to be babied. And there was that wonderful aroma again of cologne and tobacco. She heard Dorsey say good-night and the sleigh pulled away.

Inside, Jackson settled her back in Granny's rocker, kneeling on the floor in front of her to help pull scarves and robes away before wrapping her up in Granny's quilt. "Snuggle down," he whispered. "I'll stoke the fire and let myself out."

She opened her eyes and said, "That was the best Christmas present I've ever had, Private Jackson. Thank you. It's too bad Charlotte wasn't here to enjoy it instead of me."

Jackson cleared his throat. "I'm quite content with the companion I had." He started to lean toward her but stopped himself and stood up. "I'm going to get out of here before I take advantage of the situation and steal a Christmas kiss from the prettiest girl at Camp Robinson."

Laina chuckled. She waved her hand at him. "The prettiest or the pitiful-est? You've done your good deed, Private Jackson. You don't have to spin any more yarns tonight."

"Hey," he said, kneeling back down beside her. "I meant what I said about you being the prettiest girl at Camp Robinson."

With her index finger, she tapped the place on his chin where there was a dimple beneath the beard. "You made me feel very . . . special . . . tonight, Private Jackson. That's quite a feat, considering I feel like a bloated cow most of the time these days. Thank you."

He caught her hand and kissed her palm. "Any time you need to feel special, you just call on me." He got up then, stoked the stove, and poured her another cup of tea.

"You mind if I ask you something?" he said.

"Ask away."

"What do you think that verse about a person being a new creation means?" He hadn't replaced the cover on the stove top, and when Laina looked up at him he was staring down into the fire, his features illuminated by golden light. "Do you think it could mean that a person . . . well, say a person like me, with my history, could maybe have a normal life?" He looked at her. "You know. A wife, a family—the whole thing."

"I don't see why not," Laina said. "Why would God talk about a person being a new creation if He wasn't going to let him have a life that reflected the change?"

Jackson nodded and closed the stove lid. "It's just weird lately," he said. "The card playing and the drinking. I don't even want to do that stuff any more. And I *like* reading the Bible. I mean, it makes sense. It's like I just learned to read." He looked at her with a puzzled expression. "I still have trouble with swearing. But when I do, I feel bad. Is that crazy or is that how it works?"

Laina smiled at him. "I think that's how it works, Private Jackson." She asked, "Have you asked Doctor Valentine about writing to Charlotte yet? He's got to have seen the change in you."

"I did. I wrote one letter." He shrugged. "She never answered me."

"Maybe it's just taking a while for the mail to come through," Laina suggested.

He shook his head. "No. I finally worked up my courage and asked Dr. Valentine about it." He tugged on his beard. "It seems there's a Lieutenant Somebody squiring her around town these days."

Laina put her hand on his arm. "I'm sorry."

He pulled up a chair and sat opposite her. "Would you mind calling me Caleb?" he asked abruptly. "I mean, we've shared a sleigh ride. That stands for something, doesn't it? Some new kind of friendship, at least?"

Laina smiled at him. "Of course, Caleb. And you call me Laina. Please."

He nodded. Something in his dark eyes made her feel self-conscious. *Don't be absurd. It's Christmas Eve and he's thinking about Charlotte and that lieutenant. He's just lonely. So are you. It was just a sleigh ride . . . and you always did love bay rum cologne. You're smarter than this. Just control yourself.* But if Riverboat Annie knew anything about men, Caleb Jackson's dark eyes were flickering with something besides just friendship. Just as he leaned toward her, Katie and Becky, followed by Nathan Boone, burst through the door.

"He did it, Laina. He asked her!" Katie blurted out.

"Katie O'Malley!" Becky said.

"I'm sorry," Katie apologized. "I couldn't help it."

"Who did what?" Laina asked, hoping no one noticed her flaming cheeks.

Becky hung her coat up next to Katie's. When she turned around, she was blushing, too. "Harlan asked me." She giggled, "He came all dressed up as a *groom*. With a suit and a top hat and everything. And he asked me!"

"Asked what?" Laina teased, relieved that Caleb was leaning back in his chair, acting as natural and calm as if the two of them had just been playing checkers.

"He asked me to *marry* him!"

"And you said . . . ?" Laina raised one eyebrow.

"*Yes!*" Becky dropped to her knees beside the rocker. "Oh, Laina, I'm so happy, I'm gonna burst!" She threw her arms around Laina and hugged her. "Oh, I *wish* Mama and Papa and Granny Max were all here! I *wish* they knew!" She burst into tears.

"They know, honey-lamb," Laina murmured. "You can bet they know." She took Becky's face in her hands and smiled through her own tears. "Can't you just imagine them doing an Irish jig with the angels right now?"

Becky giggled and nodded. "He took me for a sleigh ride. That's when he asked me."

"Oh, really?" Laina said, looking over Becky's shoulder at Caleb, who held up his hands and shook his head back and forth as if to say, *"Don't look at me. I didn't know anything about that."*

"He said he didn't really plan that part. But he stepped outside and saw Corporal Dorsey driving by on his way to the stables, and Harlan asked him to drive us." Becky giggled. "Isn't that romantic?"

Yes, Laina agreed. It was romantic. She glanced at Caleb again, and then toward the door where Sergeant Boone stood watching them all with a scowl on his handsome face.

———

"It's Christmas Day, Miss Gray," Sergeant Boone said, stepping into the washhouse. "No one expects Soapsuds Row to operate on Christmas Day."

"You got all your men to agree to going without long johns when it's twenty below?" Laina asked. She arched her back and grimaced. "Becky and Katie are going to take over in a few minutes. The routine is good for all of us. Keeps our minds off all the people we're missing this Christmas," she said. "I let them sleep a little later since they were out so late last night." She smiled. "It took another hour to get them settled down after you left."

Nathan smiled. "When's the wedding, anyway?"

"You tell me," Laina said. "When can Harlan get some leave? He's going to want to take her back East to meet his mother and sister."

He shook his head. "Not until this mess with the Cheyenne is taken care of." He paused, then said, "Sheridan's told Crook they have to be moved back South. By force, if necessary."

"Oh, no," Laina said. "Don't those people back East know what that could mean?"

"Captain says General Crook hates it, too. Says some of the men in that barracks were with Crook last summer as scouts. Now this." Nathan shook his head and swore softly. "It's a shame. I guess Crook telegraphed last night and told Sheridan it would be downright inhuman to make them move now, in this cold."

"And?" Laina asked.

"And Sheridan said move."

Laina closed her eyes. "What are you going to do?"

"I'm going to hope that someone comes up with a better idea. Although I don't know what that could be," Nathan's voice sounded miserable. "Captain's going to do his best to talk them into going without putting up a fight."

"Do you think there's any hope they'll agree?"

Nathan shook his head. "None."

"And *then* what are you going to do?"

"Obey orders. Do the job. Try to keep anyone from getting hurt, if I can." He shook his head. "But I didn't come up here to talk about the Cheyenne."

Just then the back door to Laina's quarters slammed shut. Becky and Katie arrived, greeted Sergeant Boone, and went to work, Becky taking the paddle out of Laina's hand and Katie getting ready to rinse the load of long johns.

"Bring them inside," Laina said. "We'll hang them up in the back room to dry. I'm going to make Sergeant Boone a cup of coffee. I'll save you girls some." She patted Katie on the head. "Maybe some hot cocoa for you when these are hung up."

Together, Laina and Nathan walked through the sleeping quarters and into the kitchen. She set the coffeepot on the stove and got two cups. Nathan rummaged in his coat pocket and produced a small box. "Merry Christmas," he said, and bent down and kissed her on the cheek.

Flushing with embarrassment, Laina opened the box. Nestled inside was a pair of garnet earrings.

"Those were Lily's. I hope it doesn't make you mad. But I want you to have them."

"Oh, Nathan," Laina said, picking up one of the earrings and admiring the deep red glow of the stones. "These are beautiful." She smiled at him and shook her head. "But I can't accept them."

He frowned. "I bet you'd take them if they were from Private Jackson instead of me."

"What are you talking about?"

"I saw the way you two were looking at each other last night. You can't be serious, Laina. You *know* what he is." He was leaning forward, his brows drawn together.

"Yes, Sergeant Boone, I do. He's my friend."

Nathan snorted. "Right." He shook his head. "Wake up, Laina. You know better than to fall for that."

"I haven't fallen for anything." She put the lid back on the box and slid it toward him across the table. "As I said, these are beautiful. But I can't possibly accept them."

"What's so perfect about Caleb Jackson?" Boone demanded. He took his hat off and plunked it on the table.

"Nothing. There isn't one thing perfect about him," Laina said. *Except maybe those brown eyes. That little dimple in his chin. His laugh. I really like his laugh.*

"So what's the attraction?" He held up his hand. "No. Don't play that game with me, Laina. I *saw.* Everyone at the hop was wondering who it was that got Dr. Valentine to get his sleigh out of the shed. And who it was taking a romantic moonlight ride. It was you and Jackson. And when I brought the girls home I *saw.* What I can't figure out is how a woman who reads the Bible twice a day could possibly have feelings for a man with his history. Even though he has learned to talk religion, you know as well as I—no, you know better than I—what's really inside him."

"I'm not going to discuss my feelings for Private Jackson with you, Nathan. But what's inside him just might be a new creation. Something God promises people who come to Him. And I can tell you one thing that's very attractive about Caleb. He doesn't have any delusions of grandeur about himself. He's trying his best, and he's terrified he's not going to succeed. In fact, he knows he can't change without God's help."

"Well, I'm trying my best, too." He leaned over, resting his hands on the table, staring down at her. "I'm trying my best to watch over the girls and to get on with my life and to take care of you." He tapped his finger on the box. "What do you think *this* is, if it isn't me trying?!"

Laina bowed her head and sighed. "I'm sorry, Nathan. But your best isn't good enough."

"And Caleb Jackson's IS?" He roared the question. "And since when do you call him CALEB, anyway?!"

Laina was trembling with a combination of her own temper and fear of Nathan's anger. "I'll call him Caleb if it pleases me, and it does. And the difference between *your* 'not good enough' and *his* 'not good enough' is he *knows* he's not good enough. He knows that without God, he's hopeless and helpless."

"That's what you want? A man who's helpless?"

Laina put her hands to head and moaned with frustration. "I don't know if I want a man at all. But if I did, I'd want one who knew he was helpless and who had offered God his helplessness."

"That doesn't make any sense," Nathan muttered.

"It doesn't make any sense," Laina agreed. "Not to a man who's never once looked at himself and seen *nothing*. Sergeant Nathan Boone sees himself as a man who handles everything on his own. Who doesn't ask God or man for help. Who doesn't need anyone or anything."

"And what good does it do to ask *God* for help? He doesn't *answer!*" He pounded the table with his palms and backed away, glaring at her.

Tears filled Laina's eyes and spilled down her cheeks. "Nathan. Dear, wonderful, blind Nathan. He *does* answer. But sometimes He says *no*." Her voice was miserable. "Just like I'm saying *no*."

"I want to take care of you," he said, more gently.

"I know you do." She went around the table and, standing before him, put her hand up and patted his cheek. "I look at you, and I think I must be crazy, but I can't let you take care of me, Nathan. I tried to talk myself into it the last time this came up. I really tried. But I can't do it." She dropped her hand to her side.

"Because of Jackson," Nathan said.

Laina shook her head. "No. Because—"

He snorted. "Because of *God*."

Laina picked the earring box up off the table and handed it to him. "I owe you my life, Nathan. But I can't give you my future. And, yes, it's because of God."

———

"I won't do it." Caleb planted his feet and stared up at Sergeant Boone.

"Private Jackson, you are being *ordered* to stand guard outside that barracks."

Caleb nodded. "I understand that, sir. But I can't be trusted with the duty. First, captain's orders took away food and fuel. Then water. I won't stand guard over something like that."

"They'll be given everything they need as soon as they comply with the directive to come out and head back South," Boone said.

Caleb nodded. "Right. That's a good solution. Starve them until they agree to go back where they were starving." He pleaded, "It's been four days, sir. They've been scraping the frost off the glass to try to relieve their thirst. Can't we at least try to get the women and children out?"

"We did that while you were chasing after those ponies that stampeded. They said 'one starves, all starve.' "

"What if that was Laina and Katie in there? Would you still follow orders not to let them have any food or water? Would you let them freeze?"

Looking off toward Soapsuds Row, Nathan swore softly. "Get over to the stables and muck out a few stalls. Think about this. Think about the fact that the next time you refuse an order, you're likely ending your career."

"Sir, I could muck out stalls from now to kingdom come, and it's not going to change my mind. Put me in the guardhouse if you have to. Court-martial me. Do whatever you want. I won't be changing my mind about this." He lowered his voice. "And if I could figure a way to do it, I'd smuggle in provisions."

"I didn't hear that," Nathan said. "Now get to work. Stable duty." Nathan could barely keep his voice from trembling as he gave the order. Jackson saluted, spun on his heel, and headed for the stables.

———

"Well, now, would you look at that." Dorsey, who was stacking crates of provisions in the back of a wagon outside the commissary, motioned toward the Cheyenne barracks.

Caleb, coming out the commissary door lugging another crate of goods, set it down on the ground just in time to see Wild Hog and Old Crow come out of the Cheyenne barracks under guard and head across the parade ground toward the commander's headquarters. Sergeant Boone was one of the guards.

"Maybe they've come to terms," Caleb said hopefully. He handed the crate up to Dorsey.

Before long, there was a commotion from inside headquarters. Soldiers who'd been stationed just outside the building charged through the door. Dorsey jumped down from the wagon, yelping with pain and swearing about his knee.

"Sit down," Caleb ordered and headed for the commander's office just as Wild Hog and Old Crow were brought out in chains and led away. He hesitated and turned back toward the wagon. "Looks like things are under control. Let's get you over to have Doc Valentine take a look at that knee."

Dorsey got up slowly. Just as he started to hobble after Jackson, another warrior came outside the Cheyenne barracks and gave himself up. Several more young men spilled out the door, to be met by soldiers who quickly took up positions in front of and east of the barracks.

Two soldiers came running from the hospital with a litter. Caleb turned to Dorsey. "Did you see Sergeant Boone come out of headquarters?"

"Nope," Dorsey grunted. Just then, the men came out, carrying a wounded soldier toward the hospital.

"You go on," Dorsey said. "I can't run."

Caleb tore across the road and charged inside the hospital just in time to hear Dr. Valentine tell Sergeant Boone that he was a very lucky man.

Chapter Twenty-Seven

I said unto the Lord, Thou art my God:
hear the voice of my supplications, O Lord.
PSALM 140:6

"NATHAN SENT ME to get you all to move up to the trading post." Private Yates ducked inside Laina's apartment, but not before Laina and the girls heard the unearthly cries coming from the other side of Soldier Creek.

"What *is* that?" Katie asked, clutching Wilber's collar.

Yates pursed his lips. "You don't worry about that, Miss Katie," he said. "You just gather some things in case you end up staying the night with the Grubers."

Becky went to the window and scraped frost away so she could look outside. "There are more soldiers around the barracks," she said. "Tell us what's going on, Harlan. Please."

"They're just smashing things inside."

"What things?"

He shrugged. "Don't know. They put blankets over the windows a while ago."

"But they're singing," Katie said.

"That's a death song," Laina croaked. "Sergeant Boone told me." She had hurried to the hospital a while earlier, her heart in her throat, insisting she must see Sergeant Boone for herself, crying with relief when he smiled and squeezed her hand and told her in his own words what had happened inside the commander's headquarters—how Wild Hog had managed to stab him.

"I guess I'm not the big bad army officer I thought I was," he said, coughing and wincing with pain. "Taken out of the action by a half-starved old man."

"Thank God," Laina said, and brushed her hand over his forehead. To her surprise, Nathan blinked back tears. She sat with him until he fell asleep, leaving only when Doctor Valentine insisted that he had far too much to do to be concerned about a premature delivery brought on by her own stubbornness.

While Harlan helped Becky into her coat, Laina lumbered around gathering her sewing basket and a pile of mending. "Here, Katie," she said, "put these shirts in a sack."

"We're not going to want to do any sewing," Katie complained.

"Well, we're not going to sit up all night staring at each other worrying, either!" Laina snapped. Immediately, she apologized. "I'm sorry. I just . . . I'm not feeling very well."

Harlan grabbed Laina's coat off its hook. "Wind's blowing in, ma'am. It's gonna be a cold one tonight. Best be getting up to the trading post." He patted her awkwardly on the shoulder. Looking around the room, he said, "You ladies ready?"

Laina grabbed Granny Max's Bible off the table and tossed it into her sewing basket. She nodded, took a deep breath, and followed everyone out the back door.

At the trading post, Becky clutched Harlan's hand and began to cry. "Now, Becky," Yates said, with a degree of sternness that surprised Laina. "You stop making such a fuss. If you're going to be a soldier's wife, you got to be brave." He swiped a tear off her cheek. "I been ordered out with the troops going down to help guard Bronson's horses. Captain thinks they might make a run for his ranch first, trying to get some horses before they head north." Kissing her on the cheek, he left.

Mrs. Gruber fussed over Laina, making her put her feet up, fixing her tea, and insisting she was generally grateful for something to do to keep her mind off the horrible sounds coming from "over there."

By four o'clock in the afternoon, things quieted down at the barracks. Mr. Gruber, who'd been keeping an eye on things from just outside the store, came in and reported that Wild Hog and Old Crow had been brought back from the cavalry encampment a mile away. "Looks like they talked their families into coming out," he said. "Saw about twenty of 'em head back down to the lower camp with the guards. That still leaves over a hundred inside, though."

"I hope our soldiers sleep with their boots on tonight," Mrs. Gruber said.

"They did stable call under arms," Mr. Gruber replied. "They're ready."

"At least it's quiet," Mrs. Gruber said hopefully.

"Yes," Mr. Gruber said, "the calm before the storm."

Private Jackson came just before tattoo. "Sergeant Boone was threatening to crawl up here if I didn't come check on you." He took off his coat and gloves while he talked. "He's resting—if you can call being mad as a hornet about being sidelined resting. Doc seems to think he'll mend. But it will take some time."

"Are we gonna have to sleep here tonight?" Katie asked.

Mrs. Gruber spoke up. "I want you all here with us, Katie. At least for tonight."

Jackson nodded at Mrs. Gruber, then said to Becky, "Private Yates is the lucky one. Bronson will treat those boys well just out of thanks for having his horses guarded."

Laina stopped pretending to stitch the quilt block in her hands and tossed it into her workbasket. "All I can think about is Lame Deer and her mother trapped in a fight . . . or running off into the frigid night." She took a deep breath, trying to relax the muscles across her abdomen that seemed to be cramping. "They won't do that, will they? In the cold? In the snow? With just what they can carry?"

"I hope not," Caleb said. He bent down and asked Laina, "Could I . . . talk to you . . . in private?"

Her heart thumped. *He's got bad news he doesn't want Katie or Becky to hear.*

Mrs. Gruber spoke up. "Go right through there," she motioned, "Into the canteen." She lighted an extra kerosene lamp and handed it to Caleb.

In the deserted canteen, Caleb set the lamp on a billiard table. He pulled a chair out from a nearby poker table for Laina.

"What's wrong?" Laina asked.

Looking around him for a minute, Caleb shook his head. Suddenly, he dropped to one knee beside her. "I don't know if I can do this." He gulped. When he looked up at her, his eyes were brimming with tears. "Can you understand that? I don't want you to think I'm a coward. That I'm just running scared." His hand trembled when he rubbed the side of his jaw. He choked out a laugh. "I finally got to where I do care about things like honor and God and country. But where's the honor in what's been going on around here?"

The anguish in his voice brought tears to Laina's eyes. Not knowing what to say, she grabbed his hand and held it. When a tear rolled down his cheek and into his beard, she pulled him toward her. Putting her arms around him, she kissed his cheek. Her voice broke. "I want to pray for you, Caleb, but I don't even know what to say."

He put his forehead on her shoulder. He was quiet, but Laina could tell from the occasional shudder coursing through his body that he was crying.

Finally, he pulled away, sat back on the floor, and leaned against her knee. Instinctively, she began to comb through his hair with her fingers, something Granny Max had often done to calm her after a nightmare. "One time Granny Max told me that when she didn't know words, sometimes she just pictured the thing or the person she cared about in the palms of her hands, and she'd just silently lift her palms up to the Lord." She opened her hands, palm up, and reached around him to show him. "That's where you'll be tonight, Caleb. Right here." She touched first one palm, then the other. "I'll be holding you and Lame Deer and Nathan and Harlan . . . all night. Holding you up to God. Until we know what's going to happen. Until it's over."

Caleb grabbed her hands. He kissed her palms, the back of her hands, the scars on her wrists and then, rising to his knees, he turned around. Leaning forward, across her bulging abdomen, he kissed her lightly. "Thank you," he said, then stood up and helped her out of the chair.

"Laina, I . . . uh . . ."

She reached up and put a finger over his lips. "Let's just leave things as they are, Caleb."

"Exactly how are . . . things . . . between us?"

Laina thought for a moment. "You used to be one of my best customers," she said, smiling up at him. "Care to take a stint as one of my best friends?"

"I was hoping . . ." he said.

"So am I," she said.

After Caleb left, Mrs. Gruber lit her best hurricane lamp and set it in the center of her table. The women gathered around—Katie and Becky pretending to read and Laina and Mrs. Gruber pretending to sew. They had been there less than an hour when shots rang out. At once, they jumped to their feet, exchanging glances while they listened, every muscle tense. There was more gunfire. Katie grabbed for Laina's hand. Wilber stared at the door, whining.

"Oh, dear God," Mrs. Gruber said, "let them be safe. Let it all end. Oh, dear Lord."

Laina gasped and bent over, resting her palms on the table. "Mrs. Gruber," she said, reaching for the older woman. "What—"

There was a gush, a sensation of warmth, and then the first strong contraction.

At the first sound of gunfire, Caleb leaped off his cot and grabbed his rifle. He had followed Dorsey's example and stayed dressed, but the men charging toward the barracks were a ragtag bunch, most in a state of half-dress, some even barefooted, running through the snow, oblivious, for the moment, to the cold.

"Help! I'm shot!" a guard stationed on the west side of the barracks screeched. Dorsey knelt beside him.

Caleb rounded the front of the barracks. On the east side, warriors were spilling out the windows, guns blazing, forming a line of fire, buying time for the women and children to get away.

"I *knew* they had to have guns hidden in there!" A soldier knelt next to where Caleb had taken cover behind a wagon and cursed. He raised his rifle.

"You might hit a child," Caleb yelled, grabbing the barrel of the rifle.

"One less warrior for the next battle," the man screamed back. When he shoved Caleb away, Caleb lost his balance and hit his head against the steel rim of a wagon wheel. Stunned, Caleb watched as the soldier jumped up and charged toward the barracks. When an old woman fell in the snow, the soldier put a gun to her head and pulled the trigger.

"They're headed for the river!" someone yelled.

"Bronson's!" another voice shouted.

The minute his vision cleared, Caleb took off for the bridge. Just behind the barracks several warriors were putting up a desperate fight, to buy time for the women and children scurrying up the river toward the distant bluffs. As he took cover around the corner of the adjutant's office next to the barracks, Caleb had the odd impression of things happening in slow motion. Cheyenne rifles flashed, war cries filled the air, but then a volley of gunfire sounded from inside the barracks where soldiers had taken cover and were returning fire through the windows. The Cheyenne rear guard toppled, and the soldiers charged out of the barracks and toward the river in pursuit of the fleeing captives. Caleb thought, *It would be a different fight if the warriors had left the women and children behind. They would have crossed the bridge and headed for Bronson's . . . and some of them still might make it before we get our horses saddled and ride after them.*

"Get after them!" someone screamed.

Caleb charged toward the bridge, where he fell into a washout beside the sawmill. His rifle went flying, and he landed with a thud almost on top of two Cheyenne. With his best Rebel yell, he scrambled to his feet, pulling his pistol from where he'd tucked it into his belt, and he launched himself at the shadowy figure coming toward him with upraised arm. He discharged his pistol just as the warrior's arm came slashing down. The warrior crumpled to the earth and lay still.

As gunfire faded into the distance, Caleb whirled around, expecting another attack. Behind him, cowering in the snow, a child pleaded over and over, "Do not kill me. Please do not kill me!"

"Lame Deer?" Jackson gasped.

"Jack-Son. It is you? I begged to leave. They said we would all die together. I don't want to die, Jack-Son. Please do not kill me."

"Where's Brave Hand?" Caleb said, hunkering down in the snow next to Lame Deer.

"I not know," the child said.

"Are you hurt?" he asked.

"I not know," she said, trembling.

"Who is this?" He nudged the body with his boot.

"Pretty Horse," Lame Deer said.

Pretty Horse. The vision of a wizened old man with flowing white hair flashed in his head. He and Caleb had talked, through signs and broken language, of the old man's favorite horse, long since dead. When Pretty Horse learned of Caleb's reputation with horses, he'd insisted they smoke a pipe together. Caleb gulped.

As gunfire blazed around them, he hoisted Lame Deer like a sack of potatoes under his good arm and staggered up out of the washout, heading for the hospital. Halfway there, he stumbled and fell to his knees.

Lame Deer threw herself against him, clutching his shirt. "Don't die, Jack-Son," she screamed at him, pulling on him, trying to get him back to his feet. In the cold air, his left arm felt colder. Wet, he thought. He listened to the shouts and the sounds of gunfire, scowling when he realized they seemed far away. He looked down at his arm. Dark liquid was dripping off his fingertips, staining the moonlit snow. Lame Deer was clutching at his shirt. He thought she was screaming at him, but he couldn't seem to make out the words. The last thing he remembered was a thin line of silver glistening on her cheek as the moonlight illuminated her tears.

Chapter Twenty-Eight

And I will give thee the treasures of darkness,
and hidden riches of secret places . . .
Isaiah 45:3

PRIVATE CALEB JACKSON lifted his head off the hospital cot and tried to look around, but even the effort to do that made him sick to his stomach. He lay back down. Closing his eyes, he tried to remember. When it finally came back to him, he couldn't think why he was even here. He'd been carrying Lame Deer . . . to the hospital . . . his arm . . . His memory ran out somewhere near the stables.

He listened to the suffering around him. Doctor Valentine was at the opposite end of the infirmary giving orders about something. Even from this distance, Caleb could hear the weariness in the man's voice. On the cot next to him lay an old man. Jackson thought he'd seen him perform at one of the dances the Cheyenne held in their barracks not long after they arrived at Camp Robinson. *Fort Robinson now,* he reminded himself. The official announcement had come over the wires in December. The old man was asleep. His face was so pale, Jackson wondered if he might be dead.

I wonder if that's what I look like, he thought, and he raised his hand off the cot to look. It felt like he was straining to lift a log. His left forearm was wrapped in blood-soaked strips of white cloth. At the sight of his own blood, his stomach lurched. He closed his eyes again.

Lord. Lord God Almighty. Help. Help us all. He wondered about Yates, assigned to help protect the horse herd down at Bronson's ranch. He doubted any of the Cheyenne had made it that far. From what he could remember, they'd started that way, then had recrossed the bridge and scattered up the river toward the bluffs.

Sergeant Boone. I wonder if he's in this room somewhere, listening to all this. He wanted to get up and see if he could find him, but he couldn't even find the strength to lift his head.

Someone laid a hand on his forehead. Caleb opened his eyes.

"You all right?" Dorsey asked.

Caleb nodded. "Arm hurts."

"No wonder," Dorsey said. "Doc ain't had time to stitch it up yet." He grinned. "I poured kerosene in it. You had a few colorful words for me, but we got it wrapped up. Bleeding's stopped. Doc'll be back later to stitch it up." He looked around him. "There's others need him worse right now."

"Yates? Boone?" Caleb asked.

Dorsey shook his head. "Can't say. Yates isn't back off patrol yet. Boone's been moved over to the barracks with the ones that aren't so bad. He'll mend."

"You found me?" Caleb asked.

Dorsey nodded. "It's a wonder you didn't bleed to death."

"Lame Deer?"

He shook his head. "Wasn't nobody but you."

Caleb blinked back tears. "She was so terrified," he croaked. He told Dorsey about falling into the washout. "I thought she was shot. Do you think maybe she got away somehow?"

Dorsey looked away. He cleared his throat. "Hard to say. The chase is still going. Sleep if you can. It'll be a while before Doc gets to you."

"Do you know if Laina and the girls are still at the trading post?"

Dorsey grinned. "I reckon they are. Becky came in here some time ago asking for Doctor Valentine to come. That baby's on the way." Dorsey added, "She was more than a little upset when the doctor said he didn't have time for delivering babies."

"Is Laina all right?" Caleb asked.

"I reckon. Doc's been having me go over every so often to check on things. It's taking some time, but women know about these things. She'll be fine."

Caleb struggled to sit up. "Help me get up. I wanna go to her . . ." His head swam, and he fell back on the cot.

Dorsey was stern. "You're not goin' anywhere until Doc Valentine says it's all right, soldier. Now you lay back down." His expression softened. "That little gal's made of iron. Think what she's been through. Birthing a baby's nothin'." He patted Caleb's shoulder.

———

Had Laina Gray heard Corporal Dorsey's opinion of birthing a baby, she would have resurrected a Riverboat Annie phrase or two. As it was, she was struggling not to scream her insides out. Katie and Becky were clearly terrified. Mrs. Gruber was worried. Laina's emotions rocketed between fear, worry, and complete exhaustion. Just when she thought she'd endured the strongest contraction possible, another one left her panting and breathless. She'd begun the ordeal perfectly at peace with God's timing, more concerned with what was happening with the soldiers and the Cheyenne than herself. But as the hours wore on, as the contractions increased, as all her efforts at control and trust failed to birth a baby, she grew afraid.

Twenty hours into the ordeal, Laina no longer cared about any of the things that had worried her before. If Katie and Becky couldn't handle her moans, they could leave. If Doctor Valentine didn't get here soon, she was going to die, never knowing whether the baby looked like Josiah Paine or not. She didn't care anymore. She just wanted things to be over.

———

When Caleb next awoke, it was daylight. He lifted his arm and realized there was a new bandage. Apparently he'd been stitched up and never realized it. The throbbing was terrible. He tried to sit up.

"Whoa, there, soldier." Dorsey was immediately at his side. "You lost a lot of blood. It's going to be a while before you're back in the saddle."

"Is it . . . is it over?"

"It will be soon enough," Dorsey said. "They're holed up on Soldier Creek. Every time Wessells gets them in a tight spot, he calls a cease-fire and begs them to give up. Then somebody else gets killed or gets his horse shot out from under him and they retreat back here." He shook his head in disgust. "I just heard he's going to take artillery out to negotiate a complete surrender."

"Is it a girl or boy?" Caleb asked.

Dorsey chewed on his moustache. "Baby hasn't come yet." He held Caleb down. "Now you listen here, sonny. I've got better things to do than scoop you up off the floor. You rip that arm open again and gangrene is going to be the only friend you care about. Doc Valentine went on over. Unless you think you know more than him, you'd best stay put."

"How long has it been?" he demanded.

"Becky said things started up for Miss Gray right about the same time they started up for everybody else." He thought for a moment. "Guess that makes it nearly a full day. Sun's setting outside."

"Does it always take this long?"

Dorsey stared at him like he was crazy. "You think I know the answer to that?" He paused. "Doc'll send word. He knows Sergeant Boone and you both want to know."

"Any word about Lame Deer?" Caleb asked.

Dorsey shook his head. "Sorry, son."

"Help me up," Caleb said. "Please. Just help me get over to the trading post. I don't care if you lay me out on a billiard table. I want to be closer."

Dorsey started to protest, then relented. "All right. Here we go—"

He was conscious for about ten seconds.

———

It was dark outside when Caleb woke again. Lifting his head off the cot, he could see Dorsey sitting in a chair on the far side of the hospital, his head leaning back against the wall, his mouth hanging open.

On the cot next to him lay a Cheyenne child. *The old man must have died.* The child, a little girl with two long braids tied with bright hair ribbons, was lying on her side with her back to Jackson. When she turned over, she smiled at him.

"You saved me, Jack-Son."

Caleb's eyes filled with tears. "How? I fell in the snow."

She nodded. "I run away. Hurt leg. Go to Soapy Row. No one there."

"Are you hurt bad?" he asked.

She made a face. "Not bad."

Caleb forced another smile. He tried to get up, but realized he wasn't going to get far alone.

"You sleep," Lame Deer whispered. "Doctor-man take care of you."

Nodding, Caleb closed his eyes.

———

"Wake up, soldier. There's news."

Caleb opened his eyes and looked up at Dorsey. It was daylight.

"I'll help you get over to the trading post now. She's asking for you."

Caleb frowned. "Asking for me? Why? Is something wrong?"

Doctor Valentine came into view. "There is nothing wrong, Private. But it was a long haul. Breech. Almost lost them both." He sighed. "The keyword, Private, is *almost*. Go on over so you can see for yourself."

Dorsey helped him sit up.

Lame Deer was sitting up in bed, too, eating a bowl of grits. She smiled at him.

"I'll be back," Caleb said.

Dorsey leaned down. "Stand up slow. You're gonna be dizzy. Put your good arm over my shoulder, and do what you can yourself. My knees haven't gotten any better since you tackled me." He reached into his pocket and took out a small silver flask. "Now don't give me a sermon about the evils of drink. One swig won't kill you, and it might get you over to the trading post without me having to haul you on my shoulder. This is no different than taking a dose of Granny Max's medicinal whiskey."

"I haven't heard any bugles," Caleb said when they got outside into the sunshine. "What time is it? What day?"

"It's about seven. Sunday."

They had to stop twice and wait for Caleb to get his breath, but by the time they reached the trading post, Caleb had let go of Dorsey and was walking, albeit slowly, under his own power. He stopped just outside and took a deep breath, trying to still his nerves, wondering if, now that the baby was here, things would change between him and Laina. Dorsey had said she asked for him—she wanted *him*. He was almost afraid to find out what that meant. He wanted her, too, but he wasn't sure if they both meant the same thing.

Sergeant Boone was at the trading post, sitting at a table with Becky and Katie playing cards. Jackson stammered a string of questions. Nathan held his hand up. "Hey. You look terrible. Get yourself in there before you pass out on us." He pointed over his shoulder, then he said, "She was happy to know Lame Deer is all right. But that didn't settle her much." He smiled sadly, "I don't understand it, personally, but it seems she wants *you*."

His heart pounding, Caleb felt his way along the counter towards the door that led to the Grubers' sleeping quarters. He paused at the end of the counter to catch his breath before continuing into Mrs. Gruber's kitchen, past the table and stove, toward the doorway that stood open, revealing just the foot of a bed. He swept his hands across his hair and wiped the sweat off his forehead with the back of his hand. Instead of going in, he leaned against the door frame and peered around toward the head of the bed.

When he saw how pale she was, his heart lurched. But then she opened her eyes and smiled at him.

"They . . . uh . . . they said you wanted to see me." He suddenly felt shy in her presence.

She nodded. "Come over here and sit down before you collapse."

He sank onto the bed beside her.

She touched the edge of the bandage on his arm.

"It's all right. I just lost a lot of blood. Makes me feel weak as a kitten."

He swiped his hand across his forehead again. "Dorsey tells me he poured it full of kerosene. Sure to prevent infection."

"Dorsey's a good man."

Caleb nodded. "He helped me get over here."

"I'll have to thank him."

The awkward silence between them was broached by a faint mewling sound coming from a drawer behind him. As he turned and looked down, Laina said, "She's hungry. Again."

Caleb glanced back at Laina. "She?"

Laina nodded. Her green eyes misted over. "I miss Granny Max."

Caleb lay his hand on her cheek. "I know you do, honey-lamb." The endearment had just slipped out. He wondered if it would somehow hurt her more to hear Granny's pet name for her come from his mouth. But then she raised her hand to his and nuzzled his palm.

The baby's complaints took on a more strident tone.

"Think you can pick her up?" Laina asked. "If it hurts your arm, we can call Katie. She's hardly put her down since she was born."

Caleb reached into the drawer and lifted the infant out, barely needing his wounded arm. He looked down in wonder at the tiny creature with the wrinkled face, so swathed in blankets he could see nothing save a nose and two eyes. "She just fits," he said, cradling the baby in his right hand.

"You'd think she could have arrived with less of a fuss," Laina said, moving to her side to snuggle the baby next to her. When she stroked her cheek, the infant turned and began to mouth the knuckle of Laina's little finger.

Caleb looked from the child to Laina and back again. His heart pounded. He cleared his throat. "You're really pale. You gonna be all right?"

She nodded but didn't look at him as she said, "Thank you for coming. I just . . . I just needed to see for myself." Her cheek flushed with color.

"See what for yourself?"

"You," she said. Her voice trembled. When she finally looked up at him, he saw tears glistening in her green eyes. She croaked, "I just wanted you."

"You did?" he asked, brushing the hair away from her forehead.

She nodded. "That night after the sleigh ride—before the girls came in—I thought . . ." She looked up at him and bit her lower lip. "I thought maybe there was something . . ."

He tucked the long braid of auburn hair behind her shoulder. "There was. For me. But I didn't know about you. That's what I was trying to talk about that night in the canteen. When you said to leave things as they were. Not to say anything more."

"I didn't want to take advantage of you," Laina said.

He chuckled. "*You* didn't want to take advantage of *me*?"

She smiled. "I guess that is kind of funny when you think about it . . . considering. But it's true." The smile disappeared. "People can do crazy things when it seems like the world's going to h—" She bit her lip and corrected herself. "—falling apart. That's not a time to say things or promise things you might regret later." She looked down at the baby. "I've no right to expect . . ." She left the sentence unfinished.

Caleb cleared his throat. "Is that a hint of red I see in her hair?" he said, moving aside the blanket.

Laina nodded. "I was so afraid the baby would look like *him*. I thought I'd hate it." She blinked back tears, then gave in to her emotions and let them come. "I don't. I love her so much it hurts." She looked up at Caleb, tears streaming down her cheeks.

He nodded. "The good Lord just funnels it down from heaven. Isn't that what you told me Granny Max used to say?"

Laina nodded.

He touched the baby's hand. When she latched on to his little finger, it was his turn to tear up. He wiggled his finger, thrilled when the infant didn't let go. Then he looked at Laina and smiled. "The Lord started funneling long before this lamb was born. He's been funneling love for you into my heart for a while now. But you wouldn't let me tell you the other night." He slipped his finger away from the infant and lifted Laina's chin, waiting until she looked into his eyes. "I love you, Laina Gray. So much it hurts."

His heart nearly cracked while he waited for her to say something. She closed her eyes. Tears slid from beneath her eyelids and coursed down her face. When she finally opened them, her eyes were shining with joy. "I love you, too," she said. Her voice broke. "But, oh, Caleb . . . I don't deserve . . . I don't deserve any of it." She was almost sobbing.

"Didn't you tell me once that's what God is about—giving love to people who don't deserve it?" He kissed her, then asked, "Will you marry me?"

She nodded. "Yes."

He smothered her next sob with a kiss. Pulling away, he stroked the baby's cheek. "So what will we name the baby, Mrs. Jackson?"

"Joy," Laina said. "We'll name her Clara Joy."

———

And I will give thee the treasures of darkness,
and hidden riches of secret places,
that thou mayest know that I, the Lord,
which call thee by thy name,
am the God of Israel.

ISAIAH 45:3

Watchers
on the
Hill

Chapter One

My soul is weary of my life;
I will leave my complaint upon myself;
I will speak in the bitterness of my soul.
JOB 10:1

THEY WERE LOWERING her husband's casket into the grave, and the only emotion Charlotte Bishop could manage was relief; relief diluted with just the slightest tincture of guilt perhaps, but relief nonetheless. She had protested at first when her mother-in-law insisted on the old-fashioned mourning garb, but now Charlotte was grateful for the long black veil covering her face. If she kept her eyes lowered and refused to meet anyone's gaze, perhaps she would be able to maintain the facade and earn her Widow Who is Still in Shock moniker. Thankfully, everyone seemed to think her lack of emotion since Emory's sudden death was evidence of a vast sea of grief.

The fall breeze wafted the scent of roses her way. Charlotte closed her eyes and inhaled deeply. The boy at her side reached up and took her hand. He squeezed. She squeezed back, turning her head just enough to be able to see the dark curls cascading from beneath his wool cap and over the collar of his dark suit. Her mother-in-law cleared her throat, and Charlotte looked down again, this time noticing the shoes. Will's were impossibly old-fashioned, as were the knickers he despised.

She continued looking around the circle of shoes ringing the grave and thought about how much could be revealed about a person just by their shoes. The Colonel's two ancient uncles had donned full dress for the occasion. Their military boots shone with new polish, but still looked dated beside Major Peyton Riley's. The proximity of Riley's dress boots to Mother Bishop rankled. Charlotte suspected he would come calling under the guise of comforting the grieving widow. Probably in less than a week.

She had caught him leering at her from behind the hymnal in church. *At the Colonel's funeral. How dare he.*

Aunt Daisy's shoes weren't visible, but picturing them necessitated suppressing a smile. Charlotte had heard the shouts of agony earlier that morning as one of the servants helped Daisy cram her size-ten feet into the size-eight shoes she'd always worn to funerals "because I'm too old to be paying for special-occasion shoes." Aunt Daisy walked with a cane, so hobbling around in too-tight shoes fit the image.

Mother Bishop cleared her throat again. Charlotte started at the sound and realized the casket had landed and everyone was waiting. Taking a deep breath, she squeezed Will's hand. He squeezed back again and held out his rose, reminding her of what came next. Together, Charlotte and her son stepped forward. Together, they dropped their roses into the grave. Together, they stepped back. Charlotte bowed her head.

Good-bye, Colonel. I am supposed to be praying for your soul. Perhaps someday I shall. But not today. Today I can't seem to stop thinking you deserve a little time in hell for the things you've done.

———

"All I'm saying is"—Aunt Daisy gestured with her butter knife—"in my day children showed more respect for their elders." Charlotte's eyes followed the clump of butter on Daisy's knife as it plopped into a bowl of fresh blackberries, splattering dark juice onto the white linen breakfast cloth. In an effort to recover the butter, the elderly woman tipped her overfull teacup. Amber stains joined the deep blue ones around Daisy's place at the table.

"Please, Daisy," Ella Bishop snapped. "Between Will's pranks and your clumsiness, Edgar has just about had his fill. With all that has happened, we don't need him giving notice, too."

"Let him give notice," Daisy blustered. "In my day, people didn't allow themselves to be ruled by the help."

Mother Bishop sighed. "I'm doing my best to reestablish a peaceful home." Her voice trembled. She dabbed at the corner of each eye with her napkin. "Although heaven knows without Emory it's going to be a difficult task."

Charlotte shoved her napkin off her lap. She bent down to retrieve it instead of meeting Mother Bishop's gaze.

"I apologize if I sound harsh, Daisy. It's just that Edgar's been with us for years, and we don't want to lose him." She looked pointedly at the empty seat beside Charlotte. "I see we are once again off to a disorganized beginning to our day." She looked down her nose at Charlotte. "May I remind you, dear, that we agreed that Master Will would cease dawdling in the morning and join us for breakfast precisely at seven?"

Charlotte twisted the napkin in her lap while she formulated a reply.

"You do recall that conversation?" Mother Bishop intoned.

"Of course I do," Charlotte snapped. Mother Bishop's left eyebrow arched. Charlotte felt goose bumps rising on her arms. She touched the scar on her left wrist where the surgeon had operated to repair a broken bone. Just before Charlotte had "fallen," her husband had arched his left eyebrow exactly that way. Forcing herself to look into her mother-in-law's eyes, she replied, "I do remember, Mother Bishop. But Will had a headache when he woke this morning, and I told him to stay in bed."

A shriek from the kitchen caught everyone's attention. Will bolted like lightning from the butler's pantry, followed by the cook in hot pursuit, her cap askew, a rolling pin wielded like a sword.

Charlotte jumped up, but not before Garnet Irvin came to the top of the stairs, glided down to the landing, and intercepted Will. Small in stature but strong as a horse, Garnet wrapped one hand around the boy's shoulders. Charlotte saw her whisper something in his ear just before she let go. The cook paused to catch her breath. Will skittered up the stairs and escaped to his room at the far end of the expansive upper hall, slamming the door shut behind him.

Charlotte instinctively started to follow after him, but she sensed Mother Bishop's approach and turned around, grateful she was almost halfway up the stairs so the woman couldn't loom over her, as was her habit. Even so, her heart thumped when she saw the tightly pressed lips, the tilt of the head, the way the older woman's left hand clenched her walking stick. No one had ever been able to tell Charlotte why Mother Bishop required a walking stick, but she had an impressive collection of them. This morning, she was using the ebony one with the brass dragon head at the top. If it was going to be what Will called a "dragon-lady day," Charlotte was in for it. She backed up one step and put her hand on the railing, grateful when Garnet descended from the upstairs landing and stood behind her, close enough for Charlotte to feel her comforting presence.

"In my day, Charlotte," Mother Bishop said, her voice terrible in its studied self-control, "children were taught to be seen and not heard. My son would be appalled by the demonstration we've just witnessed. But even more disturbing would be the realization that the behavior was enabled by a lie told by the child's *own mother*." The gray hair piled atop Mother

Bishop's head trembled as she punctuated the chastisement with a tap of the walking stick on the inlaid wood floor.

Charlotte looked down at the hem of Mother Bishop's black silk dress. Across the hall in the dining room, china clinked as Aunt Daisy continued her breakfast. Good old Aunt Daisy. Nothing ever came between her and a good meal. The doorbell rang. Cook retreated to her kitchen, muttering unhappily. Mother Bishop glared at the door and waited for Edgar.

Edgar opened the door, bowed, and announced the caller. With a warning glance up the stairs to where Charlotte stood gripping the handrail and trying to suppress a sense of overwhelming dread, Mother Bishop advanced toward the entryway, her hand extended, her genteel-lady-of-the-manor expression easing into her version of a welcoming smile.

"Major Riley," she purred, "what a delightful surprise."

November 3, 1889
Detroit City, Michigan
Dearest Papa,

I received a letter from Dinah only yesterday, and she seems to be thriving in Philadelphia. It doesn't seem so long ago that I heard you lament the fact that the family tradition in medicine was destined to end with your generation and the birth of two girls. And now we have Dinah planning to seek admission to medical school as soon as she is old enough. Who would have thought that my little sister the tomboy would brave a world only recently opened to women. I, for one, am proud of her, and I hope you share that sentiment. Miss James says Dinah is applying herself well in all her studies. Aunt Hazel seems pleased with Dinah as a houseguest. Our little girl certainly has a bright future ahead.

Will and I have not been quite so fortunate in our adjustment to life without the Colonel. Of course his death was a shock. The jump was low, and how he came unseated I will never understand. It is even harder to comprehend that such a minor spill could kill a man. There are days when I wake and almost convince myself it was all a dream, and a silly one at that. But then I look around at my little room and I am forced to accept reality. Moving into the manse permanently has proven to be very different from when we used to stay here for holidays or when the Colonel was on leave. There is little more to say appropriate for my pen.

Papa dearest, I well remember what a challenge I was to you in the past. In the summer of 1879 when you said good-bye to Mama and Dinah and me, I know you were relieved to have me away from Fort Robinson. Since then I have done my best to learn from my mistakes and to become someone of whom you might be proud.

Charlotte's hand trembled. She raised the pen from the paper, but not before leaving a smudge. "Blast," she muttered. Looking up from her writing desk, she was struck once again by the recent change in the view from her bedroom window. The Colonel and she had once occupied nearly an entire wing of the house whenever they came to stay. From their sitting room, they had enjoyed a view of the distant hills forested with oak and pine trees through which ran a stream that shone like a silver ribbon at daybreak. The day after the Colonel's funeral, Mother Bishop had instructed the servants to close off that wing of the house and move Charlotte's things into the small room next to Will's.

"It will be better for the boy's adjustment to have you nearby, don't you think," Mother had asked, in the tone of voice that was not a question.

Seated at the tiny desk she had positioned in front of the only window in her new room, Charlotte looked out on the stone courtyard between the back of the house and the stables. On a clear day, she could still see the hills in the distance if she leaned far enough out the window. Today, a gray mist obscured the view of anything beyond the stables and the groundkeeper's residence. For the first time, Charlotte realized the groundkeeper probably had more space of his own than both she and Will combined. She leaned her head on her hand, thinking back to the days when she used to complain about having to share a room with Dinah.

"Why do we always have to share?"

"Will we ever get to live in a real house?"

"Nothing ever happens here."

"When I grow up, I'm leaving Fort Robinson and I'm never coming back!"

Watching the rain wash over the stone courtyard at the back of Bishop House, Charlotte sighed. Fort Robinson was certainly a far cry from this. Built on a broad valley between the White River and a ridge of high bluffs way out in western Nebraska, the fort had been little more than a collection of canvas tents that first winter when Charlotte's father reported for duty. Even when the family finally joined him the next year, Fort Robinson hadn't been much. But it grew. It had been named regimental headquarters for the Ninth Cavalry with hundreds of soldiers stationed there now—most of them the black troops called "buffalo soldiers." Father had explained the moniker, which had evidently come via the Cheyenne and had something to do with the men's thick, curly hair and what the Indians thought was its resemblance to the fur between a buffalo's horns.

Father practiced medicine in a brick hospital now. He even had his own house. And they were building a new set of officers' quarters and more barracks around a larger parade ground to the west of the one

Charlotte remembered. The railroad had arrived, and a town had sprouted up nearby.

Papa was alone now. Charlotte's mother had died only last year. Colonel Bishop hadn't allowed her and Will to travel west to the funeral. Charlotte pictured the Fort Robinson cemetery. Papa said it was fenced now and had neat rows of gravestones. He assured her that he had ordered a fine one for Mama.

Winter lay ahead, bleak and frigid in Nebraska until spring when the vast prairie would be alive with wild flowers, bursting with color. Charlotte remembered how she and Dinah had delighted in gathering them by the armfuls, adorning the dining table at home and even the men's mess hall tables, making bracelets and garlands, once even scattering petals across the front steps when Sergeant Nathan Boone came to dinner. *Nathan Boone.* Charlotte's cheeks still colored with embarrassment when she thought about her adolescent flirtations with the handsome widower. He'd been gone from Fort Robinson for years now. Papa had written news of him once, saying Sergeant Boone had been promoted to lieutenant.

Looking out through the raindrops clattering against her window, Charlotte also remembered the seas of mud that were part of every spring at Fort Robinson. Battles with mud usually subsided just in time for the hot summer wind to layer every flat surface with dust. When the wind died down, the air grew heavy with the oppressive odor of stable manure and outhouses. In spring everyone rushed to get gardens planted and then spent the summer hauling water to coax life into seedlings and transplanted trees, longing for shade in a land where a person could see the heat rising from the earth come July. *"Fort Robinson,"* Charlotte's mother used to say, *"is not the end of the earth, but you can see it from there."*

Charlotte picked up her pen, wiped off the nib, and dipping it back in the inkpot, she brought her letter to a close.

> *Please, Papa, I am begging you. Please may I come home?*
> *Always your devoted and loving daughter,*
> *Charlotte Mae Valentine Bishop*

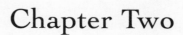

Chapter Two

Woe unto them that decree unrighteous decrees . . . that widows may be their prey,
and that they may rob the fatherless!
ISAIAH 10:1-2

SIX FEET TALL with striking blue eyes and thick blond hair, Major Preston Riley was what women called a fine figure of a man. He danced with grace and dined with the impeccable manners of a gentleman. When in the company of men, he displayed a good grasp of the chief political issues of the day, and when in the company of women, he could discuss the newest variety of roses being imported from England. He was sought after as a dinner guest, admired as a military leader, and generally expected to become great.

Charlotte Valentine Bishop was neither blind nor ignorant, and therefore she was aware of the major's assets. If it were not for two things, she would have perhaps been able to convince herself to smile more when he visited. The first thing was that Mother Bishop smiled quite enough for the both of them when Major Riley stopped in. The second was that his presence made Charlotte's skin crawl.

Mother Bishop found a need for financial advice regarding her son's estate just a week after his funeral. Major Riley knew the bank president. Of course, Emory's widow must be included in the meetings. Charlotte hated the way Riley stood behind her chair at the bank, as if he had applied for and had been hired to fill the position of The Widow's Protector. With the only man who had ever harmed her in the grave, Charlotte felt no need for protection. She resented Riley for applying for a position she had not advertised. It soon became clear to Charlotte that someone was, indeed, "advertising" on her behalf.

When Mother Bishop decided to purchase a different team of horses to draw her carriage, Major Riley assisted in the decision. This especially rankled Charlotte, who had become an expert horsewoman in her own right and knew almost as much about horseflesh as Emory had. She didn't see the need to change teams and she told Mother Bishop as much.

"A four-in-hand is just too much, now," the older woman said. "We must economize."

Major Riley arranged the sale and arrived late one December evening with flowers for both Charlotte and Mother Bishop, under the guise of celebrating the good price he had gotten for their four matched bays. "Everyone knows those horses," he said. "There was practically a bidding war." He was invited to dinner and was seated next to Charlotte.

Will took one look at the seating arrangement and declared he was not hungry. He marched out of the dining room and up the stairs to his room and did not come down again even though he knew dessert was to be his favorite, coconut cake.

As winter unfolded, Major Riley's attentions became more persistent and Mother Bishop's intention to make the match became more evident. Scarcely a day went by that mention was not made of the need to economize. Mother Bishop made the shocking suggestion that Charlotte ignore local mourning custom and attend a holiday ball with the Major.

"I'm not saying she should *dance*," she explained when Aunt Daisy expressed her dismay at the possibility of such unheard-of behavior. "But Charlotte is young. I don't think it's right for the old guard to make such old-fashioned demands on the younger generation."

Charlotte began a desperate kind of avoidance while watching the mail for the letter that would say *come home*. If only Papa would say it, she could wire him for a loan, buy a train ticket, and be free once and for all of everything about the Bishops, save the name.

———

Shortly after the New Year, Mother Bishop hinted at letting Garnet go. Charlotte's unhappiness almost reached panic mode.

"But you can't replace Garnet," she protested at tea one afternoon. "I don't know what I'd do without her. She's practically family."

"That's precisely the problem," Mother Bishop sniffed. "She's begun to think she *is* a member of the family. I don't care for her uppity ways one bit. It just doesn't do for one to become too close to one's *servants*," she said.

So that was it, Charlotte realized. It had nothing to do with finances or Garnet's performance of her duties, and everything to do with the relationship Garnet and Charlotte had forged over the years since that first time

Emory had stormed out of the house, angry again over one of his young wife's errors. Charlotte had slunk down the back stairs to the kitchen to make herself a cup of tea. Halfway down the stairs, she had heard singing. When the last step creaked, Garnet whirled around. Even when her lips were closed, the tip of one of Garnet's terribly crooked teeth tended to show. She had a habit of covering her mouth when she talked or smiled. Her hands and forearms were dusted with flour, and when Garnet reached up to cover her mouth, she left a floury imprint on her chin.

"Please," Charlotte said, "please don't stop singing. I only wanted to make a cup of tea. I . . . Emory . . . the Colonel . . ." Her voice began to tremble. Clasping her hands together, Charlotte blinked away tears.

"Yes, ma'am," Garnet said. "I know. He came through here on his way out."

"I made him so angry," Charlotte said, biting her lip.

Garnet shook her head. She turned back around and punched the dough. "Colonel Bishop has always been an angry man, missus." She ducked her head and brushed her chin against the shoulder of her apron. "I used to make the first Mrs. Bishop my special tea when the 'angries' were visiting. Would you like to try it?"

Charlotte nodded. "I would. But, please . . ." She unclasped her hands and gripped the back of a chair. "If you'll just show me where . . . Keep at your work . . . and keep singing." She forced a smile. "My mother liked to sing. It's very soothing."

Garnet nodded toward the door leading into the butler's pantry. "There's a jar on the bottom shelf. Part of the blue and white set. Says R-I-Z on it. That's my special tea."

Charlotte headed to the cupboard. While she made tea, Garnet shaped the dough into loaves, singing while she worked. Sitting at the kitchen table that day, sipping Garnet's special tea, Charlotte closed her eyes and gave herself to Garnet's music and the warmth of the sunshine pouring in the window.

After that day, whenever she and her husband were staying at the Bishop manse, Charlotte often asked Garnet to sing. She soon discovered that, contrary to her assumption, Garnet was neither illiterate nor unschooled. In fact, one of the primary reasons she stayed with the Bishop family, in addition to having been needed by the Colonel's first wife when the "angries" visited, was that Emory Bishop's now deceased father had amassed an impressive personal library, and Garnet was allowed access to the books.

Most people thought Garnet, who was small in stature and quiet by nature, was painfully shy. But Charlotte soon learned that Garnet had an independent streak and a will of iron. She moved about Bishop House with an ease that belied the complexities of pleasing a domineering older woman and her equally demanding, quick-tempered adult son. Charlotte was drawn to Garnet's inner strength. Although about the same age as Charlotte, Garnet soon took the young woman under her more experienced wing, becoming her confidante and, when necessary, her encourager. It wasn't long before Garnet was reading aloud to Charlotte while Charlotte struggled with the fancywork Mother Bishop seemed to think so necessary to a lady's résumé.

"I hate sewing," Charlotte had tried to explain to her mother-in-law. "I made one ugly quilt before I was married because my mother insisted. I'm just no good at it." She had appealed to Emory, "I much prefer riding with you, dear, to being housebound with the sewing circle."

It didn't work. Colonel Emory Bishop might command regiments but he had no talent for resisting his mother. Charlotte learned needlepoint and filet crochet. She started a quilt with velvets and satins. And had it not been for Garnet's reading aloud to her while she poked and stabbed fabric with needles, Charlotte was quite certain she would have gone *crazy* while working on her "crazy quilt."

Garnet read when Emory broke his wife's wrist. *"Lead me, O Lord, in thy righteousness because of mine enemies; make thy way straight before my face. For there is no faithfulness in their mouth; their inward part is very wickedness; their throat is an open sepulchre; they flatter with their tongue."*

Garnet read when each of the three babies died and the Colonel sent his wife across town to recover at the Bishop manse. *"I am weary with my groaning; all the night I make my bed to swim; I water my couch with my tears. Mine eye is consumed because of grief."*

Garnet read after the Colonel died and Charlotte's state of mind affected her ability to sleep. *"I will both lay me down in peace, and sleep: for thou, Lord, only makest me dwell in safety."*

Since the Colonel's death, Garnet had taken to reading aloud to Will on nights when the boy was especially upset. She could calm him like no other person in the world, simply by crooning in her low, mellow voice while Will tossed from side to side in his narrow bed.

It often struck Charlotte just how applicable the Scripture passages Garnet read were to a given event. "I've got nothing to do with that, missus," Garnet would protest. "I just open up the book and read. I'm partial to the Psalms, but I'm no preacher. If the verses mean something to you, I'm glad. Lord knows you need comfort and strength."

Garnet had, in many ways, become Charlotte's only friend. And now Mother Bishop was hinting that Garnet might be let go.

There had to be a better way.

———

No letter.

Charlotte stood in the foyer of the grand old house blinking back tears of frustration. It had been this way every day for weeks. She had given the letter plenty of time to reach Fort Robinson and plenty of time for Papa to send his reply. Why, she wondered, didn't Papa answer?

Perhaps the letter was lost. What if it had never arrived at Fort Robinson? Charlotte wondered if she should telegraph the fort. But she couldn't think of how she would explain that to Mother Bishop, especially if Papa *answered* in a telegram.

Maybe Papa was away on some kind of drill. Charlotte couldn't think of a reason for her father to be called away in the dead of winter.

There could be any number of reasons. Charlotte turned to go back up the stairs, trying not to think the worst. *Maybe he doesn't want us.*

Certainly her father had never anticipated helping his daughter raise a ten-year-old boy. He was probably looking forward to an undisturbed retirement, and here she was asking to come home. And he didn't know how she'd changed. She wouldn't be a burden. She'd be a help. She'd see to that. But of course Father didn't know her now. Emory had never allowed her to visit, not even when her mother returned to the fort, not even when she died. All Papa knew was the spoiled brat he'd sent away. But surely, Charlotte thought, surely her letters had shown a change.

Faced with yet another day of doubts and possibilities, Charlotte hesitated on her way up the stairs. The thought of another hour alone in her tiny room was unbearable. Will was at school. Garnet had left a little while ago to do the marketing. Mother Bishop and Aunt Daisy had gone to make calls. For what seemed like the fiftieth time, Mother had hinted that it wasn't time yet for Charlotte to make social calls.

"But you wanted me to go to those holiday balls with the Major," Charlotte protested.

"That was different," Mother said, tapping her walking stick as she spoke. "I didn't want to offend the Major. But I never really approved."

Charlotte had retreated from yet another confrontation. Now, as she sat on the stairs thinking, the sun came out from behind a cloud, streaming through the landing window, throwing rainbows of light all around the entry hall as it passed through the prisms set in the leaded glass. In spite of the sunshine, the grand old house seemed small and dark and oppressive.

Succumbing to impulse, Charlotte hurried up the stairs, changed into riding clothes, and was soon in the stables saddling a tall gray thoroughbred named Isaac. When the horse playfully nipped her shoulder, Charlotte shoved his great head away and tapped him on the nose. "Stop that," she said, "I know it's been a while. We've got to hurry. I don't want the Queen Mother to catch me enjoying something." She giggled at the joke and was shocked by the sound. Just how long had it been since she laughed, anyway?

She scrambled aboard Isaac and headed for the distant hills by a familiar trail, inhaling deeply as her horse minced along, eager to be given his head. "All right, old boy, let's *go*." Isaac leaped away, and for a few moments Charlotte was free of all thought of anything but moving in rhythm with the powerful animal.

Her peace of mind was soon shattered by the sight of Major Riley headed toward her, mounted on a dark bay stallion that, unfortunately, reminded Charlotte of Emory's horse.

"Good morning," the Major said. "I was just headed up to the house to inquire about you. I saw Mrs. Bishop a few moments ago and she indicated you hadn't felt up to making calls today. Obviously it was nothing serious." His horse danced sideways. "I hope you won't get a chill riding on such a cold day."

"I feel wonderful," Charlotte said. "I don't mind cold weather at all."

"This fellow's begging for a workout," the Major said. "Would you mind terribly if I joined you?"

"Well . . . I . . ."

"If it means anything, Mother Bishop gave her blessing," Riley said with a sidelong glance at Charlotte. "In fact, she suggested I lure you out-of-doors for a ride." He smiled. "I'd say this is a happy coincidence."

"Thank you, Major," Charlotte said, ignoring the man's outstretched hand and dismounting. "It's kind of you to offer to brush him down, but I prefer to tend to Isaac myself. He's been neglected since my husband's death." She patted the horse's thick neck. "I owe him some attention."

"Well then," the Major said and bowed stiffly. "I'll pay my respects to Mrs. Bishop and be going. Would I be speaking out of turn to request the honor of your company again tomorrow?" He looked up at the blue sky.

"This kind of weather is a gift this time of year. It's a shame to waste any of these lovely winter days indoors."

Charlotte ducked her head, working at an imaginary knot in Isaac's mane. "I don't know," she said. "I'm not certain what time I'll be riding. Or if I will at all," she said. "It's Saturday, and Will—"

"Ah, yes," the Major said nodding. "I remember. The boy isn't fond of horses, is he? Pity."

"Actually," Charlotte said, "I promised Will we'd spend some time together in the stables. He just needs someone with the patience not to hurry him. He had a bad fall when he was little. It's difficult to overcome your fears when you've been forced into something before you're ready."

"Quite," the Major said. He bowed again, thanked Charlotte for her company, and headed for the house.

Charlotte turned to the work of brushing Isaac and was soon humming to herself while she braided the gelding's long white mane.

Charlotte was still humming to herself when she stepped inside the back door of the manse and heard Mother Bishop's angry voice sounding down the hall and all the way to the back of the house. Oblivious to the filth caked on her riding boots, she hurried into the back hall.

"What on earth were you thinking?!" Mother Bishop was practically shouting.

"I was making something for Mother," Will replied.

Charlotte hurried up the hall and to the doorway of her mother-in-law's private parlor. Mother Bishop had Will by the collar with one hand while the other hand held a catalog of some kind. Major Riley was standing in the corner by the small fireplace, staring disapprovingly at Will.

"What's the matter?" Charlotte asked.

Mother Bishop held up the catalog without releasing Will. "THIS is what's the matter," she said.

For the first time, Charlotte noticed the neat holes cut in the top page.

Will blustered, "I didn't know it was important. I was making something for you." He tried to twist away from his grandmother's clutch.

"Stop that," the older woman ordered, shaking him by the collar.

"Please, Mother Bishop," Charlotte said. "Please let him go. He didn't know."

"He didn't know? How could he *not* know? Has he not been in this house every spring of his life? Has he not seen my rose catalogs before? Has he not been told not to bother them?"

"I thought it was an old one," Will protested.

"Well, it isn't," Mother Bishop snapped. "It just came and now it's ruined." She glared at Charlotte. "I was just preparing to show Major Riley the new variety of red we're adding to the rose garden this year."

Charlotte looked across the room at Major Riley. "Roses?" she said.

He nodded. "I have an interest. Although not nearly the knowledge Mrs. Bishop enjoys."

"You have a rose garden?" Charlotte asked.

The Major shook his head. "No. But I have plans."

Something in his tone sent a chill through Charlotte. Will squirmed and his grandmother shook him again.

"Please let him go," Charlotte begged. "He didn't know. And . . . and can't you get another catalog?"

With another shake, Mother Bishop released Will, who moved to his mother's side, rubbing his neck and coughing slightly.

Charlotte took his hand. "If you'll excuse us," she said, "I'll have a talk with Will now." She turned to go.

Mother Bishop spoke up. "Talk is precisely the problem, Charlotte," she said. "You do entirely too much talking to that boy and not nearly enough *doing*. He has no sense of duty, no sense of propriety. What's worse, he doesn't respect authority in the least." She shook her head from side to side. "What's to be done I don't know, but something must be."

Major Riley spoke up. "If it's discipline and respect for authority the boy needs," he said, "I'd recommend the Longview Academy. They excel at instilling both in their charges. And if he does well, Master Will could look forward to a fine career following in his father's footsteps." He smiled. "Many of our finest officers got their start at Longview."

"Absolutely not," Charlotte said. "I won't hear of it."

"*You* won't hear of it?" Mother Bishop said, staring at Charlotte.

"I won't go!" Will shouted. "You can't make me."

"See here, young man," Riley said. He stepped quickly across the room, and before Charlotte could intervene, he had grabbed Will's arm. "You don't talk to the women in this house that way."

Will jerked free. When Riley went to grab him again, Will kicked him and dashed out of the room.

Mother Bishop's face went white. "Major, I am so very sorry."

"It's all right, ma'am," the Major said.

Riley's tone of voice sent chills through Charlotte. She recognized that tone. It was the exact tone Emory would use—when it was anything but all right.

"Obviously the boy needs help," Mother said.

"Quite," the Major agreed.

"Would you make inquiries on our behalf?"

Charlotte protested. "Will is far too young to be sent away to school. He needs me," she said. "We need each other. It's too soon after his father's death. He's still adjusting."

"He isn't adjusting," Mother said. "That's exactly my point. He's always been a handful, but without Emory here, he doesn't even pretend to obey the simplest of rules. And now he's becoming violent. And *I*," she said, mimicking Charlotte's earlier tone, "will not have *that*. No *child* under my roof is going to be allowed to behave in such a way."

"No," Charlotte said, "I can see that. Violence is only allowed if you're an adult in this house." She rubbed her wrist.

"That is quite enough." Mother spat the words out, tapping the floor with today's selection—an ebony walking stick with a carved ivory handle.

The two women stood staring at one another for a brief moment. Charlotte wavered. "I apologize," she said. She looked at the Major. "If you'll excuse me," she said, and turned to go.

"No," Mother Bishop said. "I do not excuse you. Not until you apologize for your son's outrageous behavior toward the Major."

A dozen similar moments from the past flashed in Charlotte's mind. She closed her eyes, fighting a wave of nausea. "I . . . I'm afraid I'm going to be sick," she said. Clamping her hand over her mouth she fled the room, barely making it up the stairs and to her room before her stomach overcame her willpower.

She was lying on her bed when someone knocked softly on the door.

"It's me, Mama," Will called through the keyhole. "May I come in?"

————

"See now," Charlotte said, "Isaac *likes* you. When he turns his head to look at you like that, it's his way of saying 'welcome aboard.' He isn't rolling his eyes or snorting—"

"He is too snorting," Will said, his voice tight with fear. He clutched at the rounded edge of the English saddle.

"No he isn't, honey," Charlotte said. She looked up at the horse and, taking the reins in her right hand, touched his soft gray muzzle. "He's just breathing deeply. Getting to know your scent." She jiggled the reins. "Isn't that right, boy?"

As if in answer, Isaac grunted and nodded his head. Charlotte laughed and smiled up at Will. She was glad she had suggested they come out to the stables together. Already, she was shaking off the unpleasant thoughts she'd been harboring about Mother Bishop and the motives behind her treatment of Major Riley.

"Now you just grip with your knees like I told you. I'm going to walk Isaac around a little. *Just walking.*" She headed across the stone courtyard in the direction of the open countryside beyond the Bishop holdings. As they walked along, she told Will the story of Isaac, how he had been prancing around a paddock miles away when the Colonel first saw him and how, when brought to the Bishop stables, he had proven himself an escape artist and kept returning home until Charlotte had discovered the horse's passion for apples and won his heart. "So you see," Charlotte concluded as she reversed directions and headed back to the stables, "that's the secret with Isaac. You give him apples and he'll be your best friend."

"Is he *your* best friend?" Will asked.

Charlotte looked up at the horse, walking along as calm as any plow horse, almost as if he had understood her whispered pleas as she was saddling him earlier to *be good to Will; he needs some self-confidence*. She thought back to all the rides and the thousands of words the horse had heard on those rides, times when she had simply needed to talk about things she could not say to human ears—even Garnet Irvin's. There were times, Charlotte realized, when the horse had seemed to understand her desperate need to talk. Mornings when he'd begun a ride with energetic, playful bucks and then settled down and plodded along, his ears turned toward her voice while she talked and, sometimes, cried. Reaching up to stroke Isaac's sleek neck, Charlotte said, "In some ways, son, yes, he is my best friend."

They came back to the courtyard and walked into the stables and to Isaac's stall. Will slid down and stood back.

"Here," Charlotte said, taking his hand and pulling him forward to stand nearly beneath the horse's neck. "He loves to be patted right there." She guided Will's hand to the broad chest. As Will stroked, Isaac lowered his head and stood very still. "See how his eyes are almost half closed? That means he likes what you're doing."

"Hey there, fella," Will said. "You like that? I'll do it for you every time you let me ride you. How's that?"

Isaac turned his head and eyed the boy. He arched his neck and touched Will's chest with his nose.

"He's looking for more apples," Charlotte explained.

Will pushed the great head away. "No more apples, boy. Maybe tomorrow."

"That's good, son," Charlotte praised him. "You didn't jump away. If you stay calm, Isaac will stay calm."

Will nodded. "Can I help you brush him?"

———

"But—" Charlotte's voice caught. "You can't, Mother Bishop. Please. You can't sell Isaac. Not now. Not when Will's just beginning to learn to relax around horses. Surely you've seen how much better he's been." The two women were in the library. Mother Bishop ensconced in her favorite chair, her feet propped up on a small needlepoint footrest, her teacup perched on a tiny mahogany table at her side, while Charlotte tried in vain to untangle a knot in the embroidery floss dangling from the pillow cover Mother wanted for the guest-room bed.

"Will's improved behavior," Mother Bishop said without looking up from her book, "has nothing to do with the horse. He's simply trying to avoid Longview."

"That's not true," Charlotte protested. "He doesn't need Longview. He's feeling more self-confident and he knows he only gets to spend time around Isaac if he behaves himself."

"He is behaving himself," Mother Bishop said, glaring at Charlotte over pince-nez glasses, "because someone finally has had the fortitude to follow through with consequences." She lay her open book in her lap. "And for my part, I thank God for Major Riley's concern."

"Please, Mother," Charlotte pleaded. "Please don't sell Isaac. You'll see. All Will needs is time to grow and adjust. And Isaac can help us with that."

"It's not as if the horse is disappearing from your life," Mother said reasonably. She rattled her teacup. Charlotte jumped up, went to the tea tray for the pot and refilled Mother's cup. "I'm certain Major Riley will be more than happy to have you visit and ride Isaac any time you feel so inclined. In fact," she smiled, "he's already said as much."

Charlotte set the teapot back on its tray with trembling hands. She glanced at Mother, who had once again picked up her book, a sure sign she considered the matter settled. "But he's mine," she said. "The Colonel gave him to me."

"My dear Charlotte," Mother said, her voice laced with a kindness that was not kind, "I should have thought you would be willing to make this one small sacrifice for the good of the family without causing a stir. You have disappointed me."

"You have disappointed me." A chill went up Charlotte's spine at the all-too-familiar phrase, the one uttered over and over again after her wedding day, the one that always ultimately led to the Colonel's taking what he called *corrective measures* to ensure his wife never repeated an infraction.

Charlotte met Mother Bishop's gaze, at once chilled and repulsed by the absence of compassion in the old woman's dark eyes. She took in a deep breath, fighting back the wave of fear washing over her. *Don't panic. There's nothing left to take from you after this. Once Isaac is gone, there's nothing left.* Except there was. And now, Charlotte realized, Mother was determined to take it. Will would be sent away. It didn't matter how he behaved. Major Riley didn't like him, and that made Will the last obstacle preventing Mother from attaching herself and Aunt Daisy and the Bishop's holdings to a secure future with Major Peyton Riley, as he stepped into Emory's position as head of the household. Charlotte's feelings and desires were, she realized, irrelevant. She was expected to cooperate. She and Will were little more than pawns the Queen Mother would gladly sacrifice.

————

Finally, Charlotte knew what to do. The idea terrified her, but beneath the fear was the knowledge that it was right. Even wild animals protected their young. What she had not had the courage to do for herself, she would do for Will. And so it was that late one night not long after Mother Bishop appointed Major Riley to "make inquiries" at the Longview Academy regarding a position for Will, Charlotte climbed the narrow stairs to the third-floor garret and knocked on Garnet Irvin's door.

Garnet opened the door a crack and peered out, then quickly motioned Charlotte inside.

Charlotte perched on the edge of Garnet's mattress in a poorly lit room only slightly smaller than hers. The rough board floor was covered with rag rugs. The room smelled of soap and furniture polish and was impeccably clean.

"Do you think you could find a way to get Will's and my things packed and to the railway station without anyone here at the house knowing about it?" Charlotte asked quickly before she lost her nerve.

Garnet nodded her head. "Of course. Old George can muscle a trunk down the back stairs after Mrs. Bishop and Aunt Daisy are asleep."

"What about the rest of the servants?"

"The cook and some of the others were talking today about some doings over at the church on Wednesday night. If Mrs. Bishop gives them leave to go, that would clear the way." She added, "And I don't think anyone else would ask questions. If they do, old George can just say he's putting some of the Colonel's things in storage."

"Will you come with us?" Charlotte asked.

Garnet hesitated. "I've got a little money saved, but it's not near enough for a train ticket."

Charlotte looked down at the enormous opal the Colonel had put on her finger on their wedding day. "Just pack and be ready," she said. "And have George take the things to the station on Wednesday. But make certain he doesn't say a word to anybody."

"You can trust old George, missus," Garnet said.

"So, you'll come?" Charlotte asked, putting her hand on Garnet's arm.

Garnet smiled gently and patted the back of Charlotte's hand. She nodded. "Where exactly is it we're going?"

"Nebraska," Charlotte said. "We're going home to Nebraska."

Chapter Three

The foolishness of man perverteth his way:
and his heart fretteth against the Lord.
PROVERBS 19:3

WHO, LIEUTENANT NATHAN BOONE wondered, would have put flowers at his wife's grave. The small bouquet of wilted wild flowers gave off a faint, sweet aroma that took Nathan back to the days when Lily's had been one of only a few scattered graves in the Fort Robinson cemetery. Her tombstone had been the first granite marker. Now there were several neat rows of identical white stones. And a fence. It was a proper cemetery.

Other than Dr. Valentine, Nathan didn't think there was anyone left at Fort Robinson who would even remember Lily Bainbridge Boone. He looked around and spotted another grave with an identical bouquet of flowers. The same red ribbon. He walked over to read the marker. *Clara Maxwell.* That explained it. Laina Jackson had been here. After all these years, Laina still remembered how intent he had always been on keeping flowers at Lily's grave. *I expect I'll be seeing you sometime early in April,* Nathan had written the Jacksons from Texas. Knowing Nathan would pay his respects upon his arrival, Laina must have wanted to make sure he found evidence that someone else remembered, too.

It would have taken hours for her to ride in from the Four Pines Ranch on such an errand. He shouldn't be surprised by the show of friendship, though. Laina Gray Jackson had proven herself to be the kind of woman who would do just about anything for the people she loved. Hadn't she even said exactly that on that January morning ten years ago when he had left Fort Robinson? Hadn't she stood right at the kitchen table in her quarters down on Soapsuds Row and looked up at him with those shining green eyes and said, "Nathan, you know I'd do anything for you"?

"Anything but marry me," he'd replied, letting the regret sound in his voice.

"I can't marry you, Nathan. You've been my rescuer and my good friend. But you are still married to Lily in your heart. And for that and a thousand other reasons, marriage would never work for us. And in your heart of hearts, you know it."

"Yeah, well, I'd have argued with you about that 'til the cows came home if it wasn't for *him*." He'd waved his hand in the general direction of the post hospital where Caleb Jackson had gone to have over two dozen stitches taken out of his arm.

Laina blushed and touched the scar on the left side of her head, as she often did when she was embarrassed or unsettled.

"Don't get riled up," Nathan had said quickly. "I guess a person doesn't always have control over who they love—or don't, as the case may be."

Laina smiled up at him. "I'll always love you, and I'll always pray for you, Nathan." She cleared her throat. "I wish you were going to be here for the wedding."

"Orders are orders."

Laina nodded. "I know." She put her hand on his arm. "I'll never be able to thank you—"

"Don't," Nathan said, and touched her chin lightly. He pulled the blanket away from the face of the infant sleeping in her arms. "You take care of this little lamb," he said, stroking the baby's cheek, marveling again at the softness of her skin.

"You take care of yourself," Laina had replied, and stood on tiptoe to kiss his cheek. The baby in her arms grunted softly. "Don't let any of those—What do they call them? Buffalo soldiers? Don't let them know about this side of you for a while. Having a soft heart isn't usually seen as an asset in a lieutenant." She'd brushed an imaginary piece of dust off his new bars.

The next moment the bugler had sounded assembly. Boone put his hat back on. "Well, I guess this is it." Seeing the tears gathering in Laina's eyes, he looked away. "Laina—"

"Yes, Nathan."

"I guess I won't mind if you say a prayer now and then."

And Laina had prayed. In fact, Nathan thought as he made his way back to Lily's grave, both of the Jacksons had mentioned praying for him over the past ten years. It didn't seem possible so much time had passed. The infant in Laina's arms was a young girl now; Laina's little miracle, conceived in terrible circumstances, yet greatly loved long before she saw daylight. Laina had named the baby Joy. Clara Joy, for Clara Maxwell, the dear old woman they had all called Granny Max.

As it turned out, the baby girl was even more of a miracle than anyone realized. In the ten years since Laina had married Caleb Jackson, there hadn't been any other children born to them. Nathan could tell from their letters that Laina and Caleb were what people called "crazy in love," and when he had heard from them at Christmas, Caleb had proudly reported the news that they were expecting a baby early this summer. Still, Nathan thought it odd that the God they both believed in so strongly hadn't answered their prayers for children sooner. That, he realized, was just one more thing in a string of things he didn't understand about the way God handled people.

He certainly didn't understand how God had handled him. Ten years ago he'd still been enraged at the supposedly all-powerful God who had let Lily die an agonizing death from a snakebite. Time had apparently grown a thick layer of scar tissue around that particular unanswered question. As he stood emotionless at his wife's grave, Nathan reasoned that leaving Nebraska had been a good thing. The searing pain he'd always felt here was gone.

So many people at Fort Robinson had said things about his need to move on. Some thought he was wallowing in the past. Others just thought new scenery would be good for him. Dr. Valentine said serving with the Ninth would be a good career move. With Granny Max's death and Laina Gray's decision to marry Caleb Jackson, things just fell into place.

Since leaving Nebraska, Nathan had done what he could for the Jacksons by investing in the Four Pines Ranch. Over time, he had become more interested in ranching than he ever expected. He and Caleb wrote back and forth talking about blooded stock and future expansion. Once when on leave back east, Nathan spent some time with a group of horse fanciers, asking questions for Caleb about certain bloodlines and educating himself about thoroughbreds and Morgans.

Lately, the two men had been speculating about a stallion named Banner, wondering if bringing such a renowned animal west would enhance the reputation of the Four Pines—or bankrupt them both. In all the planning, he'd never suspected that when Fort Laramie closed, Fort Robinson would be named regimental headquarters, and he would once again find himself living in Nebraska, where everything was familiar and yet so much had changed.

He hoped the commander would agree that he'd earned an extended leave from the Ninth. There was more to his desire to visit the Four Pines than just seeing the Jacksons. Old Emmet Dorsey, his tobacco-chewing bunky from the old days, had retired and was living there. According to

Caleb, Dorsey was slowing down as his arthritic knees stiffened, but he was still an encyclopedia of common sense and good advice, and the Jacksons were happy to have him around.

And then there was Rachel and Jack. Nathan had been stabbed and was a patient in the infirmary when Rachel was brought in, half frozen, nearly starved, and wild with a combination of fear and grief. Back then, she spat out her name, Winter Moon, with a venomous snarl. Nathan couldn't blame her. She and her husband, Grey Foot, had escaped the Fort Robinson barracks along with the rest of the Cheyenne involved in what the whites were calling "the Outbreak." They had eluded the soldiers for weeks before being caught. For Winter Moon, "being caught" meant she and her husband were pursued up a narrow trail to the top of a bluff. Surrounded by soldiers, Grey Foot had pried his wife's hands from around his neck and dumped her in the snow before throwing himself off a cliff. The troops had hauled Winter Moon to the Fort Robinson hospital where a number of Cheyenne were being treated.

It nearly broke Nathan's heart to see the Cheyenne victims. It took a while, but he finally succeeded in getting Winter Moon to talk to him. Little by little, he learned her story. And at the last minute before he was transferred, he put salve on his conscience by locating Grey Foot's younger brother among the captives and then talking Caleb and Laina into taking both Rachel and Jack under their wing. It didn't take much convincing.

In time, Winter Moon changed her name to Rachel. Nathan guessed she was maybe ten years younger than him. That would make her about twenty-seven now. Nathan remembered her as a desperate, dark-haired, wild-eyed scarecrow. But he also remembered that beneath the despair was a beautiful woman. He wondered why she hadn't married Jack. Everyone said the boy was a lot like his older brother. He'd even started using Grey Foot's name as his last name—as had Rachel. It confused some people, but Nathan respected the boy for honoring his brother and for finding a way to make his name live on. It was only logical that people would assume Rachel and Jack would marry someday, but Nathan knew that logic didn't always affect reality.

Oh well, Nathan told himself, it didn't do to obsess about things a person couldn't understand. If he had learned anything in the years since he left Nebraska, it was that letting things you couldn't control occupy your mind was pointless. He had, for example, stopped obsessing not only about Lily, but also about religion. On the rare occasion when he thought or talked about God, it wasn't in terms of a personal being, but rather an unfathomable power that ruled from some remote location. He bore no resentment toward people who believed differently. Laina and Caleb's letters contained frequent references to God and to prayer. Nathan appreciated their faith and could see it had done them both good. On occasion, he even admitted to himself that he liked the idea of devout believers praying for him.

Of his men who could read, several of them had their own Bibles. Nathan still had Lily's. The difference was, Nathan kept Lily's Bible as an artifact from the past, whereas men like Private Carter Blake treated their Bible reading almost as if it was as important as eating. Nathan didn't begrudge them their faith. It was just, as he once told Private Blake, that religion had done precious little for him personally, and therefore he didn't see the point in pursuing it.

"Well, Lily," Nathan said, looking down at the tombstone, "here I am again." He crouched down and ran his finger over the lettering on the stone. It was odd to feel disconnected from his own wife, not to have words come tumbling out. He still thought of Lily often. Fondly. But he hadn't brought any flowers, and for some reason he felt awkward about that. He whispered an apology.

Standing up, he returned to Granny's marker. "I'm back, Granny," he said. "Wish I could come over to Soapsuds Row and get some of your corn bread." He swallowed hard, surprised when tears, which had not come at Lily's grave, clouded his eyes.

"I think you'd be proud of some of what I've done since I left." He laughed nervously. "But not all of it. I got away from the mess with the Cheyenne back in '79. But there was still plenty of similar things to face down in the Southwest with my men." He shifted his weight. "I did my best. The men of the Ninth are some of the best fighting men I've ever seen. I'd trust my life to them any day. Heck, there's one named Carter Blake—well, I wouldn't be standing here today if it weren't for him. You'd like him, Granny. He talks about God like you used to." He chuckled. "Although he doesn't bring it up quite as often as you." He cleared his throat. "The men of the Ninth are something, Granny. They don't get their due respect from Washington. But they stand tall and walk proud. I wish you could see that."

He stopped abruptly, shaking his head at the absurdity of talking to a grave. "Old habits die hard, Granny. I used to come up here to talk to Lily. It seems I've said all I had to say to her. Guess now it's your turn." He stood for a moment with bowed head. He could almost hear Granny's voice booming, *About time you started talking to the LORD again, Nathan Boone. No better place to do it than at my grave.*

Taking a deep breath, Nathan put his hat back on. He turned to go, surprised at the sight of a very pregnant woman and a girl crossing the bridge at the river, clearly headed for the cemetery. The girl ran ahead, bounding up the hill with exaggerated strides until she saw that a soldier was inside the fence. She stopped abruptly and waited for the woman to catch up.

Nathan recognized Laina when she paused to catch her breath and pushed her bonnet back off her head, revealing her auburn hair. The closer she came the more he realized that ten years had done nothing to diminish her beauty. If anything, she was more lovely than ever, her cheeks flushed with the exertion of the walk, her face aglow with unmitigated pleasure as she called his name.

"Nathan Boone, is it really you?" she called out.

At mention of his name, the young girl whirled back around to face him. She whispered something to Laina. They laughed.

Nathan swept his hat off his head. "It's me," he said.

Laina tugged on one of the girl's red braids. "Say hello to Lieutenant Boone," she said. "And yes, he is just about the handsomest man I ever saw—except, of course, for your daddy."

"Moth-*er*," the girl's face turned scarlet.

Nathan smiled at her. "Last time I saw you," he said, "you were about this long." He held his hands about a foot apart. "Even then you had that beautiful red hair." He thrust out his hand. "I'm pleased to meet you, Clara Joy."

"CJ," the girl corrected him.

"All right, then," he said, and shook her hand. "CJ. Pleased to meet you." He turned to Laina. "I saw the flowers."

"We came in yesterday. Caleb wants me to be near a doctor when the baby comes, and Maude at the trading post offered to put us up in her spare room."

CJ spoke up. "Pa's going to work here this summer. Then we'll have the money to make the ranch bigger."

Laina looked up at Nathan and smiled. "Who would have thought all that repair work he did with Harlan years ago would come in so handy. But CJ is right. With all the building going on here at the fort, Caleb's thinking he'll try to get on with a crew for the summer."

"What about roundup?" Nathan asked. "Isn't it almost time for that?"

"We'll do roundup like always," CJ spoke up. "Then Pa will come to work here. And then we're buying the Dawson place right next to ours."

Laina touched CJ on the shoulder. "That's enough, CJ. Why don't you go ahead to Granny Max's grave."

CJ headed off. Laina looked up at Nathan. "CJ has never ascribed to the 'be seen and not heard' version of childhood."

"She seems very bright," Nathan said.

"Sometimes too bright for her own good," Laina laughed. "But she's her daddy's right-hand man at home. Would much rather be out in the barn with him than in the kitchen with me. The two of them have talked over this plan about the Dawson place until I think they've talked it to death."

"Is it for sale yet?"

Laina shook her head. "Not yet. But the old man keeps talking about it. And he's promised to give Caleb first chance."

Nathan nodded. "How's Dorsey doing?"

"He still loves his chewing tobacco, and his knees still kill him when the weather changes," Laina said. "But all in all he's doing fine."

"Rachel and Jack?" Nathan asked.

"Rachel rode in with us. She's over at the trading post right now. We decided she could shop for roundup supplies and then head home in the morning. You should come by later and say hello if you have time." Laina added, "And you won't believe how Jack has grown. He's a man now. And the best wrangler a rancher could want." She smiled. "He talks about you like you're a legend in your own time."

Nathan frowned. "Really?"

"He says you saved his life," CJ said. She had wandered back toward Laina and Nathan and was hanging over the top of the iron gate listening.

"I did no such thing," Nathan protested.

"All I know," said CJ, "is Jack says if he'd gone with the rest of the Cheyenne to the reservation, who knows what would have happened. Anytime we hear news from there, it's bad."

"Well," Laina said, "whether you want to accept the hero worship or not, the fact is Jack and Rachel seem to be happy at the Four Pines, and we're grateful they are. Although," she added, "Jack would be happier if Rachel would take him a little more seriously."

"Oh, puh-*leeze*," CJ interjected. "Do we have to talk about *that*?"

"About what?" Nathan wanted to know.

CJ took in a deep breath and recited, "Jack keeps asking Rachel to marry him, and Rachel keeps saying no, she's too old for him, and Jack gets mad or hurt or whatever it is and goes down to the barn, and then in a day or two he's back eating with us again like always until it all happens all over again," CJ made a circle in the air with her hand. "Around and around and around. It's so *boring*."

Nathan laughed. "Sounds to me like you're smarter than most grown-ups I know," he said. "At least you know to stay out of other people's love life."

"I hear you, Lieutenant Boone," Laina said. "And I suppose that means I shouldn't warn you."

"About what?"

Laina smiled innocently. "Caleb just heard that Charlotte Valentine is back at Fort Robinson."

Chapter Four

Will the Lord cast off for ever?
and will he be favourable no more? Is his mercy clean gone
for ever? doth his promise fail for evermore?
PSALM 77:7-8

IF CHARLOTTE BISHOP expected escaping to Nebraska to solve all her problems, she was sorely disappointed. She had arrived in March, both grateful the railroad had finally reached Fort Robinson—precluding the necessity of enduring a frigid stagecoach ride—and angry that Garnet was assigned a "seat" in the baggage car. Her father, whom she had telegraphed from St. Louis, met her with open arms, undisguised joy at finally meeting his only grandson, and not a little surprise.

"But I wrote before Christmas," Charlotte said.

Her father shook his head. "I never got any such letter." He put his arms around her. "I'm so glad you came anyway, but why didn't you telegraph when you didn't hear from me?"

"I didn't want to insist," Charlotte said. She looked away. "I thought you might not want—"

"Not want you? Oh, my dear." He pulled her close. "I've been so lonely since your mother died. I wrote a dozen times begging you to come home. When you didn't answer—"

Charlotte frowned. She pushed herself away from her father and looked up at him. "*You* wrote to ask *me?*"

Her father nodded. "Many times. I thought perhaps . . . well, Mrs. Bishop wrote and mentioned a Major Riley."

Charlotte shuddered. She pressed her lips together. "*That,*" she said, "will never happen."

Her father put his hands on her shoulders. His eyes searched hers. "Well, you're home now."

"There's Garnet," Will said.

Charlotte and her father turned just in time to see Garnet smooth her hair back with both hands and, with a regal toss of her head, come their way.

That had been a few weeks ago. They had finally decided that Edgar, Mother Bishop's faithful butler, must have been "preempting" the mail, allowing only the letters that didn't mention Charlotte's moving home, to reach her. That likelihood birthed a simmering rage in Charlotte that made her short-tempered and suspicious.

Will brought his own emotional baggage from Michigan. The headmaster at the school for the officer's children declared him *incorrigible* and *unmanageable* and expelled him in short order. Will seemed determined to prove him right. And Charlotte felt increasingly incapable of controlling her son and her own emotions.

She had expected to feel better once she was home. Except Fort Robinson felt nothing like home. Reading her father's letters about the changes and living amongst them were two different things. She wanted anonymity and peace and quiet. Unfortunately, Colonel Bishop's military reputation was more widespread than she had realized. She was expected to make calls and become part of the same social structure she had left behind at Fort Wayne. For Will's sake, she reluctantly decided she must maintain the facade of The Grieving Widow of the Military Hero. The effort left her tired and out of sorts and only served to emphasize the lifetime of changes a decade had wrought.

Ten years ago, a young Charlotte Valentine would have taken advantage of a lovely April day by mincing along the picket fence near the fort's parade ground hoping to be noticed by recruits as they marched by. Now she sat in a rocking chair on her father's front porch, fighting back weary tears, hoping to be left alone long enough to decide how to handle her son's latest infraction of his grandfather's rules.

Ten years ago she would have been mentally designing a new gown for the Fourth of July ball, even if it was three months away. She would have thought it unfair that such a young widow had to wear mourning clothes and forego dancing. Now Charlotte wondered if there was any way to get out of the welcome event being given in her honor in a few days. How she dreaded the thought of making small talk with the string of officers who'd feel obliged to show Dr. Valentine's daughter and Colonel Bishop's widow her due respect.

Oh, no. Her father was crossing the parade ground with a tall soldier who would undoubtedly expect to be invited to stay for dinner. Charlotte closed her eyes, reminding herself that hospitality was not an optional part of military housekeeping. Officers' families were expected to welcome guests at a moment's notice and do so with grace and goodwill. She opened her eyes. This unexpected guest was tall, with very dark hair. As he got closer, Charlotte's heart skipped a beat. *Oh, no. Not him. It can't be.*

She would have known him anywhere. Ten years ago, the sight of Nathan Boone would have sent her through a well-rehearsed routine— smooth hair back off face, pull a tendril or two down onto collar, bite lips to redden them, smile, but not too much. Today, all Charlotte felt was a sense of dread not unlike her response when Mother Bishop first hauled Major Riley in the door.

Charlotte scolded herself. *It's not the same thing at all. Major Riley was on a fishing expedition for the Bishop money. Even if Lieutenant Boone's determination to remain alone has changed, he won't have a flicker of interest in you. Too many changes—and not one of them for the better.* Her waist was thicker. Four pregnancies in five years did that to a woman. Her eyes and mouth were outlined with fine wrinkles. Three infant burials did *that* to a woman, whether her husband drank and gambled or not. She'd stopped her various beauty routines years ago, and she knew it showed in the loss of shine in her ash-blond hair. She'd gone riding without gloves so often that freckles peppered the backs of her hands.

Oh, well, Charlotte thought. *What does it matter anyway?* She hadn't come back for the society functions. She'd come back for Will's sake and to take her recently departed mother's place in her father's household. And while she might have been a disappointment to Colonel Emory Bishop, she had no intention of being a disappointment to her father. She would find a way to settle Will down and run the doctor's household well, if it was the last thing she did. Doing the latter required welcoming her father's guests. Taking a deep breath, Charlotte pasted on a smile. She got up and went to the edge of the porch to greet Lieutenant Boone.

He swept his hat off his head with a white-gloved hand and tucked it beneath one arm. "I convinced your father to let me pay my respects before the reception," he said, smiling. "I suppose I'm taking advantage of the privilege of past acquaintance." He removed his glove and extended his hand. "Welcome back to Fort Robinson, Mrs. Colonel Bishop. And please accept my sympathy for your loss."

Being at a loss for words had never been a problem for Charlotte Valentine. But Emory had changed her. Turned her into something besides an empty-headed flirt, as Emory had called her. For her own good, Emory said. Taught her to think before speaking. Eventually taught her it was usually better not to speak at all, because saying the wrong thing in public would be corrected in private places in secret ways no one would ever suspect.

And so, with Emory's lessons still fresh in her mind, Charlotte simply extended her hand and allowed it to be swallowed up in the lieutenant's without saying anything besides "Thank you." When he dropped her hand, she clasped both of hers together behind her back and waited for her father to speak.

"This old reprobate seems to think he's learned enough in all his gallivanting through the Southwest to finally beat me at chess," her father said, pounding the lieutenant on the back. Looking back up at his daughter, the doctor asked, "Where's Will?"

"Garnet sent him to the trading post for some eggs," Charlotte said. She took a step toward the door. "I'll make you gentlemen some coffee."

"Have Garnet do it," her father said. "You keep us company."

"Garnet's gone down to Soapsuds Row for a visit."

"What about supper dishes?"

"I told her I'd take care of it."

"You're too easy on that girl," the doctor protested.

Charlotte put her hand on her father's shoulder. "Doing dishes makes me feel useful. Don't expect me to spend all my evenings doing needlepoint like some high-and-mighty lady." She patted his shoulder. "I came back to Fort Robinson to take care of you, Papa. Let me do it." She turned to the lieutenant. "Do you still like chokecherry pie?"

"You remembered. I'm impressed," Nathan said, as he and the doctor followed Charlotte inside.

"One of the laundresses down on the Row gave Garnet a jar of choke-cherries just yesterday." Charlotte looked at her father. "Garnet hurried to get the pie into the oven before she left for her little visit. It's probably still warm. I'll get you some."

While the men headed into the parlor to collect chairs and a chessboard to be moved out onto the porch, Charlotte made her way through the dining room, down the short service hall, and into the kitchen. Once in the kitchen, she took down two white china dessert plates and fired up the stove for coffee. How many times had she dreamed of serving pie to Nathan Boone, picturing how she would put a single flower beside his plate.

While she waited for water to heat, Charlotte ground coffee, thinking back to simpler days when her only problems were figuring out how to convince her mother to let her try a new hairdo or how to catch a soldier's eye at the next dance. The aroma of freshly ground coffee propelled her memories to another time. *"It's too strong, woman!"* An angry voice shouted. *"How many times do I have to tell you to measure it out more carefully!"*

Charlotte's hands began to tremble. Closing her eyes tightly, she took a deep breath, raised her palms to her cheeks and began to softly sing a song she'd learned from Garnet. "Swing low, sweet chariot, comin' for to carry me home. . . ." Opening her eyes wide, Charlotte looked around her, reminding herself, *You ARE home. It is OVER.* By the time the coffee was ready, she was calm again. She poured coffee, took up the heavily-laden serving tray, and headed back toward the front of the house.

The men were already seated on the front porch, the chessboard between them. She could hear their voices and smell the smoke from their evening cigars wafting in the open front-parlor window. She smiled to herself. Cigar smoke was a welcome change from earlier in the day when they had been downwind from the privies.

As she advanced toward the front door, Charlotte's foot landed in a pile of something just slippery enough to throw her off-balance. Two pieces of pie, two cups of hot coffee, the coffeepot, sugar bowl, and creamer went one way, while Charlotte went the other, landing with her left hand immersed up to her wrist in what proved to be a pile of manure. Shrieks of laughter erupted from behind the parlor sofa even as her father and Lieutenant Boone rushed inside.

"Emory William Bishop!" Her father bellowed, swooping behind the sofa and emerging with a wriggling boy in tow. "If this kind of behavior is going to continue . . ."

"Papa," Charlotte pleaded, grimacing with pain. She blinked back tears, almost passing out as she grasped her left forearm with her good right hand and pulled her left hand out of the pile of manure. She closed her eyes and turned her head, even as Boone knelt at her side.

"You'd better let the boy go and come look at her wrist, doc," he said, leaning closer. "Keep your eyes closed, Mrs. Colonel. It's probably not all that bad, but I bet it hurts something fierce."

Charlotte flinched, pulling away when the lieutenant tried to put a comforting hand on her shoulder. Clamping her lips together, she concentrated on breathing evenly. *You will not faint. You will not faint. Swing low . . . carry me home . . . band of angels.* Her head swam.

Her father knelt next to her on the floor. "Dear Lord in heaven," was all he said.

Charlotte spoke. "Is that . . . is that really what I think it is sticking . . . out?" Her stomach roiled.

"Don't think about it," her father said quickly. "Keep your eyes closed and concentrate on breathing. Slow, even breaths, dear. And don't you dare faint on me. I need you to hold still while I get it wrapped. Lieutenant, hand me that napkin."

"I'm not going to faint on you," Charlotte snapped. Her voice broke as she asked, "Where . . . where's Will?"

"Don't you worry about Will. There'll be time enough to deal with him later."

"He'll be scared. Scared that he's hurt me." Charlotte swallowed hard and bit her lip when her father tightened the makeshift bandage around her wrist.

"And well he should be. I'm going to knock some sense into that boy if it's the last thing I ever do," her father snapped.

"You'll do no such thing," Charlotte begged. She cried out, gasped for air, and clutched her father's arm. "Please, Papa. Promise me you won't."

Her father pulled her head onto his shoulder. "Now, Charlotte. Calm down. You know I won't. I'm just mad. Now, stop worrying about Will. We've got to get you over to the hospital."

Boone stood up. "I'll fetch a steward and get some men headed this way with a litter."

"No," Charlotte gasped. "Just get me to my own bed." She looked up at her father. "Call Garnet back from the Row. She'll know what to do. I'll be fine."

"You're going to need surgery," her father said.

"I'm *not* going to any hospital," Charlotte insisted. "And certainly not on a litter for all the world to see."

"You *are* going to the hospital."

"I'll carry you," Boone offered.

"Don't be ridiculous," Charlotte insisted. She motioned him away. "Stop fussing and let me get up." Taking a deep breath, she bit down hard on her lower lip as she pushed herself up off the floor and leaned against the wall, waiting for the room to stop reeling. She was to remember the irony of this moment for the rest of her life. As Miss Charlotte Valentine she had actually practiced swooning and falling into the arms of a handsome soldier. But it was 1890 now. She was no longer a child, and she didn't swoon. What she did was worse. The last thing she would remember was doubling over and vomiting all over Lieutenant Nathan Boone's polished boots.

Chapter Five

Depart from evil, and do good; seek peace, and pursue it.
PSALM 34:14

IT WASN'T JUST the iron grip of the molasses-colored hand clamped around his ankle—although that was surely enough to make Will's heart lurch. But once caught in the man's iron grip, he still had to look past the bulging muscles in the soldier's forearm to two scowling ice-blue eyes. He still had to hear the deep voice rumble ominously, "Just *what* do you think you are doing?!"

Usually extremely talented at squirming out of the grasp of whoever was attempting discipline, Will went limp against the straw and looked up, wide-eyed. "N-n-nothin'," he stammered. "I wasn't doin' nothing."

The soldier let go of Will's ankle and straightened up, his hulking outline filling the space at the opposite end of the stall—the space between Will and freedom. Will opted for backing away instead of trying to bolt past the angry private. He crabbed backward in the straw and plastered his back against the rough boards forming the front of one of the several dozen stalls in Company B's stable. The bay gelding Will had untied lowered his head and blew softly into the straw through velvety black nostrils, slowly shaking his head back and forth. *Great,* Will thought, *even the horse is mad at me.*

"Move over, Dutch," the soldier said, leaning against the bay's haunches. When the horse stepped sideways, the soldier reached forward to grab his lead. He looked down at Will. "I'm gonna back my horse out of here so you don't get stepped on. You stay put." The soldier didn't take his eyes off Will as he reached for a huge iron ring and hitched Dutch out in the walkway.

His horse out of the way, the soldier lounged against the side of the stall, hardly seeming to take notice of Will as he talked. "Funny thing about a man like me. You can call him every name in the book of life, and he doesn't get riled. You can refer to his race and his lineage in whatever terms you want, and he just lets it roll off; does his duty and gets on with life. You can order a march across a desert where it's so boiling hot even the rattlesnakes sweat. Order him through a blizzard and expect him to get half frozen, and a man like me, why, he'll salute and say 'Yes, sir.' Obey orders or die trying."

The man paused, reached for a piece of straw and inserted it into his mouth. He chewed on it for so long Will thought he had forgotten what he wanted to say. But then he threw the straw to the ground and crouched down, glaring at Will as he said, "But you mess with that man's horse, sonny—the horse that carried him *across* that desert and *through* that blizzard, the horse that saved his life in a fight with the Apaches down in Arizona Territory, the horse that has been all the family that man's got—you mess with that horse and you've got yourself a fight." He stood up. "So you'd better have a good explanation for why you were messing with one of the best horses the good Lord ever set on four feet, or—"

"Or what?!" Will blurted out. Hearing his own voice gave such welcome release to his emotions that Will mistook the relief for courage. "You can't do anything to me. You're just a private. My grandfather is Dr. Avery Valentine—*Colonel* Valentine to you. You wouldn't dare do anything to me!"

The soldier's eyebrows shot up in mock surprise. "Oh, so it's *you*." He pushed his hat back off his forehead. "I've heard about you."

"Then you know you'd better leave me alone," Will said, his voice wavering only a little. He'd blustered his way out of more than one tight spot with bullies back in Michigan, and it looked like maybe he was going to manage to do it again. The man was, after all, *only* a private. Will inched away from the stall wall, looking for an escape route.

"Aren't you the same boy who tied a pan to Frenchy Dubois's dog's tail the other day and sent him through the quartermaster's herd?"

Will shrugged. "Just having a little fun. Didn't hurt anything."

"And aren't you the same boy who put salt in the punch bowl at the officers' club social last Friday night?"

"So what?" Will sneered, "*You* weren't there. Didn't have anything to do with you." He inched along the back of the stall. The way the horse was standing, he just might be able to duck under its neck and dodge out the door. "And if you know all that about me then you know who my grandfather is and you know you'd better not mess with me or he'll . . . he'll . . ."

"How'd you do it?"

Will stopped short. He looked at the private, who was staring at him solemnly.

Frowning, he hesitated. "What?"

"Well," the soldier said, leaning back against the stall. "I just wondered how you managed to sneak in there and not get caught." He winked. "That was a wondrous prank. Don't know how you managed a whole *sack* of salt. How come they didn't see you do it?"

He wasn't sure, but Will thought the blue eyes might be thawing a little. Was that an almost-grin barely visible beneath the man's bushy moustache? He shrugged.

"Nothing to it. Didn't have to sneak. I just put salt in a sugar sack is all. It was easy. Frenchy didn't even know I made the switch. He's almost blind anyway. A broken-down old soldier like that is easy to fool."

"Hey!" The blue eyes grew cold again. The corners of the mouth turned down. "You don't disrespect a man who's been through what that old soldier's been through, young man. You salute him."

"What do you mean, what he's been through?"

"Oh. So you don't know about Sergeant Charles Dubois?"

"I know he's old. And he married the trader's widow, and now when he's not behind the counter he just sits on the front porch at the store and chews tobacco and spins yarns."

The soldier nodded. "Well, maybe sometime after you apologize for messing with Dutch here—maybe sometime I'll tell you about Sarge. But not now. It's too near time for parade. So you get outta here. And the next time you want to make the acquaintance of a soldier's horse, you ask the soldier first. You could get yourself hurt. Dutch is a good old boy, but some of these hacks in this stable would just as soon eat you for supper as look at you. And they could do it, too. Send you flying with one well-placed kick." The soldier stood up. "And as you've pointed out, since I'm just a lowly private and your grandfather is *Colonel* Valentine, I don't want to be held to blame for his grandson getting sent to glory ahead of schedule."

"He wouldn't care," Will said. He ducked his head, mortified by the blush he could feel creeping up his pale cheeks. "Even if he *is* looking for me, it's just to give me a walloping."

"You think you need wallopin'?" the private asked.

Will shook his head, then looked down at the soldier's boots, embarrassed by the tears filling his eyes. "I didn't mean it. Didn't mean to hurt anybody. Sure didn't mean to hurt Ma." He tried to control his breathing, tried to keep the short jerky sounds from overtaking his voice.

The soldier was quiet again. When he spoke, the ragged edges of anger in his voice had mellowed into something almost kind. "Mothers are a strange breed, son. They forget hurts faster than any creature alive. Whatever you did, if you ran off, I bet she's more worried than she is angry." He picked up a hay rake and stabbed the straw with it. "Either way, running off on a stolen government horse is no way to handle it. If that's what you were thinking of doing, you need to think again. That kind of behavior never solves anything. Just makes a man miserable for longer."

"You don't know what I did," Will said. "It's bad." He rattled off the prank, embarrassed by the tears that began to flow while he talked.

"Are you sure she broke her wrist?" the soldier asked.

"I saw the bone sticking out," the boy murmured, touching his own wrist as if to illustrate the injury.

The soldier set the hay rake aside and crouched back down. "Well your grandpa's a good doctor. I bet your ma will be just fine."

Will looked into the blue eyes. "That's not what he said. He said the manure means it'll get infected as sure as anything. He said she could . . . she could . . ." It was so horrible, he could barely make himself continue. "He said she might *die!*" The last word was said through a mighty sob that erupted from his innards and ended any hope of further speech. He crumpled back down into the straw, hid his face against his arms and let the sobs come.

"No such thing," the soldier said.

Feeling a giant hand on his shoulder, Will's first inclination was to jerk away. He went with his second inclination, though. He threw himself against the stranger's chest and for the first time in a long, long while became the frightened little boy he was. Will had learned to hide that boy beneath pranks and bluster and anger. He'd learned to keep that boy hidden all day, every day. Only once in a while had he let that boy out—and only *after* his mother had tucked him in and left him alone. Sometimes then, in the dark, Will had covered his head with a goose-down pillow so no one could hear. Because when he came out, that boy inside always had to holler and cry. Now, feeling the warmth of strong arms around him, Will let that frightened little boy cry his tears.

"You know better than that," Carter said when Will begged him to go home with him. "An enlisted man doesn't just stroll up to a Colonel's front door and knock. And besides that, first call for retreat will sound soon. I've got to get Dutch saddled and get myself ready for parade."

"Then I won't go back," Will said, the rebellion returning to his voice. "I'll hike up onto the butte."

"And do what?"

"Maybe I'll just take a run at one of 'em and be done with it," Will blurted out. "Like that Cheyenne warrior I heard about."

Carter didn't question the plan. He nodded slowly. "That's one answer. Sure would make it hard on your ma, though. She'd blame herself. Mothers are like that, you know. Whatever bad their young'uns do, they seem to take it on themselves."

"That's crazy. If I run off it's not her fault."

"She'd think it was. And she'd grieve until the day she died, wondering what she did wrong." Carter tilted his head to one side. "But the other option is for you to stand up like a man. Take the blame on yourself for what you did. Tell her you're sorry."

"She wouldn't believe me."

"She would," Blake said. "*I* believe you're sorry, and I just met you."

"Aw," Will said, kicking at the straw. "That's because I acted like a baby, crying on your shoulder and all."

"There's nothing wrong with a man crying when he's done wrong, Will Bishop," Carter said. "The fact is, it takes a better man to apologize and shed a few tears than to lock it all up inside and go out and do harm to someone else—or himself."

"You're just saying that 'cause you want me to go home," Will said.

The soldier's blue eyes narrowed. "I never lie, Will Bishop. Never. And I'm telling you the best thing is to admit your wrongs, and go see your ma. Your grandpa was angry when he said those things, and he'll be as glad as your ma to see you. Or my name isn't Carter Blake."

Looking up at the man, Will swallowed hard.

A few minutes later the looming shadow of the giant behind him gave Will courage as he stood at his grandfather's back door, doing his best not to tremble while he waited for Garnet to answer his hesitant knock.

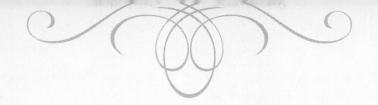

Chapter Six

Let us therefore come boldly unto the throne of grace, that we may obtain mercy, and find grace to help in time of need.

HEBREWS 4:16

WHATEVER GARNET IRVIN had expected when she agreed to accompany her widowed employer west, it did not include the sight of a hulking black soldier with muddy boots appearing at her back door with Will Bishop in tow. Of course Garnet realized that when it came right down to it, it was not *her* back door. It wasn't even Doctor Valentine's. The United States Army owned both the back door and the house attached to it. Still, Garnet Irvin had a way of sweetly, yet completely, reigning over whatever territory ended up being assigned to her by the white people who thought they were in charge. Thus, in the Year of our Lord 1890, Garnet Irvin's newest kingdom was comprised of a surgeon's residence at Fort Robinson, Nebraska—including the back door.

Reigning over the surgeon's residence meant many things. For instance, it meant that you sweetly accepted whatever your employers suggested and then quietly did what you pleased. And as long as they had clean linens and an immaculate house, they usually didn't notice. On the rare occasions when Dr. Valentine did notice and try to take issue with Garnet's rule, a freshly baked pie provided a satisfactory distraction.

Reigning over the surgeon's residence also meant doing what one could to keep young Will Bishop from completely destroying his mother's peace of mind—what little of it Mrs. Bishop had left. And so, however Garnet felt about the man in the muddy boots, she was relieved to have him haul Will home so she could send the little rascal over to the hospital. Maybe then his mother would stop worrying about Will and listen a little better to what the doctors were saying, which was that they needed to do surgery right away.

But Mrs. Bishop wasn't even considering surgery. Not until she saw Will.

"I won't have him coming in here later tonight and thinking I'm almost dead. I want to see him before you do it," she had insisted.

"Then I'll find him," that nice Lieutenant Boone had said. And he'd gone looking. Now here was Will, but no sign of Lieutenant Boone.

The private who had Will in tow seemed to have been rendered speechless. Garnet waited for him to speak, but the soldier just stared at her with eyes so blue it would be impossible not to notice them. Just as it was impossible for Garnet not to notice his physical size. Will's entire shoulder was hidden by one of the man's hands. Garnet observed it all without a word and then met the private's gaze, hoping to encourage him to say something. When Will was dragged home there was usually a lot more to it than someone just bringing Will home. People usually had complaints. Something was usually broken. Garnet waited for the telling of Will Bishop's most recent sin.

But this time there was no complaint, no tale of a broken treasure. When the giant man finally cleared his throat, all he did was introduce himself as "Private Blake, ma'am" and add "Found the boy over in the stables. He's worried about his mama."

Garnet nodded and turned to Will. "Your mama needs surgery right away to mend that wrist," she said. "But she won't hear of it until she sees you. So you need to get yourself over to the hospital. Right now."

"Is she gonna be all right?"

Garnet heard the terror in the boy's voice. When she noticed Private Blake patting his shoulder, her voice mellowed. "Your grandpa said he saw a Dr. Reed work on a homesteader who had a much worse break a few years ago. Said the man's ankle was almost crushed. He says he learned a lot from Dr. Reed, and he thinks it will be all right. But since it's been broken once before, that might make it a little harder."

At mention of the other time his ma broke her wrist, Will squeezed his eyes shut. He tried not to ever think about that night, but now it all came back. Father had been angry and shouting and then there was a loud thump against the wall separating Will's room from his parents. The next morning when Ma appeared at the breakfast table with her arm in a sling and a story about falling in the dark, Will realized that what had hit the wall the night before was not a *thing*. Not long after that Will was moved to a bedroom farther away from his parents. As time went on, he realized he had begun to hate Emory Bishop and would do whatever it took to be as unlike the man as possible. But Grandfather Valentine said he looked just like his father. And now, as he stood at his grandfather's back door looking up at Garnet, all Will could think about was how not only did he *look* like the man he hated—he was starting to act like him, too. He'd even broken his mother's wrist. He squeezed his eyes shut trying to keep the tears from flowing. When he was unsuccessful, Garnet's voice gentled even more.

"Don't cry, Will. Everyone knows you didn't mean to hurt your mama. She's more worried about you than she is about herself. So you just go on over there and ease her mind. I'll be along directly when I get this beef tea clarified."

Will looked up at Garnet's smile.

"Nothing like my beef tea to bring a body back to health."

Lieutenant Boone came around the corner of the house. Private Blake straightened up, saluted, and stepped back. "Found him in the stables, sir. In Dutch's stall."

Boone returned Blake's salute, thanked him for seeing the boy home, and dismissed him. Then he turned to Will. "Your mother won't let your grandfather do a thing until she talks to you. Let's get over to the hospital."

He hadn't expected this. Hadn't expected that Grandfather would be gone, called out to check on some fool soldier who'd shot himself cleaning a rifle. Hadn't expected Ma to be left in the hands of a hospital steward while Garnet made beef tea. Hadn't expected her hospital bed to be at the far end of a row of empty cots, surrounded by upright screens so a person couldn't even see who was there. And when he finally did walk the interminable distance to those upright screens and peer around them, Will hadn't expected his mother's face to be as pale as death.

Look what you did. It was the same voice that had so often warned Will he'd better watch himself and be ready to duck. The voice wasn't audible this evening, but Will could still hear the words as clearly as if it were Father and not Lieutenant Boone standing beside him. He startled when a hand touched his shoulder. Realizing it was Boone, he resisted the urge to twist away.

"She's just sleeping," Boone said, and crouched down beside him. "Look carefully, son. She's breathing low and even. Your grandfather likely gave her something for the pain."

Boone was right. The sheet covering his mother's still form was rising and falling with her even, deep breaths. Will felt the spring wound tight inside him relax a little.

"There you are."

It was his grandfather's voice sounding from the doorway. The spring wound tight again, and Will stepped closer to Boone while his grandfather strode up the aisle between the two rows of empty cots.

"One of my men found him in the stables," Boone said.

Will pressed his lips together to keep his chin from trembling.

Grandfather's voice was stern. "Do you have any idea how serious this is, young man? Do you know how many limbs I've amputated after injuries like this?"

Now look what you've done. They'll cut off her arm and it's your fault.

"Answer me."

Yeah. Go ahead. Tell the old man you're sorry. Whine and squeeze out a tear or two. Give the old man what he wants. You know you're too soft to be a soldier so just go ahead and cry.

Will swallowed hard. He wanted to answer, but somewhere between the spring wound up inside and the voice in his head, he lost the words. His mother's foot moved beneath the sheet next to him. Will jumped and looked back up toward the head of the bed. "Is she . . . is she . . ."

"She'll have surgery to repair the break," Grandfather said. "We'll have to put some drains in the incision to try to control the infection."

"D-drains?"

"Little glass tubes. Over the next few days they'll likely be dripping with pus." The doctor clasped his hands behind his back and shook his head from side to side. "What were you thinking, Will? *Manure*, for goodness' sake."

"Is she going to die?" Will blurted the words out past the tightly wound spring, past the voice in his head.

"Of course she isn't going to die. I won't let that happen."

The words gave no comfort. Will knew soldier-talk when he heard it. The kind of talk that made it sound like nothing was impossible. Will's father had told him battlefield stories of unbelievable things like soldiers running on broken legs to get to safety or lifting loaded wagons to free comrades pinned beneath the wheels. Even miracles seemed to be possible on the battlefield.

But not for you, Will Bishop, the voice in his head whispered. *The old man is just blustering soldier-talk. He'll have to cut off her arm in a few days. He knows she's going to die. He's just being a good soldier. She's going to die. You've killed your mother.* Will closed his eyes. A shudder passed the entire length of his body. He felt a flood of tears threatening and scrubbed his cheeks with the palms of his hands.

"Garnet went home to make some beef tea," Grandfather was saying. "You run tell her I'll sit with your mother tonight. She was talking about bringing a bedroll up here. Tell her that won't be necessary—but the beef tea is a good idea and she should bring that early in the morning. I'll keep the night watch." He leaned down and put a hand on Will's shoulder. "We need to operate soon, but I'll wait for you to get back before I take her into surgery. If she's awake at all, you can talk to her then."

Will shuddered again.

"You hear me, boy?" His grandfather's hand shoved him toward the door. "Run, now, and tell Garnet what I told you. Lieutenant Boone has evening parade to worry about. Don't be wasting any more of his time."

As he headed for the door, Will felt the spring inside him unwind a little. There was something he could do to help his mother. He might be a bad person, but here was something good he could do.

"Will," his grandfather called out.

Will stopped at the door and turned around.

"You didn't mean to hurt her. I know that. But this is serious. We still need to have a talk about your behavior."

Will nodded. "Yes, sir," he said, saluted, spun around on his heel and charged out the door, across the trail and one corner of the parade ground, and up the row of officers' quarters toward the one occupied by the Valentines.

"Run faster, you little runt. Can't you run any faster? You'll never be a good soldier. Too small for the infantry. Unfit for the cavalry. I can't believe a son of mine would turn out to fear horses. Maybe that's it. Maybe you aren't really my son after all. That would explain a lot. Run faster, you little runt. Can't you run any faster?"

"Grandfather said you don't need to come tonight," Will repeated when Garnet told him to wait a minute and then emerged from her room behind the kitchen with a pillow and a bedroll.

"I heard you," Garnet replied. She poured the beef tea into a glass jar and settled it into a basket along with some other things, including Charlotte's hairbrush and comb. Handing the bedroll to Will, Garnet headed for the back door. "Let's go," she said.

In the time it had taken Will to carry the message to Garnet and for Garnet to pack up, the evening retreat formations and drills had been conducted on the parade ground. Garnet and Will were rounding the commanding officer's headquarters building at the end of Officers Row and crossing the trail toward the hospital when the retreat formation was dismissed. Two soldiers, mounted on bays, broke away from their company and rode up.

Lieutenant Boone and Private Blake dismounted. Boone asked, "Are they going to operate tonight?"

"That's what Grandfather said," Will replied.

"Do you mind if we wait with you?" Boone asked. He nodded at Blake, "Private Blake here is something of an unofficial chaplain for the Ninth. It can't hurt to have a praying man on your side."

Will stared up at the two men. He looked at Garnet, who lifted her free hand to her mouth as she said, "It's not my place to say."

Will spoke up. "A prayer can't hurt, can it? Ma won't mind."

"Then we'll come," Lieutenant Boone said. He called on another soldier to take the two horses to the stables, and he and Private Blake fell in behind Garnet and Will.

By the time they all filed into the hospital, the sun had set and an orderly had lighted the oil lamps hanging from the ceiling. Nathan and Blake lingered at the door. "We don't want to intrude," Nathan said. "You go on. We'll wait here."

"If you think it will settle her mind," Blake said to Garnet, "tell the missus I'll be praying for her."

Nathan saw the smile Garnet flashed at the private. "Thank you, sir."

Blake nodded and perched on a narrow bench outside the hospital ward door.

Garnet took Will's hand and led him toward the corner of the empty ward, to where the portable screens shielded Charlotte's bed from view. Nathan lingered in the doorway and saw Will stop at the foot of the bed and grab one of the iron rails and hang on.

"There's my boy," he heard Charlotte say. "Where'd you run off to? I've been worried about you."

Will's breath came in little jerks. Nathan could tell the boy was trying hard not to cry as he asked, "Does it hurt terrible?" He realized he was rubbing his own wrist as he listened.

"It hurts, baby," Charlotte said. "But not as much as it hurts to think you were afraid to come to Mama. We agreed you'd never be afraid to come to me. About anything. No matter what. You remember that?"

Will inhaled again and let out a raggedy moan. "I'm sor-sorry, Mama. I didn't mean—"

"Of course you didn't mean to hurt me, baby. Come here and hold my hand."

Will moved from the foot of the bed to his mother's side and out of sight. Nathan imagined him taking his mother's good hand. Remembering his own mother's last illness, he could imagine Will laying his head on his mother's shoulder, could almost feel her warm breath as she kissed the boy on his forehead or cheek. Feeling guilty for eavesdropping on the moment, he stepped away from the door and settled on the bench beside Private Blake.

The doctor's surgical assistant must have arrived then, as there were other voices, and finally he heard Will approach, his younger footsteps echoing on the hospital's bare board floor. Will appeared in the doorway, with Garnet at his side. From behind the screens, Charlotte called, "Make him eat, Garnet. I can hear his stomach rumbling from way over here."

When Will refused to go home to eat, no one fought him. He supposed they thought he'd eventually grow weary of waiting on the bench at the hospital. But sitting still was nothing new for Will Bishop. He'd spent so many hours being disciplined with "sit still," he'd practically made a study of chairs. There was the Windsor chair in Grandmother Bishop's formal dining room back in Michigan. It had a tilted slippery seat that made a boy feel like he was going to slide right onto the floor beneath the dining room table, something Will often wished he could do when he'd been told to "sit there until you eat every last pea on that plate."

His own bedroom at Grandmother Bishop's had a plain oak chair that he liked to draw up to the window overlooking the apple orchard. After being sent to his room for spilling his milk at dinner, Will could sit in that chair for hours, watching Shep, the groundkeeper's dog, snuffle in the grass and bark at garter snakes. In spite of the reason he knew the oak chair so well, Will liked it. Being in the chair meant he wasn't going to have to face his father's belt.

The kitchen at Grandmother's held a variety of chairs. Will's favorite had once been painted blue. It was scarred and nicked and a little wobbly, but it was higher than most chairs and sometimes Garnet let Will pull it up to the counter when she made pie crust. If there was any crust left over, she'd let him dust the pieces with cinnamon and sugar, and when they came out of the oven she gave them to Will along with a glass of milk. Those were the times when that old blue chair was Will's favorite place in the world.

There were other chairs in Will's life, too. The one he hated most was red mahogany. Its back was almost a semicircle, and when he sat on that chair in the entryway of Grandmother's grand old home he felt swallowed up, not only by the chair but also by life, because being ordered to wait in that chair meant facing Father the minute he came in the door. Waiting in that chair meant admitting to disobedience of one kind or another and having Father mete out punishment. For most children, waiting for their father was probably the worst part of the punishment. For Will, the waiting was only the beginning of sorrows.

Will's thoughts were brought back to the present situation when he heard Lieutenant Boone ask Private Blake to pray for his ma. Will had never heard anything like the big man's simple prayer. It was, Will decided later, as if God were a special kind of doctor and Private Blake's good friend; as if God stopped by and was right there with them, ready and able to help the minute the private asked. Will had never heard anyone address God the way Private Blake did. He thought people were supposed to grovel at God's feet and beg for what they wanted, and that sometimes God gave it but most of the time He didn't just to remind people that He was in charge. Will wasn't sure, but he thought Blake just might be making God angry, treating Him like he was a friend or something. He hoped God wouldn't hold it against his mother and mess up her surgery.

"Do you know how to play chess, son?" Lieutenant Boone asked as soon as they all said *amen*. When Will shook his head, Boone declared that to be a shame. He left for a few minutes, and when he returned he had a leather-covered box tucked under his arm that, when opened, proved to be a portable chess set that he positioned on another chair between himself and Will. As the night wore on, Boone explained the arrangement of the pieces to Will. When he came to the figure called a knight, Will looked up at him and asked abruptly, "How'd you get to be a soldier?"

Boone continued placing chess pieces on the board. "Well, I was a little older than you when my Uncle Billy visited my parents' farm in Missouri. He was on leave from his regiment in the War Between the States." Boone shook his head back and forth. "And the stories that man could tell. I thought every soldier in the army was a hero. It all seemed so grand. And when Uncle Billy walked down the street in our little town . . ." Boone chuckled. "Well, all the women noticed. I decided being in the army was the best thing a boy could do. We were poor, and when my pa died, my ma married a man I didn't like much. So I begged and begged until Uncle Billy got me signed on as drummer boy for his regiment." Boone sat back in his chair. "And I've been in the army ever since. Never wanted to do anything else." He moved the knight on the chessboard. "What about you, son? You plan to be a soldier when you grow up?"

Will shook his head from side to side. "Father told me I couldn't."

"Why not?"

"I'm too small. Too slow. I wouldn't be a good soldier."

"So what did your father think you should be?"

Will shrugged. "He never said. Just said I wouldn't be a good soldier. It made him mad sometimes." Picking up a pawn, he murmured, "He was a cavalry officer. Like you. First thing I remember about my father is him lifting me up on Buster. Buster was a really tall horse, and he didn't like me one bit. I remember him looking around at me and rolling his eyes and snorting. Then he bucked and I fell off. It scared me when he picked up one of his big feet. I thought he was going to step on me. Or bite me. Father laughed. When he went to put me back up on Buster, I cried. It made him mad." Will bit his lower lip. "I've sort of been afraid of horses since then."

Will pointed at the rook. "What's this one do?"

Boone went back to explaining how each piece could or could not move across the chessboard.

Will interrupted him. "You ever fight any Indians?"

Boone nodded.

Will drew his legs up and wrapped his arms around them, resting his chin on his knee. "Tell me about it."

Chapter Seven

A foolish son is a grief to his father,
and bitterness to her that bare him.
PROVERBS 17:25

HAMMERS POUNDING, VOICES SHOUTING, mules braying, wagon wheels grinding—the noise of construction at Fort Robinson reached Laina's ears long before she was ready to get up. Barely awake she snuggled against her husband and moaned, "What *is* that infernal noise?!"

Caleb spooned up behind her and kissed the back of her neck. "Progress, Mrs. Jackson. The sound of progress." He slid out of bed. "You stay put. I'll get you some coffee."

Laina closed her eyes, hoping for a few more minutes of sleep. But the baby was awake, too, rolling and kicking inside her, gleefully pummeling until she sat up to catch her breath.

Caleb came in with coffee. He reached over and covered her belly with his hand. "Whoa, in there," he said, leaning down to talk. "Give your Mama a rest, son. There's plenty of time to learn bull riding and wrestling later." He winked at his wife. "Want to take a walk with me?"

Laina nodded. "As soon as the coffee takes hold."

"I'll be in the kitchen," he said. "Mrs. Dubois made flapjacks!"

In the ten years since she and Caleb had married and started ranching, Laina had visited Fort Robinson often. She'd witnessed the beginnings of an entirely new collection of buildings around a larger parade ground to the west of the original fort. This morning, as she and Caleb and CJ made their way around the West End, they paused before one of the newly constructed barracks, a frame L-shaped building with a main living area across the front and a kitchen and dining room at the back. Caleb pointed east toward the old log barracks on the opposite side of the original parade ground. "It sure is a far cry from where I lived. Can you imagine . . . running water in the kitchen!"

"Why didn't they just tear down that awful old place?" CJ asked, nodding toward the old barracks.

Laina agreed. "It has to be filthy . . . and flea infested."

"Apparently several families claimed it right away," Caleb said. "They call it the Bee Hive now. You know how the army does things. If they haul their wife and children along, enlisted men are on their own to provide shelter."

CJ spoke up. "I'm glad *we* don't have to live any place like that!"

"Well, as a matter of fact," Caleb said, "that's where you'll be going to school."

"There better not be any *fleas*," CJ retorted.

"You just see to it you pay attention in class and learn a lot," her father said.

Caleb pointed toward what he said was the administration building. "They have hundreds of library books in the post library," Caleb said, "and some of the companies even have their own reading rooms now." He shook his head. "Quite a change since I was a new recruit." He pointed south toward Soapsuds Row where Laina had once lived. "Not much has changed over there though."

"Except the view out the back door," Laina pointed out. "Stables and corrals instead of wide open country."

They walked by a huge pile of adobe bricks. "I can see why they needed ten adobe mills," Laina commented.

Caleb nodded. "Frenchy's watched them plow up the clay. Says they found a good source about four miles away, and before all the building is finished, they will have made hundreds of thousands of bricks right here on the site. Their biggest problem—other than delays in shipping—has been finding enough labor." He nodded toward the east. "Crawford's booming, too. Once I get on a work crew here at the fort, maybe I'll be able to make connections in both places. Between the ready cash from working here *and* the future market for Four Pines beef here and in town, the Jackson family should do very well."

He leaned over and spoke to Laina's belly, "You hear that, son? And it's all for you and your brothers." They walked between a maze of barns and corrals and headed east toward where the post trader's store still occupied the northwest corner of the old fort grounds, now known as the "East End."

CJ grumbled. "It's going to drive us crazy having to listen to hammering all day every day."

"I knew things were going to change, but my goodness," Laina said, nodding toward the swarms of enlisted men and civilians clustered around the work sites, some laying foundation, others hammering siding or installing windows. Dust hung in the air from the continual passing of supply and water wagons. More dust was being kicked up on the new parade ground, where a company of black soldiers performed a mounted exercise to the shouted orders of a white sergeant. "It just doesn't look like the same place," she wondered aloud.

Frenchy Dubois, the soldier who had married a widowed Maude Gruber five years ago, appeared in the doorway to the trading post. He motioned to CJ, teasing, "Ooh-la-la, *ma petite,* I will keep ze rifle close by." When CJ looked confused, Frenchy raised an imaginary rifle to his shoulder and took aim. "To keep ze soldier boys away from the lovely young woman you are to become."

CJ made a face. "Boys? UGH!"

Frenchy shrugged. "You don' like boys? Is good! Soon enough you will be changing ze tune, *non?*" He motioned everyone inside, where Maude was piling flapjacks onto a platter.

"Come in," she said and pointed Caleb to the chair at the head of the table.

"Thanks very much, Mrs. Dubois," Caleb said, patting his stomach, "but I already ate more than my fill." He leaned down and kissed Laina on the cheek. "Enjoy the girl talk. I'll be back when I have a job." He left with Frenchy.

"How are you feeling dear?" Maude asked, patting Laina's shoulder.

"Like a spring cow ready to burst." Laina settled heavily into a chair. "Or at least how I imagine a spring cow feels right before the calf makes his appearance."

"Might be a she-calf," Maude observed.

"Oh, it's a boy," Laina said quickly.

"It had *better* be a boy," CJ agreed.

"Really?"

"Caleb ordered a boy," Laina said, grinning. She patted her belly. "And I think he'll get his wish. Carrying this one has been nothing like CJ. This little guy is three times as active and he's just settled in differently. Rachel says her mother always believed that if you carry the baby lower, it's a boy. I definitely think it's a boy."

Maude arched one eyebrow. "Well, Rachel can predict and Caleb Jackson can order up all the boys he wants, but I expect the good Lord will send what the good Lord will send, and Mr. Jackson will just have to adjust."

"Speaking of Rachel," Laina said, "where is she?"

"Already up front, filling her order. I told her to help herself and just leave me a list of what goes into the wagon headed for the ranch." Maude settled into a chair and stacked five flapjacks on the plate in front of her. "Now, ladies, let's thank the Lord and get down to business!"

———

Nathan Boone groaned when reveille sounded the morning after Charlotte Bishop's surgery. He'd fallen into bed three hours ago, but it felt like only ten minutes. He had sent Private Blake to his quarters shortly after the private offered up his prayer for Charlotte's welfare and young Will's peace of mind. Nathan found Blake's concern for the latter quite touching, and evidently Garnet Irvin did, too. Nathan had noticed the admiring glance she had cast in Blake's direction as the private exited the hospital and headed for the barracks.

Nathan had stayed on through the night, playing chess and telling stories until fatigue finally threatened to send Will Bishop face first into the chessboard. "Settle here beside me," Nathan had said, patting the place next to him on the bench. "I'll tell you about the first time Private Blake saved my hide." Will had come to sit next to him and was asleep and snoring softly in less than five minutes, his head lolling against Boone's shoulder.

Not long after Will fell asleep, Doctor Valentine came through the door to report that Charlotte's surgery was finished.

"We'll be bringing her into the ward in a few minutes," he said.

"Is she going to be all right?" Will had asked, rubbing his eyes as he spoke.

"How long ago was it that she broke her wrist the first time?" the doctor had asked his grandson.

Will pressed his lips together. "I was little," he said, looking down at the floor. "I don't remember exactly."

"Well," the doctor said, "bone has a good blood supply. It should heal up just fine. I was just curious."

"But you said it'll get infected," Will said.

"Maybe not," Garnet interrupted. "The Good Book says 'the effectual fervent prayer of a righteous man availeth much.' "

"You talking about Private Blake?" Will asked.

Garnet nodded, and then Nathan noticed how quickly she changed the subject. "I've got some beef tea for tomorrow. And I brought my bedroll over."

"I told Will to tell you I'd stay with her tonight," the doctor said.

"He told me," Garnet said. She turned toward the hospital ward door. "If you men will excuse me, I'll be unrolling my pallet." She looked up at the doctor. "You let me know if there's anything special I need to watch for." She interrupted the doctor's protest. "I can't answer this boy's questions. You can. As soon as the orderly comes by in the morning I'll go home and start breakfast for you two." She'd hurried away before the doctor could protest further.

"Well," he said, shaking his head and shrugging his shoulders. "I guess she told me." He looked down at Nathan and Will. "You wait here with Lieutenant Boone, and as soon as your mother is settled you can have a look, so you know she's all right. Then we'll go get some sleep." He rumpled Will's hair as he said, "One thing I've learned these past weeks is that Garnet Irvin's gentle and quiet facade camouflages a will of steel. It does no good to argue with her."

And so it was. The men retired, leaving Garnet to tend Charlotte through the night.

———

Nathan checked in at the hospital after assembly. Garnet reported the patient had slept well, then told Nathan that her main concern was for Will Bishop and how to keep him occupied and out of trouble until his mother was allowed to leave the hospital. "Doctor says it'll be a few days," Garnet worried aloud.

"I could take him over and introduce him to the Jacksons," Nathan offered. Quickly, he told Garnet about Laina and Caleb and their plans. "CJ is going to school while Mrs. Jackson stays here at the fort."

"Doc said he was going to see to it that Will goes to that school. They won't have him at the other one. Doc said he'd be taking Will over this morning to meet the teacher," Garnet explained.

Nathan nodded. "I'll just head over to the trading post and talk to the Jacksons. Laina would want to know about Charlotte's being in the hospital anyway."

Here I am again, Nathan thought as he headed for the trading post, *taking up my old ways of trying to fix things for everybody around me.* He smiled to himself, remembering how Granny Max used to scold him. *"Never saw a man so set on helping others and so set against helping himself,"* Granny used to say. *"You'll never be happy until you spend a little time on your own troubles. Get yourself right with God. Then you'll be even better at helping the rest of the world."* Granny had told him he was a good man . . . and then reminded him that the good he did would go to the grave with him until he joined what Granny called God's family.

As the sun tipped the distant bluffs with gold, Nathan remembered Granny's talk about gold. *"You need to think less about making it better for a little while here below and more about making things better for time and all eternity, Nathan Boone. All the good you do is only so much wood and hay and stubble unless it is done for the glory of God. And you can guess what happens to wood, hay, and stubble when the refining fire of the Lord God descends upon it. You're a good man, Nathan Boone. I want to see you build with gold and precious stones . . . send things on ahead and know it will last for eternity."*

Nathan paused beside the trading post and looked toward the new West End. He could almost hear Granny Max calling him back to the same questions, the same answers, the same God. As he headed for the front door, he shook his head. Returning to Fort Robinson was surely bringing things to mind he had not thought about for a long, long time.

"Sorry to be so early, Mrs. Dubois." Nathan removed his hat just inside the trading post and called out. From the sounds of things, she was packing canned goods into a crate. He could hear the *thunk* of the cans being stacked, one on top of the other. "I was hoping to talk to—" In one instant Nathan saw the woman, took in the river of dark hair flowing over her shoulders, the huge dark brown eyes and flawless skin. In the next he recognized her.

"Hello there, Rachel," he said.

"Lieutenant Boone," Rachel Greyfoot replied. "You were looking for Mrs. Dubois." She turned sideways and pointed through the doorway. "In the kitchen. With Mrs. Jackson and CJ."

"Who's there?" Maude's voice called from the back of the trading post.

Rachel stepped to the doorway and called out Nathan's name.

"Come on back, Lieutenant," Maude called.

Rachel stepped aside. She smiled up at him.

Nathan smiled back. "Mrs. Jackson told me you were here when I saw her up at the cemetery yesterday. She said you're headed back to the ranch?"

"This morning," Rachel said. "As soon as we get supplies loaded up."

"For roundup," Nathan said.

Rachel nodded.

"You drive the chuck wagon, as I recall."

"Not this year."

"Oh, right . . . I forgot. Mrs. Jackson told me. You and Jack . . ." Nathan paused. "How *is* Jack?"

"Taller than his brother was. Healthy as a horse, as they say." She smiled up at him. "Thanks to you."

Nathan shrugged, "You both deserved a chance."

"You went to a lot of work to see that we had that chance," Rachel said. "We owe you much. Jack feels the same way."

"Well, you tell Jack that next time I visit the ranch, I'll consider the debt paid if he refrains from making fun of my attempts to be a cowboy."

Rachel laughed softly. "I'll tell him." She turned back toward the storeroom.

Nathan headed up the hall. He joined Laina, Maude, and CJ in the kitchen. He told them about Charlotte's accident, then left for target practice out on the firing range. He was halfway through the morning before he realized he had been thinking entirely too much about Rachel Greyfoot. He had, in fact, forgotten to tell the ladies that Will Bishop would probably be going to the same school as CJ.

———

Early that same Monday afternoon, a teary Laina clung to Caleb just before he climbed aboard the wagon that would take Rachel and him back to the ranch for roundup. "Now, don't cry, sweetheart," he whispered. "I won't be gone that long and you know this is for the best." He patted her belly. "I don't want us taking any chances—with you or our baby boy."

"There's a perfectly good midwife up on Hat Creek," Laina said, sniffing.

"And there's an even better doctor right here at Fort Robinson."

"I know, I know," Laina said. She closed her eyes and put her cheek next to Caleb's, inhaling deeply. She rubbed her cheek against his beard and fought back tears. "I'm sorry. But I'll miss you."

Caleb lifted her chin and looked down into her eyes. "I'll miss you, too, honey-lamb. It won't be long and you'll be in my arms again. Now give me a kiss and let me go before CJ throws up. She's watching."

Laina glanced over Caleb's shoulder to where CJ stood beside the wagon, trying not to watch her parents' display of affection. "She's really not very happy with you."

Caleb sighed. "She'll get over it." He tipped his head so he could see around Laina. "Hey, girl. Cheer up. You might like school."

"And those horses just might sprout wings and fly home," was the answer.

"Watch your tone, young lady," Caleb said, a little more sternly.

"Yes, sir. I'm sorry."

Caleb nodded. He tapped the tip of Laina's nose and winked at her. "It's going to be all right, honey-lamb. I'll miss you. Shoot, I already miss you."

"Go," Laina said. She pulled away. "I'm being silly. Go." She called to Rachel, "Thank you in advance for everything you are doing for us. I don't know how we'd manage without you."

"You are welcome, Mrs. Jackson," Rachel replied.

Laina watched the wagon until it disappeared in the distance.

The next thing she knew, Maude Dubois was leading her back inside the trading post for tea. Once the two women were settled at the table, Maude smiled and said, "I know it's hard to watch him go, dear, but be thankful you have such a hard-working husband. Many women aren't so blessed."

"You're right," Laina said. She sighed. "He has such dreams. He's even been talking about changing the name of the Four Pines. Drawing up a new brand."

"Really?"

Laina nodded. "Wants something that says Jackson & *Sons*."

"*Sons*—plural?" Maude asked.

Laina nodded.

"A little ahead of himself, ain't he?" Maude asked. "Or do you expect this is twins?"

Laina shook her head. Her expression softened. "All I expect is the Lord's blessing on a precious new life. Ten years is a long time to wait for a baby."

"Don't I know it, child." Maude raised her teacup in a mock toast. "One of my friends waited *eleven* and then had one a year for five years. So you just watch out, Laina Jackson. The Lord may be fixin' to rain babies on that ranch of yours!"

"Showers of blessings," Laina said and laughed, raising her open palms toward the ceiling. "Let it rain!"

"Amen," Maude agreed. She set her teacup down and lowered her voice. "You know, dear, you're not the only woman at Fort Robinson needing the Lord's blessing on her child. The news about Charlotte Valentine doesn't bode well for her son." Maude clucked her tongue and shook her head from side to side.

"What do you mean?"

"Well, the Widow Bishop is an odd bird to begin with." Maude seemed to anticipate Laina's response. "I know, I know, dear. You're not one to gossip. I'm not carrying tales. And I'm not holding grudges from the past, either. Charlotte's been back at Fort Robinson for nearly a month, and she hasn't made a single call. She's declined three invitations to tea. And although she's apparently quite the horsewoman, she doesn't go riding with the ladies. And I can tell you her reclusive behavior hasn't set well with the women here. And that boy of hers!"

"What about him?"

"The most mischievous troublemaker I've ever had the displeasure to know. Tormenting dogs, pouring salt in punch. I've never seen the like of such pranks." She shook her head from side to side. "No wonder Charlotte came back here to stay with her father." Maude lowered her voice, "In fact, although Lieutenant Boone didn't say so, I wouldn't be surprised if the little rascal didn't have something to do with his mother's broken wrist."

Chapter Eight

A man that hath friends must shew himself friendly.
PROVERBS 18:24

"MISS JACKSON."

CJ closed her eyes and pressed her lips firmly together, barely avoiding making a face. "Yes, *Mr.* Phelps," she replied, exactly copying the teacher's exasperated tone. The boy behind her uttered a half cough, half laugh of approval.

Mr. Phelps took a deep breath and put on a disapproving expression. "I realize, Miss Jackson, that you have come late to school—"

"I wasn't late," CJ interrupted. "I was here before you today. Remember? I was waiting outside the door when—"

"That's *not* what I meant," the teacher snapped. "I was referring to your being *unschooled*."

CJ frowned. "I haven't been unschooled. My ma's been teaching me at home. She's a good teacher and don't you say she isn't!"

"There's no reason for you to be impertinent, young lady," the schoolteacher said.

"And there's no reason for you to say my ma isn't a good teacher," CJ replied.

Mr. Phelps sighed deeply and pointed to the corner. "You may occupy the seat of honor until you have learned to respect your elders," he said.

CJ stood up slowly. Head held high, she marched to the corner, climbed onto the waiting stool, and sat facing the class.

Mr. Phelps smirked, lifting his right hand and making a circling motion with his index finger. CJ turned around, relieved to be facing away from the class full of strangers.

Since CJ's arrival at school, every last one of the fifteen students seemed to have entered into the game of "Make the New Girl Miserable." Even

Will Bishop, who wasn't even supposed to *be* at this school and was new himself, seemed to enjoy tormenting her. Ma had said there was a separate school for the officers' children. But CJ had also heard Mrs. Dubois telling Ma how Mrs. Bishop's son had been kicked out of that school. The teacher wouldn't teach Will, even though, as far as CJ could tell, he was plenty smart. Well, she could wonder about that while she stared at the corner. Time might go more slowly, but at least no one would see her cheeks flaming red with embarrassment. And no one would see her eyes fill with tears. They might think she was sad when really she was mad. CJ tended to cry when she got really, really mad. Ma was going to be angry when she heard about this. Ma didn't take disobedience lightly. And she'd been cross ever since Pa had gone back to the ranch to get things ready for spring roundup.

After an hour of sitting on the backless stool in the schoolroom corner, CJ's legs began to feel all tingly. Her back hurt. Mr. Phelps was lecturing in a droning monotone. CJ dozed off and jerked herself awake just in time to keep from falling off the stool. Several of the girls tittered with laughter. Mr. Phelps put his hand on her shoulder, pressing on a spot with his thumb until pain shot up the back of her neck. He said something about "helping her to stay awake." She mentally transported herself to the ranch, counting off the horses by name, wondering if Jack had convinced the gelding she called Rebel to eat grain out of his hand yet, if he had managed to saddle him yet, and if Rebel would really be ready to be ridden when CJ finally got to go home.

CJ tore off a piece of beef jerky and chewed it slowly, trying to shut out the sound of laughter wafting through the schoolroom window. Of course, she told herself, the girls weren't laughing at *her*. She hadn't dozed off again all morning. The girls were just having fun while they ate their lunches. They were probably talking about something else besides her. And even if she *was* allowed off this stool, it's not like they would have included her in the fun anyway.

At least half the day was gone. Maybe Mr. Phelps would let her out of the corner. Maybe, she thought, he'd sprout wings and fly back east where he belonged. It sure was obvious to Clara Joy Jackson that Phineas Phelps (she took silent pleasure in refusing to call him "Mr. Phelps" in her mind) didn't know much about teaching. And he thought he was so much better than Ma. CJ bet Phineas Phelps couldn't say one word if Frenchy Dubois started talking French. But her Ma could. She'd heard her. So who was Phineas Phelps to call her *unschooled*? Who did he think he was, anyway.

CJ could read as well as any student in the class. And what if her cipher-ing was a little behind? What did a girl need with ciphering anyway? It wasn't like she was going to run a ranch someday like her pa and have to keep track of market prices and such. All the ciphering she would ever need would be for shopping at the trading post, and didn't she already know how to do that? Calico was eight cents a yard, and she knew her times tables just fine. No shopkeeper would ever be able to cheat her.

CJ had closed her eyes and was gesturing in a mock argument with some future store owner who'd just overcharged her for calico when she heard the school door creak. She opened her eyes in time to see one of her classmates walking toward her with a dipper full of water. She held up her hands, "Don't you dare think you can throw that on me and not get pounded," she said, and held up her fists.

"I don't think any such thing," the boy said. "I'm bringing you a drink."

"*You* drink it!" CJ said. "I don't need Mr. Phelps trying to be nice, send-ing you in here after he made fun of my ma."

"Mr. Phelps doesn't know anything about this. He went over to the canteen for something," the boy said. He held out the dipper. "I spent plenty of hours on stools and chairs. A body gets thirsty. Phelps doesn't care."

CJ narrowed her gaze and sized up the boy. "Why do you want to be nice to me? Nobody else does. I've heard what they say about me. Like they're better'n me." She looked at the dipper full of water. "Well they aren't."

"You gonna drink this or not?" he said.

"You afraid you'll have to sit in the corner with the ranch girl if you get caught?"

"I'm not afraid of anything," the boy said. "If you don't want a drink then say so, and I'll go back outside." He shrugged. "It's not like they want to have anything to do with me, either. I'm supposed to be in school with the *officers'* brats."

CJ grabbed the dipper and drank the water down. It was lukewarm, but it slaked her tremendous thirst.

"Why don't you go to that other school? When my pa tells stories about the army he always says the officers and their families don't have much to do with the enlisted men and the civilians."

"It doesn't matter who my father was. They don't want me at that school anymore," the boy said, grinning wickedly. "They can't handle me."

"Exactly *what* do you think you are *doing*, Master Bishop?" Mr. Phelps must have been lurking in the narrow space just inside the door where they hung their coats. Looking over the boy's shoulder to where Phelps was standing made CJ dread what was coming. She didn't need to hear his voice to know the teacher was angry. His closed mouth was pinched shut so tightly it looked like he had deep wrinkles turned downward from the corners. It had taken CJ exactly one hour in the schoolroom to learn to fear that expression. She gripped the edges of the stool with both hands and waited.

The boy looked around. "It's not right to make her sit up there all during lunch. And it's not right for her to go thirsty. My grandfather says a man can go without food, but you take away water and he'll die. Fast."

"Miss Jackson is in no danger of dying for lack of water," the teacher sneered. "But since you are so concerned for her well-being, you may sit next to her this afternoon. You'll be much more able to monitor her condition. Be certain you inform me if you think she needs medical attention. After all, with your grandfather being a *doctor,* I imagine that qualifies you much more than the adults around you to judge these matters."

———

At the end of the day, schoolmaster Phelps delivered his well-practiced sermonette on the dangers of showing disrespect to your elders. While his teacher droned on, Will let his eyes wander to the corner of a window where a leggy white spider was scurrying up and down a slender thread, attaching more and more threads, weaving them all together in a busy dance. While Phelps talked, Will inched closer to the window. He might have learned his lesson about pranks that made adults fall down, but that didn't mean he wasn't still Will Bishop.

"Do I make myself clear, Master Bishop?" Phelps cleared his throat loudly. His arms were crossed in front of him, his toe tapping the floor.

"Yes, sir," Will said quickly. "Very clear, sir."

"Very well, then." He turned to CJ. "In light of the fact that you are in a new situation, Miss Jackson, I shall refrain from speaking to your parents about today's difficulties. But let us agree that such a display of disrespect will not happen again, shall we?"

"Oh, yes, sir," CJ said. "I won't hold it against you. You haven't even *met* my ma."

Phelps's eyes opened wide along with his mouth. With a sound of exasperation he scooped the geography book up off his desk and turned to go. He paused at the door. "Before you two leave today, I want the floor swept and the stove polished." He sniffed. "I'd stay to be certain you do it correctly, but I have an appointment. If it isn't done to my satisfaction," he said, looking back at the two children, "you'll both be taken *to your mothers* first thing in the morning." He swept out of the room, like a dictator who held life and death in his hands.

As soon as Phelps was gone, Will turned around and destroyed the spider web.

"What'd you do *that* for?" CJ said. She looked down at the window ledge where the spider had landed. "Now she has to start her web all over again."

Will looked at the girl in disbelief. He had been watching that spider all day and had devised a plan involving the brown-eyed girl who had crossed her eyes and stuck out her tongue at him. Her name was Molly Plummer, and Will hated the way she smirked when he pretended he didn't know an answer to one of Mr. Phelps's stupid questions. Of *course* he knew when the Battle of Vicksburg was fought. Of *course* he could name the states on the eastern seaboard. But right answers were boring because they were too easy. Will loved the entertainment of confounding the teacher. But snobbish Molly Plummer didn't get it, and Will had decided the spider was just the thing to get her attention. Everybody knew girls were afraid of spiders.

"I said," CJ was repeating, "What'd you do *that* for?" She was standing at the door with a broom in hand. When Will didn't answer, she shrugged. "I'll sweep. You polish the stove."

"I'm not polishing any stove," Will said.

CJ held out the broom.

"I'm not doing *anything* for Phelps."

"I'm not doing it for *him*," CJ said. "I'm doing it so he won't bother my ma." She began to sweep.

"You're afraid of your *ma*?"

"No," Clara Joy shook her head. "She's going to have a baby soon. My pa made her stay here at the fort so she'd have a doctor. She's homesick. I don't want to make her any sadder." She shrugged. "Some things just aren't worth getting into more trouble for." She sneezed and rubbed her nose with the back of her hand. "Besides, this floor *does* need to be swept!"

Will watched the girl for a minute. She kept working. Going to the the back of the room, he took a rag from a bucket on the teacher's supply shelf and began rubbing the stove top.

"You wanna come with me to the stables?" Will asked CJ as he put the finishing touches on the once filthy stove. "Lieutenant Boone is going to let me groom his horse. He's been showing me things about horses."

"What's there to show? Everybody knows about horses."

"Well I don't," Will snapped. "We had servants who did everything back home. Ma was going to let me ride Isaac—that was her horse—but then my grandmother decided to sell him. My Father's horses were half-wild stallions and they liked to eat people for breakfast. My father was the only one who could handle them, but he didn't have time to show me and then he died."

CJ frowned. "I don't know what kind of army your father was in," she said matter-of-factly. "But the United States Army doesn't let their soldiers ride wild stallions. And horses don't eat people—although we have a horse at home that has a nasty habit of biting. Jack's going to cure him of that. And when I get back home, I'm going to ride him."

"You can't ride any horse that likes to bite people," Will said.

"Well, when I ride Rebel all the way back here and come up to your back door, I'll guess you'll know I can! Just because *you're* afraid of horses doesn't mean I am!"

"Who told you I'm afraid?"

CJ pointed to Will's clenched fists. Her voice gentled. "It's all right. If your father's horses were mean, I bet you just haven't had a chance to know any good ones. You should meet my horse back at home. Pappy doesn't have a wild bone in his raggedy old body." She smiled. "I bet Lieutenant Boone has a great horse, too." She added, "*I* don't care if you're a little afraid of horses. Even if you are, it's just 'cause you haven't learned. Like you said, you didn't have a chance to learn before your pa died." She saw Will's fists relax a little. "It's funny," she said.

"What's funny?"

"Well, your pa was mad because you were afraid of horses, and my pa gets mad because I'm not. He caught me in Rebel's stall once and nearly tanned my hide good."

"Lieutenant Boone says it's dangerous to get in a stall with a half-wild horse."

"Well of course it is," CJ agreed. "But Rebel isn't half-wild. He's just afraid."

"Afraid or wild, I don't see it makes any difference. They can still smash you good."

"Rebel doesn't want to smash anybody," CJ said. "He just has to learn to trust people." Her face brightened. "And Jack's going to teach him that."

"Who's Jack?"

"He's a Cheyenne Indian who lives on the ranch. He came there with Rachel. Rachel was married to Jack's brother, but he got killed. Jack and Rachel have been there ever since I can remember." CJ leaned close. "You want to know a secret?"

Will looked at her from beneath furrowed brows. "What secret?"

CJ moved closer to him and whispered, "I'm going to marry Jack."

Will jerked his head back and looked at her in disbelief. "Go on," he said. "You're not going to do any such thing."

"I am, too."

"Why'd you want to go and marry an *Indian*?" Will went on to expound his vast knowledge of Indians gleaned from stories told by a father who'd never met one he didn't want to shoot.

"I don't know what Indians you're talking about," CJ said, "but Jack and Rachel aren't anything like that. Rachel cooks the best flapjacks ever and Jack knows everything about horses." She smiled. "Maybe you can come visit. And we could go riding together."

"My ma won't hardly let me go across the parade ground by myself," Will said. "She's not gonna let me go off to some ranch where there's Indians." He stuffed his hands in his pockets. "I gotta go. Lieutenant Boone's probably wondering where I am. You coming or not?"

Chapter Nine

Use hospitality one to another without grudging.
I Peter 4:9

FOR A LONG WHILE Charlotte wasn't sure which of the flashes in her mind were reality and which were dreams. Eventually she realized she was drifting in and out of consciousness. The hospital ward was real, as were the screens around her bed . . . Will's terrified eyes . . . her father's voice. She wasn't certain about *all* the voices. She recognized Garnet's. And Lieutenant Boone's. But there was another one she didn't know. The other surgeon, probably. Did she really hear praying? She was too tired to open her eyes, too tired to be polite to strangers, too tired to care. The only constants in all the swirling of impressions to Charlotte's brain were the throbbing pain on the left side of her body and Garnet Irvin's voice. Sometimes she would wake and Garnet would be sitting next to the bed in the simple pine chair, her head bowed over a book.

When Charlotte finally jerked awake to full consciousness and looked around, she wondered exactly how much time had passed. It was a sunny day outside. Garnet was seated beside the hospital bed, her hair bound up in a bright yellow kerchief, her head tilted back against the wall. She was napping with her mouth slightly open.

Charlotte lay still for a few moments, remembering and reciting to herself. She'd been taking coffee and pie out onto the porch to her father and Lieutenant Boone . . . and then Will . . .

Looking out the window, Charlotte wondered about Will. Where was he? She hoped her father had forgiven the boy this infraction. She hoped he had talked Mr. Phelps into taking Will into the school that met over at the Bee Hive. If only that teacher could handle him. She was almost glad Will had been evicted from the school attended by the officers' children.

Perhaps seeing how hard life could be for the enlisted men and civilians would be a good thing. She did not want her son to become a soldier.

It must be afternoon. There were no orders being barked, no drills ongoing at the parade ground—at least not as far as she could tell. In the short time since she had been at the fort, she'd grown accustomed to the incessant noise of construction and could ignore it, just as she'd learned to ignore the passing of a carriage or a stagecoach in Michigan.

She lifted her head to look down at her wrist. It was so heavily bandaged it looked nearly twice its normal size. Glass tubes protruded from the bandage. She knew those were meant to drain pus away from the wound, but there was no sign of infection or drainage and the bandage was clean. That was good—surprising, given the circumstances of her accident, but good. Maybe she could talk Garnet into taking her home. She tried to sit up. Her head swam only a little. Then pain shot up her arm, across her shoulder and up the back of her neck. She gasped and Garnet sprang awake.

"What day is it?" Charlotte wanted to know.

"It's Saturday, missus," Garnet said, rising to help Charlotte sit up.

"And I fell on Monday." She frowned. "I've been unconscious all that time?"

Garnet nodded. "Mostly. But you're doing so fine you're nearly a miracle. That's what the doctor says, anyhow."

Charlotte looked down at the bandage. She pointed at one of the glass tubes. "There's no drainage."

"There was a little at first. But nothing like what you'd expect. It's going to be a while healing, and you might have some trouble with stiffness, but they say you'll be fine." Garnet plumped a pillow and tucked it behind Charlotte's head. "No infection, missus. There's no explanation for it except the good Lord took a hand in the healing." Garnet poured Charlotte a glass of water from the white pitcher at her bedside. As she handed over the glass, she said, "Private Blake came that first night. He said a fine prayer."

"Private Blake?"

Garnet nodded. She covered her mouth with her hand, but Charlotte could see the smile in her eyes. "Yes, ma'am. A big hulk of a soldier that came hauling Will home the night you got hurt. He found Will over in Troop F stables. Scared him silly, I guess, before hauling him home. Will seems to have taken to him." Garnet turned aside and rummaged in a basket while she talked. "Then there was a preacher stopped by. You remember him at all?"

Charlotte shook her head.

"He asked the Lord to heal you. Spent a good while praying over it. Dr. Valentine knew him. Said he's been riding the circuit out this way for as long as anyone can remember." Garnet nodded. "I'd say between Private Blake and the Reverend, the Almighty just had to answer *yes*."

"How is Will?"

"The day after you fell, doctor took him over to the barracks school and handed him over to Mr. Phelps, just like you wanted. Lieutenant Boone and Private Blake have had him with them in the stables every day after school. He's keeping busy and out of mischief for the most part. He seems to be getting acquainted with one of the older horses. Name of Bones. Will talks about Bones like he was almost as important as his new best friend, CJ."

Before Charlotte could ask who CJ was, Garnet leaned close, hairbrush in hand. "You got company," she whispered, nodding toward the door.

"I don't want—" Charlotte started to protest, but then she heard a woman's voice from halfway down the hospital ward.

"I promise not to stay but a few minutes." Laina Jackson stepped between the screens at the foot of the bed. "We rode in from the ranch the same day you fell," she explained. "Nathan Boone told us about your accident the morning after it happened. But you've been too sick for visitors."

"I . . . I didn't think you were living here at Fort Robinson," Charlotte said. *No, that's not right. She told you. Something about a ranch.* She rubbed her forehead with the back of her good hand and tried to focus on what Laina Jackson was saying.

Laina talked more slowly. "We've got a ranch up on Soldier Creek." She turned sideways, emphasizing her pregnant belly. "Caleb got it in his head I should be here where your father could take care of me when the baby comes. So CJ and I are staying over at the trading post with Maude and Frenchy."

"CJ?" Charlotte feigned interest, all the while thinking how tired she was and how she wished Garnet would step in and make Laina leave.

"Clara Joy has decided she'd rather be called CJ." Laina smiled. "She's quite put out with God for making her a girl. Much prefers the open range to the kitchen. Chooses riding over stitching every time."

Invite her to sit down. Charlotte knew it was only polite, but she was having trouble staying awake. She should introduce Garnet.

Laina raised her hand to the left side of her head and tucked a ringlet of auburn hair behind her ear. "It's good to see you doing so well," she said. "I'm sorry about your husband. And your mother. Goodness but you've had to deal with a lot since we parted ways all those years ago. I know your father must be so pleased to have you back under his roof. And having Will around will keep him young."

Charlotte nodded, wearied by the litany of condolences.

"I don't want to wear you out, Charlotte. I just wanted you to know I'm praying for quick healing. And I'm grateful for your son, Will."

Charlotte roused. "Will?"

Laina nodded. "You've raised a good boy."

"Will?" Charlotte repeated, inwardly telling herself not to sound so surprised.

"Yes, *Will*," Laina nodded, emphasizing the name. "Of course we put CJ in school. We both agreed she should take advantage of the opportunity, even if I'm only here at Fort Rob for a few weeks." She paused. "At any rate, she can be quite a handful—as the young schoolmaster has discovered. And she doesn't have the gift of . . . tact. Mr. Phelps took things a bit far in the discipline department the other day, but . . . well . . ." Laina smiled. "Will was very sweet. Stood up for CJ. You should be very proud of him." She patted Charlotte's hand. "And now I really do need to let you rest. As I said, I'll be praying for quick healing."

Charlotte listened to Laina's departing footsteps echo through the empty hospital ward. She had been in the hospital for five days. How quickly life could change.

Laina and Caleb Jackson were staying at Fort Robinson. *Caleb Jackson.* Memories of a morning long ago when a young and foolish girl named Charlotte Valentine had nearly been compromised by an even more foolish Caleb Jackson flashed in her mind. *The last person on earth I want to see again is Caleb Jackson.* If she was lucky, Laina would feel she'd done her duty with this one visit.

But Will was apparently becoming friends with the Jacksons' daughter. *Laina Jackson thinks my son is sweet?* Charlotte wondered what kind of miracle that had taken.

And Garnet had mentioned that Will was spending time with Nathan Boone. Charlotte didn't know how she felt about that. She'd hoped that getting away from Bishop House would provide a positive male influence for Will. But she'd only thought in terms of her father. What would people think about Lieutenant Boone's calling at the surgeon's residence? *I am so tired of ordering my life to please other people.*

Most puzzling of all was that Garnet Irvin obviously thought more of Private Carter Blake than she was letting on. Charlotte planned to look into that. As soon as she felt better.

"Ma! Guess what! Lieutenant Boone is going to let me *ride* Bones tomorrow."

Will had been walking at the lieutenant's side as the two crossed the parade ground in the direction of the house, but as soon as he caught sight of her in the rocking chair on the porch, he ran the rest of the distance between them and blurted out the announcement.

When Boone caught up, he leaned toward Charlotte and muttered under his breath, "Bones is ancient and half lame. Don't worry."

"So will you come watch me?" Will asked as he stopped to catch his breath.

"Perhaps you can ride over here from the stables and show off to your mother," her father interrupted. He leaned back in his chair next to Charlotte's and drew on his pipe. "She's just out of hospital, and she really shouldn't—"

"Please, Papa," Charlotte said wearily, "I feel fine."

"You need your rest," the doctor insisted.

Charlotte grumbled, "It's been two weeks, Papa. If I rest any more I am going to *decompose!*" She smiled at Will. "*Of course* I'll come watch you."

"We'll be in the corral behind the first set of barracks to the east," Lieutenant Boone said. "What if I send one of the men over to pick you up?"

" . . . and then I'll walk home," Charlotte said. She looked at her father. "You said walking would be good for me. You've been talking about a 'daily constitutional' of fresh air."

"All right," the doctor grumbled. "But you take Garnet along. And use your sling."

"Hey," Will said. "You didn't have to come."

CJ climbed onto the lower rung of the corral and rested her chin on her arms. "Wouldn't miss it," she said. "Where's your ma?"

"Coming directly. Lieutenant Boone sent Private Blake to fetch her in a carriage. My Grandfather thought it was too far for her to walk both ways. How's *your* ma?"

"Grumpy," CJ replied, shrugging.

"They get that way right before a baby," Will said. "At least my ma always did." He kept brushing Bones while he talked. "She had three babies after me. I was little, but I remember enough to know Ma was real short-tempered. Every time." Before CJ could ask, he said quickly, "They died."

"*All* of 'em?" CJ wanted to know.

Will nodded, picking at an imaginary tangle in the horse's mane.

"That's awful," CJ said. She frowned. "She must have been *real* sad."

Will shrugged. "She was sad a lot when we lived with Grandmother. But she only got the 'angries' when her belly got big like your Ma's." He pondered. "Grandmother made her sit in the parlor with her feet up and do needlework."

"What's so bad about that?" CJ wanted to know.

"My ma *hates* to sew," Will said.

"My ma seems to hate just about everything right now," CJ said. "She's got what you call the 'angries' most of the time."

"That probably means the baby will be here soon," Will commiserated. "Things will get better."

"I'll say," CJ agreed. "We'll get to go *home*." She stared off into the distance. "I can't believe I'm missing roundup for *school*. With *Phineas Phelps*."

"What's so bad about missing roundup?" Will wanted to know.

"You're kidding, right?"

Will shook his head. For the next few minutes, CJ regaled him with stories about spring roundup, ending with, "And if you want a different horse from Bones, then you should get your ma to let you come out to the ranch, 'cause there'll be all kinds of Indian ponies out there. You could have your pick. Most of our horses only cost thirty-five or forty dollars."

"I wouldn't know the first thing about picking out a horse," Will said. "And we don't have that kind of money anyway. Not since my pa died. And besides that my ma would never let me go. The only time she ever let me go anywhere without her was the first time she broke her wrist. My pa sent me to stay with some friends while he took care of her himself. He said she needed peace and quiet. Wouldn't let anybody else near her—except Garnet—for a long time." Will pondered, "Since then Ma's kept me real close. Like she's always worried something awful is going to happen."

"Mothers are just like that," CJ said.

"Yeah. That's what Private Blake says, too. Mothers are like that." He chewed on his lower lip. "But I sure would like to see roundup on a real ranch."

"So," CJ explained to Laina over dinner. "Will did great today. Even his ma said he's getting good at riding. And when school gets out in June, he won't have anything to do. And since Pa's coming to work at the fort after roundup, I was thinking maybe Will could come to the ranch and help us out. He said he'd really like to."

Laina closed her eyes and sighed wearily. "I don't know, CJ. You'll need to talk that over with your father. I don't know how Jack and Mr. Dorsey would feel about having a boy to keep track of. Especially one who grew up in town. And I don't know that Mrs. Bishop would be at all eager to let her only son go off with strangers."

"We *aren't* strangers," CJ said. "Will's my best friend. And you and Will's mother aren't strangers, either."

"Don't argue with me, young lady," Laina snapped. "I said you will have to talk to your father about it."

"He won't care. He wants a passel of boys. Will's a boy."

"It's not the same thing."

"But—"

"I said you will have to talk to your father. Mrs. Bishop and I are not strangers, but neither are we friends. And as I said, I doubt she will be enthusiastic about being separated from her only child."

"We could invite her to the ranch, too," CJ said.

Laina closed her eyes and shook her head from side to side.

"Well," CJ repeated. "We could. Will says his mother loves to ride. Will says she's been sad since she came to Fort Robinson. Maybe she'd feel better if she visited us for a while. She could ride and—"

"*No*," Laina said. "Not now. Maybe later in the summer. There's just too much going on right now with a baby on the way and your father planning to come back to the fort to work all summer. It's just not a good time for us to have guests."

"I thought you said God wants us to take care of whoever comes to our door," CJ protested. "At least that's what you said when the preacher started showing up and staying for a week every spring and again in the winter. You said God gave us a nice home and we should share it with people. You said that's how Rachel and Jack and Mr. Dorsey came to stay with us. And that we should never turn people away from our door. That God expected us to show kindness to strangers 'cause they might be angels."

"Mrs. Bishop and her son have a good home here at Fort Robinson," Laina said.

"They *don't*. Will *hates* it here. And he says his ma is sad all the time. The other kids treat him awful, and he—"

"That's enough, young lady," Laina said. She shook a finger at CJ. "I've told you to talk to your father about this. And I don't want to hear any more about it."

"You don't want to hear anything about anything," CJ said, and huffed out the door. When she heard her mother call her name, she ignored it, darted across the trail, around the corner of the commanding officer's headquarters, and thus out of sight in case her mother should come to the door and call for her . . . which, CJ grumbled to herself, she doubted her mother would have the energy to do.

"Babies!" she huffed to herself. "If having 'em makes everybody so miserable, I don't know why they bother."

Chapter Ten

And be ye kind one to another, tenderhearted, forgiving one another, even as God for Christ's sake hath forgiven you.

EPHESIANS 4:32

"LAND SAKES, CJ," Laina fumed. "Does every other word out of your mouth have to be *Will Bishop*? You didn't even know the boy two weeks ago, and now you can't seem to take a breath without him." Laina pushed herself upright with a grunt and scooted back against the headboard of the bed where she had been trying to take a nap.

"I thought you'd be *glad* I have a friend," CJ said. "You said you wanted me to make friends at school."

"I was hoping you'd meet a young lady."

CJ made a face. "Can I go or not?"

"Tell me again where you're going."

CJ sighed deeply. "For a *ride*. Lieutenant Boone is going to take Mrs. Bishop for a carriage ride, and he said Will and me can ride Bones alongside the carriage." She added, "Will doesn't believe I can ride as good as I can." She smiled hopefully, "Maybe you could come, too."

Laina shook her head. "I wasn't invited. And besides, a bumpy carriage ride is the last thing in the world I need right now," she said. "Do you have any schoolwork to do?"

"I'll do it later. It's not much. *Please*, Ma. I haven't gotten to ride since we've been at Fort Robinson. *Please*." CJ went on to expound on Charlotte Bishop's recovery and Will's newfound interest in horses with more details than Laina's weary brain wanted to process.

Laina held up her hand. "All right, CJ, all right. Go. But be careful and—"

CJ disappeared, calling out a thank-you from the trading post kitchen. The door slammed, and with Maude Dubois working up front in the trading post, a welcome silence reigned. Laina closed her eyes. She tried to settle back into her nap, but could not get comfortable.

My back hurts, my knees hurt, I can hardly breathe, I'm sick of making trips to the outhouse in the middle of the night, I'm tired of waiting for the baby, and . . . Laina's eyes teared up. *I miss Caleb.* She sniffed. The walls in the tiny room seemed to move in closer. The baby rolled up against her midsection, pushing so hard she gasped for breath.

Get hold of yourself, Laina. Maybe you should have followed CJ's suggestion about that carriage ride. You know Nathan won't mind.

But the last thing Laina wanted to do was try to befriend Charlotte Bishop. *I've done my duty, Lord. I visited her in the hospital. She's doing fine. Good heavens, she's out for a carriage ride. And Maude said she doesn't socialize much, anyway. She probably wouldn't even want a visit from a ranch wife. I'm hardly the kind of person she is used to associating with.*

Remembering how a young Charlotte Valentine had ordered her around years ago when Laina worked as the Valentine's housekeeper convinced Laina she was right. It didn't matter how many years had gone by, the widow of a colonel would definitely not be interested in having tea with a former servant.

She went to the bedroom window and raised the sash. Someone down on Soapsuds Row was screaming obscenities. A wagon rumbled by, the driver lashing the team of mules to a faster pace, the mules braying in protest as they pulled. The spring breeze was blowing from the direction of the stables. Grimacing, Laina closed the window. How she longed for the peace and quiet and fresh air of the ranch, the methodical routine, the sound of Caleb's voice as he came in for supper and called to CJ to come in lest supper get cold. *He'll be back right after roundup,* Laina reminded herself. *It won't be long now.*

It almost hurt to walk, and yet she could not bear the thought of being cooped up inside the trading post for one more moment. Snatching up her shawl and bonnet, Laina decided to head for the fort cemetery—the one place she could be assured of being left alone, the one place there might be a respite from the sound of construction. *Land sakes, if I have to listen to very much more hammering and hollering, I am going to go stark raving mad.*

I'm waddling, she thought as she ducked outside and headed toward the East End. *I can't even walk right.* Once at the cemetery, Laina opened the gate and went inside, plopping down in the shade at Granny Max's grave and raking her hand through the short grass. "I miss Caleb, Granny." She spread her hand over her abdomen. "I didn't expect to miss him so much. And if it's this hard now, how am I ever going to get through the summer when he's working here at the fort and I'm back home at Four Pines?" The baby landed a kick against her bladder.

Once again, she thought of Charlotte Bishop, convalescing alone at the surgeon's residence. *She has Garnet to talk to. And I'm not fit company for anyone, Lord.* She held back a sob. "I'm a mess," she murmured aloud, and looked at the tombstone engraved with Clara Maxwell's name. "Would you believe it, Granny? CJ is preaching me sermons about hospitality and friendship." She swiped a tear away. Another followed. And another. Several minutes later, Laina was still crying, albeit more quietly.

"Well," she murmured. "Let's hope I got *that* out of my system." She scooted across the grass and leaned against the tombstone. She felt tears surging again. "I just want to go home, Granny. I never wanted to come back to Fort Robinson, and I certainly don't want to *stay* here without Caleb. I need his arms around me. Nothing is right when I'm lonesome for Caleb."

Think of what it would be like without him at all. What if you were going to have to raise this baby all alone? Like Charlotte.

The baby pushed against her belly. Laina put her hand over the place and pressed down. The baby pushed back. *It's high time you made your appearance, you stubborn little boy. Just like your father, the man who knows what is best for his family and won't consider any other way. The two of you are going to lock horns some day, and I hope I don't have to be there to witness it.* When the baby kicked as if to answer her, Laina laughed and said aloud, "You *are* a stubborn little thing, aren't you. That's just what we need at Four Pines. Another child to question our decisions and be forever asking 'why.' You know, little boy, your sister already has that job pretty well in hand."

And what about you, Mrs. Jackson? a voice in her mind asked. *You're just as stubborn as CJ. Questioning why. Complaining about Fort Robinson. Pining for home. When are you going to stop grumbling and start paying attention? Maybe you are here for a reason other than the obvious ones.*

Long ago, she had read something in Granny Max's Bible about God not liking it when His children grumbled. When she really thought about it, Laina realized she had been spending a lot of time lately telling God what she didn't like and what she didn't want. Like not wanting to pay Charlotte Bishop a visit.

It's not about you. The circuit-riding preacher who visited the ranch on occasion had once given a sermon on that very subject. He'd talked about how the Lord didn't expect folks to handle their troubles on their own and how He often ministered to people through one another. "God puts on skin," he'd said, "by working through his children to love others."

The preacher had encouraged people to be available to God. Laina had congratulated herself during that sermon, thinking how she and Caleb had welcomed Rachel and Jack into their lives and made a place for Corporal Dorsey to spend his retirement years.

Caleb had been affected by the preacher's teaching, too. Ranchers all around the Sandhills were up in arms over the influx of grangers into the area. The grangers wanted to farm. They put up fences and plowed fields and disrupted the open-range days that many of the big ranching operations depended on. Troops from Fort Robinson had even been sent out to quell range wars between ranchers and farmers. While he would never participate in the violent conflicts, Caleb had done his share of grumbling against grangers. But after hearing Preacher Barton talk about eternity and loving your fellow man, Caleb had said, "The folks coming in around us seem like a good bunch. I'll let them live in peace." He'd decided to look on the good that could come of the changes. "When they want cattle or a good stallion to breed with their mares, they'll come to the Four Pines. I fought enough battles back in the war. I don't want to fight any more."

It's not about you. Laina realized she hadn't thought about anyone else but herself for quite a while. She sighed. "I've had all these years to read your Bible and hear the preacher's sermons, but I'm still nothing like you, Granny. You always welcomed whatever lambs God brought to your door. I remember you saying that. Goodness, I owe just about everything I've become to the fact you loved me when I didn't deserve to be loved."

She had refused God's urgings to visit Charlotte again and again. At first, she had used Charlotte and Caleb's past flirtation as an excuse. She had even mentioned it to Caleb. But when she hinted that things would be "awkward" between the two families, Caleb just shook his head. "Don't be ridiculous," he said. "We were both young fools. Completely different people. What's past is past and I, for one, wish Charlotte the best, and I'll be sure she knows it if you think I should tell her." And he had one evening before he left for the ranch, walking over to the surgeon's residence with CJ under the guise of meeting Will. One part of Laina admired him for it, while another part—the selfish one, she admitted to herself—wished she could hide behind that imaginary barrier and stay away from the surgeon's residence. When CJ expressed concern for the Bishops and wanted to help, she had brushed it off. She had reminded God of how, in her youth, Charlotte Valentine had looked down her nose at people. She had assured God repeatedly that, grown up or not, Charlotte Valentine would have no interest in a visit from lowly Laina Jackson. She had reminded God that in the military economy, officers' families just didn't mix with lower-class civilians. *She was married to a COLONEL, for goodness' sake. She's probably more high-toned than ever. I did visit. And she wasn't exactly happy to see me.*

But God, in the guise of Granny Max's voice, was relentless. *It's not about whether or not she was happy to see you. She was hurting. Her boy is hurting. He's acting it out right before everyone's eyes. Don't you wonder about what's behind Will Bishop's reputation for pranks? What's he so angry about?*

Some of the things CJ had said in recent days all tumbled together.

"Will says his ma was always sad when they lived in Michigan."

Charlotte's marriage must have been less than happy.

"Will says his pa was usually mad about something."

What would it be like, Laina wondered, if Caleb were perpetually angry with her. The thought brought a knot to her stomach.

"Will didn't like his pa."

What would it take for a boy to grow to dislike his own father?

"Will had three baby brothers, but they all died."

With a grunt, Laina stood up, arching her stiff back and lifting first one foot, then the other, making little circles in the air with each one in an attempt to limber up. She would call on Charlotte Bishop tomorrow.

A voice sounded behind her. "You all right, ma'am?"

She turned around. The circuit-riding preacher was standing at the cemetery fence, hat in hand, his long white hair especially snowy as the evening sun bathed his profile in light.

"Why, it's Mrs. Jackson," the preacher said. "Just the person I've come to find."

"Is . . . is something wrong . . . at the ranch?" Laina asked, her heart pounding.

"Everything's just fine." The preacher reached into his breast pocket and pulled out a small package wrapped in brown paper. "When I told Mr. Jackson I was coming this way, he asked me to bring you this."

Laina walked to the fence and took the package, chuckling when the preacher's ancient white mare, Elvira, stepped forward, stretching her neck over the cemetery fence, and nuzzled Laina's pocket. "Sorry, old girl, I didn't know you were coming. There's no sugar for you today." She patted the mare's soft muzzle and asked, "What brings you to Fort Robinson? Caleb was counting on your usual prayer before roundup."

"Oh, I expect to get back in plenty of time for that," the preacher said. He looked toward the fort. "I was just impressed to check on a little gal I prayed for some days ago. Didn't really want to make the ride, but the Lord just wouldn't let it go. Kept bringing her to mind. The doctor was mightily worried over her. You wouldn't happen to know how she's doing, would you?" The preacher tapped his wrist. "She had just had surgery for a broken—"

"—wrist," Laina finished his sentence. "As a matter of fact, I do know she's left the hospital. Word has it she's enjoying a nearly miraculous and trouble-free recovery." She looked at the preacher, who only smiled. "If you'll come with me, I'll show you to her house. Mrs. Bishop has a son—"

"Will," the preacher said. "I remember him from the hospital. Troubled boy. So unhappy."

Really, Laina thought. *He could tell that from just the one encounter?*

"He and CJ have become good friends. As a matter of fact, they're on a ride together now. One of the soldiers apparently took Mrs. Bishop for a carriage ride."

"That would be Lieutenant Boone, I suppose," the preacher said.

"Yes. You know him?"

"We met the night of Mrs. Bishop's surgery. He was waiting with young Will." The preacher put his hat back on his head. "You take a minute to open that message from your husband. Elvira and I will wait at the gate yonder, and then, if it's all right with you, you can show me to Mrs. Bishop's."

Laina opened the box and removed the piece of paper on which Caleb had written, *Gave you this years ago. Hope you still want to keep it.*

Frowning slightly, Laina looked at the smooth, flat rock in the box. Caleb had never given her a rock. What could he be talking about? She looked at the note again. Lifting the rock from the box, she put it in the palm of her hand and ran her finger around the edge. Smiling, Laina closed her hand around the *heart-shaped* rock as understanding dawned on her. *Gave you this years ago. Hope you want to keep it.* She headed for the cemetery gate. She would stop grumbling to God about being at Fort Robinson. Her presence here was, after all, testimony to Caleb's love for her. She would have to consider the possibility that perhaps, it *really* wasn't about her.

———

When the Reverend Barton concluded his brief visit at the Valentines' house, he asked to pray a blessing. Being the well-bred woman she was, Charlotte Valentine Bishop thanked him and bowed her head. Having been trapped into staying during the visit by the preacher's assumption of a friendship where none existed, and not wanting to appear rude, Laina Gray Jackson bowed her head. The two women sat opposite one another in the Valentine parlor. The preacher stood up, held his hat in his hands, and lifted his face toward the ceiling, smiling as he prayed.

"Thank you, heavenly Father, for answering my prayers for this young lady's wrist in a positive way. And now for this friendship, Lord, I pray your blessing."

Friendship? Laina thought. *I'd hardly call it a friendship. All right, Lord. I'll keep an open mind about it.*

"You know it is hard to be a rancher's wife . . ."

Amen to that, Lord, Laina agreed. *But then I suppose it was harder for Charlotte, being married to a man who was so difficult he alienated his own son.*

" . . . and you know it is hard to be a widow."

Especially when you are supposed to be brokenhearted but you are not, Charlotte thought. *God forgive me . . . it's such a relief not to be so afraid all the time . . .*

"But you have given these women one another . . ."

Granny would call Charlotte one of her lambs, Laina admitted to herself. *I know she is one of yours, Lord. But I can't see friendship happening. We're too different.*

I doubt Laina Jackson is going to want to be my friend, mused Charlotte. *She'll never believe I've changed.*

" . . . and similar life experience . . ."

Preacher, you have no idea, Charlotte thought.

" . . . and may they shore one another up . . ."

Laina doubted.

Charlotte rebelled. *The last thing I need is another self-righteous Christian telling me what to do with my life.*

"In the name of our dear Savior, I pray. Amen."

In your name, Lord, I'll try to do what you want, Laina prayed. *I know you love Charlotte and you care what happens to her. If you want me to help, I guess I should be willing to try.*

I tried praying, God, Charlotte thought. *My babies still died and Emory still hit me. Where were you?*

The preacher put on his hat. He beamed at the two young women before him. "I don't mind telling you two ladies that I was somewhat put out with the good Lord when He insisted I make the ride to Fort Robinson. But He just would not give me peace." He turned to Laina. "And then Caleb gave me that little package and I knew I must come." He stepped toward the door.

"Surely you'll not be heading back to the ranch tonight," Laina said.

"Please stay for supper," Charlotte urged.

The preacher hesitated. "I wouldn't want to impose."

"If there's one thing I've learned from living in an officer's household," Charlotte said, "it's hospitality. One never knows when visiting dignitaries will need a place to stay. There's always extra food ready at our table, and I would never turn a man out into the night without offering him shelter, even if it's just a pallet on the floor." Charlotte smiled warmly. "Garnet's made a huge pot of beef stew. And she makes the lightest biscuits you've ever eaten." She turned to Laina. "You and CJ would both be welcome. I believe Father said something about Lieutenant Boone and a chess game this evening." She turned back toward the preacher. "So you see, we've already been expecting company. Please stay."

The preacher accepted and then left to bed down Elvira in the doctor's stable.

Laina and Charlotte proceeded to set the table for dinner.

"I remember these dishes," Laina said, setting a blue-and-white plate on the table. "Your mother was so excited when we took the top off the crate. She'd been waiting for the freighters for weeks." She set a soup bowl on the matching plate. "The folks who lived at Camp Robinson back in the seventies would be amazed at the changes now that the railroad's come."

"Mother would be so much happier," Charlotte agreed. "How she used to fuss over how long it took to get things shipped. And Father was always unhappy over the cost." She leaned down and reached toward the back of the sideboard, pulling a stack of soup bowls toward the edge. "Do you mind?" she asked Laina. "I don't think I can handle them one-handed."

Laina took the bowls while Charlotte counted out soup spoons.

"Your mother was so horrified when I didn't know the difference between a soup spoon and a teaspoon," Laina said.

"Yes," Charlotte said. "I remember." Without looking up she added, "I'm sorry."

"Don't apologize," Laina said quickly. "Just being around the people who came and went through this house did a lot for my self-confidence. It helped me stop being afraid."

"You were afraid? At our house?" Charlotte didn't try to hide her surprise.

Laina nodded.

"What on earth did you have to be afraid of?"

"Failing," Laina said. "Disappointing all the people who believed in me. All the people who'd done so much to help me." She smiled. "And I will admit I was a little afraid of you."

"Of *me*?!" Charlotte's eyebrows shot up. "Why, for goodness' sake?"

"You and your mother were real ladies," Laina said. "The kind of women who wouldn't want to be seen with someone like me."

Charlotte stopped counting knives. She looked at her own reflection in the sideboard mirror. "For whatever it's worth, Laina, that girl who treated you so poorly has had a great deal of that kind of foolishness knocked out of her . . . and hopefully some maturity knocked *in*." She turned to look at Laina. "And the woman standing here humbly apologizes for the foolish girl and anything she might have done or said to hurt you."

Laina refolded a napkin. "Oh, goodness, Charlotte—I wasn't fishing for an apology. You said it. You were a girl, that's all. As far as I'm concerned that's all part of the past. It's forgotten." *Liar. You haven't forgotten a thing. You've been holding the past against Charlotte since you first heard she was back at Fort Robinson.*

Charlotte reached up to finger the lace at her throat. "Well, whatever our differences, we can certainly agree about wanting to forget the past." She absentmindedly ran her hand over her bandaged wrist. Footsteps sounded on the front porch. Charlotte headed for the kitchen, calling out over her shoulder, "Tell them dinner will be served shortly."

———

"And how are those riding lessons coming along, young man?" the preacher asked Will.

"He's a natural," Nathan Boone said. He buttered a biscuit and then pointed the tip of his knife at Will. "He'll be an expert just like his mother in no time."

When the lieutenant turned and smiled at her, Charlotte felt color creeping into her cheeks.

"Don't worry, Mrs. Colonel," he added, "we'll start with old Bones hopping logs. I think even Bones can manage that."

"By the time you're riding again, I'll be able to come along!" Will said.

"I'll look forward to it." Charlotte wondered if she sounded too eager and worried that Lieutenant Boone might misunderstand.

"Will tells me you've become quite the horsewoman since you left Fort Robinson," Boone said.

"I took it up to please the Colonel," she explained. "Even I was surprised at how much I loved it.

"Ma had a big gray thoroughbred. His name was Isaac. He could jump *high*." Will demonstrated by raising his hand above his head. "She had a whole bunch of ribbons she won. And a trophy." Will sighed. "But we didn't have room to bring them when we left Grandmother's. We had to hurry."

Charlotte shifted in her chair. "Does anyone want more coffee?"

"Caleb's plotting to buy an entire herd of thoroughbreds from back east. Maybe you'll want to check over them if it works out. You could replace Isaac," the lieutenant said.

Charlotte was relieved that Boone seemed to understand her desire to change the subject. She shook her head. "I could never afford another horse like Isaac. He was an angel—just the right combination of power and good temperament."

"You sound like you really did take an interest in the horses," Laina said.

Charlotte shrugged. "It was something to do. I used to accompany the Colonel to sales from time to time. He bought Isaac after hearing me go on and on about Banner/Jesse Belle bloodlines." She looked down at her plate, remembering how any reference to stallions and mares and their "behaviors," as Mother Bishop had worded it in true Victorian code, had been forbidden at the Bishop table.

"Banner, did you say?" Boone asked. When Charlotte nodded, he continued, "Caleb's been trying to get me to go in with him on a stallion named Banner. I told him the price was ridiculous."

"Well, if it's the same Banner I know about, and if his owners are considering selling, I don't think you'd ever be sorry. He's magnificent," Charlotte said. "Isaac definitely took after the sire's side of his ancestry, and he was some animal."

"It really is a shame you couldn't bring him with you," Boone said.

"Grandmother said she was going to sell Isaac to Major Riley," Will blurted out. "She said she couldn't afford him anymore. And she sold the team. And she wanted Ma to marry Major Riley."

Charlotte jumped up from the table and hurried into the kitchen from where she called, "Will, I need some help out here."

Chapter Eleven

My little children, let us not love in word,
neither in tongue; but in deed and in truth.

I JOHN 3:18

NATHAN BOONE DIDN'T SPEND much time asking himself why he cared about Will Bishop. He just knew he did. Ever since Nathan could remember, it had been in his nature to care about wounded things, and Will Bishop had been wounded. Nathan didn't know all the details, but he could see the current of fear running just beneath the boy's surface. He saw the same thing in Charlotte Bishop. The things Will had blurted out at dinner the night before said a lot about where the fear and self-doubt had originated. He didn't think it was his place to help Charlotte Bishop, but fate seemed to be making a way between Will and him.

"I don't know as either one of us will really be a help to Caleb," Nathan explained to Will's mother as they stood on the front porch of the doctor's residence, "but I need to see the Dawson place before I decide about investing in more land out here, and I think Will would have a good time seeing real cowboys in action. I have plenty of leave coming, and the colonel doesn't have a problem with my being gone. Is it all right with you if Will comes with me on the roundup?"

"I don't know," she hesitated. "Do you think he can ride well enough yet?"

"Bones is as reliable as they come," Nathan said. "And from what Will tells me, I'm thinking it would do him good to get away from school for a few days. I think he's bored—and just about ready to plot some new torture for Mr. Phelps."

"Really?"

"Really," Nathan said. "Look Mrs. Colonel—"

"Would you please call me Charlotte?" she surprised him by asking.

She rubbed the back of her bandaged hand. "I really hate that Mrs. Colonel title."

"Why?" Nathan asked. "You earned it."

"Yes," was the reply. "I did. In more ways than you care to know." She stared up at him and repeated, "And I'm asking you to please call me Charlotte."

Nathan nodded. "All right, then. Charlotte. And you must call me Nathan." He took a deep breath. "The thing is, Will is just too smart for Mr. Phelps. He's bored. And he's got so much energy he doesn't know what to do with it. I realize you don't want to reward his pranks. But maybe, just maybe, if Will has some time away, maybe he'll be able to come back and settle down and finish out the school year without any more incidents."

"That," Charlotte said, "would be a miracle."

———

Getting away from the fort seemed to unwind something deep inside Will Bishop, and while he didn't gush about the past during the half-day ride to the Four Pines Ranch with Nathan, he was less guarded about it. With his guard down, he said things that revealed a lot about Colonel Emory Bishop and how he had interacted with his wife and son. What Will said birthed a seething anger in Nathan against the man, not unlike the helpless rage he had felt years ago against the worthless piece of flesh who had kept Laina Gray locked in a cellar.

As Nathan recalled the day he and Emmet Dorsey found Laina Gray, something about Charlotte clicked. He thought back to Will's prank and his mother's fall. When he'd put his hand on Charlotte's shoulder to help her up, she had reacted by pulling away. In fact, Nathan realized, she held herself apart in just about every setting he'd observed. She was slow to say much of anything. He'd chalked it up to her being physically hurt. Now he realized it was probably more than that. Living with Emory Bishop had apparently taught Charlotte to be on her guard. *No wonder she doesn't want to be called Mrs. Colonel.*

Nathan found himself wondering if Laina Jackson had any idea what was behind some of the more radical changes in Charlotte's personality. He wondered if Laina might be able to help. Maybe he'd talk to her about it when he got back to the fort. He couldn't think of anyone better to understand Charlotte's experience with Colonel Bishop. Maybe fate would bring those two together.

The boy riding alongside him this morning was really starting to come around. Nathan smiled to himself, remembering the look on Will's face a few days ago when he had finally succeeded in making old Bones trot all the way around the corral. That smile was worth a lot. Now, as they rode up the canyon in the sunshine, Will began to whistle, and Nathan was doubly glad he had talked Charlotte into letting the boy come. She seemed to trust him with Will. She'd been so pleased that morning when the boy rode Bones for the first time. Even her eyes had smiled.

"How much farther?" Will squirmed in his saddle.

"Your backside starting to ache?" Nathan teased.

Will nodded. "Yeah. And I'm hungry."

"We can take a rest if you like," Nathan offered. "I'm sure Bones wouldn't mind a chance to do some grazing."

"Naw," Will said. "I was just wondering. We can keep going." He stood up in the stirrups. "I'm a tenderfoot," he said, grinning.

"Doesn't look to me like it's your feet that's tender," Nathan said. He laughed and urged his horse into a lope.

Will finally got Bones to follow suit. Before long, they were coming up over a ridge. Nathan pulled his horse up and waited for Will and Bones. "There it is," he said, motioning down into the valley where a half dozen log and board buildings of various sizes were nestled against a low rise. "The biggest building over there is the barn, of course. The corral's out back. You can't tell from here, but it's a good strong one. Caleb wrote me about how he hauled in cedar logs for it. I think he already had a breeding operation in mind when he put it up."

"The house is big," Will said.

Nathan nodded. "They've added on. Started out with just two big rooms. Next came two more off the back. There's a huge loft. Room for his boys, Caleb said." He motioned to a small cabin next to the barn. "We'll likely sleep there tonight. That's the start of a bunkhouse for the future wranglers. You'll get to meet Jack Greyfoot."

"The Indian?"

Nathan looked at the boy. "Yes. He's Cheyenne. Why?"

Will shrugged. "I never met any before. That's all. My pa said—" He hesitated. "Never mind." He sucked in a deep breath.

"Jack was about your age when the Outbreak happened. Did your pa ever tell you anything about that?"

Will shook his head.

"Jack and his brother Grey Foot and Grey Foot's wife, Rachel, had been at Fort Robinson since October when, in January they were locked up in the old barracks south of the East End parade ground. A hundred and thirty Cheyenne in all."

"In there? But there isn't room."

"Well, that's where they had to stay. Until they said they would go back down to Kansas where they had been sick and dying."

"That's not fair," Will said.

"They didn't think so, either. And I doubt they thought it was very fair when the army quit giving them food and water."

"They didn't!" Will protested. He turned in the saddle and stared at Nathan. "You wouldn't . . . do that . . ." He frowned.

"I was in the hospital when that happened," he said, and went on to describe how he'd been stabbed by a Cheyenne named Wild Hog inside the commander's office, hours before the Outbreak. "One night the Cheyenne decided to break out and run for freedom." He went on to tell Will about the following weeks, sparing the boy the worst details, yet hoping what he said would overcome the prejudice Will had been taught. "So now you know a little bit about Jack and Rachel," he finally said. "It's been ten years since all that happened. The Jacksons are happy to have them on the ranch, and they seem happy to be there. If you want to learn how to break and train a horse, Jack is the man to get to know. Caleb says sometimes it seems like Jack can whisper in a horse's ear and get it to do anything he wants."

Nathan waited for the information about Jack to sink in a little before he went on. "You'll also meet an old friend of mine named Emmet Dorsey." Nathan added, "Now, just like you shouldn't let any of the Indian nonsense you heard back east stop you from getting to know Jack, you shouldn't let Dorsey's cranky exterior fool you. Emmet's a good man. Just don't get between him and a spittoon and you'll do fine. If you want to know how to train a horse, you ask Jack. And if you want to hear war stories, you ask Dorsey." He urged his horse forward. "Let's go. I can hear your stomach growling from all the way over here."

They rode directly to the house and dismounted, tying their horses to the hitching post that also served as uprights for a wide front porch. Just as Nathan was showing Will how to tie Bones, the front door opened and Caleb Jackson emerged, followed by two old men. And Rachel. She was smiling at him. He took off his hat. Smiled back.

"I don't believe it," Caleb said, turning to the white-haired man next to him. "Preacher Barton, meet Lieutenant Nathan Boone, who, as I told you, knows more about me than any human being has a right to know . . . and did his best to steal Laina Gray right out from under me."

"Well now," the preacher said, pumping Nathan's hand and smiling.

"That wasn't exactly mentioned over Mrs. Colonel Bishop's dinner table the other night, was it, Lieutenant?"

Nathan smiled and shrugged. Rachel turned away and headed back inside. "Guilty as charged," he said, shaking the preacher's hand. "Except there wasn't a prayer in . . . uh . . . excuse me, Reverend . . . there wasn't a chance she was going to have a thing to do with me after that moonlight sleigh ride." Nathan clapped Caleb on the back. "Let me introduce my young friend here. The reverend has already met him. This is Emory William Bishop, Jr., Charlotte's son. I talked him into coming up here to the ranch with me so I wouldn't be the only greenhorn on the roundup. That is, if you'll have us."

Caleb shook Will's proffered hand. "The boy is welcome. But I don't know about you," he teased Nathan. "Don't imagine you know a branding iron from a cattle prod."

"As a matter of fact," Nathan said, "I believe I do. But I'll try not to get in your way."

Caleb nodded. "You still good with that?" He pointed at Nathan's rifle.

"I've been known to hit a target or two."

"Well, maybe you'll bring in some game for the outfit," Caleb said.

Nathan looked at Will. "We'll do our best. Right, partner?"

Caleb nodded toward the barn. "You two men take your horses—that *is* a horse, isn't it, Nathan?" he said, peering at Bones. "Take your horses down to the barn. Jack's down there trying to convince a gelding CJ has taken a shine to that people aren't rattlesnakes." He grinned. "He's already eaten once tonight, but I bet he'll be easy to convince to come back up to the house with you for some more. Tell him Rachel is heating up the stew." He looked down at Will. "You *are* hungry, aren't you?"

"The boy's been hungry since we left Fort Robinson," Nathan said. He untied the horses, and he and Will made their way down to the barn.

Nathan was proud of Will. He might be trembling with fear and uncertainty, but the boy stuck out his hand and shook Jack Greyfoot's and looked the man in the eye.

"I told this young man you're the one to pay attention to if he wants to learn how to break and train a horse," Nathan said.

Jack shrugged. He nodded over his shoulder to where the gelding stood, his rear pressed into a corner, his front feet splayed. "Tell *him* that."

"That the horse CJ has her heart set on?"

Jack nodded. "I promised her she'd be able to ride him when she gets back."

"That must be Rebel," Will said.

"And a rebel he is," Jack said, turning around and walking to the stall. The horse snorted and tossed his head. Jack smiled. "At least he wants me to think that." He lifted his chin and directed his next words to the horse. "But I don't believe it. It's all an act."

Will's stomach rumbled. The two men laughed.

"Guess we'll put breaking Rebel on hold so you don't starve," Jack said. He reached for Bones's reins.

"Caleb said to invite you back up to the house for seconds," Nathan said.

Jack grinned. He patted his stomach and winked at Will. "Wait until you taste Rachel's fry bread."

———

"He's going to explode. That's all there is to it." Nathan looked across the room to where Rachel stood at the stove. "You'd better stop," he called out. "You're going to kill the young man with good cooking." He nudged Will, who was sitting next to him at the table, still eating after all the grown men had stopped.

Will took one last huge bite, then sat back and belched loudly. "Excuse me," he apologized, smothering a giggle.

"Good eats, ma'am," Nathan agreed, holding out his coffee mug for a refill as Rachel approached the table, coffeepot in hand. "We're going to wish we had some of that bread on roundup."

"I'll make you some," Rachel said. "You can take it in your saddlebags." She touched his shoulder lightly.

Jack pushed himself back from the table and stood up. "I have some work to get done before sundown," he said, and left abruptly.

The rest of the men sat at the table until long after sundown. Caleb wanted to know about Nathan's escapades in the Southwest. With a glance in Rachel's direction, Nathan changed the subject to ranching and the future for western Nebraska in the scheme of things. When Caleb mentioned importing a good quality thoroughbred stallion, Nathan turned to Will. "Tell Mr. Jackson what you know about Banner."

"My ma's horse Isaac was from Banner's line," he said. "I remember my father talking about Banner."

"Really?" Caleb said. "Tell me what you remember."

Will yawned. "Ma said Isaac took after Banner. He could jump higher than any horse I ever saw. Ma had a whole bunch of ribbons and trophies. She really liked Isaac. But Grandmother said we couldn't afford to keep him. It made Ma really sad. The day Major Riley came to get him, she cried."

———

The morning after Will left with Nathan, Charlotte stood on her father's back porch gazing at the bluffs in the distance.

"Don't worry, missus." Garnet's voice sounded behind her. "Lieutenant Boone won't let anything happen to Will."

"I'm not so much worried as lonely." Charlotte turned back around and headed inside. "After all of Will's mischief, who would have thought I'd be complaining about being bored the minute he's out of sight?"

Garnet poured a cup of steaming water into a china cup, measured loose tea into a silver tea ball, and plopped it in the water. While the tea brewed, she took a tray of fresh biscuits out of the oven and slid them into a basket. "Don't fret so. It won't be all that long and you'll be taking rides with Will up into the hills on a high-stepping horse. I know how you miss your rides."

Charlotte ran her hand over her bandaged wrist. "Of all the things I anticipated about coming back to Fort Robinson, missing Isaac wasn't one of them," she said wistfully. "I hope the Major is treating the old boy well."

Garnet added a lump of sugar to Charlotte's tea. "Doctor's already gone over to the hospital to make his rounds," she said. "The ladies will be making their calls soon."

"I think they've finally given up on me," Charlotte said, and sat down at the table to sip her tea.

"If the ladies aren't calling on you anymore, maybe *you* could call on *them*," Garnet suggested. "I expect that nice Mrs. Jackson could use some company."

———

The idea of calling on Charlotte would not go away. Climbing out of bed, Laina looked at herself in the mirror. *Haven't I done enough, Lord? I had dinner with her just two nights ago. And you saw—she was doing all right.*

Of course, Laina had to admit, the woman was probably a bit lonely with Will gone. Maybe even worried. Especially if CJ was right and Charlotte hadn't let the boy do much on his own.

She headed into the kitchen where CJ sat staring glumly at a bowl of steaming oatmeal.

"Are you ready to do that recitation for Mr. Phelps today?" Laina asked.

CJ shrugged.

Laina sat down next to her. "I know you miss Will, honey-lamb," she said. "But maybe you'll make a new friend in school today."

"I don't see why it was all right for Will to leave school but not me," CJ grumbled.

"Neither your father nor I are about to let you be the only female on a roundup," Laina said. "You can go this fall when things are back to normal and Rachel is riding with the chuck wagon again."

"Why does *everything* have to be different just because there's a baby coming?" CJ whined. She scooped up a dollop of oatmeal and watched it slide off the spoon and plop back into the bowl. She slumped in her chair. "And when's the baby coming, anyway? We've been here *forever*."

Laina willed her temper away. Hoping she sounded confident and not just irritated she said, "This is the way your father wants things. He would have been very unhappy with me if you showed up with Lieutenant Boone and Will without any notice. And besides that, we both want you in school, not gallivanting all over the countryside with a bunch of cowboys."

CJ's mouth turned down at the corners. She put the spoon down and dropped her hands into her lap.

"Listen to me, Clara Joy." Laina was glad to see the girl's expression in response to hearing her full name. *Good. That got her attention.* She continued, "Obedience is easy until we have to do something we don't want to do. I know you aren't very happy with things right now. The truth is, neither am I. I'm homesick for the ranch the same as you. But your pa's got enough on his mind without having to worry about you and me. So we're both just going to have to obey what he says and stay here at Fort Robinson for a while longer. That's what God would want us to do—trust that Pa knows what's best and obey him *and* God, who tells us to do everything without grumbling."

Yes, Laina. Exactly. No grumbling. So are you going to visit Charlotte today?

Laina ignored the thought. She lifted CJ's chin and turned the girl's face toward her own, insisting CJ meet her gaze. "I want to go home, too. But we can't. You have to go to school and . . ." Laina sighed. "I have to—"

"Take a nap," CJ interrupted. She turned away and stabbed at the oatmeal again, sighing dramatically. "I *know*, Ma. You're *tired*. You're always tired."

"Actually," Laina said, tugging on one of CJ's red braids, "I was going to say that I have to call on Mrs. Bishop today."

CJ perked up. She glanced up at her mother hopefully. "Really? Do you think you can get her to let Will stay at the ranch this summer?"

"I think," Laina said, "that you need to do your job, which is eating breakfast and going to school and trying not to drive Mr. Phelps crazy, and let me do mine—which includes taking care of things at the ranch." She forced a smile, and the edges of CJ's mouth turned up. "That's what I like to see." Laina stood up. "And for your information, I'm feeling quite well today. I don't need a nap. What I need is some female company. I'm thinking Mrs. Bishop is missing Will about now. She may even be a little worried. Maybe having second thoughts about turning him loose in the Wild West. So if you'll gather your school things, we'll leave together."

———

Charlotte was standing on the back porch watching Private Carter Blake sink a spade in the lumpy earth that would soon be Garnet's kitchen garden when Laina Jackson rounded the corner of the house, her sewing basket over her arm, a smile on her face.

"It doesn't seem so long ago that Frenchy Dubois was out here digging," she said.

"Yes," Charlotte agreed. "Frenchy had quite the garden in his day."

Private Blake swiped his hat off his head and bobbed a greeting to Laina. "Miss Irvin's got her heart set on a big garden." He smiled. "I told her that between the good Lord and me, we'd do what we could to make it happen."

Garnet stepped out on the porch, holding a tray with two steaming mugs of coffee and a plate of biscuits. "Breakfast, Private," she called and then nodded at Laina. "Morning, ma'am." She set the tray on an upturned barrel at the edge of the porch and handed Blake one mug of coffee before handing the shawl she had draped over her arm to Charlotte.

"You two enjoy your breakfast," Charlotte said. "Mrs. Jackson and I will just go on inside and have ourselves a cup of coffee." She turned to Laina. "If you have time?"

Laina nodded. "Actually, I was coming to see you. I thought you might be missing Will," she said and followed Charlotte inside. "The first time CJ went on roundup, I nearly worried myself sick. And all she did was ride in the chuck wagon with Rachel."

"Oh, I'm not really worried," Charlotte said. "I've no doubt Lieutenant Boone will keep an eye on him. But I do miss him." She took her shawl off and draped it across a kitchen chair.

Laina nodded at Carter and Garnet, visible through the kitchen window. "What's going on with those two?"

"I don't know," Charlotte said. "I didn't think Father asked for a striker. But I haven't been keeping track of things like I should. Garnet hasn't had a lot to say, other than that Private Blake is a 'powerful pray-er,' whatever that means. But then Garnet has always been a woman of few words." She nodded at the basket over Laina's arm. "You brought your knitting."

Garnet appeared at the back door. "I'll be right in to make you ladies some coffee," she said.

Charlotte waved her away. "We can make our own coffee. We're going to be in the parlor for a little while. Enjoy yourself." She winked at Garnet, who grinned, covered her crooked teeth with her hand, and went back to where Carter Blake was sitting eating a biscuit.

"Well," Charlotte said, looking at Laina. "I guess that answers our question." She took down two coffee mugs. "You go on and get settled in the parlor. I'll be right there with some coffee."

Once she had served up two cups of coffee, Charlotte was at a loss for what to say next. She didn't want to talk about Michigan, and she knew nothing about ranching. After a few false starts, the two women settled on the one thing they knew they had in common—their children.

"I'm so glad you decided to put CJ in school," Charlotte said. "I swear, Will thinks she hung the moon."

"I believe, given a chance, she'd try to prove she could," Laina joked. "Especially if climbing were involved." She sighed and shook her head from side to side. "That girl. Sometimes I wonder where she came from. She hates the kitchen, doesn't care about cooking. Refuses to sew. Wants to spend every spare minute she can with her father riding, hunting, herding— whatever he's doing."

"How wonderful," Charlotte murmured, staring off into the distance, "for a child to have that kind of connection with her father." She rubbed her bandaged wrist with her open palm.

"Oh, Charlotte. I am so sorry," Laina said. "That was very thoughtless of me. Will must miss his father terribly."

"Actually," Charlotte said, "they weren't all that close." She cleared her throat. "The Colonel had very definite ideas about what his son should be like. When Will didn't love horses right away and didn't want to 'play war,' the Colonel saw it as a weakness. He didn't take very well to the notion that his son didn't 'measure up.'"

"What do you mean, Will didn't measure up?" Laina said. "I know he's had his moments—but who wouldn't love Will?"

Charlotte shrugged. "I don't think it was a matter of love . . ."

"Of course not. I didn't mean it that way," Laina said.

"Of course, Will wanted to please the Colonel. Every boy seeks his father's approval. It just never seemed like Will could get it. The Colonel was always in such a hurry for him to grow up. I lost three babies after Will—"

"Oh, Charlotte," Laina said. "Will told CJ . . . and she told me, but I just didn't know what to say." She paused. "I am so very sorry."

"There's nothing else to be said," Charlotte answered. "Thank you." She took a sip of coffee to steady her voice. "They were all boys.

"It seemed like the Colonel's expectations for Will got more intense with each loss. Of course, the Colonel assumed Will would follow in his footsteps. West Point. Cavalry. When Will was only eight months old, the Colonel taught him to walk by planting Will's feet on the tops of his shoes and walking backward. Will was only two when the Colonel decided it was time he learned to ride. He took him out to the barn and set him up on one of the plow horses. The horse was gentle, of course, but Will got excited and let go of the mane and tumbled off. He broke his collarbone. After that, he didn't want to go near a horse." Charlotte looked down. "I'm afraid the Colonel didn't handle that disappointment very well."

"What do you mean?"

"Oh, he kept insisting on repeating the process. Said Will would finally get over being afraid. Except that Will didn't get over it. Finally, one day the Colonel was carrying Will out to the barn, and Will was screeching for me—" Charlotte closed her eyes, trembling with emotion at the memory. "I intervened. I just couldn't listen to my baby screaming like that."

"Of course not," Laina said quickly. "What mother could."

"Exactly," Charlotte said. "So I put a stop to the 'riding lessons.'"

"Good for you," Laina said. "I hope the Colonel learned his lesson."

Charlotte was quiet for a long time. "The Colonel wasn't very open to learning lessons. He was more the kind of man who *taught* lessons." She looked down at the clenched hands in her lap. When she finally looked up, Laina was watching her carefully.

"But that's all done with." Charlotte forced a smile and shrugged.

"Things are better now. Between Lieutenant Boone and Private Blake and my father, Will's finally getting to be around men who can set a good example. I'm thrilled he's finally learning to ride. I'm hoping that will help focus some of his boundless energy. He's a strong-willed child. Unfortunately, after the Colonel died, I didn't have the emotional strength to discipline Will. The Colonel's mother tended to be too strict. Will's been bouncing between my leniency and Mother Bishop's unreasonable demands for so long. . . . Sometimes I worry he's been ruined."

"Don't be so hard on yourself," Laina said. "It takes time to heal after loss. Especially a sudden loss like you've had. Will's going to be all right. You'll see. The older I get, the more I am convinced it's just part of parenting to worry over our children and to feel guilty about decisions we've made. I worry about CJ all the time."

"Why?" Charlotte asked. "She's terrific. Bright and funny and sweet."

"Sweet?" Laina said. "No one's ever called CJ *sweet*."

"Well, she is," Charlotte said. "She's taken time with Will. She's looked past the pranks and the streak of mischief—"

"Oh, I don't think she's looking past it as much as looking *for* it and *participating* in it," Laina quipped.

Charlotte laughed. "They *are* quite a pair. Maybe we should just arrange a betrothal now."

Laina worried aloud. "That'd be fine. Because I don't personally know any boys who are particularly attracted to a woman who wants to wear pants most of the time and can ride and rope with the best of the cowboys. CJ's still pouting that I didn't let her go on roundup with the men. It didn't help any when she overheard Nathan offering to keep an eye on her if I wanted to change my mind." She shook her head from side to side.

"I'm so grateful Lieutenant Boone has taken an interest in Will," Charlotte said. "The Colonel was all barking orders and discipline. I don't want my son to grow up like that. He needs to learn that a man can be gentle and still be a man. Will is lucky the lieutenant makes the effort he does to spend time with him."

"I don't think he sees it as a terrible sacrifice," Laina said gently. "After all, getting to know Will has put him in the company of Will's mother."

Charlotte spoke up. "I came back to Fort Robinson with one thing in mind, and that is to raise my son. All I care about is doing what's best for Will. And I'm quite certain that's all Lieutenant Boone has in mind, as well. I'm grateful he's in our lives—for Will's sake. But I am also quite certain that his spending time with me is just an unavoidable part of the package that comes with Will Bishop."

"Yes," Laina said quietly. "I'm sure you're right. It was Will he was thinking of at dinner the other night when he mentioned escorting you to the officers' ball next month."

Charlotte got up and went to the parlor window. She closed her eyes, absentmindedly running the palm of her good hand back and forth across the strap of her sling. "I'd appreciate it if you'd not tease me about that. Lieutenant Boone was being polite. That's his way."

"I'm not teasing. It would be good for both of you to be friends. I've been praying for Nathan since he left Fort Robinson ten years ago. Praying that God would heal his heart and draw him closer. Praying that maybe, just maybe, Nathan would someday open that great heart of his to friendship with someone—maybe to more than friendship."

"Well," Charlotte said, "I empathize with your concern for Lieutenant Boone. I know he was deeply hurt when his wife died so young. I was too self-centered to see it then, but on this side of grief, I do feel for those who experience tragedy." She turned around and looked at Laina. "And I can also tell you from this side of grief, that the last thing Lieutenant Boone needs is for well-meaning friends to meddle in his personal affairs. When I think back to the way I behaved toward him in those days, I could cry with shame. It's a tribute to his character that he will come near us at all. I don't intend to do or say anything that would risk Will's benefiting from Lieutenant Boone's investment in his life."

Laina focused on her knitting. Silence reigned for a few minutes. Finally, Laina lay aside her needles and stood up. She arched her back and grimaced. "Your father keeps insisting that walking is the best thing I can do for myself and the baby. I've been promising myself I'd take another bouquet of flowers to Lily Boone's and Granny Max's graves. Care to join me?"

Grateful for something to do besides wonder how Laina felt about her impromptu sermonizing, Charlotte jumped up. "I've been lax about tending my mother's grave. I'll get some ribbon." Rummaging in the sideboard drawer, she pulled out a length of yellow ribbon and cut three pieces before tucking it into her sling.

Together, the two young women went out the front door and headed across the parade ground, past the barracks and stables, and finally across the bridge spanning the White River and into the field beside the cemetery. They picked wild flowers for several minutes, then made three bouquets and entered the cemetery.

"You know," Charlotte said as she bent to place the first bouquet at

Granny Max's grave, "I have a lot of regrets about things that happened here at Fort Robinson when I was a girl. But one of the greatest is that Mother and I let *where* Granny Max lived keep us from getting to know her." She sighed. "That was yet another mistake I made in the old days."

"I learned a lot from Granny," Laina said.

Charlotte pulled her shawl around her. "I suppose I owe Granny Max a thanks, if she's the reason you came to visit today. And the reason you put up with my paranoia about Lieutenant Boone."

"It isn't paranoia," Laina said. "And you're right. I should mind my own business." She smiled. "You said it very tactfully—and from experience— and I appreciate that."

"Thank you for trying to understand," Charlotte said. "I do appreciate your company." She sighed. "I fear time is going to pass very slowly while Will is gone." When Laina was silent, Charlotte walked to her own mother's grave and placed a bouquet there.

"I was sorry I didn't know about your mother's death until after the funeral," Laina said. "I would have come."

Charlotte shrugged. "I wasn't here, either. The Colonel wouldn't allow it."

"Why on earth not?"

Charlotte sighed. "We weren't getting along very well. The Colonel was very unhappy with me."

"So he took revenge by preventing you from coming to your own mother's funeral?"

Charlotte stared down at the grave. "I think he knew that if he let me come, I might never return to Michigan."

Laina put her hand on Charlotte's arm.

Charlotte took in a deep breath. She blinked back tears. But she couldn't stop the trembling. "We should go," she said. "I don't want to wear you out."

"Let's go over and sit in the shade awhile," Laina said. "If you don't mind."

The two women made their way to a place just inside the fence where a cottonwood tree was throwing its shadow. They settled on the grass. Finally, Laina spoke up. "You know, Charlotte, one thing I learned from Granny Max is that humans aren't meant to handle all their troubles alone. God puts people in our path to help us. Sometimes He sends people who've had experiences that enable them to understand us in a way no one else could." She paused. "Granny was able to help me first of all because she loved God. He gave her supernatural love for me long before I was anything near loveable. So it was definitely God at work that enabled Granny Max. But from a human perspective, it surely didn't hurt that she had once had an experience like mine." Laina briefly told Charlotte about Granny's nightmare experience as a girl. "Knowing she had been through that really helped me trust her." Laina put her hand on Charlotte's arm. "I don't know how much of my story you heard when you were here before. I always imagined it was common knowledge."

Charlotte answered, "I don't know about common knowledge. But Mother, God rest her soul, wasn't exactly the best person about keeping confidences. And there was a time she thought you were competition for Lieutenant Boone's affections—which, as you will recall, she was intent on turning toward me." She sighed. "I probably know more than I should."

"It's all right," Laina said. "The thing is, Granny Max used to tell me that someday I would see the reason behind that awful time. That I would actually be able to see God using what happened in that dugout with the monster who kidnapped me." She put her hand on Charlotte's shoulder. "I have to admit, that as much as I loved and respected Granny, I never really believed her." She squeezed Charlotte's shoulder before letting go. "But I'm thinking now I do."

Charlotte looked down at her sling where she had tucked the last bouquet of flowers. She pulled it out. Together, they walked to Lily Boone's grave.

"Do you think . . . do you think it's possible Will won't be . . . damaged . . . permanently?" Charlotte fought for control, determined not to break down. "The Colonel tended to be . . . strict. Demanding. Sometimes he lashed out." She sucked in a wobbly breath.

"You mean he hit you," Laina said.

Charlotte pressed her lips together. She shrugged. "Not so often." She murmured, "What matters is Will. Do you think Will can get past it?"

"I think," Laina said gently, "that God promises to make all things new. And, unlike we humans, He keeps His promises."

"I don't have much confidence in God," Charlotte said.

"I understand how you could feel that way," Laina said. "I did, too. For a long time." She took Charlotte's hand.

Charlotte didn't pull away.

———

It was late afternoon before Laina Jackson and Charlotte Bishop stepped out onto the back porch of the doctor's residence together.

"Look at that," Charlotte said, pointing to the tips of the distant bluffs, still brilliantly illuminated by the setting sun. "Nebraska can be a beautiful place." She surprised even herself by hugging Laina. "Thank you for what you did for me today. I'll never forget it."

Laina protested. "All I did was listen."

"Well," Charlotte said, "you're a good listener."

Laina stepped down off the porch. She had only gone a short distance when she turned around and called Charlotte's name.

Charlotte came back to the edge of the porch. "Yes?"

"If he enjoys roundup, maybe you'd consider letting Will spend some time at the ranch this summer."

Charlotte nodded. "I imagine he'd love it."

"And," Laina added, "I'd like it even more if you'd consider coming with him. I think you'd enjoy it, too." She smiled. "Who knows. Maybe God brought you west to turn you into a cowgirl."

Chapter Twelve

A man's heart deviseth his way:
but the Lord directeth his steps.
PROVERBS 16:9

IT HAD BEEN ten years since Winter Moon and her husband, Grey Foot, fled the barracks at Fort Robinson as part of what would be called the Cheyenne Outbreak; ten years since Winter Moon had taken the name Rachel Greyfoot and come to live at the Four Pines Ranch with Laina and Caleb Jackson; ten years of internal struggle to come to terms with the contradictions that were her life. On the one hand, if it were not for the soldiers pursuing her husband, he might still be alive. On the other hand, if it were not for soldiers like Caleb Jackson and Nathan Boone, *she* might not be alive. If it were not for greedy white gold diggers and homesteaders and ranchers, Rachel's people might still be free to live in the old way. But if it were not for white ranchers like the Jacksons, she might be living in poverty on the reservation. Some whites she hated. Others she loved. Some whites talked about God all the time and then stole from their own the minute they had the chance. Others who rarely said the name of God were honorable and trustworthy.

It had taken most of the past ten years, but Rachel had finally learned to live in the place of tension between two opposing forces. She had found a measure of internal peace and was determined to see each person as an individual and to do her best not to judge them for either their skin color or their name for God. Most of the time, she was content with her life on the Four Pines Ranch. She worked hard for the Jacksons, who had proven themselves to be both kind and fair, and she grew to be genuinely fond of CJ.

On days when living suspended between two colliding worlds threatened her inner peace, Rachel found solace in climbing alone to the summit of a hill. Sometimes she watched clouds or stars cross the ancient sky and let her mind wander into the past. Sometimes she closed her eyes and listened. She heard the rustle of the grass when a rabbit poked its nose out of a clump of wild sage along with the buzzing of grasshopper wings. She heard the wind in the pines. Sometimes there was the far-off cry of an eagle or the less noble cawing of a crow. Most of the time, her moments up on the hill watching or listening helped her recapture herself and re-create the feelings of enforced contentment. She worked hard, was never hungry or without shelter, and was almost at peace.

Lately, Rachel had even begun to think maybe Jack was right, that they should be married. Everyone agreed that Jack was, like his brother before him, a good man. Even if he was four years younger than Rachel, he loved her with a desperate, youthful emotion that, even if she could not return it, Rachel at least appreciated. A woman could do much worse than being loved by Jack Greyfoot. She wasn't getting any younger, and she did not want to grow old alone.

But then Rachel accompanied the Jacksons to Fort Robinson and saw Lieutenant Nathan Boone. For the past ten years she had thought of him only as the hero who saved her life. He was one of the good soldiers, a tall, handsome white man with dark hair. He had been wounded before the Outbreak, and when they brought her to the fort hospital, he made sure she got good care for her frozen feet. Before he left, he arranged for her to stay with the Jacksons instead of being taken to the reservation. He even found Jack, Grey Foot's younger brother, and convinced Caleb Jackson to give him a home, too. Boone left Fort Robinson before Rachel was well enough to thank him.

She heard news of him from time to time. Sometimes the Jacksons talked about him over dinner. He had helped Caleb buy the ranch. He wrote about cattle and horses. Sometimes Mr. Jackson read one of his letters aloud after dinner while she and Mrs. Jackson worked in the kitchen. Boone wrote of the army and the buffalo soldiers. He was promoted to lieutenant. He described the land he was in. It sounded barren and lonely. He wrote of other native people. Sometimes, Rachel thought, there was a cloud of sadness over his words. Time blurred her memory of him, but it did not erase her sense of a debt owed.

And now he was back. In the few moments she'd seen him at the fort trading post, she had noticed that time had aged the lieutenant more than she would have expected. There was white in the hair at his temples. She also noticed that, to any woman's eyes, Lieutenant Nathan Boone was still a handsome man. When he arrived at the ranch with a boy in tow, something stirred inside Rachel. She didn't know if the lieutenant sensed it, but it did seem to her that as she moved about the kitchen, his brown eyes were on her every time she looked up. When she offered to make fry bread for Boone to take on the roundup, Jack reacted. He must have sensed something, too—something that made him jealous. At least it wasn't her imagination. That night, Rachel's nightmare returned.

Grey Foot was dragging her bodily up the face of the impossibly high butte. Rachel wanted to help, but her frozen feet would not obey. "Leave me," she begged him over and over again, but he would not. Pretending he didn't hear, he kept moving, scrambling up the same narrow crevice their people had used for generations, dragging her with him between vertical walls of earth jutting up out of a broad valley toward the icy gray sky.

The sound of approaching hoofbeats from behind fueled his ascent. He grasped her around the waist more firmly. She tried to help, tried to push off from the rocks, to be something less than dead weight. The blue coats from the fort were hesitating. As she watched, a soldier mounted on a huge buckskin charged the cliff. The horse scrambled valiantly before sliding backward. The soldier shouted an order, and all his men dismounted and began climbing on foot, their boots sending a shower of rocks behind them.

A blast of cold wind shot up the crevice and Rachel shivered. Her best beloved loosened his grip momentarily, pausing on a thin ledge to suck air into his lungs.

"Leave me," she repeated, trying to pull away.

Grey Foot's dark eyes stopped watching the pursuers. They focused on hers. "I will never leave you," he said. He bent low, putting his windburned cheek next to hers for just an instant before once again encircling her waist and resuming the desperate climb.

She clung to him, focusing on the great bird soaring above them, wishing the two of them could leap off the cliff and ride on the wind like the bird that seemed suspended in the air above them. Another blast of icy wind pelted them. The bird screeched, flapped its wings, and disappeared over the ridge.

With a grunt, her husband surged upward, over the edge, onto the summit. Together they fell to the earth, shuddering when their thinly clad bodies made contact with the snow. He got up onto his knees with his back to her. She knew what to do. How many hundreds of times had he knelt just like that when the two of them were children. How many times had she dreamed of the day when a son of theirs would clamber onto his father's back so the two of them could gallop through the tall grass, the father trumpeting like a wild horse. She fell forward, clasping his shoulders even as he pinned her thighs against his waist and staggered to his feet.

Grey Foot had gone only a few feet when mounted soldiers emerged from the pine trees ahead of them. He darted to the left. More soldiers. He spun around to

look behind them. Soldiers poured from the crevice, their breath rising like plumes
of smoke in the frigid air.

"Our family is dead. We should go to them," she whispered in his ear. Her
right thigh tensed against his waist, signaling him as she would a horse, knowing
that even as they had always seemed to think as one, he would read her thoughts
now. She felt him take in a breath, felt his elbows press against her knees, sensed
his message of love even as he lunged to the right and ran straight for the edge of
the cliff. She clutched his shoulders, closed her eyes, waited for the soaring through
the air, wanting what would come next. Just as she thought her heart would burst
with love, he ripped her hands from his neck and flipped her off his back and into
the snow.

Soldiers shouted. A gun went off. She screamed. Everything seemed to slow
down. Grey Foot turned around and put his clenched fist to his chest, even as his
dark eyes sought her face. He smiled. Nodded. And then, as the blue coats launched
themselves toward him, he spun away, spread his arms, and jumped.

She gasped as someone grabbed her shoulder. She tried to fling the hand away,
to struggle up from the cold, but the soldier was strong and wouldn't let go. She
screamed and started kicking, but the giant man with dirty blond hair wrapped
his arms around her and held tight. The smell of him made her gag.

Rachel woke with a start. She raked her hands through her long dark
hair and swiped at the tears she had cried in her sleep. She lay awake for
a few moments, staring at the ceiling. Her breathing returned to normal.
Still, she could not shake the sense of terror in her heart. Finally, she got
up, dressed, and went outside.

She was headed for the hill, the way so familiar she needed no daylight
for the journey, when Jack's voice sounded in the night. He must have been
leaning against the barn, just out of sight of the house.

"Are you all right?" he called, barely loud enough for her to hear. He
came to her side and touched her shoulder. "You tremble," he said.

Rachel shook her hair back over her shoulder. "A dream. It's nothing.
I was going to take a walk."

"*The* dream?" Jack asked. "I thought you said it had left you."

"I thought it had," she said. She shivered a little and crossed her arms,
hugging herself.

"Seeing Lieutenant Boone has brought it all back for me, too," Jack
said. "You had the dream. I couldn't sleep at all." He pointed toward the
distant hill. "I just kept remembering what it was like trying to run with
frozen feet. And the hunger. I remember the hunger."

"Don't." Rachel put her hand to his chest. "Don't go to that place. We
are here. Safe."

"*Safe.*" Jack seemed to taste the word. He looked around him. "Is that all you want, Rachel? To be safe?"

She didn't answer. She waited, dreading the next words, which she knew would come.

"I want more."

"I know you do," Rachel said. She moistened her lips. Swallowed. "And you should have more. But—"

He smothered her words with his lips, and she answered, refusing to shrink away and yet unable to respond with the same unspoken longing he displayed. When he released her, a breeze blew her hair across her face. She didn't try to push it away. She didn't want him to see her face in the moonlight. He started to apologize, but Rachel put her fingertips to his mouth. "Don't," she said. "Don't." She leaned toward him, resting her forehead against his chest. "I'm sorry, Jack. It isn't you. You're a beautiful man. A good man." She stood away and looked up at the sky. "It isn't you."

"Yes. I know." The words he said next wrenched her heart, for he turned them to their real meaning—the truth that he had always refused to acknowledge. "It isn't me." He walked away toward the bunkhouse. Rachel stood and watched him go, saw the sliver of golden light pour into the night from the open door, saw it disappear, heard him latch the door. The wind rustled her hair again. She went back to the house, back to her bed, but not back to sleep. Lying awake in the dark she argued with herself. *Brown eyes and a uniform are NOT what you have been waiting for. They are NOT.*

————

"Where's your war bag, sonny?" Emmet Dorsey asked. He sent a stream of tobacco juice into the dirt at Will's feet.

"What?" Will asked, looking at Nathan Boone for help. Nathan raised his eyebrows and shrugged. Apparently he didn't know what a war bag was, either.

Dorsey retreated to the barn, emerging with two empty feed sacks. "Your war bag," he said, handing one to Will and one to Lieutenant Boone. "You put a change of clothes in there. A towel. Your toothbrush and your hairbrush." He winked at Will. "Not as if you'll use 'em, but it'll please your ma if you can tell her you took 'em along."

Will and Nathan went to the bunkhouse and stuffed the required items into the sack. When they came back out, Dorsey was waiting. "Toss 'em in the big wagon along with the others," he said.

Rachel came walking down the path from the house carrying a sugar sack. "Pemmican," she said, handing the sack to Lieutenant Boone. She flashed a smile at him and then turned to Will. "You'll like it," she said.

"Thanks," Nathan said. His cheeks turned a curious color of red.

As Rachel turned to go, Dorsey chuckled and spit a stream of tobacco.

Nathan glowered. "Don't say a word," he muttered. "Come on, Will. I'll show you how to tie your bedroll on behind your saddle." He put his hand on the boy's shoulder. "You'll look like you grew up on a horse before we're finished with you." He glanced back at Dorsey. "And Rachel's right. You'll like her pemmican. It's like jerky, only better."

Dorsey called after them. "You think that sorry excuse for a horse you got this boy riding can keep up with Jack's outfit?"

"Bones isn't much to look at," Nathan said, "but he and Will have an understanding. They'll do fine."

Just as they arrived at the barn, a dozen or more Cheyenne rode in. Will inched closer to Nathan Boone, who put his hand on the boy's shoulder while he called out to get himself and Will hooked up with Jack's outfit.

Will saddled Bones with shaking hands. He'd never felt so excited and yet so frightened at the same time. It was one thing to get to know Rachel and Jack, but another thing entirely to be in the middle of what seemed to him to be an entire tribe of Cheyenne. The forty or so men milling around the ranch house were a diverse lot. Some were quiet, almost sullen. Others laughed and joked as they went about the task of lassoing their mounts and saddling up. All of them had an air of bravado and confidence that made Will want to be like them—except, of course, for the fact that they cursed a lot, which would displease his mother.

"You go ahead and get mounted up," Lieutenant Boone instructed Will. "We're greenhorns enough. No need for the rest of these men to have to wait for us." He took his horse's reins and headed for the house.

"Where you going?" Will wanted to know.

"I forgot something," Boone said. "I'll catch up."

Dorsey chuckled. He looked up at Will and winked. "Forgot his sugar."

Nathan hesitated just inside the front door of the ranch house. Rachel was nowhere in sight. He looked around, scratched his beard, then turned to go.

"Is that you, Mr. Jackson?" Rachel called from the loft. Nathan looked up in time to see her look down. He was pleased to see the smile light up her face when she saw it was him. "Mr. Jackson wanted me to sneak another blanket in the chuck wagon for Dorsey."

Nathan grinned. "I take it the old coot still won't admit to needing a little extra attention for his knees."

She shook her head. "We all just go behind his back to try and take care of him. Did you need something?"

"Uh . . . no." Blast it. He felt as awkward as a schoolboy. "I'll . . . uh . . . take the blanket down to the chuck wagon if you like. Dorsey will think it's for the boy."

Rachel nodded. "I'll be right down."

He heard her footsteps scurrying across the loft and back to the ladder. She tossed a blanket down to him. He caught it *and* a glimpse of Rachel's bare legs as she descended the ladder and lighted so close he could smell the freshly washed scent of her hair. "Thanks. I'll . . . uh . . . I wanted to thank you. For being so nice to the boy. He's a good boy." *You sound like an idiot.*

"He is," Rachel agreed. "A sad boy. But a good one." She smiled up at him. "Not unlike a certain man I know." Without warning, she reached up and touched the crease between his eyebrows. "This is new in these ten years." She touched the gray hair at his temples. "And this."

He shrugged. "The years catch up to a man. We can't always hide the things we've done that we aren't proud of." He looked down at her and swallowed the lump in his throat before saying, "I always wanted to tell you how sorry I was."

She shook her head. "That's for others to say. Not you. You gave us a life. You know what it would be like for Jack if you hadn't found him. You know where I would be." She gestured. "Look around you, Nathan Boone. It is not for you to say you are sorry. It is for us to say *thank you*." She stood on tiptoe and brushed his cheek with a kiss.

"Hey, Lieutenant," Will called from the door. "Everybody's leaving!"

Nathan spun around. "Then let's get going," he said. With a nod toward Rachel, he headed outside.

The men rode north, away from Four Pines Ranch, up into the buttes. Before long they had broken off into several groups of four or five, each group heading in a different direction. Will followed Nathan Boone, Jack Greyfoot, and three other Cheyenne cowboys, riding north and west.

Gradually the landscape began to change. Verdant pastureland gave way to splotches of white chalklike stone jutting up from the earth. Little by little, the grass disappeared completely and the men were riding single file through outcroppings of strangely formed rock. The horse's hooves echoed loudly as they rode along. For all the strangeness of the landscape, Will noticed masses of blooming plants clinging to the tops of some of the rock formations. He thought about how his mother would smile if he brought her some of those flowers, then looked around him guiltily, as if the men might read his mind and call him a "mama's boy" for the thought.

"Your mama would like those," Lieutenant Boone said, nodding toward a clump of orange flowers. "Too bad you can't take her some." He grinned at Will's look of surprise. "You give her flowers, and she might not worry so much about what you're learning from this bunch of cowboys."

Will peered at Boone from beneath the brim of his oversized hat. "Thank you for talking her into letting me come. I never thought she would."

"As I recall," Boone said, "mothers sometimes have a bit of trouble letting their boys do what boys got to do. Mine certainly did." He smiled. "She threw a fit when I left home."

Will commiserated. "Yeah, mothers are like that." He added, "Mine said to make sure I didn't try to rope any cows. She was afraid I'd forget to put on my gloves and get rope burns on my hands." Will looked down at the soft hands holding Bones's reins.

Boone burst out laughing. He leaned over the saddle horn toward Will. "I'm thinking you'd better learn to rope while we're out here or you'll feel like you've missed the perfect opportunity to rebel." He urged his horse forward. "Let's see if we can't find ourselves a couple of strays. I can't rope worth a darn, but maybe we can manage to at least herd them this way."

Will flapped his boots against the old gelding's sides, and Bones galumphed forward with a sound of protest. By the end of the day, Will and Lieutenant Boone had ridden until Will could no longer feel his backside. Jack and the others, with only a little help from the two greenhorns, had managed to round up a dozen cattle. Will thought they were ornery critters, bawling and protesting and not wanting to go toward the ranch at all. He watched the men drive the recalcitrant animals with growing respect for both the men's riding ability and their horses.

"It's like the horses know what the cow's thinking," Will said at one point while he rode alongside Jack.

"Well, in a way, they do," Jack said. "A good cow horse does, anyway." He patted his horse's withers. "Wait until you see this one cut."

While he was certain whatever Jack was talking about had nothing to do with a knife or scissors, Will had no idea what a horse could do that would be called *cutting*. But he nodded as if he understood. As the cowboys drove the cattle ahead of them, Will and Lieutenant Boone enjoyed the scenery and mostly tried to stay out of the way.

One day Lieutenant Boone shot an antelope and that night they all had steak for dinner. More than once Boone gave chase after a bolting cow at the same time Jack did. Boone's army horse was strongly built and the lieutenant was an expert rider, but it was always Jack's tightly muscled little gelding that made the final move that turned the old cow and her calf back into the herd. Will watched such things from his safe seat aboard old Bones, his own muscles tensing, his arms reining left and right as he pretended to be Jack Greyfoot.

———

Will and Nathan rode with the Four Pines outfit for over a week. They gathered up strays until, when they finally headed for the ranch, they were herding nearly a hundred cattle ahead of them. Will thought he would never be able to describe it all to his mother. He wouldn't have words for the smell of dust and manure and leather, the sounds of hoofbeats and yelling men and ropes whistling through the air. When the outfit neared the ranch, and they were greeted by the sight of nearly a thousand cattle milling around in the valley below, Will's mouth fell open.

Boone nodded. "We've only been working the north. There have been other outfits doing the same thing west, east, and south. Now the real work begins."

"Cutting?" Will said.

"Cutting, branding, heading for market," Boone said.

"And now you'll see what I meant when I bragged on this fella," Jack said, urging his horse down into the valley. "At least two hundred of those beeves belong to the Four Pines. Let's go get 'em."

For this part of the roundup, a frustrated Will Bishop was ordered to watch from the relative safety of the chuck wagon seat. Over the next few days, he saw horsemanship like he had never imagined. It was nothing like the fancy stepping of his father's horses in a military parade, nor was it anything like the steeplechasing his mother liked. To Will, it was better because it wasn't just for show. Just as Jack had said, the cutting horses were amazing. Will was on his feet for most of the day, standing on top of the wagon seat, watching as the horses bobbed and wove their way through the herd, turning this way and that, singling out a cow and her calf and giving chase until both were separated from the herd.

Now that they were camped near the ranch house, Rachel came down every day to help the chuck wagon cook. Will noticed that Lieutenant Boone showed up at the wagon more often. One day when he was standing nearby, Will said, "Oh, I *wish* I knew how to do that!"

Boone looked up at him, squinting into the bright morning sun. "You'll be riding as good as any of them soon."

"No, I won't," Will said, slumping down onto the wagon seat. "Bones is a good old horse, but he's too slow."

"You won't be riding Bones forever," Boone said. He nodded toward the string of horses belonging to the wranglers. "You'll have a good pony like one of those."

"Mother would never let me have a wild ranch pony. She'd be afraid I'd get hurt."

"Well now," the Lieutenant said, "I think the word you have to avoid with your mother is 'wild.' Mr. Jackson has plenty of fine working ponies that don't have a wild bone in their body. That's the kind you'll need first."

Will just shook his head.

"Don't get discouraged before you even get started," Boone said. "And don't let anybody tell you that you can't. Because you can."

"I can what?"

"Just about anything you set your mind to. Think about it. A boy who was afraid of horses just spent the last two weeks on a roundup. And he handled his horse just fine. And tomorrow—"

Caleb Jackson rode up. "Tomorrow is branding," he said. "And you can help."

Will hardly slept. Lieutenant Boone didn't spend much time in his bedroll, either. Will suspected it had something to do with Rachel Greyfoot.

Branding lasted only a day. Will was up early, watching Jack and a few other men build a large fire in the predawn light, and helping them plunge several branding irons into the hot coals until they glowed red hot.

When the lassoing began, Will once again admired Jack's and Caleb Jackson's abilities with a twirling rope. Once again, he admired the cow ponies, who seemed to know what to do without any signal from their rider. As soon as the ropes hit their mark, the ponies began to back up, straining against the struggling cow until the bellowing creature was stretched full out.

Will winced when the first brand was applied. After the cows were all branded, the men began to work with the calves—roping them only around the hind legs while cowboys wrestled them to the ground. Lieutenant Boone waded right in, laughing and joking while he sweated and strained with the other cowboys. At one point, Rachel came down and perched on the top board of the corral and watched for a while. Will sat next to her, surprised when she was able to explain as well as anyone what was going on and why.

"It's your turn," Lieutenant Boone finally said. He moved toward where Will and Rachel sat, taking off his leather gloves as he walked and slapping the dust out of them against his thigh. "You want to brand or wrestle?"

"Neither," Rachel teased.

Lieutenant Boone laughed.

"Both," Will said. "I want to do both."

Boone nodded and tapped the brim of Will's hat. "Well then, cowboy. Let's get you out there." He winked at Rachel.

Rachel had long since gone back to the chuck wagon to start cooking supper when Will finally succeeded in wrestling a calf to the earth without help. He held it down with all his might until the branding was done, then leaped up, extending both hands to the sky and yelping with joy. The men around the corral burst out laughing. Will felt himself starting to blush, but then Caleb Jackson came forward with a red-hot branding iron and said, "Brand the next one, and you're a real cowboy, Will Bishop."

Will worked alongside Lieutenant Boone this time, applying the brand as soon as Boone threw the calf. He winced in sympathy as the smell of burned flesh filled the air, but then the same men who'd laughed when he wrestled the calf to the ground cheered. The feeling that he was being laughed at was replaced by a sense of camaraderie the boy had never experienced before.

By the end of the week, Will Bishop had heard more swearing than in all his life put together. He'd overheard jokes that would have made his mother gasp, been offered his first chaw of tobacco, and been teased until his cheeks were flaming red. He had also been rescued from an angry bull, taught to lasso a pole, and allowed to ride one of Jack's horses—a pretty little mare with more energy than old Bones had probably ever had in his entire life. He had decided that while he couldn't speak for the entire Indian nation, the Cheyenne certainly were nothing like the Indians his father had told him about. He had learned that men who swore could also be generous and kindhearted and brave. And he had decided that no matter how long it took to convince his mother, he was never going to be in the army. Will Bishop was going to be a cowboy.

———

Roundup was over, the calves all branded, the herd culled, the various outfits scattered to the half dozen Sandhills ranches around Fort Robinson. Will stood in the dark with his arms crossed atop one of the corral boards, admiring a gray pony.

"You look almost like a ghost," he said aloud. "In the dark I can hardly see your black legs or your mane or tail. It's like you're floating above the ground." He extended his hand inside the corral. "You hear me, Spirit?" He was amazed when the filly stopped milling around with the other horses and looked at him. "Is that your name, then? Are you Spirit?" Will said, his heart pounding.

The horse snorted and tossed her head.

"Oh, yeah, you're something," Will said. He wiggled his fingers. "Afraid of a little boy. What's that about, huh? You afraid of me? I'm not going to hurt you."

The horse pawed the dust with one black hoof. She shifted her weight from one foot to the other and back again before taking a step toward him.

"Come along, then," Will said, thinking surely the pony could hear his heart pounding. Surely she would be afraid of the unusual sound and whirl away. Any minute now.

But she didn't. As Will talked, the little horse inched her way across the corral until Will could feel her warm breath on his open palm.

Afraid to move, Will kept talking. "My name's Will." Just as he said the name, the filly thrust her muzzle into his palm. When he didn't snatch it away, she took his fingers between her velvety lips and nibbled gently. "Hey," Will said quietly. "That's not food. That's my hand." She let go and stood, looking at him.

Bones rambled up to the corral fence, thrust his big head over the top rung and shoved Will playfully. "Hey, now," Will protested. "I'm talking to Spirit. You go on."

As Bones stood at the fence, the gray horse edged closer until she had sidled alongside him, and the two horses stood side by side, listening to Will talk.

From the darkness behind him, Lieutenant Boone's voice sounded. "What'd I tell you? She doesn't have a mean bone in her body. She just needed the right person to pay her some attention. And a little courage borrowed from old Bones."

"What should I do now?" Will asked.

"I don't think you need any advice from me," Boone said. "Seems to me you're doing just fine. That little gal won't come near me, and here you've got her nibbling on your fingers. I'm thinking she's picked you out to be the one she trusts."

"Why'd she do that?" Will wanted to know.

"Guess she's the only one that knows that," was the answer. "But one thing's for sure, she trusts you and Bones. You think you've got the patience to break her in? She's going to take a little extra time. But I've got a feeling she'd be a good horse for you."

"F-f-for me?" Will stuttered at the idea.

"That's right," Boone said. "For you."

"Ma wouldn't let me," he said.

"Your ma's a first-rate horsewoman," Boone said. "She'll take one look at this little gal and know she'd make a good ride for you. Maybe we could ride out here with your ma next week and show her."

"I don't have money to pay for a horse," Will said.

"Can you haul hay and clean out stalls?"

"Sure."

"Then I imagine we'll be able to work something out with Mr. Jackson," Boone said. "You've been talking about wanting to be a cowboy. Maybe you can start this summer."

"I'd work hard," Will said.

"Tomorrow at breakfast I'll give you some sugar cubes so you can give her a treat." It was Rachel Greyfoot. Will hadn't realized she was with the lieutenant.

Boone spoke up. "See to it you stay *outside* the corral, you hear? She likes you, but she doesn't know you well enough yet. Getting kicked in the head is no way to start your career as a cowboy."

Will nodded. "Yes, sir," he said. "I'll stay here. I'll just talk to her. Get her used to my voice."

"That's good. She likes listening to you. Look at her now. Those little ears are taking in every word."

Boone's and Rachel's footsteps retreated toward the house.

"That's Lieutenant Boone," Will said to the horse. "He's nice. Maybe you'll let him help me put a halter on you tomorrow. I met him because he came to see my ma." He pondered for a moment. "But I think he really likes Rachel."

———

"First we rounded 'em up and then we lassoed 'em—I can lasso a pole but not a calf yet—and then we branded 'em, and I branded one, and everybody cheered and even the Indians were nice, Ma. And there's something I got to ask you, Ma. . . ." Will, who had wrapped both arms around his mother's waist, leaned back and looked up at her, his face flushed with joy.

"Hold on, Will," Charlotte said, gasping for breath.

Will jumped back and let go. "Did I hurt your arm? Oh, gosh, Ma— I'm sorry."

Charlotte put her open palm on the boy's cheek. "No, you didn't hurt me," she said, smiling. "I just can't take it all in. You've rounded up and lassoed and branded and met nice Indians—and I want to hear more." She stepped to the edge of the porch and smiled at Nathan who was waiting, still mounted on his horse, holding the reins to Bones. With his free hand he reached up and raked his fingers through his scruffy beard.

"I'll take Bones on over to the stables, Will," he called out.

"No," Will protested. "Wait!" He looked up at his mother. "I should take care of my own horse, Ma. You understand. Right?" He was already scampering off the porch and climbing into the saddle. "We're starved," he called from the saddle. "Does Garnet have any pie?"

Nathan spoke up. "Never mind the pie for me."

"Just because it isn't chokecherry," Charlotte said, "doesn't mean you won't like it." She interrupted before he could object. "It's the least I can do to say thank-you."

"Thank-you for what?" Nathan asked.

Charlotte pointed at Will, who had already turned Bones around and started to ride toward the stables.

Nathan shrugged and tugged on the brim of his hat. "Ranch life agrees with him." He headed for the stables. Halfway across the parade ground he looked back over his shoulder. Charlotte was still standing on the front porch. He tugged on the brim of his hat. She waved.

Chapter Thirteen

I am weary with my groaning:
all the night make I my bed to swim;
I water my couch with my tears.

PSALM 6:6

"NOT BREATHING."

Charlotte held back her own tears as she watched Laina touch her baby's perfectly formed nose, then brush a fingertip across the closed eyelids. Only moments ago, as Charlotte cheered her on, Laina had made the final tremendous effort to birth her son. The two women's eyes had locked as they shared an instant of rejoicing. And then Charlotte's father frowned. Charlotte held Laina's hand while they waited for the cry that never came. She remained motionless when her father pronounced the two words that brought a weight of grief into every corner of the little room.

"Not breathing."

"I'm so sorry, my dear," Charlotte's father spoke again. "But there's still more work to do. Push now." Gently he directed Laina to the completion of the birth process.

While her father worked with Laina, Charlotte wrapped the baby boy in a blanket. Somehow, she found the strength not to collapse into sobs. How well she remembered this helpless, empty feeling. She had felt it three times, the third time no easier than the first.

Leaning back against her pillow, Laina closed her eyes. "Caleb," she said. "I want Caleb."

"I'll see to it," Charlotte said, handing the baby to the doctor and heading for the kitchen where she motioned for Nathan.

"Where's CJ?" she asked.

"Outside with Will."

Charlotte took in a deep breath. "The baby." She closed her eyes, unable to say the words.

"Oh, no," Nathan said. He shook his head.

"She's asking for Caleb."

"He'll be here in the morning," Nathan said, and left.

"What's wrong with my ma?" CJ came to the door.

"Your ma's fine," Charlotte said. Her voice wavered. "I'm afraid your baby brother . . ." She swallowed hard. "He's in heaven."

CJ grabbed Will's hand and held on. "Can I see him?"

Charlotte's father entered the kitchen. He shook his head. "I think your mama needs to be alone for a little while, CJ."

Charlotte's eyes filled with tears. Her presence seemed so accidental. Will and Lieutenant Boone had returned from the Four Pines Ranch at sundown, bedded their horses, and came back to Dr. Valentine's house to be treated to a piece of Garnet's fresh gooseberry pie. Charlotte marveled as Will recounted the details of his first western roundup, described his adventure with an enthusiasm Charlotte had never seen in him before. He was demonstrating branding, by standing over an imaginary calf, when CJ pounded on the back door in search of Dr. Valentine. Before anyone had time to think, they were all clustered in the kitchen at the trading post, trying to assuage CJ's fear and waiting half the night while Dr. Valentine came and went.

Not far into the night, Charlotte had been surprised when her father came out to the kitchen and said Laina was asking for her. Laina was apologetic. Charlotte was touched. As the hours went by, she applied cool compresses to Laina's furrowed brow and stroked her arms. At one point, she even sang a hymn, joking about her wobbly voice until Laina actually smiled.

Now the birthing was over, Laina in mourning, and Will's best friend, CJ, was clutching his hand in fear while she tried to process what had happened.

Charlotte took charge. "You come on home with us, honey." She held out her hand to CJ. "You can come back after your ma has had time to rest."

Maude DuBois spoke up. Turning to Charlotte she said, "You're exhausted, too. You don't worry about a thing. I'll check in on Mrs. Jackson from time to time. That elixir your father gave her will keep her asleep, likely until mid-morning tomorrow."

CJ allowed Charlotte to lead her away to Dr. Valentine's house. As they walked along across the darkened fort grounds, Charlotte put her arm around the girl's shoulders. "It'll be all right, CJ," she whispered. "Don't worry."

———

Charlotte rose at dawn. She roused Garnet and asked her to delay CJ as long as possible, then headed to the trading post to be with Laina. She stroked the back of her friend's hand while they talked. "I've been through this three times, but I don't know of anything I can say that will help. I wish your Granny Max was here. Maybe she'd know what to say."

Without opening her eyes, Laina recited, " 'I don't understand it, honey-lamb. No, I don't. But I know God is still on His throne. We just got to trust Him.' " She looked at Charlotte. "That's what she'd say."

Charlotte nodded. "That sounds good." She patted Laina's hand. "I can tell it's helping you."

Laina pulled her hand away. She shook her head. "I know God's ways are not our ways. I know He is the Potter and I'm the clay. But right now, those things just sound like empty words." Her eyes filled with tears.

"I don't understand why this has happened," Charlotte said. "If any-one deserves happiness, it's you. It seems to me you've been through enough."

Laina snorted. "Apparently not." She shook her head. "The only thing I've asked God for in quite a while is sons for Caleb. He wants sons so badly." She stared at the foot of the bed, talking to no one in particular. "What could possibly be wrong with that? Why on earth would God say *no*?" She reached over and touched the edge of the blanket that still held her baby. Tears rolled down her cheeks.

"I'm so sorry," Charlotte said. "Try to get some sleep. I asked Garnet to keep CJ occupied as long as possible so you would have some time to yourself. And Caleb should be here soon."

"I know Maude's worn out from keeping watch last night," Laina said. "Would you . . . could you . . . stay. . . ."

"Of course I'll stay," Charlotte said, stroking her arm. "Try to get some sleep. I'll be right here."

Once, Laina woke with a jolt. "The baby! Where's the baby?"

The panic in her voice brought tears to Charlotte's eyes. "Right here, Laina. Right here at your side."

"Why isn't Caleb here? What's taking so long?"

Charlotte looked out the window. "The sky is really overcast. Maybe he had to wait out a cloudburst."

Laina looked down at her baby. "Oh," she moaned softly, bringing her hand to her breasts as her body awakened the timeless response of a mother to its child.

"I'll be right back," Charlotte said. She slipped out and returned with a length of muslin from the trading post shelves and tore it into strips. "Let me help you bind yourself," Charlotte said. "It will help."

"How do you know about this?" Laina asked.

"I've been through it."

Laina closed her eyes. "I'm sorry. I forgot." Tears streamed down her cheeks. "It hurts."

"I know," Charlotte said.

———

At last, Caleb arrived, his footsteps muffled by the rag rug on the floor. Laina stifled her sobs and opened her eyes just in time to see Charlotte pat Caleb's shoulder and slip out of the room. For all their married years, Caleb had always had a way of soothing her woes. His hands were large and rough, but when he stroked her forehead, following her hairline down one temple and to the tip of her chin, he was as gentle as Granny Max had ever been. She'd once told him that his touch was like being soothed by God. When he stroked her that way, he always hummed a raggedy melody. Off-key. Then he'd stretch open his fingers and massage her head, easing the tingling along the left side of her head where a bullet had once sliced her scalp, leaving a wide scar. Whatever old wounds or fears assaulted her, Caleb's presence had always stilled them all, bringing her back to the present and to a place where she was safe and loved and as secure as any woman could be.

It was only natural for Laina to expect that Caleb would reach out to her that way again, show his love without saying a word, stroke her forehead, maybe trace a line between her eyebrows to the tip of her nose. She closed her eyes. *It's all right, baby girl* he would say.

But instead of reaching out to her, Caleb touched the edge of the baby's blanket. "Let me hold him," he said.

She knew that voice. It was low and gravelly—the voice he used when he was having trouble controlling his own emotions. She heard it when a calf was found half eaten by wolves or a prized mare died or when he didn't know if they were going to be able to make the next payment on the ranch. She'd heard it at the worst times of their lives.

When she held the baby out to him, Caleb took the bundle and stood up and went to the window. He turned his back to her. She saw his shoulders shaking. He must be crying. But he didn't share his tears with her.

The quiet in the room nearly smothered her. The tension came back to her midsection and a weariness settled over her. Pulling the covers up to her chin, she closed her eyes.

"Not breathing."

The night before, Laina had thought hearing those words was the worst thing she would ever have to endure. As Caleb left with the baby without saying a word to her, she realized she was wrong. Dreaded words could rip a woman apart inside. Words could break a heart. But sometimes silence was worse.

——

Caleb and Laina Jackson buried their infant son on a bleak May morning made even more dreary by a cold wind heavy with moisture. Laina stood beside her husband, thanks to an herbal tea supplied by Garnet Irvin and CJ's clinging to her hand. Taking Caleb's proffered arm brought her no comfort. Before his son died, Caleb always walked with his arm around her waist, not caring about the shocked looks such a public display of affection garnered them both. But that was then. And this was now. In the hours since his son's death, Caleb Jackson had undergone a transformation.

Dr. Valentine was reading the Shepherd's Psalm. But Laina could not listen. All she seemed to be able to hear were the words he had spoken a short while ago when, after a brief examination, he summoned Caleb to his wife's room.

"As I told you yesterday," the doctor had said, looking apologetically at Caleb, "I had some concerns after the delivery. There is good news. The bleeding has stopped. That's a good sign in regards to *your* health, my dear." He patted the back of Laina's hand. "I think it will be all right for you to ride in the carriage over to the cemetery for the service. However," he continued, "I am very sorry to have to say this, but future pregnancies are no longer possible."

"What?" Laina said. She looked at Caleb, who was staring out the window. She looked back at the doctor. "What do you mean? I'm fine. Of *course* there will be more babies. We're building a ranch to pass on to our children. Our *sons*. We expanded the house to make room. Maude knows a woman who didn't have a baby for years and years—but then she had five in the next five years. That's what we want, isn't it, Caleb? Tell him. Tell him we're going to have—"

Caleb turned around and faced her. He shook his head. "No," he said. "We're not." He stayed by the window, barely looking at her. "Tell her, Doc," Caleb said. "Tell her how you explained it to me."

At least he walked over and put his hand on her shoulder while Dr. Valentine explained things. Tissue had been expelled in the delivery, he said. And the loss of that *tissue* made it impossible for her to conceive again. "I recall, Mrs. Jackson, that when Clara Joy was born I told you she was something of a miracle. Having also attended this birth, I can tell you that with even more certainty. He turned to look up at Caleb. "And I can also say that you are blessed that your wife survived this birth."

They still call it birth. How odd, Laina thought.

"Will she be all right?" Caleb asked.

"She needs rest and time to heal. But she'll be fine," Dr. Valentine said. He issued a few more directives, encouraged Laina to rest, to spend most of her time in bed for the next week, then to gradually take short walks until her energy returned. He complimented Charlotte's "binding," and offered to bring over one of his women's medical books if Laina thought it would help answer her questions. And then he left.

Caleb looked down at her. "You must be exhausted. I've got to check in with the commanding officer. He promised to put me to work right after roundup." He patted her head twice. Kissed her on the cheek. Left without another word.

"Will she be all right?" Caleb had asked. Dr. Valentine had said she would be, with time. Now, while the doctor's voice droned on through the reading of the Shepherd's Psalm at her baby's graveside, Laina thought how very wrong Dr. Valentine had been. She might heal physically, but something had happened to make Caleb pull away. And Laina was quite sure she would never be all right again.

———

CJ Jackson told Will she had never experienced having her parents barely speaking to each other. Will had never experienced anything else. "Don't worry," he said. "My folks practically lived in different parts of the house sometimes. At least yours aren't fighting."

CJ frowned. "You don't understand, Will. It's not like that for Ma and Pa. I mean, they were *embarrassing* the way they always acted around each other, always kissing or hugging or just—you know, just *looking*. Like they had a secret or something." She was sitting on the side porch at the doctor's residence with Will. "It's been a week. Ma sleeps most of the time, and

Pa . . . well, Pa is always working. He hasn't even had supper with us." CJ stifled a sob. "I'm scared."

It felt awkward, but Will made himself put his arm around his friend. "Don't be afraid," he said. "Things will work out." He added, "You can eat with us tonight. Lieutenant Boone is coming to talk to Ma about Spirit."

———

Dinner at the Valentines' residence was over, and it was nearly sunset when Nathan finally found Caleb, still at work installing windows in one of the new buildings on the West End. "I had dinner with Charlotte and Will and the doc tonight," Nathan said after a quick greeting. He cleared his throat. "CJ was there, too. She's worried about her family."

Caleb frowned. "According to the doc, there's not going to be much family." He went on to tell Nathan what Doctor Valentine had said.

"I'm the last person in the world to preach any sermons to you, and I know it," Nathan said brusquely. "But, Caleb—you do need to take a look around."

"At what?" Caleb said. "At the loft back at the ranch that's going to be empty? At the new brand I'll never need?"

Nathan scrubbed his jaw with a closed fist. "How about you take a look at the tombstones over in the cemetery. Start with the one that says Lily Bainbridge Boone. Realize everybody loses people they love. Everybody has dreams they didn't manage to live."

"And I suppose the fact that your wife died makes you an expert in this kind of thing," Caleb mumbled, taking one of the nails from between his lips and nailing a board in place.

"Hey," Nathan said. "You've already got a preacher in your life. You don't need another one, and I know that. But blast it, man—" Nathan looked away. "Laina *survived*. You've still got a beautiful wife *and* a terrific daughter. And they need you. Charlotte can't even get Laina to go for a carriage drive. CJ tells Will the two of you hardly talk. She says Laina spends most of the day in bed." He cleared his throat. "I know you don't want to hear this—neither did I when Lily died. But when it comes right down to it, your problems aren't all that special. God sends rain to fall on the just and the unjust."

Caleb placed another nail, speaking before he hammered it down. "I hear what you're saying. And I know I've got things to be thankful for. Dorsey rode in this morning, and once he quit grumbling about his bum knees, he said Jack has a good start on breaking three colts. Rachel's garden is coming along well. We're going to have a good crop of foals. And with me working here at the fort, we'll have money to expand the herd, maybe even bring Banner out, and put a down payment on the Dawsons' place if they decide to move into Crawford. Things are looking good for the building of a ranch." He hammered another nail, then another, before looking up at Nathan.

"But blast it, man, what's it all *for* if there's nobody to leave it to? We've done nothing these past ten years but dream about building something that's worth passing on." His voice was bitter. "And now this." He bent the nail he was trying to drive. Swearing under his breath, he pulled it out and held it down as he hammered it back into shape. When Nathan still didn't speak, he finally grumbled, "I know. I know. And you're right. I got to get my thinking straight." He shook his head. "I *really* got to get it straight when the man who doesn't talk to God is quoting Scripture at me."

"Scripture? What are you talking about?"

" 'God sends rain to fall on the just and the unjust,' " Caleb replied.

"I was quoting Granny Max," Nathan said.

Both men chuckled. Caleb shrugged. "Well, you're right, anyway." He stood up straight and looked at Nathan. "I appreciate you caring enough to walk over here tonight. Really, I do. And I'll be all right. But I need some time."

"Then take time," Nathan said. "But don't let Laina *see* how you're struggling. She'll blame herself. It'll kill her."

Caleb shook his head. "That's where you're wrong. She's strong. And it's not like she doesn't know what's going on inside me. It wasn't just my dream. It was hers, too."

Tattoo sounded. "I've got to get going," Nathan said. "I'm sorry, Caleb. You two deserve better."

"I'm inclined to agree with you." Caleb nodded. "But we'll be all right. Laina's strong. She'll bounce back. We all will."

Chapter Fourteen

Trust in the Lord with all thine heart;
and lean not unto thine own understanding.
PROVERBS 3:5

IN SPITE OF WHAT her husband said about her, Laina Jackson showed no sign of being strong. And those who knew her best saw that she was far from being "all right."

Charlotte invited her on a walk every day. Laina was too tired.

Maude Dubois suggested Laina check over the new bolts of calico in the trading post and get started on a new dress for the Independence Day festivities. Laina declined, saying she doubted they would attend this year.

Caleb wanted her to go with him into Crawford. Laina didn't feel strong enough for such a long drive.

Charlotte suggested they attend a women's tea together. Laina had no energy for "small talk."

Garnet Irvin offered her special healing tea. Laina claimed she was healing just fine and left most of it in the cup.

CJ asked for her help with a school assignment. Laina told her to ask her pa.

Nathan Boone offered to have Private Blake drive Laina and CJ back to the ranch. Laina wasn't ready to go.

Caleb began to work longer days and took to sleeping in a tent on the East End instead of "coming in late and disturbing you, honey."

Everyone was concerned, but no one knew what to do.

Charlotte wondered why Laina's faith, which had seemed so real, did not help her more.

Nathan wondered why Caleb's faith, which had seemed so real, did not help him more.

———

"I'm really worried about her," Charlotte said to Nathan Boone one morning several weeks after the funeral. He and Will and CJ had arrived at the Valentines' back door without Laina, who had once again refused an invitation—this time a ride up into the hills for a picnic with the children.

Nathan had dismounted and come to the door to fetch Charlotte. "She won't come." With CJ and Will out of earshot, he lowered his voice and added, "She's never cared much for riding, but I really thought she'd come for CJ's sake."

"I thought part of the problem was her being homesick for the peace and quiet on the ranch," Charlotte said. "You'd think she'd welcome an afternoon away from all the construction noise."

Garnet spoke up. "No reason you two shouldn't let Will and CJ have their outing," she said.

"Bess isn't anything so fine as you're used to riding," Nathan said. "But she's gentle. And it *is* a beautiful day."

"Come on, Ma, *please*," Will begged. He'd jumped down off Bones and come inside. He looked back over his shoulder. "CJ needs cheering up."

Looking past Will to where CJ waited aboard a rangy spotted mare, Charlotte nodded. "All right. Let's go."

They rode north and picked up a trail leading toward the high bluffs overshadowing Fort Robinson.

"Even old Bones can feel summer coming," Charlotte said to Nathan as Will kicked the horse into a canter and sped away. "I didn't think Bones could move that fast. Will has been complaining about the old boy's stubborn tendencies."

Nathan said, "Have you had time to think any more about Spirit?"

"The gray filly at the Four Pines?" Charlotte said. "Will can't go a day without mentioning her. She sounds pretty."

"She is," Nathan said. "Black legs, long black mane and tail. Interesting face." He drew an imaginary line diagonally across his own face. "Half white, half black."

"You said she's *feisty*—I think it was—at dinner the other night."

Nathan nodded. "But there was definitely a connection between her and Will." Nathan went on to describe the scene he'd witnessed the first night Will noticed the horse.

Charlotte nodded, murmuring, "I know what that's like."

"Isaac?" Nathan asked.

"Yes. Isaac." She looked into the distance. "I do hope Major Riley is treating him well."

She looked over at Nathan. "Will said he calls her Spirit because she looked like she was floating above the ground that night he first noticed her. I assume that means her movement is good."

"She has a beautiful, fluid gait. I definitely think you'd approve." Nathan nodded at the trail, which was narrowing to where they would begin to climb single file. "You sure this is all right?" He nodded at her still-bandaged wrist.

"Of course," Charlotte said, and nudged her mare forward. From above them, they could hear CJ and Will calling to one another, laughing and screeching as their horses climbed the steepest part of the trail.

"Get on, Bones, get on!" Will shouted.

Charlotte smiled at Nathan. "I'd say his confidence level is definitely improving."

For a few minutes they both gave their attention to the steep ascent. Finally, they emerged at the top to find that CJ had already spread a cloth on the ground and was opening her saddlebags to unpack the lunch Garnet had sent along.

Nathan reached up to help Charlotte down. She blushed as his hands encircled her waist. As soon as her feet touched the ground, she mumbled a thanks and walked toward the edge of the bluff. "I'd forgotten how breathtaking the view is from up here," she said. "When Emory used to tell his mother about Nebraska, he only mentioned the barren hills. It was as if he'd never seen this." She pointed to the valley below.

"The Colonel came out here?" Nathan asked.

Charlotte nodded. "Once. When Will was a toddler."

"You didn't come?"

Charlotte shook her head. "The Colonel didn't want the distraction."

"Lunch is ready!" CJ called.

After lunch CJ and Will headed off to explore.

"I'm thinking a horse to train might be just the thing to keep Will out of trouble," Nathan said. He leaned back on his elbow and stretched out his long legs. Turning his face up toward the sky, he closed his eyes.

"Heaven knows he's going to need something to keep his attention now that school is ending," Charlotte agreed. "And you're right—he has definitely outgrown Bones."

"I've put in for an extended leave," Nathan said. "Once the school session closes, if you approve, I thought maybe Will and I could head back up to the ranch for a few weeks. He could work to earn the horse. I'd have time to visit the Dawson place and talk to the old man about buying him out."

"I didn't know you were interested in ranching," Charlotte said.

Nathan shrugged. "I don't know that I am. Land is a good investment, whether I'm personally living on it or not. And I don't think it would be too hard to get someone to work the place."

Charlotte smiled. "You're talking about Rachel and Jack," she said. "Will told me about them. So do you think Rachel is closer to saying yes?"

Nathan hesitated. "I don't know if Jack has asked her recently."

Charlotte looked at him. "I wasn't talking about Jack." She smiled. "Will's young, Lieutenant. He isn't blind." When Nathan didn't respond, she apologized. "I'm sorry. It's really none of my business." She sighed. "And here I've been congratulating myself on how much I've changed from that little gossip Charlotte Valentine used to be. For whatever it's worth, Lieutenant, I haven't said anything to anyone, and I won't."

"Good," Nathan said. "Because there's nothing to say." He turned and looked at her. "Rachel Greyfoot is a good woman. I like her. The same could be said for any number of women I know. Including the one sitting next to me watching the clouds from this hill."

Embarrassed, Charlotte got up and went to look for Will and CJ.

———

The Reverend Erastus Barton III, who was simply known as Preacher Barton by his supporters and friends, had spent most of spring ministering to the outfits working roundup, among them the boys hired by Caleb Jackson for the Four Pines Ranch. He'd spent two weeks at the Four Pines, making no headway at winning Rachel, Jack, or Corporal Dorsey over to Christianity. He'd also failed to get a positive response from Lieutenant Nathan Boone during their late night discussions, and he'd left the area feeling defeated, except for having witnessed the blossoming friendship between Mrs. Jackson and the surgeon's daughter at Fort Robinson. Barton could sense that the Widow Bishop needed to hear about the Savior. *Trust that to Mrs. Jackson, old man. Her faith is sure.*

With roundup concluded, Barton had thought about heading for Fort Robinson again to check on the Widow Bishop and to follow up with Nathan Boone. He and the lieutenant had had some good talks around the campfire. Talks about eternal things. Thanks to his deceased wife and his association with a woman he called Granny Max, Boone seemed to have a lot of head knowledge about spiritual things, but he was holding a grudge against God. In the end, Barton had decided he didn't have the wisdom to argue the young lieutenant into the kingdom. He would instead pray that Boone would read the book of Job, as Barton had suggested, and perhaps think more on God's omniscience and less on his own human understanding.

So, in spite of the coming heat of summer, Barton decided to head up to the Black Hills. But then his faithful horse, Elvira, threw a shoe, and for some reason he could not quite discern, he felt he should visit Crawford before heading north. In all his years of wandering around the Sandhills, the Reverend Erastus Barton III felt he had accomplished very little for the kingdom of God. He was, he often thought with a sigh, long on persever-ance and short on results.

In Crawford, Barton walked the streets for the better part of a morn-ing, arguing with God about the wisdom of street-corner preaching in such a rough town. The fact was it scared him spitless. He wondered if the apostle Paul had been nervous on Mars Hill and chastised himself for the thought. Paul might have mentioned preaching with "fear and trem-bling," but Barton doubted he would have minded being laughed at by a few drunken cowboys, which was probably the worst thing that would happen in Crawford.

This morning, the boomtown buildings served to funnel a cool wind down the main street, penetrating his threadbare wool jacket and making him shiver. It took all his willpower to step up onto the crate he'd dragged out of a pile of rubbish and upended in the space between two unfinished buildings. Barton cleared his throat and began to recite words his aging eyes could not see in the small book in his trembling hands. Two or three men who had been on the opposite side of the street crossed over.

"Preach it, brother!" one of them yelled.

Barton blinked. *Did you hear that, Lord? Mocking. They don't want to hear from you.* The wind ruffled the pages of the book. The old man didn't hear a voice, but his heart recited familiar words. *"Blessed are ye when men shall revile you and persecute you."* He held the book closer, blinking, squinting, hoping the print would come clear. When it didn't, he held the little book farther away with the same unsatisfactory result.

Two men snickered.

Preacher Barton looked up. Both hecklers had better than a day's growth of stubble on their faces—although it was hard to tell where beard ended and dirt began.

More memorized words came to mind. *"Therefore thou shalt speak all these words unto them; but they will not hearken to thee: thou shalt also call unto them; but they will not answer thee."*

All right, Lord. All right.

The familiar words of Scripture, and an added fleeting prayer, helped steady the old man's hands and quiet his pounding heart. Odd, he thought, how, after all these years, he still got so nervous. He would have thought by now his skin would be thicker.

"Love your enemies, bless them that curse you, do good to them that hate you, and pray for them which despitefully use you, and persecute you."

The preacher recited another familiar passage of Scripture. He called upon the gathering of men to do something he called "consider Christ."

One drunk nudged the other and hollered "Amen!" The effort made him stagger sideways. Losing his balance, he fell to the ground. When his partner tried to help him get up, the drunken man waved him away. "I can hear jus' as well from down here. 'Sides . . . I'm closer to hell down here, which is where I b'long—ain't it, preacher?!" The man guffawed, slapping his leg.

The preacher hesitated. Was he just casting pearls before swine after all? More words came to mind. *"If ye love them which love you, what reward have ye? Do not even the publicans do the same?"* The wind blew the long white hair away from his face. He gave up trying to adjust the book so he could read the words. Instead, he recited yet another passage from memory.

"This morning I declare unto you the gospel . . . the good news . . . by which ye are saved. . . . How Jesus Christ died for our sins according to the scripture; and he was buried, and he rose again the third day. . . ." He looked at the drunken man sitting on the ground. "And that, my boy, is the best news you'll ever hear. And as to whether you are closer to hell or to heaven, I say that's up to you this very minute and how you answer this question: What will you do with Christ?"

The drunk was leaning against a barrel, his eyes closed. He drawled, "I'm not doin' anything with 'im, preacher-man. I ain't seen Him all morning. Guess He heard about a change in the weather and had the good sense to stay home."

A few of the men laughed. One let out a loud belch and started to walk away.

Preacher Barton raised his voice, "That's where you're wrong, boy. Christ is here, even now. He was raised from the dead, and He is here, calling you to himself."

"He *is*?" One of the men held up his hand to his ear. "I must be going deaf! I can't hear a thing! Heal me, preacher! Heal me!"

"Now settle down, boys," Barton said. "And listen. Someday we're all going to be called out of our graves, and there's only one thing that's going to matter"—he raised the little book up over his head—"and that will be what we did with Christ. It says right here, 'That if thou shalt confess with they mouth the Lord Jesus, and shalt believe in thine heart that God hath raised Him from the dead, you shall be saved.' "

The drunk hollered, "I don' need savin'. I'm jus' fine, thank you very much."

"You listen up, son," the old man said earnestly. "You won't be fine at all when Judgment Day comes. That's what I'm trying to tell you." He looked around him at the small group of men. "None of us will be all right on Judgment Day unless we have Christ."

"Yeah, yeah, yeah," one of the bystanders yelled. "I heard all that before. At my mama's knee."

Someone else made a vile joke about mothers. Before Barton knew what had happened, a brawl had started and was gaining momentum. Someone got knocked against the crate he was standing on, and he fell, tumbling to the ground, clutching his arthritic knee.

"You all right, Preacher?" Someone was reaching down to help him up. Someone with whiskey on his breath. Grabbing his small testament, Barton allowed himself to be hauled upright. He looked behind him, relieved to see the brawl was dying down fast.

"Come on. Let's find Elvira. Get you something to eat."

"Give me a minute, son," the preacher said. After leaning for a moment against the one finished wall of what a sign claimed would soon be Crawford's *Newest and Best General Merchandise Mercantile,* he bent over to catch his breath, straightened his rumpled collar, and tucked the testament in his breast pocket. Looking into his rescuer's face, he started to say *thank you,* but instead he blurted out the man's name. "Caleb? Caleb Jackson?"

Caleb looked away. "Not proud of it. But it's me."

Barton put his wrinkled hand on Caleb's forearm. "Elvira is at the livery just up the street, son. She threw a shoe, and I'm getting her a whole new set, thanks to your generous pay for the little work I did on roundup."

Caleb nodded. "Good."

"You come with me," Barton said. He took hold of Caleb's arm. "We'll both have breakfast. Strong coffee and something in your stomach will do you as much good as it will me."

By the third cup of coffee and his second plate of eggs, Caleb Jackson was feeling clearheaded enough to be ashamed of himself. "I don't know what got into me," he said. "I came into town yesterday for supplies for the foreman." He put his coffee mug down. "Too much time to think on the way in, I guess." He looked out the window. "They told me the order wasn't due until today, so I started back to the fort. Then I saw Mr. Dawson headed into the saloon. I've been wanting to talk to him about buying his place, so I followed him in. Didn't think there was anything wrong with having one drink."

"It's not one drink that got you into trouble, son," the preacher said.

"I know it. I never should have gone through those doors in the first place." Caleb shrugged. "I thought my drinking problems were enough years ago that I didn't have to worry. I should have known better. Especially now." He took his hat off and raked his hands through his raggedy beard.

"What do you mean . . . especially now?" the preacher asked.

Caleb's eyes filled with tears. "We lost our baby, Preacher. Our *son.*"

The preacher leaned forward. "I'm so sorry. Is the missus all right?"

Caleb shook his head. He leaned forward and put his elbows on the table and his head in his hands. "No more children." His voice broke. "That's what the doc says, anyway."

"But Mrs. Jackson is all right?"

Caleb lifted his head. He nodded. "Physically."

The preacher stared at him. "Let's hear it, son. Let's hear it all."

"I know it rains on the just and the unjust. I know everyone has tough times. A man has to expect his share. But . . ." He took a deep breath. "Every time she looks at me I feel it. And I can't stand it."

"You feel what?"

"Like I've done something wrong. Something to hurt her. Like she's waiting for me to say something. Only I don't know what I'm supposed to say."

"Well, in my short-lived experience as a married man," Barton said, "I found that *I love you* goes quite a ways."

Caleb shook his head. "Laina knows I love her. It's not enough. I've tried to love her. She pulls away. That's how I ended up sleeping in the tent with the crew. It got to where I couldn't stand the way she was pressing against the wall on the opposite side of the bed. Like she couldn't stand to be near me."

The preacher took a sip of coffee, then spread butter on a biscuit. Presently he cleared his throat. "I am claiming no special expertise with the species of creature Adam named *woman*, young man. But I do have some knowledge of *love*. And I believe God defines it pretty well. My testament uses the word *charity*." Barton recited, " 'Charity suffereth long, and is kind. Charity doth not behave itself unseemly, seeketh not her own.' Do you understand what that means, young man?"

"I thought I did. But obviously I'm missing something."

"Well, I'd say that's fairly obvious even to the casual observer," Barton said. "Does it look like love for you to be sleeping on the opposite side of Fort Robinson from your grieving wife?"

"I'm grieving, too," Caleb said.

"Of course you are. Both of you are in a time of mourning. So is CJ, I'm sure. But that's not my point, son. My point is that 'charity seeketh not her own.' This may be a time when your faith is being tested to see if you can look past your own hurt. Don't wait for Mrs. Jackson to turn to you. If she's learned she can't give you sons, she's probably frightened to death."

"Frightened?" Caleb asked. "Why would she be frightened?"

"For the past few years, every time I've visited your ranch, you've talked about your plans for the future. You've literally raised the roof about it—getting that loft ready for more children—a passel of boys, I believe you said. Mrs. Jackson has been told she can't give you your dream. And you're sleeping in a tent clear across Fort Robinson. What's she supposed to think?"

Caleb scratched his beard, then ran his hand across his chin to smooth it down. "I haven't handled this well. I just don't understand what was so wrong with our dream that God had to rip it away."

"Wasn't necessarily anything wrong with it," Barton said. "Sometimes God takes away good things so He can replace them with something *better*."

"I don't see any way that having only CJ could be better than a loft full of boys," Caleb protested, but even as he said the words he heard how "only CJ" sounded and realized how his behavior must look to his daughter. He'd hurt her, too. God forgive him.

"Don't be so earthly minded, son," the preacher was saying. "Those of us who claim faith in God are supposed to look at life differently. Whether you have a passel of boys or not won't matter in twenty thousand years. What will matter is whether or not you trusted God. If you and your sweet wife can find it in yourselves to trust and obey now, you will be enjoying rewards for that trust long after the Four Pines Ranch is nothing more than a memory in some Dawes County history book." Barton smiled. "And I'd better be right, because the belief that the next life is more important than this one is the only motivation strong enough to make me climb up on a crate and preach Jesus to a bunch of drunken cowboys."

Caleb took a deep breath. He looked across the table at the white-haired preacher. "I want to trust and obey. But . . ." He swallowed hard. "He was such a beautiful boy, Preacher. You should have seen him." His voice wavered.

"Trust and obey doesn't mean you don't hurt, son."

"So, where do I start?"

Barton leaned forward and put his hand on Caleb's forearm. "Hold on to your wife and daughter. And don't let go."

Caleb nodded. "I'll try. The supplies should be arriving soon. I'll head back as soon as we get it loaded." He folded his napkin and put it on the table before standing up.

The preacher paid the bill and together they headed toward the door. Barton reached out and put his hand on Caleb's shoulder. "And be fore-warned, young man. I can lasso *you* as easily as I can a steer, and if I get wind of you near a saloon again, I'll be obliged to prove it."

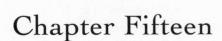

Chapter Fifteen

A good man sheweth favor, and lendeth.
PSALM 112:5

FOR A MAN who had spent more than a decade avoiding women, Lieutenant Nathan Boone had more than his share of female troubles.

Laina Jackson's situation was the most pressing. He was not going to stand by and do nothing while her life fell apart. If her husband and God weren't going to do something for her, then he was.

Because of Laina Jackson's problems, Nathan also had concerns for Clara Joy. The usually feisty young girl had become unusually subdued in recent days. Her heart was breaking over the difficulties between her parents. And because CJ's heart was breaking, Will Bishop was a simmering pot of trouble just waiting to happen. Whether Laina would go or not, Nathan decided he had to find a reason to get CJ and Will away from Fort Robinson and back to the ranch.

Then there was Charlotte Bishop. He had originally called on her out of respect for Dr. Valentine. Circumstances had continued to throw them together. He'd done his duty and been a gentleman. That was all. It was Rachel Greyfoot who was stirring up feelings he thought had died with Lily. But then roundup was over and he came back to the fort. He and Charlotte took CJ and Will on a picnic, and a simple thing like putting his hands on Charlotte's waist to help her down from a horse changed everything. Charlotte said she was happy for him and Rachel. And he didn't know why, but he didn't really want Charlotte to be so approving of the idea of Nathan Boone and Rachel Greyfoot being together. He began to catch himself thinking about Charlotte with a kind of gentle sadness. He noticed the way she smiled. And that it happened all too infrequently. He realized that a light shone in her eyes when Will hugged her that made her almost beautiful. He decided he had misread Rachel's response to him. She was grateful to him for the past. That was all. He decided he was grateful for the attention, though. Rachel's smiles had awakened a part of him that had been sleeping for a long, long time.

Ever present in all of Nathan's musings about the women causing him to lose sleep was the memory of Granny Max and the knowledge that somehow he was failing her because he had yet to make his peace with God. He felt differently about all of that these days. Like maybe it could happen. In all the years he'd been away from Fort Robinson, he had remained closed to the idea of God. But the words of Granny Max kept coming to mind. He'd even quoted her to Caleb Jackson and been surprised when Caleb said it wasn't just a *Granny-Maxism,* but something out of the Bible. Believers kept coming into his path—people like Private Blake and Preacher Barton. The preacher had told him to read the book of Job. Nathan was doing it.

Barton was like no other preacher Nathan had ever met. During the roundup he worked as hard as any of the wranglers and was a passably good cowboy in spite of his advanced age. In the evenings around the campfires he laughed and joked. He never acted sanctimonious or self-righteous, even when some of the men slipped up and swore in his presence.

Between Carter Blake, Erastus Barton, and Job, Nathan had been getting very close to reevaluating his opinion of God. And then the Jackson's baby died, Laina fell apart, Caleb fell apart, and Nathan began to wonder. The seemingly unanswerable questions loomed again. Where was God at times like this? If He could control everything, why didn't He protect his children from pain?

Job had asked the same questions. As far as Nathan could tell, the only answer he got was "Where wast thou when I laid the foundations of the earth?" Which, Nathan decided, was God putting Job in his place. Once put there, it seemed like Job stayed humbled. "I will lay mine hand upon my mouth," he said. No more questioning God. "I repent in dust and ashes," Job said. As nearly as Nathan could tell, the answer to *why* was pretty much, *because I'm God and you're not, you speck of dirt.* He wasn't sure he was ready to be a speck of dirt. But he was beginning to realize that the people who lived by faith—who accepted things they didn't understand and still trusted in a loving God—were, for the most part, happier than he. They weren't perfect. They had their moments. Like Caleb and Laina. But, Nathan reasoned, he'd been bitter and miserable for more than enough years. He was getting a little tired of demanding answers to questions God had decided not to answer.

In the midst of all his wonderings, Boone decided to follow through with plans to help Caleb expand his ranching operation, and he rode into Crawford intent on a meeting with a local banker. At the first livery stable on the edge of Crawford, both front and back sliding doors were open, giving a clear view of the blacksmith's yard out back. Nathan peered through the open doors and caught sight of a white horse chowing down on a pile of oats while the blacksmith filed her rear hoof. *Elvira.*

The sight of the preacher's horse and the idea that he had "just happened" to ride into Crawford and see her in the livery stable gave Nathan an odd feeling. In one of their campfire talks on the roundup, the preacher had made it clear he didn't believe in coincidences. In his reading of Job, Nathan had been challenged to think about the idea of what the preacher called God's sovereignty. He remembered something Charlotte had said just the day before.

"I wish we had a regular chaplain at Fort Robinson. The Jacksons might benefit from a visit. That night Preacher Barton showed up at Fort Robinson to see how I was doing, he said the Lord just impressed on his mind that he should come and check on me. That was strange. But it really was the beginning of my friendship with Laina. If he's still in tune with whatever powers that be, maybe he'll be impressed to head back this way before too long. The Jacksons surely could use a visit from him right about now."

Of course, Nathan thought, as he headed up the main street of Crawford in search of a white-haired preacher, it was only a fortunate coincidence that he had seen Elvira. The old horse had thrown a shoe. Surely not something God would use to plant the preacher in his path. *Or was it?* He knew Granny Max would have told him not to be so sure.

He must be crazy. Completely. That was the only explanation for Nathan's interrupting his search for Preacher Barton to step inside a general store and look at things like hair ribbons and lace.

"May I help you?" The shopkeeper approached from the opposite end of the store. Nathan pulled his hand back like he'd been burned. He could feel a blush crawling up the back of his neck.

"Shopping for the missus?"

Nathan frowned. He shook his head. "A girl." He stretched out his arm and indicated CJ's height. "This tall."

The shopkeeper looked confused.

"The daughter of a friend."

"Ah," the shopkeeper nodded. "How old is the young lady?"

"Ten, I think."

"Well, this," the shopkeeper said, indicating a wide lavender velvet ribbon, "should make her eyes light up with pleasure."

Picturing CJ Jackson with lavender velvet hair ribbons almost made Nathan laugh. He looked around the shop. "Just some candy," he said, crossing the store to where a row of glass jars displayed sweets of various shapes and colors. "Those," Nathan said.

He was about to leave with the sack of candy when a small figurine in a glass display case caught his eye.

"Those just arrived. Fine craftsmanship. Hand-carved ivory."

Nathan bent over to inspect the small, intricately carved figure of a white horse.

"That," he said. He'd give it to Will. The minute he thought of it, he had another idea. Exiting the general store, he headed for the telegraph office.

After sending the telegram, Nathan combed the east side of the town of Crawford looking for Preacher Barton. He was crossing back to the west side when he caught a glimpse of shoulder-length white hair just as the man beneath it ducked out of sight between two buildings. Hurrying up the street, Nathan slipped between the same two buildings and yelled, "Preacher! Preacher Barton!"

The preacher emerged from the rear of the building, holding his hand up, palm out, as he tried to block the sun and focus on Nathan's face.

"It's Lieutenant Boone, Preacher Barton."

"Well, my boy, if this isn't the day for meeting up with old friends." The preacher pumped Nathan's hand.

"Am I ever glad to see you," Nathan said.

"Why? What's happened, son?" the preacher asked. He frowned. "It's not Mrs. Bishop, I hope? She was doing so well—"

"No, not her," Nathan said. "Laina Jackson. Both of the Jacksons, actually. The baby died. And they aren't doing well. Caleb's sleeping in a tent on one side of the fort, and Laina's barely left their room at the trading post for weeks. Charlotte and I have tried everything we know to—"

"Calm down, son," the preacher said. "I just came from having breakfast with Caleb."

"Caleb is here? In Crawford?"

The preacher nodded. "We had a fine talk over breakfast." The preacher patted his stomach and belched. "Too much of a fine breakfast for me." He grimaced. "Anyway, Caleb is heading back to Fort Robinson to see Mrs. Jackson. And I believe things are going to be all right."

"Laina just hasn't been herself," Nathan said.

The preacher nodded. "I promised Caleb I'd head their way as soon as Elvira gets shod." He smiled. "The Lord works in mysterious ways, doesn't He? Elvira threw a shoe. I took a detour from my planned route to visit the blacksmith. Decided the Lord might have me say a word on His behalf while I was here. Caleb scooped me up out of the middle of a brawl—"

"What?"

"My sermon wasn't too well received," the preacher said. "But Caleb came to the rescue. Seems he'd come into Crawford for supplies and then had a meeting about adding on to his ranch. At any rate, he spent the night in town and was there to rescue me. We had breakfast over at the hotel, and I sent him packing. He was going to talk to the bank about expanding his operation and then head back to the fort. What brings you to Crawford, Lieutenant?"

"I thought I could maybe help the Jacksons if I talked to the bank. Thought I might ride out to the Dawson place and talk to them about the sale." Nathan noticed the preacher looking at the package tucked under his arm. "Trying to cheer CJ up," he said, "and something for Will."

"Well, Lieutenant Boone," the thick-waisted banker reached across his desk and pumped Nathan's hand. "Glad to meet you in person. What brings you to us this morning?"

"I want to ask you to think about something," Nathan said. "Something involving the Four Pines Ranch."

"Strange how things happen," the banker said. "I haven't heard from the Jacksons in weeks, and now everyone I see is talking about the Four Pines."

"Really?" Nathan said.

The banker nodded. "Yep." He chewed on the stub of the cigar jutting from the corner of this mouth. "Too bad."

"Too bad?"

"Hate to hear those things about a good man."

"Excuse me?"

The banker looked around as if checking for eavesdroppers. "See here, Lieutenant, I know you're a friend of the Jacksons. Maybe you can do something. I had a meeting first thing this morning with Elmer Dawson." He motioned for Nathan to sit down, then followed suit, extinguishing his cigar stub in a shallow ash-littered tin bowl on the corner of his oversized oak desk. Leaning forward, he motioned to Nathan to do likewise before he said, "I've always liked Caleb Jackson. He's always been good to do business with. You know anything about his recent problems? I like to give a man the benefit of the doubt."

"You mind telling me what it is you're talking about?"

"Like I said, Elmer Dawson was in here this morning. It seems your friend followed him into the saloon last night. And had more than one too many."

"Caleb and Mrs. Jackson have had a tough couple of weeks," Nathan said. "They've had a personal setback. But things are looking up for them both. And if Mr. Dawson wants to sell then we want to buy."

The banker switched back into business mode. "What terms were you thinking of?"

Nathan smiled. "Cash." He pulled out his copy of his telegram. "And I have another matter I'd like you to handle."

Chapter Sixteen

The Lord is nigh unto them that are of a broken heart;
and saveth such as be of a contrite spirit.

PSALM 34:18

"LAINA? ARE YOU AWAKE?"

Laina turned away from the door. She had taken to putting Caleb's pillow lengthwise against her side, so that during the night his absence was not quite so evident. Now she wrapped her arms around it and pretended she was still asleep. But Charlotte did not take the hint. Instead of giving up and going away, she came into the room and put her hand on Laina's shoulder.

"Laina." She shook her gently. "You need to wake up. There's something you need to attend to."

"Get Caleb," Laina mumbled. "He's working just across the—"

"Caleb went into Crawford yesterday to get supplies. His foreman said he isn't back yet," Charlotte said. "There must have been some kind of delay."

"Can't it wait until he gets back?"

"No. It can't."

Sighing, Laina turned over and opened her eyes halfway. Charlotte had retreated to the doorway and was standing behind CJ, her hands on the young girl's shoulders. CJ was a rumpled mess. Laina lifted her head and blinked. The drapes were drawn across the window, but it was daylight and enough light filtered through the thin fabric to illuminate CJ's dress . . . with tattered hem . . . her rumpled hair . . . and . . . Laina sat up.

"What happened? You look like you've been in a fight!"

CJ pressed her lips together and stared at her mother, defiance in every muscle of her dirty face. "So what?" she blurted out.

Laina sat the rest of the way up. "You're going to have a black eye."

"So?" CJ said. One eyebrow arched just slightly. The girl's expression caught Laina's attention. This was more than defiance. It almost appeared to be . . . dislike.

"Speak up," Laina snapped. "What have you done now?" She pressed two fingers against her forehead, wishing the headache would go away.

"What do you care?" CJ spat out.

"Don't use that tone with me," Laina said again. "Or you'll find yourself waiting on the stool in Mrs. Dubois's kitchen until your father comes home."

"Hmpf," CJ said. "I won't hold my breath." She looked at the floor.

Laina looked past CJ to Charlotte. Charlotte shook her head slightly from side to side and cast a warning glance in Laina's direction.

Laina took a deep breath. "Please tell me this didn't happen at school."

"This didn't happen at school," CJ recited in exact replication of Laina's weary tone.

"School's been out for several days now, Laina," Charlotte said gently.

"Where, then?"

"Behind Troop F's stable," Charlotte replied.

"All right, young lady," Laina said. "You go on out to the kitchen. I want to talk to Mrs. Bishop. I'll be out directly." She pushed the quilts aside and slid to the edge of the bed, calling after CJ, "And you'd better have a very good explanation for such outlandish behavior."

Laina heard a chair scrape the kitchen floor as CJ pulled it out and sat down. Standing up, she asked Charlotte, "Do you know anything about this?" Laina wobbled to the dresser across the room and looked in the mirror, then moved closer. She hardly recognized the creature who stared back at her. Matted hair framed a pale face marred by great, dark circles beneath her eyes. *You look almost as bad as that creature Granny Max brought back to sanity.*

Charlotte leaned against the doorframe. "Private Blake broke up the fight. He wasn't too clear on the particulars. Said it was something said about Caleb. I don't know exactly what. Private Blake wouldn't tell me."

Laina leaned closer to the mirror, looking at Charlotte's reflection. Taking a deep breath, she reached up and shoved a matted piece of hair out of her face. She looked around at the room. Her gray shawl and yellow sunbonnet were still hanging on a hook by the door. Wrapping herself in the shawl, she headed up the hallway toward the kitchen, where CJ was sitting at the table, head bowed, her right leg crooked up off the floor, her right ankle positioned on her knee, her foot jiggling constantly.

Charlotte passed through the kitchen ahead of Laina, closing the curtain that separated the kitchen from the trading post.

Laina slid into a chair opposite CJ. She was trembling just from the effort it had taken to get out of bed. When had she gotten so weak? It hadn't even been a month since the baby—*I've been in bed for nearly a month?* It didn't seem possible. The past weeks were a blur. She forced herself to focus on CJ. "Well," she said, "I'm waiting."

CJ raised her chin and stared back. "For what?"

"I am waiting for you to tell me what happened."

CJ shrugged. She tilted her head to display her puffy left eye. "Pretty obvious, isn't it?"

"Don't be impertinent," Laina said. "Or do you prefer to wait on that chair and talk to your father instead of to me?"

Silence.

"Well?"

Silence.

Laina took in a deep breath. Coffee. She needed some coffee. Standing up, she went to the stove and poured some. She took a sip. Sat back down. "I need to hear your voice," Laina said. "Am I going to be getting a visit from the other girl's mother?"

CJ curled her lip. "I wouldn't fight with any *girl*," she sneered.

Pondering the information, Laina took another deep breath. She forced herself to sound calm. "All right, then. Am I going to be getting a visit from some young man's mother?"

"Or his ma *and* his pa," CJ said abruptly. Her hands curled up into fists. She made a little boxing motion with each hand. "Because he's gonna have *two* black eyes."

Maude came to the doorway that led to the trading post. "Excuse me, Laina, but Private Blake is here to talk with you."

Blake's hulking frame loomed behind Maude, who let him pass before she retreated into the trading post. Laina motioned him into the kitchen. "Please," she said, indicating a chair. "Sit down. Can I pour you a cup of coffee?"

"No thank you, ma'am," Blake said. "I was just checking on the little one here. Wanted to see if she's all right."

"She'll be fine. Until her father gets hold of her," Laina said. She looked at CJ. "What's it going to be, young lady? Are you going to tell me what happened, or am I going to have to rely on Private Blake to fill in the blanks?"

CJ shrugged. "I told Farley to shut up. He wouldn't. So I shut him up. That's all."

"Farley?"

"Farley Hopkins," CJ said.

"And who, pray tell, is Farley Hopkins?"

CJ rolled her eyes. "I *told* you this before."

"Well, I don't remember."

CJ shook her head. " 'Course not. You never listen."

"That will do, young lady," Laina said and popped the back of CJ's hand.

CJ snatched her hands off the table and put them in her lap.

"Now tell me about Farley Hopkins."

"He hates me. Almost as much as he hates Will."

"You can't get in a fight with people just because they don't like you. You know that."

"I didn't," CJ said.

"You didn't . . . what?" Laina set her coffee mug firmly on the kitchen table, hoping CJ would read the signal that she was nearly out of patience.

"I didn't get in a fight with Farley Hopkins because he doesn't like me. I got in a fight because of what he said about—" CJ stopped abruptly, pressed her lips together. She looked up at Carter Blake with wide eyes that suddenly filled with tears. Taking in a deep, ragged breath, she paused again.

"Honey-lamb," Laina said as she moved to the chair beside CJ and put a hand on her shoulder. "Tell me. Please."

The minute Laina's hand touched CJ's shoulder, it was as if a floodgate opened. "He said his father was in Crawford and he saw Papa go into the saloon. He said . . . things. About Pa."

Laina looked across the table at Private Blake, who nodded agreement with CJ's version of the fight. "Well," Laina said. "I'm sorry. But that doesn't mean you had to get into a fight."

"Well, he wouldn't stop saying them, and he started calling Pa names, and so I told him I'd stop him, and he said I couldn't, and I said I could and to meet me behind the Troop F stable. And he did." A shudder coursed through CJ's body. "And I stopped him."

"Where was Will when all this was going on?" Laina asked.

"He went riding." CJ cast Laina an accusing look. "With his *mother*."

"Laina," Maude's voice sounded at the door again. "Mr. and Mrs. Hopkins are out here, and they want—"

Laina sighed. She looked at Private Blake. "You don't suppose you could try to find Mr. Jackson, could you? And ask him to hurry over here?"

"I would, ma'am. Gladly. I tried to find him earlier. Miss Irvin knew you'd want him to handle this." Blake shrugged. "But he's not back from town yet."

So it was true. Caleb had gone into Crawford. And he had stayed overnight. A sense of dread washed over her. What else was true? Had Caleb really gone into the saloon? She closed her eyes. *Lord, have mercy.*

"You come with me, CJ," Laina said, and stood up. Relieved when she didn't feel quite so wobbly, she managed to smile at Carter Blake. "Thank you for coming to check on CJ. And thank you for rescuing her."

"Wasn't any rescuing necessary," Blake said matter-of-factly. "Unless it would be the Hopkins boy. Little missy here had him down on the ground when I came around the corner."

"Well, then," Laina said, "thank you for rescuing her from herself." *Please, Lord. For CJ's sake. Help me. Rescue me. From myself.*

Blake put on his hat and turned to leave.

"Private Blake, would you please ask Mr. and Mrs. Hopkins to give me a few minutes?" Laina said. She took CJ's hand. "We need to clean up a bit."

Back in the bedroom, Laina had CJ sit on the edge of the bed while she poured clean water into the washstand bowl.

Laina wiped her own face, then handed the towel to CJ while she reached up and began to remove her hairpins. "Remember when you used to comb my hair for me when you were little?" Her hair fell down her back in a tangled mass of auburn waves. On impulse, she took the used towel from CJ's outstretched hand and replaced it with her hair comb. She sat down on the edge of the bed. "When you were little, you used to like to comb my hair for me. That always felt so nice." Closing her eyes, she waited, giving an inward sigh of relief when CJ crawled up behind her. She tilted her head to one side and then the other while CJ worked out knots and tangles.

"That's all I can get out," CJ said, and handed her mother the comb before scooting against the headboard of the bed and clutching a pillow to her midsection.

Laina stood up. She could almost hear Granny Max's voice offering advice. *Just do the next thing, honey-lamb. Just do the next thing.* She got dressed and braided her hair, then wrapped the braid around her head. She perched back on the edge of the bed. Without looking at CJ, she said quietly, "Will you take a walk with me when I get back?"

"To where?"

"Oh, anywhere. Just a walk. I need the fresh air." She inhaled and made a face. "It stinks in this room. Stale air." She went to the window, threw back the drapes, and raised the window. "So . . . what do you say?"

"Sure," CJ said. "We can take a walk." Her tone was resignation, laced with a measure of doubt. And who, Laina thought, could blame her.

"You get changed while I talk to Mr. and Mrs. Hopkins. Leave your dress out so I can mend it," Laina said. She paused at the door. "I'm weak as a kitten. It's past time I started building up my strength. Don't you think?"

CJ only nodded.

Laina did what she could to calm Farley Hopkin's parents. She apologized for CJ. She promised it wouldn't happen again. When she went back to her room, CJ lay asleep on the bed. Her face was scrubbed clean, and she had pulled her hair into two separate bunches, one tied over each shoulder with a length of red string, much like the way Rachel Greyfoot wore her hair. Her torn dress lay at the foot of the bed. She had pulled a clean smock over her petticoat before falling asleep.

Laina leaned over the bed. At her touch, CJ roused. "Shhh, shhh, honeylamb," Laina whispered. "You take a little nap. We'll talk later." Pulling up the bottom of the quilt so it covered CJ and formed a kind of bedroll around her, Laina leaned down and kissed her daughter's cheek before taking the yellow sunbonnet down from its hook and heading outside.

I did the next thing, Lord. Now what?

She made her way down the trail toward the river, past the log hospital, past Soapsuds Row. She walked along the riverbank, disappointed when an old familiar picnic spot proved to be overgrown. Out of breath, she settled on the grass and leaned against a red granite boulder jutting out of the earth beside a bend in the river. Lifting her face to the spring sunshine, she closed her eyes, thinking back over the recent weeks. *I've been like Jacob. Running away. Wrestling with God. Only there's been no ladder sent down from heaven. No answer.*

The mental image of Granny Max's Bible sitting on the dresser in her room at the trading post flashed in her mind. It had been weeks since she'd opened it. She remembered the saying Granny had written on the cover page. *I want to master this book so the Master of this book can master me.*

It had been weeks since she'd prayed anything more than *help me, help me, help me.* In recent days, she'd stopped saying even that.

How did it come to this, Lord? Where did it all go? The strength to manage life. I lost it. And now . . . look what's happened. That dirty face . . . the torn dress . . . the swollen eye . . . the defiance. The mental image of CJ curled up asleep on her bed brought tears.

Laina wrapped her arms around her legs and rested her chin on her knees. *Caleb.* How she longed for Caleb's arms around her. *Do the next thing, honey-lamb. Do what you can. Give God the rest. Give Caleb to God. Give your love for him to God. Trust and obey, honey-lamb. Trust and obey.* She was back to the same place she'd been all those years ago when Nathan Boone first brought her to Granny Max. Maybe not half crazy . . . but certainly at the end of herself.

"Ma!" CJ's voice called out.

Laina sat up and looked around.

"Ma!"

She scrambled to her feet, calling and waving, "I'm over here!"

CJ came running. In the space between the trail and Laina's arms, she started to cry. In the time it took for her to sob out all her fears, Laina started to cry, too. "I'm so sorry, honey-lamb," she finally whispered. "I won't go away again. As long as God gives me breath, I promise you, I won't go away from you again."

The sigh of relief that coursed through her daughter's wiry young body pierced Laina's heart. *Do the next thing. Just do the next thing.* For the first time in a long time, Laina knew what the next thing was.

"So tell me, CJ, how a girl your size manages to get a hulk like that Hopkins boy on his back in the dirt?" Laina asked. They were walking along, hand in hand, making their way around the parade ground and toward the doctor's residence.

"I watched Jack," CJ said.

"Jack Greyfoot taught you to fight?"

"Of course not," CJ said quickly. "Jack wouldn't do that. But he likes to wrestle with the other Cheyenne who come on roundup. Sometimes they have wrestling matches."

"And the men on roundup let you watch these things?"

"No. They make me go to the chuck wagon. They told me it isn't fitting for a lady to see such things," CJ said glumly. "But I climbed up on top of the wagon and watched anyway."

"I see," Laina said. "Well, there will be no more fights with the Hopkins boy. Or anyone else, for that matter."

"I won't let him talk about my pa that way." Stubbornness sounded in the girl's voice.

"We're going home," Laina said.

"What?"

"I said," Laina repeated, "we're going home."

"When?"

"Now." She motioned toward the doctor's residence. "And we're going to see if Mrs. Bishop and Will want to come with us."

"Did Pa say we could?"

"I haven't talked to your pa," Laina said. "But I'm sure he won't mind. We'll leave him a note. And when he's finished with his work here at Fort Robinson, he'll come home." *Or not. What if he doesn't come home?* The inner doubt clutched at her midsection. Laina took a deep breath and forced a smile.

CJ bounded ahead of her, around the doctor's residence and up to the back porch. She was already knocking on the door when Laina caught up.

———

"Is Will here?" Lieutenant Boone stood at the front door holding a small package wrapped in brown paper.

Charlotte looked at the package. "You've been to town," she said. "Did you find Caleb?"

Nathan shook his head. "Just missed him. But I saw the preacher. He'd had breakfast with Caleb. He thinks things are going to be all right."

"Lieutenant!" Will called a hello from the hallway. He looked at Charlotte. "Did you tell him, Ma?" Without waiting for her to answer he blurted out, "We're going to the ranch!"

Nathan looked at Charlotte, who nodded. "Laina invited us."

"When are you going?"

"Later today," Charlotte said.

Will broke in. "Ma's going to see Spirit. And maybe we'll buy her. And I'm going to learn how to lasso. Spirit will be my cow horse! What's that?" Will pointed to the package in Boone's hand.

Nathan held it out. "For you," he said to Will. "But I want you to take it back to the kitchen while I ask your mother something. And don't come back in here for a minute."

"Secrets?" Will asked.

Boone nodded. "For now."

The boy pounced on the package and exited the room.

"What happened in Crawford? Is something wrong?"

From the kitchen came a whoop of pleasure. Will called out. "I'm gonna go show CJ!" The back door slammed.

"So tell me, what went wrong in Crawford?" Charlotte repeated.

Nathan smiled. "Actually, things went great. I didn't find Caleb, but I did run into Preacher Barton." He told Charlotte what Barton had said about Caleb. "Both of them should be back here before you all leave for the ranch." He smiled. "I think things are going to be fine."

"Laina needs to hear that."

"I agree . . . but not from me. I've put my nose as far into that business as I think I should." He paused. "For all I know, Caleb's at the trading post right now."

Charlotte shook her head. "It's amazing. The timing of it all is just amazing." Quickly, she told Nathan about CJ's fight and the effect it had had on Laina. "It seems to have jolted her back to life."

Nathan nodded. "That plays into what I wanted to ask you. I've mentioned it before, but I'd like to know what you've decided about Will maybe staying at the ranch this summer and working toward owning Spirit. To tell you the truth, I was just going to buy the horse and surprise him, but—"

"I couldn't allow that," Charlotte said quickly.

"Yeah," Nathan said. "I realized that. So . . . will you think about this other idea? I'll ride out to Four Pines in a couple of days. By then you will have seen Spirit. If you're agreeable, then I'll talk to Laina and Caleb about Will spending the summer on the ranch."

"I don't know what to say."

"*Thank you* would work." Nathan smiled down at her.

Charlotte looked away. She stepped back and put her hands behind her and nodded. "I'll think about it." She turned back to him and smiled. "And thank you."

Chapter Seventeen

Now faith is the substance of things hoped for,
the evidence of things not seen.
HEBREWS 11:1

"HE HASN'T COME," Laina said. She was standing outside Charlotte's back door clutching her shawl around her. A gust of wind caught Laina's hair and blew it around her face. She brushed it back with a trembling hand.

Charlotte opened the back door and pulled Laina inside. "With that storm brewing," she said, "he probably decided not to drive the team back. You know how it is, Laina. There's a shortage of good teams, and some of them are barely harness broke. He probably didn't want to head into the face of a storm. And I imagine Preacher Barton thought the same thing. Especially with that old mare he rides. I remember you said he treats her almost like his child. He probably would save her from a storm if he could." She pulled out the kitchen chair and motioned for Laina to sit down.

Laina shook her head. "No, no . . . that's all right. I just wanted you to know."

"I understand. Will and I can visit the ranch another time. It'll give us both something to look forward to."

Laina smoothed her hair back. She looked out the kitchen window. "I didn't walk over here to tell you we aren't going," she said. "I haven't changed those plans. Nathan stopped by a while ago. When he didn't find Caleb he headed back into town. Said the men are going on maneuvers tomorrow." Laina paused. "That means if we don't go today, we might not have anyone available to drive us. Now, I'm a determined woman, but even I'm not fool enough to head out across the prairie alone. Unless"—she forced a smile—"you have experience with a rifle I'm not aware of."

Charlotte smiled back. "As a matter of fact," she teased, "in another life I was a sharpshooter in a Wild West show. However," she said, holding up her bandaged wrist, "I'm a bit off my game at the moment. So a soldier with a rifle is probably a good idea."

"We might be in for a real drenching. On the other hand, if we can scoot up the trail, the worst of it might just blow over. It's hard to say."

"Father has an old oilskin. We can hunker down under that," Charlotte said. "If you're really going, I'd still like to come along now. Will would never forgive me for keeping him away from Spirit. And I don't want to have to be left here worrying about what mischief he might think up without CJ around."

"I never thought of CJ as a mature voice of reason," Laina said.

"Compared to Will, she's twenty-five. She's undoubtedly kept him out of more trouble than I care to know about."

"Maude thinks I should wait for Nathan to round up Caleb," Laina said abruptly.

"You have to do what you think is best. And I'll support you no matter what you decide." Charlotte patted her friend's hand. "I'm the last one on the earth qualified to give marital advice. It only took me about six months of being Mrs. Colonel Bishop to realize I had no idea what I was doing."

Thunder rumbled. Laina headed for the door. "I want to go home. I've prayed on it and asked God, and I still want to go home." She inhaled sharply. "And when Caleb is ready . . . he'll know where to find me."

"Then let's get going," Charlotte said. "Maybe the rain will wait. Or blow over. If it doesn't, we won't melt."

———

Caleb Jackson went to the hotel room window and moved the lace curtain aside so he could see up the main street. Clouds on the horizon promised a good drenching was on its way. Someone knocked on the door.

"What in blazes do you think you're doing?!" Nathan Boone sounded off as he shoved past Caleb into the hotel room. He was brought up short by the sight of Preacher Barton lying in bed, his white hair spread out on the pillow, his chest rising and falling in rapid, shallow breaths.

"How'd you know I was here?" Caleb said.

"Saw the preacher. Saw the banker. Thought you were on your way to your wife, so I headed home. Then you didn't show up. Laina didn't know what to think, so I told her I'd come back into town and check on you. No sign of you or the preacher. The guy down at the livery suggested I check hotel registries. What's going on?"

Caleb motioned to where the preacher lay. "I was on my way back to the fort when I found him doubled over in Elvira's stall."

"What's wrong with him?"

"Bad meat. That's what the doctor here in town thinks, anyway."

"Just be glad you didn't order the steak for breakfast," the preacher spoke up, his voice barely a whisper. "I'm sorry . . . son, but I need—"

Caleb swooped across the room, grabbed the chamber pot, and assisted the preacher, wiping the old man's mouth and offering him a drink of water before he said to Nathan, "I couldn't exactly leave him alone. The doc's so busy with calls he couldn't stay." Caleb shook his head. "I sure am glad this hotel isn't serving Four Pines beef. Half the town is sick according to the doc." He walked back to the window and nodded toward the west. "Looks like we're in for it." He shook his head. "I don't like the idea of Laina sitting at the fort worrying."

Nathan recounted Laina's plans to go to the Four Pines. "Blake's driving them. They'll be all right," he said, then smiled and winked. "And you can enjoy a reunion at home."

Caleb smiled back, nodded, then cleared his throat and changed the subject. "You said you talked to the bank? Was it Wade Simpson?" When Nathan nodded, Caleb took in a deep breath. "Oh, brother. What did he have to say?"

"He said you're a good man and he hopes things are all right."

Caleb let the surprise he felt sound in his voice. "Really?"

"Really."

"Well, that's a relief."

"I imagine the fact that I said we can pay cash for Dawson's place helped his attitude a little."

"We?"

"Sure," Nathan said. "If you still want me for a partner."

Thunder crashed and the skies opened. The preacher moaned.

———

It was near sunset when the Jacksons' farm wagon finally topped the last rise and headed down the gentle incline toward the Four Pines Ranch.

"That's the farmhouse," Will said, and proceeded to give Charlotte a verbal tour of the ranch, from barn to bunkhouse to corrals to hen house. "Lieutenant Boone and I stayed there in the bunkhouse with Dorsey and Jack." He prattled on about Dorsey and Jack Greyfoot, and then, as the wagon drew closer, he began to talk about Spirit. "Jack said he'd keep her in the barn and gentle her some."

The minute the wagon pulled up to the ranch house, Will started to jump down, then hesitated and looked doubtfully at Charlotte.

"Go on," she said. "I can wait a few minutes to use your muscles. But don't be gone long." Will and CJ shot down the trail toward the barn without a glance behind them.

Private Blake helped Charlotte and Laina down from the wagon. He nodded at Rachel when introduced, but didn't waste any time moving the women's two trunks to the edge of the wagon in preparation for unloading. In less than an hour, Rachel and Jack had moved CJ's things into the loft and Charlotte's trunk into CJ's room. Jack took Will's small trunk down to the bunkhouse and returned for the team.

"If you don't mind, ladies," Private Blake said, untying his horse from the back of the wagon. "I'll be going now."

"But don't you want some supper?" Laina said. "You've never eaten stew until you've tasted Rachel's."

"I believe you, ma'am," Blake said, smiling. "But as you know, you've never eaten pie until you've tasted Miss Irvin's. And she promised me a piece if I get back before taps."

———

"You were right," Charlotte said the next evening. "The silence out here is wonderful. If you could can it and sell it, everyone in Detroit would likely want some."

"I thought you might find it . . . boring. You aren't used to this kind of life." Laina settled on the rocking chair next to Charlotte's. "And shelling peas all day isn't exactly mentally challenging."

"That's what I liked about it," Charlotte said. She flexed the fingers of her left hand. "There's something comforting about the simplicity of it. And I really do think my fingers benefited. They ache—but it's a good ache, if that makes any sense." She leaned her head back against the rocker and closed her eyes. "And we certainly do have something to show for the day's work. Something much more useful than two yards of lace for a tablecloth no one needs." She opened her eyes and looked at Laina as she explained, "Mother Bishop worshiped at the altar of the cult of domesticity."

"What?"

She laughed under her breath, "That just means that while the servants did the real work, Mother and I sat by the fire and did fancywork."

"I didn't think you liked to sew."

Charlotte murmured, "What I liked or didn't like was never much of a concern to the Bishops."

"You really were miserable, weren't you?"

"I was," Charlotte said. She held up her right hand and swept it toward the horizon. "But I'm not now. This is . . . astounding. I can see why you love it."

———

"What are you doing out here in the middle of the night?" Charlotte said. "I heard the front door open." She walked to where Laina was standing beside Spirit's stall and touched her friend's shoulder. When Laina glanced at her, Charlotte could see the tears.

She took a deep breath. "I said all the right things. I believe them. I have to raise CJ and do what's right . . . regardless of Caleb's choices." Her voice wavered and she swiped at another tear. "But now I'm home . . . and the bed is empty . . . and I didn't really think I'd have to *do* it . . . without him."

Charlotte put her arms around her friend.

"I'm sorry," Laina apologized.

"For what?"

"I'm not being a very good . . . example."

"I don't know what you're talking about," Charlotte said.

Laina sniffed and wiped her nose. She turned around to the stall and scooped up a hand of grain. Spirit's black ears went forward. "Here, girl," Laina said, and held her hand out. Spirit stepped forward and accepted Laina's offering, then stood quietly while Laina rubbed the filly's ears and stroked her soft muzzle. "I'm not a very good example of faith. I mean, if I really believe that God is in control of my life, I shouldn't be such a mess."

"Don't be so hard on yourself," Charlotte said. She thought for a few minutes before speaking again. "That first night you visited me in the hospital, do you remember how I reacted?"

Laina shrugged. "You were hurting."

"I was just on the edge of rude to you," Charlotte corrected her. "Because I thought you were just doing your Christian duty by visiting me. I never expected you to call on me again, and the last thing I wanted was another hypocrite checking me off her list of things to do like I was a chore."

"Ouch," Laina said. "It sounds like you have experience with that."

"The Bishops were very involved church members," Charlotte said. "But their religion never really had much to do with what went on inside the four walls of that house. With one exception. The Colonel was fond of quoting the proverbs about meting out corporal punishment just before he disciplined Will." She swept her hand across her forehead. "But you, Laina . . . you aren't self-righteous. Your faith is real. Even in your worst moments, you cling to it."

"Like a cat clinging to a tree limb—just barely hanging on," Laina said, mocking herself.

"Did you really expect God to spare you the pain of the loss when your baby died? I always thought people were religious so they could hang on to God while they were going through bad times. Not so He would make them not feel the pain. He didn't even do that for His own son—at least not according to the Sunday school lessons I remember."

Laina's eyes widened. "I haven't thought about it that way. Ever. I didn't think I would hurt as much when hard things happened. Because I believe." She paused, speaking slowly. "You're right, Charlotte. I had things all wrong. It hurts just as much. The difference is, God provides the strength instead of my having to go through it on my own." She sighed. "Except I didn't really tap into His strength."

"How would you have done that?" Charlotte wanted to know.

"Praying. Talking to Him. Reading the Bible Granny Max left behind. You wouldn't believe how marked up that book is. I remember Preacher Barton saying you could tell a lot about people by looking at their Bible. He said sometimes a Bible will almost fall open to a person's favorite passage. Granny's Bible doesn't fall *open*. It's falling *apart*. She has things underlined, and even some notes written in the margins. Dates, too. I always wished I knew what those dates meant." Laina shook her head. "Anyway, I suspect that if I'd been reading those words like I should have, I wouldn't have been quite so helpless. But I was so angry, I stopped. We both did, Caleb and me. And then we stepped away from each other and stopped talking." She sniffed again. "And now he's . . . gone." Her voice broke on the last word.

"Don't give up," Charlotte said. "I can't imagine God has it in mind to break your heart again." Charlotte put her hand on her friend's shoulder.

"I hope you're right."

———

Caleb—CJ and I are going home. Please forgive me for failing you. It breaks my heart to think that I can't fulfill your dreams. I will do my best to understand whatever decision you make about the future.

Charlotte Bishop and Will have gone with us. Will is so sure he wants Spirit, and Charlotte needs to see her. I hope you won't mind. CJ was very excited about it, and it was good to see her smiling again. It's been a while since any of us have smiled, hasn't it? You may have wondered, but I have never stopped loving you.

Your L

As he stood at the trading post reading his wife's note, Caleb frowned. He looked up at Maude. "I sent a note with Nathan Boone for Laina. Did she get it?"

Maude shook her head. "I don't know anything about a note. Lieutenant Boone left on maneuvers. He and Private Blake and all of Company B headed out to Chadron for the readiness drill two days ago."

"But I sent word," Caleb repeated. "Nathan would have seen to it that someone else got the message to her, even if he couldn't do it himself."

"Maybe you'd better take it in person next time," Maude said. "And not make her wonder."

Caleb nodded. "You're right."

"You bet your britches I am," Maude said. "Now get going!"

Caleb swung back into the saddle. He rode to the hospital and was pleased when the preacher stepped out and swung onto Elvira at his approach. "Doc says I'm fit as a fiddle," the old man said. "Let's get you home."

———

Charlotte grabbed the saddle horn with her right hand and hauled herself astride a rangy dun mare Jack Greyfoot had assured her was the perfect horse for her. She looked down at Laina, grinning. "Mother Bishop would be appalled."

"No doubt," Laina agreed. "But we don't own a sidesaddle, so this is the only way."

Charlotte rubbed her palm against her denim pants. She hugged the horse with her knees and flexed her feet in the too-large boots Emmet Dorsey had loaned her. "Slow down, CJ," she called to the girl who was mounted and waiting outside the corral. "Give me a chance to get the feel of things here in the corral before we head out, okay?"

Charlotte nudged her horse into a trot. In a few minutes, she was moving with the animal, sensing its rhythm—and feeling in control.

"That's it, Ma," Will encouraged. He was riding an ancient buckskin gelding—after a protracted discussion with Jack, who would not agree that Spirit was ready for trail riding.

"Are we having company?" CJ asked, and motioned toward the top of the rise in the direction of Fort Robinson.

Laina turned to look into the distance.

"Hey . . . it's the preacher!" CJ called out. "I can see his white hair . . . and . . . Pa!" CJ squealed. "It's Pa!" She whirled her horse around and set off.

Charlotte walked her mount to the side of the corral where a pale-faced Laina waited with her hand at her throat. Charlotte found herself casting a *Help her, Lord,* toward heaven, even as she watched CJ ride up next to her father and lean over and hug him without ever leaving the saddle. "That girl's a good rider," she said.

Laina nodded. "I told you she'd rather be in the saddle . . . helping her Pa . . . than in the house with me any day of the week." She reached up to touch the left side of her hair.

"You look fine," Charlotte said, waiting alongside her friend, her own heart beating rapidly as she hoped for the best and feared lest it not happen.

Caleb and Preacher Barton headed for the house, but then Caleb saw the women out at the corral and detoured. He rode up to Laina, swung down off his horse and swept her into his arms.

Charlotte heard very little of what Caleb Jackson said to his wife as he buried his face against her neck, but she knew they were both crying, and she knew it was good. A pang of emotion shot through her as she rode out of the corral and to where Will and CJ were waiting. She frowned at the next thought, which was the image of Lieutenant Boone in his dress uniform. *Even if it were possible, which it is not, the last thing on earth you would want is another soldier. The very last thing.*

"Let's go," she called to CJ and Will, and led the way.

Chapter Eighteen

He that trusteth in his own heart is a fool.
PROVERBS 28:26

CJ WOKE WITH A START.

It was time.

She couldn't believe she had let Will talk her into such a crazy plan.

For over a week now, things at home had been wonderful. She didn't understand all the details, but she'd overhead snippets of a talk between the grown-ups that hinted at a lost letter from Pa. A letter that would have made Ma feel better those couple of days after they got home and before Pa and the preacher arrived. Apparently something had happened to the paper as it passed from Pa to Lieutenant Boone to another soldier who was supposed to deliver it to the ranch. There had been orders to go on maneuvers and the letter was lost. But it didn't matter now because Pa was back home and Ma was smiling again.

Even Mrs. Bishop, usually quiet and subdued, had laughed aloud at dinner last night. Lieutenant Boone had gotten his leave and was staying at the ranch for a while, and he and Pa spent hours together, talking about horses and land. Even Will seemed happier these days. When Pa complimented Will on being such a good worker, CJ could see how pleased Will was. Jack Greyfoot claimed that Will's hard work in keeping the barn clean freed him up to spend more time breaking and training Rebel and Spirit. CJ figured Jack's extra time with the horses must be the reason why he never ate meals with them at the house anymore. CJ was proud of Will, although the closest she got to telling him that was when she said his riding was "not too bad, for a city boy."

It was in the midst of this same week that CJ and Will had started planning an adventure based on something Will had seen on their ride with his mother the day Pa came home. When CJ told him it was too dangerous, it seemed to make Will all the more determined. "Ma's birthday is coming up. She's never even seen an eagle egg." Will went on to describe the glass dome at their home back in Michigan that had once protected a beautiful, decorated ostrich egg from dust and fingerprints. "It was a present," Will said.

"Well, it might be all right if we can get someone to help us," CJ finally said. "And maybe we could go into town and get some pretty buttons and beads and things. We could decorate it for her."

Will nodded. "That's a great idea. I bet Lieutenant Boone would help us."

"I bet he would," CJ said, grinning. "He likes your ma."

Will frowned. "Sure he does."

"No, I mean he really *likes* her. How would you feel about getting a new pa, anyway?"

Will looked at CJ like he thought she was crazy. "I don't know what you're talking about."

"Well," CJ explained, "My ma was telling Pa just last night how she's been praying for them both, and she thinks it would be just fine if God would 'open their eyes and make them realize what's really going on.' " CJ took a breath, "and what she *means* is they like each other. Only they don't seem to know it yet."

Will shook his head. "That's crazy. Lieutenant Boone is being nice, that's all. He was making eyes at Rachel all during roundup. She came out and watched him bulldog the cattle. And they took a walk together. In the dark. Your pa even teased the lieutenant about it."

"Grown-ups!" CJ said. "My folks talk about how God is in control all the time. But they sure spend a lot of time making sure God is doing things right."

Will returned to the subject of the eagle egg. "My father broke the ostrich egg Ma liked so much."

"Why?" CJ said.

Will shrugged. "I dunno. Captain Danley gave it to her. He liked to dance with her. She told Pa it didn't mean anything. But Pa got mad and broke the egg the captain sent her."

"Your pa was jealous," CJ said matter-of-factly.

"I guess he was," Will said. "But I don't know why. He never let Ma go anywhere without him."

CJ shook her head. "I'll never understand grown-ups. Ma and Pa think your ma should marry Lieutenant Boone, and you think Lieutenant Boone likes Rachel. And Jack likes Rachel, and—"

"He does?" Will said.

"Of course," CJ said in a tone of an adult explaining something to a child. "Why do you think Jack quit eating with us?"

"So he could spend more time with Rebel and Spirit," Will said.

CJ shook her head. "Naw. That's not it. That's just an excuse."

"How do you know all this?" Will asked. "I haven't seen anything different."

"Well, tonight at dinner you watch. Rachel makes sure Lieutenant Boone's cup is always full of coffee. And she sneaks him extra biscuits. And pie. She makes sure he gets two pieces."

"My ma doesn't do any of that stuff when Lieutenant Boone eats with us," Will said.

"Maybe not," CJ said. "But Ma says your ma smiles more when he's around. And she's happier."

Will thought for a moment. "She does like to go riding with him," he said. "But she always liked to ride."

"I thought you said she hated riding with that Major Riley."

"That was different."

"Of course it was," CJ said, rolling her eyes. "Because she didn't like Major Riley. Honestly Will, for a smart boy you can be really, really dense sometimes."

"I don't care about all that stuff," he said.

"Maybe you should," CJ said. "You just might be getting a new pa. So, I'm asking you again, what do you think about that?"

"Ma wouldn't do that."

"She might. With somebody nice like the Lieutenant."

Will was quiet for a minute. He looked at CJ. "Ma's been sad for a long, long time. Lieutenant Boone makes her smile. He even made her laugh the other night. If he can make Ma laugh, then I'll be glad to call him Pa. But I still want to give her that egg. And I don't want any grown-up help, either. Lieutenant Boone isn't the only one who likes to see her smile."

Will had insisted and planned and schemed until CJ was ashamed of her fear and overcame her reluctance.

Even so, this entire night had been one of waking, looking for daylight, trying to fall back to sleep, and then tumbling into a dream from which she woke again. Lying in the dark, CJ listened, half fearing she would hear Rachel or her father moving around in the kitchen, half hoping she would get caught. But it was so early even they weren't stirring yet. CJ sat up in bed. Bending over, she felt beneath her bed for the gunnysack Will had given her the night before.

"You'll need pants and a shirt," he'd said as they went through his trunk in the bunkhouse. "And my extra boots. And some socks. How you going to sneak them into your room?"

CJ had assured him it wouldn't be hard, and indeed it wasn't. For the first time in her life she saw some practical use for skirts and petticoats as she had tucked the bag out of sight up under her petticoat and headed for the house. Once inside, she made some excuse about needing something from her room and walked past Laina and Rachel and Will's mother, all three hard at work in the kitchen canning green beans. She quickly tucked the gunnysack beneath her bed and then went back to the kitchen to offer help with the harvest. As far as she could tell, no one suspected a thing.

And now the time had finally come. Dawn was breaking, and she needed to hurry and find a way to sneak out. She put on socks and pants while still beneath the covers, then sat up, pulling her nightgown off and Will's flannel shirt on. Arranging her pillows to look as much like a sleeping girl as possible, she pulled the covers back up and, with Will's extra boots in hand, crept to the door, looking each way to make certain no one was stirring.

Just as she stepped out into the hall, she heard the front door creak open. *Blast.* Rachel must have already gone down to the barn to get fresh milk. CJ ducked back in her room. Hoping no one heard the scraping of wood against wood, she raised the one small window she had closed when the night breeze proved too cold, slithered through the opening, and dropped to the ground. Slipping around the corner of the house, she made a dash for the chicken coop. Her heart pounding, she made another dash for the thickest stand of cedars behind the coop, scrambled across the steep incline behind the trees, and ducked into the canyon where Will waited astride . . . *Spirit.*

"This is a bad idea," CJ said immediately.

"It's an easy ride," Will retorted. "You said so yourself."

"I don't mean going after the eggs," CJ said. "I mean you and Spirit. She's not ready." As if agreeing, the little mare tossed her head and side-stepped.

Will reached down and patted her neck. "She's fine," he said. "She's just excited to finally get outside the corral."

"My pa or Lieutenant Boone or Jack would've already had you going for short rides up into the hills if they thought Spirit was ready," CJ said. "You should trust them. Pa says a rider and a horse have to be a good team. You and Spirit aren't a team yet. She knows more than you."

"I'm riding Spirit," Will said. "Now are you coming or not?"

CJ stared up at her friend. His jaw was set, and even in the dim light she could see the familiar glint in his eye that meant he was set on something and it was futile to contradict him.

"What if I go wake up Jack or the lieutenant?" CJ threatened. "They'll stop you."

"Go ahead," Will said. "Just don't ever expect me to talk to you again."

CJ hesitated. If she went along, she could at least make sure nothing bad happened. "Oh, all right," CJ said, and took the reins of her horse, Pappy, as Will held them out. Together they headed west. Morning light had just begun to gild the tips of the bluffs looming above them when CJ noticed a gathering of dark clouds on the distant horizon.

"Hey," she called to Will's back.

Will pulled on Spirit's reins and waited for CJ to come alongside.

She pointed at the dark clouds.

Will shrugged. "Probably nothing."

"That's rain. Or hail," CJ said. "You haven't been out here long enough to know, but I sure do. Weather moves in fast. And if it comes this way—"

"If it comes this way, we'll hightail it back to the ranch," Will said. "We can probably outrun it. And if we don't, we'll get wet. You afraid to get your new duds wet?"

CJ looked down at Will's flannel shirt. "Of course not," she said. "But you haven't sat out a hailstorm. Believe me, we don't want to get caught. Out here you can't always outrun a storm."

"Maybe Pappy can't," Will said. "But Spirit can."

"There's prairie-dog holes and all kinds of things. You—"

"Stop lecturing me," Will said abruptly. He was frowning. "I'm not afraid of a little rain or hail."

"I'm not talking about you, silly," CJ said. "I'm talking about Spirit. Pappy's an old army horse. The soldiers fire blanks over their heads to get them used to gunfire. Pappy's not going to be scared of a little thunder. But Spirit—"

"I should have known not to ask a *girl* to come with me," Will said. "I should have known you'd chicken out. You just don't want to climb up to that cliff."

The gauntlet had been thrown down, and CJ picked it up. Kicking Pappy's sides she said loudly, "Don't you worry about me, Will Bishop." She called over her shoulder, "You just worry about keeping up!" She urged Pappy into a run and tore away.

Spirit leaped after Pappy the second Will touched her flanks. Dodging this way and that, the surefooted pony quickly caught up with and passed Pappy. It was all Will could do to cling to the little horse's back. Suddenly CJ was yelling from behind him. Grabbing Spirit's reins, Will finally managed to pull the horse up, albeit with much prancing and foaming at the mouth and a couple of stubborn little bucks that nearly unseated him. CJ was waiting far behind him, gesturing and pointing up above her.

"Gosh you're fast," Will said to Spirit, patting her sweaty withers even as he tried to make his own voice sound calm. "Just settle down now," he said, relieved when the horse's black-tipped ears twisted toward his voice. Spirit shook her head and arched her neck, dancing sideways. "Whoa there, now. We're done running. CJ's found the nest. Let's go back and check it out." He barely touched Spirit's sides, and the horse leaped ahead, trying to run again. With great difficulty Will managed to keep her in check, almost getting thrown off again when Spirit gave an enthusiastic hop with her hindquarters that put daylight between Will's backside and the saddle.

"Whew," Will said when he was finally alongside CJ. "She likes morning runs!"

"I warned you." CJ nodded toward the west again, where a mountain of dark clouds was piling up, obscuring the familiar buttes in the distance. "And I'm telling you, if that turns into a bad storm that comes this way, Spirit is going to—"

"If you'd stop yapping and start climbing we'd have the egg and be home before anybody even knows we're gone," Will snapped.

CJ jumped to the ground. Letting Pappy's reins drop, she headed up the incline that lead into a cleft in the bluff and a narrow rocky trail.

"Hey," Will called, "aren't you going to tie Pappy?"

"He *is* tied as far as he's concerned," CJ called back. "It's called *ground* tying. Jack taught her. As far as Pappy knows, when his reins are down like that he's tied to a post. He's not going anywhere." She paused and put her hands on her waist. "But since you couldn't wait until Jack worked with Spirit more, you'll have to figure something out for her if you expect her to be within a mile of here when we're done." She turned back around and began to scale the rocky trail.

Will looped Spirit's reins over a low-growing bush three times and scrambled to catch up to CJ, oblivious to Spirit's nervous snorting.

CJ and Will climbed together, finally reaching the first ledge. Above them, sticking out from the bluff, was a narrower ledge barely visible beneath the impressive pile of sticks and brush gathered by two eagles over years of nest building.

"There," Will said, pointing upward. "There it is."

"I'm not blind," CJ snapped. Her next step on the trail sent her sliding backward. Rocks tumbled down, bouncing off the sides of the bluff. Below them, they could hear Spirit snort.

"It's okay, girl," Will called down. "Just a bunch of rocks. Nothing that will hurt you." He held his hand out to CJ. "Come on. I'll help you up."

CJ brushed her open palm against her jeans. Inspecting it, she spit on the skinned place and wiped the blood off on the backside of her borrowed jeans. She pretended not to hear Will and, ignoring his proffered hand, scrambled back up and past him.

Thunder sounded in the distance. "That's not good," CJ said.

Will looked toward the oncoming storm. "Maybe it'll blow by."

"I don't think so," CJ said.

"Well, maybe it'll go south of us," Will said. "Lots of storms do."

CJ shrugged. "If it doesn't, we're in for a drenching."

"I don't care," Will said.

CJ looked at him soberly. She looked down the trail and then back at the clouds. "All right," she said. "Let's go." She turned around and began to scale the rocky trail again.

Will protested. "Wait for me," he said. "This was my idea. I should get to go first."

"Fine," CJ said, and hunkered over to the side of the trail, clinging to a seedling tree while Will scrambled past. There was barely room for him to pass between her and the vertical wall of the bluff.

"That's rain," CJ called after Will. She reached up and felt the crown of her head. As she did so, another drop of rain landed on the back of her hand. She turned around. "Oh brother," she exclaimed. "Here it comes."

"Well, hurry on up," Will said, climbing harder. "We can sit out the storm on the ledge."

CJ hurried, pulling herself onto the ledge just as the storm broke.

"Is it always like this?" Will shouted above the roar of the storm. They were hunkered together against the looming wall of the bluff in a sliver of space left open in the amassing of the great nest before them.

"It's been abandoned," CJ shouted after an especially loud peal of thunder.

"How do you know that?" Will shouted back.

"See those two broken eggs?" CJ said. "Something got at them. And that one"—she pointed to the lone remaining egg—"must be infertile."

"What?" Will asked.

"City boy!" CJ shouted. "It won't hatch. So they left it."

"Why didn't it get broken, too?" Will said, as he picked up the egg to examine it.

CJ shrugged. "So some fool boy could come steal it, I guess." She wrinkled her nose. "You aren't going to like the way that smells when you try to empty it out for decorating."

The storm grew even more intense. Water came down in sheets. They could no longer see beyond the edge of the ledge.

Will shivered. "How long do these storms usually last?"

"Don't be afraid," CJ said. "I've seen worse."

"I'm not afraid!" Will said. "I just wanted to know!"

At that moment a flash of lightening revealed the valley floor below.

"The horses," CJ said.

"What about the horses?"

"They're gone. Even Pappy."

Will shrugged. "They'll run home."

"Of course they will," CJ said. "But then everyone is going to worry about us, and we're going to be in trouble."

"Not if we hurry back right now," Will said.

"We can't," CJ said. "I don't even know how we're going to get back down the trail after this rain. Look at it!" She pointed to the narrow trail, now a mud slide running with water.

"Just sit on your backside and slide!" Will said. With the next flash of lightening, he stood up and, stepping forward, clutched the egg. Just at that moment a roaring wave of water spilled from above them. One second CJ could see Will clinging to the nest, the egg cradled in his hands, the next he was gone. She screamed his name and leaned forward. A second wave of water took her over the edge, too. The last thing she remembered was the sensation of something cold slashing at her as she rolled over and over and over—down, down, down.

————

Jack Greyfoot landed inside the ranch kitchen door to report missing horses at the same time Rachel came rushing out of CJ's room after discovering the pillows positioned to look like a sleeping child.

"Will," they both said at the same time, and hurried out of the house, down the trail to the bunkhouse.

Just as they neared the door, Nathan Boone emerged. "Will's—"

"—gone." Rachel finished his sentence for him. "CJ too."

"On Pappy," Jack chimed in. "And Spirit."

"Spirit?" Nathan frowned. "I told that boy Spirit isn't ready for trail riding."

Jack nodded. "We all did." He looked toward the west. "And if they get caught in that . . ."

"Spirit will throw a fit, dump Will, and hightail it home." Nathan dragged his fingers through his beard, then scratched his head in frustration. "That boy," was all he could say, even as he headed for the barn.

Jack followed him.

Rachel turned to go back to the house, calling out, "I'll tell everyone else and get some warm blankets ready. They'll be drenched," she said.

Within minutes, Caleb joined Nathan and Jack. The three men had no sooner set out when the rain hit them like a wall, coming down in such thick sheets they were momentarily blinded. Pulling their hats down over their eyes, they gave their horses their leads and were soon standing sidled up to a clump of cedar trees.

Just as quickly as it came, the storm was gone, leaving in its wake broken branches and rivulets of water gushing down every crevice in the bluffs. The meandering creek that wound its way through the Four Pines had become a rushing torrent of water. About the time the men managed to force their mounts through the raging water, Spirit and Pappy came charging toward them, heads high, tails flying in the wind. Spirit leaped over the raging creek with one easy bound. Pappy screeched to a halt and eyed the water suspiciously. Deciding not to cross, he dropped his head and began to graze.

"Well, wherever they are," Caleb said, "those two are going to get a talking to."

Nathan shook his head from side to side, muttering, "What were they thinking?"

"They weren't thinking," Jack said.

"You have any idea what kind of plan they'd hatched up?" Caleb asked.

Jack shook his head. "We all told Will that Spirit wasn't ready for trail riding. We didn't have to tell CJ. She knew that. The only thing I can figure is CJ went along because she couldn't stop Will."

The longer the men rode, the more quiet they became. Nathan swore at the rain. "Washed out any hope of tracking them," he muttered. He pulled up, took his hat off his head and flailed it against his thigh, then rolled up the brim, pressing the excess water out. "Ruined my new hat." He swore again.

"CJ! CJ Jackson!" Caleb called.

"Will Bishop!"

Their voices bounced back at them off the bluffs. Unanswered.

With the departure of the fast-moving storm, the prairie glistened in the morning sun. Droplets of moisture dripped from every pine needle and every leaf. The heads of blooming flowers bowed down with the weight of water, painting the prairie floor with a mass of subdued color. As they rode, the sun came out and began to dry off the rain, the flower heads lifted toward the light. Still, there was no answer to the men's repeated shouts for CJ and Will.

———

CJ rolled over onto her right side and looked around. The sun was shining brightly, making the droplets of water on the pine boughs looming above her sparkle like jewels. It made her head hurt. Squeezing her eyes shut, CJ grunted and raised her hand to her forehead. "Will?" With her eyes closed, she tried to listen, hoping to hear the sound of a horse grazing nearby. "Pappy?" *You dumbbell. He's back home by now.* The idea sent a chill through her. She was going to be in so much trouble.

She managed to pull herself to a sitting position, grunting again with the pounding of her head. Slowly, she turned and looked up the bluff, shivering a little when she realized just how far she'd fallen. She looked at the trees around her. If she'd hit one of those . . . Carefully, she checked her wrists, shrugged her shoulders, turned from side to side, lifted first one leg, then the other. Every muscle screamed, just like the time she kept getting thrown by a rambunctious pony. She'd climbed back on, over and over and over again, until the meanspirited varmint gave in and let her stay on its back. Once she'd conquered the beast, she decided she didn't want to ride it anyway and had hobbled home. The next morning she'd felt a lot like she felt right now, which was sore but not permanently hurt. There was a difference though. After conquering the pony she'd felt proud. Right now she felt ashamed. And a little frightened.

"Will . . . ? Will Bishop? Can you hear me?"

An eagle screamed and CJ looked up. She caught a glimpse of the great bird soaring high above and, for a moment, felt a pang of regret on behalf of the bird. Maybe that was the one whose nest got washed away. She imagined how it would feel to have the ranch house swept away in a flood. Looking up at the bird, she murmured, "Sorry."

Will. She had to find Will. He'd gone over the ledge before her, which meant he might be farther down the hill. Or did it? Calling out his name, CJ bent over and pushed herself to a standing position, surprised at how dizzy she was. She blinked and brushed the back of her hand across her forehead. Finally, she leaned against a tree. Which way was home? She didn't even know that . . . and she *never* got lost. That fall must have addled her brain. It sure hurt enough for something to have shaken loose.

Breathing in deeply, CJ looked around her. The horses were gone, that was certain. If she stayed put, someone would eventually come looking for them. But what about Will. What if he was hurt? What if—

Stumbling a little, CJ stepped away from the tree and reached for the next. She made her way down the incline groping her way from tree to tree. When she'd gone what seemed an impossible distance, she slid to the ground to rest. She just couldn't seem to clear her head. No matter how much she blinked, everything seemed fuzzy.

"Will? Can you hear me, Will? It's CJ."

Deciding to lay down for a minute, she leaned over. That was when she caught a glimpse of red sticking out from beneath the low-hanging branches of a cedar tree. Rubbing her eyes, CJ tried to focus. There was a *hand*!

"Will!" CJ shouted. "Will!" She rose and scrabbled across the few feet between the pine trees, across a small clearing to where the boy—yes, it was Will's hand—had come to the end of a long tumble down the mountainside.

CJ called his name again and again, but Will didn't answer. Afraid to pull on his arm in case it was broken, CJ lay close and ran her hand underneath the branches, along his sleeve, up his back. She could barely touch his neck, but the feel of something warm and sticky made her shudder. Blood.

"Will," she shouted. "Will, can you hear me? Please answer me!" She began to cry. She shook his shoulder. He moaned. "That's good, Will. You just keep breathing. You hear me, Will Bishop? You keep breathing! I'm bringing help and . . . and . . . and you've got to help us break Spirit. You hear me? You keep breathing, Will Bishop!"

Stumbling and crying, CJ made her way down the incline into a clearing. Her head was pounding and she still couldn't focus. Which way? Which way was home? She looked skyward. Nothing looked familiar. Nothing looked—

Wait. Calm down. Look around you. Isn't that what Jack Greyfoot had taught her when she begged him to show her how to track animals? "I can't see anything," she had whined. Jack had told her to wait. To calm down. To look. Inhaling deeply, CJ closed her eyes. She listened. She waited. She calmed down. When she opened her eyes again, she looked around. For a few moments nothing made any sense. *Find the sun, stupid. You headed west. Home is east. Where's the sun?* Looking east, CJ saw the sign she was looking for. The thinnest plume of white streaked the sky in the distance. Someone might have mistaken it for a cloud, but CJ knew it wasn't. That was Rachel's cooking fire. That was *home*.

She wanted to run. But she couldn't. Every muscle in her body screamed every time she moved. She did her best, though.

"You listen to me, Will Bishop," she called back up the hill. "I'm running home and I'm bringing help and you'd better be ready to get moving because I'm not growing up without you. You hear me? I'm not!"

CJ headed east, tears streaming down her dirty cheeks.

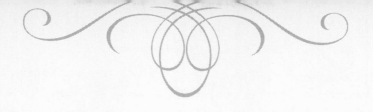

Chapter Nineteen

He hath shewed thee, O man, what is good;
and what doth the Lord require of thee,
but to do justly, and to love mercy,
and to walk humbly with thy God?

MICAH 6:8

KEEP WALKING. Keep going. Don't stop.

CJ stumbled along, wiping tears, rubbing her aching head, talking to herself. Her entire body ached. She'd taken off her coat and tied it to Pappy's saddle before the climb, and now the damp morning air made her shiver.

Keep walking. Keep going. Don't stop.

The mental image of Will lying unconscious beside a cedar tree kept her moving in spite of the urge to stop and rest. Finally, the wind carried a voice. Voices. Calling out. Calling . . . her name. Will's. CJ paused, squinting into the distance. Movement. Three dots on the horizon. Strength came from deep inside, and she began to run. She forgot her aching head, her sore muscles. She kept running, pumping her arms, sobbing, crying out loudly, "Here! I'm here!"

Pa and Lieutenant Boone and Jack flung themselves down off their horses all at once and ran to her, encircling her in their arms.

"Are you all right?" Pa asked. He put his hand to her skinned forehead.

CJ nodded. "My . . . my head hurts. But . . . Will." She began to sob. "Will's hurt."

"Where?" the men said in unison.

"Back there. By the . . . the split tree. Under a . . . cedar."

"Catch your breath, CJ," Pa ordered. "Calm down a bit."

CJ inhaled deeply. Her heart slowed enough for her to talk. She looked from Jack to her father. "You know the big tree. The one split by lightning last year. And the ledge. The eagle's nest?"

They nodded.

"We climbed up . . . the storm. There was a big *whoosh*. It washed us down." She gulped. "He isn't moving. I couldn't get him to . . . answer . . . me." She began to sob again.

The men mounted their horses. Pa leaned down, his arm extended. CJ wrapped her arms around his and hung on while he hoisted her up. "Hang on," he said. "Tight."

CJ clasped her hands around her father's waist.

"You ready?"

"Ready," CJ said.

The horses leaped forward. Together, they charged across the wet earth. CJ squeezed her eyes shut and pressed herself against her father's back, grasping the horse with her legs. *Just hold on. Just hold on. Don't let go. Don't let go, Will. Don't let go.*

It seemed to take forever to get to the split tree, but when they finally did, Jack leaped off his pony first, calling Will's name.

"Show us," Pa said, helping CJ down while he searched the area with his eyes.

"There," CJ said, running toward the cedar tree.

Will lay curled up like a baby, his hands pulled in toward his body, his eyes shut.

Lieutenant Boone ducked beneath the cedar's low-hanging branches and hunkered over him. He leaned down and listened. "He's breathing," he said.

"Will," he said loudly. "Will Bishop. Wake up, son. It's Lieutenant Boone. Will? You hear me?"

Will didn't move.

Gently, he checked the boy's arms and legs. "I don't think anything's broken," he said.

Will moaned softly.

"I'm gonna pick you up, son. We're going for help. You hear? You just stay with us, son. You're going to be all right."

CJ stood back while Jack and Pa used their bodies to press some of the cedar branches out of the way. Lieutenant Boone scooped Will up into his arms. Halfway to his horse he asked Jack to check the side of Will's head that lolled against his shoulder.

When Jack lifted Will's head he grimaced. "He's bleeding. Not bad, but it's swollen up. Looks awful."

"Is he gonna be all right?" CJ asked.

"I don't know," the lieutenant said. He looked at Jack. "He needs a doctor. The question is, do we wait the half day it will take for one of us to ride and fetch him on horseback, or do we take Will to the fort."

"Just get to the house," Pa said, and once more climbed into the saddle and reached down for CJ. "Maybe we'll know more when we can take a closer look."

The minutes it took to get to the house seemed like hours. Nathan held Will close and wondered again how such things could be allowed to happen. First Laina and Caleb, and now Will and Charlotte. Sometimes it just seemed to him that the worst things kept happening over and over again to the nicest people. How, Nathan wondered, was Charlotte Bishop going to get through this. Just when it was beginning to seem like things were going to be all right.

———

Charlotte took one look at her unconscious son and said, "We're going to the fort."

"Do you think we should put him through that?" Nathan said. "It's a rough ride."

"I'm not sitting here for half a day waiting for someone else to rescue my son," Charlotte said.

"Are you sure?"

"I'm not sure of anything," Charlotte's voice wavered. She closed her eyes and inhaled deeply. "But I remember my father talking about things like bleeding on the brain. I don't know if that's what's causing the swelling, but if it is . . . then time means a lot."

Laina was already moving around the house gathering blankets and quilts. "We'll cushion it as much as possible," she said. Rachel joined her, emerging from her own room with two blankets and her pillows. CJ ran for her room and followed suit. Jack and Nathan headed to the barn, hitched the wagon, and rumbled up to the door. The women climbed into the back, spreading first their pillows, then all the blankets on the wagon bed. Nathan lay Will atop the mound of feathers and blankets. Charlotte climbed in and perched herself at the head of the makeshift bed, elevating Will's head gently, pulling a pillow into her lap, then positioning herself so she could stroke her son's forehead.

Rachel handed Laina a bucket of water and a cloth.

When CJ put her foot on the wagon wheel to climb aboard, Laina held up her hand. "Honey, you should st—"

"I'm going," CJ said. "I can help." She plopped down beside Will.

With a glance at Caleb, Laina nodded. "All right."

"I'll catch up," Caleb said, and headed for the barn to saddle his horse.

Nathan gathered the reins and lashed at the team. The wagon lurched ahead, sloshing water out of the bucket onto CJ's dress. She dipped the cloth her mother had handed her into the water, wrung it out, and passed it to Charlotte, who did her best to wash Will's face clean.

"It doesn't look bad," Charlotte said. "Not that deep. May not even need stitches."

"So why doesn't he wake up?" CJ asked.

Charlotte closed her eyes and bent down to briefly press her lips to Will's forehead. "I don't know, CJ. I don't know."

———

They reached the fort in record time.

It felt like it had taken a lifetime. Nathan wanted to lash the horses and make them run full out, but he forced himself instead to watch the trail and try to keep the ride as smooth as possible while pushing the team at a steady lope.

As promised, Caleb had caught up with them, shouted he would alert the doctor, and raced ahead to the fort. Orderlies were waiting with a litter when the wagon pulled up to the hospital. They moved Will inside, the doctors examined him. Dr. Valentine came out into the hallway and explained the situation. He used words like *hematoma* and *trepanning*. Nathan had once seen a surgeon open a box containing the tools for that procedure. He'd winced at the sight of the drill and the saw. And now it was Will's skull they were drilling. Nathan's stomach reacted to the idea. He almost reached for Charlotte. Instead, he put his hand on his hip and shook his head. Apparently she knew the details, too, because when the doc said "trephine," she went pale and sat down on the bench in the hallway. She looked up at Nathan, then reached for Laina's hand, leaned her back against the wall, and closed her eyes.

"C-could we pray for him?" CJ asked, her voice distorted by fear and barely controlled sobs.

Without opening her eyes, Charlotte said, "Please."

"Help us," Caleb prayed. "God, help us. We're afraid. Doc said there's blood pressing on Will's brain. That sounds bad to us, but you are the Lord, and we are asking for a miracle. Guide Doc's hands to the right spot to drill. Let it be all right."

"Please," Charlotte said aloud. "Lord God, help my boy." She swallowed hard before adding, "I haven't asked you for anything in a long time, Lord. But Will's just getting started. Please, Lord. For my boy's sake. Please."

Even Dr. Valentine prayed. "It's my grandson, Lord. And I love every mischievous bone in his body. Please take my hands and help me help Will. Bring him back to us."

Charlotte took in a deep, ragged breath. Laina took her hand and whispered a prayer. The words were simple, but so natural, so heartfelt.

When even CJ talked to God, Nathan found himself wishing he knew more about praying for other people. Given a moment longer, he thought he might have tried it.

But then Dr. Valentine put his open hand on the top of his daughter's head and spoke aloud. "You keep praying, daughter." He looked at Laina. "Thank you for being here." With a pat on CJ's shoulder and a nod to Nathan and Caleb, he hurried off down the hall.

"Would you mind, terribly . . ." Charlotte opened her eyes and looked at Nathan.

"Anything," he said. "Just say it."

"Garnet."

Nathan hurried outside.

"Oh, my Lord." Garnet Irvin raised her hands to her face, one palm against each cheek. She stood just inside Dr. Valentine's back door, staring at Nathan. "Will he be all right?"

"God knows," Boone said.

Garnet reached for the shawl hanging beside the back door. As she stepped out on the back porch, she asked Nathan to find Carter Blake. "He'll want to know."

Grateful to have something more to do besides sit and wait, Nathan went to find Private Blake.

Nathan found Carter Blake and sent him to the hospital. He drove to the trading post and told Maude Dubois about the accident. Then he unhitched the team, took them into the stable and rubbed them down. All the while his mind raced, second-guessing the decision to move Will, thinking of ways they could have made the trip easier on the boy, wishing he would have heard CJ and Will ride away early that morning, wondering if somehow he'd neglected to fully warn Will about taking Spirit out on the trail, thinking back over the last week, asking himself if he'd missed some hint at what Will and CJ were planning.

When he ran out of things to do, Nathan stepped outside the stable and looked up at the sky and said aloud, "If anything happens to that boy . . ." He scolded himself. *That's good, Lieutenant. Threaten God. That's worked so well in the past. Surely God trembles when Nathan Boone talks.* He took his hat off and raked his hands through his hair. *He probably doesn't even listen. And why should He? By now He's probably tired of hearing you blame Him for everything that's wrong in the universe.*

Thinking back to the scene at the hospital made Nathan reluctant to return. It had been strange standing in that circle of people, listening to everyone else but him say a prayer for Will. He'd always felt uncomfortable around that kind of thing, but this time, something was different. His discomfort wasn't because he thought they were wasting their time. Today he was uncomfortable because he was the only one who didn't pray. It bothered him not to be able to offer Charlotte the same kind of comfort the others had. He'd seen the change that came over her while they prayed. She visibly relaxed. The concern didn't disappear from her lovely face, but the deep lines of agonizing fear seemed to recede. Nathan wished he could have been part of that. Part of helping Charlotte.

Something else niggled at him. He realized that of all the people around Charlotte Bishop, he was the only one who had reacted with anger toward God. Everyone else had seemed to just naturally turn to Him for help. Will's situation had him—just a friend of the family—pacing back and forth in a stable while Will's own mother sat quietly on a bench over at the hospital, no less concerned . . . but much more in control.

"All right then," Nathan said aloud. "If it makes any difference to you, I'm asking. I don't expect you to listen. But just in case you are, I'll ask. Is that what you want me to do? Ask you?" He looked into the distance. The morning storm was moving east. Bright blue sky was beginning to appear between thick clouds on the horizon toward the west, and the tip of Turtle Butte was bathed in sun while off to the east, low-hanging storm clouds still obscured the tip of Crow Butte. Nathan looked toward the ribbon of blue in the west.

"I'm not asking for me. It's for them. For Charlotte and Will. Please let Will live." Nathan pulled his hat back on, started to go to the hospital, then stopped again and looked up. "And if there's anything I can do—" His voice broke. "I really like that kid, God." Sniffing, Boone looked around him to make sure no one had heard or seen the embarrassing display of emotion. He pulled his hat back on. He didn't know what else he could do. But one thing he did know. He couldn't stay away from the hospital any longer.

By the time Nathan Boone got to the hospital, Will had been brought out of surgery and moved into a small back room at the far end of the ward. Dr. Valentine was leaning over him listening to his chest with a stethoscope. When Nathan looked in, the doctor glanced up and shook his head in reply to Nathan's questioning look, then his eyes directed Nathan's attention to where Charlotte sat, her head bowed, her eyes closed, her hands clutching a black book.

Nathan didn't recognize Granny Max's Bible until he sat down next to Charlotte and she held it out. "Laina said she grabbed it at the ranch as we were leaving. She said it might bring me some comfort."

"You know where to read for that sort of thing?" Nathan asked.

Charlotte pointed at the Bible. It lay open, and many passages on the two pages Nathan could see were heavily underlined. It looked, he realized, a lot like Lily's Bible.

Charlotte read aloud, " 'God is our refuge and strength, a very present help in trouble. Therefore will not we fear, though the earth be removed, and though the mountains be carried into the midst of the sea; though the waters thereof roar and be troubled, though the mountains shake with the swelling thereof.' " She paused, put her finger on the text, and repeated the words, " 'God is our refuge and strength. . . . Therefore will not we fear.' "

"Does that bring you some comfort?" Nathan asked.

Charlotte's eyes filled with tears. She nodded. "Yes," she croaked. "It does."

"Then keep reading," Nathan said.

Moistening her lips, Charlotte looked back down. " 'The Lord of hosts is with us; the God of Jacob is our refuge. . . . Be still, and know that I am God. . . . The Lord of hosts is with us; the God of Jacob is our refuge.' "

Charlotte looked up at Nathan. "I haven't tried making God my refuge in a long, long time." She smiled through her tears. "I had sort of decided the people were right who say God started it all and then just sat back to watch. I used to picture Him sitting up on a hill somewhere just watching." She shook her head. "I don't want to believe it's that way anymore. I want to think He was in the operating room guiding my father's hands. And that He's in this room right now."

Nathan only nodded.

Doctor Valentine finished his examination and pulled a white sheet up to his grandson's chin before turning toward them. "Caleb and Laina went over to the trading post to get CJ cleaned up and so they could all get some supper," he said. "I'm glad you came back, Lieutenant. I need to check on another patient, but I didn't want Charlotte left alone."

"What about you?" Nathan said to Charlotte. "You need to eat, too."

"Garnet's bringing me something," Charlotte said.

"Garnet's a good woman," Nathan said. "A good friend."

"Yes," Charlotte agreed. "She is." She took in a deep breath. "You know, she didn't have to move all the way out here with me. I sure am glad she did." She paused, then said quietly, "She prayed for Will. You should have heard her." She swiped at a tear.

Doctor Valentine put his open palm on Will's bandaged head. "He did well through the surgery, sweetheart," he said. "Now, we wait." He stepped across the room to kiss Charlotte on the cheek. "I'll be back directly." He headed for the hospital ward.

"Is there anything else I can do?" Nathan asked, and started to stand up.

"Wait," Charlotte said. "We have to wait."

Nathan sat back down.

"I didn't mean *you* have to stay," Charlotte said. "I just meant that's all that's left to be done." She ran her thumb over the printed page of Granny Max's open Bible.

"You must be exhausted," Nathan said.

"I'll be all right." Charlotte lifted her chin and straightened her shoulders. She tilted her head from side to side and arched her back. Finally, she laid the Bible on the bench, stood up, and went to the tiny window that looked north toward the trading post and the distant bluffs. "We told Will not to ride Spirit outside the corral yet," she said. "We told him it was too dangerous." She rubbed her hand across her forehead. "I didn't think to add that he shouldn't be climbing rocky ledges in the rain." She closed her eyes. Her shoulders slumped. She began to cry.

Nathan got up and went to her side. Feeling awkward about it, he put his hand on her shoulder, half expecting her to flinch and pull away. When she didn't, he stepped closer. "I haven't prayed in a lot of years, Charlotte. But I prayed for Will. And you."

"Thank you," Charlotte said. She closed her eyes. "I appreciate that. I'm grateful for all you've done for Will. He loves you, you know."

"I'm flattered," Nathan said.

"Don't be flattered," Charlotte said. She looked up at him, her eyes shining with tears. "Just don't give up on him." She looked over to the bed where Will lay motionless.

"I won't," Nathan said. He lifted her chin and looked down at her. "On either of you."

Offering Charlotte a shoulder to cry on was the manly thing to do. Offering her his strength and his friendship made sense. What didn't make sense, Nathan thought as he wrapped his arms around Charlotte, was the way his heart thumped when she lay her head on his chest and gave in to her tears.

"Don't let go," Charlotte said, closing her eyes as she leaned against him.

"I won't," Nathan whispered.

———

"I don't know."

"Time. He needs time."

"We released the pressure. But we can't know yet."

"It all depends."

"All we can do is pray."

"I've seen remarkable recoveries."

"Give it time."

"We don't know."

"There's no way to know."

"Only God knows."

A week after her son's accident, Charlotte was no closer to knowing his fate than she was two minutes after his surgery. Laina and Caleb and CJ had reluctantly gone home, with a promise to return as often as possible to visit.

From her place at her son's bedside, Charlotte had heard snatches of the Independence Day festivities at the fort. Through the open window of Will's hospital ward, she'd caught glimpses of the dozens of Sioux in full regalia who had ridden down from the reservation for the celebration.

Nathan took up his soldiering responsibilities again. "Will and I can go back to the ranch together when he's better," he promised.

Charlotte's father said that every day was a step in the right direction. To Charlotte, it looked like every day was a step into nothingness. And yet, in the moment of her life that she should feel most desperate, there was a voice of reason. Somewhere deep inside her, hope flickered and would not be extinguished. The knowledge that half a dozen strong believers were praying for Will brought comfort. Charlotte read the forty-sixth psalm so many times she could recite it from memory. She went on to read other psalms, and began to cling to the God revealed in them.

One morning while she was sitting beside Will's bed, Charlotte fumbled through the unfamiliar pages of Granny's Bible trying to find a string of verses Granny had written on the inside cover of the old book. They talked about God being holy and just. They mentioned sin and the sacrifice Jesus made because of it. Charlotte read phrases like "whosoever will may come." She puzzled on the verses and asked Garnet about them. Garnet said they had talked about such things before.

"I know," Charlotte said. "But this time your answers make sense." Charlotte decided to step forward with what she thought of as a trembling kind of faith—cloaked in things she didn't understand but would trust to God. As a result, God was no longer a remote spirit watching from a distance to her. He became a "refuge" and her "present help in trouble." She was still terrified about Will. But in the midst of the fear was a sense that she was no longer alone.

The days took on a routine. They moved Will home. Garnet stayed in his room at night. Every morning Private Blake, who was officially a striker for Dr. Valentine now, carried Will into the kitchen, where a makeshift cot had been set up near the window.

"I just want him to hear our voices and be part of the family," Charlotte said. "I can't explain it, but I think it has to be good for Will to hear us talking."

Garnet, who had long since stopped reading aloud to soothe Charlotte's mind, took up the habit again, reading every afternoon from books Lieutenant Boone brought from the post library. And she sang. She filled the kitchen with music, sometimes accompanied by Carter Blake on a mouth harp.

Will did not open his eyes, but he could swallow, and between Charlotte, Garnet, Carter, and Nathan, his young body took in a steady stream of gruel and fresh milk. One day nearly two weeks after Will's surgery, Charlotte was feeding Will fresh applesauce.

"Mmm."

Charlotte's eyes widened. "You like that, honey? That's an apple. I put cinnamon and sugar on it."

"Mmmm. Mmmmhmmm."

"If you can hear me, Will . . . if you know what Mama's saying, could you show me? Do you think you could open your eyes, sweetheart?"

And there they were. The most beautiful gray eyes in the universe.

Chapter Twenty

A friend loveth at all times, and a brother is born for adversity.
PROVERBS 17:17

FOR ALL HIS EXPERIENCE with chairs, Will Bishop had always thought of the mahogany chair in Grandmother's entryway back in Michigan as the worst. That was the chair where he waited for his father to come home on days when he had been particularly naughty. He thought he'd never hate any chair as much as that one. He was wrong. As the weeks went by after his accident, and he was able to sit up and be more aware of his surroundings, Will grew to despise the rocking chair on his grandfather's porch more than any chair he'd ever inhabited. He couldn't get out of it on his own because it wobbled. And he couldn't rock in time to anything, so the creaking sound it made was irregular—just like his body and brain since the accident. He hated being trapped in the chair, and he hated the way it talked to him, reminding him how different things were.

Even if he did walk oddly now, Will couldn't see the reason why he had to just sit on the porch or hobble around the house. Loot Boone had said as much one night when they thought Will was asleep. He'd almost argued with Ma, asking her how Will was going to learn to walk any better if he was never allowed to exercise. Loot Boone had said Will ought to be walking around the parade ground every day, even if it took all morning. He argued that the walk would be good for him and maybe he'd get better. Will thought that made sense. But he couldn't quite figure how to get down the three stairs between him and the ground. And then how to get back up to standing so he could take a step. That was a puzzle he hadn't solved. He had to be able to do it fast, too, before Ma found out, or she'd throw a fit. But he was determined to do it or die trying, because if he had to spend many more days in that rocking chair on Grandfather's porch, he was going to lose what was left of his mind.

Everyone treated him differently now. Even Ma. Although she still stroked his head and said she loved him, she was different. Always hovering, as if there was some unseen evil just waiting to hurt her baby. Will tried to show her he was still Will inside, but every time he tried to talk, she interrupted him. "It's all right, honey," she'd say. "Don't upset yourself." And she'd pat his hand and give him something to eat. He was beginning to hate cookies.

When he tried to take a walk, Ma called him back and said he had to wait until she could go with him. And when she called his name, her voice was laced with fear. If he could form the words, he could tell her it was all right. That he knew he couldn't do the same things as before. That his mind still worked pretty well, except that he couldn't find words any more. At least not the kind he could say. His tongue just wouldn't do it. And for some reason when he tried to write the words down, his fingers wouldn't act right either. But the words were still in his head. He remembered the way to the Four Pines Ranch, even though he hadn't been there in a long time. He remembered all the faces from before and the names that went with them, although sometimes he suspected a little part of the names might be scrambled. *Loot Boone* didn't seem quite right, but that was the best he could do. He wondered if he were allowed to walk around the parade ground like Loot Boone had suggested, if that would make his brain work better so the names would come back just right.

If he had the names, Will thought, maybe people would stop treating him like he wasn't there. Sometimes when people came to the house and saw that he was sitting on the porch, they walked right past him. Like he was invisible. Even if he looked right at them, they didn't even nod. He could have been a giant doll for all the attention they gave him. Didn't they see his eyes? Couldn't they tell he was smiling? Didn't they hear his voice? Even if it was only a grunt, surely they realized he was grunting at them. They should talk back. But they didn't. Most of them glanced at him, averted their eyes, and knocked hastily on the door, looking around nervously while they waited for Garnet.

There were exceptions. Loot Boone always slapped him on the shoulder and said hello. So did Private Blake. Will understood everything they said. He wished he could talk back. But he could only lift one corner of his mouth and try to smile—and he always slobbered when he did it. It was embarrassing. Especially when he was so awkward with his hand and couldn't always manage to wipe his own mouth. He looked away when that happened. Sometimes people sighed with the sound that said they pitied him. That made him mad.

It was the *pity* that finally got to Will. He couldn't stand all those sappy women walking by him to knock on his mother's door. News of his accident had spread fast, and the women at Fort Robinson had turned out in droves to comfort his ma. From the things they said, you would have thought Will couldn't understand a word. Surely, he thought, if they knew he understood them, they wouldn't have said the things they did. Sometimes they lowered their voices so he couldn't hear the words, but he remembered that tone. It was the same tone women had used in their murmurings when Father's body was laid out in the dining room at Grandmother's back in Michigan. Such voices had made his mother cry back then, and they made her cry again now. Will was sure of it, although Mother never let him see the tears. But he saw her red eyes often enough. She talked about God helping them and she prayed now before they had a meal. But she still cried. A lot. It made him want to scream. Except he couldn't. It made him want to run away. Except he couldn't do that either.

One July morning Will finally got them to listen without his having to talk. Ma had decided to have a quilting, which was a first, since Ma hated to sew. Will suspected it was another way for her to provide entertainment for him. She seemed to think that hearing other people talk would somehow help him get his own words back. She and Garnet scurried around all morning, moving the parlor furniture back from the middle of the room and setting up the quilting frame so they would be ready when Mrs. Barstow from up on Officer's Row arrived. Mrs. Barstow was the one bringing the quilt top. It would be put on the frame along with some filler and back fabric, and the women were going to "tie" it, Ma had explained. That meant they would be there all day, putting needles with yarn on them through the fabric layers and tying a million knots before it was finished. It also probably meant Will would be ignored all day. He could hear the scraping of chairs on the floor inside and the excitement in Ma's voice as she and Garnet got ready. They had taken Will out onto the porch to "enjoy the sunshine."

Just about the time the aroma of fresh coffee wafted through the windows, making his mouth water so that a bit of saliva ran out the corner of his drooping lip and made a dark spot on his blue shirt, the women started to come. Mrs. Barstow was the first, followed by five more. And not one of them said a word to Will as they paraded past him. Mrs. Barstow hugged her quilt top to her body and frowned as she walked by. Another glanced at him and then looked away, shaking her head. Another one made that clicking sound against the roof of her mouth he hated so much. The last two were quiet, but when they got onto the porch they sort of drew their skirts aside. As if Will might have lice or something. Those skirts were the last straw.

Sitting in the rocker, Will realized that if he waited for his mother to understand or for anyone else to listen, he was going to be sitting in this rocker on Grandfather's porch for the rest of his life. He was going to see those looks and endure those sounds of pity unless he put a stop to it, and he *was* going to stop it. He would show them. Ma would stay occupied with her guests, and Garnet would be busy in the kitchen, and that would give him time.

The first problem was getting himself out of the rocking chair. He inched his bottom to the edge of the seat and looked down at the porch, thinking he might as well be peering over the edge of a cliff. He was going to fall, no doubt about it. But if he could break the fall so he didn't land with too big a thud, then he would be able to roll to the edge of the porch and tackle the next big hurdle, which was the steps. Leaning over as far as he could, he felt the blood rush to his head. With a grunt, he pitched forward so that the top of his head was the first thing to land on the porch. Quickly, he rolled his head to one side, feeling the pull of the muscles as first his shoulder, then his entire right side landed on the porch. He lay quietly for a minute, breathing hard, waiting for Ma's screech. But the only thing he heard was laughter from the women inside.

Rolling toward the steps took another few minutes. But he made it, and even managed to sit up after a few tries. That was when he realized something wonderful. His legs were long enough to stretch across the top of all three stairs. His feet almost touched the ground. Bracing himself with his hands, he pushed himself forward until his bottom slid onto the top step and his feet were resting on the earth. If it weren't for the stair rail, he could have swung his feet to the side of the stairs and pushed off and been standing up. But the stair rail was a problem. Unless . . . Reaching up, Will lobbed his hands across the top of the rail, dismayed when his bad left hand was too weak to grip firmly enough for him to pull himself up.

How long it took, Will didn't know, but Ma caught him just as he had managed to get himself to the bottom step, wrap his forearms around the stair railing, and inch his torso along the rail until he was positioned at a crazy angle—half sitting, half standing—and completely worn out.

"Will Bishop!" she called out from the doorway. "What do you think you are doing?"

Will couldn't get his head turned around to see her, but he didn't have to look to imagine every woman at the quilting standing behind her, looking at Widow Bishop's idiot son. Closing his eyes, he could hear their sympathy. It made him mad. So mad that when his mother's hand touched his shoulder he tried to shrug her off. He shook his head angrily, becoming even madder because of his inability to speak. *No no no no no*. Why couldn't his mouth even say *that*. Angry tears sprang from his eyes.

"What is it, baby," Ma was saying, "what hurts? Did you twist your ankle? Does your back hurt? Show Mama, darling." And without even waiting to see his answer in his face, she was calling for Garnet.

Garnet came, her face a mask of kindness, a hint of apology in her eyes as she helped Will stand upright. "Put your hands on my shoulders, baby," she said. "Then you can lower yourself back onto the stairs while I get Carter to help us."

No no no no. Will struggled, lost his balance, fell back, crashing onto the edge of a stair. Pain shot up his back, making him even angrier. The tears flowed. The women came out onto the porch. With monumental effort, Will pushed himself to sit up, raised his fists to the side of his head and sat, his eyes scrunched shut, the tears flowing.

"Run get help, Garnet," Ma was saying. She sounded out of breath.

Will leaned against the railing, his hands clamped over his ears, trying to shut out the clucking and murmuring of the women behind him. It seemed like it took ten years for the murmurings to stop. Even after Ma suggested the ladies go back inside and quilt, and even after they did, he could hear their voices through the window, imagine the things they were saying, and picture their pitying looks—like hens clucking over a wounded chick.

Ma was leaning over, looking up at him, rubbing his back, trying to calm him down when Loot Boone's voice sounded. "Is everything all right?"

Ma's answer made Will mad. "Of course not," she almost snapped. "Will's fallen. He must have been trying to walk again. Alone. Garnet's gone for Father."

"Doesn't look to me like you need a doctor," Loot Boone said.

"Help me get him back up to the porch, will you?" Ma asked as she stood up.

When she reached for his arm, Will pushed her away, shaking his head. He looked at Loot Boone, and then at the parade ground and back again.

"Why don't you let me take him for a walk?" Boone said. "I've got nothing pressing this afternoon. You can go back to your quilting, and Will and I will just take a stroll." Loot Boone looked at Will. "That all right with you, son?"

Taking a deep breath, Will did his best to smile. He knew it came out as more of a grimace, but Loot Boone must have seen the intent rather than the result, because he said, "See, Charlotte? I've got it right. A walk is what the boy wants." He glanced past Will toward the parlor window. "And it's no wonder, with him having to listen to a gaggle of women all morning long. That would wear any boy out."

Ma opened her mouth to protest, but Loot Boone interrupted her. "You can trust me, Charlotte. I won't let anything happen. But you can't expect the boy to spend the rest of his life in a rocking chair on his grandfather's porch." He went on without giving Ma a chance to speak. "Now go on back inside with your women friends and enjoy the afternoon." In one easy movement he hauled Will to his feet. "Will and I will be just fine. I'll bring him back to you for dinner, and I predict he'll be hungry as a mountain lion."

Ma closed her mouth. Will saw the doubt in her eyes. She looked back up toward the parlor and back at Loot Boone.

"Trust me, Charlotte," Boone repeated, his eyes never leaving Ma's.

Ma looked up into Loot Boone's eyes, and Will could see that something inside her let go. The effect was not unlike what Will had sensed happening when Father left on an expedition. The minute he was gone, Will stopped tiptoeing around the house and Mother smiled more. Just like she was smiling now as she said, "All right, Nathan. If you're sure."

"I'm sure," Boone said.

Ma nodded, smoothed her apron, and turned to go. But not before she pulled a kerchief from her apron pocket and swiped the place at the corner of Will's mouth where the spit sometimes rolled out.

"All right, young man," Loot Boone said, the minute Ma was out of sight. "Think you can make it all the way around the parade ground?"

Will nodded eagerly, and took a step, grunting with dismay when his right foot refused to step and he nearly toppled to the ground.

Boone was quick to catch him. "Whoa, there," he said. "What if you just slide that bum foot along without trying to pick it up. Can you do that?"

Sweat broke out on his forehead with the effort, but inch by inch, Will managed to slide his bad foot forward, throw his weight on it, and bring his good foot alongside.

"Outstanding," Loot Boone said, clapping him on the shoulder. "That will work for now. Let's go." Cupping his left hand under Will's right elbow, Boone stepped forward, bracing himself and holding tight while Will struggled to take another step.

Will sighed with dismay and looked up at Boone, who grinned back. "Want to give up?"

Will frowned and shook his head.

"Didn't think so," Boone said. "Not much fun sitting in a rocking chair, is it?"

Will shook his head again.

"Well then," Boone said, tugging on Will's sleeve. "Let's keep moving."

———

It took the better part of the afternoon for Will to walk the perimeter of the parade ground. Halfway around, Loot Boone made Will sit down on the front stoop of one of the new barracks. "Wait here," he said. "Catch your breath. I need to run over to the trading post for a minute. I won't be long."

While Boone was gone, Will watched Company G of the Ninth run through their drills on the parade ground. He frowned suddenly, wondering what had happened to Carter Blake's bay gelding named Dutch now that Carter was Dr. Valentine's striker. The fact that he even had the thought thrilled him. He'd forgotten a lot and he knew it. Garnet had taught him how to button his shirt, but try as he might, he could not figure out how to tie his own shoes. Still, with all the things he'd forgotten, he remembered Carter Blake and Dutch. Looking across the parade ground toward the stables in the distance, Will promised himself that the minute he was able to walk that far, he'd visit Dutch. Maybe he'd even hide a lump of sugar in his pocket. No, that wouldn't work. His hands didn't operate nearly well enough for him to dig a lump of sugar out of his shirt pocket. He'd have to ponder that. Maybe he could invent a way.

"Here you go," Loot Boone was saying, as he held out a brass-handled cane. "Frenchy has a half dozen canes behind the counter at his store. He was happy to loan us one. Now here's how he said it works," Boone said, and demonstrated how Will should step forward with the cane and his good foot, then drag the lazy foot up alongside. When Boone did it, it didn't seem hard, but when Will tried, it took all his concentration to move even half a foot. Looking ahead of him to the long walkway that ran in front of the row of barracks, Will hesitated.

"Too far?" Boone asked.

Will pondered. Taking a deep breath, he grasped the cane with his good hand and shuffled forward, carrying himself away from the barracks, away from his mother's quilting party and—thank you, God—away from that blasted rocking chair.

Chapter Twenty-One

There is a friend that sticketh closer than a brother.
PROVERBS 18:24

HE NEVER WOULD have thought it possible, but one day in late summer Lieutenant Nathan Boone realized that he was actually beginning to see the United States Army as an intrusion in the life he wanted to live. Or *lives* as the case seemed to be. He was getting increasingly confused about what the future might hold. Back in June he'd been at the Four Pines when Troop F was sent to Beaver Valley east of Chadron to check into rumors of "Indian depredations." Nathan was glad he hadn't had to be part of the "expedition" that spent several days finding nothing. Spending time as a cowboy had been great. And getting to know Rachel Greyfoot had been nice, too.

In July, when Troop I had been sent north to intercept Chief Red Cloud and some followers who had left the Pine Ridge reservation up in South Dakota, Nathan hadn't had to go with them either. As it turned out, the Sioux returned to the reservation long before they reached Soldier Creek—where the troops were headed. When the men rode back into the fort, grumbling about the wasted time, Nathan realized he felt his work with Will Bishop was more important than charging up to Hat Creek to do nothing. Dining with Will and his mother was becoming increasingly comfortable, too.

A new spiritual movement among the western tribes was ratcheting up the tension in the West. Periodically, all the men from Fort Robinson were ordered to "fall out" and camp just outside the post "to test their readiness for field service." Nathan had no choice but to participate, but every time he was gone from the fort he caught himself wondering how Will and Charlotte were doing in his absence. Every time he returned, he looked forward to seeing Will's lopsided grin and Charlotte's welcoming smile.

In spite of visits from nervous citizens who were certain the Ghost Dance religion spreading through the western tribes was going to result in a renewed Indian war, life at Fort Robinson continued to be ruled by 5:30 A.M. reveille and a routine number of bugle calls throughout each day until taps sounded at 9:15 every evening. Nathan began to resent the rigidity of military life. He got in the habit of checking in on Will every night after taps. Sometimes they played chess, with Nathan encouraging Will to use his "bad hand" to move the pieces, and sometimes they took a walk. Boone grew to look forward to the sounding of taps and the lamplight in the window at the surgeon's residence that meant they were expecting him.

Nathan's negative feelings about the direction his own life was headed reached a new high early in August when an expedition from Princeton University in the East arrived at the fort. The leader of the expedition, a Professor Scott, stayed as the houseguest of Commander Tilford, and the rest of the expedition members were treated almost like visiting royalty. Nathan didn't see why Dr. Valentine had to invite some of them to dinner every blasted night. Especially the one named Gabriel Moser.

Moser had an opinion on everything from what he called "the Indian problem" to the origins of man to the future of Nebraska in the national economy to the impossibility of earning anything approaching a respectable living in ranching. In spite of Nathan's personal resentment of the man's high opinion of himself, he was glad about one thing. Moser knew a specialist back east who might be able to help Will. But even that caused Nathan's hackles to rise, just because of the way Moser put it. "If anyone knows how to return the boy to normal, it would be Doctor Faucett."

"I don't think anyone who knows Will thinks of him as not being normal," Nathan said, staring across the table at Moser, who was seated next to Charlotte. Nathan got up and excused himself before Moser could respond. He went outside to join Will, who had long since excused himself from the table and headed outside.

When a few minutes passed and the sound of Charlotte's laughter lilted through the parlor window to where Nathan and Will sat talking, Boone stood up. "It's all right if you'd rather stay here with your company than come with me," he said to Will. "We can always ride tomorrow."

In response, Will pushed himself upright and grabbed his cane.

Boone nodded. "All right, then. I'll just tell your mother, and—"

The door opened and Charlotte came out, followed by the fresh-faced man Nathan and Will didn't like. She turned to shake his hand. "Thank you again, Mr. Moser. I'll write Doctor Faucett tomorrow."

"Be sure to mention my name," Moser said. "He and my father studied together."

"Not following in the old man's footsteps?" Nathan asked abruptly.

Moser shook his head. "No. I always had my heart set on Princeton, where my grandfather studied." He motioned to the new buildings of the West End. "Professor Scott is very impressed with the improvements made here since his first visit." Moser looked around. "He said it was quite primitive back then."

"Well," Boone said, unable to stop the sarcasm in his voice, "we had to cope with the buffalo and the Cheyenne and the Sioux, you know. There wasn't a lot of time to hang wallpaper."

Will nudged Nathan's arm and smiled up at him. He nodded toward the stables.

"We'd better get going," Nathan said. "Will wants to climb aboard old Bones before it gets too dark."

"Are you sure this is going to be all right?" Charlotte asked.

"Why don't you come and see for yourself?" Nathan said.

Charlotte hesitated.

Moser spoke up. "Why don't we all go."

Will frowned. Nathan sighed.

"That's a wonderful idea," Charlotte said. "I'll get my bonnet and my shawl and be right out."

———

"You're . . . what?" Nathan didn't think Charlotte Bishop could surprise him.

"We're going with the Princeton expedition. Father is to be their surgeon. You should see him. It's given him a new lease on life to be part of the project."

"Do you think Will is ready for something like that?" Nathan asked. "And do you have any idea how miserable it is up in that country in *August*?"

"I don't mean we're going fossil hunting," Charlotte said. "We'll only go as far as Four Pines and stay there while Father is gone."

"But *I* was going to take Will to the ranch as soon as I get back from my trip east."

"Well, now you won't have to. It's all arranged." She looked up at him. "I'd think you'd be happy Mr. Moser came up with the idea. Now you won't have to hurry back just because of us."

Nathan chewed his lower lip while he formulated a reply. The fact was, he didn't understand what it was about Charlotte and Will's going to the ranch without him that should make him so upset. *She'll be right where you want her when you get back. It's perfect.* And it would have been perfect. If only Gabriel Moser wasn't in the picture.

———

"Please, Laina," Charlotte said. "Give it a rest." The women were sitting on the front porch at the ranch. "You were mistaken about Lieutenant Boone and me, pure and simple. He's written to Will twice since he's been gone, and I'm grateful for that. The fact that he *didn't* write to me is evidence enough."

"You're wrong," Laina insisted. "Nathan's just . . . slow about letting his feelings show."

Charlotte closed her eyes. "This is embarrassing," she said. "I wish you would just drop it. He's a good friend, and I'll always appreciate that. But that's where it ends."

"You can't tell me you don't feel . . . something." Laina objected.

Charlotte flexed the fingers of her left hand and went back to snapping the green beans in the bowl in her lap. She and Will had been at the Four Pines for two weeks now. The summer garden was bearing vast quantities of food, and the women worked hours every day preserving the bounty. "All right. If it makes you feel better, yes, I feel something," Charlotte said. "And I'm grateful God woke up that part of me. I really thought the Colonel had probably destroyed every last trace of that kind of thing for me. It's nice to know he didn't. That's probably what God intended when He brought Lieutenant Boone back into my life. I'll admit that lately I've been hoping it might be more. But I'm determined to be content with whatever happens." She smiled at Laina. "And I believe a certain Mrs. Jackson is the one who first said that kind of thing to me about being content with whatever God provides."

"I did no such thing," Laina snorted. "I never wanted you to give up on Nathan."

"That's not what I meant," Charlotte said. "I mean the idea of contentment and letting God be in charge."

"Oh . . . that," Laina said. She looked at Charlotte. They both burst out laughing. "You mean that little item of eternal importance. Trusting and obeying God."

Charlotte nodded. "Uh-huh."

Laina sighed. "All right. I repent. But I still have to say one more thing about all of this. And that is . . . you cannot possibly tell me you are truly interested in Gabriel Moser."

"Why not?" Charlotte asked. "Because he's a few years younger than me?"

"Charlotte," Laina said. "He's a *century* younger than you when it comes to life experience."

"And I find that refreshing," Charlotte said. "But lest you worry, I'm not interested in him the way you think." She lowered her voice. "But, Laina, for the first time in a long time, someone sees me for myself. To Mr. Moser, I'm Charlotte Bishop. I'm not 'Will's mother.' That's nice. And now," she said with a flourish, "could we please talk about something *besides* my nonexistent love life?"

Laina laughed. "All right. Jack put a saddle on Spirit weeks ago. She's going to be a wonderful little ride."

Charlotte sighed and shook her head. "I don't know if Will will ever be ready for Spirit. I was amazed when Nathan got him up on Bones a few weeks ago."

"Don't give up on that," Laina said. "Being around Spirit just might spark some part of Will's willpower you haven't tapped into yet."

"Or it could discourage him to the point he'll give up," Charlotte said. She sighed. "I don't know what to do. It's taking so *long*."

"What does that doctor out east say?"

Charlotte shook her head. "I haven't heard from him. But there was an article in one of my father's medical papers not long ago. The latest research, supposedly. And it reiterated exactly what my father has been telling me. Every case is different. They see miracles every day. Don't give up hope. Keep him working at everything. Fine-motor skills come back last. He could eventually be completely normal . . . or he might never talk again. There's no way to know what was destroyed permanently or how much he might be able to relearn." She blinked back unexpected tears.

"You," Laina said, "are a wonder of patience and love, Charlotte Bishop."

"I," Charlotte said, "am tired." She sighed and closed her eyes.

"Which is why," Laina said, "you belong here. New scenery. Rachel and Jack and old Dorsey to help. Who knows, we might just witness that miracle your father prayed for that first night before surgery."

"I don't think I'm standing in the right line for miracles," Charlotte said.

"What do you mean?"

"I mean, that some people get miracles . . . and other people get the patience to handle things without the miracles. I'd like a miracle, don't get me wrong. But if God isn't going to do the miracle, he'd better pass out some patience and perseverance."

Laina nodded. "He does."

"I know," Charlotte said. "He has. 'It is of the Lord's mercies that we are not consumed, because his compassions fail not. They are new every morning: great is thy faithfulness.' " Charlotte smiled. "See? I took your advice. I'm reading the Bible."

"Has it helped?"

"Oh my goodness *yes*," Charlotte said. "Just when I fall on my face and tell God I can't, He picks me up. And I can. Most of the time. Although," she said, with a grin, "I did almost lose my head and run off into the badlands in search of fossils with my young lover."

"Charlotte Bishop!" Laina looked appropriately shocked. She brought her hand to her chest in mock horror. And they giggled like schoolgirls.

———

The hardest thing, CJ thought, was that Will couldn't talk to her any more. That was the thing she missed most. She didn't mind so much that he walked with a jerk or that he drooled a little. And his crooked smile was almost cute. Anyone who knew Will at all could see he was still *in* there, behind those gray eyes. But he didn't talk. And she couldn't get him to try.

"Please, Will," she'd say. "Just try. I don't care if you can't say it good. But it's like walking. You had to have a cane when Lieutenant Boone first took you around the parade ground. And now you barely need it. I bet you won't even have a limp by Christmas. I bet it would be the same way with talking. If only you would try."

Will would listen, press his lips together, and shake his head. He was staying in the bunkhouse with Jack and Dorsey, just like always. But as far as CJ could tell, he didn't try to talk to them, either. It drove her crazy.

———

Late in August, the expedition from Princeton was back at the ranch before heading for Fort Robinson and the railroad and the long ride back east. The Jacksons hauled their bathtub out to a place behind the barn and, one by one, the members of the expedition washed the grit and grime of weeks in the badlands from their sunburned skin. Will sat on the front porch of the ranch house grinning as he listened to the whoops and hollers as the men doused one another with ice-cold well water. The fossil hunting had been a success, and the students and Professor Scott were in high spirits.

Behind him in the ranch house, Mrs. Jackson and Will's mother and Rachel were preparing food and bringing it out to the table they had set up on the porch. Toward evening, one of the more energetic students hauled out a violin and began to play. Before long, someone suggested a dance. Even CJ was invited to join in, which she did, much to Will's amazement. He had almost forgotten that CJ was a girl. Seeing her dancing reminded him. Made him wish he could dance, too. From where he sat on the porch watching, Will tapped his foot to the music. He nearly laughed aloud when the old soldier Emmet Dorsey did an arthritic version of a jig that had everyone rolling with laughter—including Dorsey.

He was having a wonderful time until he caught a glimpse of his mother. Dancing. With that Gabriel Moser. He did not like the way his mother looked up at that man. *"You might get a new pa,"* CJ had told him. He'd said that was all right with him. And it was. As long as it was someone like Lieutenant Boone. *Lieutenant. See? He knew the right name now. It wasn't "Loot Boone" anymore. He was normal. Boone knew it. Why didn't this Moser guy?*

The music ended. Moser held on to Ma, and she didn't seem to mind. Will got up and shuffled toward the barn. He leaned his cane against the door and continued inside, making his way to the last stall on the right where a gray filly stepped forward and thrust her head over the top board. She watched him approach with her wide dark eyes, her ears both brought forward to take in every sound. As Will came up alongside her, Spirit put her head down. She kept it lowered while Will buried his face in her mane and reached around her neck. Spirit didn't move. She didn't bob her head up and down, as was her manner. She stayed very still, except for a gentle whicker that vibrated her black muzzle.

Will slid his hand down her face and to the muzzle. Spirit opened her lips and nibbled. Will laughed.

"S-s-s . . . pir-r-r-r . . . it-t-t," Will whispered. "Hey, gir-rl-l-l-l."

Spirit whickered again and nudged Will gently. She took in a deep breath and sighed.

Chapter Twenty-Two

The Lord is good unto them that wait for him, to the soul that seeketh him. It is good that a man should both hope and quietly wait for the salvation of the Lord. It is good for a man that he bear the yoke in his youth. . . . For the Lord will not cast off for ever: but though he cause grief, yet will he have compassion according to the multitude of his mercies.
LAMENTATIONS 3:25-27, 31-32

EARLY IN SEPTEMBER, Charlotte and Will returned to Fort Robinson. Charlotte's energy and attention were given to the planning and execution of a wedding between Garnet and Private Blake. Dr. Valentine solved the quandary over the availability of living quarters.

"Why, you'll live at my house, of course," he said.

Blake, who had lost sleep over the idea of moving his bride from the relative luxury of the room behind the surgeon's kitchen into a shack down by the White River, offered his sincere thanks, to which the doctor replied, "Don't thank me, Private. I don't want to lose my cook and my striker."

Caleb Jackson rode into Fort Robinson and made sure Charlotte knew they expected both her and Will for a long visit soon. "Jack has Spirit trotting around the corral. She's just waiting for Will." He also told them that Nathan Boone was having great success out east, rounding up a good string of mares for the ranch, and that after protracted negotiations it looked like the stallion named Banner might be headed west to stand at the Four Pines, after all.

Charlotte answered Gabriel Moser's latest letter and enclosed Dr. Valentine's notes on Will's accident and surgery for Dr. Faucett's review.

Early autumn colors began to dot the bluffs in the distance, and the flat land around the fort turned golden as the grasses dried out and went dormant. The cavalry and infantry companies at the post made a long march and fought practice battles along the Niobrara River.

Charlotte did not hear from Nathan.

Dr. Faucett wrote that he had reviewed Will's case and could offer little more information than what Charlotte already knew about Will's prognosis. *I would, of course, be happy to evaluate your son here in my clinic.* Charlotte wavered between wanting to pack up and leave immediately and her desire to be at the fort when Nathan Boone returned.

But before Charlotte could decide what to do, the fervent prayers of many were answered. Will began to speak with words again. It came about when Garnet handed him a book one day, saying, "I've got work to do, young man. Suppose *you* do the reading from now on." As a result, Will's once impossibly garbled speech improved to the point where anyone could understand him. He continued to choose his audiences carefully, though, once he realized that strangers often assumed him to be mentally slow.

Lieutenant Boone wrote to Will. He was funny and took time to share anecdotes of the "city folk" he encountered who didn't know a "cattle prod from a rifle." Will laughed uproariously when he read the letter, telling his mother it was a "private joke." Charlotte scolded herself for being jealous of the two of them having private jokes. She admitted to wishing Nathan would add a note for her at the bottom of Will's letters.

But Charlotte didn't hear from Nathan.

———

On a crisp September day, when frost dotted the landscape, Private Blake started the first fire of the season in the parlor fireplace. Charlotte was in the kitchen, helping Garnet load a basket with pies and cakes for a masquerade ball being planned for the officers' families, when footsteps sounded on the back porch. Charlotte felt the blood rush to her cheeks as she anticipated seeing Nathan Boone.

"Hello, Mrs. Bishop," Preacher Barton said, removing his hat and waiting to be invited in. "I'm on my way to the Four Pines and just wanted to check in on that boy of yours. Is he at home?"

Charlotte hid her disappointment and invited the preacher in. She made him coffee and coaxed him into letting her cut into one of the pies. She told him all about Will's recovery, ending with, "but you'll be able to judge for yourself. He's just over at the stables with Private Blake for a little ride. They should be back before long. Will wants to keep his riding skills sharp. We've been waiting for Lieutenant Boone to get back with a new string of horses for the ranch before we head that way. The lieutenant has written Will, and said he can help him deliver the new horses." She paused and poured herself a cup of coffee. "You'll have to be sure and ask

Will about Spirit. He's really excited to see what Jack Greyfoot has been able to do with her."

The preacher stood up. "Well, if you'll excuse me, I think I'll just hurry on over to the stables and check in with your boy right now."

"I'll come with you," Charlotte said.

The preacher held out his hand. "There's no need. No need for that at all." And he hurried off, so abruptly that Charlotte was a little hurt by the obvious. The preacher did not want her along. She wondered why.

———

"Tell me the truth, Emory William Bishop," Charlotte said firmly.

Will looked down at the piece of apple pie on his plate. He sighed. He picked at the roll of crust at the edge of the pie and pursed his lips. Finally, he said, "Yes, I s-s-saw him-m-m."

Charlotte looked away. "I don't understand what all this secrecy is about. Have I done something to offend Lieutenant Boone that he didn't even stop to say hello before he took the new horses to the ranch?" She paused. "I thought you were supposed to help him with that." She sighed. "I'm not angry with you, Will. You didn't do anything wrong. The same goes for Lieutenant Boone. I just don't understand his behavior." When Will looked at her, Charlotte said, "You're hiding something behind those beautiful gray eyes, William Bishop. I don't like it when you keep secrets from me."

Will picked up the piece of pie crust and put it in his mouth. He chewed so slowly Charlotte wanted to scream. "He tol' me not to tell. It's a s-secret."

"People who love each other don't keep secrets that hurt others," Charlotte snapped.

The corners of Will's mouth went down. His gray eyes grew wide and sad. "I sorry Ma. He coming back. S-soon."

Will looked ready to cry. But it was obvious to Charlotte that he wasn't going to betray Lieutenant Boone's confidence. Jealousy over Nathan entrusting Will with something fairly important gave way to irritation with him for burdening Will with something that erected a wall between Will and his own mother. She would speak to Nathan about that.

"All right, Will," Charlotte said, and reached across the table to pat the back of his hand. "Don't worry yourself about it. I'll just have to wait until the lieutenant decides to come back."

She changed the subject abruptly and asked Will about the day's ride up the bluff. "I'm so proud of you," Charlotte said, "how you just climbed back aboard Bones and learned everything again." She hesitated, then decided to tell him. "The lieutenant's not the only one who has a secret, you know." She winked at Will. "I plan to make certain Mr. Jackson understands that we intend to buy Spirit."

Will's eyes grew wide. They filled with happy tears. He laughed. *Laughed.* It was a jerky, sort of sobbing noise, but to Charlotte it was a lovely sound. She sent a prayer of thanksgiving to heaven. Whatever Lieutenant Nathan Boone was up to, whatever disappointment was on the horizon for her personally, her boy was getting better, and that, Charlotte decided, was quite enough happiness for one woman.

———

It came clear to her later that night. She was glad it had come to her while the world was quiet and she was alone. It gave her time to absorb the truth and rid herself of her own petty and unfounded emotions. She should have realized the truth when Nathan took care *not* to address her in any of his communications with Will while he was back east. It was so obvious, Charlotte scolded herself for being so dense. Hadn't Will even said that the lieutenant and Rachel spent time together during roundup? Hadn't everyone mentioned that Jack wanted to marry Rachel, but she repeatedly refused his attentions? That was it. Nathan wasn't hurrying to the ranch with the horses as much as he was hurrying to Rachel Greyfoot. That had to be it. His absence must have made him realize his true feelings for Rachel.

He hadn't written to her because he knew she had misinterpreted his actions during Will's injury and recovery. Knowing Charlotte cared for him, he didn't want to hurt her. So he didn't write. And he also didn't come to see her as soon as he got back. He was sending her a message. He cared for Will. He had seen Will. And he would see her . . . but in a more casual way. It took Charlotte the better part of the night to talk herself past the hurt and into a state of semi-acceptance.

Dear God, she prayed, *I've let my mind fly to ridiculous places since Nathan has been gone. I was so sure you sent Mr. Moser to awaken the possibilities to me so that when Nathan—*She caught her breath. *Thank you for Nathan's love for Will. Help me not to do anything stupid that might come in the way of their friendship, which I know is a blessing straight from your hand.*

———

"R-r-riding," Will said at breakfast. "I wanna go riding."

It was as if he had read her mind. Or her mood. Charlotte wondered if the boy could sense her inner turmoil. She had prayed a long time last night. She had come to a place of peace. And then, with the rising of the sun, the questions and inner turmoil had come back. *You do not love Nathan Boone,* she had told herself while she brushed her blond hair and assessed herself in the mirror. Ten years ago she had had a twenty-two-inch waist. Ten years ago there hadn't been a single fine wrinkle around those big gray eyes. Sighing, Charlotte turned away from what she saw. *No wonder he wants Rachel Greyfoot. She's been through hard times, too, but she has that long river of dark hair. And that cinnamon skin.* Charlotte sighed. Fair skin certainly didn't weather the west very well. She looked down at the backs of her hands and shook her head, then made fists and closed her eyes. *Get hold of yourself. You have a son to raise.* She had looked outside at the blue sky and decided, if ever there was a morning for becoming a "watcher on the hill," this was it.

And so, after breakfast, with Will over at the stables with Private Blake, Charlotte went to the barn out back, saddled one of her father's horses, and headed away from the fort. She'd realized weeks ago that things took on a proper perspective when she rode to the top of a bluff. This morning was no different. Looking at the vast expanse of the scenery before her, Charlotte preached to herself. *Creation does not revolve around Charlotte Bishop.* She looked down at the fort, expanded to almost twice the size it had been only a few years ago. *It doesn't even revolve around that busy fort.* She gazed at the massive granite boulders jutting up from the earth, the white rock exposed on the sides of the buttes. *These rocks have looked down on that valley for centuries, and when Fort Robinson is little more than a pile of rubble on the valley floor, they'll still be here. The sun will still rise and make Crow Butte glow red in the morning, and the face of these cliffs will still glow golden on clear summer evenings.*

Charlotte smiled, remembering when riding up here and looking out on the scene had made her feel small and unimportant and alone. She looked up at the blue sky. *And now I come up here to be reminded that you, Father, who made all of this, are mindful of Charlotte Bishop and her future, and of Will and his physical challenges. You own the cattle on a thousand hills. You know when the mountain goat gives birth, and . . .* She smiled to herself. *You know whether or not Charlotte Bishop needs a husband, and if she does, you have one in mind. And, Lord, I don't want a man in my life who doesn't belong to you. So that means . . . I shouldn't want Nathan Boone. Fine as he is.*

Charlotte envisioned Boone's square shoulders, his thick dark hair.

A handsome man by anyone's standards. A good man, full of caring and gentleness. *Good as far as his own humanity can take it.* But that wasn't enough. Not now. She wanted what Caleb and Laina had. The kind of love that sprang from a source beyond humanity. The kind that weathered storms. It didn't matter that Laina and Caleb had struggled so with their baby boy's death. In fact, Charlotte realized, it was almost comforting. They weren't perfect. Having real faith didn't mean people became perfect. Charlotte liked that. You could be a true believer and fail, and God didn't let go.

Don't let go. She had said those words in Nathan's arms while Will was in surgery.

Her eyes filled with tears. Caleb Jackson had let go. For a while. She supposed life could throw things at men that would make even the strongest of them tempted to let go. But in that entire awful time in the Jacksons' lives, when it looked like they might let go of each other, God had not let go of them. *That* must be what that Bible verse about the "everlasting arms" means. People let go. God never does.

———

She was trusting God in a new way, but that didn't mean Charlotte's heart didn't thump a little harder the day Nathan Boone finally appeared on her doorstep. There he stood, his hat in his hand, his dark hair rumpled, his beautiful mouth smiling. He'd shaved his beard. She didn't remember that cleft in his chin. He was even better looking than she remembered. *Don't let go, Father. Don't let go.*

"Come in, Lieutenant," Charlotte said, hoping her smile looked natural. "I'll call Will in from the barn. He's brought Bones over from the stables for the day." She hesitated. "Or would you rather just walk on around to where he is?" She put her hands behind her back and looked away. *This is harder than I thought it would be.*

"Actually," the Lieutenant said, "I'm kind of glad Will isn't here. I needed to talk to you first."

Charlotte took a step back. "Should I make coffee? Garnet and Carter have gone over to the Bee Hive to visit some friends, but I can surely—"

"No," Nathan interrupted her. "That's all right. I don't want coffee. I'm wondering if you and Will can get ready fast enough for us all to head to the ranch."

"What? When?"

"Now. Today." He cleared his throat. "As soon as possible. I mean, Laina said you were planning a visit. I was hoping you might be packed.

I brought the wagon. For your trunk. Will's things. We can take Bones, too, if you want. He's mostly retired from the army. I'm certain nobody will mind."

Charlotte had never seen the lieutenant so nervous. He was half apologetic. This would not do. She cleared her throat. "Nathan. Please. Calm down. I've been looking forward to a visit to the ranch. And I'm very happy for you and Rachel. So please. Relax. You don't owe me—"

"Lieutenant Boone!" The back door slammed in concert with Will's exclamation.

"Hello there, pard'ner," Boone said. He grinned at Will and winked.

"Ready to go," Will said. He looked at Charlotte. "Right, Ma?"

"Not completely," Charlotte said. Will made a face. She smiled. "But I can *be* ready to go. In an hour?" She looked up at Nathan. He nodded. "How about you two go on over to the Bee Hive. Find Carter and Garnet and let them know. Then go to the hospital to find your grandfather." Will nodded eagerly. "And I promise to be finished packing by the time you get back."

Charlotte felt like the drive to Four Pines Ranch from Fort Robinson took about three years out of her. She asked about the trip east. Nathan had little to say, other than that the string of horses he'd brought back was fine and, yes, Banner was a magnificent animal, and he hoped the price they had paid wasn't the downfall of their relationship with the banker Wade Simpson. "I've saved up," Nathan said, "but I didn't have the money for that kind of horse, that's for sure. And Caleb used all his savings for the rest of the horses. But Wade said 'all right' to fronting us enough to get Banner. He'll take his interest in breeding some of his mares soon."

"You took out a *loan* to buy a horse?" Charlotte said.

"I know what you're thinking. I hate debt, too. And initially I didn't expect to need it. But things just didn't go according to plan."

"Forgive me, Lieutenant," Charlotte said. "It's really none of my business. And I'm certain you were prudent in whatever risk you were taking."

"Please. Call me Nathan," he said. "We're friends, remember?"

"Here they *come*!" CJ could be heard shrieking with joy from the minute they got within earshot of the house.

"Well, she certainly had faith in our willingness to come at a moment's notice," Charlotte laughed as the wagon rumbled along.

Nathan only nodded. He had become increasingly silent the closer they got to the ranch. Now, as she looked down at his hands, Charlotte realized he was gripping the reins so hard his knuckles were white. She was going to have to pull him aside as soon as possible and wish him and Rachel happiness. And she was going, by God's grace, to do it with a sincere smile and not a tinge of regret in her voice. She hoped they wouldn't have to endure an awkward meal before she could clear the air.

Laina came at once, hugging her, laughing, a strange tone in her voice that made Charlotte think even Laina was nervous about the announcement that would be made about Rachel and Nathan.

"Where's Rachel?" Charlotte asked. *Might as well get it over with.*

"Rachel? Oh, she and Jack are over at the Dawson place," Laina said. "They'll be back later."

Nathan's plans were really moving forward. He'd already bought the neighboring ranch. Rachel was probably settling in. Poor Jack. It would be hard for him, too.

Nathan hauled Charlotte's trunk in and set it in the room Charlotte knew had originally been intended for the new baby. They all went back out to the front porch as Nathan and Will departed for the bunkhouse. As they walked down the trail, Charlotte watched as Nathan put his arm on Will's shoulder. They must have been sharing a joke because Will looked up at Nathan and nodded and smiled.

Thank you, Father. That's such a beautiful thing to see.

"That's a wonderful sight to behold," Laina said aloud, echoing Charlotte's thoughts.

Charlotte nodded. "Praise God, from whom all blessings flow." She turned toward the house. "Put me to work. What can I do?"

"You," Laina said, smiling, "can sit right there in that rocking chair and enjoy the view until the men come back from the bunkhouse. And then . . . we'll see." She grinned. "I'll be back in minute."

Charlotte could hear Laina inside, working in the kitchen. Once she went to the door, but Laina would not hear of her helping at all. "Just go sit down, Charlotte. Really. I want to do this on my own. I'm preparing a celebration. And I have a surprise or two."

"You didn't have to do that," Charlotte said.

"Yes," Laina said. "I did. Now behave yourself and do as you're told."

Charlotte turned around to see Nathan coming up the trail. Alone. He was walking with such purpose, Charlotte realized. *We're going to have THE TALK.* She took a deep breath and whispered a prayer.

"Can we . . . talk?" Nathan said.

"Relax, Lieutenant . . . Nathan," Charlotte said, hoping her smile was reassuring. "It doesn't have to be as serious as all this. I'm happy for you. Honestly, I am. Whatever you thought—"

"Down there," Nathan said, nodding toward the barn.

"What?"

"Thought you'd want to see the new horses. Thought you'd want to get a look at Banner for yourself," Nathan said.

She didn't want to go. Didn't want to walk alongside Nathan Boone and be tempted to imagine the impossible. Didn't want to be trapped in the barn and have to retreat to the house if her emotions didn't follow her intellect. She really *was* content in the role God had assigned her. Life was full. She really was going to be all right. But being alone with Nathan Boone didn't seem like a good idea. Not right now.

"Please, Charlotte," Nathan said, "just . . . just come and see."

She gave in. *Lord guard my heart. This is just looking at a few horses. Then make him leave me alone. Send him over to his own ranch. To Rachel. Please.*

"All right." She nodded toward the door. "Laina insists that she won't let me help anyway." She stepped off the porch, uncomfortably aware of the way he towered over her, remembering that night at the hospital when he had held her. How safe she had felt. "So," she said as they walked toward the barn, "tell me about these amazing horses that required a special trip east."

"Well," Nathan said, "actually, there's only one who's all that special. He's in that stall down there next to Spirit. Thought the two of them should learn to get along." He gave a low whistle. There was an answering whicker, low and . . . familiar.

Impossible, Charlotte thought, even as the occupant of the stall put his great, gray head over the stall door and looked their way.

Charlotte grabbed Nathan's forearm to keep her wobbly knees from collapsing. "Oh, my . . ."

"Major Riley took some convincing to let him go. He's a fine animal, but there seemed to be more to it than his just hanging on to a good horse."

"Isaac? You . . . found . . . Isaac?" She tried to keep herself from running to the stall. She wanted to maintain her dignity. But it was *Isaac.* He was bobbing his head, and when she spoke his name, he lifted his upper lip the way he always did and greeted her with his signature snort. When she came within reach, he pressed against the stall and thrust his head at her. He leaned down, and when Charlotte scratched just behind his jaw, he gave such a huge sigh, tears came to her eyes. She bowed her head and rested her chin against the place between the horse's ears. Tears rolled down her cheeks. Without looking at Nathan, she said, "I can't imagine how you managed to convince Major Riley to let Isaac come back to me—"

"Oh, I didn't let on that I knew anything about the horse or its previous owner," Nathan said. "I asked around at Fort Wayne a bit before making contact with the illustrious Major Riley, and I knew better than to mention your name."

"He's bitter then," Charlotte said.

"Only about losing the Bishop money," Nathan said, then immediately apologized. "I'm sorry, that sounded—"

"—truthful," Charlotte said. "You aren't telling me anything I didn't already know." She swallowed hard, rubbed her tears away with the back of one hand, and finally looked up at him. "However long it takes me," Charlotte said, "I will pay you back for this." She looked up at Isaac. "Thank-you just isn't enough. Words just don't begin to express—" She took in a deep breath.

Nathan cleared his throat. "He was expensive," he said. "I mean, *really* expensive."

"I can imagine," Charlotte said. "And he's a gelding. So he really is just a pricey toy."

"No," Nathan said. He took a deep breath. "Actually, he's a present. Sort of a . . . uh . . ."

"Good-bye." Charlotte interrupted him. "I know. It's all right, Nathan. Goodness, you didn't have to go to so much trouble or expense. You don't owe me such extravagance. If I gave you the impression I was . . . assuming . . ." She felt her cheeks color. "I'm sorry. I'm happy for you and Rachel, Nathan. Really, I am."

"If you'd be quiet for just a minute," Nathan said, "I'd like to finish what I was saying."

Charlotte stepped away from him. This was going to be harder than she thought. He had to make a *speech* about it all. *Help, Lord. Help me allow him to do whatever it is he has to do to feel better about all this.*

"First of all, I want you to know. I love Will."

"I know you do, Nathan. You don't have to tell me that."

"Well, the thing is . . ." He cleared his throat. "There was a time when I thought I should propose to you. For Will." When Charlotte said nothing, he sighed. "I'm not very good at this."

"You're doing fine, Lieutenant," Charlotte said without looking up at him. "You love Will. Like the son you never had." She drew herself up, put her hands behind her back. "And I am very grateful for that. I see it as a gift straight from the hand of a loving God. And I guess I understand how your convoluted brain could have convinced you that you should marry the mother . . . as a necessary accessory to your ongoing relationship with a boy you care about. But really, Nathan, I hope you know I'm not so shallow as to allow that."

"I don't—"

"Because," Charlotte took a deep breath, "I have been there and done that and I'm not ever making that mistake again."

"You've done . . . what?"

"Been a convenient accessory to a man's life."

"But it's more than that," Nathan said. "I *liked* you. I admired you. You're strong. You've got more guts than some of the men I've commanded."

Desperate to lighten the serious weight of regret pressing down on her, Charlotte saluted. "Thank you, Lieutenant, sir. I'll take that as a compliment, sir."

Nathan put his hands on his hips. He grunted. "I'm making a mess of this. Could we . . . could we sit down?" He waved toward the end of the row at a pile of hay bales.

"Really, Lieutenant, you are making such a mountain out of a very small hill. This is not necessary."

"I'd appreciate it if you'd let me . . . just . . . talk." He sounded almost annoyed.

Charlotte closed her eyes. *Help, Lord. Help.* Later she would mull over the never-ending speechmaking and try to make some sense of it. God certainly chose odd times to teach a woman patience.

Nathan didn't sit, he stood, pacing back and forth as he talked. "I've been attracted to you for a long time. First, it was just . . . admiration. For the way you've handled Will's accident, for the way you've handled everything that's come your way. When Lily died, I got bitter. When bad things happened to you, you got stronger." Seeming to anticipate her protest, he held up his hand. "I know, I know. It took a little while. But you did grow stronger. And then I loved Will. And so I hatched this plan to go east and get Isaac and make you love me. And marry me." He stopped and looked down at her. "For all the wrong reasons."

Charlotte nodded. Good. He realized it. Why he had to beat her over the head with it, she didn't quite understand. But at least he realized it. Maybe he had to say it so he'd be comfortable continuing his friendship with Will. Maybe he needed to clear the air.

"All these years I've been bitter and angry at God," he said. "But God didn't give up on me. He kept putting true believers in the ranks below me. Men like Carter Blake. He kept bringing Preacher Barton around at the most amazing times." He paused. "This last time . . . well, I realize there aren't that many choices when a man wants to return to Fort Robinson, so it isn't all that much of a coincidence, and yet . . ." He paused. "The preacher and I shared the train ride back here from St. Louis," Nathan said. "He was returning from the annual meeting of his missions board." He shook his head. "And you know the preacher. He's never been one to miss an opportunity to talk about God. Except this time, all those people I've been meeting over the years and all the little pieces of truth I've been hearing . . . Well, all my excuses just disintegrated." He swallowed. "I . . . uh . . . I decided to try it."

"Try . . . ?"

"Getting over myself and giving things up to God. And seeing what He could do about it."

"Do about what, Nathan?"

He swallowed. His dark eyes filled with tears. "This great big lump of . . . garbage." He made a fist and hit his midsection. "This gut full of—" He took a deep breath, a heart-wrenching sob. He looked at Charlotte and smiled through his tears and shrugged. "He did it. He took it. I'm . . . uh . . . well, I'm changed. Inside."

"Oh, Nathan," Charlotte whispered. "I'm so *glad.*"

"I don't even know what happened," Nathan said. "It's like a lamp just . . ."

"Went on?"

He nodded. "Yeah. I realized my plans were all wrong. Marrying you for Will was just . . . wrong."

"Yes," Charlotte said. "Completely wrong." She started to get up.

"But . . . marrying you . . . for *me,*" Nathan said. "That"—his voice lowered—"would be completely, absolutely, totally, *right.*"

Charlotte sat back down. She frowned. "What?" She looked up at him. *Don't do this. Don't—do this. You are too beautiful and too near, and I am not strong enough to—*

"The truth is, Charlotte, I finally got things figured out. I don't love you because you're Will's mother. I love you because . . . you're . . . you."

"Stop it," Charlotte said. She raised her hand to her hair. "You're being kind and I appreciate it, but you aren't looking. You aren't seeing."

"I'm looking," Nathan said. He crouched down before her and touched the hair at her temple. "And I'm seeing."

"What?" She laughed bitterly and looked away. "A widow who's aged before her time? A woman with lines and freckles."

"Stop it," Nathan said. He ran his finger along her jaw, touched the corners of each eye. "Every one of those things is a medal, Charlotte. A badge of honor. Proof of victory in battles waged in the most difficult place possible." He pointed to her heart. "Right there. And you fought them alone. And you won them."

She shook her head. "I didn't," she said, almost whispering. "*He* won them. God. Not me."

Nathan lifted her chin. He looked into her eyes. "I haven't been able to sleep, or eat—with thinking about how to say all these things to you. Knowing you wouldn't want to believe it. Fearing I've waited too long." He smiled at her. "The thing is, Charlotte, the horse is a gift. With a catch."

"A catch?"

His smile grew. "You have to take a retired cavalry officer along with him."

"Retired?"

He nodded. "I . . . uh . . . bought the Dawson place. For us. What do you think?"

Charlotte inhaled. "I think," she said, "that this is overwhelming. You've never shown . . . even tried to kiss—"

"I made up my mind, Charlotte, that the day I kissed you it had to be with a clear conscience. I had to come out here first. To talk to Rachel."

"Then I was right about her," she said.

Nathan shook his head. "We talked. And walked. And had some nice evenings together during roundup. Maybe we even flirted a little." He shrugged. "But the fact is she's happy for us. Even a little relieved, I think. She doesn't have a heart for anyone but Grey Foot." He reached over and covered her hands, which were clenched in her lap, with his own.

Avoiding his eyes, Charlotte murmured, "I've spent most of the past few weeks trying to convince myself that I have a very good life without you, Nathan Boone."

"You do have a good life," he said. "I just want to make it better."

"Well," Charlotte said, nodding towards Isaac. "You're off to a very good start."

Nathan leaned over to kiss her.

She didn't lean away.

———

Perhaps, after all, romance did not come into one's life with pomp and blare, like a gay knight riding down; perhaps it crept to one's side like an old friend through quiet ways; perhaps it revealed itself in seeming prose, until some sudden shaft of illumination flung athwart its pages betrayed the rhythm and the music; perhaps . . . perhaps . . . love unfolded naturally out of a beautiful friendship, as a golden-hearted rose slipping from its green sheath.

L.M. MONTGOMERY

Footprints
on the
Horizon

A Word from the Author

OF THE DOZEN NOVELS I have in print, *Footprints on the Horizon* is my first historical novel set in the twentieth century. I never expected to be interested enough in events beyond 1900 to want to read the dozens of books and newspaper articles I usually ingest before tackling a new project. That changed a few years ago when I encountered the WWII exhibit at the Fort Robinson Museum in western Nebraska.

My overactive imagination had already been at work during my stay at the fort as I learned about Dull Knife and the Cheyenne Outbreak and stood, weeping, on the spot where Crazy Horse was killed. But then, on the second floor of the museum, I came around a corner and was startled by the figure of a man asleep on an army cot. Of course it was only a museum exhibit, but it was a realistic one, and it immediately drew me in (this was back in the day before museums had to shield exhibits behind Plexiglas boxes and barriers).

When I returned home I began reading about German PWs in America. (The term was PW then . . . not POW.) Preliminary research raised the "what if" questions I have come to recognize as the seeds of a story I want to tell. What was it like, I wondered, for the very people whose sons were fighting against Germans in Europe to have Nazis working on their farms and ranches? How was it, I wondered, that these people interacted in such a way that more than a few of the prisoners returned to Nebraska after the war and became American citizens? How could lifelong friendships be forged between former enemies?

The book you hold in your hands is the result of my personal journey into the not-so-long-ago past in search of answers to these and a hundred other questions. But because it is a work of fiction, it combines experiences and accounts from many places in the United States where German prisoners were interred. For example, according to Tom Buecker, author of *Fort Robinson and the American Century*, a personnel shortage at Fort Robinson prevented the prisoners held there from working on the farms and ranches in the surrounding community. But in his book *Prisoners on the Plains*, Glenn Thompson tells of prisoners from other camps throughout Nebraska being transported—sometimes by farm wives—to jobs in their respective communities where they did everything from working in town bakeries to harvesting apples and sugar beets. Therefore, your author's disclaimer is this: While documented precedent does exist for the events in my story, details regarding exact locale have been adjusted to accommodate the fictional lives of my imaginary friends.

Prologue

March 1945
Four Pines Ranch

PEOPLE WHO MAKE a point of "wanting the plain truth" fall into two categories: liars and fools. And that *is* the truth or my name isn't Clara Joy Jackson—which, of course, it is, even if most of Dawes County, Nebraska, doesn't know it. I've been called CJ for over half a century, so most of my neighbors don't even know what that C and that J stand for, which is fine with me. I never liked the name Clara and it's been sixty-six years since I was what my mama—may the good Lord rest her soul—called her "little bundle of joy."

But back to the topic at hand, that being "the truth." The main truth that controls my every waking moment these days is this: America is at war. The impact of that bit of truth didn't really hit me personally until Johnny showed up at the ranch-house door in a United States Army uniform. Before that moment, calving and foaling and gentling yearlings and mending fence and putting up hay and the thousand other things on my rancher's chore list kept the war literally "over there."

Before Johnny enlisted, I did what I could to avoid thinking about the war. The good Lord said to "be anxious for nothing," and I seem to have the ability to do that. If I can fix it, I do. If I can't, I don't worry over it. I may wear out my knees talking to the good Lord about a thing or two, but once I've done that, I'm usually able to leave it where it belongs—with Him. And that's how I had handled the war up until Johnny enlisted. Every Sunday in church I prayed right along with everyone else for an Allied victory. I contributed old machinery to the iron drive and used kitchen cookware to the tin drive. I saved grease after reading a formula in the *Crawford Tribune* that told us how many tablespoons of fat yielded how many pounds of dynamite and such. Who would have ever thought that draining the grease off bacon could be patriotic? Shoot, I even sacrificed my ration card to my niece, Jo, so she could get herself some of those nylons she likes so much. Oops . . . there I go . . . talking about "the truth" and bending it in the same speech. The truth is, giving Jo my ration card didn't take a bit of sacrifice on my part because one thing this old girl does not have a need for is nylon stockings. I only own one dress, and when I put on my dress boots with it I don't show any leg at all. No, I don't need any nylons—that's for sure.

As I was saying, until Johnny showed up in that uniform, I was doing my best to let the Lord handle the big picture while I continued to breed the best horses I knew how and raise the best beef possible—which is no different from what we've done here at the Four Pines since my daddy, the late Caleb Jackson, bought the place. As far as I was concerned, God and the army could take care of Hitler and Mussolini and company. But then Johnny signed on—along with his best friends, Paul Hunter and Delmer Clark—and that brought the war off the front page of the newspaper and right to my front door in the panhandle of Nebraska.

John Boone Bishop is the kind of boy every woman dreams about when she daydreams about her grown son. He's good-looking and respectable, strong and loyal. Shoot, I'm making him sound like one of those dogs over in the K-9 corps at Fort Robinson. Don't think that. Johnny's about half full of mischief and trouble. But he's not at all meanspirited. Just spirited. Which, I suppose, is why he aimed for the air corps. He wanted to be a pilot, but instead he's part of the crew. On a B-17.

I shouldn't be surprised at his wanting to fly. I can remember way back to when he had to climb up on a tree stump to get aboard his horse. Before we'd go riding up into the bluffs, Johnny would look into the distance—a person can see halfway to heaven from atop one of our bluffs out here in the Pine Ridge area—and he'd watch the eagles riding the wind and then hold out his arms and pretend to do the same. He thought it was fun to get right to the edge of a cliff and look down on where the mountain goats had made a path along the rim of a drop-off. It scared me to death the way he always wanted to climb up to the highest point and go to the edge. That's because years ago his daddy, Will, darn near got killed when he and I climbed higher than a human ought to climb. But Johnny never got hurt. He always has loved the heights, and now he has his wings. Will and I are proud and scared to death all at the same time.

I fell in love with Johnny the day he came to live at the Four Pines. Will stepped down from his pickup with a bundle in his arms and limped up onto the porch. Will always limps when he's burdened down—whether it's bone-weariness or heart-weariness, doesn't matter. Anyway, Will limped up onto the porch and pulled the corner of the blanket back so I could see that baby boy's face, and that was it for me. You see, Johnny looks just like his daddy, and it's no secret that I've loved Will Bishop all my life, so there was nothing to do but love Johnny, too.

"Well," Will said slowly, like he always talks when he's got a lot to say. "Here we are, CJ."

"Welcome home, Will," I said. My eyes still fill up with tears just thinking about it, even though that was nearly twenty years ago. I had a huge lump in my throat, and I couldn't say anything else right then, but I patted Will's shoulder and led him inside. We had coffee—strong and black, just like Will likes it—and then we headed down to the cabin my old foreman, Ted Cramer, had just vacated, and both Will and Johnny have been here at the Four Pines ever since.

Now the liars in Dawes County would have all kind of things to tell you about Will Bishop and CJ Jackson if you were to ask to "hear the truth." They would say I kicked Will off the ranch when he took a liking to a little slip of a woman up the line in Whitney. Or they would say that Will and Mamie were never really married and they only stayed together because there was a baby coming, and they'd probably say that I took Will back because it was the only way I could have a child to raise.

The fools of Dawes County have a different version of "the truth," which is much more entertaining than the liars' version, but no less foolishness.

So I will tell you the real truth about Will and Johnny Bishop and CJ Jackson. As I said, I have loved Will Bishop for as long as I can remember. I loved him so much that when he asked me to marry him I said "no." Because I knew that the one sure way to kill our friendship was for us to get married. The Good Book says that wives are supposed to submit to their husbands, and I am here to tell you that the man who has what it takes to make CJ Jackson submit to male foolishness has yet to be found on God's green earth. I am as good a rancher as ever owned land in Nebraska, and I don't need a man telling me what pasture to use or which stallion to breed to my mares or how to negotiate a better price for the hay I sell to the remount at Fort Robinson. I just don't need the interference—even from a man as good as Will Bishop.

So when Will proposed marriage, I looked him square in the eye and said, "Will, I love you with all the heart God gave me to love a man. But I won't marry you. Now don't bring it up again." And, to his credit, Will didn't. He didn't moon about, either. It did surprise me a little when, a few months later, he married Mamie. But Will is neither a fool nor a liar, and he knew he'd heard the truth when he proposed to me the first time, so there was no need to make a big fuss.

Just about the greatest heartbreak of my life is the knowledge that Mamie Parsons never had one whit of appreciation for what a wonderful man she had. Mamie was one of the fools who wanted a truth of her own making. Will told her he wanted to ranch. Mamie heard, "Just give me a few more years to save up and we'll move to town." Will told her that sometimes he was slow and tired because of the accident. Mamie heard, "I'll only be able to dance two or three dances at parties." Will told her she'd have to be careful with money. Mamie heard, "We'll have to buy last year's model instead of a brand-new car."

Right from the start, Mamie's foolishness rearranged Will's truthful words. No one realized how bad it was. Mamie got pregnant right away. Now don't be shocked because I said that word. I know there are some women who just don't think it's polite. But for heaven's sake, I breed horses. Pregnant is a *good* word. Usually. But Mamie Bishop's reaction to pregnancy made me worry for Will. She said all the right words when people congratulated her, but I could tell something wasn't right about it.

Johnny was barely weaned when Mamie disappeared. Will took it bad. I stayed away, not wanting people to gossip. Of course, that didn't do a bit of good. It only hurt Will, and the gossip didn't stop. But not everyone in Dawes County is a fool or a liar, and thankfully, someone did the right thing. My phone rang one night and a voice said, "Will Bishop and that baby need you." *Click*. That was it. I don't know who called, but I'm glad they did because the next morning, when I went to Will's place, I saw how right they were.

Johnny was screaming with a combination of hunger and hurt. He had the worst case of diaper rash I'd ever seen. Well, all right. I'd never really seen all that much diaper rash, but Johnny's was bad. Will took one look at me and burst into tears. He was so low he didn't even try to talk, just handed me Mamie's note.

I cannot live the way you want me to live. Do not try to find me.

That was it. Not even a word about her own child.

"I've lost the ranch, CJ," Will said. Blubbered, really. "I've lost my wife and my ranch."

I didn't believe the last part, but it turned out to be true. Will was mortgaged to the hilt—and trying to please Mamie did him in.

"Plenty of people have lost ranches, Will Bishop," I snapped back. "You get yourself straightened up and get this baby into town to see Doc

Whitlow. And when you've got whatever it takes to fix that boy's raw bottom, you get packed up and come home. Rachel's as old as dirt, but she's spry as they come and she will love having a baby to tend." Rachel Greyfoot, may God rest her soul, was Lakota Sioux, and she came to the Four Pines with my parents and never left. "I'll have Ted moved out in an hour and the place will be ready for you. He's worthless and I need you."

I need you. When Will heard those words, his shoulders heaved and his whole body shuddered. Then he raised his chin and stood tall. He didn't look me in the eye, but he said, "I told you Ted didn't have what it takes."

Of course I was tempted to throw those words right back at him because that was exactly what I had said to him when he told me about Mamie. *"She doesn't have what it takes to be a rancher's wife, Will. And you'd know it if you could see past that tiny little waist and those big blue eyes and look into her soul. That girl's all fluff and no substance."*

I could tell Will was remembering the very same thing, because he literally took a step back and his jaw began to work like he was clenching his teeth to prepare for a blow.

My friendship with Will probably turns on three moments in our lives. The first was when Will, who was an officer's child and therefore from a world I had no part in, chose to do a kindness for "the ranch girl" who was the school outcast. The second was when I said no to his proposal of marriage. And this was the third. It took everything in me to do what I did next, which was to nod my head and say as softly as I could—softness just doesn't come naturally to me, you know—"Yes. You did. I should have listened."

Will blinked a few times when he heard me say that. Tears welled up in his eyes again, and for a minute I thought I was going to have to snap him out of it—again. But he gave a little shake of his head and swallowed hard. "If we don't drive in tonight, don't worry." He looked around him, and I think maybe he had the feeling of waking from a bad dream. He put his hand on the edge of the table that was piled high with dirty—and I do mean dirty—dishes and said, "I want to clean this place up. It won't do for Chase to see it this way when he comes out to look it over for the bank sale."

"I'll do it while you're in town at the doctor's." Of course it was only natural for me to offer, but the minute I said it I wished I hadn't. Sometimes a man needs to clean up his own mess, and I realized this was one of those times.

Will just shook his head. "I'll see to it." He looked around some more. "May take a while." And then Will Bishop surprised me—which isn't easy for a friend to do when you've known each other nearly your whole lives. He laughed. "May take a long while."

"You don't know the first thing about cleaning a house or doing up laundry," I protested.

"Sure I do," he said. "Learned how to do it all since I got married."

Apparently Miss Mamie was even less of a ranch wife than I had thought.

He went to Johnny then, and as soon as that baby saw his daddy, he smiled all over himself. Will reached out his finger, and Johnny latched on to it with his little hand. And so, the next morning the Bishop men came home to the Four Pines ranch. And Johnny took possession of the corners of my heart that hadn't already been given over to Will.

The fools and the liars of Dawes County are right about one thing: The bond between Will Bishop and CJ Jackson is enduring. They just don't know the details, which is fine with me. If there's one thing I can't stand, it's people putting their nose into business that isn't theirs to be in. Which is exactly what I said to Will the other day when he told me he thought I was little better than a traitor to my country and our Johnny if I did what I planned to do.

Chapter One

THE FACT THAT Will Bishop had loved Clara Joy Jackson for over half a century made raising his rifle and taking aim at her kitchen window harder than he expected it to be. His hand shook as he peered around the cab of his truck. He'd argued with himself half the morning about it. Even after he saw CJ leave for town, he hesitated. But he couldn't come up with anything better to get the bullheaded woman's attention. So here he was, crouching down, resting the rifle barrel atop the truck-bed siding and closing his eyes, wishing he could think of another way.

He'd argued until he was blue in the face all through the winter—which was something, considering he rarely said more than three or four words at a time. He'd even called her Clara Joy just like her mother used to when CJ was in real trouble. But no amount of arguing could make the foolish old woman change her mind.

Their biggest blowout had occurred a few days ago. "I don't care if they're blue-skinned orangutans from the North Pole," CJ had said. "The remount depot has a few thousand hungry horses and mules depending on Four Pines hay, and there's a long line of neighbors just waiting for me to give up so they can put their name on the dotted line." CJ slammed her coffee mug down and went to the window—the very window Will was now planning to shoot out. With her back to him, she said, "Last fall I had to ask *Clarissa and Ben* to come out and lend a hand with the haying, Will. I was that desperate. And it's only going to be worse this year. The war just keeps going and more local boys keep leaving. There's no other way." She nodded toward the southeast, where, little more than a dozen miles from the ranch, a prisoner of war compound had been added to the

Fort Robinson remount depot operation. "If the Germans will work, I'll be glad to have 'em."

Will brought up what he thought was his best argument yet. "Our own United States War Department says the Nazis are fanatics who would rather kill themselves than be captured. Now, I know that's likely a touch of propaganda, but, CJ, we just can't have them roaming the farms and ranches out here. It's too far from one place to the next—too far from help if there's trouble."

"They won't be roaming. And there won't be trouble. It's not forced labor. The Geneva Convention wouldn't allow that. They'll be paid for their work."

"And you feel all right about that?" Will argued. "Paying the enemy?"

CJ snorted. "You were at the meeting when they explained how it works. They don't earn cash. It's just coupons to spend at the post exchange."

"Don't matter," Will said a little louder than he was wont to talk. "It still ain't right."

She turned around and faced him. "You stuck by me through the dirty '30s, Will. You were there when we had to slaughter cattle because we couldn't feed 'em, when the oats didn't grow and corn was little more than a dried ear with no kernels. Nature is finally beginning to smile on the Sandhills again, and I can't believe you want me to lose out because I don't have the manpower to manage nature's blessings."

"Folks won't stand for it, CJ. You can't expect them to forget what they've been told. You can't expect them to have forgotten the last war, either. It wasn't that long ago."

"Abel Wilson from Phelps County was up here at the last remount sale, and he's already been using PW labor from Camp Atlanta. Hasn't had a bit of trouble. His own wife picks the prisoners up and drives them back at the end of the day. They eat at the same table with the Wilson family for lunch. Shoot, Will, half the people around here have roots in Germany. People know better than to think every PW is a Nazi." CJ ran her fingers through her short gray hair and adjusted her glasses. She always adjusted her glasses when she was being stubborn—almost like she appeared to be considering another person's viewpoint when what she was really doing was waiting for them to see things her way. Will could almost imagine a stubborn teenager inside her. "It's my decision," she said. "I'm turning in the request forms Monday."

"I won't stand for it," Will said, raising his voice just a little to make his point.

CJ's blue eyes were cold. "You don't have to agree. But you do have to be civil and work alongside 'em. Or . . . or else." She snatched her hat off the hook by the back door and left.

After the door slammed behind her, Will had watched out the kitchen window. She headed across the road to the old barn. He could picture her storming around in there, jerking up buckets of oats for the horses, mucking out stalls, muttering to the memory of her father who had built the barn with his bare hands . . . and giving a thousand reasons why she was right and "that old fool Will Bishop" was addled. The more he thought about CJ and that "or else" she'd tossed out, the angrier he got. He could take a lot from CJ Jackson. Most of the time he liked her spit and fire. But when she drew *that* line in the Sandhills, a man had to do what a man had to do. Love the woman or not, love the land or not, he was not going to stand around while some Nazi cut hay in the very field where his Johnny had learned to ride. Times might be tough and help might be scarce, but hiring Nazi prisoners was *not* the right answer. It just couldn't be.

So Will followed her out to the barn.

"What are you going to say to Johnny?" he blurted out just inside the door. "He's over there right now in the line of fire. What are you going to say when he comes home and finds out you hired the very men who might have killed his friends?"

For a moment, Will thought he'd finally gotten through to her. She tossed a pitchfork full of hay into the corner of the empty stall, and when she looked at him she had tears in her eyes. She swallowed. But then she took a deep breath and said in that quiet voice that was worse than shouting, "I'm gonna throw my arms around him and say welcome home. I'm gonna tell him I did what I had to do so that he'd have a home to come back *to*." Anger flickered in the blue eyes. "And I'll thank you not to try to use the blood of my friends and neighbors to coerce me."

Now as Will crouched behind his rusting blue pickup and replayed the scene over in his mind, he couldn't help feeling bad. The old woman was right about one thing. Bringing Johnny and the other boys from Dawes County into it probably wasn't fair. And while Vernon Clark had said he'd shoot his herd and burn his fields before he'd let one "Kraut" set foot on his place, there were other people just as firm in their beliefs that it was only practical to use the labor that was available, no matter what language it spoke. But Will agreed with Vernon Clark, and it was Clark's blustering that gave Will the idea to fake a little vandalism on the Four Pines.

Maybe, he reasoned, if CJ understood how strong some folks felt about things, just maybe she would reconsider. So he'd waited for her to head into Crawford with her paper work requesting prison labor, and then he whitewashed *Nazi Lover* across the front porch. At the last minute he decided that maybe shooting out a window—which he would fix before nightfall—would put some muscle into the protest. He knew it was a desperate thing, and he felt bad about it, but he was compelled to convince CJ that the boots that had clicked together to the sound of "Heil Hitler" should never be allowed to touch Four Pines soil.

Grunting softly, Will raised his rifle and took aim. He'd been squatting for a while, arguing with himself about whether or not he was going too far, and his weak leg pained him. Just as he was about to squeeze the trigger, his leg went out from under him. His chin hit the edge of the truck bed so hard he saw stars. As he slid to the ground the rifle went off, harmlessly aimed toward the sky. His ears were still ringing when he realized someone was coming up the road. He saw a flash of red top the hill on the horizon. Scrambling to his feet, he limped the two steps to the cab of his truck, but he was too slow.

CJ had barely skidded to a stop when she hollered out the passenger side window of the red pickup she called Sadie, "What's going on?"

As both his vision and his hearing cleared, Will slapped the dust off his backside and stepped to the front of his truck. Staring across the hood of his own truck, he stammered, "I tho-tho-thought you went to town."

"Left one of the forms on my desk," CJ grumbled as she started to climb out of the truck. Then she paused halfway out, holding the door, staring in the direction of the house . . . and the whitewashed lettering just to the right of the front door. Her mouth fell open. Closing her door, she walked toward Will's truck and peered in the bed of his truck . . . at the can of whitewash and the paintbrush. She stared at Will, then at the rifle still in his hand. Turning around to face the house again, she ran her fingers through her hair. She adjusted her glasses before turning her head to glare at Will.

In that moment, Will would have given everything he'd ever owned to make up for what he had done, which, he could see in CJ's eyes, was to hurt her to the very core. "You've just got to listen to me, CJ," he begged. "You cannot do this. You will alienate neighbors for miles around, and no matter what you think, you will never be able to explain it to Johnny in a way he'll understand. We can't have Nazis on the place, girl. Why can't you understand that?"

CJ just stood there. She, who was never one to mince words, didn't say anything. After too many moments of brittle silence, she set her mouth, lifted her chin, straightened her shoulders, and headed for the old barn. She emerged with a bucket in one hand and a rag in the other.

"I'll do it," Will said, and reached for the bucket. CJ ignored him. She walked across the road to the cistern, filled the bucket with water, stepped up on the porch, and began to scrub at the whitewash. As the lettering melted into milky streaks, Will turned away and, rifle in hand, headed along the well-worn path to the only place in the world he had ever felt at home. Inside his cabin, he sat down at the table and put his head in his hands, trying to muster up the energy to pack.

Clara Joy

If my heart hadn't already been broken into a thousand pieces by that whitewash on the house, it would have broken the next morning when Will knocked on the back door. He *knocked,* mind you. Like some stranger. As if I hadn't been sitting at the kitchen table watching him walk up the path from his cabin, knowing something was on his mind because his bad leg was dragging a little. As if I hadn't been there since 5:30 A.M., like I've been every morning since I was a young girl waiting to tag alongside my papa when he made his way down to the barn or out to the herd.

Will knocked like he was a visitor, and after that there just wasn't much to say. I went to the door and stood there hating how awkward things felt between us and wishing Will would cross over the divide and end it. Shoot, I don't even know if I needed to hear an apology. I hadn't delivered the papers yet, and I was beginning to think maybe I wouldn't. The truth is, if he would have just come in and poured himself coffee like always, I probably would have buried the whitewash issue and thrown out the papers requesting PW help, and never brought it up again.

But Will knocked. So I went to the door and stood there and waited for him to say what was on his mind.

"C-called up Bill Harker over at the remount," he said. "They've got trainloads of horses coming in for resale. Said he'd be happy to have me."

I think he was waiting for me to ask him not to go. To say I'd been wrong. I didn't.

He cleared his throat. "So I'll be headed out come Monday."

"No need to wait," I said. "Might as well get yourself settled before you start work."

We stood there staring at each other for a minute, like two old boxers waiting to see who was going to start the next round, and finally Will turned and headed for his cabin. I went back inside and sat down at the kitchen table. I couldn't quite get my mind around the idea that Will and Johnny's cabin was going to be empty come Monday morning. I suspected Will would probably leave while I was at church Sunday. All of a sudden I wondered where he'd be leaving *for*. From what I'd seen down at Fort Robinson the last time I checked in with the head of the breeding program, they were hard-pressed to keep roofs over the heads of the soldiers coming in, let alone add a civilian to the mix. Things had really changed in recent years. Back in the '30s, it wasn't unusual for a married man and his wife to end up with a six-or seven-room officer's house all to themselves. But that had changed since Fort Robinson was named the central remount station for the cavalry. Horses by the thousands were being cycled in and back out again as the army switched over from hayburners to gas hogs. As if the Remount Division wasn't enough, the army decided to train its war dogs out here, too. That meant a whole new compound full of buildings, kennels for over a thousand dogs, and the staff to run it all.

And with the addition of a prisoner of war camp, Fort Robinson just plain ran out of beds. Men were taking rooms in towns as far away as Chadron—and that is twenty-eight long miles away, especially in the winter, when snow can drift over the two-lane highway in less than an hour. I wondered just where the animal superintendent thought he was going to put a civilian employee.

I got up and went to the kitchen door and opened it. "Will," I called. He was halfway down the path by then. When he stopped he cupped his left ear with his hand so he could hear me better. "There's no need for you to move out. The Four Pines has been your home all this time. You can drive the forty-five minutes to work. We've got the gas allowance to do it, even with the rationing."

He seemed to consider the idea, but then he shook his head. "Bill's assigning me to training and conditioning. Says he needs a good hand with a couple of the stallions they want put out to civilians in the breeding program. He said there's one for sure that needs some sense worked into his head. I'll probably set up camp in one of the barns so's I can keep an eye on things." He shrugged. "It's for the best."

To hear Will Bishop say he preferred a barn to his own home on the Four Pines hurt so much it made me mad. "All right, Will," I said, "whatever you think." And I slammed the door as soon as I said it. I didn't even watch Will walk away. Instead, I tore out the front door and headed off up the road, walking as fast as I could while I told God exactly what I thought of Will Bishop and Vernon Clark and all the other idiots in Dawes County who couldn't see beyond their own prejudice against Germans to notice God's own answer to our concerns about the manpower shortage on our ranches and farms.

"They're like that fool on the roof in the flood, Lord," I said out loud. I tend to talk out loud to the Lord when things are really churning inside me. "You know the story I mean. Those folks are on the roof watching the water swirl around them and praying for help. And a man comes by in a leaky boat and they turn him away because God is going to answer their prayer. And then they drown and go to heaven and ask you why you didn't answer the prayer and you say, 'I sent you a boat! Why didn't you get in it?' That is not me, Lord. I've got the faith to ask you for help and the sense to see when you send it and I don't *care* how it's dressed. Whether it says *PW* on their shirts or not, they are young and strong and I need 'em. Now why can't Will see that?"

And there I was, walking my Sandhills, talking to God, crying. I cry when I get mad. And I was *mad*. Finally, I said, "Well, Lord, I guess I can thank you I had the sense to stay single, because you surely know I would never have submitted to this foolishness about not using German manpower on the Four Pines." I turned around then and looked back down the hill toward where my ranch lay, nestled beside a spring-fed pond in the low spot of a thousand hills of sand.

Now a lot of folks from the city come out here and think all they see is nothing. "It's so empty," they say. But it's not empty. Not to someone who has the eyes to see. A person can see nearly all the way to heaven from the top of the ridge that looks down on my ranch. There's not a tree or another house in sight. Just miles and miles of rolling hills where the soil is mostly sand and only the toughest grasses stick. It's that tough grass that makes the best grazing in the world. And it's the fact you can see where you are that makes me love it so.

The sun was high in a bright blue sky, and the pond was glowing like one of them sapphires you see in the fancy jewelry shops. I closed my eyes and took a deep breath, inhaling the sweet aroma of warm earth that promised prairie blossoms in the near future. Then I looked toward the old barn my papa built right across the road from the house, remembering how I held some of the boards in place while he nailed them up. The house is the work of his hands, too—at least most of it. There was a little two-room cabin made of cedar logs when Papa and Mama moved onto the place with their new baby, Clara Joy, but Papa added a big open loft.

He always wanted a "passel of boys" to fill up that loft, but the Good Lord only gave Laina and Caleb Jackson two children, and both girls at that. It frustrated Mama somewhat that I was more interested in being Pa's right-hand "man" than I was in learning to cook, but sixteen years after I was born, she finally had another little girl who was exactly what Mama thought a lady should be. That's Clarissa, and never were two girls more different than my sister and me. I won ribbons at the county fair for my calves while Clarissa won ribbons for her fancy work.

When Clarissa started to date, she never gave the local ranchers' sons a glance. She went for town boys all the way, and she finally landed one—and a preacher at that. My ma and pa took their religion very seriously, so they were thrilled when Ben Hale proposed to Clarissa. And I must say that, while I don't have the fancy words Ben has, I know in my heart what's right and what's not, and I look forward to Sundays and Ben's sermons. He has a way of saying things that brings a little bit of heaven itself right into the church. There have been times I have gone to church more out of duty than anything else—and to avoid Clarissa's Monday morning phone call wondering where I was—and right when I expect it the least, God speaks to me the most.

Anyway, I stood up on the hill looking down at my ranch and the work of my father's hands—and mine, too, because I've added a bigger barn and more corrals by the south spring—and a new head wrangler's cabin. For Will and Johnny. But Will was leaving the Four Pines. Maybe for good. I felt like I had just been kicked by a yearling foal—which, if you have ever experienced such a thing, you will understand is a powerful kind of hurt. All of a sudden, I wasn't mad anymore. I was just hurt, with a deep-down kind of hurt that only a man can give a woman when she loves him. Now, I remind you—I know I love Will. So that wasn't the thing that made me cry. It was just the whole business that we couldn't come to agree—or at least to agree to disagree—and get on with the business of ranching together.

As I stood there, looking down on my ranch, a kind of loneliness settled over me such as I hadn't felt since Will married Mamie Parsons. *"What will you say to Johnny?"* Will had asked. And right now I wanted to ask him the same thing. What would he say when Johnny came home and found his papa had moved out of the only real home they had ever had?

Being all emotional about things and talking about feelings and such has never been my cup of tea. But I can tell you that right then, standing up on the hill and looking down on the only part of the world that had ever mattered to me, I blubbered like a baby. It just seemed like I was caught between two impossible things. Not having enough help might mean losing the Four Pines. But not having Will and Johnny on the place . . .

So I told God I would delay delivering the papers requesting PW help until tomorrow, and I asked Him to change my mind—if it needed changing—and to give me wisdom to know what to do and the courage to admit I was wrong—if I was, which I doubted. And then I made myself stop crying and headed toward the old barn. I told myself I just wouldn't think about it anymore, and for most of that afternoon I managed to keep my mind on the ranch and off Will. And it worked—mostly—until supper, which I ate alone because Will just didn't show up.

I was standing at the kitchen window washing my plate when I saw the light come on in Will's cabin, and in spite of all the pep talks I'd given myself that day, I considered walking down there and begging him to stay. I considered tearing up the request forms I was set to deliver to the county agent the next morning. I lay awake most of the night, asking God over and over again about what I should do. Part of me wanted God to convince me I'd been wrong. Part of me wanted to walk down to Will's place and knock on the door and say I was wrong. But then it was dawn, and as much as I had tried to think of a way around it, I could not think I had done anything wrong in accepting the help I felt God had provided in answer to my prayers.

And so, when morning came, I climbed into my old Chevy pickup and headed into the county agent's office in Crawford and filed my request for German PW help. I didn't stop by Clarissa and Ben's. I had had enough arguing and just did not need any more advice, which Clarissa would feel obligated to give. When I got back to the ranch, Will was gone. He had left a note on the table. All it said was *You can reach me at the remount if you need anything. Will you please make sure I get Johnny's letters?*

It rankled me that Will felt he had to ask me to bring him his own son's letters. As if I wouldn't. I sat and stared at the note for a long while before walking down to Will's cabin and going in. I had already decided I would leave Johnny's things in his room so that when he finally came home he could pick right up with ranch life. Maybe he would want to be my head wrangler. Maybe by then Will would have come to his senses and moved home.

I headed into Johnny's room, thinking I'd use his bedding to drape the sofa and such—to sort of close things up temporarily, like families do to their summer lake houses and what not. But I never went into Johnny's room. I just stood at the doorway and stared at the empty walls and the empty place under Johnny's bed where he had kept an old footlocker full of treasures. Empty. Empty. Empty. Will had emptied the place of any trace of himself and Johnny, save for the faint aroma of Old Spice aftershave.

It made me so mad I cried.

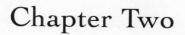

Chapter Two

The angel of the Lord encampeth about them that fear him,
and delivereth them.
PSALM 34:7

"I WON'T HAVE IT!" Clarissa Hale slammed both palms down on the kitchen tabletop and leaped out of her chair.

"Now, Mother—"

"I am *not* your mother, Benjamin Hale!" She glared, first at her husband and then at Jo. "Do you *hear* what your daughter is saying?" She reached up and swept a once-blond curl off her once-smooth forehead. "She doesn't see a problem with her going to the ranch? She doesn't see a reason for us to worry?!" Touching her own graying hair brought Clarissa's attention to Jo's golden tresses. The unruly tumble of curls that made Clarissa feel slovenly transformed her daughter's face into a gilt-framed Renaissance portrait, which irritated Clarissa even more.

"How many times do I have to ask you not to come to the table looking like Tarzan's Jane?!" Clarissa motioned toward the doorway that led first into the living room, and from there into a small back hall and two bedrooms. "Go fix your hair and calm down. We'll talk later."

The girl frowned. "*I'm* not the one who needs to calm down," she said beneath her breath—just loud enough for her father to hear.

Benjamin Hale suddenly seemed to have trouble with his pipe. He withdrew it from his mouth, inspected the bowl, and then tapped it gently on the edge of the table.

"Don't you dare take her side against me," Clarissa said. "And stop fussing with that pipe." She reached for the pipe, then thought better of it and sat back down. "It's just not right for you to smoke, and you know it. What would the congregation think if they knew their pastor was a secret smoker?"

The Reverend Benjamin Hale took a maddeningly long time to fiddle with his pipe. When he finally spoke, he didn't address the smoking issue. "I can't say as I see any reason Jo shouldn't spend her summer out on the ranch, same as she has every summer of her life."

Clarissa's cheeks blazed red. "You can't be serious."

"Oh," Benjamin said, leaning back and smiling at his daughter, who had just returned from combing her hair and was standing in the kitchen doorway fluttering her eyelashes at him, "but I am."

"You two," Clarissa said. Jumping up from the table again, she went to the stove and, lifting a lid, took a taste, made a face, and added salt before replacing the lid. "I never could do a thing with either of you."

"Don't cry, Mama," Jo said, and settled back at the table.

"I'm not crying!" Clarissa opened the oven door, retrieved a pie, and straightened back up. She glared at her husband. "I suppose you'll spend our gas ration taking her out there, too."

"No need," Ben said. "CJ can take her home with her some Sunday after church."

Clarissa plunked the pie onto the hand-crocheted hot pad in the middle of the table.

"Mmmm," Ben said, inhaling deeply. "Smells wonderful."

"Humph," was all Clarissa could say.

"You make the best apple pie in the county, Clarissa Jackson." Ben got up from his chair and wrapped his arms around his wife.

Clarissa pretended to struggle. "Just because that line got you a date when I was single doesn't mean it will work now. And this isn't apple pie, anyway. It's soda crackers and spices."

"That's my girl," Ben said, nuzzling her hair. "Doing her part to conserve and still winning blue ribbons at the fair."

"Where are you going now?" Clarissa said to her daughter, who was headed for the back door.

"Out to do *my* part—plant the victory garden."

The door slammed shut before either parent could respond.

"That girl," Clarissa said, sitting back down at the table, "is out of control. Entertaining at the Servicemen's Club, coming in late, running around with Delores Black. Last week Josephine wanted to go over to the Sioux Theatre and see a matinee. On *Sunday*."

Ben offered up his plate for a slice of cracker pie. "It was Ronald Reagan and Ann Sheridan." He grinned up at his wife. "Even *you* like Ronald Reagan. And I don't see how singing 'America the Beautiful' at the Servicemen's Club on a Saturday evening is going to lead Jo down a wrong path. There's nothing wrong with giving the boys from Fort Robinson a wholesome way to spend their free time. Crawford doesn't have much to offer in comparison to New York City, and according to Tom Hanson, a lot of the new recruits are from big cities. He said they step off the train out at the fort and look around like they've just landed in the wilderness. Which, I guess, if you are used to Manhattan, it is."

"All the more reason to keep Josephine away from them," Clarissa said, "and probably the reason Delores is so interested. That girl is trouble waiting to happen."

Ben shrugged. "High-spirited, maybe. A trifle under-disciplined, probably. But Mrs. Black has not had an easy time raising a daughter alone. Tom seems to think she's done a good job of it."

"Tom Hanson's judgment about Stella Black has been blinded by a twenty-two-inch waistline and a permanent wave."

"Now, Clarissa—"

Clarissa returned to her original subject. "Josephine has no business being out at the ranch this summer, Ben. Not with my sister insisting she's going to hire prison labor." She shivered. "Will Bishop certainly had a thing or two to say about it, and Josephine is not even his child. I cannot begin to understand how her own father can just glibly wave good-bye and let his little girl go."

"Will's thinking is colored because of Johnny. I can't fault him for that, but Tom has been working at Fort Robinson since the first load of prisoners arrived nearly two years ago. He knows Jo goes out to the ranch every summer. He'd say something if he thought we should change that."

"Have you asked him?"

"Well, not directly . . . but he's been my deacon for years, and I know he'd say something. And as far as CJ's decision goes, for her to risk losing her hay contract won't do a thing to help John or the war effort. In fact, the argument could be made that Four Pines is essential to *winning* the war."

Clarissa snorted. "Right. So for my sister to dine with Nazis is patriotic."

"She won't be dining with Nazis. She's hiring some prisoners to do chores. Don't be so dramatic. And as for Jo, she's eighteen years old, and the more we try to tether her to a hitching post, the more she is going to struggle to break free. We've got to loosen the reins. Let her take the bit in her mouth and run a little."

"She's not a horse, Benjamin. She's a young woman."

"The analogy fits," Ben said. "If we try to keep her here in Crawford all summer, she just might hop a train and head out some morning with Delores for WAAC training at Fort Des Moines."

"I *want* her to hop a train," Clarissa said. "For Lincoln and the university this fall. But until then, I don't see anything wrong with a mother wanting her only child to spend her last summer at home."

"The ranch *is* home to Jo," Ben said. "She's got her own room out there, CJ adores her . . . and we're going to let her go. Word has it they may not have enough guards to let any of the prisoners work off the military reservation anyway. But even if they figure a way around that, CJ told me herself she wants them mostly for cutting hay. That's far enough away from the house and the barns that Jo won't so much as see the *PW* painted on their shirts."

Clarissa glowered at him. "They are *Nazi war criminals.*"

"Maybe some are," Ben said. "But a lot of them—according to Tom— are just young boys who got drafted and did what they were told. Tom says most are pretty much model prisoners. They aren't at all what he expected. He almost likes one or two of them. Goodness, honey-lamb, one of them got off the train and recognized a guard. The two of them lived next door to each other in Brooklyn."

"Well then," Clarissa sniffed. "If you and Tom think they are so wonderful, let's just invite a few up for Sunday dinner after church next week. I'll make sauerkraut and sausage."

"That's not my point, and you know it," Ben said. "Everything in Jo's world has changed in the last year. No high school girl expects her friends to be in danger for their lives. But not a day goes by that she doesn't worry over John Bishop. No high school girl expects her friends to die. But Delmer Clark and Ron Hanover did. The war has changed what we eat and where we go and what we pray about. There's one thing it doesn't have to change, and that's Jo's time at the ranch. She loves it. And I want her to have it—not just on the weekends she sometimes spends out there now. I want her to have her summer."

Her husband didn't lay down the law very often, but Clarissa recognized this as one of those times. "If she loves that ranch so much," she mumbled, "maybe she should just move there. Then she wouldn't have to even talk to me. Ever."

"Now, Clarissa, you don't mean that."

Clarissa got up and headed to the sink with her pie plate. She hadn't wanted to play dirty, but a mother had to do what a mother had to do. Without turning around she asked quietly, "And what about Mia? What's her summer going to be like with Josephine gone?" Through the window she could see her daughter as she bent over in last year's shorts to cover the row of seeds she had just scattered. "Josephine Hale!" Clarissa called through the torn screen. "You get in here and put on some slacks. The entire neighborhood doesn't need a girlie show!"

Josephine stood up, arched her back, and raised her hands to the spring sun, then minced to the next row and began to thin out seedlings.

Ben brought their coffee cups to the sink and stood just behind his wife. "She didn't hear you," he said.

"Oh, she heard me," Clarissa muttered, yanking the hot water faucet on. "She likes knowing half the neighborhood is watching those long legs strut around the garden." She slid the pie plates into hot water and grabbed the dishrag, scrubbing as she said, "I don't know where I went wrong, but somewhere along the way I forgot to teach my daughter modesty. I *told* her she'd outgrown those shorts when she dragged them out a few weeks ago."

"She's young," Ben said. "Don't be so hard on her." He tugged on one of his wife's errant curls. "Wasn't all that long ago I was watching your legs while you—"

"Stop that!" Clarissa said, blushing as her husband ran his hands over her hips.

"This evening when Jo's helping out at the Servicemen's Club, we'll have the house to ourselves—mm-hmm." Ben reached around her waist.

"Reverend Hale, you behave yourself!" Clarissa pretended to struggle, but she leaned back against her husband and kissed his cheek before grabbing his hands. "You have a sermon to polish."

"All right," the preacher said and backed away. "I'll behave. Until Jo's gone." He twitched his eyebrows at her. "But my sermon is just about as polished as it is going to get." He winked at her from the doorway.

"You," Clarissa scolded, "are a naughty boy." Snatching the teakettle off the stove, she poured herself a cup of hot water and called after him, "And you didn't answer my question. What about Mia Frey?"

———

Crouching over the seedling garden, Jo pretended she didn't hear her mother telling her to put on pants. The vague murmur of her dad's voice from inside made her smile. She stood up. Arching her back she stretched, brought both hands up to her eyes, and pushed her hair back as she lifted her face to the sun. It had been such a long winter. She could not wait to be finished with school and head for the ranch. She was sick of indoor life, and very soon now it would be over.

Another door somewhere up the block slammed. At the sound of two angry voices, Jo pursed her lips. The neighbors must be at it again. Just as she stepped over a row of seedling snow peas, a child emerged from behind the garage and, nestling her chin in the niche created at the top of the picket fence, stood mutely watching her.

"Hello, Mia," Jo said, glancing up at the girl's unnaturally pale face and equally pale, mournful eyes.

The child didn't answer.

"You want to help thin out a row?" Jo asked. She looked back over her shoulder toward her mother's kitchen. "I bet there's a cookie left in the cookie jar."

Mia unlatched the gate. Slipping inside the yard, she went to the row next to Jo and stooped down. The two worked their way up and down the garden rows side by side. Once in a while Jo would make a comment or ask a question. Mia's one-word answers told Jo more than tears or childish tales could have, for Mia Frey had once been a talkative child—before her daddy returned from the war. Henry Frey had volunteered the minute war was declared on Germany and been badly burned in a crash on one of his first missions. After a little over a year in a foreign hospital, he came home. As far as Jo knew, almost no one in Crawford had actually *seen* Hank Frey since his discharge. Rumors abounded, but being the preacher's daughter and thus a frequent topic of rumor herself, Jo was disinclined to believe anything she'd heard—except what came out of little Mia's rosebud mouth. Hank Frey had a hook instead of a right hand and a disfigured face that frightened his daughter.

When the weeding was done and Mrs. Frey still had not come to fetch Mia, the girls set to folding the laundry hanging on the clothesline positioned between the rickety garage and the back of the house. Finally Jo said, "Why don't you stay the rest of the afternoon? You can have supper with us."

Mia glanced at the Hales' back door with such longing Jo had to swallow to keep the tears from her eyes. "I'll have to ask Mother. She might want me to stay home."

Mother. The Frey family was one of the reasons Jo found herself questioning her father's insistence that God's angels kept track of everything and everyone in Crawford, Nebraska. If that had ever been true, Jo was positive some angel had forgotten to transfer *Frey* to the next page of his—or her—book of Families to Watch Over. As far as she could tell, things had gone steadily downhill for that family since Mia's father came home and practically barricaded himself inside the house. Not long after that, Mia started referring to the woman who had been *Mommy* as *Mother*.

Beyond mentioning the hook and the scarred face, she never talked about her father, and whenever Jo spent any time at all in the Hales' backyard, Mia appeared, pretending to busy herself in the alley, scratching in the dirt, singing to herself, pulling the earliest dandelion bloom, waiting, hoping for a chance to come into the Hales' yard. Only when Jo's father stepped out on the back porch and called "Hello, Sprite," did Mia's face light up. Even Mama, who was not given to hospitality, had a soft spot for Mia.

And on this Saturday afternoon in early spring, with only a little encouragement from Jo, Mia slipped out of the Hales' yard and up the alley and was back in record time, her pale cheeks flushed and her eyes sparkling with happiness. "Yes," she panted, leaning against the fence. "Mother said I can stay. Long as I want." She pointed to the laundry. "I'll fold the rest if you'll take them down. I can't quite reach the clothespins yet."

Promised supper at the Hales, the real Mia Frey emerged, and Jo realized once again how fitting was her father's nickname for the child. Like a sprite, Mia flitted across the yard, infused with such energy she couldn't stand still. Running to the clothesline pole, she grabbed it and spun around it until she collapsed on the grass laughing, "I'm dizzy!"

"Are you hungry, too?" Clarissa called from the back porch. She nodded to the girls. "Come have some milk and a cookie while it's still warm." She set a plate at the edge of the porch and went back inside.

Mia ran to the porch ahead of Jo and had devoured her cookie and drunk half the glass of milk before Jo arrived. Jo grunted, "I'm too full from lunch," she said, and looked down at Mia. "Any chance you can eat another cookie?"

Mia took the cookie. "We're out of our sugar ration for this month," she said. "A prisoner that works in the office gave Mother some—Mother said they don't have rationing up at the fort. But Father found out where it came from. He was mad. He threw it out."

"Well," Jo replied, "we've still got sugar. And all the milk and butter we want, thanks to Ella."

"Ella's a good old cow," Mia said as milk dribbled down her chin. She swiped it away with the back of her hand, then burped loudly.

"Mia Frey!" Clarissa scolded from just inside the back door.

"Sorry, ma'am," Mia said, stifling a grin when Jo pursed her lips and puffed out her own cheeks pretending to burp soundlessly.

"You girls get the laundry folded and come on in. You can set the table while I start dinner."

"Yes, ma'am," Jo said. Together, they headed back to the clothesline. When they were finished, Mia grabbed one handle of the overflowing wicker laundry basket and Jo took the other. Once inside the back door, they set the clean laundry atop the table on the back porch. They washed up and set the dinner table, and by the time the Reverend Hale got home from making his hospital visits, Mia Frey was no longer the pale, frightened child who lived two doors up. She was Ben Hale's "little sprite."

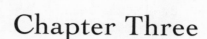

Chapter Three

Hath God forgotten to be gracious?
hath he in anger shut up his tender mercies?
PSALM 77:9

AS SHE TURNED SIDEWAYS to see if her slip was showing from beneath her polka-dot dress, Helen Frey thought she heard the floorboards in the hallway creak. Relieved that it was Friday and Mia had already left for school, she stepped away from the mirror and reached for the gray felt hat perched at the foot of the bed. Bowing her head, she settled the hat in place and worked at the pin with her eyes closed, hoping that if Hank flung the door open he wouldn't notice that she'd moved the dressing mirror so he wouldn't see himself if he came in.

When no one came to the bedroom door, she sat down on the foot of the bed and spun to the side so she could see herself. It surprised her when she really looked at the woman in the mirror these days. How could someone so worn out on the inside still appear somewhat . . . attractive . . . on the outside? How could someone about to burst with sorrow look so trim? How could she possibly still look like the girl who had kissed her high school sweetheart good-bye and stood waving as his train pulled out? But she did, and that proved that you really could not judge a book by its cover.

Her gaze drifted away from the mirror to the window and a view of Mia's tire swing.

"She's too little to use it," Helen had said when Hank decided to hang an old tire from a limb of the giant hackberry tree in the backyard. "She'll fall off."

"Come here, Spridget," Hank had said, sweeping his six-year-old daughter into his arms and showing her how to balance inside the tire. "By the time Daddy gets back home, you'll be so good at swinging you'll be wanting to try out the trapeze when the circus comes to town!"

Was it really only two years ago, Helen thought this March morning—only two years since Mia giggled and screeched with pleasure while her Daddy swung her on the old tire? She'd grown so much since Hank left that now she preferred draping her gangly legs over the top of the old tire while she spun around and around and around, hanging on to the rope with one hand while, with the other, she leaned down and traced circles in the grass. Helen closed her eyes, thinking how much her own life had become a blur, just like Mia's view of the world from her spinning tire swing.

She looked back at the woman in the mirror. She and Hank had had such plans. How naïve she had been, Helen thought, crying and begging him not to volunteer to go to war. She was so afraid he would be killed. How childish she had been. She had never suspected that worse things could happen than a man getting killed in battle.

Stop it, stop it, stop it, stop it. Helen jumped up off the bed. *Her* bed now. That, at least, was not her fault. She hadn't done a thing when Hank came home but smile and throw her arms around him. She'd kissed the side of his face that was nothing but scars and cried and whispered *"I love you, darling."* For a fleeting minute she'd thought maybe it would be all right. But then Hank turned to Mia.

Helen had tried so hard to prepare their little girl. "Daddy's been hurt, honey. He may not look the same. But underneath the blanket he's still your daddy." She had thought herself creative to come up with that analogy. Underneath a blanket was a soft mattress, and underneath the scars was the same daddy who loved them.

If only Mia could have playacted. Just a little. But she was too young to understand. "Take that off," she demanded, pointing to the right side of her father's face. "Take that blanket off. I don't like it."

Just as Helen had tried to explain, Hank tried to understand. He smiled down at his daughter. "It's not that kind of blanket, sweetheart," he said. "I can't take it off." When he reached for Mia, she slunk behind her mother.

Helen took Mia's hand, and looped her other arm through Hank's. "It'll be all right, darling," she whispered, "just give her a little time."

Hank nodded. Then he shook her off. "Haven't learned to manage this hook yet. Need to pick up my duffel."

He had forbidden her to tell anyone he was coming home. As she saw the looks people at the train station cast their way, she was grateful. They walked home in silence with Hank leading the way. When Helen joked that he'd forgotten his hometown and tried to lead him toward Main Street, he shook his head. "Don't want to see anyone." Then he snorted, "And they sure don't want to see me." The walk home stretched before them like a marathon to a weary runner. Even though it was unseasonably warm, Helen had shivered beneath her wool coat.

At home, Mia exchanged her coat for a thick wool sweater and went to her tire swing in the backyard. Hank dropped his duffel inside the front door and then walked through the house to the back. From just inside the screen door he called to her. "Be careful, Spridget."

Helen smiled at him as she set the table for supper. Surely it would help for Mia to hear the special nickname. What happened next broke Helen's heart. Mia lost her balance and fell to the ground with a thud. Instinct sent Hank out the door and across the yard to help the daughter who had always wanted her daddy when she was hurt.

But Mia screeched. "Get away! Don't . . . don't—"

Helen went to the door just in time to see the last remnants of the man she had loved torn away. Mia was sitting with her back pressed against the hackberry tree trunk, her face hidden in her hands.

Hank must have been trying to reassure her. He must have said "It's Daddy," because Mia shouted, "I want a new daddy! I don't want this *ugly* daddy!"

Helen saw his broad shoulders slump as he turned back toward the house. When he came in the door, she reached out to put her hand on his shoulder, but he pulled away and stumbled toward the stairs. She heard his feet landing on each one with a thud as his heavy footsteps retreated.

Holding back her own tears, Helen went outside to calm Mia. By the time Mia felt better and brave enough to see if that really *was* her daddy inside the wounded body, Hank had locked the bedroom door.

Helen and Mia had dined alone. Through the door, Hank told Helen he needed to rest awhile. She should go on to Wednesday evening services and choir practice.

"Take Spridget with you," he said through the door.

Helen went. Mia joined Jo Hale in the Sunday school rooms, helping keep track of the choir members' children while their parents practiced. Helen plastered on a big smile and said yes, Hank was home and no, they didn't want visitors yet because he was just bone-weary and needed to rest. The young women seemed to believe her. Only old Mrs. Koch didn't. She nodded and squeezed Helen's arm.

"I have prayed for you every day, Helen. I won't stop." She blinked a few times and then leaned close. "The women at home have to be heroes, too." She gave Helen a quick hug and hurried away.

At home Helen discovered that while she and Mia were at church,

Hank had moved out of their bedroom and up the rickety stairs to the attic. Late that night, she heard him descend.

"Sweetheart," she said, and headed into his arms.

"Don't," he said, his voice hollow.

"But—"

"I said," he repeated, "don't. Don't call me sweetheart. Don't pretend you're happy. Just . . . don't. Now go back to bed. I won't bother you and I don't want you bothering me. You'll need to keep your job out at the fort. This hook they gave me . . . I don't know what I'm still going to be able to do at the garage." He paused. "I doubt folks are going to want to come to a freak show every time they need their oil changed."

Feeling as though she'd been punched in the midsection, Helen stammered, "All right, dear." She retreated to her bed and lay wide-awake for the rest of the night.

That had been weeks ago. For the next few days, Helen didn't know whether Hank was alive or dead. She worried about the cold up in the unfinished attic. She told Mia her daddy was sick and that he didn't want them to "catch it," but at night, when she heard him on the stairs, she lay listening . . . longing . . . wishing he would open her door and whisper her name and take them both to places in the dark where they could forget. One time he did. Helen's spirits soared. Finally, she thought, they were finding each other again. Lying in his arms, she thought that maybe things were going to be all right. But early the next morning Hank pushed himself out of bed into the cold room . . . and *apologized*.

Helen wanted to scream. What had she done? Didn't she welcome him completely? Hadn't their love been sweet? For Mia's sake, she had pretended to be asleep. Best to say nothing, she told herself as her husband crept back up to the garret.

And now both Helen and Mia had accepted the fact that Hank lived in the attic. Helen learned to lie. She made up stories about things Hank said or did at home. She made excuses. She warned Mia not to talk about Daddy, and after a few weeks, people stopped asking. She avoided Mrs. Koch, who, as far as Helen Frey knew, was the only woman in Crawford who suspected that the army had been wrong when they said Hank Frey survived the crash of his B-17.

Thank God for the Hale family. Helen had never really liked her pastor's wife. But since Hank's return, Clarissa and Ben and their daughter, Jo, had become a lifeline for Helen and Mia. If it hadn't been for the Hales and old Mrs. Koch, Helen didn't know what she would have done these past weeks. She wondered what she would do when school was out and

Mia was supposed to be at home all day. She'd thought she would be able to quit her job out at the fort as soon as Hank came home. She'd expected life to be normal. She'd been such a fool.

The sound of a car honking jolted her back to the present, and she hurried out into the hallway and, with a glance up the stairs at the closed attic door, made her way downstairs and out onto the front porch just in time to see Tom Hanson across the street holding his car door open for Stella Black. She felt a pang of jealousy as Stella minced down her sidewalk toward the car. Before sliding into the seat, she called to Helen.

"I'll miss you today, honey."

"Thank you," Helen replied. "I'll be back tomorrow."

Helen waited for the car to head out before descending the porch steps and going down the sidewalk toward the street. She couldn't risk Stella Black noticing that Helen Frey, who had said she was taking the day off to be room mother at Mia's school, was walking in the opposite direction of the school. While she waited for Stella's ride to round the corner and head for Fort Robinson, she glanced up at the garret window centered above the porch. Was it her imagination, or had there been a flicker of movement just then? Her heart pounded. It wouldn't do for Hank to be asking questions. Not today. Inhaling deeply, she headed downtown. By the time she arrived at the cottage Doctor Whitlow used for his office, Helen Frey was herself again—the hardworking wife of a war hero.

———

Shortly after lunch on Saturday, Jo crossed the street and headed for Stella Black's front porch, where Delores waited, ensconced on the porch swing reading a magazine. At her approach, Delores turned the magazine around so Jo could see a full-color photograph of Betty Grable. "Looks like you," she said.

Jo plopped down on the porch swing with a sigh.

Delores closed the magazine. "So?"

"So I can't go," Jo said. "I already knew I couldn't. I should have told you. Asking only made my mom angrier."

"Why not? What could be wrong with Charlie McCarthy and Edgar Bergen?" Delores asked.

"It's not the movie. It's the day. Remember? No movies on Sunday." She looked sideways at her friend. "I could have gone to the matinee today. But now it's too late."

"Of all the dumb things," Delores Black said. She closed the magazine and dropped it on the concrete.

"You go ahead," Jo said. "I heard it's really good."

"Naw," Delores said, shaking her head. "I'll wait for you. We can go next week." She hopped up. "Let's go downtown and get an ice cream, anyway." She jangled the change in her pocket. "Before this burns a hole." Touching Jo's arm, she whispered, "We don't have to walk straight home. The sooner we get back, the more chores they'll have lined up for us."

Jo grinned. "That's what I like about you, Delores. You're always thinking." With a laugh, she headed off toward the park with her friend.

"Why'd you have to go and be a *Baptist,* anyway?" Delores asked as they walked along. "They *never* have any fun. You should just tell your parents you're going to be Methodist or Episcopalian—or Catholic. Why not Catholic? We can do whatever we want." Thunder pealed from the clouds that had been gathering all day. "Come on," Delores said, looking up at the sky.

"You can *not* do whatever you want," Jo retorted. "Not and be on good terms with God." She pointed toward the thunderclouds swirling in from the west. "We're gonna get drenched."

"Not if you hurry," Delores said. She turned around and called over her shoulder, "And I'm on *great* terms with God, thank you very much. I go to confession and do my penance and attend mass. If that doesn't get me points with God, what would?"

Jo picked up the pace. Lightning crackled out of the clouds. "It's not what you *do* that makes the difference." She pointed to her heart. "It's what's in here." She hurried up the steps to the park shelter. Together the girls leaned on the railing along the edge of the shelter and watched the storm approach.

"Is that you talking or the Reverend Mr. Hale?"

Jo frowned. "It's me. Why?"

Delores tossed her head. "Well, if it's not what you *do* that makes the difference with God, how come you have that long list of things you can't do?"

Jo looked down at her petite friend. She expected to see the now-familiar grin that said Delores was only teasing, but the girl's dark eyes were serious. *I should have an answer,* Jo thought, feeling a little ashamed, for if the preacher's daughter didn't have the answer to a basic question like that, there was something wrong. "I don't know," Jo finally said. Her face brightened, "But if you really want to talk about it, we could go over to my dad's office and ask him."

"Oh right," Delores rolled her eyes and made a face. "That's *just* what I need to do. Can't you just hear my mom after someone tells her that her only daughter has been checking out the Baptist church?" She perched atop the railing that bordered the shelter. "She'd have a heart attack. And besides, there's going to be a downpour any minute."

"I thought your mother liked me," Jo said, pretending to pout.

"She does. But I don't think her enthusiasm quite extends to the rest of your clan. Call it cautious acceptance. And don't push it." Delores swept her straight black hair back off her shoulders and pretended to make a ponytail. "So. You can't go to the movies tomorrow. Can you work in the club kitchen with me tonight?"

Jo sighed. "I want to—*so* much. But Mother had a fit the last two times I helped out."

Delores dropped her ponytail. "You sang 'America the Beautiful' to cheer up the soldiers," she said. "What could possibly be wrong with that?"

Jo shrugged. "I don't get it, either. I was going to ask Dad to work on her, but he already stood up for me when she objected to my spending the summer out at the ranch. I don't think we'd better push her about anything else just now."

"My gosh, Jo, is there anything your mother *isn't* upset about right now? You always spend your summers out there."

Jo shrugged. "And every summer she hopes I won't."

"You can't help it if you take after your Aunt CJ instead of her," Delores said.

"I know," Jo murmured. "But she just doesn't think it's ladylike to work a ranch. She doesn't think men find it attractive."

"You're ladylike enough to have one of the cutest boys from our class writing you practically every day," Delores said. "It's not like you aren't already practically engaged."

Jo sighed and shook her head. Sometimes it bothered her the way everyone assumed things about her and Johnny Bishop. But that was not information she could trust to Delores, as much as she liked her. "I can't help it if I hate sewing and cooking. I've loved horses ever since I knew what one was. Daddy says horses are in my blood on both sides. His grandpa raised racehorses back in Kentucky."

"It's fate," Delores said.

"Maybe you're right," Jo agreed. "I just wish Mother wouldn't take it so personally that I'd rather go out to the ranch and work for Aunt CJ than stay in town this summer." She bit her lower lip and stared into the distance. "Sometimes in the winter when the sky's been gray and we're all snowed in—sometimes I feel like I can't breathe. Like if I don't get out into the wide open spaces I'm going to suffocate." She tossed her head and inhaled. "I feel *alive* when I'm at the Four Pines. Honestly, just about everything else I do is filling time until I get to go back there. I'd move right now if I could."

"Well, I'd agree with your mom that you should graduate first, but then—why can't you? Move right after graduation. Make it permanent. Everyone knows you're going to end up out there after Johnny gets back."

Jo sighed. There it was again. As if her future was already mapped out for her. "I promised I'd go to the university in Lincoln," she said.

"What for?"

"Mother's got her heart set on me getting an education," Jo said. "That's all she talks about. How women are going to have all kinds of opportunities once the war is over. How the world isn't going to be the same now that people have seen what women can do." She raised her left arm and struck a Rosie the Riveter pose, flexing her bicep.

"Now let me get this straight." Delores paced around the bandstand gesturing while she talked. "Your mother is all excited about opportunities for women—she wants you to go to school so you have more than the usual choices women have . . . but she's counting on Johnny to see to it that you make the usual choice and get married?"

Jo laughed. "Exactly."

"So she wants you to choose . . . to make the choice she would have made . . . if she had had a choice . . . when she chose."

"All right, all right," Jo said, waving at Delores to be quiet. "I get the point. It doesn't make sense to us. But it does to my mom." Jo frowned, "She likes Johnny a lot. But I think sometimes she wishes she hadn't gotten married so young."

"You're not your mother," Delores interjected.

"You can say that again."

"Maybe *she* should go to the university," Delores said. "And let you be what you want to be."

"I don't mind the idea of going to college," Jo said. "Aunt CJ says there's nothing wrong with a woman rancher being educated." She looked off into the distance. "And Mother means well. It just seems like it's going to take so long to get back here." She hopped down and smoothed her skirt. "And Aunt CJ isn't getting any younger. There's a lot I've got to learn from her. Stuff you can't find in books. Things Aunt CJ just seems to have a sixth sense about."

"Like what?" Delores blew a bubble and popped it.

"Like how to tell if a mare's going to have it easy or tough when she foals. And how to calm down a nervous mama. And breeding. Aunt CJ's always had an uncanny talent for pairing up the right stallion with the right mare."

Delores's face turned bright red, and she laughed nervously. "Josephine Hale, shame on you!"

Jo, whose face was almost as red as her friend's shook her head. "Well, gee, Delores. It's part of the job."

When huge raindrops began to fall on the shelter roof, Delores looked at her watch. "Shoot!" she shouted. "I've got to get going. I promised Mom I'd clean house today. She's working overtime."

"I'll help," Jo said, just as the heavens opened. "Come on!" she said, "nobody ever died of a good soaking!" She started down the steps. The spring rain was cold. With a shriek, Jo skittered back under the leaky metal roof of the park shelter. Tiny hailstones began to fall amidst the raindrops. Lightning cracked and both girls squealed and jumped.

"That hit nearby," Delores yelled.

Jo nodded. The girls huddled together. While they waited, a train approached from the east. Delores's eyes grew wide. "Prisoners!" she said, and nodded toward the train. Its windows had been adjusted from the outside so they could only be opened a couple of inches.

Delores leaned closer. "Nazis!" she whispered.

As the rain diminished, the sound of squealing brakes joined the receding thunder. Slowly, the train came to a stop within shouting distance of the park shelter.

A guard stepped out on the platform between the two cars nearest the shelter. Lighting a cigarette, he looked to his right and to his left, and then descended to the opposite side of the tracks.

"Come on," Delores said, grabbing Jo by the elbow. "Let's go take a look. That guard was cute."

"Don't be ridiculous," Jo said sharply. She drew back. "My mother would have a cow if—Delores!"

Delores was already down the shelter steps. At the edge of the park, she crouched down behind a row of bushes from where she looked back toward the park shelter, motioning for Jo to join her.

Jo looked from Delores to the train car and back again. She shook her head. Delores waved, then made a gesture as if she were praying. Jo scuttled across the grass. "What on earth do you think you are *doing*?"

Together they stared. A dozen faces were looking in their direction.

Jo grabbed her friend's arm. "Let's go. We shouldn't be here. I don't know why the train's stopped, but that guard is gone and—"

Delores pulled away. "Don't be silly. They aren't going anywhere. Look!" She nodded toward the train. "They're waving hello."

It was true. A couple of the men held up their hands in greeting. Delores waved back.

"What are you *doing*?!" Jo said between clenched teeth.

"Diplomacy," Delores said. She smiled toward the train. "Wouldn't you want people to be nice to Johnny if he was on his way to a PW camp somewhere?"

"Don't even *think* about that!"

"Well?" Delores shrugged. "You know you would." She nodded toward the train. "Look at that one. He can't be a soldier. He looks like someone's little brother."

If Jo hadn't known better, she would have thought the round-faced soldier with the big eyes was frightened. Another face leaned closer. It was not so young. And not friendly. "The one with the short hair looks mean," Jo muttered.

"Yeah," Delores agreed. "But look at the one next to him. Wow."

Delores's "wow" was just that. Blond hair, square jaw. Jo couldn't see his eyes too well, but she imagined them as being a gorgeous blue.

"Beautiful American girls . . . can you please tell us where we are?"

The handsome blond was being shouldered away from the window by someone with dark hair and a moustache. He repeated the question. "Please, dear ladies. Have the kindness of the angels that you resemble."

"That does it," Jo said. "We're leaving."

"Nebraska," Delores called out. "You're in Nebraska."

A rumble of voices erupted on the train car.

"My uncle lives in Boston," one of the German prisoners called out.

"We have cousins in New York," another said.

"Do you have any cigarettes?"

Suddenly the guard who had jumped down on the opposite side of the train reappeared. He stomped out his cigarette and scrambled up the stairs, across to the park side, and down the steps.

"You! Girls!" He came charging toward Delores and Jo. "What do you think you're doing?"

"What do you think *you're* doing?" Delores said, lifting her chin. "You're the one who was supposed to be guarding them. I saw you jump down to have a cigarette, so don't act all high and mighty."

The soldier stopped. When he spoke again, it was with less anger. "Hey, it's all right. I just don't want you to get hurt, that's all."

Delores made a face. "That would be kind of hard, wouldn't it? Since the windows are nailed practically shut?" She nodded toward the train. "And what's wrong, anyway? They never stop in Crawford."

The guard shrugged. "Something on the tracks up ahead. We'll get moving before long." He looked at the sky, then gazed toward the buttes in the distance. "You know how much farther Fort Robinson is from here?"

"My mom works there," Delores said. "It's about ten miles."

"Finally," the soldier said, shaking his head. "Never thought we'd get here." He nodded toward the train. "Some of those men have been accusing us of running the train through a maze. They don't believe we could be going in a straight line. Sometimes I wonder if they're right." He smiled down at Delores.

"Where you from?" Delores asked.

"Brooklyn." He looked in the direction of the buttes again. "I thought Nebraska was all flat."

"You probably thought we still have fights between the cowboys and Indians, too," Delores said, nudging Jo.

"Don't you?" the soldier grinned, and Jo couldn't tell if he was teasing them or not.

"Not very often," Jo said.

"What does anyone ever do around here, anyway?" the soldier asked. "I mean, it's so . . . empty."

"There's a movie house," Jo said. "And some churches. And a Servicemen's Club on Main Street."

Delores spoke up. "Jo here sings for the variety show out at the fort sometimes."

Jo glowered at her. Voices up the line caught the soldier's attention.

"So . . . if I come to the Servicemen's Club some night, any chance you'll be there?" He was looking at Jo.

Delores linked her arm through Jo's and spoke up. "You never can tell," she said.

The train began to move. The private jogged back to the car full of German prisoners, grabbed a handrail, and hauled himself aboard. As the train picked up speed, he leaned out and yelled, "Franco Romani."

Inside the train car, hands were raised as if to say good-bye. Jo saw the older short-haired soldier sit down. The youngest prisoner stood staring at them. Jo barely noticed him. She could not take her eyes off the tall blond, who did not look back but sat with his profile to the window and his nose in the air. Now there was a Nazi a girl could hate.

As the train receded into the distance, Delores nudged Jo. "So, Mrs. Four Pines Ranch, you gonna sing in the variety show again or not?" She leaned against Jo's shoulder. "Private Romani from New York might be there."

Jo shook her head. "Mother would throw a fit." She paused and looked down at her friend. "And Private Romani is *not* my type."

"Oh, right. And what, pray tell, is your type?"

"Hmm," Jo said, and turned to walk toward Main Street. "More Cary Grant, less Eddie Bracken." She giggled. "And no Fred Astaire."

Delores rolled her eyes, "Do the 'no-dancing' Baptists have a rule against pouring punch?"

"Of course not, silly."

"Well then, come and pour punch." Delores leaned toward her. "That Private Romani was real cute. And he liked you." Delores nudged her. "Come on, Jo. Mrs. Blair is going to be the chaperone. She's as upright a citizen as could ever be."

"Maybe," Jo said. "But Mother and Mrs. Blair had words at the county fair last year, and Mother's not too keen on her."

"Honestly!" Delores exclaimed. "It was only jelly for goodness' sake."

"*Only* is not a word my mother uses when it comes to whether she brings home a blue ribbon or not."

"She got blues for pie and pickles," Delores said. "It's not like she had a baby in the 'Beautiful Baby' contest and Mrs. Blair said the little thing was ugly."

Jo laughed. "All right, all right. I'll ask. That's all I can say. But I don't think I'll mention Mrs. Blair as chaperone. Deacon Jones's wife is going, too."

Delores laced her arm through Jo's. "Good plan. Everyone knows Mrs. Jones can't bake her way out of a paper bag. So maybe your mother will approve of her."

———

"Absolutely not!" Clarissa exclaimed over supper. "I can't believe you'd ask such a ridiculous thing."

Jo saw her mother look across the table and send an unspoken plea in her father's direction. When Daddy didn't pick up the hint, her hopes soared. "It's not ridiculous. It's . . . it's something I can do. For the war. For Johnny."

"For Johnny? Oh, please." Clarissa rolled her eyes and shook her head. "The fair citizens of Crawford and Chadron just cannot wait to put their daughters on display in hopes some soldier will marry them. Those variety shows out at the fort are little more than a . . . a . . . farm sale. It's disgusting, and I won't have you participating."

"Where's the harm in smiling and trying to cheer up a homesick soldier? You already let me go once. Some of them are from New York City. They've got to think they came to the ends of the earth when they came way out here. I bet they don't know which end of a horse eats and which end—"

"Don't be crass, Josephine," Clarissa said.

"I'm sorry. But I want to go." She turned to her father. "Aren't you the one who's saying we should all do our part?"

"You planted the garden," Clarissa said. "And you've participated in every drive we've had. You are doing your part."

"You pray for President Roosevelt," Ben added. "You write to John and keep his spirits up."

"I want to do more," Jo said.

"Maybe once you've graduated," Clarissa answered. "If there's a war still on, God forbid."

"Next year—it's always next year," Jo muttered. "When are you ever going to let me grow up?!"

"If growing up means you rebel and tell your parents they don't know what's best for you, I hope you never grow up."

Jo pressed her lips together firmly. "I'm eighteen years old. I'm going."

"I happen to know," Clarissa said, "that Mrs. Blair requires parental permission when she collects young women for the events at the fort. And you do not have parental permission. So you will not be going."

Slamming her hands down on the table, Jo opened her mouth to protest.

"Josephine," her father said. " 'Be angry, but do not sin. Children, obey your parents in the Lord, for this is right.' "

" 'Fathers, provoke not your children to wrath!' " Jo blurted out and, jumping up, she charged out the back door, down the porch steps, across the yard, and through the gate. Plopping in the damp spring grass and leaning her back against the garage wall, she let the angry tears come.

"Hey, Jo," said a familiar voice.

"Oh . . . hi, Mia."

"What's wrong?"

Jo shook her head. "Nothing too serious."

"You're crying," Mia said. She extended her index finger and touched a tear.

"Yes," Jo said, and forced a smile. "But not anymore. You cheered me up! What are you doing out here in the alley, anyway?"

Mia looked back over her shoulder toward her own house. "Waiting for Mother to come home."

"Want to wait with me?"

Mia grinned. "Can I have a horse story?"

"You bet," Jo said, and patted the ground beside her.

Chapter Four

As we have therefore opportunity, let us do good unto all men,
especially unto them who are of the household of the faith.
GALATIANS 6:10

Clara Joy

THE THIRD SUNDAY after Will left, Ben Hale asked me to meet with him in his office after the Sunday service. Now that made me nervous. I couldn't remember a time when Ben had treated me like I was a regular member of his congregation, and I didn't hear much of his sermon after he asked for that meeting, which was disappointing because I had driven into Crawford hoping for some comfort, what with Will deserting me in my time of need and all. It didn't help calm my nerves to see that Jo and her mother were upset, too. Clarissa missed more than one note when she played the offertory that morning, and I could tell by the way Jo sat turning pages that my niece was none too pleased with her mother.

I headed for Ben's office right after the service, but it took a while for Ben to arrive, since he and Clarissa always stand at the back of the sanctuary to shake hands as people leave the church. The longer I sat in front of that blasted brass desk plate with *Reverend Benjamin T. Hale* engraved on the front, the more fidgety I got. I never did understand why on earth my sister had that thing made. As if everyone in Crawford didn't already know who Ben was. It got more annoying by the minute, so finally I got up and went over to the window, which Ben had opened, I assume, to let in the spring morning air.

Now Ben's office window is just to one side of the front steps, but I did not eavesdrop on one conversation. I did notice Mrs. Frey send Mia on ahead while she paused to talk to old Mrs. Koch, who is the oldest member of our congregation and a war widow—from the Great War. It was the first time I really thought on the fact that I hadn't seen Hank Frey since he came home. I pondered that for a while, but by the time Ben came in I was back in the "inquisition chair" just about to twist the handle off my purse with my fidgeting.

"I'm about to ask you a favor," Ben said, settling behind his desk. He folded his hands over his ink blotter and smiled. "And I don't want Clarissa to know it was my idea."

I relaxed a little. If Ben was up to something that would make Clarissa mad, chances were it would be something I'd like. "Ask away," I said.

Ben cleared his throat. "Well, Clarissa is dead set against Jo going to the ranch this summer," he said. "That business with using PW labor has her riled."

I opened my mouth to say something snazzy, like maybe Clarissa would like to drive the tractor fourteen hours a day to help me out. But before I could, Ben said, "Now don't get your hackles up yet, CJ. I'm on Jo's side— and yours—and Jo will be coming. Although the fact that Will's moved out of the cabin isn't going to help matters much."

"Who told you about Will?"

"Deacon Hanson. He's been doing a lot of work at the fort lately."

"For the remount?" I snapped—mostly because I hate gossip, and the last thing I wanted was for the fools and liars of Dawes County to pull my own pastor into another round of "the plain truth" about Will Bishop and CJ Jackson. Of course I knew Tom Hanson was a good carpenter, and it was no surprise he was working out at the fort—along with a lot of other folks from Crawford. But Fort Robinson is really three different places—a PW camp for the German prisoners of war, a K-9 division for training war dogs, and the U.S. Army Remount Service Headquarters, which is what everyone just calls "the remount." I knew enough about the way things worked over at Fort Rob to know that the three divisions were mostly kept separate, even if they did all coexist on the flat prairie between the White River to the south and the long string of rocky buttes to the north. And I also knew Tom had been hired to help build the PW camp.

"As a matter of fact," Ben said, real calm—and I will admit that Ben Hale's voice is probably one of the reasons my sister fell in love with him— "even though he works at the PW camp most of the time, Tom put in some extra hours on Saturday helping the remount get ready for the next horse sale. Something about refitting the arena to make things go more smoothly. Anyway, Tom said that Bill Harker was going on about how great it was to have someone with Will's experience helping condition and test the new arrivals."

I kept my mouth shut. When Will decided to come to his senses and come home I didn't want him thinking I was talking behind his back.

"Anyway," Ben said, and leaned back in his chair, "I expect Clarissa will get wind of Will's departure soon enough, and when she does, there will be yet another stir. But—" he smiled at me—"I can handle Clarissa. In the end, she'll realize that Jo needs the ranch like a fish needs water."

Now that helped me relax even more. Even if he is your brother-in-law, you don't want to be in trouble with your pastor. That just isn't a good feeling no matter how you cut it. But apparently I wasn't in trouble. "And the ranch needs Jo," I said as quick as I could. "She'll be a big help with gentling the yearlings. And I appreciate your standing up to Clarissa. You know I'd die before I'd put Jo in harm's way. Now let me explain how it'll work with the PWs. When—"

Ben raised his hand. "There's no need," he said. "I trust you, CJ. That's not what this little meeting is about at all."

"It isn't?"

He shook his head. "Nope. Actually, I was wondering if you'd be able to take on more than just Jo this summer."

I sat back and adjusted my church hat. "Who?"

"Mia Frey," Ben said.

Now, while it is true that most of my maternal instincts have been spent on four-legged babies, I am still a woman, and even Clarissa, who is about as far from a soft touch as a woman can be, has affection for Mia. I had prayed for Hank Frey—just like I did Johnny and the other boys in Crawford who were in uniform—and I had just been wondering about him, so while Ben was saying things like he realized Jo would have to agree to keep track of Mia and it was asking a lot, I blurted out, "We'll take her," so abruptly I surprised myself. And then I said, "As long as it's all right with her parents. And they have to know about my plans to hire labor from the fort."

Ben nodded.

"Doesn't Mrs. Frey work out there?"

"She does. She's one of the secretaries at the prison camp headquarters."

"What about Hank? Will he agree to it?"

Ben was quiet for a minute while he studied the back of his hands. "Hank is . . ." He paused. It was one of the few times in my life I'd seen Ben Hale at a loss for words. " . . . struggling. He's badly scarred from what I hear."

"You haven't been to visit?" This was not like Ben Hale, who took his job as a shepherd so seriously he once cancelled a family vacation so he could take old Fred Davenport to see a heart specialist in Lincoln.

Ben shook his head. "I haven't wanted to cause a stir. Hank's been reclusive." He sighed and looked out the window. "To tell the truth, CJ, about all I know is what Mia hints at. I think her mother has told her not to talk about it." He looked up at me. "And Mrs. Frey has been avoiding me. I'm going on what Mia has said and the rumors that started way back when Hank first got home." He grimaced. "At first I thought it was a good idea to give him some time to adjust. But I've let it go too long. It's something I intend to spend some time on. After Mia is gone."

Sometimes what a person doesn't say is more profound than what they say. I may be old, but I like to think I'm still quick mentally, and I could see what Ben was getting at. He wanted Mia happily tucked away while he tried to help her parents.

"We'll make it seem like camp for her," I said. "She can learn to ride. Ned will be perfect for her. He's twenty-six years old and swaybacked and he wouldn't hurt a fly. The old boy's bulletproof." I stopped. "What? What are you smiling at?"

"You, CJ. For all your bluster and attempts to appear to the contrary, you really are a very caring woman."

If there is one thing I hate, it is sentimental talk. So I made a face and told Ben Hale to hush. Which, I suppose, is evidence enough I was no longer intimidated by the desk or the pastor's office or the brass plate. Fact is, I plumb forgot about all of that. It was just Ben and me talking about how to help out a little girl who needed some time away while her parents figured out how to cope with what the war had dealt them.

"Think you can get Mia and her mama to join us for lunch today?" I asked. "If you think Clarissa can handle two more for Sunday dinner without blowing a gasket, I'll take it from there."

Ben laughed. "I'll take care of it."

And he did. But I never suspected he would avoid getting Clarissa upset over unexpected guests for Sunday dinner by making her mad about something else.

My sister doesn't have false teeth, but if she did, her upper plate would have landed in her cherry pie when Ben asked Mrs. Frey her opinion about his holding a chapel service for the prisoners. Clarissa's mouth dropped open and she—a pastor's wife who is usually very aware of her duty to remain quiet and support her husband—well, she just blurted it out. "You *cannot* be serious!" It got quiet real fast around that table. "The Lutherans and the Catholics already have services out there. That's enough."

Ben patted the back of Clarissa's hand, which was his signal to her to behave herself. He turned to Mrs. Frey. "Tom Hanson tells me some of the prisoners are employed in your office. What do you think? Would they be interested in a chapel service led by a Baptist?"

"Well, I-I don't know. You'd have to clear it with Captain Donovan," Mrs. Frey said.

"Of course. And I will," Ben reassured her. "I'm just curious as to your insights about the prisoners themselves. I've talked to my deacon about it, but I'd like to take advantage of your woman's intuition. Have you observed any evidence of a spiritual awareness?"

When Ben glanced Clarissa's way I understood what he was doing. His wanting to sow the gospel in the mission field beyond the barbed wire was sincere, but he had additional reasons for bringing it up over Sunday dinner. I have to say I didn't realize Ben Hale had it in him. I mean, with one lunch he was trying to win Clarissa's support to start a new ministry, stop her protests about Jo coming to the ranch by getting Mrs. Frey's assurances that the PWs weren't dangerous, and prepare the way for his talking to Hank Frey without Mia being around for whatever might happen. Clearly, there was way more to Ben Hale than I had ever given him credit for. Pondering all the complexities of my brother-in-law's mind took my own thoughts away from the dinner table for a while, and when I came back Mrs. Frey was talking about the PWs working in her office.

"The two in the office right now are new. I don't know about what you are calling spiritual awareness. I don't think either of them has gone to the other services. But that doesn't mean they won't. The younger one seems especially vulnerable—almost like a schoolboy who's shocked to find himself in this situation.

"Schoolboy?" I interrupted. "How old is he?"

"Fifteen, according to his *soldbuch*," Mrs. Frey said.

"His what?" Clarissa asked.

Jo spoke up. "It's a book they all carry. Like an identity card. Except it tells all about them—birthplace, parents, medical history, military train-ing . . . all kinds of things."

"That's right," Mrs. Frey said, nodding.

"And how do you know about these . . . these . . ."

"*Soldbuchs,*" Jo repeated. She looked around the table. "Johnny wrote me about it. One of the men in his unit had one he was keeping as a war souvenir. Something he'd found in a ground campaign. Johnny was wondering about the man who lost it. . . ." Her voice gentled. She looked down at her hands and almost whispered, "Whether he's alive. Or dead." She sighed. "Johnny said it made the war—the things he's doing—more . . . personal. It bothered him to read about Helmut."

"Helmut?" Clarissa said.

"That was his name. The German soldier." Jo looked at Mrs. Frey. "He was really young, too."

"What kind of monster drafts children to fight a war?" Clarissa said.

"Private Bauer's entire class from school was forced into the service and trained to ram tanks with bangalore torpedoes," Mrs. Frey said. "Apparently not many survived for long. He seems grateful to have been captured."

The quiet around the table was more than a little uncomfortable. There we all were, praying for our boys to be successful . . . and suddenly it seemed strange because maybe what we had prayed for would mean boys like Private Bauer—and Helmut Whoever—were getting killed. The more a person thinks about things like that, the more confusing it can get. I was beginning to wish I could have kept the war "over there" while I kept my nose to the grindstone out on my ranch.

Mrs. Frey tried to make things less serious. "One thing about Private Bauer is he's eager to please. I expected to miss the PW he replaced—he wanted to work in the K-9 area—but since Private Bauer arrived, you could eat off the floor in our office." She chuckled. "I think his mother must have had something of a general inside her. When I compliment him, he ducks his head and blushes just like a schoolboy—which, I suppose, he still is in some ways." She looked almost apologetic. "All the PWs who have worked in our office have challenged my idea of what a German soldier is like." She shook her head. "I haven't wanted to like them, but it's been hard not to—with one or two exceptions."

And there we were again, sitting around the table with an awkward silence. For myself, I was realizing that praying for victory over the enemy gets a little strange when you realize you are asking God to help the boys you love kill the boys someone else loves. The generic enemy is easy to hate. But who wants to hate the fifteen-year-old who empties your wastebasket?

"You said you have two prisoners working in your office," Clarissa said. "What about the other one?"

I looked at my sister and wondered if she was just being polite or if she was looking for evidence to shore up her case against the PWs.

Mrs. Frey looked down at her plate. "Dieter Brock," she said. She picked up her knife and started to butter the biscuit on her plate while she talked. I could sense there was something different about the way she felt about this prisoner.

"Well?" Clarissa prodded. "What's he like?"

"Different from Bauer," Mrs. Frey said. "A little older. More reserved." She rubbed her forearms like she was cold and asked for more coffee—which I did not understand because from the color of her cheeks it looked to me like she was plenty warm. "He's asked me to help him get transferred to a remount work detail. He doesn't like office work much," Mrs. Frey said. "Apparently his father was quite the equestrian. He's very frustrated to have landed in a place where there are thousands of horses and not be able to work with them." She looked around the table and gave an odd little laugh, "I've tried to explain to him that the remount horses are a far cry from what his father rode, but—"

"Not all of them are," I said. "Jenny Camp is a world-class jumper."

"And Dakota," Jo chimed in.

"If Dieter knew about them, he'd be even more frustrated cooped up in the office," Mrs. Frey said. "But Captain Donovan insists that Sergeant Brock is needed to interpret for new arrivals."

"He speaks English?" I was getting more interested in this Dieter Brock person all the time.

Mrs. Frey nodded. "And four other languages, according to his file."

I wanted to know more, but Mrs. Frey claimed she didn't know much more, which didn't make any sense when she'd just spouted off all that information, but then Ben interrupted. "Do you think he'd interpret my sermons?"

"He certainly *could*," Mrs. Frey nodded. "His English is flawless." She was looking down at her plate like she wanted more food, but when Clarissa offered it, she said no thanks.

I decided there was something funny about Mrs. Frey's reluctance to talk about Dieter Brock, but I also decided not to pursue it at the dinner table. Maybe I'd check in with Tom Hanson before leaving Crawford. Maybe he'd know more about Brock's interest in horses. I was going to be using more horsepower than gas during haying, and if there was a PW who knew horses and was motivated to work around them, I was intrigued.

Ben changed the subject then by patting Jo's arm and saying, "Your aunt CJ is looking forward to having you on the place this summer. She told me this morning she wanted to talk to us about it."

That was my cue to speak up about Mia, but it was an awkward segue, and I wasn't prepared. I did notice that the minute Ben mentioned Jo leaving Crawford, Mia Frey's little cherub mouth puckered up and she ducked her head.

When I didn't speak up, Ben charged ahead. "I can't believe summer's almost here," he said and winked at Mia. "No more school for you soon, Sprite. Freedom!"

Mia sighed. Her mother tousled her hair. "Mia's going to visit her grandmother in Omaha this summer," she said.

I could tell from the expression in Ben's eyes, he hadn't expected that.

"Sounds like fun," I said. "I always wished I'd had a grandma to spoil me."

"My mother isn't exactly the spoiling kind of grandma," Mrs. Frey said, laughing—a little too loudly, I thought. "But I have to work, and Mia's daddy just isn't well enough to watch over her all day every day."

I was sitting next to Mia, and I could see her little hands balled up into two fists in her lap. I could almost feel the air around her fill up with dread.

"Too bad you don't like horses," I said quickly. "I've got an old nag that could use some attention. I don't have the time for him."

"Ned?" Jo asked. Bless her, I think she was catching onto the plot.

"Ned," I said. I spoke to Mia, although she didn't look up at me. "Yep. He's a swaybacked old cow horse. Just stands around looking sad all the time, thinking about the good old days when there was somebody riding him every day."

"I could do that," a voice barely above a whisper said. Then Mia repeated it a little louder. "I could. I could do that." She looked up at her mother. I couldn't see her face, but I didn't have to. One little hand was reaching up to touch her mama's arm.

"Don't be silly, Mia," Mrs. Frey said. "You don't know how to ride a horse."

"I could learn," Mia said. "I like horses. Really. I do. I draw 'em a lot," she said, and turned and looked at me. Her face was shining with excitement and her pale blue eyes were pleading.

"Well now," I said, "I used to do that, too. My bedroom was covered with drawings of horses. Wasn't it, Clarissa?"

"Horses on the walls. Bugs in jars. Snakes in cages." Clarissa shuddered. "Never knew *what* you were going to find in CJ's room."

Mia giggled. Mrs. Frey smiled.

"Well, my little artist," I said to Mia, "what do you say? Would you like to spend some time helping an old lady with an old horse?" I looked at Mrs. Frey. "Do you think her grandmother would mind so much if she came to the Four Pines for a while?"

"Please, Mrs. Frey," Jo chimed in. "Say yes."

I noticed Clarissa looking very strangely at Ben. I think she knew something was going on, but she couldn't guess what. "But the Germans," she said, turning to Mrs. Frey. "CJ has filed the paper work to have *prisoners* working on the place."

Mrs. Frey smiled. "I know when the first trainload arrived back in '43, everyone was a little nervous about the whole idea. I had my own doubts—especially when the commander said he was going to hire a couple of them to clean the offices. But honestly, after having several different men rotate through our office to help out, I think most worries are unfounded."

"If the German army is made up of fun-loving linguists," Clarissa said dryly, "I don't understand why there's still a war going on."

Mrs. Frey didn't get riled. "Well, of course not all the prisoners are like Private Bauer and Sergeant Brock," she said. "Some of them—especially the first arrivals—were hard-core. But most of the more uncooperative ones have been transferred down to the camp in Oklahoma. And only the most trustworthy would be assigned to work details off the military reservation—if it's allowed at all. I think there's a question about having enough guards to allow it—and they won't take any chances with that." She tried to reassure Clarissa. "Really, Mrs. Hale. You needn't worry in the least if PW crews end up working on your sister's ranch."

At that moment I really wished Will Bishop was sitting at the table. I wouldn't have *said* "I told you so," but I would have thought it.

"Well, that's fine, then," I said.

Mrs. Frey looked down at Mia. "But we *will* have to ask your daddy."

It was probably my imagination, but I could have sworn little Mia actually *shivered*.

Clarissa got up from the table. I probably should have helped her with something out in the kitchen, but the truth is I didn't want to listen to her rant. She was upset about the PWs, and now she would be upset that Mrs. Frey had called the Four Pines *my* ranch when, in fact, Clarissa was part owner. She had happily relinquished the running of the place to me, but every once in a while she liked to remind me that our daddy had left the place to the both of us. And to have Mrs. Frey assume otherwise was likely to be an irritation. It might, in fact, just result in Clarissa's trying to force her will into the PW issue. So I didn't give her the chance to start ranting. There's no rant in the world like a Clarissa Jackson rant. How Ben Hale has stood it all these years, I don't know. Then again, maybe he's found a way to charm even that out of her.

———

"Did I hear right? Did Daddy just tell me that Uncle Will has moved off the ranch?" Jo had followed me to the car.

"He's working at the remount," I said. "Leastways that's where he was headed when he drove out."

"But . . . ?"

I shook my head—my way of warning Jo not to pry. I forced a laugh. "Don't worry yourself over it. We had a disagreement. Will doesn't want the Germans. I need them. It'll blow over. He'll come home."

"He'd better," Jo said. "Johnny would have a fit if he thought you two were on the outs."

"And don't you be the one to write and tell him," I said. "We don't want Johnny worrying over things at home. Remember what they told us about that. Only good news from home. No complaining."

"I won't say a word," Jo promised.

I hitched up my dress and slid behind the wheel of my truck. Jo's hand was on the door and I patted it. "Glad you fell in line with the plan at lunch today, hon. It'll be fun to have another blondie on the place."

Jo grinned. "Wait until you see the real Mia Frey," she said.

"The real Mia?"

"You'll see," Jo said.

"I expect I will," I replied, and started the truck. It coughed and sputtered a minute.

"You should have Daddy look under the hood for you," Jo commented.

"Not on Sunday, Jo. Can't have the preacher working on the Sabbath, now, can we?"

Jo laughed. "Guess not." She leaned into the truck and kissed me on the cheek. "I love you, Aunt CJ," she said.

"Pshaw," I said, and swiped my cheek. "What's got into you, child?!"

Jo grinned. "You don't fool me one bit, you old softie."

I put the truck in reverse. "See to it you keep that to yourself," I said, then let out the clutch and headed toward home. As I drove by the Frey place, Mia was standing at the front gate. She waved and blew me a kiss. It did my heart good to think about Mia and Jo occupying the two empty bedrooms at the Four Pines. And old Will Bishop could stay at Fort Robinson for as long as he wanted for all I cared.

Of course, I did. Care. But I wasn't about to let Will or anyone else know.

Chapter Five

Rebuke a wise man, and he will love thee.
PROVERBS 9:8B

WILL BISHOP HADN'T been at Fort Robinson for a week before he admitted to himself that he was miserable. It was, of course, completely the fault of one CJ Jackson. The woman turned up everywhere he went. Not in person, but since Will and CJ had grown up together in and around Fort Robinson, just about everywhere he looked he encountered a memory. As the weeks passed he tried not to think of her, but what could a man do? If he watched the sun rise, he was looking toward the old parade ground and the officers' quarters where he and his mother had come to live after his father died. While he lived in that house, he and CJ had played more pranks than a grown Will Bishop would ever own up to.

In the evenings, when the sun set over the bluffs in the distance, he was reminded of his and CJ's adventure up in those bluffs—and the fall that nearly ended his life. When he reported to the animal superintendent at the remount service, he walked past the very building where his own grandfather had performed the surgery that saved his life. And even though the fort had grown many times over from the days when Will and CJ were children here, the place was still one big memory album for the aging wrangler.

It wasn't just his childhood memories of the fort that bothered Will. Every morning when he got up and headed to the mess hall for breakfast, he couldn't help but think about CJ drinking coffee all alone in the Four Pines kitchen. He wondered if she missed him at all.

Every day, as he went about the business of trimming manes and filing hooves, of mucking out stalls and evaluating horses, something inevitably happened that made him wonder about one horse or another on the Four Pines. He knew those horses as well as a parent knew their own children, and it bothered him, not being the one who fed and watered and monitored their well-being. The idea of another wrangler handling "his" herd was something like what Will imagined it would be for a man to have his children answer to another daddy. He hadn't expected to worry over them so much.

Every night, when he bedded down on a cot outside a row of stalls so he could keep an eye on the horses, Will looked up at the roof above him and wished it was the familiar ceiling at home. He would never think of anyplace in the same way he did the Four Pines. The path between the Four Pines owned by Laina and Caleb Jackson and the Rocking B Ranch owned by Nathan and Charlotte Boone was so well-worn by the time CJ and Will were teenagers that people in the area began to call it the Jackson-Boone Trail.

Will had ridden that trail by moonlight to be with CJ the night her mother died. CJ flew up the trail bareback to get to the Rocking B when Jack Greyfoot brought the news that Will's parents had been killed in a train accident back east. He and CJ had gone east together to bring the bodies of Nathan and Charlotte Boone back home. They had stood side-by-side when Jack Greyfoot's body was lowered into the grave beside Rachel's. Every Decoration Day they made sure Jack got his due as hero of the Great War even as their fathers were remembered for their service in the Civil War. And while he would never admit it to anyone but himself, Will knew that none of those family ties or memories were what made the Four Pines home. No, Will realized, the Four Pines Ranch was home because CJ Jackson was there, and he missed her—so much that the first Sunday after he left, he darned near went to church just so he could sit in the back pew and see that scruffy black straw hat of hers up near the front.

Thinking about the straw hat set Will to grinning—it being something of a private joke between him and CJ ever since Clarissa Hale tried to banish it from her sister's wardrobe.

"Say it straight out, Clarissa," CJ had snapped the Sunday Clarissa hinted at CJ's need to "keep up appearances" since she was part of the reverend's own family. "You know I don't like it when you hint."

"That hat," Clarissa had said, pointing to the hook by the back door where CJ kept her Sunday-go-to-meetin' hat, "is a disgrace."

"Really?" CJ said, glancing in Will's direction.

Will had to turn away to hide his smile, because he could see in the old gal's blue eyes that CJ Jackson had just decided that she would probably wear the black straw hat until the day she died.

"Yes," Clarissa said. "It's out of style by about fifteen years."

"Really?" CJ repeated.

Will wondered at Clarissa's oblivious perseverance when she offered to help CJ shop for something more stylish. Then he renamed oblivious perseverance "stupidity" when Clarissa went on to say, "And while we're at it, we really should get you a decent pair of shoes. Ben wouldn't say it, but it just isn't fair for his own family to be the laughingstock of the congregation."

Will saw CJ's cheeks grow red. Ordinarily he would have hightailed it out to the barn at that moment, but since he wasn't the cause of CJ's impending temper tantrum, he lingered.

"Laughingstock," CJ repeated. "I didn't know."

"Well, of course not," Clarissa said, practically falling over herself to be kind. "I know you'd never deliberately embarrass Ben. But really, CJ . . . cowboy boots with a dress?" She snorted. "And the same hat every Sunday, winter and summer . . . for years?"

CJ went to the back door. "Ben Hale," she called. When Ben peeked out from beneath the hood of his Nash, CJ waved him up to the house.

"Clarissa says I'm the laughingstock of the congregation. She says I've embarrassed you by wearing my boots and my straw hat to church." CJ pointed to the hat. "Is that true, Ben Hale? Do I embarrass you?"

Will had never seen the Reverend Hale at a loss for words until that moment when the preacher raised his eyebrows and looked in disbelief at his wife. When he finally spoke it was to order his wife to help with the car outside.

For a moment, Will wished he could have wielded the kind of power over Mamie Parsons that Ben Hale apparently held over Clarissa, for at her husband's command the woman meekly ducked her head and scooted out the back door. Will couldn't resist going to the window over the kitchen sink and watching to see what would happen next. Once at the car, Clarissa slid into the passenger seat while Ben leaned against the driver's side and spoke to her through the open driver's side window. Will had never seen the reverend so animated. His entire upper body shook with the force of what he was telling his wife.

Will chuckled, but just when he turned to describe the scene to CJ, he was astonished to see that, while she was sweeping the kitchen floor, she was also crying.

He cleared his throat. CJ swept faster. "Come on, old girl," he said. "Don't you give her the satisfaction of seeing she's made you cry. She'll take those tears for a personal victory."

"I never meant to embarrass Ben," CJ muttered. She allowed Will to put his arms around her, but she didn't let go of the broom.

"And you never have," Will patted her on the shoulder. "You know how men are. They don't even notice such things."

"That's nice of you to say, Will. But it's a bald-faced lie."

"Is not," Will repeated.

"Is too," CJ insisted. "Just ask Mamie Parsons."

Will couldn't help his reaction to that name. He tensed up. CJ pulled away. He put one hand on each of the old girl's shoulders and looked her square in the eye. "You listen to me, CJ Jackson. Reverend Ben Hale is a real man—not a fool like I was when I was a young pup. And he wouldn't care if you wore your flannel shirt and your ten-gallon hat to church. And if you'll just take a look outside you'll know I'm telling you the truth." He gave her a little push, and she went to the kitchen window. Her tears stopped flowing as she watched Ben lecturing his wife.

Presently, Clarissa and Ben came to the door.

"I'm sorry," Clarissa said.

Will thought it sounded almost sincere.

"I wouldn't know what to do if that black straw hat wasn't in the third pew on the right every Sunday," Ben said.

Will knew that was sincere.

"I can only wish that half my congregation had a heart as good as yours, CJ," Ben said. He looked at his wife. "Go down to the barn and fetch Jo," he said. Clarissa went.

As soon as she was out of earshot, Ben said, "CJ—"

Will was never prouder of CJ Jackson than at that moment, because instead of dwelling on the hurt, the old girl rose to the occasion. "You know what, Ben," she interrupted. "The first time Clarissa brought you out to the Four Pines, I thought she'd corralled herself a real looker. Guess it's about time I told you that I'm very grateful for the fact that she also got herself a real man." She brushed the last of the tears off her cheeks—or maybe it was a fresh batch. Will couldn't be sure. Either way, she brushed them away and smiled up at Ben Hale, and while no more was said aloud, Will knew that volumes had been spoken.

It was memories like those—memories of CJ—that made him regret that Fort Robinson had been chosen as a site for a PW camp. If the Germans hadn't come . . . he'd still be at home. Pondering that thought, Will looked up from his chores and off toward the northwest, halfway thinking that if he could figure a way to salvage his pride . . .

"Mr. Bishop."

The voice at his side came so unexpectedly it made Will start. "What?" He sounded grumpy—which, he realized, was how he felt most of the time these days.

"Bill Harker wants you to meet him at the stud barn."

Will set the empty feed bucket in his hand on the ground and headed off in the direction of the barn where the stars of the remount's breeding program were housed. As he walked along, he passed a half-dead cotton-wood tree. He remembered the first time it had been struck by lightning. It was the first time he had allowed himself to be coaxed outside after his accident. It had taken a lot of effort for Will to once again be able to stand up straight, and even longer to make his legs work well enough to make it out the front door and into his grandpa's rocking chair to watch the incoming storm clouds.

Just when CJ had gone inside to get Will a pillow to prop up his weak side, lightning had struck the ancient tree. There was a magnificent flash of light, and a *pop* that echoed all the way to the bluffs behind the house and back. When CJ charged back out to the porch, Will was so excited he forgot to be ashamed of his faltering speech. "You sh-sh-shoulda seen it, CJ!" he blurted out.

Walking by the once-towering tree that still showed the damage from that long-ago night, Will thought back to all the hours CJ had spent helping him recover, encouraging him to walk, patiently waiting while he learned to talk again. She'd even stuck by him when he had that "spell of stupid" with Mamie Parsons. It made it hard not to have the old gal around. Real hard.

————

"He's a great steeplechaser and has incredible bloodlines," Bill Harker said as he and Will made their way along the row of box stalls in the stud barn. "But he's a regular prince of darkness to handle and most of the boys around here won't go near him after their first encounter. I'm glad you decided to come on board. If anybody can figure out a way to humor him, I expect it'll be you."

Will followed Harker down the row of stalls to the last one on the left where the alleged prince of darkness had resided since being kicked while servicing a mare. While the effects of the injury were no longer visible, the animal was obviously disinclined to reacquaint himself with any other living flesh. Will had heard the creature snorting and stomping at the sound of their approach. Now, as the two men stood outside the stall, the horse bared his teeth and charged the stall door. Then he wheeled away and gave it a solid kick with both hind feet punctuated by a shrill whinny that Will could only describe as a scream.

"Whoa." Will backed away, almost stumbling over his bad foot. He leaned against the empty stall on the opposite side of the walkway and stood watching the stallion, who had plastered his rump against the back side of his own stall and stood there, rolling his eyes and alternately pawing the straw and tossing his head.

"We let him out twice a day—alone, of course—just long enough to muck out the stall, give him fresh water and oats, that sort of thing. You can see from the condition of his coat that he hasn't been brushed in a long time. And he isn't getting any calmer as the days go by."

Will tilted his head as he studied the animal. Without turning his gaze from the horse, he asked, "You got plans for that stall next to him?"

"We need it, but we can't use it. I thought maybe all he wanted was a stablemate, but that was a disaster. He nearly tore himself up trying to tear the wall down last time we put another horse in there. You should see him when we let him out in the corral." He paused. "I tried to get Bob Hanover to take him over to his place. He was thinking it over when he got word about his boy Ron getting killed. I'm not going to bother him with remount troubles right now."

Just the mention of Ron Hanover's death on Iwo Jima put a knot in Will's stomach. He hadn't had a letter from Johnny in a week. Or had he? Maybe CJ was being bullheaded about that, too.

"The truth is, Will, I would have asked you first, but this is definitely a hands-on project and I just never dreamed you'd be open to coming on here."

Will shrugged. "Times change." He studied the horse. "I'll just stand here a bit and see what I can see. If you don't mind, that is."

"You do whatever you think will help," Harker said. "I probably should have put him down weeks ago. He's just not the kind of animal we need around here. But . . . look at him. He's one of the most gorgeous pieces of horseflesh I've had the privilege to try to handle. And he's smart. If we can find a way to work the cussedness out of him, we'll put him up at the sale and hope for the best."

"You know how I work," Will said. "I'm not gonna hog-tie him. It's going to have to be his decision whether he trusts people or not. And that could take a while."

As the men spoke, the stallion began to move again, tossing his head and snorting. He kicked the side of his stall. Harker jumped. "I've never been afraid of a horse before, but I'm close to it with that son of a gun."

Will nodded. "He's got the evil eye, that's for sure." After a minute he added, "Can you keep the other boys out of this end of the barn for . . . oh, say, an hour or so?"

"I'm shorthanded as it is. They'll be more than happy to let you have him to yourself for as long as you want it." He sidled along the stall opposite the stallion's. Only when he was out of the horse's sight did he step to the center of the walkway. At the far end of the barn he turned and said, "Glad to have you, Bishop. Hope you stay on."

Will slowly raised his left hand to acknowledge the comment. When he did so, the stallion let out another scream and half-reared, flashing his front hooves. "Ah, shucks," Will said in a monotone. "Stop that nonsense, you big galoot. You aren't scaring me, and you're just making yourself ugly."

The horse screamed again and pawed the straw.

"Uh-huh, uh-huh. Keep being stupid. See if you don't end up dogmeat for the K-9 corps."

The horse snorted and tossed his head. He stared at Will.

Will stared back. After several minutes, the horse looked away and then back at Will, who watched the animal's ears flicking about. *You just keep listening,* Will thought, but he didn't say it aloud. Instead, he leaned back against the empty stall behind him and, hooking his thumbs through the belt loops of his jeans, kept watching the horse.

———

For the greater part of the next three days, Will did little more than stand opposite the stallion's stall watching his every move. When the "Prince of Darkness" was let out into the corral and the stall door closed to keep him out, it was Will who mucked out the stall. While he worked, he ran his hands along the iron bars forming the top half of the stall walls. He handled the water bucket and, after he poured oats into the horse's feed bucket, sifted the grain through his hands until everything the animal came in contact with bore Will Bishop's scent. At first it drove the animal into a frenzy. But by the third day, when the horse charged back inside his stall and lowered his head, he walked from place to place, snuffling.

"Yeah, that's right, Buster," Will said from his observation post—which, by now, was a kind of couch formed from bales of hay stacked out in the walkway. "You learn that scent, Buster Boy. That smell is connected to every good thing you get. Water. Oats. Fresh straw. There's nothing good coming your way without that smell on it. And this voice. You learn this voice, too. Your life depends on it, Buster."

———

"Uncle Will?"

Will lifted the shovel full of horse manure and turned around just in time to see Jo appear in the walkway outside Buster's empty stall.

"Well, well," Will said, "what brings you to the fort on a Wednesday afternoon?" His heart thumped. "Something wrong out at the ranch?"

"Daddy's talking to Captain Donovan about doing a chapel service for the PWs," Jo said. "And yes, there is something wrong at the ranch." Jo put her hands on her hips. "You moved out."

Will shrugged. "Oh, that." He reached for Buster's water bucket and headed up the walkway toward the water spigot.

"How could you, Uncle Will? How could you leave *now*? When she's already shorthanded?"

"She won't be shorthanded for long," Will said. "She's got herself a fine plan to take care of that."

"The PWs," Jo said. "I know. She told me. Us. Mama's having a fit over me going out there."

Will nodded. "I'm not surprised."

"Mrs. Frey set them straight, though." At Will's questioning look, Jo explained. "She's been working here at the prison headquarters as a secretary. They have a couple of the PWs working for them, and Mrs. Frey doesn't think there's anything to worry over. In fact, she's letting little Mia come out for a visit, too." Jo frowned. "Things aren't going very well for them right now."

"Hank still not back to work?" Will asked.

Jo shook her head. Quickly, she told Will all she knew about Hank Frey's homecoming.

"That's a shame," Will said. "A real shame." He hung the water bucket back in the stall and went for oats. On the opposite side of the back stall wall, Buster landed a thump on the door and snorted. "You just calm down, you big galoot," Will called.

Jo headed across the stall and put her hand on the door. "I'll—"

"No!" Will lurched across the stall to stop her. When Jo snatched her hand back and looked at him, Will explained. "I've got myself a real holy terror to try to handle. Nobody around here wants a thing to do with him. If I can't gentle him—at least make him manageable—he's gonna be dog food."

"Can I at least see him?" Jo said.

It was then that Will noticed the door was actually open a crack. Through the crack he could see a dark bay coat. Buster was standing quietly. If Will hadn't known better, he would have thought the horse was actually listening to their conversation.

"Say something," Will said, pointing to the crack in the door.

Jo followed his gaze. "Hi there, boy," she said gently. "What's all the fuss about, anyway? Are you so bad?"

From the other side of the door Buster snorted and stomped. But he stayed near the door.

Will pursed his lips and watched. He looked at Jo. "Come with me." Leading her out of the stall, he closed the door and latched it. At the water spigot he said, "You wait here. I'm gonna let him back inside. But don't you move until I tell you."

While Jo watched, Will went into the stall next to Buster's where he pulled on the rope he had rigged up to operate the sliding door at the back of Buster's stall so that anyone could let the horse in and out without getting near him. As soon as the door slid open far enough, Buster charged into his stall and to the door. He kicked the wall and snorted, going through the now-familiar routine of snuffling around for Will's scent on everything, tossing his head, and generally causing a ruckus. Will retreated to the walkway just outside the stall and took his seat on the hay-bale sofa.

"Now, Jo," he said, without looking her way, "tell me again what's new with you."

Jo swallowed. "All right," she said, her voice a low-pitched monotone. "I said you've got to come back to the Four Pines. For me."

At Jo's first words, Buster snorted and tossed his head. Both his ears pointed in the direction of her voice.

"Keep talking," Will said.

"It just won't be the same without you. Aunt CJ doesn't say anything, but she misses you. I can tell."

"Keep talking," Will said as Buster stepped to the corner of the stall, obviously trying to see the owner of the female voice.

"And what would Johnny say if he knew you two were fighting like this?"

Will held up his hand. Without taking his eyes off Buster, he motioned her toward him. "Walk this way. Real slow. You've got this monster curious. Let's see what he thinks when he can take a look at you. But you stay on the far side of the walkway, and if he puts up a fuss you hightail it right back out of sight, you hear? He can't hurt you, but I don't want him hurting himself banging around in there, either. Now keep talking as you come this way."

"You once told me that Aunt CJ stuck by you through what you called your 'spell of stupid,' and I understand how you wouldn't want to be around German PWs, but honestly, Uncle Will, don't you think you could stick with Aunt CJ through what you think is *her* 'spell of stupid'?" Jo was standing next to Will by now. She came to a halt and stopped talking. "Wow," she said abruptly. "He's . . . wow."

Will nodded. "I'd say 'wow' about says it." He chuckled softly. "All this time trying to gentle him and all I had to do was introduce a female. Seems he's partial to the ladies."

"That just might be the most beautiful horse I've ever seen," Jo said.

Will nodded. "I tend to agree with you."

"Imagine what he'd look like if a person could only groom him."

"Not a chance of that . . . yet," Will said. "He's earned the name Prince of Darkness from everyone around here, although I'm partial to calling him Buster."

"Buster," Jo said, and stepped toward the stall.

Buster tossed his head, and, whirling around, presented his hindquarters and smacked the stall wall with both feet.

Jo jumped back, laughing nervously.

Buster snorted and tossed his head again, then plunged his muzzle into the bucket of oats hanging in the corner of his stall, and began to eat.

"He's big on letting humans know he's a tough guy," Will said, smiling.

"Just like you," Jo quipped.

Will frowned. "What?"

"Oh . . . you know what I mean. You make a point and then drive it home." She motioned to the barn. "We already knew you're a tough guy, Uncle Will. You can come on home now."

Chapter Six

Wives, submit yourselves unto your
own husbands, as unto the Lord.
EPHESIANS 5:22

JO HALE WAS BEGINNING to believe that her father had some unusual form of the gift of healing. It sure did seem to her that miracles happened when Daddy "laid on hands" under the hood of the 1935 Nash Aeroform sedan he had been driving for as long as Jo could remember. There just had to be a supernatural component to the way the old rust bucket simply would not die, something beyond the known fact that the Reverend Benjamin Hale was an anomaly—a preacher with mechanical skills. As a child, Jo had been present more than once when Hank Frey's predecessor at the garage on Main Street had fiddled and wiggled and shook his head and told the preacher that "this was it," and he had better be looking for another car.

"Well," Daddy would say, as he put his hands on his hips, "I guess it had to happen sooner or later." And he would close the hood. But later Jo would peek in the garage window at home and there Daddy would be, tinkering and trying, and sure as the sunrise, the next morning Daddy would announce at breakfast that the Lord had decided to revive the old Nash yet again.

But on the Sunday afternoon when the Nash seemed to balk at the idea of taking the family out to Fort Robinson for the first PW service, Jo almost wished the car's guardian angels were on vacation. For the first time in her memory, Daddy had not been able to cajole Mother into having a good attitude about something against her will, and as Clarissa climbed silently into the front seat of the car with icy compliance, Jo's stomach did a flip-flop.

Just because Mother hadn't made a big fuss over last week's Sunday dinner—probably because Mrs. Frey was there—didn't mean she was going to give up, and she had taken more than one opportunity in the past week to protest. Even when everyone was in shock over the sudden death of President Roosevelt, Mother was not distracted from her goal. "Our beloved president is dead, Ben. It's the worst time imaginable to appear to be soft toward the enemy. The neighbors will shun us," she said.

When that did not sway Daddy, she tried another tack. "What about poor Hank Frey? How do you suppose he'll feel, knowing his own *pastor—*"

"Forgave the enemy the way the Bible says we should?" Daddy interrupted.

Mother pursed her lips and shook her head. "We can't be expected to obey every single jot and tittle. Not at a time like this."

"I suspect God knew about World War II when He wrote His book, Clarissa. And of course we are expected to obey. *Especially* at a time like this." Jo's dad tilted his head and looked at his wife. "I've tried to ignore the still, small voice inside telling me to do this. I can't ignore it anymore."

"Well, I'm not going," Mother said firmly.

Jo had seen very little of what her father had sometimes referred to as a "tendency to bullheadedness in my youth," but she got a glimpse of it then. "You are going," Daddy said quietly. "I'll need you to play the piano." Then he turned and looked at Jo. "Both of you are going. It will send a more positive message, both to the community and to the prisoners." He looked steadily across the table at his wife.

As her two parents warred across the dinner table, Jo watched, expecting her mother's chin to tremble and her eyes to fill with tears. Mother cried when she was angry. When no tears materialized, Jo's midsection tightened. It was a serious fight when Mother didn't try to wheedle and Daddy didn't joke. His face was gentle, but his usually clear blue eyes were stern as he stared down his wife. It seemed like hours before Mother swallowed, cleared her throat, and said, "All right, Ben. If that's what you want."

Daddy gave a little nod. "Good." He stood up and went to the door. "I'm going to go across to my study and work on my sermon," he said, then turned back. "It's not about what *I* want, Clarissa. It's the Lord who wants it." He glanced at Jo. "From all of us. The Lord's compassions are new every morning. He extends them to *all* men. We can do no less."

Jo rose to help her mother with supper dishes, but Mother waved her away. "Does that long black skirt still fit you?" she asked.

Jo frowned. "What?"

"The long black skirt you wore to Mr. Koch's funeral last year. Do you still have it?"

"I suppose so. Somewhere."

"Well, dig it out." Mother looked at her. "And I'll be getting you up early in the morning to tame that mane of yours. I won't have those—" She swallowed hard, then drew herself up. "We'll be dressing very conservatively," she said.

Jo retreated to her room, where she dug out the despised black skirt. The tension in her mother's voice was spilling over into her own mood, but when she thought about it, she realized that part of the tension was a tiny thrill of danger and adventure. She was going *inside* the prisoner compound. She was sick of hearing about Michelle Brighton from Whitney and how she'd volunteered for service. She'd just read an article in the local newspaper touting the "local girl serving her country," and there was Michelle's face plastered on the front page. Now Delores said she was going to be a WAAC, too. Well, Jo thought, let Michelle and Delores go off to Fort Des Moines, so what. Neither of them would get so much as a glimpse of the enemy in Iowa. When they came home on leave it would be Josephine Hale who'd seen the Nazis, not Michelle Brighton or Delores Black.

What, Jo wondered, perching on the foot of her bed, would it be like? Would they goose-step in? Would they have hateful stares when Daddy got up to preach? A lot of people in Crawford had opinions and ideas about the Germans, but Daddy kept saying it was all based on rumor and not to be believed. Mrs. Black said they didn't know what Jell-O was. A guard at the fort had told her the German cooks mixed Jell-O in hot water and drank it. Jo pictured the round-faced PW on the train drinking Jell-O. What, she wondered, did they think about Nebraska? What kind of people were the Germans, anyway?

The only thing Jo knew for sure about the German prisoners was what Mrs. Frey said about the two working in her office. And the only real "old-country German" Jo had ever known was Mrs. Koch, who was about as far from a square-jawed Nazi as a person could imagine. Mrs. Koch was more like everyone's favorite grandma. Her special cookies had become an expected part of every Christmas Eve celebration at the church, and she was always crocheting a baby blanket or knitting slippers for someone.

For the first time since the war began, Jo wondered if Mrs. Koch, who spoke English with a thick German accent, had relatives back in Germany. Had someone she knew lived in Dresden? Had they been hurt in the air raids? Johnny had been part of the mission back in February that destroyed three-fourths of that city. Jo didn't like the feeling it gave her to think about Germans as something other than "the ones who are trying to kill Johnny." And after tomorrow she was going to have more than just the muddled impressions from the train car. She was curious and excited and a little bit afraid.

Grabbing the black skirt and a blouse of her own choosing, Jo headed out to the kitchen to set up the ironing board. "Is this blouse all right, Mother?" she asked as she plugged in the iron and sprinkled the skirt with water. She added before her mother answered, "And can I wear a hat?"

"Of course you should wear a hat," Mother snapped.

"Are you . . . afraid, Mama?" Jo asked.

"Of course I'm not afraid!"

Jo knew her Mother was not only afraid, but also more angry at Daddy than Jo had ever seen. As Jo pressed the wrinkles out of the black skirt she'd declared "hopelessly frumpy" a year earlier, she pondered the idea of a God who told Daddy to go to the prison camp and preach. She didn't doubt that Daddy was sincere. He really believed he was doing God's will. What she didn't understand was why, if God spoke so clearly to Daddy, He didn't take a minute to give Mother the same message.

And now here they were, loaded into the car, and Jo wasn't sure if she wanted it to start or not. Maybe, Jo thought, Daddy had misunderstood the message from God. While Daddy rolled up his sleeves and jiggled parts under the hood, Mother and Jo retreated to the kitchen. For nearly half an hour Mother sat drinking tea and thumping the tabletop with her fingers in a nervous rhythm.

Footsteps sounded on the back porch. "Josephine," Daddy called, "Come out and help me!"

Jo climbed behind the steering wheel and followed her father's instructions and finally, with a backfire that sounded like a gunshot, the car rumbled to life. Daddy's blue eyes sparkled with joy as he closed the hood and winked at her. "Praise the Lord!" he said, and headed inside to wash his hands. Jo slid into the backseat, almost grateful for the unfashionable length of the black skirt that would hide most of her bare legs. Aunt CJ's ration notwithstanding, a girl had to be careful with nylons, and Jo was not about to waste a good pair of nylons on a bunch of prisoners who probably smelled of sauerkraut.

The ride westward to Fort Robinson passed in unnatural quiet. Mother was taking pains to let Daddy know exactly what she thought of his idea. She sat with her head turned so she could see out the side window. She seemed to be studying every detail of the bluffs that formed a ridge looming above Highway 20 as if she'd never seen them before. As the Nash turned off the highway that divided Fort Robinson into "new" to the north and "old" to the south and wound its way past the old fort parade ground and toward the prison compound erected not far from where old Red Cloud himself had made camp and traded with the white men invading his ancestral home, Jo's pulse quickened.

When they came to a gate Jo relaxed a little. None other than Deacon Tom Hanson was waiting outside the guardhouse to greet them. When he leaned down and tipped his hat to Mother, you would never have known she was anything but excited about serving the Lord among the German prisoners of war.

"You got a beautiful spring day for your drive out, Mrs. Hale," Deacon Hanson said.

"Indeed we did," Mother replied. She even nodded inside the fence. "I didn't expect to see spring flowers planted here."

"There's a lot that's unexpected about these men," Deacon Hanson said. "You could have quite a choir depending on who shows up. There are some true musicians inside this fence. Back in '43 we had the entire 47th Infantry Regiment Band, but they were transferred out. Still, just last Christmas Eve the band that plays for their variety shows lined up just over there and serenaded their guards. I wasn't here, but Sergeant Isaacson said it was quite beautiful."

"Now you're making me nervous," Mother said, laughing as if she didn't have a care in the world. "I'm just here to plunk out the four parts written in the hymnal."

"I'm sure they will appreciate it," Deacon Hanson said warmly. He looked past Mother at Daddy. "Captain Donovan said to park over there by headquarters." He gestured toward the building, and Jo recognized the deacon's car. "I'll wait for you here."

"You didn't tell me Tom was going to join us," Mother said as Daddy parked the Nash.

"I wasn't sure if he would be able to come."

"We should have given him a ride."

"I offered. He said he'd rather drive out on his own."

Jo was relieved when Mother waited for Daddy to get out and walk around to her door. Things were thawing.

Daddy held out his hand. Mother took it, and he wrapped it through his arm. "Josephine," Daddy said, "carry the hymnal for your mother."

Jo felt a shiver go up her spine at the thought of walking right through the prison compound, then a pang of regret when Deacon Hanson motioned them toward the chapel just a short distance away. It wasn't much of a walk.

Still, they were inside the fence, and all around them were guard towers. It was at once comforting and unnerving.

"What did I tell you?" Daddy said to Mother, patting her hand. "There's nothing to be afraid of."

"I'm not afraid," Mother snapped. "I'm mad. What on earth a man could be thinking to bring his wife and daughter into this—"

"Look over there," Daddy said and nodded toward a trio of WAACs making their way toward the K-9 compound. "They have their own two-story barracks, a mess hall—even their own beauty shop—all right across the road behind the new officers' quarters."

"What woman in her right mind would want to be a WAAC?" Mother mumbled.

"Delores does," Jo spoke up.

"Exactly my point," Mother snapped.

"I think it would be fascinating," Jo said.

"Well, I don't know how fascinating it is," Daddy replied, "but they perform all kinds of important jobs. Secretarial, motor pool, all kinds of things."

"Join the army and drive a truck," Mother said. "Just what every mother dreams for her little girl. Unless, of course, she can be housed within a mile of a thousand or more Nazi prisoners. That's even *more* special."

"Tom said one of responsibilities of the WAACs is driving the trucks that take the prisoners back and forth to their jobs over at the remount depot. You know the men can't be dangerous or that would never be allowed."

"Well, thank you, Reverend Hale," Mother said with exaggerated sweetness. "I feel so very much better." She looked at Jo. "We'll sign you right up, honey, soon as we get back to town. Who needs a college education when they can *pump gas* for the *motor pool*?!"

Things were quiet as the three headed up the steps and went inside the chapel. Deacon Hanson followed them up the center aisle. "It's hard to imagine that not so long ago some of the PWs were worshiping in Lutheran churches in beautiful neighborhoods."

Jo was surprised when Mother grumbled again at Daddy—this time within Deacon Hanson's hearing, "Let's just get this over with and get home."

Chapter Seven

The way of a fool is right in his own eyes. . . .
PROVERBS 12:15

RELAX, MAN. JUST RELAX. Inwardly, Private Franco Romani crossed himself and begged the Blessed Virgin to keep his voice from shaking when he made his announcement to the mess hall filled with hungry PWs. He scanned the room, watching the prisoners while he reviewed all the reasons not to be nervous.

You expected that Private Bauer to come at you with his fists the first time you talked to him. Did it happen? No.

Romani remembered the incident as if it had happened this morning instead of weeks ago. A burly sergeant had sent him to stop a prisoner from rummaging through a barrel of items they had been ordered to hand over. When the prisoner stood up with a shaving kit in his hand, he towered over Romani. The prisoner started to babble and gesture, and a voice said, "He's trying to explain," and there was an Aryan poster boy looking at Romani with clear blue eyes and an unreadable expression. Feeling surrounded by the enemy, Romani barely managed to stifle the urge to step back as he barked, "Orders are to leave personal items in the barrels."

The boy began to babble again. Romani could hear the pleading tone even through what he considered to be the almost animalistic sounds of the German language.

"He asks you to take pity," the blond poster boy said. "He begs you to let him keep the shaving kit. It was a gift from his sister. She died just before the war."

The giant looked from Romani to the poster boy and nodded. It was getting embarrassing. The kid was almost in tears. "Give it here," Romani blurted out, and snatched the shaving kit away. He opened it. Looking over his shoulder, he saw the sergeant who had ordered him to handle the situation striding toward a much more threatening-looking collection of prisoners on the other side of the holding room. "Here," he said, and thrust the kit toward the kid. "But get moving." He gestured toward the poster boy. "Both of you. Over there."

"Danke, danke, danke," the kid said, bobbing up and down, and bowing as he lumbered to where Romani directed him. To keep from being called to help with a group of prisoners that looked hardened enough to have been Hitler's own staff, Romani pretended to shuttle the kid and his friend to the opposite side of the room.

And now here they were, a train ride, a delousing, and two weeks of imprisonment later, having caused no trouble at all. So why, Romani wondered, couldn't he get rid of the knot in his gut?

Not even Gunnar Stroh, who looked like he would relish the idea of eliminating Franco Romani from the earth, had caused any trouble. He grumbled in German once in a while behind a guard's back, but that was all. However, Romani was certain that one of the homemade weapons found in last month's sweep of the prison compound belonged to Stroh. The man still bore watching.

While Romani congratulated himself on getting "his" prisoners to Nebraska without incident, he pressed his back against the mess hall door and clenched his hands. He was certain his military bearing was part of the reason he'd had no trouble. He had determined to be gruff and unapproachable ever since he escorted the men through the delousing process in New York and then past the doctor who plunged a very long needle into their backsides with relish. As long as he could keep them thinking he was a no-nonsense kind of guard, maybe he'd make it through. As he stood looking out over the mess hall, he could feel sweat trickling down his back between his shoulder blades. The men must never know how poorly Franco Romani had done in basic training.

Nothing happened on the train, he reminded himself. *Nothing has happened here in Nebraska, either—unless you count the dead cow lying across the tracks when we went through town.* Romani almost sighed audibly. His image of life in the army had never included living in a place where the biggest news of the day might be a cow getting struck by lightning and stopping a train for a few minutes. Although talking to those two girls had definitely been a good thing. If those two were any indication, they grew them pretty out west.

The quiet in the mess hall brought him back to the moment. He was supposed to make an announcement. How long had he been daydreaming by the door? He cleared his throat and barked out, "Attention! Those who wish to attend the afternoon church service should be ready to fall out at exactly fourteen hundred hours. I will escort you to the chapel. As we have announced, the service will be conducted by the Baptist minister from Crawford."

Darn. He had forgotten to ask Dieter Brock to translate. But without even a nod from Romani, Brock stood up and shouted German. Romani could only assume it must be the announcement about the new chapel service. Being in a room full of babbling prisoners got on a man's nerves after a while. Tiring quickly of standing still, Romani sauntered down the row of tables while the men finished eating. As he walked, conversations stopped, then started up again after he had passed. Nothing bothered him more than when they mumbled behind his back. Well, he thought, as he walked the perimeter of the room, that wasn't exactly true. Army food bothered him. And the boredom. And, he thought, as he walked past the Aryan poster boy . . . the fact that Angelina hadn't written. Not once. He could not suppress the fear that in spite of her promise to him, Angelina had kept going to the club for servicemen just around the corner from the apartment she shared with four other girls back home in Brooklyn. He was writing her every day—and Franco Romani was not a man who wrote letters. He was not, for that matter, a man to wear his feelings on his sleeve. But thinking of Angelina was one of the few things that kept him sane. Angelina thought he was brave. Angelina was proud of him.

Beloved Angelina, he had written only the night before.

Imagine nothingness and still you cannot imagine the place to which I have been sent. This part of Nebraska is called the Sandhills, but from what I have seen there is much more sand than hills. The view from the train was very discouraging, although there is a ridge of bluffs not far from the military reservation with some interesting Indian legends attached to them. I will save those for another letter.

It is very hard to look at the mounds of food on these prisoners' plates and think of how you must count stamps in a ration book. They have German cooks and no rationing. Sausage and sauerkraut and rye bread and those little cookies called pfefferneusse. (Remember that old couple who ran the bakery around the corner? They made piles of those things at Christmas). And plenty of butter and sugar and whatever else they want. Well, not everything—but still.

How I miss my girl! The citizens of the nearby town have tried to make a Servicemen's Club, and while it is well intentioned, it is not much to a boy from Brooklyn who is used to dancing his weekends away with the prettiest girl in town. And besides, if I have asked you not to go to the club in New York, the least I can do is stay away from the female company in Crawford.

I could tell you many stories of the train ride out here, but the most amusing was when one of the men accused us of running the trains in circles. He couldn't believe America was so big. I must admit I almost agree with him. I didn't think it would take us so long to get out here. Nor did I think things would be so desolate. Why anyone would choose to live in Nebraska, I cannot say. Honestly, one expects Indians to come charging across the prairie at any moment. Do not worry. I have not seen a single Indian yet, although Sergeant Isaacson says there are some Sioux employed as wranglers over on the remount part of the post.

The Germans are interested in the western legends. One day when a very spirited debate was going on, my translator said they were talking about a German writer named Karl May who wrote about the American West. He is the favorite writer of some of these men, and they seem to actually be excited about being out here. "It would be wonderful to ride a stallion across the prairie," one of them said. Of course they are thinking of riding to freedom, although after being a Nazi they don't know what freedom is. But they don't know that they don't know. The materials in their reading room are designed to introduce them to the idea. And there are classes on American government and democracy. I am surprised at how many of them attend both these classes and the church services. Yes. Church. There was a weekly Lutheran service and a weekly mass already in place when I arrived with my prisoners, and now the Baptist minister from Crawford is coming on Sunday afternoons. Never fear, America—the Nazis are getting overdoses of religion during their stay in our fair country.

Fort Robinson is actually three different places with separate military headquarters and organizations to run each one. In addition to the prisoner of war camp, there is the remount service and the K-9 corps. Remount takes in all the cavalry horses from the army and sees that they are "remounted" by civilians. There are thousands of horses just across the road. They arrive by the trainload and horse sales take place every few weeks. Some of the men want to learn to ride while they are here, but I am not one of them.

In addition to horses, we have dogs, dogs, and more dogs. Over a thousand are being trained as sentries, scouts, or messengers. The K-9 has separate barracks and mess halls from us, so I don't have much to do with them. But I hear them. Every night—barking and yapping and baying at the moon. When I think I have it bad being assigned to guard Nazi prisoners, I realize I could be slaughtering horses to feed the dogs or shoveling manure by the ton. If only you could convince your parents to let you take the train to visit me, I would have nothing to complain about.

The Germans aren't too bad. Of the men in my compound I am only concerned about one or two who have hung Nazi flags over their beds and seem to *be waiting for America to be invaded by the German navy. The other day one of the men was taking the eagle off his uniform to barter for something, and a hardcase named Gunnar Stroh told him he'd better keep it, that he would need it for the occupation. I only know this because it came out after we broke up the fight that ensued. Don't worry. Stroh is in the minority. Others are almost friendly, although I am keeping my eye on my translator. Sometimes I think that beneath his blond hair is a mind plotting escape.*

––––

While his mind wandered, Private Franco Romani was the center of attention for one table of prisoners in the mess hall where he was supposed to keep order. Seated at a table with five other men who, if not friends, were at least a loose association of men who had walked through the prison experience together, Gunnar Stroh nodded his almost bald graying head toward the daydreaming guard and muttered, "He's gone again." He shook his head. "If I would have spent as much time as that idiot does in another place, I'd have died in the first week of battle."

"He's never been in a battle," Dieter Brock offered. "You should have been in our car on the train. He held his rifle like we used to hold sticks when we were children playing at war."

Across from Brock, Rolf Shrader twisted around and peered toward the door, then leaned forward and whispered to the table of six men, "Ten American cents says five minutes."

Stroh shook his head. "Too easy," he said. "They'll be calling us all to line up and fall out soon. He'll have to stop daydreaming."

"All right," Rolf said, sighing. "*Ten* minutes. But you have to bet twice as much." He looked around the table. "And you ALL have to bet."

Bruno Bauer's eyes grew wide, and the young giant shook his head. "Not me," he said. "I need my money."

"What for?" Rolf said. "It isn't real money, anyway. It's not like you can take it home."

Bruno shrugged. "Maybe not, but I can buy soap at the canteen and take *that* home to Mama. And all my cousins."

Stroh looked at the younger man with disdain. "Taking soap home to Mama, are you? What a good little boy you are." He reached over and pinched Bruno's earlobe.

"Hey!" Bauer pulled away.

When Stroh reached for the other ear, his hand was stopped in midair by Dieter Brock's palm. "Leave him alone," Dieter said.

Stroh stared at Brock for a moment. When the other man didn't back down, he rattled off a few choice names for both Bruno—whom he called a weakling among other things—and Dieter.

Brock stared at Stroh, unmoved by the man's string of profanities. "Leave him alone," he repeated. "Just because you don't have a mother in Germany waiting for you to come home doesn't give you a reason to make fun of Bruno." He paused and then said diplomatically, "And you will agree that Germany will need its mothers and sons to rebuild."

"Right," Shrader chimed in. "And the mothers and sons will need soap or . . ." He made a comical face and held his nose.

"You," Stroh said with a disgusted grimace. "Always joking."

"That's me," Shrader said, and bobbled his head from side to side, "your favorite comedian." He peered at Stroh out of the corner of his eyes and worked his eyebrows up and down.

Bruno burst out laughing.

"You there!"

At the sound of Romani's voice, the men at the table glanced at the clock at the front of the mess hall.

"Three minutes," Stroh said and held out his hand toward Shrader. "You lost the bet. Pay me."

Romani's voice, thick with its own accent from the land of Mussolini, sounded across the room. "I repeat . . . those attending chapel must form up outside their barracks at fourteen hundred hours."

While the men didn't need an interpreter to know what was said, everyone pretended not to understand. Gunnar Stroh looked around his table in smug satisfaction as the young Italian guard's face flushed with the realization that he had failed—again—to ask Dieter to translate for him.

Dieter stood up. He repeated the order and grabbed his tray. "Come on," he said to Rolf Shrader. "We can get in a game of table tennis before the service starts."

Gunnar Stroh frowned. "You? Church?!"

Dieter shrugged. "It's better than sitting around the reading room all afternoon learning about this battle and that battle and surrender."

"It will change," Gunnar insisted, looking around him. "You will all need your uniforms again one day."

"Yes," Rolf said. "I personally am planning to sell mine to the first American soldier who wants a souvenir."

Stroh looked ready to explode.

Dieter maneuvered his lunch tray between them. "I take it you aren't going to church?" he said to Stroh, who shook his head. "Then let us by.

And as for the guard, we'd all better hope he never figures out what we're talking about when we bet on his lapses. I don't think he would find that amusing."

"Quiet!" Romani shouted. *"Mach schnell,* ladies." He looked at Dieter and smirked. "You won't need to translate *that.*" He laughed at his own joke. No one joined in.

Chapter Eight

A broken and a contrite heart, O God,
thou wilt not despise.
PSALM 51:17

HAVING THE COURAGE to die had never been a problem. But whether or not he had the courage to live had been eating away at Dieter Brock since the day his unit surrendered in the desert. When Hitler changed his orders from "fight to the last man" to "fight to the last shell," men all around Dieter had begun breaking their shells. Dieter was so enraged he almost grabbed a rifle and shot them all. Instead, he made a speech about the fatherland and glory. But this time, his musical voice had no effect on the men. This time, they stared at him like lifeless dolls, unswayed by his patriotism.

"Look down there," Unteroffizier Von Runkle said, nodding toward where they could see the British swarming the estate where, only hours ago, the very men on the hillside had been living in luxury. "Do you think our resistance has any point at all? Africa is lost. Rommel is gone. You will have to find glory on another battlefield, Brock."

"We could escape," Dieter insisted. "I told you how."

"Oh, yes," Von Runkle snorted. "I heard you. Right into the belly of the enemy. Convince the British we are Russians. The Americans we are Dutch." He shook his head. "It's over."

Someone else spoke up. "My father was treated well by the Americans in the last war. It's only reasonable to expect the same this time."

"You aren't being captured by Americans," Brock snarled. "And we've dropped enough bombs on England to destroy most of the country. I don't think you should be expecting satin pillows and plates piled high with plum pudding. And if they give us to the French—"

"If they give us to the French, you'll be doing the same thing you've been doing since the war started," Von Runkle said. "You speak French, too, so you'll be valuable to them. You have nothing to fear."

"I'm not afraid!" Brock snarled.

"And no one said you are." Von Runkle leaned close. "Listen to me. You have the scars and the medals to prove you are one of our best. But it is *over* for us." He gripped Dieter's forearm. "Now it is time to turn our minds toward the future. To waiting until we have the opportunity to help rebuild our beloved fatherland." He nodded toward the British down below. "Once they are finished with us, we will be needed at home. And you, *Herr* Brock, will be among the best of the best. Listen to me. Do not fall in love with your hatred. I know it has given you strength in the past. More than once it kept you silent under interrogation. But this time you are *not* going to escape. Face it." He paused. "You have had the courage to die. Now you muster another kind of courage. The courage to live. Obey their orders. Eat what you are given. Preserve your strength. Germany will need you again. When she does, be ready."

All across the Atlantic, when he had been too seasick to do anything but lie in his berth and vomit into a biscuit tin, Dieter Brock had pondered Von Runkle's words. Von Runkle was gone, dead of an illness that swept the mud-soaked prison camp long before the prisoners boarded the ship that would take them to America. But his words echoed in Dieter's mind. They continued to sustain him off the ship, onto the ferry, and then to the train—which was not a cattle car, after all, but rather a first-class Pullman—and all across the vast expanse of America to the desert called the Nebraska Sandhills. He had learned about the American West by watching Tom Mix movies. But he had never heard of Nebraska. When he stepped off the train and looked around him, his heart sank. Except for a low ridge barely visible against the distant gray sky, the land was flat. Except for thick, tall grass and an occasional small tree, the land was barren.

They were treated surprisingly well. Dieter had expected to be nearly starved, but on the train and since the arrival in Nebraska, they had been fed mountains of food. He had expected they might end up living in tents—Rolf Shrader, who admired Karl May, said it would be fun to live in tepees like the American Indians—but instead they were escorted into clean new barracks. They had their own showers. Hot water. Soap. Even mirrors. Dieter had expected the guards to be surly and hateful. But with one or two exceptions, they treated their charges well. A few like Private Romani seemed to relish the chance to prove themselves "tough" with the prisoners. But men like Sergeant Isaacson, who had actually seen battle, treated them with the honor code understood by true warriors.

And now here Dieter was, twenty-one years old and still hoping that what Von Runkle said was true, that he would have the opportunity to serve his country again. More than a personal code of honor fueled his determination. He would never tell another living soul, but every time he was tempted to despair—and he had considered ways to end his own life—every time, the face of his little mother stopped him. *"You will be my first thought in the morning and my last thought at night, mein schatz,"* she had said the morning he left to enlist. *"And with each thought,"* Mama said, *"will be a thousand prayers."*

Prayers. Personally, Dieter didn't see the point. But Mama did. That was what was important. If praying for her son made his leaving bearable, then Dieter hoped his little mother "prayed without ceasing," as her Bible told her to do. At night, when the dogs barked and the coyotes howled and he could not sleep, Dieter lay in his cot looking up at the ceiling as he pictured his little mother clinging to the letter he had written her. They had been told what to write the first time:

I have been taken prisoner, and I am well. My new address is Fort Robinson, Nebraska, Box 20, New York.

There was room for Mama to answer on the very same card. But no reply had come.

He had written again, this time using the code they had devised so she would know where he was. If she didn't trust the Red Cross card, she would know from his letter it told the truth. The first letter of every sentence in the letter spelled his location in America. N-E-B-R-A-S-K-A. Still, no reply came.

As he made his way up the steps to the compound chapel, Dieter thought again of his mother. He imagined her gray head bowed over a scrap of paper as she scratched out a letter to her brother Konrad, who lived in Chicago. She would be wishing she and her only boy had come to America when Uncle Konrad invited them after Papa died. She would be blaming herself for Dieter's predicament.

As he filed up the center aisle of the prison compound chapel, Dieter wished there were some way for Mama to know that her boy was in church today. She would be pleased. Was there any more beautiful smile in the world than the smile a mother gave the son she loved? As he sat down between Bruno Bauer and Rolf Shrader, his eyes began to water.

"Thank you for agreeing to translate for me," a voice said. "My grandparents were German, but I didn't learn to speak the language."

Dieter looked up. The American pastor was extending his hand and introducing himself as Ben Hale—not even using the title Reverend or Pastor. That was strange. Dieter stood up and shook the man's hand. He had a firm grip and looked Dieter in the eye.

"We'll sing a hymn first," the preacher said. "Would you come and stand beside me after that? I'll say a short prayer and then a message." He smiled. "It won't be a long sermon."

Dieter thought the pastor seemed a bit nervous. But he was sincere. Not condescending.

"As you wish," Dieter said.

"This is my wife," the preacher said, motioning toward an attractive woman sitting at the piano. "And my daughter," he said.

Nod, but don't look at their faces. While he wasn't above using his broad shoulders and square jaw to get what he wanted, Brock had learned the hard way that being what Gunnar Stroh called a "poster boy" had its problems. People tended to assume things about the most innocent of gestures or remarks. Even now, Dieter could feel Romani watching him. It wouldn't take very much for the overzealous guard to decide he had done something inappropriate. Romani might depend on Brock to translate for him, but he also loved excuses to write him up for discipline.

Dieter looked at the floor and barely nodded in response to the pastor's introduction—until the hymn started. Once the wife was playing the piano, and Romani moved to the back of the chapel, Dieter looked up.

———

Jo stared out the rear window of the Nash until she could no longer see the prison compound gate. "Are we coming back next Sunday?" she asked.

"Your mother and I will," Daddy said.

Jo saw her mother inspecting her in the rearview mirror.

"I liked helping," Jo said, hoping she looked pious. "It made me feel good—like I'm doing something important." She looked out the window so her mother couldn't see her face. "Was it . . . odd . . . to have to wait for the interpreter to put your words into German?"

Daddy grinned. "Not so much odd as disquieting. I kept wondering if he was really translating what I said, or if he was making some kind of morale speech for the Fuehrer. He certainly had the voice for it."

"Do you think—Do you think he . . . or any of them . . . believe like we do?"

"I don't know. I imagine most are Lutheran, if they are anything at all."

"So why'd they come to a Baptist service?"

"Boredom," Daddy said. "Entertainment. A chance to see Americans. I suppose there were as many reasons as there were men."

"I didn't want to appear to be staring at them," Mother said, "so I didn't get a count, but Tom said he guessed about thirty came."

"Maybe we'll have more next week," Jo said.

"Maybe," Daddy nodded. "Lord willing." He paused before adding, "But I don't think we'll have you come again."

"Why not?"

"Aunt CJ needs you more at the ranch than we need you for the chapel service," Mother chimed in. "I'm going to call her when we get home and tell her to plan on you coming out to visit after church next Sunday morning. With Mia. You can introduce Mia to Ned, and then your father and I will drive out and pick you up after the service at the fort."

"But—" Jo started to protest.

"You heard your mother," Daddy said. "The subject is closed."

Jo fumed. She was glad Mother wasn't angry anymore, but now her parents had that "united front" thing going again.

Daddy slid his hand across the front seat and squeezed Mother's.

Mother looked at Daddy with *that* smile.

Jo sighed. The subject was definitely closed.

————

"So," Ben said once they were upstairs in their room changing out of their church clothes. "Was it so bad?"

"It was fine," Clarissa said. She sat at the foot of the bed and slipped her shoes off.

"They certainly liked your piano playing."

"Thank goodness Tom knew to suggest 'A Mighty Fortress Is Our God,'" Clarissa said. She smiled. "I certainly never expected to find myself hearing that grand old hymn sung in German—loudly, and off-key in some cases."

"Except for the translator," Ben said. "He has a nice singing voice."

"Yes," Clarissa murmured. "He is quite the . . . exception."

"I think they were all trying to show their appreciation for our coming," Ben said.

"Even after hearing Mrs. Frey describe the PWs who work in her office,

I never expected them to be so . . . human." She sighed. "The one standing beside Brock during the singing had such a boyish grin. He seemed so eager to be nice. I don't know what I expected . . ." she said, her voice trailing off. "But that wasn't it."

Ben slid his tie off, hung it up on a nail inside the closet, and began to unbutton his shirt.

"Your sermon was wonderful," Clarissa said.

Ben nodded. "Thank you kindly. I'm surprised you listened."

"I have come to bring to you the Word of God in your troubled existence," Clarissa recited. *"Jesus Christ did not differentiate between people. You are here as prisoners of this terrible war, but all men are prisoners on this earth until the Lord makes them free. Do not give up your hope in God. He has not forgotten you here. The new life that is springing up all around us on this beautiful spring day is proof. It may be hard for some of you to believe in God because of what has happened to you. But he who believes in God will be free, even though he may be surrounded by barbed wire, and those who do not believe are prisoners wherever they may live. 'If the Son therefore makes you free, ye shall be free indeed.' "*

"What's this?" Ben said, going to his wife and swiping a tear off her cheek.

Clarissa swallowed hard and sniffed. "The tall one with the sweet face. I know we can't see the heart, but—his face beamed when he was singing. Like he was somehow oblivious to the circumstances. It made me think of Johnny, and Ron Hanover, and all the others who haven't come back yet . . . or never will." She looked down at her hands and touched her wedding ring. "And of our neighbor."

"Hank?"

Clarissa nodded. "He's *home*—free to go to work every day, free to hold his wife, free to play with his child, to talk to his neighbors, and yet—"

"He's in a prison of hatred and bitterness," Ben said.

Clarissa sighed. "It's so sad." She stood up and headed for the closet, then turned around. "I'm proud of you, Ben. I didn't want to go today. I hated the idea. I hated *them*. But then . . ." She smiled and shrugged.

"Does this mean you'll play the piano for me again next week?" Ben said.

"Just try to keep me away," Clarissa smiled, but added quickly, "but please keep saying no if Jo hounds you about 'helping.' "

Ben nodded. "Not to worry, Mother Hale." He winked. "I saw it, too. She was quite taken with our translator. Which probably means nothing more than she is a normal girl. But I also saw something you didn't. The guard at the back of the room couldn't take his eyes off her."

Clarissa sighed. "I can't believe I'm saying this, but I am glad she is going to the ranch for the summer."

"Me too, although she would be following her mother's lead concerning men in uniform if she were to be attracted to Private Romani," Ben teased as he wrapped his arms around her.

"Just because it worked for you and me doesn't mean it's right for our daughter."

"Of course not," Ben said, and nuzzled her cheek.

"And she already has a man in uniform in her life. His name is John Boone Bishop."

"You're right," Ben said, tracing the lines of her face and neck.

"She should have an education."

"Absolutely," Ben said, and nibbled at her earlobe.

Clarissa struggled. "I need to get changed."

"Let me help," Ben said.

———

"So?" Delores's face was alight with excitement as she opened the screen door to admit Jo.

Jo stepped across the worn threshold and leaned over, peering into the kitchen.

"Mom's at work," Delores said.

"On *Sunday?*"

"On any day when she can earn a buck. I think there's trouble with the bank," she said. "Chase Young's been sniffing around lately. Mom's stressed."

"I'm sorry," Jo said.

"Me too. But . . . hey!" Delores pulled Jo down beside her on the worn gray couch. "We can talk about that later. Tell me about it. What was it like? Did you see any dreamy boys? How many came? Were you really inside the barbed wire?"

Jo tilted her head. "If you'll be quiet for a minute, I'll tell you."

"Oh . . . sorry." Delores sat back and primly folded her hands in her lap.

"First, when we drove up to the gate . . ."

Half an hour later, the girls had poured themselves iced tea and were sitting on the front porch swing. "So," Delores said as she turned sideways to face Jo. "Let's hear it."

"Hear what? I told you everything."

Delores sighed. "This is *me*, Josephine. Delores. Remember her? Your best friend? The one you tell everything?"

Jo could feel the color rising up the back of her neck. No matter what she did, it would creep around her collar and up to her cheeks. She closed her eyes. She shook her head. "I can't," she said. She sighed. "It doesn't matter, anyway. I'm never going back there."

"So . . . what does he look like?"

"Who?"

"*Him*—who. Him who you didn't talk about. Him who isn't the guard. Him who you noticed but won't talk about."

Jo held up her index finger and waggled it back and forth. "Exactly. What you said."

"What did I say?"

"Won't talk about. But I've got other news. I think maybe Mother will change her mind and let me help out at the Servicemen's Club here in town once in a while. Maybe."

———

There were some days, Dieter realized as he lay in his cot Sunday night, in which he did experience moments when he thought life might be worth living after all. No one suspected that he had ever questioned the value of his life, of course. Everyone looked at his pleasing exterior and made assumptions. Because they looked up *at* him physically, they tended to look up *to* him emotionally. He kept quiet, and they thought he had some kind of hidden wisdom. He defended Bruno Bauer, and they thought him courageous. He stood up to Gunnar Stroh, and they took that as a sign of strength. He wondered if he would have any friends at all if they knew the truth.

He kept quiet because these days he wasn't sure what he believed. He'd been reading some of the materials left in the reading room about democracy and other subjects, and it was beginning to make sense. But the idea that he had nearly died for a false ideal filled him with self-loathing. Could he have been so stupid?

He defended Bauer because the American guard Romani was a weakling and it was easy. Anyone could have done it. With his big ears and wide grin, Bruno had reminded Dieter more of a faithful German shepherd dog than a soldier of the Third Reich. If he'd had a brother, Dieter reasoned he could have done worse than Bruno Bauer. And so he'd fabricated the story about the dead sister and the shaving kit. It had nothing to do with courage. It was more about having a small victory over the American who was bullying Bauer.

He stood up to Gunnar Stroh because he wanted to prod Stroh to expound on his beliefs. He wanted to understand the man. Part of him respected Stroh, who hung a Nazi flag above his cot and gave the salute whenever he could. Part of him pitied the old soldier, who was so blinded by his loyalty to the Fuehrer that he would not believe the American news reports. It bordered on being pathetic. But it was intriguing. You had to admire someone who was so sure of what they believed. Gunnar's faith in the Fuehrer was just as strong as the American pastor's faith in God.

But there was an edge of cruelty to Gunnar Stroh that Dieter couldn't stand. He took obvious delight in giving the Nazi salute—especially in Sergeant Isaacson's presence. Once, when Dieter apologized for it, Isaacson told him not to. "He's just following the orders of his high command as should you," he said. Which made Dieter think less of Stroh . . . and more of Isaacson. The irony of that was almost funny.

And now there was this Pastor Hale, who seemed to have a sincere belief in God that Dieter had not seen since he was living at home. Apparently the Baptist minister would be returning every Sunday to conduct chapel services. The idea that he could look at a beautiful girl and hear a speech on religion at the same time was attractive to him.

No one knew how close to despair Dieter Brock had been in recent months. Things had continued to spiral downward for him until, just recently, with everything in Germany being destroyed and the future so uncertain, he had come to realize that if it were not for his little mother, he would have found a way to stop thinking. Permanently.

Twice a month he was allowed to write home. And while he had not heard from his mother, he knew he must not give up on her. And so he wrote, *The Americans are treating us well. I am using my time as a prisoner to learn. I am safe, eating well, and attending chapel services every Sunday.*

Mama would be pleased.

He did not mention the pastor's beautiful daughter.

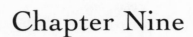

Chapter Nine

What man of you, having an hundred sheep,
if he lose one of them, doth not leave
the ninety and nine in the wilderness, and
go after that which is lost, until he find it?

Luke 15:4

IN TWENTY YEARS of marriage, the Reverend Benjamin Hale had never strayed from his devotion to Clarissa. Not that he hadn't had opportunity. Their marriage had had its moments. But Ben was a man who kept his word, and when he promised his bride "for better or for worse," he meant it. However, Reverend Benjamin Hale was not blind, and as he stood at his church office window on Monday morning watching Helen Frey walk down from her front porch and slide into the backseat of Deacon Tom Hanson's Pontiac next to Stella Black, he noted that Helen Frey was a lovely woman—albeit under a great deal of stress.

The talk in Crawford about the Frey family was more about Hank's unfortunate war experience than anything else. People were curious about when Hank was going to open up his auto repair shop again. They gossiped about the extent of his wounds. Ben and Clarissa had practically been nominated for sainthood for taking an interest in Mia. No one seemed all that worried about Helen, who had a smile for everyone who asked about Hank. She was cheerful and positive and, unless a person was her pastor or old Mrs. Koch, they might not recognize the signs of trouble behind Helen's sunny disposition. But Reverend Hale had a gift of mercy that enabled him to see right through Helen Frey's smile to the slight stoop in her posture and the sadness in her eyes that had never been there before.

Today, Ben thought, there was more than a little hesitancy in the way Mrs. Frey turned back to wave at the house before getting in the car. Once in the car, she leaned forward and, as the Pontiac rolled away, looked up at the house. Following her line of sight, Ben was convinced at least one rumor about Hank was true. Helen Frey was waving at the attic window.

As the Freys' pastor, Ben had waited in vain for Hank Frey to feel "well enough" to come back to church. As a family friend, he had watched little Mia change until rarely did the sprite in her personality appear. The final impetus for what Ben was about to do had happened just yesterday, when old Mrs. Koch knocked on his office door.

"I come to you with a concern," she said. She didn't come all the way into the pastor's office. She declined Ben's invitation to sit down. Instead, she stood with her back to the door and her hand on the knob.

Ben leaned forward. "What is it, Mrs. Koch?"

"Henry Frey," she said.

"Yes," Ben replied, "I've been concerned, too."

"You will go see him, then?" When Ben hesitated to answer, Mrs. Koch nodded. "I know. It is awkward. You won't know what to say." She shrugged. "Maybe there is nothing. But you must try, Pastor. For the wife and the child, you must try."

Looking into the aged saint's watery eyes, Ben was ashamed that he hadn't already visited Hank. It was the first time in all his years as a leader of this congregation that old Mrs. Koch had even come close to "suggesting" that the pastor do something.

"You're right, Mrs. Koch," Ben said. "As soon as Mrs. Frey leaves for work tomorrow I'll go over to their house."

Mrs. Koch nodded. "Good." She smiled at Ben. "I will pray for you, Pastor."

As the door closed behind Mrs. Koch, Ben had cross-examined himself. Why, he wondered, had he been so willing to lead a chapel service for the Germans . . . and so lax about shepherding his own flock? Even Clarissa, who made no claim to any gift of mercy, had shed a tear over Hank Frey's situation. Why hadn't he done something?

I'm afraid, he realized. Scripture came to mind. *"There is no fear in love; but perfect love casteth out fear."*

I don't know what to say, he thought. *What if it's completely wrong? I could make things worse. I don't know the first thing about what Hank's going through.* Once again, Scripture came to mind. *"If any of you lack wisdom, let him ask of God, that giveth to all men liberally . . ."*

I'm ashamed, he confessed. *Here I sit in my comfortable little community with my family intact . . . when all the boys in our town are going through hell on earth.* A verse from his recent study in the book of Romans came to mind.

"Shall the thing formed say to him that formed it, Why hast thou made me thus?" Ben bowed his head and prayed.

And here he was on Monday morning, with sweat collecting on his brow as he anticipated walking toward the front porch steps of the little whitewashed bungalow where Hank and Helen Frey had started their married life.

The Pontiac turned right at the end of the block and disappeared from sight.

"Well, Lord," Ben whispered. "Here I go. You said I could pray for wisdom. I have. I still am." Rumors had transformed Hank Frey from a local boy who knew the cars in Crawford as well as most men knew their children, into a deformed monster who lurked in his attic and slunk along the back alleys of town after dark, half-crazed with hatred for the Germans who were responsible for his destroyed life. Ben knew the rumors were just that, but it didn't keep his heart from pounding.

Ben didn't know exactly what he expected, but whatever he thought might happen, it wasn't the booming "GO AWAY!" that answered his knock. The words were so forceful Ben stepped away from the door.

Mrs. Koch's words came to mind. *"I will pray for you, Pastor."* The idea that the widow of a Purple Heart recipient was praying for him brought comfort. And accountability. Ben had no doubt that Mrs. Koch would soon knock on his office door again and ask if he had visited Henry Frey. He must be able to say yes. If he couldn't say yes, when she asked, that would bring an entirely new level of shame—one he wasn't willing to endure.

He stepped back to the door and peered through the locked screen door.

"Hank! It's Ben Hale."

After a long silence, footsteps sounded on the stairs, just visible off to the left of the door. A pair of rugged work boots and then two legs clad in what looked like overalls came into view. "Helen's already left for work," Hank said, stopping on the stairs. "Mia left for school a little while ago. Is something wrong?"

Good. The edge in Hank's voice meant his bitterness hadn't smothered his protective instincts when it came to family. "Nothing's wrong with Mia or Helen," Ben said quickly. "I came to see you."

"Trust me, Preacher. You don't want to *see* me."

Not knowing how to answer, Ben said nothing.

"You've done your duty," Hank said. "You've made your call. Now you can go."

Through the screen, Ben could see Hank start to turn around. He was heading back upstairs.

"It's my car, Hank. The old Nash." *Now where did that come from?* Ben wondered.

"Take it to Jack or Bill," Hank said without turning around. "It's not like there aren't any other mechanics in town."

"Jack means well, but he's in over his head when it comes to the Nash. And Bill retired while you were gone." Ben cleared his throat. "The thing is, Jo and Mia are supposed to go to the Four Pines with CJ after church on Sunday. Then Clarissa and I are supposed to bring them home in the evening. Will Bishop is working at the remount now or I'd ask him to bring them home. I just hate to disappoint them, but I'm not comfortable with the Nash the way it's running these days. Can't you take a look at it for me?"

"I've got no right arm."

Ben hesitated, despairing when the words that first came to mind amounted to little more than what he'd come to call a "comfort cliché." *What do I do now, Lord? What do I say?*

"Hank, you know as well as I do that you've forgotten more about Nash Ramblers than Jack ever knew. You used to say you could fix any car better than Jack could with one hand tied behind your back. But you don't have to prove that. You've got a hook. Right?"

"So?"

Ben blurted out. "I'll . . . I'll . . . leave my garage unlocked and you can come up tonight. After we're all in bed. Please, Hank. I need your help." Ben looked away from the door. A flash of movement caught his attention. He glanced at the next house where a climbing rosebush on a trellis obscured most of the front porch. He looked back inside the Frey house. Hank's lower half was still visible. He had turned back around. That was something.

"Well, you think about it," Ben said. As he watched, the toe of Hank's right boot seemed to inch forward, almost as if he were thinking of coming down. Ben held his breath. But then Hank turned around and, without a word, headed back up the stairs.

At the foot of the Frey porch, Ben looked toward the neighbor's house. "Good morning, Mrs. Bohling," he called out to the trellis. "Hope you have a nice day."

As he walked down the sidewalk, across the street, and back to his office at the First Baptist Church, Ben prayed.

Please help Hank Frey . . . because it doesn't look like I can.

"Ben . . . Ben!" Clarissa shook him awake. "Wake up, Ben! Someone's trying to steal the car!"

"Wh-what?" Ben grunted and opened his eyes.

"Someone's broken into the garage. Listen." Clarissa pressed herself against his back. "Is the back door locked?" She was waiting, breathless, her mouth poised about an inch from his ear.

Ben listened, then relaxed into his pillow. "It's all right. I asked Hank to work on the car."

"But you just brought it back from Jack's," Clarissa protested.

"It still needs a thing or two."

"That we can't afford," Clarissa replied. "And those are your very words, Reverend Hale." She rolled away from him and lay on her back staring up at the ceiling. "You never mentioned talking to Hank."

Ben sat up and shoved his feet into his slippers. "Think I'll go on out there and see if he needs any help." He pulled on his bathrobe. Just as he was about to open the bedroom door, Clarissa called his name.

"Yes?" Ben turned back toward where his wife lay on her side, her left arm bent, her head cradled in her open palm.

"Would you like it if I put a thermos of hot coffee and some cookies out on the back porch? Just in case you and Hank get hungry?"

Ben smiled in the darkness. "That'd be real nice, honey," he said. He opened the door.

"Ben?"

"Yes?"

"I love you."

"And I love you, baby girl."

Ben paused just inside the screened back porch and looked at the yellow spot on the backyard lawn where light was spilling through the garage window onto the grass. *I don't know what I am doing.* It was a good thing the garage door opened toward the alley. It wouldn't do for Hank to look up and see his own pastor hesitating like a coward.

Finally, after he had asked the Lord for help a dozen times, Ben heard Clarissa's footsteps behind him in the kitchen. He ducked his head back in the kitchen.

"Just leave it on the top step and go on back to bed," he whispered. "Don't want to scare him off."

Clarissa nodded. "I'll go right back up to bed," she said, "soon as I set it out."

Ben went back out to the screened porch. Still, as he contemplated walking down the path alongside the garage, he didn't know if he should open the single door right at the front corner near the house or not. Finally, he opened the porch door, stepped outside, and closed it behind him. Again, he paused, listening to the crickets chirping, looking up at the stars, and sending silent messages toward heaven. Taking a deep breath, Ben walked to the window and peeked in.

Hank had opened the hood and was intent on working something loose with the hook that was supposed to serve as his right hand. As Ben watched, he jiggled something, reached for it with his left hand, then went back to working with the hook. Finally, he held it up to the light—and Ben saw the ravaged face. He inhaled sharply and closed his eyes. Then he adjusted his approach so that, when he came around the corner and leaned against the doorframe, it would be the uninjured part of Hank's face that he saw.

"I appreciate this, Hank," Ben said. Hank's reaction brought tears to his eyes. The man started, raised his hand, palm out, as if to ward Ben off, and stepped back away from the car. Ben hoped his voice sounded calming when he said, "Now don't run off just because I came out here to make sure it was you and not someone stealing my car. I'm very relieved. Anybody trying to steal the Nash would have to be crazy as a loon."

Hank pulled his hat down over his eyes and stepped back into the shadows. But he bantered back. "Well, I can't promise I'm not crazy, but I'm mostly harmless except for the fact that I scare my own daughter," he said.

Ben ignored the comment. "Got any idea why it's misfiring?"

"Not yet. Got some things I can check"—he held up the hook—"but I'm clumsy. Everything takes twice as long. Some things I can't do at all."

Ben shrugged. "Take all the time you need. I imagine it's just like preaching."

"What?"

"My first few sermons were awful—and that's being kind. I still have no idea why they hired me." He grimaced. "But, with practice, I like to think I've gotten to where I actually form complete sentences and make sense—most of the time." He nodded toward the hook. "I imagine learning to use that will be the same. At times you'll think it doesn't make any sense at all. But as long as you keep trying . . . it'll come to you."

The gasket Hank was holding slipped from the hook's grip and went rolling under the car. Hank swore and slammed the artificial forearm on the top of the car's fender.

"I'll get it," Ben said, and walked toward the car.

"No!" Hank raised his hand.

Ben stopped. "Clarissa was the one who heard you out here first. When I told her I was pretty sure it was our mechanic, she made a thermos of coffee—along with some of those oatmeal cookies everyone raves about. Said she'd leave it on the top step."

"She didn't have to do that."

"Well," Ben said, "that's exactly what I told her. But she insisted. And I've learned—since that first horrible sermon and my first mostly horrible year of marriage—that when Clarissa has it in her mind to do something, it's best to let her have her way and get to it." As Hank continued to stand where the metal shade on the overhead bulb cast a shadow across his face, Ben felt a tug toward the house. *It's a good start. Don't push it. Say good-night.* He cleared his throat. "You help yourself to some cookies and coffee," Ben said. "Let me know what you think about the old girl." He nodded toward the car, then shook his head. "What is it, do you suppose, that makes a man think of a car as a woman?" Without waiting for an answer, he turned to go.

"Pastor Hale," Hank said.

"Yes?"

"You come up to the house tomorrow after Helen's gone to work and I'll tell you what I find out here tonight. I'll let you know if I think she can run any smoother. I'm fairly certain it'll be fine to drive 'er out to the ranch, but I'll let you know for sure."

"I appreciate that," Ben said. "Good night, now."

Ben heard the grunt as Hank bent down to retrieve the gasket from beneath the old Nash. As he passed the garage window, he resisted the temptation to look in.

"You have a nice talk with Hank last night?" Clarissa asked as she came in from the back porch, thermos and empty plate in hand.

Ben sat down and opened the paper. "Just said hello and thanks and came back to bed. Glad to see he took a break."

"What did he say about the car?"

"Said to stop by this morning after Helen goes to work. He'll tell me what he thinks."

"Did he . . . did you . . ."

"You still have that material you wanted to use to make a window curtain last year?"

Clarissa paused. "Why?"

"Well, after talking to Hank last night it came back to me. How I made fun of you for wanting to make curtains for a garage." He ducked behind the paper, pretending to pay more attention to his reading than to the conversation. "Didn't mean to hurt your feelings, Clarissa. Sorry if I did. Fact is, a curtain at that window might be nice."

It was quiet in the kitchen for a while. Ben glanced up a time or two, but his wife was busy cooking breakfast. When she set the plate of bacon and eggs in front of him, she kissed him on the cheek. "I'll take care of it this morning," she said, and squeezed his shoulder. "And you tell Hank I'll make him some of my Boston brown bread and leave it out there for him tonight. In case he takes a mind to work on the car again. He always liked my brown bread."

Chapter Ten

And I will restore to you the years
that the locust hath eaten. . . .
JOEL 2:25

"WHAT IN BLAZES did they do to you, boy?"

The voice from the direction of the dark alley caught Hank by surprise. He started, raised up, clunked his head on the hood of Ben Hale's car, and did his own share of swearing as he backed into the shadows.

"Now don't bolt," the voice said. Vernon Clark stepped into the light. "I just came to . . ." His voice wavered. He shoved his hands in his pockets and gulped. "Just came to see . . ." He sighed. His voice trembled. "I didn't understand why you weren't at Delmer's funeral. You were one of his best friends, Hank. Didn't understand why you weren't there."

"I expect you got your answer just now," Hank said.

"I'm sorry. Really, I am." Vernon lingered in the doorway, alternately clenching and unclenching his hands. Finally, he nodded toward the car. "Getting back into the business?"

"Just paying a debt," Hank said. "Preacher's been good to my family." He cleared his throat. "Sorry about Delmer, Mr. Clark."

As Hank watched, Vernon's face contorted. The man shuddered. "I always thought there'd be a Double C Ranch for at least a couple of generations." He choked the words out, then swallowed and seemed to get control of his grief by uttering a string of epithets against the general who, according to Vernon, sent Delmer into a "death trap," against God, who could have kept the boy safe, and most vociferously against the Germans.

Hank shrugged. "There's nothing to be done." He slowly stepped forward and went back to work, all the while being careful to keep his head turned so as to hide the worst from Mr. Clark.

"Well, I'm not sure you're right about that, friend," Vernon said. He stepped into the garage and perched atop a barrel next to the door. "Say . . . you're pretty handy with that hook."

Hank paused. He stared at the hook, almost as if he hadn't looked at in a while. "Now that you mention it, I guess I am getting better at it." He put the tool he was holding into his flesh-and-blood hand. "It's getting to where I'm better with the hook on my right side than the real hand on the left."

"Well, you were right-handed before. Weren't you?" Vernon asked.

"Yeah," Hank said.

"Guess your brain didn't forget."

"The doctors said that. I didn't believe them. Been knocking stuff over with it for so long I didn't expect it to change."

"Glad it has," Vernon said.

Hank stopped what he was doing and straightened up. Without looking at Vernon, he said quietly, "Hard not to feel like somebody made a mistake sending me back—like this—and losing track of Delmer that way."

"There's no sense to who lives and who dies," Vernon said. "It's all a game. Like poker. Some win, some lose. No rhyme or reason." He reached into his pocket. "Mind if I smoke?"

"Help yourself," Hank said.

Vernon lit a cigarette and took a long draw. His exhale was a great sigh. "Guess there's some comfort in that your family doesn't have to figure how to get on without you. At least Marge and me don't have a daughter-in-law and grandchildren to worry over." He swallowed and his voice wavered again as he said, "It's just the two of us missing Delmer and trying to make sense of it all. Marge's gone back home to visit for a while."

"It's not just the two of you missing Delmer," Hank said quickly. "I miss him. All those months I was in the hospital I spent a lot of time thinking about the good times at home. Delmer was part of a lot of them. So don't think you and Mrs. Clark are the only ones missing him. You aren't."

Vernon looked off into the dark. "Thank you, Hank. I appreciate that." He flicked the cigarette into the dirt and stomped on it. "It's been hard seeing how quick folks are to forget about what they done to Delmer." He swore again.

"I'm not sure I know what you mean," Hank said.

"You haven't heard? Folks around here are standing in line for the opportunity to welcome the Nazis to America."

"What are you talking about?"

"Prison labor. The preacher's own family was some of the first to sign up."

"Sign up?"

Vernon nodded. "That's right. CJ Jackson put in for an entire crew of the Krauts." He shook his head. "Can you imagine it? Nazi's swarming all over the fields at the Four Pines while Johnny Bishop fights for his life overseas." He paused. "Rumor has it Will Bishop up and quit the ranch when he couldn't talk sense into her. He's working over at the remount now. And good for him, is all I can say. I told him I'd burn my place down before I'd let one of 'em set foot on the property." He jumped up and began to pace. "I just can't believe the way folks around here forget their loyalties. All for the sake of the almighty dollar." He gestured wildly, "Let the hay stand in the field if it has to. Let the whole darned crop rot. That's a darned sight better than hiring the Nazis to do what our own children ought to be doing!" He stopped pacing abruptly. "Sorry, Hank. I get carried away when I think about it." He reached in his pocket, pulled out a silver flask and took a sip. "Want some?" He held the flask out for Hank as he said, "You don't have to hide from me, son," he said. "I saw it all in the first one. Mustard gas, arms and legs flying around, burned flesh. I saw it all."

"I appreciate your stopping by, Mr. Clark," Hank said, pretending not to notice the flask. He reached up and pulled the chain dangling over his head, turning the light out. "I'm finished for tonight. Need a part from up at the shop."

"Mind if I walk with you?" Clark asked. "Can't seem to sleep much these days."

"Suit yourself," Hank replied. He lowered the preacher's garage door.

The two men headed up the alley toward Hank's auto repair shop. As they walked along, Vernon reached up and patted Hank on the back. "It's good to have you home, Delmer," he said, "good to have you home."

It was an honest mistake, Hank thought. Wanting to avoid embarrassing Delmer's dad, he didn't correct the old man. He let him ramble on . . . about townspeople . . . and the preacher's daughter . . . and . . . Mia. His own little Mia.

———

"I am telling you, sir, these Bolsheviks really have discipline. The barracks is so clean, even my mother would find nothing wrong!"

Helen smiled to herself as she heard Private Franco Romani and Sergeant Isaacson come into the office on Wednesday morning. She had grown accustomed to Romani's attempts to camouflage his personal insecurity with a cover of bluster and high volume combined with posturing that sometimes had her and Stella turning away to hide their smiles.

Today, the younger man's hand trembled as Helen handed him the stack of transport documents she had been typing. "I just wish they would do a little less Heil-Hitlering," Romani said. "We'd be a lot less nervous about transporting them off the post."

"Any of our men who are nervous about transporting work teams can request to be reassigned," Sergeant Isaacson said. "There's plenty of work to do right here on the post. The remount is begging for help."

"Well, sir," Romani said, "I know that's true. But some of the men are more nervous about horses than Hitler."

Helen turned toward Stella's desk to hide her smile. She made another paper/carbon/paper sandwich and fed it into her typewriter.

Isaacson nodded. "Would you be one of those men?"

"What?"

"One of the men more nervous about horses than the Heil-Hitlering prisoners."

Romani shrugged. "Maybe."

"As you know, Private, these aren't goose-stepping, polished-boot Nazis. They are captured men anxious to see their families again. I realize there are exceptions, but if you report any troublemakers, we can see about having them transferred."

"Brock," Romani blurted out.

Helen got up and crossed the room. With her back to the men, she opened a file drawer.

"Who?" Isaacson asked.

"Dieter Brock. Compound A. Wants to be transferred. And I'd feel better without him around."

Isaacson frowned and looked down at the papers on his desk. "Brock is quiet, but I don't think he'd cause trouble."

True to form, Helen noticed that Romani was eager to agree with his superior. She filed a document.

"Oh no, sir. I agree, sir. I didn't mean we should worry about Brock," Romani shook his head back and forth. "What I meant was, he'd be happier and less likely to cause trouble if we gave him the work assignment he wants."

"And just what would that be?"

Now apparently eager to display his knowledge of "his" prisoners, Romani rattled on. "Well, sir I've been watching them all real close, just like you said I should. The other day when they were huddled up together in the reading room, I made Brock tell me what was so interesting in the paper. Turns out they were talking horses. Brock was bragging about his father. Seems he was in the Olympics in his day. Anyway, Brock seems to hanker for mucking out stalls and clipping manes instead of helping process new arrivals." Romani shook his head. "Imagine."

"So why doesn't he ask?"

"Doesn't want to draw attention to himself."

Helen heard Isaacson's chair creak. That meant he would be leaning back, with his hands folded across his belt as he stared out the window.

"Do you know of any problems with Brock? Has he instigated any trouble?"

Helen watched Romani out of the corner of her eye. He shook his head, then waxed long about his charges. "Just the opposite. The other day Gunnar Stroh said something behind my back. I didn't know what it was, but coming from Stroh—and the way he said it—I figured it wasn't anything too friendly. I know it's against regulations, sir, but I let my temper fly. Told the man exactly what I thought about Hitler and his German army and where he could put that flag pinned over his cot. I was so mad . . . and it all just flew out of me. In my mother tongue, of course." Romani smiled and shrugged. "So no harm done, right? Stroh didn't even know what I said."

"But Brock did," Isaacson said.

Of course he did, Helen thought.

"Of course," Romani agreed. "And later he comes over to me, says he is personally sorry about the war and 'any inconvenience' it might have caused me. Imagine that!"

"So . . . if most of these guys are so amicable, why are you so nervous about transporting them to work on a ranch?"

Helen exchanged silent smirks with Stella before closing the file drawer and returning to her desk. She saw Romani shrug.

"Filthy Bolsheviks."

"Nazis, Private," Isaacson said, "Not Bolsheviks. And I'll thank you to control your tongue in the presence of the ladies." He nodded toward Helen and Stella, who both nodded back and looked down at the work on their desks.

Did he know she wasn't doing anything productive? Helen wondered. *Could he read her as well as he obviously read Private Romani? Dear Lord, she hoped not.*

"Bolsheviks, Nazis . . . all the same."

Isaacson shook his head. "Not the same at all, Private." He launched into a lecture on European history.

Helen could tell that Romani was trying to pay attention, but she could also see his eyes glaze over. Issacson must have sensed it too. Helen could see him eyeing Romani as he concluded, " . . . and that's why most of the prisoners are really nihilistic Lutherans instead of lying Baptists."

Romani blanched and blurted out, "Lying? I'm no liar, Sergeant. Every word I said about Stroh and Brock is the truth. You told me to keep an eye on them, and I'm keeping an eye on them."

"Forget it, Private," Isaacson said, sighing. "I was just pulling your leg."

"Pulling the leg?"

Issacson glanced at Helen, but she quickly covered her mouth with her hand and turned away.

"Do they even *speak* English in your part of the world, Private?"

"Some," Romani shrugged. "Not much, though."

———

"So," Sergeant Isaacson said after Private Romani left the office, "do you have anything to say, Mrs. Frey? Mrs. Black?"

"About what?" the women replied in unison.

"Private Brock. You've had opportunity to observe him closely for a while now. Has he been satisfactory in the office?"

Stella spoke first. "He's smart. Respectful. And gorgeous. I like having him around, and I don't care if he's a Bolshevik or a Nazi—although I doubt he's either. I think he's divine." She pretended to swoon. "But if he's unhappy being around two dolls like Helen and me, then I'd say send him on his way. Get us someone who appreciates us."

Isaacson laughed. "Mrs. Frey? Do you have anything to add?"

Helen could feel herself blush as she cleared her throat. "I agree with Stella," she said, hoping it sounded normal. "You know what the captain says . . . 'A *working prisoner is a happy prisoner* . . . ' and it can only be better if they are working at something they enjoy."

Stella and Helen exited headquarters and walked toward the canteen. From across the compound of tar-papered buildings came a chorus of shrill wolf whistles. Helen ducked her head. Stella waved.

"Don't encourage them," Helen said.

"Why not, honey? It's harmless fun, and I'm going to be getting precious

little of that in the near future. I've got to do some serious belt tightening
if I want to keep my house." She laughed and batted her eyelashes, "And
it just wouldn't do to give up Tara. If it weren't for the gossips in town, I'd
rent Delores's room when she leaves for Des Moines to one of these guys."
She gestured toward the parade ground swarming with new soldiers. "The
longer this war goes on, the more money I realize I've missed out on by
being so *upstanding*."

Not knowing what to say, Helen was quiet.

"It's all right, honey. You don't have to show any righteous indignation
or anything. I know I shouldn't have a male tenant. But honestly, these boys
are young enough to be—" she giggled—"well, my little brother, at least.
Take Romani. He's darling and completely harmless. Why couldn't I just
adopt him?" She led the way to the lunch counter.

"Because then you couldn't charge him rent," Helen joked.

"Actually," Stella said, "when it comes to Romani, the army would owe
me a big thanks if I gave the boy a home and he settled down."

"What are you talking about?"

Stella put a finger to her lips. Once the women were seated where no
one could eavesdrop, she said, "I overheard a call he made the other day.
To Brooklyn."

"On the post phone?"

Stella nodded. "I know. Strictly against regulations."

"He could get put in the stockade for something like that."

"Yeah," Stella said. "He was almost frantic. It seems his best girl hasn't
answered any of his letters. He was threatening to jump aboard the first
train home."

"You overheard someone threatening to go AWOL?" Helen frowned.
"That should be reported."

"Not a chance." Stella took a bite out of her sandwich, then gulped it
down. "I'd have to admit I was eavesdropping, and I'd lose my job." She
hesitated. "But I do have an idea. . . ."

Helen shook her head. "You leave me out of whatever it is you're
plotting."

"Just listen," Stella said, leaning forward. "If the problem is he's homesick, then he'd probably welcome a little taste of home, wouldn't he? I bet
a lot of our boys would love to have somewhere to go besides the Servicemen's Club for a change. I could offer a home-cooked meal for, say, fifty
cents. How many of the boys do you think would go for that? 'Sunday
Dinner at Stella's.' What d'ya think?"

"I think," Helen said, "that you are out of your mind. And that you already work hard enough." She glanced down at her watch. "And we need to get back to the office."

Outside the mess hall, Stella pulled out a pack of cigarettes and lit up, smoking as they made their way back to work. "You can't tell me you are rolling in the dough now that your hubby's back. Maybe you could help me out. We can split the profits fifty-fifty. Wouldn't your old man be impressed with that!"

At the mention of Hank, Helen blinked tears out of her eyes.

"Oh, honey . . . I'm sorry. I didn't mean to make you cry." Stella waved her cigarette in the air, tossed it on the ground, and stomped it out. "Hey, I was just kidding before. But honest, why don't you help me once Mia's gone to the ranch?" She raised both eyebrows and winked. "You'd be protecting my reputation. Come on. . . ."

"I don't know." Helen shook her head.

"Think about it."

"All right," Helen said. "But don't say anything to anyone yet."

The only person Stella mentioned Sunday Dinner at Stella's to was Private Romani . . . who mentioned it to someone . . . who mentioned it to someone. . . . And by the end of the day, the first Sunday Dinner at Stella's was promised to six homesick soldiers.

Stella beamed.

Helen sighed. She would have to tell Hank. As soon as she told him about Mia going to the ranch for the summer. As if he would care.

Chapter Eleven

Say not thou, I will recompense evil;
but wait on the Lord, and he shall save thee.
PROVERBS 20:22

HELEN FREY HAD just fallen asleep on Wednesday night when Hank threw open the bedroom door.

"Is it true?" he asked, his voice deadly quiet.

"Wh-wh-what?" Half asleep, Helen clutched the blankets to her chest as she sat up.

"Delmer Clark's dad stopped over at the Hales' last night while I was working on the reverend's car," Hank said. "And he tells me CJ Jackson is hiring Germans to work the Four Pines. And I also heard from him that my own daughter is going to visit the ranch with Jo Hale on Sunday—and maybe stay for the whole summer. Tell me you didn't know about the Germans. And when were you going to tell me about my own daughter's summer plans, anyway?"

"I . . . I . . ." Helen ran her hand through her hair.

With a glance up the hall toward Mia's room, Hank stepped into the bedroom and closed the door behind him. "You knew about the Germans!" he said. "I can hear it in your voice. You *knew*!"

"Th-there are rules. Strict rules. Guards. And no fraternization. CJ wouldn't let . . . Jo wouldn't . . . Mia won't go anywhere near—"

"I don't want her there," Hank said.

"But I've already promised—"

"Well *un*promise!" Hank ordered. "I won't have my daughter—"

"No." Helen could hardly believe the sound of her own voice. "I won't disappoint her."

"What did you say?"

Helen took a deep breath. "I said . . . no. There's nothing to worry about. The Grants over on the White River ranch have a work team of prisoners and—"

"I know all about the Grants and their little lunches with the Nazis," Hank said. He spat out the word. "Vernon Clark has just the word for them. Traitors."

"They are no such thing," Helen said. She gained courage. "And whatever you are thinking about the German boys who have been sent to Nebraska—it's wrong. We've had a couple working in our office. They are educated. Respectful. Honestly, Hank, they are so *relieved* to be out of the fight. So *thankful* to be in America."

Hank stepped back as if he'd been hit. "I can't believe my own wife has forgotten—"

"Don't you say that. Don't you *dare* say that to me!" Helen barely managed not to yell at him. "I haven't forgotten *anything*. I remember . . ." She choked the words out, "I remember all the way back to the night before you left . . . and the whispers."

"Stop," Hank said. He raised his hand to his scarred face.

Helen couldn't stop. "I remember your promises . . . and the way your hand stroked my neck . . . and then . . ." She was sobbing, blubbering, out of control. "I remember my wonderful husband. . . . Where is he? What happened to him?" She looked up at him through the tears, oblivious to the scars. On her knees, she reached for him, clutched the front of his shirt. "Sometimes I think he must be in there—beneath the scars—somewhere." She jerked on his shirt. "And if I can only be patient . . . maybe, just maybe my Hank will come back to me."

Hank grabbed her hands. Forcing her to let go of him, he backed away.

"Don't you dare run up those attic stairs!" Helen screeched. She slid to the edge of the bed. "Who *are* you? Where's my Hank? Where did he go?"

He turned his back on her and put his hand on the doorknob. Speaking over his shoulder he said calmly, "I don't want my daughter at the Four Pines."

"She's going," Helen said. "Think about what you're saying, Hank. Think about what you're asking. Do you remember her laugh? When she talks about the ranch, her face lights up with joy. You can't want to take that away." Swallowing hard, Helen said, "You can do whatever you want to *me*, Hank. I'm your wife, and I'll keep my wedding vows. I'll take it. But I won't make Mia stay in this house. I won't."

Hank leaned his forehead against the doorframe. "Wh-what do you think I'm going to do to you, Helen?"

"I . . . I don't know." She gulped and whispered, "I don't know you anymore. I never see you. You never let me—"

"You want to see me? Is that what you want?" He whirled around, flipped on the bedroom light, and pulled off his hat. "There," he said, thrusting the scarred side of his face toward her. "Is this what you want? Take a look. Take a real good look." He pressed closer and closer to her, until Helen's back was against the wall, her hands above her head. With Hank's hot breath and barely controlled rage roaring around her, she put her hands over her ears. "Stop," she begged. "Please, Hank. You'll wake Mia. Please stop."

"NO!" He reached across the bed and pulled her hands away from her ears. "I won't stop. You want to see your loving husband? Well, here he is, in all his glory! Take a good look, Helen. Tell me what you see. Do you see your loving husband? Here he is, honey. Back from the war!"

The warmth of his hot breath on her cheek and the smell of whiskey and motor oil and sweat was overwhelming. She could defend Mia with all the ferocity of a she-bear, but when the attack shifted and she was the target of Hank's rage, all of Helen's courage melted. She cowered against the wall, weeping, while he raged on and on about fire and peeling skin, about pain and kind nurses, about stepping over smoking bodies and lifting a man's head to comfort him and finding it was no longer attached to a body. Horrors and more horrors, made even worse because they were uttered in an eerie stage whisper. When she could bear no more, Helen balled up her hands into two fists. She intended to hit the scarred face. Instead, she fainted.

Helen's first thought when she woke early the next morning was that she had had a nightmare. Only when she sat up in bed and saw the grease stains on the once crisp white sheet did she have to face the truth. *Not a nightmare. Reality.* Closing her eyes, she remembered every harsh and ugly word, every whispered threat. She could feel Hank's breath on her cheek and smell the whiskey. And the scars. She saw the scars as they had been— dark red because he was so angry.

She slid out of bed. Clasping her hand over her mouth, she tore out of the room, down the hall, and to the bathroom where she leaned over the sink, retching. Once finished, she rinsed out her mouth with cold water and stood, grasping the cold edge of the sink with both hands, peering at her pale face in the mirror. She couldn't leave Hank. Not now. But she felt she had to go. For a while. For Mia. With trembling hands, she washed up, then retreated to her bedroom. It took only a few minutes to throw her own clothing into a suitcase. She woke Mia.

"We're going to visit Stella," she said, opening Mia's drawers and throwing her clothes into the suitcase with her own. "Get up and get dressed. We can talk about it later, but right now I want you to hurry. And be quiet."

Mia obeyed, her eyes wide with uncertainty. She clung to Helen's hand as they went downstairs. As they passed the kitchen, Helen put the note she had agonized over since dawn at the bottom of the stairs where Hank would see it.

Helen was calm until her friend's front door opened. Stella took one look at the suitcase and pulled them both inside. Her kindness overcame Helen's resolve to be calm for Mia. She put her head on Stella's shoulder and let the tears come.

———

Clarissa waited until Helen and Mia crossed the street and were inside Stella Black's house before she stood up. She'd been stooped down trying to retrieve Ben's morning newspaper from where it landed nine mornings out of ten—beneath the spirea bush.

———

Before the sun came up on Thursday morning, Hank had crept down the attic stairs in the night and stood outside what used to be their bedroom door, wanting to knock, longing to beg for forgiveness. When he put his hand to the doorknob, it was cold against the skin of his left hand. He looked down at his right hook. He leaned his head against the doorframe. If she said even one nice thing . . . he pictured sweeping her into his arms . . . and the hook . . . and her expression of revulsion. Hank headed back to the attic and lay awake, staring at the beams supporting the roof. He'd have to pick the right one. And strong rope. He was a big man. It wouldn't do to pick the wrong beam.

When Hank woke again, Mia had left for school and Helen had gone to work. His stomach was rumbling. He couldn't remember everything he'd said the night before, but from the way his head was pounding, it probably hadn't been good. Helen always left his breakfast on the counter. If he had to make his own breakfast today, it would serve him right.

At the bottom of the stairs he saw the note:

When Stella Black first offered to let Mia and me stay with her for a while, I preached her a sermon. I still believe everything I said, but I have to think of Mia.

She didn't even sign it. Hank read the note over and over again. He carried it with him to the living room, where he sat down and stared out the window that faced Stella Black's house. Things were beginning to green up. Funny he hadn't really noticed. The pots where Helen usually planted pansies were still on the wicker table in front of the window. Empty.

He got up and went into the kitchen where a small mirror hung over the row of coat hooks beside the back door. Maybe if he raised his collar. Maybe if he—Who was he kidding? For the next few minutes, he paced around the kitchen, alternating between grief and anger, guilt and blame. Helen would probably go to the preacher, he finally thought. She would tell him all about last night. About how Hank had acted. Shameful. Frightening her. And the preacher with the perfect skin and the perfect family and the perfect life would take her side. As would everyone else in this town.

Someone knocked at the back door. When he saw who it was, Hank crumpled the note into a tight ball and shoved it in his pocket. If that was the way she wanted it, so be it. He would be the villain, so she could be the saint. Maybe that would be better for everyone, anyway. It sure would make things easier for Spridget.

Hank opened the back door. Vernon Clark had a plan. A way they could do a little payback on behalf of Delmer and the men like Hank whose lives had been ruined by the Nazis.

Hank listened.

Chapter Twelve

An hypocrite with his mouth destroyeth his neighbor.
PROVERBS 11:9

"GIVE IT A WHILE LONGER," Will said, trying to downplay Buster's most recent fit. "He's bound to come around. I've got a few tricks up my sleeve yet."

"I've got to be honest with you," Bill Harker said. "I'm running out of patience, time and—more important—budget money for a stallion that's too unmanageable to stand at stud."

"That's why you hired me," Will said with a smile. "I've got the patience and the time to get Buster to contribute to the budget instead of draining it."

"Are you sure it's worth it?"

Will nodded toward the horse. "Look at him, Doc."

"All right," Harker agreed. He headed off toward Barn 3. "Keep me posted."

Will nodded. "You bet."

Harker was at the end of the row of stalls before he turned around and said, almost as if he were apologizing, "You do know, Will, if I was running my own ranch, I'd do whatever it took. He's from the Imperial Prussian stud, for goodness' sake. But the remount isn't a ranch. We just don't have the luxury of catering to problem animals."

"I understand," Will said. "I can't take forever." He smiled his slow, easy smile. "But I can take a while longer, right?"

Harker nodded. "I'm trusting you to prove my instincts right about this one."

As Harker exited the barn, Will turned around and began a conversation with Buster. While the horse had nothing to say, he did listen, his dark eyes locked on Will, his small, perfectly shaped ears alert.

"Now, you," Will said, "better behave yourself or you *are* gonna be dogmeat. I bought you some more time, my friend." He stepped toward Buster's stall. "But—" The horse half-reared, snorted, and landed a kick on the side of his stall. Again. Scratching the back of his neck, Will backed off and sat down on the hay bales across from the stall.

He'd said he still had a few tricks up his sleeve. It wasn't exactly a lie. There must be a trick up one sleeve or the other . . . if only he could think of one. Sighing, Will slapped his knees. Buster jumped. "Oh, settle down," Will said. "I'm just going to feed some of the more well-mannered critters around here." He got up and walked into the stall next to Buster's. "And while I do, you see if you can't trot some of the meanness out of those flashy legs of yours." Knowing what was about to happen, Buster walked expectantly toward the sliding door at the rear of his stall. Will let him out, closing the door behind him.

Mucking out stalls had never bothered Will before. It was part of the business of horses, and he loved the mix of aromas in a barn—even when manure was part of the mix. But the work here at Fort Robinson was becoming increasingly tedious. The fact was, Will admitted to himself, he was tired. Bone-tired. Weary. Homesick, even. The endless series of remount chores were mindless stuff for an old wrangler. Trimming manes, trimming hooves, feeding, watering . . . and rising again to trim more manes, clean more feet, muck out more stalls. Thousands of horses and mules needed the same thing, and there was precious little about the work that was interesting, except for Buster.

Will was at the end of his rope with the horse. For the first time in his life, it looked like he was not going to be able to solve the mystery of a hard-to-handle horse. While the prospect of Buster's demise was depressing, that wasn't the main thing making him grumpy. He missed CJ. Blast it. He did.

"Hey, wrangler. There's a wild horse in the stud barn that needs your attention."

Will had been slower than usual making his rounds. Between the cloudy sky and thinking about the Four Pines, he was feeling low. The sound of Jo's voice was music to his old ears.

"Hey, cowgirl," he bantered back. "Who let you loose today?"

Jo threw her arms around Will and hugged hard.

"Whoa." He pretended to be smothering and pushed back, looking around him to see who might have seen Jo's display. He tugged on the brim of Jo's cowgirl hat. "You can't just hug a man in plain sight like that. You'll have these wranglers thinking I'm a soft touch."

"Like they don't already know," Jo said.

"Know what? That I'm touched?" Together they laughed.

"Daddy's over at the PW camp making plans for a weeknight Bible study," she said. "If you can imagine that. Apparently some of the prisoners have expressed an interest."

"I'll just bet they have," Will said and turned away to grab another forkful of hay.

"I know, Uncle Will. It's probably not from real interest," Jo said. "Daddy already said that. But he also said that if the Lord can use a talking mule to accomplish His purposes, He can probably use boredom." She linked her arm through her uncle's. "So how's Buster the wonder horse?"

"No 'wonder' to that lame-brained critter," Will grumbled.

"Can I see him?"

Will shrugged. "Sure."

As they crossed the parade ground and headed between a row of barracks toward the stud barn, Jo told her Uncle Will that she and Mia would be leaving earlier than expected for the Four Pines. When Will expressed surprise, Jo told him about the Freys. "Daddy and Mother just think it's best for Mia to have something good in her life right now." She smiled. "And the Four Pines is it."

"You gonna miss graduation?" Will said.

Jo shrugged. "Probably. But I don't really care. Delores will be gone before that. It's just a walk across a stage and a piece of paper. Daddy went over and talked to the principal, and I'm going to keep up the schoolwork on my own, and they'll mail me my diploma. Honestly, with the war and everything, no one's much in a mood to celebrate, anyway."

Will patted her on the back and told her he was proud of her. Together they entered the stud barn.

"Buster's out in his corral behind the barn. Come on through with me, and we'll pick up some sugar. He likes you. Who knows, maybe he'll even get within three feet if you have a treat for him. He's probably pacing back and forth at the door right now, giving it a good kick now and then, wondering when he's going to get back in."

But Buster wasn't kicking the door. He wasn't even *at* the door. With Uncle Will behind her, Jo pried the door open just enough to see Buster poised in the middle of his small exercise pen staring at someone standing at the fence. She motioned for her uncle to come. Buster tossed his head. Will opened his mouth to warn the intruder, but stopped short when

Buster shook his head from side to side and whickered . . . and then took a step forward toward . . . the PW.

"I know him," Jo whispered. "He's the one who translated Daddy's sermon last Sunday. And I'm pretty sure he'll be doing it again tomorrow. Buster seems to like him," Jo said.

Will said nothing.

———

"Yes . . . you. Beautiful. *Liebling.*" He sang a line of a lullaby before saying, "So you like German music . . . ? Maybe that is why you have been so much trouble—no German music. You remind me of my father's horse. Almost I think you have some of those bloodlines. How about it? Are you demisang like Renzo? Would you jump to the skies, if only they would let you . . . ? Is that what you are trying to tell them—that you want to jump . . . ?"

His heart pounding, Dieter held out his hand, amazed when the infamous stallion from the stud barn didn't come charging at him. He'd heard about the creature from some of the men in Compound A who had volunteered to work over in the remount. When their romantic Karl May-fueled images of stables and cowboys and Indians were smothered by rancid hay and manure, most philosophized that at least the days passed by quickly. They kept at it, happy to embellish their work for the ears of anyone who would listen.

"Jenny Camp?" Dieter said one evening in disbelief. "You must check again. Jenny Camp cannot be in this place." But she was. The famous Olympic mare was stabled just across the road. Brock grew even more impatient with office work. But today Rolf Shrader was sick, and Isaacson had appointed Dieter to substitute for him. He had not yet seen Jenny Camp with his own eyes, but here he was watching a magnificent stallion dancing around a too-small corral. He was feeling almost content. Earlier in the day, Isaacson had asked him about working with the horses.

"Your education merits a better job, but Romani told me that you'd like to work over at the remount. If that's true, there are a lot of the stable crew on furlough right now, and they are screaming for help."

"I have never wanted anything more than to live and work around horses," Dieter said.

"Romani mentioned your background." Isaacson frowned. "But there's nothing in your file about a knowledge of horses."

Dieter shrugged. "Perhaps Private Romani has not yet filed my requests."

"Requests? What requests?" Isaacson thrust his chin forward as he spoke—a sure sign he was concentrating on something besides what he was saying.

"I have asked many times to work in the remount," Dieter said. "Private Romani said that you said I am needed in the office."

Isaacson's gray eyes narrowed. The fine muscles around his mouth pulled the corners of his mouth downward. "I see," he said.

"I . . . I don't mean to speak ill of the private from New York," Dieter said. "Please, I do not want any trouble."

"There won't be any trouble," Isaacson said. "At least none that can be traced back to you."

Once again, Isaacson understood—a fact that both surprised and confused Dieter. During the long journey to America, he and his comrades had wondered what would happen once they were delivered, body and soul, into the hands of their enemies. That would be bad enough. No one imagined they might be at the mercy of a member of the most hated race in the fatherland. When they first arrived at Fort Robinson and Isaacson introduced himself, the hair on the back of Dieter's neck stood up. Surely this was the essence of being without protection in the land of the victors. But, like many things in America, Sergeant Isaacson was not as expected. He reprimanded another guard who was unnecessarily rough with the prisoners. "It is not a crime to be German," he said. "May I remind you that America is heavily populated with Germans. Did you know that even our great President Lincoln had a German on his cabinet?" Even the prisoners like Gunnar Stroh, who didn't trust Isaacson because he was Jewish, eventually came to view him with grudging respect. Other, less prejudiced prisoners, soon came to seek him out when they had a request, knowing that Isaacson was less inclined to say no.

An intelligent Jew, who was both generous and kind, was confusing to the boy who had never owned any creed deep in his soul. Standing alongside his little mother in church, Dieter was a good Lutheran boy. In the Afrika Korps, he was a Nazi. Now he was in America, and everything he had experienced reminded him that Dieter Brock had no idea what he really believed. His parents had taught him to be truthful and to fear God. In the Hitler Youth he was taught to love the Fuehrer and fatherland. But here, in a prison camp in America, where Jews deserved respect and newspapers were allowed to criticize the government, things were becoming increasingly unsettled in his mind. Everything in the world was upside down.

Rolf Shrader had teased him about his impatience with office work. "Wouldn't you miss this?" He motioned with his hands down his body, adding curves in the air and batting his eyelashes.

"Being around females is—"

"Delicious?"

Dieter shook his head. "Disturbing."

Gunnar Stroh snickered. "What's the matter, Brock? Not used to being in the candy store and not being able to have all you want?"

For all his crudeness, Stroh had hit on a truth. Being around the American secretaries was beginning to fray on Dieter's nerves. It was only natural for a man to be attracted to beauty, but his attraction to any American woman could only lead to catastrophe. He was used to holding out his hand and having what he wanted fall into it.

Now, as he looked at the beautiful horse before him, his heart soared. Here, too, was beauty. And just like a painting or a piece of sculpture, this was beauty that could be openly admired. Others might think it a small thing, but to a man coming from battlefields to prison, even a small window of beauty was a gift to be treasured. To have a creature such as the one before him come to him of its own free will would be something of a triumph.

Dieter knew the animal's reputation. Even the professional cowboy who worked in the stud barn was having difficulty with Buster.

"If only they spoke German," he said to the horse. "That is the key, *ja*?" While he talked, he reached into his pocket and retrieved a small, square biscuit and put it in his open palm. Instead of reaching out toward Buster, though, he rested his hand on the top railing of the corral and waited.

Buster's nostrils flared.

Dieter could almost see the horse thinking. "Sure. You smell that? That was the favorite treat of my father's horse. You think that smells good?"

Buster shook his head and took one step forward.

"Sure. You smell me, but you smell that, too. You can't have that delicious treat unless you trust the man holding it." As the horse watched him, Dieter began to sing quietly. Buster took another step forward. Dieter sang. Another step. Dieter kept singing. "You should come ahead," he sang, abandoning the lullaby's words and conversing instead with the horse. "Because soon it is time I must go back to my barracks."

The stallion tossed his head.

Two blasts on the post horn announced the end of the workday and summoned the PWs to their truck. Dieter stopped singing. "All right, you," Dieter said in German. He put the *pfefferneusse* back up on the fence post.

"That's good enough for today, then. You don't kick, and you don't charge me . . . so you get the treat." As Dieter walked away, Buster whirled around and whinnied a protest. He pranced toward the fence, snatched up the small cookie and stood watching Dieter retreat, pawing the earth and whinnying.

———

From their vantage point just inside the barn, Jo and Will looked at one another in disbelief.

"I've never seen anything like that," Jo said. "It was like they were actually talking to each other."

Will nodded. "And Buster just told him to come back," he said, as Buster danced along the far edge of the corral watching the German walking away and trumpeting loudly. The German didn't stop and look back. Instead, he jogged away in the direction of the parade ground.

The minute the German was out of sight, Buster whirled about, shook his head, and, trotting to the sliding stall door, gave it a quick kick.

Jo jumped back. "Well," she said, laughing nervously. "The old Buster's back." She headed out of the stall with Will, and together they rolled back the door to admit Buster.

"Give him some sugar," Uncle Will said. "See if his sweet mood comes back."

Jo spoke to the horse while she perched a sugar cube atop the side railing of his stall and stepped back. Buster minced forward, inhaled, snorted, and pushed the sugar cube off the railing.

"You brat!" Jo said, shaking her finger at the horse and laughing. She turned to Uncle Will. "Apparently he only speaks German."

———

"You're kidding, right?"

Will thought Bill Harker could at least try to hide his amazement. "No, sir. I saw it with my own eyes. My niece says he translated the sermon last Sunday afternoon. Could you find out if he'd want to work in the stud barn?"

"Isn't *avoiding* the German PWs what brought you to Fort Robinson in the first place? Because I've had to be pretty creative to keep them out of your area."

Will shrugged. "I appreciate that. Really, I do. But you asked me to take special care of Buster. I'd be cheating you *and* the horse if I didn't say—or do—something about what I saw yesterday."

"But, Bishop, if you're going to work with PWs, you might as well have—"

"Yeah. I know. I might as well have stayed on the Four Pines." Will took his hat off and pretended it needed shaping. He looked up. "I told you I had a trick or two up my sleeve. I guess I'm the one being tricked." He chuckled softly. "By a dadgummed *horse,* of all things."

Harker slapped his knee and began to laugh. "I can't believe it. A stallion that speaks German."

"And likes whatever it is that guy had in his pocket," Will added. "Don't forget that."

Harker stopped laughing. "Are you sure you want him working in the barn with you?"

Will shrugged. "You asked me to try and save the horse, and I think the horse is worth saving." He stood up. At the door of the vet's office he turned around. "Just make sure this guy understands that my boy's in the air corps. If he's got any brains at all, he'll know I'm not exactly predisposed to make friends. And he'd better not give me any trouble."

———

No one in Crawford, Nebraska—least of all Helen Frey—would have imagined Clarissa Hale as their angel of mercy. Helen's prewar opinion of Clarissa had been forged in the fires of the women's sewing circle that met twice a week in the fellowship hall of First Baptist Church. And it was perfectly clear to anyone attending, that from the day she married Ben Hale, Clarissa Jackson had demonstrated a peculiar talent for annoying the women at First Baptist Church.

Helen could recite—although she never did—an impressive list of reasons why the women spoke about their pastor's wife with raised eyebrows. Mrs. Hale had the blue ribbons to prove she was a good cook, but she never volunteered to make a meat loaf for the church supper. Mrs. Hale could stitch circles around any woman in the church sewing circle, but she avoided the weekly meetings in favor of "important" projects like making curtains for her *garage* of all things. Once her own child was raised—and she had only one, which was a shame, the women said, given the fact that Ben Hale was such a wonderful man—Mrs. Hale quit volunteering to work in the nursery on Sundays and gave up helping with vacation Bible school. No, the women agreed, Clarissa Hale was nothing like what a congregation had a right to expect. It was widely agreed—and often discussed—that if Pastor Hale weren't such an exceptional man, the deacons would likely have formed a search committee and sent the Hales packing long ago.

Which was why, once she had been forced to stop attending the sewing circle and go to work at Fort Robinson, Helen Frey was amazed when Clarissa Hale had become her angel of mercy. The first time Helen retrieved Mia from the Hales' backyard, the child was working alongside Jo in the garden, manhandling a hoe twice her height and chattering away about mama's job at the fort.

"I hope she wasn't a bother," Helen said.

"A bother?" Jo replied. "She's a hard worker." Jo patted Mia on the head. "Mia's welcome as often as she wants to come. I always wanted a little sister."

And now, as the days went by and Helen didn't move back home, she got a taste of what it was like to be the main topic of discussion among the women of her town. It was a subtle thing—the change that Helen came to view as her fall from grace. There were strange silences when she shopped around town. Meaningful glances. Cold shoulders. It was hurtful. But it led to Helen's conclusion that when the chips were down, she could trust exactly two women in town: Clarissa Hale and Stella Black. At least she had been able to trust them so far. Helen didn't know what they would think when—and if—she told them the complete truth about herself and Hank. Wondering about it kept her awake. Doubting kept her quiet. And hope kept her sane.

———

"Thank you for seeing me, Mrs. Hale," Harriet Bohling said.

Clarissa, who had been dreading this moment since Hettie's phone call right after lunch on Saturday, opened her front door and stepped outside. How she wished she had gone with Jo and Ben out to Fort Robinson.

"Let's just chat here on the front porch, shall we?" she said when Hettie arrived. There was no way she was going to get trapped in her own home. "It's so pleasant out here, don't you think?" She guided Hettie to one of two lattice-backed rockers. "That's the reverend's favorite chair, and I'm sure you'll see why. Isn't it comfortable?"

Yes, the chair was comfortable, Hettie agreed, perching on the edge of the seat like a nervous bird. Yes, it was nice to be able to finally enjoy the porch again now that spring was here, but you never knew when a late snowstorm would ruin it all. "You know how it is out here in the Sandhills," Hettie said. "We've only got the two seasons—winter and July."

Clarissa smiled politely and waited for the real reason for the visit. It wasn't long in coming. People, Hettie began, were concerned for Henry Frey.

"So are we," Clarissa said, rushing to defend her husband from the implication that the pastor was somehow not doing enough. "Ben is doing what he can."

As usual, Hettie was more interested in what she had come to say than what Mrs. Hale could contribute. Why, did Mrs. Hale know that Mrs. Frey was going to have to keep her job out at Fort Robinson?

"It would be a hardship on her fellow workers if she left right now," Clarissa said. "Mrs. Frey says they are almost drowning in paper work. Did you know there are something like fifteen forms to be completed for every PW?"

Did Mrs. Hale know that little Mia was afraid of her own father?

"Mia is a delightful child."

It was wonderful, of course, that young Josephine was good with children and that Mia had a place to go. And it was certainly an answer to everyone's prayers that Mr. Frey had taken to working again, but didn't Mrs. Hale agree it could not be good for the family for Hank to be "in there" at night with all the shades drawn. And Vernon Clark—who everyone knew had simply not accepted Delmer's death and had taken to drinking—was hanging around Hank's garage.

"I wonder," Clarissa said, "if it's ever possible to *accept* the death of a child. I just don't think the English language has words for what's going on in our world right now."

Hettie plunged ahead without commenting on Clarissa's comment. As far as anyone knew, she continued, Vernon Clark was the only one in Crawford who had actually *seen* Hank Frey. And that couldn't be good for Hank. What if he took to drink, too? He was already acting strange. And people had heard the two of them ranting about the Germans.

No one was blaming Mrs. Frey, of course, but Hettie had heard that "just the other day the poor woman was seen crossing the street, suitcase in hand, and taking refuge—" Hettie leaned forward and lowered her voice before almost hissing—"at Stella Black's. And we all know what that will lead to!"

"I-I'm afraid I don't know what you're talking about, Mrs. Bohling." Clarissa felt as though she were swimming through mud. Hettie had come

up for air, but Clarissa didn't know how to break the surface of all the dirt
that had been slung in the last few minutes.

"Sarah Fosdick told all of us at circle. She was sweeping the front
walk and she saw it for herself. Helen Frey came out her front door with a
suitcase, walked across the street, and went into Stella Black's house. Then
the two of them came out a little later and got into the back of Deacon
Hanson's Pontiac just like always and headed off. And then, when they got
back from work, Sarah just happened to be out on the front porch doing a
little mending, and she saw them go inside together, and Mrs. Frey never
came out. So don't you see? She's left her husband. I can't imagine what's
to become of Mia."

Hettie leaned forward a little farther. Clarissa found herself wishing
the woman would just slip right off the edge of Ben's rocker.

"I knew you'd want to know," Hettie said. "So the reverend can finally
do something about the Freys."

It was the word *finally* that gave Clarissa the courage to interrupt Hettie.
Finally? What did she mean *finally?* As if Ben had been ignoring the pain in
his flock? Who did the old hen think she was, anyway? Clarissa stood up.
"Mia will be staying with us for a few days. In fact, she and Jo are going to
enjoy an early summer break. My sister is delighted to have them at the
ranch, and my husband has arranged it with the school."

"Good for him," Hettie said. "We've been concerned."

"I beg your pardon?"

"Now relax, Mrs. Hale. . . ."

I would if you'd get your claws out of my back.

"No one is criticizing the reverend. . . ."

*Of course, no one is . . . but about a half dozen of you just can't help your-
selves, can you?*

"Josephine is an adult, after all. She can certainly look after herself,
but are you quite sure your sister is equipped to handle a child by herself?
I hear Mr. Bishop is no longer—"

With supreme effort, Clarissa resisted the urge to go inside and slam
the door in Harriet Bohling's face. Instead, she sat back down. "I'm afraid
I don't understand," she said, "what you are talking about."

"The *Germans,* Mrs. Hale. The *Germans.*" Hettie's eyes grew large and
she nodded with what Clarissa could only take as an unsuccessful attempt to
look like a sage. "Everyone knows your sister has requested workers. Which
is, of course, her prerogative. It's not like she's the only one. But—"

My husband . . . my daughter . . . the Freys . . . and now . . . CJ? Clarissa
snapped. She stood up.

"Of course, your sister has always been eccentric, but—"

"I-I believe I hear my phone. Excuse me." Clarissa let the door slam behind her. She did not know how long Hettie waited on the front porch, but by the time Clarissa had finished crying and assured herself her eyes were no longer bloodshot, her husband's rocking chair was vacant. And then the phone really did ring.

The way CJ shouted into a telephone had always irritated her. But today, Clarissa smiled as she listened to her sister's enthusiastic plans for Jo and Mia.

"Sis?" Clarissa finally interrupted.

"Yes?"

"I love you."

Chapter Thirteen

Be ye therefore merciful as
your Father also is merciful.
LUKE 6:36

KNOCKING ON STELLA BLACK'S front door was one of the hardest things Clarissa had done in years. She was shaking all over when Helen Frey pulled back the window curtain to see who was there.

"What . . . what's wrong? What's happened? Is it Mia? Is she hurt?" Helen's face had gone white and she was clutching Clarissa's arm.

"No, Mia's fine. Ben took her and Jo downtown for a treat. The girls are all packed, and Mia was about to implode from excitement. I just—" Clarissa put her hand on Helen's shoulder. "Helen. Calm down. Really. Everything's fine."

Helen's dark eyelashes fluttered away the tears of relief while Clarissa talked.

"I just talked to CJ, and she has all kinds of plans for the girls. She was asking me if Mia liked this or that, and what her favorite foods are—all kinds of questions. She is so excited about having her. I wanted you to know." She paused. "It's going to be all right, Helen."

Helen took a deep breath and let it out. She brushed her forehead with her open palm. Then she forced a smile. "Maybe you could let Mrs. Bohling know."

Clarissa feigned innocence. "What?"

Stella appeared at the doorway to the kitchen. "Are you kidding, honey?" She flourished the wooden spoon in her hand. "There's a big old *nasty* grapevine that crawls all over this town. Helen landed on my doorstep at 7:30 Thursday morning, and I can pretty much guarantee that by 7:45 most of Crawford knew."

Helen ducked her head.

Clarissa sighed audibly. "I know. I'm sorry. I was hoping maybe the grapevine would have died back—just a little."

Stella snorted. "Dream on. Mrs. Fosdick up the street almost broke her neck trying to watch when Helen and I got home from work yesterday." She strode to the front door and out onto the porch. Clarissa and Helen exchanged horrified glances as they heard Stella holler, "You go on in and cook supper, Mrs. Fosdick. The preacher's wife is on the case. Helen's staying here for a few days. And say hello to Mrs. Bohling when you talk to her!"

Stella marched back inside. She paused at the kitchen door. "You're welcome to share my mostly beans chili, if you want to hang around," she said to Clarissa.

"Thank you, but, actually—"

"What was I *thinking*?" Stella brought the back of her hand up to her forehead in mock horror. "The Baptist minister's wife can't be caught dining with a 'mackerel snapper.' " She retreated, laughing, into the red and yellow kitchen.

Clarissa, who had always wanted a red and yellow kitchen, called after her. "Actually, I came over here to invite both of you to come with us to the ranch tomorrow evening." She looked at Helen. "I'm thinking you'd like to see just where your little cowgirl will be."

"Is this an invitation to the ranch or an invitation to the ranch with church strings attached?" Stella reappeared at the kitchen door.

Clarissa smiled. "It's an invitation to the ranch. No strings."

"All I have to do Sunday is go to mass," Stella said. She winked at Clarissa. "With all the flirting I do out at the fort, I have to get my regular dose of forgiveness. But then you've probably heard all about that from your husband's deacon."

Clarissa didn't know where the next thing she said came from. The only thing she had prayed for before walking across to Stella's house was that Mrs. Fosdick would tell Mrs. Bohling that Pastor Hale's wife had done her duty and visited Mrs. Frey . . . and then leave Ben off the gossip tree for a while. But what came out of her mouth seemed to be inspired by someone other than herself. "The grapevine spares no one," she said. "Not even the preacher's wife." She looked past Stella into the red and yellow kitchen and then back at Stella. "So we'll expect you to join us, Mrs. Black?"

"Stella."

"All right. Stella. As long as you call me Clarissa. Now tell me about Delores. How does she like it in Des Moines? When the paper ran that picture of this year's Easter bonnets and included the women's military hats, I was trying to picture her in her new uniform. Do you have a photo yet?"

As Stella tipped her head sideways and looked at her, Clarissa had the unwelcome feeling of being measured and weighed. Judged. Again.

"Why don't you come back here and have a cup of tea while I finish this pathetic chili?" Stella laughed. "I think I've already worn Helen's ears off bragging on my daughter. And yes, I have a picture. She's far too pretty in that uniform, by the way."

In the kitchen, Stella put a water-spotted teakettle on to heat. And friendship climbed out of the primeval ooze of tea leaves, hot water, and lemon.

———

Clara Joy

The woman who climbed out of Ben Hale's Nash earlier this evening looked like Clarissa, but she didn't sound a thing like her. She seemed almost proud of the Four Pines. "You'll have to ask CJ," she said when Stella Black asked a question. "She's the rancher in the family. I'd be good at feeding the wranglers, but I don't know the first thing about horses or haying."

"CJ had that built," she said, pointing out the new barn down by the spring. "Of course, in the old days when our papa had to be able to get to the barn in a blizzard, he wanted the barn close to the house. But when we outgrew the old barn, CJ decided to put a new one closer to the bunkhouse so it would be easier for the men to do chores." Clarissa laughed, "They still have to be able to get to the barn in a blizzard, but CJ always thinks of her wranglers when she improves the place. That's how she keeps hands for so long."

Now, all of what Clarissa said today is true, but she's never let on like she cared about a bit of it. Shoot, in the '30s when the oats didn't head up and the high meadow spring went dry, Clarissa did everything she could to make me sell the place.

"Half of it's mine," she yelled one night, "and half of a worthless ranch is just that: *worthless*. Sell it now and get what you can and be *done* with it!"

"So that's it," I snapped. "It's the money." And I really let her have it. Of course, I was scared to death about losing the place and I really wasn't myself or I wouldn't have said everything I did. I called her a coward and a goody-two-shoes. I accused her of not caring about Mama and Papa's dream and all they'd done to give us a home. It was a terrible row. We didn't speak for nearly a year.

Finally the weather broke. I was feeling pretty smug when I got the hay contract down at Fort Robinson. In fact, I actually joined the line of people shaking the preacher's hand one Sunday just so I could hand Clarissa her profit-sharing check in a semipublic way. I thought it would feel real good to do it, too. But it didn't. God sort of nudged me about how prideful that was. I hung around to apologize and, while the rest of the congregation passed by, God really got my attention. I once heard someone say that "crow is a tough old bird," and they were right. I've eaten my share. But one of the biggest helpings I ever ate was that day when I apologized to Clarissa for being so prideful.

Since then, we've managed what I like to think of as a peaceful coexistence. She doesn't give unsolicited advice about how I should run the ranch, and I come to church. Oh. And Jo comes to live with me every summer. Between the obvious fact that living with Ben Hale all these years has mellowed Clarissa and the years living alone have mellowed me, we get along all right. Now and then when there is a glitch in our sisterly relations—like that thing about me wearing boots with my Sunday dresses and the same hat for all those years—we work it out. Or Ben does. Once in a while, Will Bishop even has a hand in keeping the peace between Clarissa and me. Although I guess that won't be happening anymore.

Now there I go again. It just seems like, lately, no matter what I'm thinking about, it always ends up turning to Will Bishop. I've gotta stop that.

———

"Watch me, Mama, *watch* me!" Mia screeched with delight as she bounced along astride the swaybacked old gelding CJ Jackson called Ned.

"I'm watching, baby!" Helen called back.

"Giddy*up*, Ned," Mia said, rattling her reins and flopping her legs. "Giddy*up*!"

At Helen's side, CJ chortled. "Ned lost the 'giddy' in his 'up' about five years ago."

Helen smiled. "He doesn't seem to be minding all the commotion in the least," she said.

"Ned never did mind commotion. He's one of those old cow horses that has more sense than most of the cowboys who ever rode him. He'll be perfect for your little blondie. They'll be best friends in no time."

Helen leaned against the corral pole and watched her daughter. Jo Hale was standing in the middle of the corral with a long lead attached to Ned's bridle. The old horse grunted in protest when Jo said, "trot," but he obeyed. When Mia lost her hold on the saddle horn and started to slip to one side, Ned stopped.

"Is he actually waiting for Mia to right herself?" Helen asked in disbelief.

"I think he is," CJ said. "Ned's always had a sense about things. Even as a two-year-old he had a talent for adjusting his behavior to his rider. Of course, back then 'adjusting' sometimes meant taking advantage of an inexperienced rider. All horses will test a rider now and then. But Ned's past that. You don't have to worry. I wouldn't let Mia near any animal I didn't know was safe."

"I'm not worried," Helen said. When Mia climbed down, she stood beside the old gelding, patting his neck and talking to him. When the horse lowered its head and nibbled the top of the little girl's head, Mia pulled away.

"Hey," she said, then laughed and said, "I'm not *hay!*"

Her daughter's laughter brought tears to Helen's eyes. "I don't know how to thank you," she said to CJ. "For letting Mia come."

CJ shook her head. "No thanks needed. Blondie's welcome to stay as long as she wants." She paused. "Do you want her back home before the labor crew from the fort starts here?"

"I've got enough to worry about without adding imaginary problems to my life," Helen said. "I guess it's lucky I've been working in the PW headquarters. I know there's nothing to worry about with that. And I don't know when—" Helen swallowed, and thought *or if . . .* "I don't know when we'll be ready to bring her home."

"I'm sorry," CJ said, "about Hank's . . . difficulties." She cleared her throat. "After Johnny got that worthless old car of his, he used to haul Hank out to the ranch to work on it. Used to irritate me, sometimes, the way Hank could always see the silver side of a cloud."

Mia grabbed Ned's reins and walked over, playacting the cowgirl.

CJ kept talking. "Will was wishing Johnny would just let him haul the old thing out to the junk pile in the canyon, but Hank always had something else to try . . . and he always found a way to make it run again."

At the mention of her father, Mia lost her smile. She looked sideways up at her mother. "I don't want to go back home."

Helen blinked back the tears that were all too close to the surface these days. "I thought you were going to show me how much you know about taking care of horses," she said abruptly. "I don't know a lot, but I know there's a lot more to it than just jangling reins and yelling 'giddyup.' And if Miss Jackson is going to let you stay out here, you have to be ready to help."

On the opposite side of the corral, Jo was opening the gate.

"Come on, Ned," Mia said, leading the old horse to the barn. She called back to her mother, "I'll help. I'll work *hard*."

Helen took a step toward the barn.

"She can stay as long as you need her to," CJ said, just loud enough for Helen to hear. "And I mean it."

Helen nodded, swiped at her eyes, and headed after her daughter.

As Reverend Hale drove his old car over the winding road that led from the Four Pines Ranch, up the ridge, and back down into the valley where Fort Robinson and the city of Crawford nestled beside the White River, Helen stared out the passenger-side rear window of the old car, purposely tuning out the conversation around her and the concerned stares being exchanged between Clarissa and Stella. When Pastor Hale pulled the Nash over to the curb in front of Stella's house and let the ladies out, Helen thanked him, hoping that Mrs. Bohling and Mrs. Fosdick were watching. They would likely be upset at the idea of Pastor Hale and his wife supporting her new abode, but it still gave Helen a warm feeling when Pastor Hale even opened the gate that led up the sidewalk to Stella's front porch, and he and Clarissa lingered to talk.

"Thank you," she said. "I feel so much better knowing Mia is happy." She looked across the street. "I know Hank and I have to . . . do . . . something. But I don't know what. Having Mia gone is best for now."

"You don't have to know what you're going to do, honey," Stella said and slipped her arm around Helen's waist.

"I agree," Pastor Hale said. "Take some time. Watch and pray. I might have an idea . . . but I'm not sure. . . ." He smiled at Stella. "Be thankful for friends. And keep busy."

Stella nodded. "There's a dance at the Servicemen's Club tomorrow night. I promised Mrs. Blair I'd help chaperone." She turned toward Helen. "You should come with me," she said. "It'd do you good to get out."

"Oh, no," Helen said. "I couldn't."

"Of course you could," Clarissa spoke up, then looked at her husband. "Couldn't she?"

"Why don't all three of you go," Reverend Hale said. He smiled down at his wife. "I could use the time to get an early start on next week's sermon."

———

Just inside the back door Clarissa emoted. "Do you *want* to get fired?"

"What are you talking about?"

"I can't go to a dance at the Servicemen's Club."

"You aren't going to a dance," Ben said. "You know Mrs. Blair will shuttle you into the kitchen the minute you show your face. No one can possibly take issue with you doing your part to help the men from the fort have a wholesome evening instead of frequenting the bars." He kissed her cheek. "Clarissa Hale is the best cook in Dawes County, and everyone knows it. Those boys from Fort Robinson have no idea what a treat they are in for. If you like, I'll even walk the three of you to the club," he offered.

"That's all right, honey. You said you wanted to get started on next week's sermon."

"And I will. But . . . I was thinking I could just happen by Hank's garage on my way home."

Chapter Fourteen

My little children, let us not love in word, neither in tongue;
but in deed and in truth.
1 JOHN 3:18

Clara Joy

WHEN THE PHONE rang Monday morning, I could not believe my ears.

"You coming to the dispersal sale next week?"

"Wh-what?"

"I said," Will repeated, "are you coming to the sale next week? Here. At Fort Robinson."

"Wasn't planning on it,"

"Think you should," Will said.

My old heart thumped at the idea the old fool might actually be missing me. He'd only been gone for a little over a month, but it seemed like a year, and I was hoping he felt the same way.

"There's a horse you should see. Demisang. Gorgeous head. Good bloodlines."

The old fool wasn't missing me. He was talking horses. I let him hear the irritation in my voice. "If he's so perfect, why's he going on the sale? Bill Harker's always been willing to make room for new blood—at least for a season or two."

"Too much fire. Needs special handling."

"All men do," I snapped, "and most aren't worth the trouble."

Will cleared his throat. "Buster is."

"Buster?"

"The stallion I want you to see."

"See? Or buy?" There was no reason for me to drive to the dispersal sale just to look at a horse.

"Buy," Will admitted.

"With a name like that I'll be expecting a plow horse."

"There's not a drop of plow horse in Buster. You come to the sale, and you'll see what I mean."

What was he thinking? "Will, things have changed since you left, and the very last thing I need at the Four Pines right now is a hard-to-handle stallion. Jo and Mia are already here."

"I know," Will said. "Jo told me about it. Sad about the Frey family."

"Well, if you know about it, you know I've got my hands full, and I don't need any more challenges at the moment. No more wranglers have sprouted from the rocks since you left." He was quiet for so long I thought the line might have gone dead. "Will? Hello? Are you there?"

"I'm here," Will said.

He was talking very slowly, which meant he was about to say something real important. I am not a patient woman, but once in a while I give Will Bishop the benefit of the doubt. So I hung on and waited to hear what he would say.

"If you come to the sale . . . and you want the horse . . ." Will cleared his throat. "I'd be willing to take him on as a special project." More silence. Then, "He's w-worth it, CJ."

"My work request was approved, Will. I'm getting fifteen PWs to help out around here. And I'm not waiting until July. I've been talking to the Walkers. Margaret says that other than the fact they don't like sweet potatoes and prefer rye bread to white, there hasn't been one thing happen that's anything but great. In short, my work crew is coming before haying season, and if they are any good at all, I'll keep them coming for as long as I can get them."

"Ask for one named Dieter Brock."

"What?"

"I said," Will repeated, "ask for Dieter Brock. He's got a way with horses. Especially Buster." Will swallowed. "You need me to spell his name for you?"

It was my turn to hunt for words. "Am I hearing you right?" I finally said. "You want me to come to the sale and risk . . . I don't know, probably a hundred dollars on an unknown horse named Buster—"

"It might take more," Will said. "Vic Dearborn was watching the German work with him the other day. Seemed pretty impressed. I think he's coming to the sale."

I couldn't resist being just a little sarcastic. "So I should pay serious money at a sale that usually brings about fifty dollars a head. . . . And if I do, you'll move back on the place . . . and you want help, but not just any help—you want *Nazi* help?"

"He's not really a Nazi," Will said.

"Really? I seem to recall you saying they all are." Of course, I knew more about Dieter Brock than I was letting on. The minute Will said the name, I remembered Helen Frey talking about him over lunch at Clarissa's. But I wasn't in the mood to make things easy on Will. Not yet.

"Well, I was wrong," Will said. "Brock is . . . I don't know. He doesn't act like a Nazi, anyway. I haven't really asked him about it."

"I expect not, unless you've been studying German." I am ashamed to admit that I carried things this far with Will. Helen Frey had made a point to tell us all that Dieter Brock spoke English real well, and of course I knew he was translating for Ben's services. But I was taking a sinful kind of pleasure in making Will squirm. I am not proud of that, and I have repented. But I'm also telling it straight, and that is what I did.

"He . . . he speaks English. You get him on the crew," Will said, "you won't have anything to worry about. He talks better than me. 'Course that's not s-saying m-much." He paused before saying, "I-I'm sorry, Ceeg. I was wrong."

Will hadn't called me *Ceeg*—pronounced like *siege*—in years. But my stubbornness wasn't about to fold yet. "Did I just hear you say you're sorry?"

"You did."

That did it. "Come on home, Will. I've missed you."

———

On Monday night, when Hank let himself into his auto repair shop via the alley door in the back, he kicked what proved to be a set of keys across the floor. Someone had used the key drop. Again. It had started happening soon after he'd worked on the preacher's car.

He used his flashlight to find the keys, then, checking to make certain the front door was locked and all the blinds were drawn on the windows up front, he settled on a stool behind the front counter to read the note from Bob Hanover.

Need Ron's old Buick running good before we sell her. Call before you do the work. Don't have much cash.

After staring at the note for a few minutes, Hank made his way to the back door, opened it, and peered out into the dark alley. Assured there was no one lurking there, he raised the garage door, went to Ron's old car, started it up, and pulled it into the first of two bays.

As soon as he raised the hood, a knock sounded at the back door. Hank ignored it.

"It's me," a now-familiar voice yelled. Hank sighed and went to unlock the door.

Once inside the shop, Vernon perched on a metal stool to watch Hank at work. On occasion, he retrieved a wrench or a belt.

"You're getting good with the hook," he said at one point.

Hank shrugged. "They told me not to give up with it. Said before long it would be second nature. Almost like a hand."

"Looks to me like you're there," Vernon offered. "You could open up again. The way you keep getting night visits, it's pretty obvious folks are glad you're back."

Hank said nothing.

"A man needs to know he's worth something," Vernon said. "That he can provide for his family."

"I've got no family," Hank said. "Not one that wants me, anyway. Helen took Mia and moved out."

"I heard," Vernon said. "Never figured her to quit on you like that."

Hank propelled himself out from under the car. "She didn't quit," he snapped. "She did what any woman would. Mia's afraid of me. And who can blame Helen if she can't stand to look at me. It's not her fault."

"Calm down, man," Vernon said. "I'm on your side, remember? 'Course it's not her fault. Pretty little gal sends her high school sweetheart off . . . and look what happens." He spun off center again into a colorful litany of now-familiar curses against the Italians and Mussolini, Hitler and the Krauts.

Hank scooted himself back under the car. When Vern offered him a drink, he turned it down. As the minutes passed, Vern drank the little silver flask dry.

"It's not enough anymore," he said, holding the flask upside down, then bringing it to his mouth to lick away the last drops. He stood up. "Got to get some more."

"G'night, Vernon," Hank said without sliding out. "You be careful walking home now, y'hear? Maybe go home and get some sleep."

"Sleep," Vernon said. "Wouldn't that be something? To actually sleep."

From beneath the car, Hank listened for the *click* that meant Vernon had locked the door behind him. When it didn't come, he slid from beneath Ron's car . . . just in time to see Reverend Hale come in.

"Evening, Hank," Ben said.

"E-evening," Hank said, pushing himself quickly back under the car. His heart was thumping. The preacher had looked straight at him. He hadn't even flinched, and Hank didn't know what to make of it.

"Just came by to let you know we drove out to the ranch yesterday," the preacher said. "Thought you'd like to know Mia likes it out there. Jo is teaching her to ride one of the old horses on the place."

Hank lowered his arms from the car's exhaust system and tried to picture Mia on horseback. "She used to draw horses all the time. Made me read *Black Beauty* to her until I was sick of it." After a minute he said, "I imagine she can read it for herself by now."

"I don't know about that," the preacher said. "Maybe you should ask her."

"That would be a little difficult, seeing as how she screams and runs away every time I come near her. And then there is the fact that she's out at your wife's ranch getting to know the Germans up close and personal." He went back to banging on the rusted muffler. His stump was beginning to ache from the impact. He paused, waiting for the preacher to defend his wife.

"I don't imagine you care to hear my thoughts on that," the preacher said, cool as could be. "But I can tell you that CJ Jackson would never do anything to risk Mia or Jo's safety." He paused. "If you like, I'll drive you out to the Four Pines myself. You can check it out."

"Maybe I'll take you up on that," Hank said. "Just as soon as hell freezes over."

The preacher cleared his throat. "If you change your mind, you let me know. In the meantime, I stopped by to tell you I walked Clarissa and Stella Black and your wife to the Servicemen's Club tonight. Helen's going to help Clarissa in the kitchen once in a while. I wanted you to know it was my idea. In case the town gossip burned your ears with another version."

The rusted muffler finally gave way. Rust flew into Hanks eyes. He shot out from under the car and ran for the lavatory. With his back to the preacher he rinsed out his eyes and dried his face. "I know you mean well,

Preacher. But . . . why don't you just up and say why you really stopped by?"

"Why do you think I stopped by, Hank?"

Hank leaned against the doorframe with his good side facing the preacher. "Don't tell me you haven't been working on a speech. Everyone has a speech. Helen has her 'I love you and it doesn't matter' speech. Vernon Clark has his 'the sons-a-blanks destroyed your life and you should take revenge' speech. Don't you have a Romans 8:28 speech?"

"There'd be no reason to give that one," the preacher said. "You already know the verse. And I can't answer the question."

"Which question is that?"

"The one about how good is going to come from your situation." The preacher pointed to the stool recently vacated by Vernon Clark. "Mind if I take a seat?"

"Suit yourself," Hank said.

The preacher sat down. "Bob told me they were going to sell Ron's old car."

"So you *are* the reason I keep finding cars behind the shop." Hank grabbed a new muffler and headed back toward the car. "Thanks for that."

"You've got the wrong one," Ben said.

"What?"

"The wrong muffler. It *is* for a Buick, but Ron retrofitted his exhaust system before he went overseas. Put a Plymouth muffler on it."

Hank looked at the muffler in his hand. He shook his head. "Forgot about that." He looked toward the shelves where a pitiful array of car parts had waited for the garage owner's return from the war. "Darn," he said.

"Jack'll have one." The preacher rushed to add, "I could stop up there in the morning before I go into the office for you. Pick one up. If that would help."

"It would," Hank said. "And thanks." He reached into his pocket and withdrew a roll of bills with his hook.

The preacher stood up. "Forget it. Wait 'til we know for sure Jack has the one you need. Prices have been crazy since you left. You can pay me back when I deliver a new one."

"Whatever you say." Hank shoved the roll of bills back into his pocket.

The preacher rose to go. "Want me to lock the door behind me?" he asked. "Or is Vernon coming back? I saw him leave just as I rounded the corner at the other end of the alley. He didn't seem to be feeling well."

Hank shrugged. "He's probably at home sleeping it off." He hesitated, then added, "To tell you the truth, I don't think he would welcome a visit from you, Preacher."

The preacher sighed. "Which is an indication that that may be exactly what he needs." He shook his head. "That's the hardest part of my job. And the part I like the least."

"What part is that?" Hank asked.

"Chasing after folks who not only don't want to hear what I have to say . . . but are openly hostile about it."

"Don't take it personally," Hank said. "As far as I can tell, Vernon's openly hostile to just about everybody these days." He lifted the hood of the old Buick. "I never gave much thought to the idea of a preacher not liking his job."

"It's no different from any other job. Parts you love. Parts you don't. I love studying God's Word," the preacher said. "And I like the idea that maybe once in a while something I say from the pulpit does somebody some good. Hospital visits are all right, too."

"You wouldn't have liked visiting the hospital I was in," Hank said.

"Why do you say that?"

"Every last one of us burned, and no one knowing much to do about it beyond putting on bandages and waiting for the scars to heal it over."

The preacher was quiet.

"It's a strange thing to be on fire," Hank said. He looked past the preacher as his mind retreated into the past. He told the preacher more than he ever planned to tell anyone, but the man listened without any hint of revulsion. "Anyway," he concluded, "I ended up in a hospital outside London. Mostly Royal Air Force. They took me there because the burns were so bad. Said to get me to some doctor they called 'The Maestro.' " Hank grimaced and pointed to his face. "This was the best he could do. And believe it or not, this is pretty good, given what he had to work with." He tried to laugh. "Some of the guinea pigs needed what they called 'total reconstruction.' At least I have half a face left."

"I can't begin to imagine what you've been through, Hank. I don't even know what to say."

That was different. A preacher who didn't know what to say—who wasn't spouting clichés.

"You know," Hank went on, "we were forced out into the village every chance we got. Doctor said it was part of our therapy. Soon as we could. They called it 'the town that didn't stare.' Folks were used to seeing burned soldiers. Then I came home." He looked down at the floor. "And all I get is stares."

"People can be cruel," the preacher said. "I wish I could change that." He stood up. "When should I bring you the muffler? Tomorrow morning?"

"Night," Hank corrected him. "I'm a creature of the night now."

When the preacher had gone, Hank went to the front of the shop. Pulling a shade away from one of the windows just enough to peer out, he looked up the street toward the Servicemen's Club. He waited for a long time. Finally, Helen came out arm in arm with Stella. Two men walked alongside them. One of them was Deacon Tom Hanson. The other one was in uniform. Young. Handsome.

———

After the preacher delivered the muffler for Ron's car, word seemed to travel even faster about the rather unique reopening of Hank's Garage. The next few nights several cars appeared in the back alley. And the notes people left with their keys weren't just about what needed fixing. They were personal notes to Hank:

> *Glad to have you back.*
> *Sure missed you.*
> *Finally—a mechanic who knows what to do with a Hudson!*
> *We prayed for you every day you were gone.*
> *Crawford is proud of you.*
> *Welcome home, hero.*

He folded each one in half and tucked it in his pocket, and when he went home—always before dawn—and climbed the steps to the attic past the closed door to Helen's empty bedroom, he would take out the note and tape it to the wall along with the others.

He kept his garage doors locked and the shades drawn. He put cash in an envelope for Helen and left it on Stella Black's back stoop, weighted down with a rock. Mr. Clark stopped in nearly every night to perch on a barrel in the corner. Some nights he was quiet, others talkative. His talk centered around the Germans at Fort Robinson—although he had much more colorful terms to describe the prisoners of war. Did Hank know

Jim Grant's wife invited them into their ranch house and served them like members of the family?

Hank did not. And, no, he did not think that a good idea.

Did Hank know that CJ Jackson was going to have them cut hay for her?

Hank knew.

"Did you know they're over there in the prison eating steak while most of us are still counting ration stamps?" he grumbled. "Somebody ought to do something."

———

On Thursday night when Vern entered the shop, he gripped Hank's shoulders, and said, "You know what I think? I think people need to see what the Krauts did to you. Maybe a few of 'em would wake up."

"It wouldn't make any difference," Hank said. But it made him think. The doctor in England had had them wear their uniforms when they went out—and he had insisted they go out. He believed civilians should see the price being paid for their freedom.

After Vernon left the shop that night, Hank went into the little washroom tucked into the back corner of his shop and turned on the switch. A hundred-watt naked bulb washed his face with bright and unkind light. Hank lifted his chin, turned from side to side. "Face it," he murmured. When he realized the play on words, he smiled—with only half his mouth. The other half barely moved. He reached up with his index finger and lifted his upper lip. The scar tissue was numb.

He remembered when it hadn't been numb. He remembered the screams of the crew pinned inside the wreckage. . . . *Welcome home, hero*. Staring in the mirror, he whispered the words aloud as he reached up and covered the scarred part of his image with his hand, so that all he could see was the good side . . . the side washed with tears. He wasn't a hero. All he'd done was run for his life . . . and roll on the ground to put the flames out before he passed out. If the people who had written that note knew what followed in the hospital—how he screamed with every bandage change, how he begged not to be immersed in the saline bath—they wouldn't call him a hero.

And after all the suffering, still no one wanted to look at him. Even if he did put on his uniform and stroll through town, people wouldn't be encouraged to hope their husbands and sons might come home, too. They might manage to smile—in time—but at home, late at night, they would get on their knees and beg God. He knew the prayer, because he'd prayed it himself. "Let them die."

Hank turned out the light. He'd finish working on Stinson's Buick tomorrow.

Before stepping into the alley, he looked both ways. It was growing light. With his heart pounding, Hank ran for home.

Chapter Fifteen

A righteous man regardeth the life of his beast.
PROVERBS 12:10

"WILL WE SEE lots and lots of horses at the sale?" Mia asked Jo on Friday afternoon as she bounced up and down on the front seat of Aunt CJ's pickup.

"Hold still," Jo laughed. "You'll kick Sadie out of gear."

"Huh?"

"Sadie," Jo said, tapping the dashboard of her aunt's old pickup.

Mia looked up at Jo. "I wish I had a hat like yours."

"Your mother might not approve. Mine hates it when I wear flannel shirts and denim jeans."

"My mama doesn't care," Mia said. "I'm asking for a cowgirl hat for my birthday."

"When is your birthday, Blondie?" Aunt CJ asked.

"August 18," Mia said, frowning slightly.

"What's the matter?" Jo asked.

"Nothing."

Aunt CJ patted Mia's leg. "Nothing is something. So tell us what's the matter."

"Will you come to my birthday?" Mia said. "No matter what?"

CJ and Jo looked at each other. "Of course we will," Jo said. "In fact, I bet my mama would bake your favorite cake if I ask her. What kind do you like the very best in the world?"

"Angel food," Mia said.

"Well, you are in luck, because my mama won a blue ribbon last year at the fair for her angel food cake."

"I know," Mia said.

"Really?"

"Uh-huh. Mrs. Bohling that lives next door to us got the red ribbon. She was *mad*." Mia went on to describe Hettie Bohling coming home with her red-ribbon cake in such a way that both CJ and Jo were red-faced trying to stifle their laughter.

"Well," Jo said, "you can count on it, Mia. Angel food cake for your birthday in August. Anything else you want?"

"To have my party at the ranch."

After a long pause, Jo changed the subject. "You're gonna see more horses than you can count today, Mia."

"How many are we gonna *buy*?"

"Only one," Aunt CJ answered. "And I'm not even sure about that one. But Will says he is one of the prettiest you'll ever see."

Mia pretended to hold a horse's reins. "I wanna ride him!"

"You won't be riding this one," Jo said.

"Why not?"

"Well," Jo replied, "because Ned would get jealous. You don't want to make Ned sad, do you?"

Mia shook her head. She looked up at Jo. "Are *you* gonna ride the new horse?"

"No." It was Aunt CJ's turn to speak up. "If we get him, he won't be for riding."

"What's he for?"

"Making baby horses."

"That's *all*?"

Aunt CJ nodded.

Mia fumed. "Can I at least *pet* him?"

"We'll see."

Mia sighed loudly.

"What's the matter?" Jo asked.

"When grown-ups say 'we'll see' . . . it always means 'no.' "

As they walked toward the holding pens where hundreds of sale horses milled about, Mia wrinkled up her nose. "Phew," she said.

Jo laughed and tugged on the child's ponytail. "If you're gonna be a cowgirl, you've got to get used to that."

Mia made a face, then pointed to a horse in the pen nearest them. "What do you call the gold ones?"

"That's a buckskin," Jo said.

"I thought gold ones were palominnows."

"Palo-*mee*-no," Jo corrected her. "See the dark legs and the dark stripe down his back? That's a buckskin." She scanned the horses milling around in the pen. "I don't see a palomino. We probably won't. Aunt CJ told me once that the army usually preferred dark colors—and solids."

"Why?"

"So they didn't draw attention in battle."

"Why?"

Jo sighed. Aunt CJ had gone to find Uncle Will and to see Buster close up . . . and she had made a lame excuse as to why Jo and Mia couldn't come along. But Jo knew the real reason. Dieter Brock was likely to be the one handling Buster, and Aunt CJ had promised to keep both she and Mia as far away from the Germans as possible. It wasn't fair. And it was silly. She had watched Brock's face when he translated Daddy's sermon. She had seen how gentle he could be when he talked to Buster. She had heard him sing a lullaby. Whatever he might be, Jo was convinced that Dieter Brock posed no threat to anyone in Nebraska, least of all anyone Will Bishop cared about.

"Look! That one looks like Black Beauty!" Mia pointed to a horse in the far holding pen.

"That *is* a pretty one," Jo said, tugging on Mia's hand and leading her away. "We'd better get Aunt CJ's seat saved for her."

"I wanna sit up high," Mia said as they climbed the grandstand, and Jo led the way into a row halfway up.

Jo shook her head. "Aunt CJ will expect to find us here. She likes to sit in the same place."

"Why?"

"Well," Jo said, taking a deep breath and forcing herself to stop scanning the holding pens for a tall, blond PW, "the auctioneer knows her, and he'll look her way when a horse comes up he knows she might like."

"How's he know what she likes?"

"Aunt CJ is pretty well known around here. And I think she and the auctioneer went to school together."

Mia frowned. "I never thought of Aunt CJ going to school."

"Of course she went to school," Jo said. She pointed into the distance, "In fact, her school was right over there in a log house by the old parade ground. But the building's gone now."

"Did Aunt CJ like school?" Mia wanted to know.

"I don't think so. Not very much."

"I don't like school, either," Mia said. She grinned. "I'm glad we got to quit early this year. Aren't you?"

"Uh-huh," Jo said.

"You aren't listening," Mia said, tugging on Jo's sleeve.

"Sure I am," Jo said. "I just want to watch for Aunt CJ and make sure she can find us."

"You said she always sits here," Mia replied.

Jo sighed. "You're right." She forced herself to stop looking for Dieter Brock and smiled down at Mia. "So . . . what should we call the gray one in the first pen?"

"Sneezy." Mia giggled as the horse in question let out a wheeze.

Jo laughed. "That's a good name. Do you see one we could call Dopey?"

Mia nodded and pointed to a dun mare with her head down. They had named horses for all seven dwarves and several other fairy-tale characters before Aunt CJ finally arrived.

"Will stayed over in the barn with Buster," she said.

"Well? What do you think?" Jo prodded her.

"I think he's a looker and a troublemaker."

"So . . . you don't want him?"

Aunt CJ sighed. "What I want is for Will Bishop to come home."

Jo looked sideways at her aunt.

CJ looked back. "What?"

"You old softie," Jo said, and nudged her shoulder.

For the next two hours, except for two brief breaks, Jo and CJ and Mia watched horses sold at the rate of three per minute.

"I bet Uncle Will is tired of trimming hooves," Jo said.

"And manes and tails," Aunt CJ muttered. "He should have known his old back wouldn't take it." She looked at Jo. "But don't you tell him I said that."

"Don't worry," Jo said, "I learned to stay out of your squabbles with Uncle Will when I was in fourth grade."

"Is that so?" Aunt CJ said, feigning irritation.

Jo nodded. "It is. I was really upset when the two of you were fighting over where to build the new barn."

Aunt CJ looked down at the sale bill. "I didn't realize you knew anything about those disagreements."

"It's all right," Jo said. "I learned something about you and Uncle Will."

"Really?"

"Well, not then. But since then."

"I cannot wait to hear this," Aunt CJ said. As she spoke, she reached up and jerked on her hat brim.

"I see you, Miz Jackson," the auctioneer said, "and you're in for five."

Aunt CJ's eyes got big. She looked down at the sale ring. "Oh no!" She muttered, "Just what I need. A charity case."

"Way to go, CJ," a voice sounded from above them.

Looking back over her shoulder, Jo saw Vic Dearborn sitting a few rows above them. "Oh, brother," she whispered.

"What's wrong?" Mia wanted to know.

Jo shook her head.

"Sold!" the auctioneer said.

"And a bargain at five dollars," Dearborn teased.

"Did we buy that horse?" Mia said.

"Suppose you tell me what you learned about Will and me?" Aunt CJ said.

"Well, Mama said that love looks different to different people. That it's a lot more than a feeling you feel when you feel like you're going to feel a feeling you haven't felt before. And that between you and Uncle Will, sometimes love looks like a spat. But it's still love and it's still strong. And then she said, 'It's the same way with your aunt CJ and me. She is stubborn and so am I, and we have had more than our share of words, but don't you ever doubt that we love each other. We may not be soul mates but we are sisters, and that's a bond no man can break. And it's the same between your aunt CJ and uncle Will. They have had their share of words over the barn, but don't ever doubt that they love each other.' "

"Your mother said that?" Aunt CJ asked.

Jo nodded.

"Well, let's go get some lunch," and with that, Aunt CJ stood up and headed off in the direction of the pickup.

———

Clara Joy

I spent the entire walk to the truck alternately fuming over being tricked into buying the dun mare the girls had named Dopey and Vic Dearborn's rubbing it in. I never have liked that man. He was in school with Will and me, and as a boy he always took an evil kind of joy in teasing Will about his slow speech and his bad leg. And when Will lost the ranch, Vic was right there at the sale, lowballing the bid and winning it. Thanks to his daddy's money he waltzed into a good deal, and he struts around Dawes County like he's the biggest shot in the Sandhills. I cannot stand him. So when he intercepted the girls and me on our way to get our picnic lunch out of the truck, it didn't take much to get my goat.

"You starting a new business out at the Four Pines?" he said, and gave me that grin that he thinks makes him looks handsome.

"Why?"

"That last purchase. Thought maybe you were building a glue factory."

"Ha. Ha. Ha. Ha." I said the words with a space in between. He got the point.

"Heard I'll be up against you for the bay stallion," he said.

"What bay stallion?"

"The one Will couldn't handle. The one that's partial to Nazis."

If I have ever wanted to throttle a man it was then. I am not exactly a petite woman, and honestly, I think maybe I *could* have, I was that mad. But I cry when I get mad, and I could feel the tears threatening as he stood there bad-mouthing one of the best men that ever lived. But Jo interrupted.

"Dieter Brock is no Nazi," she said. And there was fire in her blue eyes.

"Is that so? And what would you be knowing about it?"

Thank goodness I had the presence of mind to notice Will headed our way. "We've got a letter from Johnny in the pickup for Will," I said real quick. "He asked to be transferred to the Pacific. We're hoping it will say where he ended up. Marion didn't ask to be transferred, did he?" My reference to his little prissy son pretty much got rid of Vic Dearborn.

As it turned out, Johnny's letter was old news, but assuming that Jo was always eager for news from John Bishop, Will did the kind thing. He read the letter aloud.

Every time Jo was mentioned—which was often—I'd glance up at her. Most of the time she was listening, but once or twice she was looking over toward the holding pens. I figured she might be watching for Buster, but Will had already told her that he was going to be handled a different way and that Dieter Brock would be walking him from the barn, hoping that maybe that would keep him calmed down.

When Will read Johnny's reaction to President Roosevelt's death, I felt like we ought to have a moment of silence out of respect, it was that moving.

I cannot tell you how many times hearing his voice on the radio or encountering his personality on the newsreels rallied my confidence and reminded me why I am fighting. Losing him is almost like losing a member of my own family. We were counting on him to help us shape a new peace after our work over here is done. Now that he is gone, I wonder who will step into those great shoes.

"I do believe that boy could have written the president's eulogy," I said, and looked over at Jo, figuring she would be sharing in my moment of pride in our boy. But she wasn't. She was daydreaming about that horse again.

––––––

"Well," Uncle Will said, folding up Johnny's letter and tucking it into his shirt pocket. "Best be going. Time to convince Buster to put on a halter."

"Mr. Brock doesn't even have him halterbroke yet?" Jo asked.

"Well, of course he does. Sort of. He puts the *pfeffernuss* in his fist, and when Buster puts his nose through the halter, he gets the treat."

"I don't have time for baking pfeffer-whatevers," grumbled Aunt CJ.

"We'll do it," Jo offered. "Mia and me." She turned toward her uncle Will. "Where do *you* get them?"

"The PW kitchen," he said.

"Do you think Mr. Brock can give you enough to get him into his new stall?"

"I reckon," Will said. "Buster's coming up right away in this next group," he said, looking at Aunt CJ. "Don't be late."

"He sure is vocal," Jo said, leaning across Mia to whisper in her aunt's ear while Dieter led Buster into the sale ring.

Aunt CJ nodded. "Vocal. And gorgeous."

Jo agreed mentally—about both males in the sale ring. She scolded herself and scanned the crowd. Vic Dearborn was no longer sitting behind them. Now he was positioned on the opposite side of the grandstand in about the third row.

"Are we going to buy him?" Mia asked.

"We're going to try," Aunt CJ said.

The bidding began at fifty dollars. At a sale where most horses sold for thirty, it was a lot.

"Don't forget the horse comes with Uncle Will," Jo said. She could have sworn Aunt CJ blushed. The thought that maybe the horse would come with a certain PW made *her* blush. *What is* wrong *with you? Didn't Uncle Will just read you a letter from Johnny?*

Aunt CJ raised her hand and took the bid up to one hundred and twenty-five dollars.

Jo looked across the arena as the bidding continued. "It's Vic Dearborn," she hissed. "Don't let him win, Aunt CJ."

"Don't worry," CJ said between clenched teeth. She nodded again.

"One hundred and seventy-five dollars. Do I hear one-eighty?" The auctioneer was looking toward Dearborn, who had apparently motioned that he wanted to take a closer look.

Dieter tried to signal the rancher to stop, but Dearborn kept moving in on Buster. Uncle Will stepped up to the edge of the sale ring and spoke to Dearborn. He didn't listen.

"Why won't he listen to Uncle Will?" Jo muttered.

"Vic Dearborn's never had any use for any of us, and his ego sure isn't gonna get any smaller in front of all his cronies," Aunt CJ said.

Buster tossed his head, sidestepped, and snorted. When Dearborn stepped over the fence into the arena, Dieter barked, "Stop!" Dearborn ignored him The closer he got, the more Buster danced. When Dearborn tried to take the lead rope out of Dieter's hands, Buster let loose, ripping the rope out of Dieter's hands, spinning around, and letting fly with both rear hooves. As the men ducked, Buster spun back around and launched himself across the dirt toward Dearborn with bared teeth. He skidded to a halt at the edge of the sale ring just as Dearborn flew over the fence to safety, but even with Dearborn gone, Buster wasn't finished. He reared and pawed the air while Uncle Will stood on one side and Dieter on the other, their arms at their sides.

Dieter began talking loudly—reciting something, Jo thought, something rhythmical—a poem? Whatever it was, it got Buster's attention. He came to a halt in the center of the sale ring, his head lowered, his front legs splayed, his velvety ears at attention. He was ready to lunge away at any moment, but he was listening to Dieter. He pawed the dirt nervously, but he listened. When Dieter finally took a step forward Buster didn't move.

"Has he got *magic*?" Mia whispered.

"I'm beginning to think so," Aunt CJ answered.

Absolutely, Jo thought, as the gorgeous man reached out a huge hand toward the gorgeous horse. Finally, Buster stretched out his beautiful head, his dark muzzle quivering with anticipation. Dieter slowly reached into his pocket. When he held up what Jo knew was a small square cookie, the horse whickered and loped toward him.

"What about it, Vic?" the auctioneer said quietly. "One-eighty?"

"I wouldn't give one dollar and eighty cents for that monster," was the answer.

"You still in, Miss Jackson?"

Jo looked at her aunt, who seemed to take forever to nod.

"Sold!"

Aunt CJ looked at Jo. "I hope we aren't going to have to tranquilize him to get him into the trailer. You take Blondie here in search of 'the facilities' and meet us at the truck," she said. "I'll hook up with Will and the German. I want Will to be sure that man is part of my work crew. I love the way he handles a horse."

As if to prove Aunt CJ right, "the German" got Buster loaded without a hitch. While they watched him work his magic, which amounted to a combination of gentle prodding and bribery with *pfefferneusse,* Aunt CJ turned around and winked at Jo. "Maybe I should'a tried that on your Uncle Will a few years back," she said.

Jo laughed and took Mia's hand. Dieter Brock was going to be working on the Four Pines. She finally had something interesting to write Delores about.

———

"Not me," Rolf said, shaking his head back and forth. "Not in a million years."

"Me, either," Bruno Bauer agreed. "I'm afraid of horses."

"Come on," Dieter argued. "Don't you want to see what Karl May was writing about? Don't you want to get outside the barbed wire?"

"I've already been outside the wire," Rolf said, "and I saw what May was writing about from the train. I'll get off this place as soon as the war is over and we can go home. Which may not be long, from what we are reading. The Allies approach from the west, the Russians from the east, and . . ." Shrader marched his hands toward each other through the air and clapped. "Bam! Germany is split in two! The fatherland is being battered into fragments. Soon it will be over."

"And so you are happy shoveling manure in the stables?" Dieter said.

"What's the difference where I shovel manure?" Rolf wanted to know. "At Fort Robinson or on some ranch. It's all still manure and it all stinks."

Bauer nodded agreement.

Rolf closed the magazine he had been reading and leaned forward.

"And just because they want you on that work crew doesn't mean they will take us, anyway. Look, Dieter, you go ahead. I understand. Really, I do. They want you, and you want to work with the horse. But I don't know the first thing about—"

"It doesn't matter," Dieter said. "Miss Jackson suggested I might know who would be better workers from our compound." Dieter looked from Rolf to Bruno. "And you are two of the hardest workers I have ever known. And you said you thought the prairie was beautiful."

Rolf sighed. "I didn't mean it. I was just trying to annoy Gunnar Stroh. It always made him angry when we said anything nice about America."

"Look," Dieter said, "It's all kinds of work. Cutting hay. Working in the field. I don't know what else. But I do know that Company D comes back every night talking about the huge meals the rancher's wife cooks for them and—"

"That's against the rules," Rolf said.

Dieter looked toward Bauer. "Piles of potatoes. Pie. Beef. And they even had orange soda."

Bruno Bauer smiled and patted his belly. "I'm convinced," he said. "I'll go if you can get permission."

Dieter nodded, "That's good." He turned to Rolf. "Come on, Rolf. We've been together all along. Why change it now?"

"I'll protect you from the runaways," Bruno joked.

"Oh, all right," Rolf said. He threw his magazine at Dieter. "I guess it will be better than crawling around in the dirt planting flowers with the theatrical troupe."

———

"There they come!" Mia said, and pointed to a plume of dust rising toward the sky.

"Good eye, Sprite," Jo said. She peered toward the horizon through the dormer window of Aunt CJ's nearly empty loft.

Jo put her arm around the child. "We'll go out and saddle Ned as soon as the truck goes by," she said.

"There she is. There's Sadie!" Mia said just as the cab of the old red pickup came into view.

It looked like a guard was seated next to Uncle Will. In the back of the pickup was the cage he had built so he could haul a few calves to the railroad depot or a sale without hitching up the big trailer. The cage was now packed with denim-clad PWs. Jo squinted, but the truck flew past too fast for her to see if the one Buster liked was among them or not.

———

Jo stood at the far end of the barn doing her best not to show any kind of uncertainty as she stared into Buster's brown eyes. She swallowed. "Mia," she said quietly. "You back out—slowly—and run get Aunt CJ."

"She's gone out to the fields to see about the prisoners," she said, as she backed away from the horse that had somehow gotten out of his stall.

Shoot. I knew that. "Oh, right," Jo said quietly. "Well then, walk slowly toward the back door and just go on up to the house and wait for me."

"What are you gonna do?"

"I'm going to get Buster back into his stall."

"That's too dangerous," Mia said. "He kicks. And bites. Unless you've got *feffer-noses*."

"It'll be fine," Jo replied. "But you go on up to the house. Just move slow." She didn't take her eyes off Buster as Mia slipped away.

"So," she said as calmly as possible. "Care to tell me how you got out of your stall?"

Buster snorted and tossed his head.

"Don't you laugh at me," Jo said, pleased when Buster didn't seem inclined to rush her. "We had no idea you were an escape artist."

Buster seemed to lose interest in the conversation and turned toward Ned's stall.

"That's Ned," Jo said. "He's old and harmless. No challenge to you at all. Be nice to him. He's Mia's horse for the summer."

Buster pawed the earth outside Ned's stall, then lifted his head and touched noses with the aged gelding. Jo watched as they snuffled and whickered and nipped, just as if they were having a private conversation. While Buster's attention was on Ned, Jo inched her way along the wall of stalls. Her heart pounding, she opened the door to one stall and then the one across from it, hoping Buster would not rush the opening between the doors where she stood. To her amazement, Buster not only didn't rush her, but when she opened the stall next to Ned, he walked in. As Jo stepped carefully to close the door, Buster waited quietly. When the door clicked, his ears came forward, and he nodded his head.

"You old meany, you," Jo teased. "Is that all it takes to calm you down?" She rested her arms on the top of the stall door. "Who would have guessed that all you needed was a baby-sitter named Ned?"

She waited for a long time watching Buster and Ned. When she heard hoofbeats coming up the road, she hurried outside just in time to see Aunt CJ dismounting over at the house where Mia was jumping up and down on the porch, gesturing toward the barn.

"It's all right," Jo called. She trotted across the road.

"Did he really get out of that stall?" Aunt CJ asked.

"He did," Jo said. "But he had a reason."

"Which is?"

"He wanted a pet," Jo said, laughing.

———

Clara Joy

I have known a lot of horses in my time, but not a single one like this Buster. Sometimes I am tempted to check for evidence that he really is a stallion, because now that he has a stablemate he acts like a big baby half the time. When Jo saddles Ned so Mia can take a ride, Buster throws a fit because he doesn't want to be left behind. And that is how we got Buster really and truly halterbroke. Ned took Mia for a ride, and Buster practically pushed Will over to get trussed up and taken for a walk. Actually, it was more Buster taking Will for a walk. Straight out of the barn and straight to the corral where our little Blondie was riding. It was comical. Buster screamed at Ned. Ned answered. And that was that. Buster gave a big old sigh and lowered his head and practically went to sleep. Ever since then, whenever we turn Buster into the corral we let Ned out, too. The two are like a couple of old soldiers telling war stories.

If Vic Dearborn gets wind of what a big baby Buster has turned out to be, he is going to think the whole thing at Fort Robinson was staged between Will and me and Dieter Brock. Which would be a violation of the "Instructions for Persons Using Prisoner of War Labor in Your County." And everyone who knows CJ Jackson knows she is a stickler for following rules.

That is a joke, by the way.

Chapter Sixteen

Be ye angry, and sin not.
EPHESIANS 4:26

IT HAD BECOME almost a ritual. On Saturday nights, Clarissa brought over cinnamon rolls and helped Helen and Stella prepare the little bungalow for Sunday Dinner at Stella's. This night, Stella grabbed the cinnamon rolls from Clarissa and motioned her onto the porch swing beside Helen. "I've got news," she said. "Now you both wait right there while I get us some tea." She grinned. "I am taking a sinful amount of pleasure in noting that Mrs. Bohling keeps finding excuses to come out onto her front porch—and I want her to see that the Mrs. Reverend Hale herself is gracing my porch swing." With a little laugh, she disappeared inside.

"Do you have any idea what on earth she is talking about?" Clarissa said.

"Just look," Helen replied, motioning with only her eyes toward Mrs. Bohling's house.

"Not that," Clarissa said. "I mean the news."

"Not a clue," Helen said, and settled back to wait.

Stella reappeared with a tray of cookies and three iced teas. "To Chase Young," she said, raising her own glass in a toast.

"The banker?" Helen said. "You're toasting the banker?"

"You bet I am," Stella said, laughing. "That poor boy is going to swallow his tie on Monday." She pointed at Clarissa. "You had better be saying a prayer for him. He just may have a heart attack."

"What on earth are you talking about?" Clarissa asked.

"On Monday morning, May 7, 1945, Stella Black is going to sashay into the Farmers Bank in Crawford, Nebraska, and make her house payment in *cash money*." She hooted with joy, raised her arms in the air, and danced a jig.

"Praise the Lord!" Clarissa said.

"Amen!" Helen agreed before adding, "So . . . maybe you won't need to have a soldier rent a room here after all?"

"I've got a roomer all lined up, and the wolf is still at the door," Stella said quickly. "But he's gonna have to make tracks if Stella's little board-inghouse keeps it up." She sat down and lit a cigarette. "Look, honey," she said to Helen, "the hens in this town have been serving me up for dessert ever since Charlie flew the coop when Delores was a baby. Whether I do or don't or will or won't doesn't really matter. I think it's my mission in life to provide fodder for the feeding frenzy. I cared when Delores was little—for her sake—but she's all grown up now and I don't care anymore." She punctuated her defense with smoke rings. "If you don't want to see it through, I understand. You're a married woman with a child to consider."

"You can stay with us," Clarissa said to Helen from her chair beside the trellis. "You can have Jo's room." She looked at Stella. "And I don't mean that as judging you. Really, I don't. It's just another option for Helen."

"I understand," Stella said.

"And it frees up another room for you," Clarissa added. "If two dollars a week is a big help, four dollars a week would be even better. Am I right?"

"Mrs. Hale!" Stella said, putting her hand to her throat in mock horror. "Can you possibly be suggesting what I think you are suggesting?"

"What?" Clarissa said. "That you actually make *two* house payments *in a row* . . . without being rescued by a man?"

"Talk like that will get you in trouble with your husband," Stella said.

"Talk like that got me a husband," Clarissa shot back. "Ben never was one to be attracted to a shrinking violet."

"Good for him," Stella replied. She lifted her iced tea glass again. "Here's to strong Baptist men. Long may they reign."

———

Helen could hear Stella singing the minute she woke up the next morning. "Uncle Sam ain't a woman, but he sure can take your man."

Slipping out of bed, she dressed quickly, made her bed, and headed for the kitchen. Unaware of Helen's presence, Stella continued singing at the top of her lungs while she added to the mountain of pancakes already in the warming drawer that made up the right half of her old gas stove.

"You let me sleep too late to be of much help," Helen said.

Stella whirled around, "Oh, honey, I'm sorry. I didn't know you were standing there." She apologized. "That's just a dumb old song I used to sing after Charlie—"

"It's all right," Helen said. She forced a smile. "There's a lot of truth in it."

Stella tipped her head and looked past Helen into the living room.

"Is that what I think it is by the front door?"

Following Stella's gaze to where her suitcase stood by the front door, Helen nodded.

Stella frowned. "I was hoping you'd stay."

"It's past time for me to go," Helen said.

"I told you I'd understand," Stella said. "And I do. You've got a reputation at stake. Mine's already—"

"No. It's got nothing to do with your decision about boarders—except that it maybe nudged me in the right direction sooner than I would have gone on my own." She sighed. "I'm not making any sense, am I?" She took a deep breath. Her voice wobbled as she sang, "Uncle Sam ain't a woman and he's *not* gonna take my man. . . ." Her voice gave out and she blinked back tears. "At least I'm going to try to see to it." She swiped the tears from her eyes and cleared her throat. "I have to go home. I can't raise two children on my own. I just can't."

Stella's eyes opened wide and tilted her head. "Two? Oh, honey." Pulling her skillet off the fire and turning down the burner on the sausage, she went to Helen, took her hand, tried to lead her to the kitchen table. "Come and tell me all about it."

Helen pulled away. "Not now. I can't. I just didn't want you to think it was anything you'd done that sent me out the door." She looked behind her at the suitcase. "But I've got to go—before I lose the courage. I've go to try to get my family—my life—back." She put her hand over her abdomen.

Stella hugged her. Hard. "You know where to come if you need . . . anything," she said before asking, "Does Clarissa know?" Stella said.

"No one knows. Except Doc Whitlow. And now you." She bit her lip. "I don't want anyone knowing. Not even Hank. Not yet."

"Not even Hank?"

Helen shook her head. "We have to fix . . . us first. If we can't be fixed, then I don't want—" Her voice cracked. "I don't think I can raise two children on my own, but if I can't have my Hank back because of *love* . . . I couldn't bear to have him back out of *duty*."

Stella nodded. "All right, honey. Whatever you say. Does Clarissa know you're going home this morning?"

Helen shook her head. "She and Pastor Hale will have walked across for church by now. I don't want to upset their morning."

Stella put her hands on Helen's shoulders. "Are you sure about this?"

"I'm not sure about anything. Except, if I don't try I'll spend the rest of my life wondering."

"Wondering what, honey?"

"If I did everything I could. If the Hank I fell in love with was in there all the time . . . and I just didn't fight hard enough to bring him back to me. To give my children a daddy."

Stella stood looking into her friend's blue eyes for a long minute. She squeezed her shoulders. "I won't say a word. And I'll light a candle for you at mass this morning." She laughed self-consciously. "I know you don't think that means anything—"

"It means you care."

The women hugged and Helen went to the front door. She picked up her suitcase and then turned around and called Stella's name.

"Yes, honey?"

"Light a dozen candles."

"Consider it done."

———

How long was it going to be before he stopped having these dreams? Helen having a baby, Helen cleaning house, Helen swimming in their favorite swimming hole, Helen . . . frying bacon? Hank opened his eyes and inhaled. He listened. Someone was clattering around the kitchen. He had to put a stop to Mr. Clark's treating the place like he lived here. It was good to have someone to talk to, but he didn't need a roommate, and some of the old guy's talk lately had been a little too crazy for Hank's taste. He almost wondered if he should say something to Pastor Hale.

Coffee. Vernon Clark didn't even like coffee. Is this what it had come to? Hank Frey and Vernon Clark living like two old bachelors? The idea gave Hank the creeps. He sat up on the edge of the cot and grabbed his work pants, oblivious to the grease stains from the long night of work in the garage. At the base of the attic stairs he paused and called out, "Mr. Clark? Is that you?" before continuing down to the first floor where he closed his eyes and inhaled again, this time catching the lightest scent of . . . perfume?

"No, it isn't Vern," Helen said. "It's your wife." She didn't turn around as she said, "Now go back upstairs and make yourself presentable. Breakfast will be ready in about ten minutes. I'm waiting for the biscuits."

He turned to go.

"Hank," she said.

"What?"

"I'm sorry." Her voice was trembling.

"What?"

"I said, I'm sorry." She turned around and looked at him.

He held his hand up to hide the bad half of his face. "I don't want your pity." He turned away.

"I'm not offering you pity," she said. "I'm apologizing."

He looked back at her with his good eye. "What do you have to apologize for?"

"I didn't get mad enough soon enough."

"I'd say you got plenty mad," Hank said. "You moved out." He dropped his hand, but turned so that what she could see was scarless—mostly.

"I wasn't mad when I moved out, Hank. I was frightened."

He shrugged. "Can't blame you for that. Between the way I look and the way I acted that night—"

"Well, I'm past being frightened and back to being mad." Her voice had a new tremor behind it—of strength.

"So why'd you come back if you're still mad?"

"Because I'm not mad at you. I'm mad at the whole world. The whole blasted bunch of people who are so sinful and so selfish and so lost that they let things like this happen. Wars and rumors of wars that destroy men's lives and tear up everything important. But you know what? I've decided something. The enemy and the Allies and the good guys and the bad guys can take everything I own and everything I hold dear, but as long as there is one breath left in this body they are *not* taking my family.

"People are overseas fighting for freedom and democracy and all those high-sounding words. I can't understand it all, and I never will. How is it that *German* can mean something as harmless and lovable as old Mrs. Koch to us and then become something awful and hideous like Hitler? How is it that one minute children can be playing in the street and the next minute be dead because someone looked at a map and said to drop bombs there? How is it that one minute I can send the only man I've ever loved off to fight for everything I care about and the next . . . Well . . . that's where it ends. I can't stop the bombs. I can't fight the battles. But there's one battle I can fight, Henry Frey, and that's this one.

"I sent a beautiful man off to war and I got back a scarred man who's anything but beautiful to look at. But I am here to give notice to the enemy: I DON'T CARE! I AM GOING TO FIGHT, AND YOU AREN'T GOING TO WIN. You don't have to look at me and you don't have to visit our bed, Hank Frey. But I'm not leaving and I'm not giving up. I'm going to cook breakfast in *my* kitchen and hang out laundry in *my* backyard and clean *my* house.

"That's who I am, Hank. I am Helen Frey, your wife and Mia's mother. It's the only job I ever wanted. And I'm going to do it, and there's not a single Nazi in this world who is going to tell me I have to stop. So you go upstairs and wash that face of yours, and come back down here and sit across the table from me and drink your coffee. If you want to cover up the scars, then figure out a way to do it. But you will get your behind in that chair and treat me like a human being. This is *my* war we are fighting now and I am *not* going to lose it."

She had begun to cry in the middle of the speech, and now, with tears streaming down her face, Helen whirled around and retreated to the kitchen sink while Hank retreated upstairs. With shaking hands, he washed his face and put on clean clothes. When he came back downstairs and sat at the table, she was waiting to pour him coffee. Her hands were shaking so badly she sloshed it all over the table. How he longed to reach out and hold those hands in his. But he dared not. He sat so she couldn't see most of the scars.

She handed him the morning paper. "Here. Clarissa says Ben hides behind the sports page every morning. What's good enough for the preacher is good enough for you."

Chapter Seventeen

Be ye therefore merciful, as your Father also is merciful.
LUKE 6:36

THE AFTERNOON SUN poured through the panes of the dormer window in Aunt CJ's loft, warming Jo to the point of drowsiness and making her golden hair glow with soft light. Aunt CJ had been worried when Jo declined a ride to visit her parents while she and Uncle Will attended a meeting in Crawford—until Jo mentioned a new letter from Johnny. Then, with a knowing smile and a pat on the shoulder, Aunt CJ collected Mia and was gone.

Jo puttered around the house most of the morning, baking enough *pfefferneusse* to fill two half-gallon canning jars, putting a load of kitchen towels and feed-sack aprons through the old wringer washer and hanging them on the line to dry, and all the while leaving Johnny's letter unopened on the kitchen table.

She went to the barn right before lunch and spent a full two hours with Buster, brushing him down, cleaning his already clean feet, handling him for the pure joy of running her hands over his gleaming coat.

"Uncle Will told me that Dieter says you are built for jumping," she whispered in the horse's ear. Buster turned his head and nibbled at her sleeve. "I'd like to know how it feels to sail over a jump with you."

Ned thrust his head across the top of his stall and grunted.

"Sorry, old man," Jo said, and reached out for him. "You want equal time, eh? Uncle Will said that Dieter thinks you're like a tranquilizer for this guy." She patted Buster's neck and then went back to scratch behind Ned's ears.

She sighed. Dieter Brock was in her thoughts a lot these days, and she didn't like it. It wasn't like the man had ever said a word to her. Of course, even if he wanted to, he wouldn't dare, not with Private Romani watching like a hawk to make certain the "Rules for Those Employing Prisoner of War Labor" were followed. Which was funny, because plenty of those rules had been broken in the first few days the PWs were on the place. In fact, when Aunt CJ posted the rules on the kitchen wall beside the back door, she had made it a grand joke.

"Listen up," she had said to whoever might be listening, "because these are things we need to know. Things we would not have thought of on our own," and in a tone of mock seriousness she read, " 'Do not help a prisoner of war escape.' "

She turned around and shook a finger at Uncle Will. "So you stop making plans right now, Will. It's against the rules."

"Now don't be that way," Will said. "It's a serious subject."

Aunt CJ looked at the list again. " 'Do not accept any written communication from a prisoner of war.' " She grinned at Jo. "So you'd just better throw away all those love letters."

When Aunt CJ said that, Jo was grateful she was able to quickly turn back to washing dishes so that no one saw her cheeks grow red. Why she was blushing she didn't know—or at least didn't want to admit.

Uncle Will was not amused. "There has to be rules, CJ. You think you can do better, maybe you should be working for the government."

"I already am," Aunt CJ said. "I'm raising hay for half the remount and employing their prisoners to keep them out of trouble."

"Then you better be following the rules," Uncle Will said.

The rules were making Jo crazy. Even now, as she grabbed a rake and began mucking out stalls, she was reminded how like her Aunt CJ she was. Rules and regulations drove her to distraction.

Do not give a prisoner of war anything. As if, having discovered the key to Buster's antics they were going to stop supplying Dieter Brock with *pfefferneusse*. As if they were going to expect the men to work on the paltry lunch they were provided by the PW kitchen.

"Now you listen to me," Aunt CJ had said when Private Romani first objected to the family-style lunches Aunt CJ and Jo served under the cottonwood trees near the back door of Aunt CJ's house. "If these men are good enough to sweat for me, they are good enough to eat my food. You may call a hunk of rye bread and a piece of meat a decent meal, but I do not. So you just have yourself another pile of mashed potatoes and hush."

Romani hushed. The young private from Brooklyn who didn't know a horse from a house was no match for Aunt CJ. Thinking back on it, Jo wished she knew what it was that gave Aunt CJ such power over people.

If she knew, maybe she would be able to get a certain male to break a rule or two and at least acknowledge her existence. Why that was important, she didn't understand, but the fact that Dieter Brock was working with Buster every day and knew the horse better than anyone, just drove her crazy. She wanted to understand what he knew. What secret understanding enabled him to charm Buster into doing those amazing gaits she had observed from the dormer window? It was more than *pfefferneusse*. Of that, Jo was certain.

Coming out of the barn, Jo shaded her hand from the sun and looked up the hill. Being alone on the ranch had always been some of Jo's favorite times, a time to daydream about the day when maybe, just maybe, she would be Aunt CJ's right-hand "man." Today, she was restless, alternately listening for the pickup and watching the horizon.

The letter on the kitchen table called to her. Sighing, Jo walked across the road. Inside the house, she grabbed the letter and climbed the ladder to the loft. Tucked into her usual spot beside one of the double-hung windows, she picked at the flap of the envelope. Beside her was the fabric-covered box her mother had given her.

"I saved all your daddy's letters in a box just like this one," Mama had said when she presented it to Jo.

"Thanks," Jo had said . . . and hoped she sounded sincere, although what she was really feeling was that tightening of her midsection. The sensation had become familiar. Everyone who knew John Bishop and Jo Hale assumed that once the war was over and "Johnny came marching home," Jo would give up her silly ideas of independence and become the rancher's wife she was born to be. And the closer the world moved to that day, the more often Jo's stomach hurt.

Sighing, she took the newest letter out of its envelope and looked down at Johnny's familiar scrawl.

> *Air power—that's me, Jo—has destroyed a lot of their transportation system and the war industry. We've put the oil refiners out of business . . . we are only suffering a one percent loss now . . . the tide has turned.*

She knew Johnny was right. She had been pouring the PW named Bruno Bauer a glass of milk when a car roared in and Sergeant Isaacson walked over and read the announcement. That had been on Monday, May 7.

*"The war in Europe has ended. The German Army has surrendered uncondition-
ally. The German Reich has ceased to exist. The German army is no longer bound
by the oath of loyalty to the Third Reich. From this point on the wearing of the
German uniform is forbidden. The same goes for the wearing of all emblems,
insignia, and medals of the German National Socialist Regime. Conduct against
these directives will be met with severe punishment. The German prisoners of
war in the United States of North America will be returned as soon as necessary
transports are available."*

The men had barely recovered from the news that Hitler had committed suicide at the end of April. Of course, they must have known things
were ending, but still, Jo would never forget the quiet around the lunch
table after Sergeant Isaacson told the men. She could hear the buzzing of
a horsefly as it hovered over the table. Bruno Bauer let the tears flow. Rolf
Shrader, the clown in the group who could make even Dieter Brock laugh,
sat with his head bowed. Sergeant Isaacson encouraged the men to "look
toward the future, continue your good work for these good people, and
keep your faith strong."

Aunt CJ grabbed Mia's hand and together, along with Jo and Uncle
Will, they left the men to themselves for a while. When Aunt CJ went out
and told them she would understand if they didn't want to work anymore,
Dieter Brock said they would take Sergeant Isaacson's advice. It would help
no one for them to sit idly in their quarters.

It was Saturday now, and as she sat in the dormer alone, Jo wondered
what the PWs were doing. Would more of them come to Daddy's service
tomorrow seeking answers from God, or would they be angry with Him
and leave Daddy to preach to an empty room? She hoped not. She should
pray that Daddy would know what to say, but she had not really prayed for
a long time. Since Delores left for Fort Des Moines she hadn't even thought
much about God. Maybe that was part of her problem.

She looked down at the letter again. Of course she wanted Johnny
and all her friends back home. She wanted them safe. She wanted the
war to be over and life to get back to normal. Except she wasn't sure
what normal was anymore. The war was changing everything. Thinking back over the past few weeks, Jo realized the effects of the war had
sent tentacles into just about every area of life in her part of the world.
Because of the war, the Frey family would never be the same. Because
of the war, Jo's best friend had left Crawford. Because of the war, most
of the boys she knew were gone—two were dead. Because of the war,
Mama was coming out of her shell and helping down at the Servicemen's

Club. She was even friends with Stella Black across the street, which was nothing short of a miracle. Because of the war, Uncle Will had almost left the Four Pines for good. And, because of the war . . . Jo Hale was confused.

Being around Bruno Bauer and the others had changed the way she read Johnny's letters. When he wrote *victory*, Jo saw a destroyed city and wondered about the PWs' families. Dieter Brock was from Dresden. He had confided in Uncle Will that he had not heard from his only living relative since February, when wave after wave of night raids reduced Dresden to a fiery inferno. Bruno Bauer was from Berlin. Johnny said the center was gutted. Rolf Shrader was from Essen. She had seen newsreels at the picture show of the damage. Eventually, she began to dread reading Johnny's letters. She didn't want to know about more German cities reduced to rubble.

Over the past few weeks, the PWs had worked hard and Dieter Brock grew tan beneath the prairie sun, Jo began to long for the end of the war for new reasons. And to dread it, too. Johnny would be *coming* home. The PWs would be *going* home.

As the afternoon sun spilled into the dormer window, Jo leaned her head back against the wall and closed her eyes. Her daydream involved a soldier climbing down off the train and coming toward her with outstretched arms and a beautiful smile. She opened her eyes and looked toward the empty corral. She called herself a fool. The soldier in her dream was not John Bishop.

———

Clara Joy

I did not like the idea of leaving Jo alone on the ranch all day Saturday, and I did not believe for a minute that she wanted to be alone to pore over Johnny's letter. Jo is like me and she does not *pore*—she *scans*. But whatever it was that made her want to be alone was something I decided to respect for the moment and investigate later, and so Will and I met Helen Frey at Clarissa's and left Mia there before heading to the school auditorium for a meeting with other ranchers interested in using PW labor. Of course the meeting was after the fact for Will and me, but Captain Donovan had rung me up and asked if we would come to help "allay any fears" in the community. At first I didn't think there would be any fears left. I mean, other work crews have been out and about for a while now, and there hadn't been any trouble. I figured folks would have calmed down. Was I ever wrong.

"I do not know for the life of me what all the fuss is about," I said, after the third person got up and protested. "First of all, Crawford is thriving, thanks to all the soldiers swarming into town for rooms and entertainment. And as for the PWs themselves, if the ten men they sent me are any indication, people have nothing at all to worry about and a lot to be thankful for. They haven't been a minute of trouble, and they've been a lot of help. They've mended fences and begun to build a new corral, and they seem to be grateful for whatever they get."

"If they're so grateful, why won't they eat our corn?" someone called out from the back of the room.

"They think it's for pigs," I said. "Found that out the hard way." I sat down. Of course, that caused some stir when they realized that if I knew the PWs don't eat corn that meant I'd been feeding them. But Deacon Tom was running the meeting and he helped get me out of that spot by changing the subject to reading the pamphlet of rules. Of course, I break those rules just about every day in one way or another.

For example, Dieter Brock has been helping Will with Buster. Will isn't as spry as he once was and Jo seems to have a notion that she'd like to ride Buster—at least once. There are all kinds of competitions and exhibitions in the panhandle every year, and Jo seems to have her heart set on showing off on Buster. I don't think that will work out, but the more sensible Buster is the more valuable he will be to me, so I agreed to the idea of seeing how far Buster would like to go in developing his skills. Getting Brock involved makes sense because the horse likes him. The first couple of days I told Jo that she and Mia would have to stay up at the house for the hour or so that Dieter was in the corral with Buster. I even posted the rules by the back door. But the girl is a lot like me, and posting the rules just seemed to encourage her to find a way to bend 'em. And just a few days later, Jo and Blondie were standing by my side at the corral watching Will watch Brock and Buster. I am old, but I am not dead, and there are few sights more beautiful to behold than a beautiful man and a beautiful horse getting along.

It's more than that, though. I did not want to let myself care about them, but some of these prisoners are likeable. We serve them lunch under the cottonwood trees out back. They are respectful and seem sincerely grateful for the home-cooked food. Bruno Bauer can eat more than any human being I have ever known. He doesn't care what we feed him, he loves it. Rolf Shrader likes fried chicken. Dieter Brock is partial to cherry pie.

Private Romani had a problem at first with Dieter breaking off from the crew and going with Will to handle the horse, but that worked itself out when Jo sweet-talked him into letting Dieter help with *her* horse. I didn't put her up to it. She's got her heart set on showing Buster, so she figured out a way to get Romani to let Brock help with the training. Of course, if Romani knew that Jo and I watch the sessions, that would probably all fall apart.

As for Dieter Brock, he is quiet, but now that I have been around him some, I don't see it as ominous at all. I think he is just careful, especially around women. He doesn't even look at Jo. He will talk to me, if I speak to him. But get him to working the horse—or talking to little Mia—and that handsome face of his lights up. He has a beautiful smile.

Dieter's got Buster behaving on a longeing rein like he was born doing it—the horse, not the man. I almost think maybe Jo wasn't crazy when she mentioned riding Buster last week. But there is no way I will tell her that. I'm not about to risk losing Jo's summers at the ranch by letting her do something crazy. And if Clarissa ever got wind of me letting Jo within earshot of one of the PWs, that's exactly what would happen.

The rule about using German labor that makes me laugh the hardest is the one that says *Do not, under any circumstances, allow women into any field where there are prisoners of war.* I'm real careful about it with Jo and, of course, with little Blondie, but honestly, it's my ranch and no one can tell me not to have anything to do with the men working for me.

In the end, most of the ranchers at the meeting down at the school had good, honest questions. I think the air has cleared and things are going to be all right. The only one I'm not sure about is Vernon Clark. The man just gives me a bad feeling. At today's meeting I had a little speech all prepared, and I finished it with this: "So here's the deal about the Four Pines: I know we are at war. I love John Bishop like he was my own son, and he's over there right now. Hiring these men to work our places isn't anything like 'fraternizing with the enemy.' At worst, it's a necessary evil. At best, it's an answer to our prayers for help until our own boys come home. Don't let your personal feelings interfere with your neighbor's right to run their place the way they see fit. If you are German, the fact is that their fatherland and yours is the same country. And remember that, when it's all said and done, the PWs are somebody's sons and husbands, too. And those mothers and wives love them just as much as we love ours."

Vern Clark wasn't impressed. When he got up it was plain as day that he'd been drinking. "Any of you here seen Hank Frey since he's been back?" he asked. Of course no one had. "Didn't think so." He belched. Didn't even excuse himself. "Well, I have. And I can tell you straight up, if you'd seen what I have, you wouldn't be coddling the—" I can't repeat the rest of what he said in polite company.

Vern Clark worries me.

Chapter Eighteen

Now we exhort you, brethren, warn them that are unruly, comfort the feebleminded, support the weak, be patient toward all men.

1 Thessalonians 5:14

LORD GIVE ME STRENGTH. Hank grabbed the newspaper off the kitchen table on Monday morning and opened it wide. If only Helen had known what she was saying a week ago when she handed him the paper and said that if Pastor Hale could hide behind the sports page, so could he. What Helen didn't know was that while Pastor Hale might use the newspaper as a shield against his wife's moods—which were no secret to the citizens of Crawford—Hank needed to shield himself from temptation. Didn't she realize it drove him crazy when she put her hair up like that? He could see the blond streak that grew just at the nape of her neck. And all those little curls. Didn't she know what the scent of her perfume did to him? When she turned around with the platter full of breakfast and headed toward the table, Hank raised the newspaper high.

"Stella and I have to work a little overtime tonight," she said. "Tom Hanson has to stay, too. Something about repairs to a roof that leaked the last time it rained. He said he'd drive us home."

Deacon Tom. Hank pressed his lips together. Who would have suspected?

"They decided they need *two* originals for all those work requests," Helen sighed. "As if we don't have enough to do. Is it all right with you if I go out to the ranch Saturday afternoon? CJ's invited us."

Us. Like they wanted him to grace the table. "Go ahead."

"Are you going to work that night?" she asked. "I could come over after I get back. Let you know how Mia's doing."

"Sure. Fine." Maybe it would be easier to be around her at the shop. Especially if Mr. Clark was there when she came.

"Are you feeling all right?"

"I'm fine," Hank said. He put the paper down and began to eat.

"Because there's a bad flu going around. Can't imagine it this time of year."

"I'm fine."

A horn honked. "There's my ride," Helen said. She got up and untied the apron.

Hank could not take his eyes off her waist.

She bent to kiss him on the cheek—the scarred side.

He heard the screen door slam shut. Heard the deacon call a greeting. Heard the car door shut . . . the engine rev . . . the departure. He sat at the kitchen table with his good hand curled into a fist.

———

"Honey, you can't keep this up," Stella said, opening her purse and passing a handkerchief to Helen, who sat crying in the backseat of Tom Hanson's car.

Helen thanked her and dabbed at her nose. "I have to," she said. "I can't think of any other way."

"It's tearing you up." She leaned closer and whispered, "You've got to tell him."

Helen shook her head. "This is what God wants me to do," she insisted. "I know it." She looked out the window, fighting back another round of tears. "If only I can do it." She looked toward Tom Hanson for support. "What's that verse about being strong when we're weak?"

"When we are weak, then He is strong," Tom quoted, glancing at her in the rearview mirror.

"That's it," Helen said. She looked at Stella. "The Lord will be strong for me. He already has been."

"Sure He has," Stella said, looking out her window. "That's why you blubber all the way to work every day."

"Not every day," Helen said. She inhaled sharply. "Let's talk about something else. How are things at Stella's Boardinghouse?"

"Great," Stella said. "Private Romani is very neat, he doesn't mind helping out once in a while, and he's completely respectful." She glanced at Tom Hanson. "It drives me crazy."

Helen laughed.

"I mean it, honey. He treats me like I'm his *mother*. Even cried on my shoulder the other night when he got a 'Dear John' from some little number named Angelina." She grunted. "I'm not *that* much older than him!"

Helen arched one eyebrow.

"Oh, all right," Stella waved at her. "I am old enough to be his mother. Still, a girl doesn't like to be reminded."

Tom Hanson opened Helen's door first, then went around to Stella. Helen heard him clear his throat before he said, "I was wondering . . . would you . . . could you . . . ? Any chance you'd go to a movie with me? Matinee on Saturday? It's *Arsenic and Old Lace*. I think I remember you like Cary Grant?"

"Honey, every woman in America that ain't six feet under loves Cary Grant." Stella looked toward Helen, then back up at Tom. "You're blushing," she said. "That's adorable. Completely." She patted his shoulder. "Sure. I'd love to go."

"You . . . uh . . . won't have too much work to do for the Sunday-thing?"

"You trying to back out now that I said yes?"

Tom shook his head. "Of course not. I could . . . help. If you . . . wanted me to, that is."

"I'm frying chicken," Stella said. "Sort of a one-woman job."

"And I'm making the biscuits," Helen said.

"What about trout? Or walleye?"

"What *about* them?"

"Think they'd like some? With the chicken? On the side? I'm going fishing with the preacher early Saturday morning."

"Tom's a great fisherman," Helen said.

"Really?" Stella smiled. "Well"—she looked up at her suitor—"as long as you clean 'em *before* you bring 'em to the house." She held her nose and exaggerated a nasal voice. "Stella doesn't like fish guts by the back door. It bothers the customers." She looked toward Helen. "Ain't that right, honey?"

"Right," Helen agreed.

Tom laughed. "I'll do better than that." He followed the women inside headquarters. "I'll filet 'em."

"You do that, honey. And I'll give you your own little skillet."

As the deacon went out the door, Helen said, "You'll likely have fish filets coming out your ears, Stella. Those men know how to fish."

"Like Deacon Tom is really going to show up," Stella said as she plopped down at her desk.

"What do you mean? Why wouldn't he?"

"Think about it, Helen—a Baptist deacon and a nominal Catholic, if she's anything? And he's going to be with the preacher Saturday morning? If Ben Hale catches wind of this, he will have a fit."

"Don't be so sure," Helen said. "Although you can probably count on a call from the preacher next week."

"Great," Stella said. "Just great. Maybe I'll invite Father Jennings over and the two of them can duke it out for my soul." She balled up her fists and boxed the air.

———

The nights were the worst. Hank left at sundown for the garage. He always went up the alley. Helen always watched him from the kitchen window, hating the way he moved—almost like a thief skulking between the neighbors' garages, hoping not to be seen.

She wasn't afraid to be alone, but she still spent long hours lying awake, listening to the house, hoping to hear footsteps on the back porch stairs . . . the creak of the screen door . . . the now-familiar sounds that would say Hank had come home early.

As light began to glow in the east, she slept lighter, almost as if her closed eyes could see the change in the sky. She always heard the click of the alley fence gate. Her heart would start pounding as she heard him come up the stairs. Sometimes he went to the kitchen first. She'd hear him open the icebox door. Sometimes he sat at the table to eat the cold supper she left every night before going to bed, sometimes he carried a plate upstairs with him. Whether he stopped in the kitchen or not, she would lie listening as he mounted the stairs and passed by her door.

Please, she would think. *Please.*

But he never turned the knob. Sometimes he paused. If it weren't for that, she wouldn't have any hint that he even missed being married. What they had now was not marriage. It might *look* like marriage to the community. But it was little more than a pitiful ruse. And the strain was beginning to show. Like the crying jag in the car this morning on the way to work. Stella said Helen she couldn't go on like this. She was beginning to think Stella might be right.

Helen had been so sure she was doing what God wanted her to do. Not long ago Reverend Hale had preached a sermon on the Israelites leaving Egypt. He described the terror all the Israelites felt on the shore of the Red Sea when they realized Pharaoh was coming after them. Reverend Hale had made the congregation laugh when he held up both his arms and paraphrased God's words to Moses. " '*Who told you to park it?' God asked. 'I said* go. *So* go.' " Helen had taken that sermon to heart. She'd thought God was using Reverend Hale to tell her to go home. So, instead of "parking it" at Stella's, she moved forward into her own Red Sea of raging waters. She came home. But God wasn't parting any waters, and more often than not, Helen felt like she was drowning.

Sure, Hank came to the table and ate with her, but he still held her at arms' length. He almost cringed when she kissed him on the cheek. He never initiated a conversation. Other than bringing her the money from the shop, he had nothing to do with homelife at all. A particular hurt was that he didn't even ask about Mia. Didn't he miss her?

Mia was still afraid to come home. Helen could see it whenever she went out to the ranch with the Hales. Everything was strained until she heard Helen say, "Daddy said to say hello and he loves you and you can stay at the ranch as long as you are a good helper to Miss Jackson—as long as you come home in time for the beginning of school." Only when Mia knew she didn't have to go home did the smile spread from her mouth to her eyes. Sometimes Helen could literally feel the little girl relax in her arms.

"They that wait upon the Lord shall renew their strength; they shall mount up with wings like eagles; they shall run and not be weary, they shall walk and not faint." Helen was clinging to that promise for all she was worth. There were days when she claimed it every few minutes. There were nights when she felt the baby's featherlight movements and she lay in the dark, her hand on her abdomen, tears rolling down her cheeks. If something didn't happen soon, she was going to faint because she was weary. Oh, how weary.

She began to leave the bedroom door open. Maybe that would send the message. Maybe then he would respond. Every morning at dawn, she awoke when Hank's tread sounded on the bottom step. In the glimmering shadows of dawn, she hoped. And night after night, Hank paused . . . and climbed the attic stairs.

————

Hank had barely gotten started on Chase Young's Cadillac when someone banged on the garage door. Hank ignored it. They banged again. Wiggled the doorknob on the locked door. Banged again.

"You want me to get that?" Vern Clark offered from his perch on a stool beside Hank's tool bench.

"Let 'em be," Hank said. "I've got too much to do as it is. And if they don't know how I operate these days, I'm sure not gonna enlighten 'em at ten o'clock on a Friday night."

"Come on," Vern said. "You're under a car. Who's gonna see? Who's gonna care?"

"All right," Hank said. "See who it is. Tell 'em I've got everything I can handle until next Wednesday. Tell 'em to leave the car in the alley and drop a note through the key hole in the door Tuesday night. And get rid of 'em."

When Vern opened the back door, Hank heard an aged female voice exclaim "Eez goot" with a thick German accent. "Praise to God," Mrs. Koch said. "He has brought your business back."

Hank called a greeting from beneath the car. "I am booked solid, Mrs. Koch. At least through Tuesday." He reached for a bracket before saying, "Didn't think you were still driving."

"Twenty years ago they said I was too old. Probably, they were right."

From beneath the Cadillac, Hank heard the old woman tell Vern to get out of the shop. "I have business with Hank that is not yours. You will please go!"

Part of him thought he should do something to stop her from treating poor Vern that way. But part of him could barely keep from laughing at the vision of bullheaded Vern Clark being shooed off his stool by an elderly woman. Hank was tired of Vern, who was too seldom sober and too often ranting—if not against the Germans, then against God. The irony of Vern's being turned out of the shop by a German who was undeniably close to God was too rich. Hank didn't interfere. Amidst protests, Vern apparently obeyed, because Hank heard the door close and the latch catch. Outside, Vern was hollering something unintelligible.

Mrs. Koch shouted back. "You leave whiskey flask here! Maybe Hank will pound it flat. Go home. Sleep. Pray to God!" In a moment, she said, "Slide out from beneath the car, Henry. I wish to talk to you."

"I can hear you just fine," Hank said. Suddenly the old woman's domineering attitude wasn't so funny. And she was calling him Henry. Just like his mother used to when he was in trouble. He could see her shoes and the tip of her cane from beneath the car. Her ankles were so puffed up they literally flowed over the tops of her shoes. She tapped the side of his leg with her cane.

"I will look into your eyes when I speak."

When Hank didn't move, the shoes stepped away. The cane tapped its way toward Vern's usual perch.

After a minute of silence, Mrs. Koch said sternly, "You cannot outwait me, Henry Frey." She paused. "Come," her voice gentled. "Don't be afraid."

"I'm not afraid," Hank snapped.

"Good," Mrs. Koch said. "Because it makes no sense to fear being seen by an old woman whose husband's face was burned in the *first* war. Before they knew their Tannafex only made things worse."

"I may have only been about five when he died," Hank replied, "but I remember your first husband. He didn't have any scars on his face."

"You speak of Adolph," the old woman replied, "and you would be right. He had beautiful skin. But he was *second*. I am speaking now of Jakob—the first." She chuckled softly. "*Ja. Tree* times I have been married. Is surprising, I know. But I am an *amazing* cook."

Hank smiled in spite of himself.

"My Jakob," Mrs. Koch went on, "oh . . . what a handsome man. Until the test flight when he crashed. Then he was no longer handsome. No ears. No nose. Of course, *you* know what he endured. What you do not know, is what the wife endured."

"I can imagine," Hank said.

"No," Mrs. Koch said quietly. "I think that you cannot. And that, dear Henry Frey, is why I am here."

Hank heard her grunt as she stood up. Once again the shoes appeared in his line of sight. This time, she bent down and grasped the edge of the creeper and pulled.

"Come out, now. If you have a nose, I have seen much worse. So come."

Was he really going to make a scene and struggle with a woman who was probably ninety years old? And what did it matter, anyway? He did have a nose and ears. Apparently she *had* seen worse. He slid out from beneath the car.

Mrs. Koch didn't pay any attention to his face. Instead, she reached for him. "Give me your arm. Do you see my ankles? Humor an old woman."

Hank stood up and offered her his arm. Together they walked toward the front of the shop where Mrs. Koch sank onto the old gray sofa with a sigh. "Sit," she said to him, patting the spot next to her. Even though the blinds were down, when the streetlight just outside the shop door came on, the room was brighter than what he liked. Instinctively, he raised his hand to his face.

Mrs. Koch caught his hand in hers. "Ah, my dear," she said, "It's all right." She patted the back of his hand. "From me you do not hide."

Still avoiding her gaze, Hank let her hold his hand.

"My dear," she said, "My poor, poor dear." She cupped his scarred cheek in her free hand. "Look at me, Henry. Don't be afraid."

Annoyed, growing angry, defensive . . . Hank glared at the old woman. The list of reactions he had come to expect was long. It included things like horror, fear, pity, repugnance, and one he thought of as "pretend." That was the one where they couldn't stop staring at the scars even while they attempted to carry on a normal conversation.

None of these things shone in Mrs. Koch's gray eyes as she held his face in her hands and said, "I am so sorry for the price you have paid, my dear Henry . . . but oh, how I bless you for it." She let go of his face, and kissed the back of both his hands. "Because of you and others like you, I can worship my God where I please. Because of you and others like you, I am safe today." Tears flowed from her eyes. "You must stop hiding, Henry." She dabbed at her eyes with a handkerchief. "Let people stare. When they see you, they see the price that has been paid for their freedom. Yes, some will *say* stupid things. So you explain you were burned in the war. Yes, some will *do* stupid things. So you walk away. Or you make a joke." She smiled gently. "You say, 'Don't worry. Is not contagion.' "

"You mean contagious," Hank said.

She shrugged. "Whatever. You are smart boy. You will find better words. But you see what I am saying." She smiled at him. "Dear Henry, for every *one* that does or says these stupid things, a *thousand* would get down on their knees and bless you . . . if only they had the courage." She put her hand on her heart. "They feel it here. They don't say it, but you are still the hero."

Hank shook his head. "Don't," he said. "That's not—I'm not—I wouldn't—"

Mrs. Koch finished his thought. "You are not feeling so much like the hero. I know. But you *are*. Don't hide. Let us thank you." When she spoke again, her voice was gentle, the voice of a grandmother advising a child. "You listen to me, now. *Listen*. There are people right here in Crawford who care about you—who want to help. But even better than friends, Henry, is the wife who loves you."

Hank shook his head. "I can't face her." His voice broke. "I love her . . . but . . . LOOK at me!" Hiding his face in his open hands he began to sob.

Mrs. Koch put her arms around him. "There, there, little one," she crooned, "you cry now, *ja*. There . . . there." She waited for him to calm down before speaking again. "Think, Henry—think. If you lose your family and your life, then for what did you suffer?" She nodded. "Take them back, Henry." She held out her hands before her, palm down and made two fists and jerked them toward her as she spoke. "Take them *back*." She patted his knee. "Your Helen was gone for a while. But she is home again. She came back to you. Now it is for you to come back to *her*."

"You don't understand," Hank said.

"But I do. I know she waits for you because she told me. 'I went home,' she said. 'And I will wait for him.' She offers you the gift of her love. Open it, Henry. Take your family back."

"Is that what Jakob did?"

Mrs. Koch sighed. She shook her head.

"Sometimes I think Helen and Mia would be better off if I had died, too."

Mrs. Koch frowned. "You misunderstand. Jakob did not die in the crash. He came home. But he refused to see anyone. He slept in the attic." She paused. Her voice trembled as she said, "And that is where I found him."

"Found him?"

"Dead. Hanging." Mrs. Koch dabbed at her eyes. "Of course, he was dead long before he did that to himself. But as you can see, Henry, all these years later and after two happy marriages, I am still wondering what could I have done . . . what did I not do . . . was it my fault?" She waggled a finger at him. "You have a good woman, Henry. Love her. Let her help you. Let her keep the promise she made to God when she married you."

Hank shook his head. "Even if Helen would have me back . . . Mia. She's afraid of me."

"I don't know about Mia," Mrs. Koch said. "God did not bless me with motherhood." She pointed toward the sky. "But you can ask Him." She reached out and patted him on the head as if he were a little boy. "So much pain, Henry. So much pain. Make it matter for *something*. Don't give those—" She paused, seemed to consider, then used a swear word to label the enemy before going on. "We are winning the war. Everyone knows it. But what does that matter to you if you lose the battle you must now fight to get your life back?"

Hank was so shocked that sweet old Mrs. Koch had said a swear word, he just sat on the couch while she unlocked the front door and left. He leaned forward and rested his elbows on his knees, his head in his open hands. He closed his eyes and ran his fingertips over the scars. After a few minutes, he got up and opened the front door. Up the street someone had opened the windows at the Servicemen's Club. He could hear laughter and music. He wondered if Helen was working up there tonight. She hadn't said anything about it. But she wouldn't. They hadn't had a real conversation in—how long? He couldn't remember. The thought of her just up the street, laughing—of someone else seeing the dimple appear in her left cheek . . . He closed his eyes against the idea and weariness washed over him. He should go back to work on the Cadillac, but he stretched out on the couch and fell asleep.

He woke at dawn. His first thoughts were of Helen. Mia. His family. And what Mrs. Koch had said. If he lost them . . . then the enemy had won. Slowly, he got up and went to the door. His hand shook as he set the cardboard clock to tell people he would open at 9:00 A.M. on Monday. With his hook, he rolled up the window shades to let in the early morning light.

Chapter Nineteen

The steps of a good man are ordered by the Lord: and he delighteth in his way. Though he fall, he shall not be utterly cast down: for the Lord upholdeth him with his hand.
PSALM 37:23-24

HELEN SAT AT the kitchen table trying not to panic. She'd been there since dawn, her ragged emotions alternating between anger at Hank for not coming home and fear that there had been an accident at the garage. She would wait ten more minutes and then—She yelped at the jangle of the phone. More fear. Something *had* happened. She glanced at the clock.

"I fell asleep on the couch in the shop," Hank said. "In case you wondered."

His voice was different somehow. Less defensive, Helen thought. She swallowed the anger. "I was worried."

"I'm sorry. I'll . . . I'll be home in a little while."

"I'll scramble some eggs," she said, preparing to hang up.

"Helen . . ."

She put the phone back to her ear. "Yes?"

Silence. She waited.

He cleared his throat. "I-I'll be home soon."

Helen hung up the phone and tried to calm herself down. She told herself she was reading too much into a phone call. Too much into his voice. He would come home, eat breakfast, and head upstairs to sleep on the cot in the attic. He would hardly look at her. She had to expect that, because she might not be able to stand much more hope. She should just stay in her bathrobe and leave her hair a mess. What did it matter, anyway?

Helen told herself these things all the way up the stairs. She preached to herself as she brushed her teeth . . . combed her hair . . . slipped into the housedress that he used to say made her skin look like peaches and cream . . . and dabbed cologne behind her ears. It wouldn't matter. It wouldn't make any difference at all.

Her hands trembled as she buttoned the dress.

————

It was 9 A.M. and Hank felt sick. There was no way he was going to be able to eat breakfast at home. He had a good plan, but as he slunk up the side of the building toward the sidewalk that led to the store's front door, his courage was failing fast. He paused at the sidewalk and looked around the corner of the building. Up the street, a cluster of ranchers was headed into the donut shop for their Saturday morning round of coffee. Sweat gathered on the part of his forehead that wasn't scar tissue as he hurried up the sidewalk half a block and put his hand on the doorknob of the western store. He swallowed. *Lord give me strength.* He opened the door and went in. *Whew.* The store was empty.

"Can I help you?" A female voice rang out from the back. He didn't know whether to be glad or not that he recognized Mrs. Jarvis's voice. "Isn't this a beautiful spring morning?"

"Sure is," Hank replied, feeling awkward. A normal conversation was not something he was used to. "I'm looking for a hat. For my daughter." He went to the wall of hats and stood with his back to the shopkeeper.

"How old?"

"Six. No . . . eight." He shook his head. "I've been gone. Guess I didn't think she'd grow while I was . . . gone." He forced a laugh.

The silence behind him made him uncomfortable. What was it Mrs. Koch had said . . . ? Something about making a joke to put people at ease, even though you were the one who was terrified. "Guess you've heard plenty about me," he said, "but don't worry"—he turned to face Mrs. Jarvis—"it's not contagious."

"Hank?" She looked at him—really *looked.* Her eyes filled with the tears. She came to him and gave him a hug. "Welcome home. It's so *good* to see you." She smiled. "We've lost so many. It's good to get one back."

Hank held up his hook, "Well, part of one, anyway." He shrugged.

The woman patted his shoulder. "If you're getting a cowgirl hat, I presume Mia must be liking life out at the Four Pines."

At his look of surprise, she smiled, "I help out over at the Servicemen's Club on Tuesdays. With Helen." She nodded. "She's so proud of you and Mia. We've heard all about the little cowgirl's adventures."

As the woman reached for a small straw cowgirl hat, Hank frowned. Had he heard right? Did she say Helen was proud of *him*?

"How's this?" Mrs. Jarvis asked, holding up a straw hat with a red strap.

Hank nodded. "I should think that will be just fine."

He had paid his money and was waiting for the package when the door at the front of the shop opened. Two girls came in, stopped, stared. Whispered.

"Good morning, girls," Mrs. Jarvis called out. "Is something the matter?"

One of the girls shook her head. The other could not seem to take her eyes off Hank's face.

When Mrs. Jarvis handed him the sack holding Mia's cowgirl hat, Hank reached for it with his hook. He could see the girls take another step back from him. As he walked by them, he nodded. "Don't worry," he said. "It's not contagious. Unless of course you know how to fly a B-17. Then you might catch it."

The girls looked away.

He left the shop, but paused just outside the door to collect himself. Behind him, he could hear Mrs. Jarvis's voice. Lecturing. He was shaking all over. Looking down at the sack in his hook, he realized that while it had taken guts, it had also taken love. He had both. He just hadn't had them both at the same time in a while. Surviving the injury and all the operations had taken more guts than it had taken to man the B-17. And it was going to take even more courage to reclaim his life. Funny how he hadn't thought about that. He'd had the courage to die. Now the question was did he have the courage to live? He looked down at the sack in his hook again. He had love. If he hadn't completely stamped it out. And he didn't think he had. Helen was, after all, still leaving the bedroom door open. He looked up the street. Even though it was still quiet at this hour, he ducked up the alley and headed for home. As he walked along, he wondered exactly how long it would take for word about Hank Frey's new face to get around town. He jogged home, hoping Mrs. Jarvis hadn't called Helen yet.

———

"Why would Mrs. Jarvis call me?" Helen asked as she ground coffee for breakfast.

"She said she works with you at the Servicemen's Club. I figure she knows all about—"

"I don't talk about you behind your back, Hank." From the way she said it, Hank could tell she was miffed. This was not the way he had hoped their first almost-normal conversation would go. "Well, I take it back. I do talk about you. I make up all kinds of wonderful things about the two of us." She paused. "It makes things easier."

"I wasn't trying to pick a fight," he said. "I just thought she might want to be the first to tell you."

"Tell me what?" She turned around and looked at him.

He held up the sack.

"I don't understand," Helen said, setting the empty coffeepot down on the counter.

He cleared his throat. "I . . . uh . . . stopped by her store on my way home." He held out the sack. "Take it. I know how to let go."

Helen reached for the sack. Hank released the hook.

"Does that . . . uh . . . is that . . . weird?"

"What?" Helen looked at him. All he could see was confusion in the beautiful brown eyes before she glanced down at the sack.

He inhaled. "Taking something out of a hook like that. I'd think it would be . . . weird. Maybe kind of repulsive."

Helen shrugged. "Actually, I've been wondering how it works."

He showed her. Then he said, "Now take a look. In the bag."

Helen pulled the hat out.

"It's for Spridget. Do you think it's the right size? Mrs. Jarvis thought it would be about right."

"I think so. She'll love it when you give it to her."

He shook his head. "*You* give it to her."

"But—"

He shook his head. "Not yet. I . . ." He sighed. "I want to talk to her. But, I've got to figure out how to explain this." He pointed to his face. "So she won't be afraid."

"She's over that," Helen said, putting the hat back in the bag. "Of course, it would help if she could actually *see* you."

"She deserves to know what happened. How. And . . . that the way I look isn't going to improve much, but that I'm still here—underneath it."

Helen was looking at the floor, her brow furrowed. She swiped at her cheeks. Cleared her throat. "*Are* you?" She looked up at him again with those eyes—those amazing brown eyes.

"Am I what?" His voice was hoarse.

"Still . . . here?" She put her hand over her mouth and looked away, trying—unsuccessfully—to control her emotions.

"Oh, baby . . . I am. But—"

"What'd I do?" She sniffed and reached into her apron pocket for a handkerchief.

"What do you mean, what did *you* do?"

"Wrong. What did I do wrong? To make you so angry. To make you hide—to not want—" She shook her head and gestured around the room. "This . . . us. . . ."

"Is that what you think?" Hank said. He remembered Mrs. Koch's words. Even to this day, the old woman still wondered what she could have done differently. Exactly what Helen was saying now. "Oh, baby. It's not you. It's never been you. It's me. This . . ." He turned away from her. "No woman in her right mind could love or want a man who looks like this."

He felt her come up behind him, press herself against him, wrap her arms around his waist, lay her cheek against his back. He raised his flesh-and-blood hand and laid it over her arm. He wanted to caress her skin, but he didn't dare. He wouldn't be able to stand it if she pulled away.

But she didn't pull away. She held on tighter. "Then," she said, "call me crazy." She stood on her tiptoes and barely managed to reach high enough to kiss the back of his neck just above his collar. "I asked for God's help to know you were still in there. To see the butterfly . . . not the cocoon. Oh, Hank . . . I love you so."

She let go of him and ducked under his arm. She pulled his arms open and tucked herself up next to him with her cheek on his chest and her hands around his neck. She didn't look up at him. His heart quickened. He started to tell himself that she probably couldn't bear to look up. But then he realized this was just the way Helen had always snuggled up against him—her cheek on his chest. He had always had to lift her chin to get her to kiss him. His heart was pounding as he lifted his hand and touched her chin . . . and lifted it. Again, she didn't resist him.

"Let me see you, Hank. Really see you."

His entire body tensed. What an end to an almost-moment. Everything in him screamed no. But he followed her to the kitchen table, sat down opposite her, took off his hat, and let her look. He could not, however, bear to watch. He still had those memories of the tenderness in those dark eyes. He wouldn't trade those for what he knew he would see now.

She began to cry softly as she ran her finger from the tip of his nose, between his eyes, across the bridge of the eyebrow, along the cheekbone, into his hair . . . down the jawline.

"It doesn't hurt," he said. "It's numb mostly. Burns that deep take the nerves, too."

"Shh," Helen said. "Shh."

While he sat, waiting, he thought about old Mrs. Koch and wondered if this is what she had wanted to do. He was trying. He was frightened. And he was back to the subject of guts and love. When Helen started to cry, he knew he couldn't handle it any longer. The scent of her cologne and the memory of the hug would have to be enough. He raised his hand to brush her away, but she caught it, and then she was climbing into his lap, kissing the scars, crying harder, and finally . . . kissing his mouth. His arms went around her. He jabbed her with the hook and she jumped.

"Ouch!"

"Sorry." He felt so clumsy.

But then she laughed. She wrapped her arms around his neck. And kissed him and laid her head on his shoulder and sighed. "I love you, Henry Frey," she said.

"I love you, too. But—"

"But?" She sat up.

"There are still so many things to figure out."

"I know," Helen said. "And I don't know or pretend to know the answers."

"Mia," Hank said.

Helen shook her head. "I don't know. I think we should ask Ben and Clarissa. Maybe . . . there is someone we can talk to who's . . . Doesn't the army have someone we can talk to? Who's been through this?"

"We'll ask," Hank said.

"We'll figure it out," Helen said.

The phone rang. Helen hopped up and answered it. "Yes," she said, smiling at him as she talked. "Thanks, Mrs. Jarvis. I'll tell him." She had just finished telling him that Mrs. Jarvis wanted to make sure he knew Mia could exchange the hat if it didn't fit when the phone rang again. "Really? Well, if the sign says Monday morning, then it's Monday morning. Yes. Much better. I'll tell him you're bringing in the Buick."

She came back to his lap. "News is out." She kissed his cheek.

"That a monster is roaming the streets of Crawford?" Hank said.

Helen made a face. "That Hank Frey bought his daughter a cowgirl hat—and that he'll be open normal business hours on Monday." She wrapped her arms around his neck. "What happened?"

He sighed. "Mrs. Koch happened." He told her about Mrs. Koch's visit, concluding, "She was right. About everything. After she left, I realized I was turning into Vern Clark. All he does is spout hatred and resentment, and that just makes me sink deeper. I've thought I lost everything for so long. Mia ran away to the Four Pines. You went to Stella's. For a long time, it seemed like Vern was right. The Nazis took everything I had, and people around here were feeding them steak. But then . . . you came back. And you left that door open." He pointed up the stairs.

"But you never came in."

"I couldn't, honey. I wanted to—"

"Do you still?"

"Do I still . . . ?" He read the message in her eyes.

"You don't have to prove anything," Hank said. He looked away.

"Don't tell me what to do, Henry Frey," his wife said. She untied her apron.

———

Helen skipped Sunday School on Sunday morning.

"You have to go to church," Hank said, nuzzling her cheek and then pulling back the blankets. "I gave this town enough to talk about yesterday just by going into Jarvis's for Mia's hat."

When Helen opened her mouth to ask him to come, too, he put his finger over her lips and tapped gently. "No," he said. "Not yet. Someday. But not yet." He stretched. "But I *will* make breakfast for you before you go."

At church, Clarissa Hale was waiting just inside the door. She slipped her arm around Helen's waist and lowered her voice. "Thought maybe you'd want to sit with me this morning." Helen looked toward the sanctuary, suddenly aware of the eyes watching her. Apparently the phone lines of Crawford had been buzzing. She smiled at her friend. "God bless you," she said.

Sunday Dinner at Stella's began with a hug and a laugh as Stella said, "All I can say, honey, is thank you for taking some of the heat off me. No one seems to care if I'm housing soldiers or not. Mrs. Bohling hasn't spoken to me since Private Romani moved in. But she flagged me down right after you left for church this morning to ask if I knew Hank had been shopping downtown."

As the days went by, Helen was increasingly thankful for her two girl friends, because things were not easy. People were still stupid, and Hank didn't always tell her about it right away. When he tried to bear it alone, he inevitably withdrew from her, and although she tried to be patient, it hurt her feelings. He resisted the idea of visiting Mia. "It's too soon," he said. But they talked. In the morning, before work, Hank descended to the kitchen and made coffee. He took it back upstairs and they talked. In the evenings, they lingered at the supper table to talk. And each night, lying in one another's arms, they talked some more.

For Helen, it was like getting to know her husband all over again. There were things inside him now that hadn't been there before—negative things, like bitterness and fear. But as they fell in love again, Helen discovered that everything new about Hank wasn't bad. He seemed to cherish her more than ever—and he told her. He savored his food more slowly, took time to inhale the aroma of his morning coffee, and noticed when she filled the planters on the front porch with pansies. He was, Helen decided, a man trying to celebrate life even while he bore the scars of death.

Friday night, one week after Mrs. Koch had invited herself into Hank's garage, the Freys invited her for dinner. "Three steps you take forward," she said, "two you take back. But you don't give up. Two out of three husbands taught me this, and we were happy."

On Saturday, Hank called up Pastor Hale and asked him to stop in whenever he had time. "I know you're busy today . . . but maybe one evening next week?"

But Pastor Hale knocked on the front door half an hour later, Bible in hand. Helen thought she would burst with love for Hank as he sat on the living room sofa holding her hand, and said, "I want my life back, Preacher. But I can't do it by myself. So I'm listening."

"I will tell you right up front," Pastor Hale replied, "that I don't have any experience counseling wounded veterans. But I've got plenty of experience looking for comfort for myself." He paused, looked at Hank, cleared his throat. "I don't have any visible scars, Hank, but I was in the other one." Helen realized she had forgotten that. Ben Hale was a veteran himself—of what they had called The War to End All Wars. How sad that it wasn't. She saw something pass between the two men. The preacher cleared his throat. He looked down and pulled a piece of paper out of his Bible. "These are the things that helped me. After a while. After a long, long while."

Hank took the piece of paper.

The preacher said, "I promise to pray with you and for you. And I want you to know that I feel very humble right now, that you'd even listen to me after what you've been through."

Helen noticed the preacher's eyes get red as he swallowed and drew in a breath. He cleared his throat. "I'll likely say some stupid things and do some stupid things, but when I do, I'd appreciate your letting me know, and I'll try to do better. I guess that's all I can promise. Humans fail each other all the time. But God never fails." Pastor Hale spread his open hand over the Bible. " 'The grass withers and the flowers fall, but the word of our God stands forever.' That's not just a Bible verse, Hank. It's the truth. The true truth."

Hank nodded. And he asked the preacher to pray for them.

It was early June before Hank would sit out on the front porch with his wife, but when he finally did, the people of Crawford began a parade by the house. They didn't come up the walk, but they made it a point to call a greeting and wave hello. At first, Hank said it made him feel like he was in a zoo. Helen worried that he would withdraw again. But he didn't. Stella came over a couple of evenings. It took her about three minutes to make Hank laugh . . . and Helen cry, because she had forgotten what Hank's laugh sounded like. She loved Stella even more.

Hank said maybe, just maybe, he would go to church soon. "I like a man who doesn't pretend he knows all the answers," he said about Pastor Hale, "but is really convinced that God does." He looked at Helen and smiled. "I think we're going to make it. And . . . I think I may have a way to reach Mia." They were sitting on the front porch. He got up and went inside. When he came back, he handed Helen a handmade book. "Tell me what you think."

When Helen had finished the book, she leaned back in her chair and closed her eyes, clutching it to her chest. "It's wonderful," she murmured. "Perfect." The baby fluttered. She opened her eyes. "Mia can read it to her little brother—or sister—when the time is right."

Hank's mouth fell open.

Helen nodded.

He slid to his knees in front of her.

Trembling, she took his hand and spread it over her abdomen.

"Are you sure?" he croaked.

"I'm sure."

"When?"

"In the fall." She tilted her head. "Is it . . . is it, all right?"

"It's . . . miraculously wonderful," he whispered, and pulled her into his arms. Right there. On the front porch. In front of Mrs. Bohling and anyone else who might be watching.

———

Mia burrowed into the corner of Ned's stall and sighed happily. She loved the way the barn smelled. She didn't even mind the manure smell, which was never all that strong because she and Jo worked hard to keep all the stalls in the old barn clean. Buster and Ned and the other horses had it good. And they seemed to know it. They were happy. Mia could tell. Even now, Ned and Buster were out in the corral, nose-to-tail, heads down, dozing in the sun, lazily brushing flies away from each other's heads the way horses always did.

"How'd they learn to do that?" Mia had asked once when she first came onto the ranch.

"God taught 'em," Aunt CJ said.

Now Mia looked down at the book in her lap. Daddy had written on the cover, *God Teaches Henry*.

Mommy had brought the book out a few days ago. Around the dinner table, no one said very much about Daddy, which was nothing new. Except that something about the way they *didn't* talk about Daddy made Mia think they had things to discuss she wasn't supposed to know about. It wasn't like before, when they didn't talk about Daddy because it made everyone sad. Now it was as if they didn't talk about Daddy because they all had a happy secret. Mia knew one thing was for sure . . . Mommy was smiling more.

Another thing that was different was that Mommy had stopped trying to talk Mia into coming home for a visit. That made Mia wonder what was going on, too. And then, right before she left, Mommy had pulled a big envelope out of her purse and handed it to Mia. "This is from Daddy," she said.

At first Mia was disappointed. She'd liked the cowgirl hat and the boots and the candy and the bracelet. Daddy was good at picking out presents. But when she opened the book and saw it was something Daddy had *made*, Mia couldn't help but pout a little.

Mommy didn't seem to notice. She just kissed Mia good-bye and got in the car with the Hales and drove away. Mia ran into her room right away and read the book. Then she read it again. And again. In less than a week she had it memorized. But she still liked to look at it. She'd brought it out to the barn and put it behind the loose board in old Ned's stall, and in the afternoons, when Jo was talking on the phone or writing letters and Aunt CJ took her nap, Mia liked to come out to Ned's stall and read her book.

Once there was a man named Henry. He had a wife and a little daughter and he loved them very much. There was a drawing of a woman and a girl and a daddy.

He loved his country, too. An American flag.

Far, far away, a man named Adolph Hitler decided he wanted everyone to do things his way. A Nazi flag.

Henry was afraid. He didn't want to leave his family to fight Hitler. But when his country asked him to, Henry went. He didn't want Hitler to take away people's freedom. A family in jail.

When Henry joined the army, they said he should help with the airplanes. Henry was excited! He liked flying and he felt proud to be helping his country. An airplane with Henry waving out the window.

But one day when Henry was flying, his plane caught on fire. The plane with flames all around where Henry is sitting.

Henry parachuted out of the airplane, but his face and his hands hurt very bad. Henry and a parachute floating toward the ground. Henry's face and hands are black.

In the hospital, a doctor tried to make Henry better. But his skin couldn't go back to the way it was. Ever. Henry felt very sad. Henry's face with a frown and tears.

Henry went home. But Henry is ugly now. People stare at him. They make him feel very sad. Henry wonders if anyone loves him anymore. Sometimes people are afraid of him just because his face is ugly. This makes Henry feel sad, too. Don't they know he is still Henry inside? He wants to tell them. But he is afraid they will only laugh and say, "Get away from us! You are ugly!"

So Henry hides. A picture of Henry looking out the attic window of his house.

Henry wants to tell his little girl that he loves her very much. He is ugly, but he still wants to swing her on the tire swing. He wants to see her ride horses. He would like to hug her, but he doesn't want to scare her.

So Henry wrote a story to tell his little girl what happened, so that maybe she won't be afraid anymore.

Daddy had drawn a heart at the end of the book. Inside the heart it said, "Daddy loves Mia."

Sitting in Ned's stall, Mia pored over the book. She spent a long time looking at the page with the plane on fire.

Chapter Twenty

The sacrifices of God are a broken spirit: a broken and a contrite heart,
O God, thou wilt not despise.
PSALM 51:17

DIETER WAS IN a nightmare and he could not climb out, so he closed his eyes and waited for it to go away. But it didn't go away. Every time he opened his eyes they were there—the skeletal bodies, the shrunken heads, the barely human forms—some smiling, some weeping . . . alive and yet appearing dead. There were dead ones, too. Piles of them. Open mass graves with bodies lined up waiting for the earth to cover them. He wished the earth would fall on him. Then he wouldn't have to find a way to live with this nightmare.

He didn't know. They wouldn't believe it . . . but he didn't know. Bruno Bauer was sitting next to him in this nightmare in the dark with the flashing lights on the screen at the front of the room. Dieter could hear him breathing, barely controlling the sobs that racked his body. Rolf Shrader was here, too . . . and every other German PW held at Fort Robinson. It was a nightmare, but one the men must endure while awake. They had been crowded into the room and told they were going to see a film . . . so that they would know what the Reich had done.

Dieter didn't want to know. Not about this. He hadn't been completely ignorant, of course. He knew people who disagreed with Hitler were taken away somewhere. To labor camps. He knew about the Jews. In labor camps. But . . . dear God in heaven, would anyone ever believe he didn't know . . . about this? Not this. He ducked his head. Waited for the nightmare to end. Wondered if he would ever again be able to look Sergeant Isaacson in the face.

Twenty minutes of nightmare ended. The film was over. The Allies had freed them all. Places Dieter had heard of . . . and forgotten. They had been only names. Auschwitz. Buchenwald. Only names. But not anymore.

Now they were nightmares. He would have them forever. He deserved it, he supposed. He had worn that same uniform. What would he have done if he had known? The questions and the horror and the shame swirled in his mind as Romani flipped on the light and the German PWs were left to sit and think. *This is your army. This is your Third Reich. This is you.*

No, Dieter thought. This is not me. I would never—And then he thought of his little mother. What would he have done, he wondered, if they had threatened to put her in such a place because the son resisted the call to fight for the Reich? What would he have done if they had decided the residents of Dresden were the undesirable elements of German society, not fit to be part of the new order?

The room was silent. He could almost hear the men breathing. Thinking. Trying to absorb such a hideous truth. At Dieter's side, Bruno Bauer was scrubbing the tears off his face while he stared blankly down at the floor. Around him men sat in stunned silence. They were ordered to form up. The sounds of chairs scraping the concrete floor were harsh. Still, no one spoke. No one looked up.

Later, after lights were out in the barracks and he lay looking up at the ceiling, Bruno Bauer called his name in a stage whisper.

"What is it?" Dieter growled.

"What can we do?" the young prisoner asked.

"About what?"

"About . . . that."

Dieter took in a deep breath. "I don't know."

"I feel so ashamed," Bruno whispered.

The words caught in the boy's throat, and Dieter could tell he was trying not to cry. Again. "Go to sleep, Bruno."

"Can God forgive even that?" the boy whispered.

It was too much. "Am I your confessor?" Dieter said. "Go to sleep. If you want to talk about God, ask the minister on Sunday. But for now, go to sleep and leave me alone." Bruno didn't ask any more questions. And Dieter lay on his cot, staring up toward the ceiling, ashamed to be a member of the human race.

On Sunday afternoon, three times the usual number of men filled the pews in the chapel. The pastor spoke of things Dieter had known all his life, only now he drank in the words like a man dying of thirst. *Forgiveness. Mercy. Steadfast love. Never ending. New. Every morning. New.* While his human mind said such good news could not be true in light of the newsreels . . . his broken heart prayed it was.

Jo heard the yells long before she saw the man. It had been a long, hard day for the PWs. Given the chance to work longer than usual and help with a new fence in the west pastureland, the men elected to stay, working madly beneath the broiling sun with relentless purpose. Aunt CJ took them water, filling two old crockery coolers from the well and driving Sadie up and down the fence line while the men toiled. The work was appreciated, Jo knew, but she also knew that Aunt CJ was concerned. The men were quiet. Not sullen, just quiet.

"You'd be quiet, too," Private Romani had said a few days ago, "if you'd just been shown what your army did to the Jews."

For the first time in Jo's life, that she could remember, Aunt CJ had nothing to say. Jo shuddered. The news was just now coming out . . . news that was so horrible her own mind couldn't quite believe it. How, she wondered, could this same sun that shone on the peaceful ranchland she loved so much, also shine on men who did such things? She tried not to think about it. But every morning, when the PWs arrived, it came to mind. *It wasn't you,* she wanted to believe. *You were far away from that. You didn't know. Did you?*

Daddy said his chapel services had doubled in size. The men were quiet there, too. He said he was keeping things simple. Good news about Jesus and assurance that forgiveness was offered freely by the Lord who loved them. He didn't know if any of them had accepted that forgiveness, but Daddy said he had done his best to be kind—and to forgive in his own heart.

And now, someone was shouting. The sun was low in the sky, and Uncle Will's pickup full of silent PWs had driven by the house and disappeared over the first hill half an hour earlier. Aunt CJ had driven into town with Mia to deliver a letter the child had written to her daddy. And so Jo stood at the kitchen sink washing dishes, enjoying the scent of fresh earth and the June breeze, trying not to think about the news, when she heard shouting—in German.

A running man came into view, and she sidestepped away from the sink to where she would be hidden behind the lower half of Aunt CJ's feed-sack cafe curtains. Her heart thumping, she stood with her head down, listening. When the shouting subsided she peered around the curtain just in time to see Dieter Brock snatch the cap off his head and stomp on it. He stood for a minute looking around, then headed for the old well where he hauled up a bucket of water, plunged both his hands into the icy water, and splashed it over his face. He ran his hands through his blond hair and began to pace. Jo could almost see his mind working as he looked down the road, paced, paused, looked up the road, paused. When he started across the road toward the house, Jo's hand went to her throat. The thing she feared—and yet longed for—was about to happen, and she was alternately thrilled and terrified. When Brock hesitated in the middle of the road, Jo glanced toward the door.

She looked at the phone, then through the window at Brock, who clearly did not know what to do. Back at the phone. How could this possibly have happened? Romani counted everyone several times a day. Had he been daydreaming again and miscounted? Even if that was what happened, why didn't Rolf Shrader or Bruno or one of the other PWs say something? For a second, Jo contemplated the possibility they were all part of an escape plot. Isn't that what the authorities had warned? *Do not think a PW likes you. He does not. Do not think a PW will not try to escape. He will.* But if Brock were trying to escape, he wouldn't be standing in the road right now trying to decide what to do. He'd have quietly saddled a horse and ridden away.

Romani. Jo had heard him call Dieter "pretty boy" behind his back. Romani made sure Dieter got the hardest jobs—the least savory. For his part, Dieter always shouldered whatever it was without complaint and without comment. Romani had been especially hateful these past few days since that newsreel had come to the fort. Aunt CJ had even threatened to report him for shoving one or two of the men when they were unloading in the morning or when they didn't do something as quickly as he thought they should. "You should follow your sergeant's example, young man," Aunt CJ had said to Romani. "You were there the same as me when Bruno Bauer tried to talk about that newsreel. You saw how Sergeant Isaacson put his hand on that boy's shoulder and said revenge was God's business and not his."

Romani had seemed to get the point, but Jo never had liked him, and now . . . Had he somehow engineered this to look like an escape attempt . . . just out of spite? She wondered what was done to prisoners who tried to escape. Would anyone believe Dieter Brock over the word of an American soldier?

She looked back toward the phone and the wall next to it where Aunt CJ had posted the "Instructions for Persons Using Prisoner of War Labor in Your County." Number three was clear. *Do not talk about the prisoners of war over the phone.*

Once again, she looked through the window. Brock had put his hat back on. He was walking up the road after the truck. As she watched, he broke into a jog. Fearing that if she thought about it a minute longer she would talk herself out of it, Jo shrugged out of her apron and hurried outside.

"Herr Brock!" she shouted. He didn't seem to hear, so she hurried to the front of the house and cupped her hands around her mouth. "Herr Brock!" When he stopped and turned around, her heart thumped again. After all her daydreaming and all her wondering, the impossible had happened. Here he was. Here she was. And no one to stop them from talking. No one to stop them from anything.

———

This could not be, Dieter thought as he looked down the hill toward the house. Logic told him he had better run away and fast. But something else tempted him to wait and see if she came closer. If she came closer, he would have a chance to really see her—to really listen to her voice without wondering who was watching and what they would think. He had day-dreamed about this happening. Sometimes, as he lay awake in his cot at night, thoughts of her came uninvited. Even now. Especially now. Thoughts of a lovely girl were a welcome diversion from the nightmare. He had told himself a thousand times that thinking about women was pointless and only made him restless. But thinking about this young woman seemed to be something he could not control. And now, here she was, calling after him, with no one to see and no one to object. He was . . . terrified.

As she hurried up the hill toward him, his heart began to pound a rhythm that was unrelated to his short run. Perhaps, he thought, it was fear. For surely he should be afraid. She could say anything and she would be believed. She could ruin him. Nothing positive could possibly come from this moment. He should run. He should. But his feet seemed to have grown roots into the sandy soil. He could not move. Was she walking or floating? Either way, she was moving toward him, that glorious fringe of golden hair shining in the evening sun. . . . *Evening!* He had to get back. He had to do something.

"Stop!" he said, more harshly than he intended, but at the sound of his voice the girl hesitated. "Don't—come—here." He waved her toward the house. "Call . . . someone. Tell them what has happened. That I am coming."

She kept walking toward him. "Exactly what *has* happened?"

He gestured after the truck. "I don't know. I don't understand. Private Romani sent me into the barn." He waved toward the new barn down by the spring. "He said Herr Bishop needed help up in the . . . where the hay . . . ?"

"In the loft." She supplied the word.

"Yes." He nodded. "In the loft. But when I climbed up there, I heard the truck start, so I jumped down and . . ." He clenched his jaw to keep himself from swearing.

He allowed himself to look into her eyes. For a moment he said nothing, so acutely aware was he of the miracle of the moment as a beautiful American girl stared at him with no emotion other than concern. There was no hint of dislike, no fear . . . only . . . Dare he think Josephine was able to look past the PW painted on his work clothes and see only a man?

"Romani!" she said in a tone that hinted of less than respect. She shook her head, then looked back at the barn.

"You must go back in the house," Dieter said. "Please."

"But you're going to be in terrible trouble," the girl protested. "And I'm not afraid."

"I know you aren't afraid," he said. "You are, I think, like your aunt—and more likely to load a rifle than run away when you face something you fear. But you are right that I am in trouble. It is I who am afraid." He turned up the road. "If you could please call and—"

"I can't," Jo blurted out. "It's against the rules."

"Rules?"

She nodded. "I know. You haven't read them. One of the rules is we can't let you read the rules. But anyway, we aren't allowed to talk about problems with PWs over the phone." She seemed to be thinking about it anyway, but then she said, "and it's a party line, so I don't dare break the rule. There'd be a full-scale mobilization."

"Party line?" He was trying to picture what a gathering of Americans at a celebration had to do with Josephine calling the fort about his predicament.

She held one hand before her mouth and with the other she appeared to be holding something to her ear. "The phone," she said. "Anyone can pick it up at any ranch sharing the same line." She pointed to where a wire went from the house to a pole . . . and another pole . . . and on across the hills of sand into the distance. "If I call about you, everyone will know."

"That's bad," Dieter said.

"Yes," Josephine answered. "Very."

"If someone calls *you* . . ."

Jo shook her head. "It's the same. Anyone could listen."

He was wasting time. He had to get moving. "Thank you," he said. "I will go now."

"You can't run all the way to Fort Robinson," she said. "It'll be long after dark before you get there."

"Someone will come," he said. "I must be trying to get back. Maybe there is a chance they would believe me."

"Of course they'll believe you," she said. Her lovely voice had taken on a crispness that, if it was on his behalf, he liked. "I'll tell them exactly what happened. And they'll believe us. Please, wait. I-I've wanted to talk to you. To know about you. Can't you wait? Can't we just . . ."

The nightmare returned. The sadness descended. "Ask me," he said. "Whatever you want." He steeled himself for the questions about the Jews. It would be miniscule penance, but he willed himself to accept it, just as he had willed himself to beg Sergeant Isaacson's forgiveness a few days earlier. He could only hope this beautiful young woman would be half as kind.

"How did you know Buster was a good horse?" she blurted out. "I saw you that first day at Fort Robinson. By the corral. And you knew. I could see it in the way you approached him. You sensed . . . But how?"

He was dumbfounded. She wanted to talk about horses. Only horses. Thank God—*horses*. He tried to smile. "If only we had met in another place. In another time," he said. "Then I would gladly share with you all that my father taught me."

"Your father?"

"He was the great horseman in our family. From him I learned everything. Because of him I knew to be amazed at Jenny Camp and Dakota, even though when I first saw them at the fort they had been rolling in the mud. They looked nothing like when I saw them back in 1936."

"You *saw* Jenny Camp win that medal?"

He nodded. "My father was there. Riding for the German team."

"How? Where?"

"He died right after that. A riding accident," Dieter explained.

"I'm sorry," Jo almost whispered. She had moved closer to him while he talked, and now, she was standing almost close enough that they could be having a normal conversation anywhere. Almost. She smiled up at him. "Do you have other family?"

"Only my mother." He looked away from her toward the horizon and shook his head. "I don't know if she is . . . alive. I write. She does not answer."

"I'm sorry," Jo said. "Really." She sighed. "War confuses . . . everything." She looked down at the ground. "I hope she's all right."

"Thank you," he said. "And I hope your John Bishop returns home."

Jo jerked her head up and looked at him with a little frown.

His smile was gentle and warm. "Mr. Bishop told about his son at our first meeting. He let me know his own feelings about the war." He took in a deep breath. "And since this news, he has been . . . so kind. I cannot believe that he is so kind."

Jo sighed. "Uncle Will has strong opinions. But he's a good man at heart." She paused and bit her lower lip before adding, "I don't know what to say about that . . . other."

Dieter nodded. He looked back up the road and then toward Jo. "Thank you."

"For what?"

"For these minutes." He looked down and pointed to the white PW painted on his shirt. "For these minutes when you looked past this."

"I've wished—" Jo stopped. Her heart was pounding again. He reached out and with the tip of one index finger he touched one blond curl just above her left eyebrow. She closed her eyes. She could just barely feel the curl move beneath his gentle touch. Before she opened her eyes again he was gone, running . . . running . . . up the road, his footprints leading him away from her and toward the sunset horizon.

———

Vern Clark could not believe his good luck. He'd been watching the Four Pines for days now, formulating his plan, and now the golden boy of all the PWs on the place was about to be delivered right into his hands. He had to clamp his hand over his mouth to keep from shouting with joy. He'd have to hurry. The German was young, and Vern wasn't spry as he used to be. Sliding away from the ridge where he'd been watching and planning, he headed for the pickup he had driven across the hills and parked in a gulley about a quarter of a mile from CJ Jackson's barns.

Vern arrived at his truck with burning lungs. As he bent over and tried to suck in enough air to catch his breath, he pondered how lucky it was he never went anywhere without his rifle. A person just never knew when he'd have a chance to clip a coyote or two. As he climbed into his truck, Vern grabbed the rifle out of the truck bed and laid it across the dashboard.

"An eye for an eye, a tooth for a tooth," he said aloud.

———

Dieter swiped at the sweat on his forehead with the back of his hand. Bending over, he tried to catch his breath. His stomach was growling, and he was thirsty. But even through the discomfort, he had to smile a little. From the top of the hill where he stood, the Four Pines Ranch was little more than a dot in the distance. Josephine would be back in the house by now. Her reaction to him had lifted the clouds of shame a little more. Dieter imagined he could see a tendril of smoke climbing into the sky from just about where the ranch house would be. He pictured her in the kitchen. Maybe she was baking *pfefferneusse*. Or maybe she had gone across to the road to tend the horses. She was pretty. Spirited. Lively. Like the heroine in a Wagner opera. *Idiot. What good does it do to think about women? Think about your predicament. What are you going to do?*

He broke into a lope, discouraged by how quickly it was growing dark. *More running, less thinking.*

There was nowhere to go and nowhere to hide. And someone was coming. On horseback. The moon had risen. Once, Dieter thought he heard a pickup truck, but it made no sense because, according to what Will Bishop had said, the ranches in this part of America occupied vast tracts of land and there were no other roads for miles. Dieter didn't think there was a road in the direction from which he thought he heard the truck. The Sandhills, he concluded, must play tricks on a man's hearing. That had to be the explanation for what he thought sounded like the hoofbeats of more than one horse on the road behind him.

———

Clara Joy

Will has been telling me for years that I have a lead foot when I drive and that someday it was going to get me into trouble. Of course me being the gentle and easygoing thing I am, I have been telling him for years to mind his own darned business. But that night in early June of nineteen and forty-five, I almost made Will's prophecy come true. Almost. Thank God that Dieter Brock is the horseman he is and that Buster is the horse he is—because I came flying up over a hill and had no time whatsoever to react to the unexpected sight of my niece and Dieter Brock riding horses in the direction of Fort Robinson. And bareback at that.

Of course *they* had heard me coming and had seen the headlights, so it wasn't all that much of a close call. Except for me. By the time I got Sadie slowed down and onto the side of the road, I was shaking all over. Mia, who had been asleep beside me, was sitting up asking what was wrong, and when I couldn't answer her right away—the cat really did have my tongue, I guess—she got scared. So I was busy calming Mia down and didn't even hear Jo and Dieter Brock ride up until they were right at the side of the pickup.

"What in tarnation is going on?!" I boomed.

"Romani tricked Dieter into getting left behind at the Four Pines," Jo said.

"I was walking back," Dieter said. "Since you are not allowed the use of the phones and the celebration line to call for trouble."

"He means we aren't allowed to use, the *party* line to call for *help*," Jo said quickly.

I was more than a little surprised to see that Buster was tolerating a night out on the prairie with no saddle between him and his rider, but apparently that unseen communication between Buster and Dieter Brock was real, because the reins were loose, and Dieter was relaxed—about the horse, anyway. He was absolutely bonkers about everything else.

As I have said before, I am good in a crisis, so in about two shakes I had Mia behind Jo on her gelding, and Jo and Mia leading Buster back to the house, while Dieter climbed into the truck beside me, and away we went toward Fort Robinson. Dieter Brock was quiet, and I let him be. When Sadie backfired, I nearly jumped out of my skin. I really do need to get Hank Frey to look her over. One of these days, when I really need a truck, she's gonna give out on me, and then I will be sorry.

Chapter Twenty-One

Be not hasty in thy spirit to be angry:
for anger resteth in the bosom of fools.
ECCLESIASTES 7:9

THEY WERE LAUGHING. It made him sick. Healthy young men driving machinery, bundling, picking up bales and tossing them on the truck, stacking and creating mountains of hay. They had no right to be healthy. No right to be here. Someone had to make a point of it, wake people up—make them see the wrongness of it all. Just watching them made Vern cry for Delmer.

Delmer should be driving that tractor while Johnny Bishop threw bale after bale aboard the flatbed trailer and Ron Hanover stacked them high. Those boys always worked together, and where were they now? Ron buried up on Walnut Hill, Delmer buried only God knew where in Europe, and Johnny . . . Well, who knew where Johnny was? The Pacific, Will Bishop said. He was fine, Will insisted. But Vern knew better.

The world was messed up, and that was all there was to it. The good boys dead or in prison camps while the very enemy that had done it all strode tall and healthy beneath a blue Nebraska sky, baling hay for CJ Jackson.

He'd missed his big chance that night when the golden boy got left behind. He'd been watching the Four Pines, waiting for a chance, and he thought that was it. But then things got too complicated. The preacher's daughter provided the horse, and then CJ herself drove up—and then he missed. He never was a very good shot. It was just as well, though. Now he knew why God let that happen. There was a better way. A bigger way to send a message than killing only one. Thanks to those newsreels about the concentration camps, he wasn't the only one who knew what they were really like.

Of course, people like CJ Jackson and that preacher in town were already talking about forgiveness. Saying that the PWs in Nebraska had nothing to do with that—didn't know about it. Felt awful. Well, Vern thought, maybe they had been quieter than normal for a few days . . . but now they were right back to their old selves as far as he could see.

He'd had to be so patient, waiting for the sun to do its work first and dry things out. Letting God prepare the fields for harvest so Vern Clark could do his part. Right after the German surrender, the PWs were put on half rations. Vern rejoiced when he heard that some of them had lost a lot of weight. Served them right. But then Hank told him that CJ Jackson said it was wrong for their rations to be cut, and she began feeding them even more, trying to make up for what she called "bad treatment."

It was just one more thing to convince Vern he was right to make an example of the PWs on the Four Pines. Make an example and send every last PW working out on the ranches back inside the barbed wire where they belonged. Hank Frey was the only one Vern had ever been able to get to listen to him, and lately even he wasn't listening too good.

He couldn't blame Hank, though. He had enough troubles as it was. No one could blame him if he said he was done with the Krauts and didn't want to fight anymore. One look at that face and you knew he'd done his share.

It was time, though, for someone to step up and show them. Make them pay. Send the message. The day was perfect for it. He never would have thought he could be thankful for the heat and lack of rain, but all through July, when it didn't rain and the fields got dry and the heat kept on, Vern was glad. And now, sitting here on the hillside watching the Krauts in the field below him, he was ready. And he knew God was on his side.

He wiped the sweat from his brow and took another drink from the silver flask. He waited. The heat and the liquor made him sleepy. That was all right, though. He had time. They had to be gone for lunch before he could do the first thing.

When he first heard how good CJ Jackson treated them, it made him so mad. But now her craziness helped his plan. The PWs were in the habit of old Will Bishop picking them up in the field and bringing them back to the house so they could eat in the shade of the cottonwood tree. At the very picnic tables where the boys used to take their lunch breaks in better times. The Krauts weren't worthy to sit in the dust beside those tables. He laughed to himself. Old CJ Jackson wouldn't be treating them to lunch after today. Nodding happily, he closed his eyes. He had time. Time to wait.

"Hey, Dad."

Looking into the sun, Vernon couldn't quite see the face. "Delmer? That you, Delmer? Where you been son? They told me . . . told me you were dead."

"I'm gone, Dad . . . but you aren't. You can do it for me. . . . You are doing it. Thanks, Dad."

In the last couple of days, Vern had had trouble telling what was real and what wasn't. Delmer was dead. Delmer couldn't talk to him. But every once in a while, when he nodded off, it seemed like Delmer had things to say. Vern couldn't be sure, but he thought Delmer was the one who came up with this idea. Maybe. Maybe not. Either way, Delmer was pleased with the way things were going. That made him feel good.

Vern started at the sound of a gunshot. The sound terrified him as he wondered if the Krauts were after him . . . or Will Bishop, who had somehow gone from knowing what was right to moving back to the Four Pines. Rolling over on his stomach, Vern separated the tall grass and peered toward the work crew. The old blue pickup must have backfired as she hauled them out of the field. There they went, out of sight. Gone to get lunch. Gone. Gone. Gone.

Vern stood up. His legs were stiff. He stretched and looked around, marking where the baler was parked. Where they were stacking. He nodded while he stood on the hill surveying. With a grunt, he bent down and grasped the handle of the can. He had a long way to walk. A long way to walk and just a little while to walk it. He hurried down the hill. At a certain spot, he unscrewed the lid. He began to sprinkle the dry grass.

Lightly. Lightly. Make it last. Make it last . . . a better blast . . . make it last. He walked along, smiling as he worked. *Smell it, boys? Smell it? That's death. See how you like that. See how it feels to be on fire. What you did to Hank Frey and my Delmer . . . to all the boys. . . . See how it feels.*

By the time the can was almost empty, he was jogging, laughing wildly, pouring generously. When the last drop came out it was exactly as he had prayed. He could lay flat out in the dip in the earth, and they would never see him . . . never see the match . . . never know . . . never guess. The only thing that could be more perfect would be if God let the wind come up. That would transform his creation into a true thing of beauty . . . a perfect masterpiece from a sincere patriot.

———

When Rolf Shrader slipped off his seat at the lunch table and fell to the ground, moaning and clutching his head in his hands, Dieter dropped his spoon. "Poison! They poison us!"

Next to Dieter, Bruno Bauer's face went white as a sheet. He bent over and spat his ice cream onto the ground.

Rolf sat up and made a face. He rubbed his head with his hands. "Never mind," he said. "I only ate too fast. Too much cold on a hot day . . . makes the brain . . . freeze!" He popped up off the ground and held out his bowl to Miss Jackson, batting his eyelashes and pleading for more.

Laughter echoed around the picnic tables beneath the cottonwood trees as first one, then another of the PWs who formed the work crew at the Four Pines pantomimed the joke on Bruno Bauer.

When Bruno looked at Dieter, and Dieter shrugged and took another bite of ice cream, his face went from white to red. For a moment, the laughter subsided while the men waited to see if Bruno's red face meant rage or embarrassment. Rage could be a problem in a man the size of Bruno Bauer.

With Bauer leering at him, Rolf shinnied up the cottonwood tree. He was perched high in the tree when Sergeant Isaacson came driving in. "Here comes the infantry," Rolf quipped. "And Isaacson likes me, so you don't dare hurt me."

"I don't want to hurt you," Bruno said good-naturedly. He grabbed Rolf's bowl. "But I do want your ice cream."

Isaacson strode up to the table where the men were seated. Dieter noticed the serious look in the sergeant's eyes.

"I know, I know," Miss Jackson said. "It's all against regulation. But it's hot, and they work hard." She grabbed a bowl. "Sit down, and I'll dish some up for you."

Isaacson shook his head. "It is over," he said, looking around the table with a grave face.

Rolf dropped out of the tree. The men all sat staring at the guard they had grown to trust and respect. Isaacson continued. "I am informed that the Japanese have agreed to unconditional surrender."

"What does that mean—for us?" Dieter spoke up.

Isaacson shook his head. "I am sorry to say it may not mean much, at least for the immediate future. They will begin compiling transport lists, but I haven't seen any. Other than the fact that certain classes are no longer optional, your daily schedule will not vary for now."

Bruno whined. "More classes? What classes?"

"They want us all to be champions of democracy before they let us go home," Rolf said. "It wouldn't do if we all go home and become communists."

"As long as the Americans don't set up some terrible regime," Bruno said, "they don't have to worry." He changed the subject. "Whoever gets home first must immediately visit the families of the others."

"What are the classes we must take?" Rolf asked.

"Knew you'd ask," Isaacson said, and reached in his pocket for a rumpled piece of paper. "We aren't supposed to know. But I sort of . . . found this . . . in the trash." The men around the table applauded. He held up the paper and read, "The Democratic Way of Life. The Constitution of the United States. Political Parties, Elections, and Parliamentary Procedures. The American Economic Scene. Why the Weimar Republic Failed. The World of Today and Germany. New Democratic Trends in the World Today."

The men shrugged. Rolf sighed. "If I promise not to be a communist—if I swear on my mother's grave—will that relieve me from all those hours in a classroom?"

"Your mother isn't dead," Bruno said. "You've been stockpiling soap to take to her. And haircombs."

"The haircombs aren't for his mother," someone else sang out and looked around the table with a grin. "Unless his mother is named Ellie and has the blond hair of our kind hostess." He nodded toward the ranch house porch where Jo had just come out and was heading toward the tables.

Dieter turned his back on her and suggested they get back to work.

Quietly, the men followed Dieter's lead, stacking their used dishes on the tray at the end of the tables and going with Will to the blue pickup truck.

Miss Jackson teased, "You're welcome to lend a hand with the haying, Sergeant."

Isaacson smiled. "I have another work crew to check on in Crawford." He gave a half-salute and headed for his jeep.

"You'll be going home," Jo's voice sounded so near to him, Dieter was startled. Before he could step away, he was looking down into her blue eyes.

She was smiling. "You must be feeling wonderful about that."

Miss Jackson moved toward the two. "You must write to us, and let us know how you are," she said. "I hope your time here hasn't been too awful."

Dieter shoved his hands in his pockets. He took a couple of steps toward the pickup before turning back. "That March day when we climbed down off the train, and it was so cold, I looked at these bluffs looming above the fort, and I thought it must be the most desolate place on earth. Now, when I look at them, they remind me of the castles on the Rhine. When I think of returning to bombed cities and a countryside over which men have stretched barbed wire and barriers . . ." He shrugged and forced a smile. "My country will need good men to rebuild. To find our way out of the mess left behind. I will do my best for her." He glanced at Jo. "But I will never forget you." He nodded toward the old barn and the pasture where Buster was rolling in the dirt. "I thought I might be able to take him over a jump someday soon." He sighed. "The world is turned upside down when the prisoner dreads being free."

Will honked the horn. The men shouted for him.

"Thank you for being so good to us," he said. "Knowing people like you still live in this world helps me realize it is worth trying to rebuild a better one."

Will honked again.

Dieter turned on his heel and ran to catch up with the field hands. Maybe, just maybe the nightmare was over.

———

Finally, they were coming back. If only there was more wind . . . but the gasoline should help things along. Vern struck the match, smiling as a beautiful little orange flame licked at the first blade of grass, consumed it, advanced, and—*Swhoooosh!*

He backpedaled out of the way so quickly he fell on his backside. He lay on his back looking up at the wall of flame. He could have sworn he saw Delmer in the flames. The boy was smiling.

———

Dieter had his back to the row of men and was tossing a bale of hay up into the wagon when he heard a loud pop and felt a rush of hot air. He whirled around just in time to see a stream of fire erupt, almost as if it were following a prescribed trail along the ridge looming just above the field.

"Fire!" Someone screamed. For a moment, everyone hesitated.

Dieter was the first to move. Running to the team of draft horses, he grasped their halters and began to turn them away from the advancing fire.

Bruno stood transfixed, watching the fire advance like a soldier paralyzed by fear in the face of an oncoming enemy.

"Go to the truck!" Dieter screamed at him, barely managing to keep on his feet as the horses caught the scent of smoke.

Will had lowered the tailgate and was yelling for the men to climb into the back.

Dieter flung himself up on the wagon and, grabbing the reins, headed the team away from the fire. He heard the truck come to life. It barreled past him as he lashed at the team, driving them out of the field. Up the hill in the distance, he could see the truck skid to a stop at the house. Miss Jackson came out, looked toward the field, then charged for the old barn just across the road from where the truck had stopped. As the team tore into the yard, Dieter caught sight of Jo headed inside the ranch house with Mia on her heels. Throwing his entire body weight against the reins, he barely managed to stop the horses from charging right past the old barn where the PWs were already at work, some hauling empty barrels out and lining them up in the bed of the pickup while others turned on a spigot and began filling the barrels with water.

"Are there more barrels?" Dieter called out.

"Water tanks," Miss Jackson called, motioning back the way Dieter had come with the team. "Down in the new barn."

Dieter yelled for Rolf and Bruno, instructing them to jump into the back of the wagon while he turned the team around. Miss Jackson climbed up beside Dieter, and he lashed at the team and charged back down the hill. Under her direction, they loaded a water tank in the back of the wagon and collected burlap sacks.

When they saw Will heading back their way with the pickup, Miss Jackson shouted to Dieter, "Just do what Will says. Tell him I'm gonna plow a firebreak," she said, and ran for the old tractor.

"Will it start?" Dieter called out.

"God only knows," she answered, then looked up at the sky. "Please!"

Will's pickup shot past, with PWs clinging to the running boards, PWs seated beside Will, as he drove them toward the flames.

————

"Hello?"

"Mrs. Hale?"

"Yes. This is Mrs. Hale."

"Thought you'd want to know," the operator said. "There's been a fire call. For the Four Pines."

Clarissa set the phone down and wiped her trembling hands on her apron. She stared for a moment at the rows of cinnamon rolls Helen Frey was frosting for Stella's Sunday dinner.

"What is it?" Helen wanted to know.

The women tore off their aprons and ran for the garage, where Hank and Ben had been all afternoon, trying to once again resurrect the Nash.

Dieter and Bruno were climbing into the wagon, preparing to follow the truck into the burning fields, when Jo and Mia ran down the hill.

"Where's Aunt CJ?" Jo yelled.

"Trying to start the tractor," Dieter answered. "Do you know why?"

"She'll plow up the dirt around the house . . . to save it from the fire."

Rolf grabbed Dieter's arm and nodded toward the horizon.

"It'll be here. Soon," Jo said, looking around her helplessly.

"Take Mia back to the house," Dieter said. Just as Jo headed off, he heard the old tractor come to life. It came into view and headed up the hill, stalling halfway to the house. But it was only partway up the hill. Behind them they could see flames licking at the horizon now. Miss Jackson had climbed down off the tractor and was standing beside it, frantically wiggling its parts. Dieter yelled at Bruno to drive the wagon after Will and help fight the fire. "You don't have to know anything," he said. "Just do this." He demonstrated slapping the team's rears with the reins. Bruno nodded. Rolf let out an authentic cowboy "yee-hah!" and the horses took off.

Dieter ran to the tractor.

"Climb aboard," Miss Jackson shouted. "When I say go, see if you can start it. Just pretend it's a truck."

It seemed to take a maddening amount of time for the thing to sputter back to life. When it did, Miss Jackson shouted for Dieter to get the horses out of the new barn. "Just get them out and turn them loose," she said, nodding toward the horizon where the flames seemed to have skirted the firefighters. "I'll get them back."

Will's truck appeared at the top of a hill in the distance, men clinging to the running boards and the back. As Dieter watched, Will Bishop swung the truck around and headed east. Behind him, Miss Jackson threw the tractor into gear and sputtered toward the house.

He tore down the hill and to the corral. Flinging open the gate, he charged into the milling horses, waving his hat, slapping rumps, running about wildly until the last skittish horse, a white yearling, finally darted away. The horses made for the south en masse. Heading into the new barn, Dieter opened the stalls, sending every horse out the wide door in the same direction as the herd.

He ran uphill toward the house where Jo stood on the porch, gesturing wildly up the road. "Help is coming!"

Looking over his shoulder, Dieter realized that help might be too late.

It looked like the rest of the men might be surrounded by flames. Miss Jackson drove the tractor into view. She had just completed the last turn around the house. A wide swath of earth ringed the house, but as she headed across the road toward the old barn, the tractor sputtered again and died, right in the middle of the road. Once again, Dieter climbed aboard, and once again, Miss Jackson wiggled this and waggled that. But this time, try as they would, they could not get the tractor started.

The flames marched toward them.

"There's still a chance it'll turn," Miss Jackson said. As she spoke, the truck appeared in the distance, this time driving ahead of the wall of fire, picking men up as it drove in a crazy pattern across the earth. From a distance they could see someone trip and fall . . . two others help him up . . . and another running for his life with tongues of fire in pursuit. The flames reached the edge of the old corral, consuming the aged wood instantly and then beginning to lick at one corner of the old barn.

As Jo screamed Buster's name, a car roared over the hill, drove across the plowed earth and skidded to a stop right next to the house. Four people jumped out. Dieter recognized the pastor and his wife. The other man he had never seen. His mind registered scars . . . and terror on the face of the woman beside him. He turned back toward the barn just in time to see . . . the little blond-haired Mia . . . disappear inside.

The women screamed. The men yelled. Suddenly nothing in the world existed for Dieter Brock but the barn door. He raced through it, into the darkness, toward the screams of Ned and Buster, into the hot breath of death. Flames climbed the walls. Above him, they licked at the shingled roof, then at the first of the massive beams supporting it. Thinking Mia would go to Ned, Dieter headed for that stall. The door was open. He thought he saw Ned's bony rump up ahead . . . but where was the child? He bellowed her name. He begged her to come to him. There was no answer.

Buster was whirling, screaming, banging the walls and door of his stall. Dieter ignored him until the stall door opened. There was a flash of golden hair—and Buster shoved the door aside. He slipped, his hindquarters landing full against the stall door. Dieter ran forward, grabbed the horse's halter, and dragged him toward the wide door, aware that as Buster followed him and the stall door swung wide, Mia's still form crumpled to the earth.

The beams began to fall. One landed between Dieter and Mia. He shoved Buster away, bringing his hands down on the animal's rump with all his might and screaming for the horse to "Go-go-go!" Everything swirled about him. He staggered, then regained his footing and leaped across the burning beam and scooped up the unconscious child. The roof was going—everything happening slowly. Flames and smoke . . . and quiet. Unbelievable, peaceful quiet. He was aware of the roof falling behind him . . . or was it ahead . . . ? Which way to run . . . which way . . . ? He propelled himself forward, not certain if he was running into the flames or away. . . . But there it was . . . a patch of sun . . . light . . . the roof falling . . . blazing beams. . . . With all his might he threw the burden in his arms toward the light.

Chapter Twenty-Two

Trust in the Lord with all thine heart;
and lean not unto thine own understanding.
Proverbs 3:5

JO CLUNG TO the porch railing and watched what was taking place around her as if in a dream. Helen Frey was at the edge of the burning barn, screaming and alternately fighting and clinging to Hank. She would hide her face against his chest and then push away and look at the smoldering remains, all the while babbling "Oh, God, no . . . oh, God, no. . . ."

While those two tried to absorb or avoid what they were facing, Uncle Will drove up with a truck full of scorched men. As they climbed out of or off the truck, one or two stumbled. Others helped them up. They didn't seem to know what to do, and for a split second they stood, reeling, looking around uncertainly.

Aunt CJ took charge. "Here, boys," she said, taking one by the arm, "you come right on up here on the porch. Clarissa, we're gonna need water and lots of it. You all right, Will? Good. Then get some bandages. You can tear a sheet up if you need to. Ben, you help Will."

The new activity roused Jo enough that the memory-film of what she had just witnessed rewound and replayed itself, and as she looked toward the barn she began to tremble. Helen was still yelling into her husband's chest. Jo had noticed Hank before, but she hadn't really seen him, and now that she did, the horror of what might be found beneath the red-hot ruin that used to be the old barn hit her full force. She raised her hand to her mouth to stifle her own cries. In the beehive of activity around her, Bruno Bauer stood motionless, blinking as if just now awakening. His eyes were like candles on a dark night as he rubbed smoke away and began to call Dieter's name.

Aunt CJ went to him. She put her hand on his shoulder and nodded toward the barn.

As the reality of what he was being told sunk in, Bruno roared like an angry bull. He charged the barn, pacing back and forth, calling Dieter's name. Finally, he grabbed the uncharred end of a blackened beam and, roaring with emotion, staggered backward. The effort threw him off balance and he landed on his backside in the dust. He put his head in his hands and began to sob.

Rolf Shrader went to him.

Jo's feet found wings. She ran to the two men, knelt in the dust, wrapped her arms around them, wept, overwhelmed by the awfulness of this moment, the sense of loss. She could not bear to think of Mia . . . could not stop thinking of Dieter.

At some point, Daddy arrived. He wrapped her in his arms. She could not look up at him, but she could feel his body quaking. He was crying, too. She had never loved him more than at that moment . . . when she thought she might have lost her own love.

––––––

When the preacher ran out to comfort his daughter, Hank turned away. He became a soldier again, doing what had to be done, not thinking about himself, denying his own feelings in favor of duty. His little girl would never need him again. The searing pain of that reality had to be put away—for now—or he would be of no use to Helen, who was clinging to him, mewling like a stricken kitten.

"Come on, sweetheart," he whispered, turning toward the house. "You come in and lie down. I've got to help these men."

Helen followed him inside. At the doorway she faltered and he swept her into his arms, carried her down the hall and hesitated at the doorway of the room where childish drawings of horses were tacked to the log walls above the bed. Physical pain shot through his heart. He turned away.

"I'll stay with her."

It was Clarissa Hale. Hank lay Helen on the bed in the next room. Clarissa sat down next to her, took her hand. Helen was pale, almost unresponsive.

"She's in shock," Hank said. "Put her feet up on a pillow. Maybe get her to drink some water." He looked toward the hall. "Wish there was a doctor."

"My sister called for help," Clarissa said. "I imagine Doctor Whitlow is on his way. He'll check everything. I'm sure it's all right. The baby will be fine."

Hank bent to kiss Helen on the forehead. He whispered love for her and their unborn baby into her ear. By the time he stood back up he was a soldier again, leaving his charge with someone else, returning to duty.

Out on the front porch, men were coughing, moaning, sighing . . . staring at the smoldering barn. Hank moved among them, hardly aware of their stares. Their burns weren't bad. He was glad for them.

Will Bishop came up. "I don't know much about this kind of thing," he said. "But if you can tell me what to do—"

"That's not as bad as it looks," Hank said, pointing to a forearm. He forced a smile at the terrified soldier looking up at him. "I know it hurts, but it won't look like this." He pointed to his own scars and shook his head no. "You'll be fine. Doctor's coming." Whether it was his tone of voice or the actual words, the man nodded and seemed to relax a little.

Hank moved from man to man, assessing their burns. Most were only superficial. He was more worried about the lungs of the ones who were coughing. "They need the doctor worse than the ones with scorched skin," he said, frowning.

"On the way," Will said. He looked toward the horizon. "Sure wish he'd hurry."

————

Somehow, her daddy knew not to make her move. He sat with her in the dust and let her cry. When her tears finally subsided enough for her to think of someone besides herself again, Jo reached out and took Bruno Bauer's massive hand in both of hers. Rolf Shrader got up and stumbled back to the porch, leaving Jo and Daddy and Bruno looking at the smoldering ruin of the barn.

Jo saw her first. She dropped Bruno's hand and scrambled to her feet, rubbing her eyes, thinking it must be a dream until she heard Mia crying; Mia, stumbling into view from the back of the barn, sniffing and sobbing as she came toward them.

Jo was the first one to reach the little girl, to fall on her knees before her, to hear the sobbing account. "I wanted to get Ned. And the man . . . he . . . came . . . and he grabbed me up . . . and the barn was falling and he . . . he . . . *threw* me out. He . . . spinned around and around and he *threw* me out—and then . . . ." She hid her face against Jo's shoulder.

"What," Jo pleaded. "Then what?"

"It fell," the little voice said. "It fell down."

Seconds later, Jo heard Mia whisper "Daddy?" and Hank Frey pulled her out of Jo's arms.

Bruno Bauer came back to life. He got up and ran around the back of the barn, out of sight. Jo could hear him calling Dieter's name, over and over again. Her tears returned. Shouts of joy over Mia behind her made the disaster before her seem even worse. She closed her eyes, trying not to think. It only made her think more. She looked up at the sky. *Where were you? What were you doing? You saved Mia. . . . Why couldn't you save him, too? What about his mother . . . Bruno . . . Rolf. . . . They need him. Please. Help.*

Bruno was bellowing something. Jo launched herself toward the sound . . . terrified, hopeful, and—when she saw . . . when she smelled it—terrified once again.

————

Ben and Clarissa arrived first. Their only daughter was seated on the grass crying. She had lifted Dieter Brock's head into her lap and was leaning low, whispering to him, caressing his hair.

"Josephine." Clarissa went to her, and as Ben watched his wife minister to their daughter, his heart nearly burst with love. He would never forget the smell. When Hank strode up, he heard the man take in a ragged breath and realized the news would be bad.

"Is he alive?" Hank asked.

"Yes." Jo looked up at them. "I can feel . . . his heart, feel . . . his breath." She swallowed hard.

Ben watched his little girl's tears wash a clear path down her smutty cheeks. At Jo's side, Clarissa knelt, one hand on Jo's shoulder, the other on Dieter Brock.

"We need to support that leg," Hank said, and began to peel off his shirt to be used as a sling. "Especially the foot. The beam must have landed right on it."

Ben wondered if there still was a foot beneath what looked like a blackened stump.

Hank spread his shirt out on the grass. "I'll lift his leg. You pull my shirt underneath. It'll do for a sling to get him to the house." As he bent down he swore softly. "Where's the doctor, anyway?"

Hank looked at Clarissa. "You take Jo and go on up to the house. Have a couple of the men drag a mattress out on the porch . . . to keep him more comfortable. Get some water." He waited for Jo to lower Brock's head to the earth. When Clarissa had pulled Jo to her feet and he was sure they were out of earshot, Hank looked at Ben. "Don't you drop him. No matter what happens when we pick him up, don't drop him."

"What could happen?" Ben said.

Hank swallowed. He looked up at Bruno and then back toward Ben. "Look, Preacher," he said. "I'm not sure if that foot is even going to stay *on*." He nodded toward Bruno. "Wish I could say that in German."

Ben shuddered. He tasted bile and clenched his jaw. He nodded. "All right."

Bruno knelt beside Brock's unconscious form. Hank lifted the leg. Ben slid the shirt beneath it. They did what had to be done. The foot stayed on. The charred skin did not.

————

Watching her daddy help Hank and Bruno carry Dieter to the porch, Jo once again retreated emotionally. She sleepwalked through the next half hour. She could not understand why they didn't bandage Dieter's leg . . . why they kept it covered and didn't try to treat it. Asking that question was the only thing she managed to say aloud. Hank Frey answered. "We're protecting it as best we can."

The military ambulance arrived. They didn't even move Dieter off the mattress the men had hauled out for him. They picked the whole thing up, put him in the ambulance, and drove away. Bruno Bauer almost self-destructed before Sergeant Isaacson intervened and Bauer was allowed to climb inside the ambulance with Dieter. A medic checked the other men. Jo didn't think he looked very interested in their condition. He waved them toward Uncle Will's pickup.

When Jo moved toward the truck, her mother tried to stop her.

"I'm going," she said.

Daddy came forward and took her arm. He guided her toward the pickup and climbed in beside her.

————

"I wish—" Seated between her father and Uncle Will in the hospital corridor, Jo bit her lip.

"You wish what?" Daddy slipped his arm around her shoulders.

"I wish I spoke German," she said, laughing sadly and swiping at the tears that came and went without warning. She cleared her throat. "Bruno seems so sad. If we could talk to him. If you could . . ." Her voice became a hoarse whisper. "Maybe you could say something that would help."

Daddy pulled her close. "All I'd do is pray with him. I don't have any magic words for times like this, honey. Look at me. I don't even know how to comfort my own daughter."

"Oh, Daddy," Jo said, putting her head on his shoulder. "You're doing it."

"I didn't realize—" He cleared his throat. "I didn't know how you felt."

"Neither did I," Jo said. She lifted her chin and looked up at the ceiling. She shook her head. "It's been a muddle. Still is."

"Since when?"

"I don't know. It just kind of sneaked up on me." She looked at Uncle Will. "I'm sorry, Uncle Will. I didn't mean for it to happen. I still love Johnny, too."

Uncle Will patted her hand. "I know you do. Don't you upset yourself about that, now." He stood up slowly and stretched. "I'm gonna get some fresh air. Maybe stretch out in the truck for a rest. You take all the time you need," he said. "I'll take you back home when you're ready."

Jo watched him go, feeling more miserable than ever.

"Don't worry about Uncle Will," Daddy said. "Things will work out. They always do."

"Dieter hasn't done anything . . . wrong. I don't want you to think—"

"I don't," Daddy said. "But I also don't want my little girl to get hurt. And . . . you . . . and him . . . It's impossible, you know."

Jo nodded. She looked toward the hospital ward door, which might as well be a stone wall.

———

Jo woke with a start, to the sound of creaking hinges and quick steps. She pushed herself upright, off her father's shoulder.

"I didn't realize you were still here, Reverend," the doctor said.

Daddy stood up. Jo followed suit. "I've gotten to know Brock these past few weeks. He translates my sermons on Sunday afternoons. He's been a good worker for my sister-in-law, as well. I was hoping you'd have some good news for me." He looked down at Jo and put his arm around her again. "For us."

The doctor shook his head. "Too early to know much. It's a bad injury. Broken bones in addition to the burns. We'll do all we can."

"But he's going to live," Jo said.

The doctor shrugged. "As long as we can control infection."

"Can we see him?" Daddy asked.

"That's against regulations."

While Daddy tried to invoke "pastoral privilege," Jo slipped away. She was through the ward door before the doctor could turn around. Ignoring the amazed looks that came her way from the other hospital beds, Jo hurried toward the bed in the far corner of the hospital ward—the one with screens surrounding it. Bruno Bauer sat in a chair fighting sleep. When he saw Jo, he stood up and stepped back, pressing himself against the wall, a silent sentry.

Dieter's face looked deathly pale against the crisp white pillowcase. There was a tent erected above the burned foot. He was too long for the bed. His good foot protruded through the railing. Jo curled her hands around the bedrail, watching him breathe, wondering if he was drugged, thinking he must be.

Bruno said something in a low, and surprisingly gentle, voice. When Jo looked up at him, she realized he wasn't talking to her.

"Jo," Daddy said behind her. He put his hand on her shoulder. "You can't be in here."

"I know," she said, her voice miserable. "I just wish—" Impulsively, she reached into her pocket.

The ward nurse approached with a frown. "You have to leave," she said. "Now."

Bruno stepped forward.

The nurse looked up at him. "Set yourself down, you big galoot," she said in a voice that belied her stern face. "I've spoken to the doctor and told him I need an extra pair of hands."

"So I am medic?" Bruno said in English.

Jo's mouth dropped open. "You . . . ? When did you learn English?"

Bruno's index finger went up. "In America." He nodded toward Dieter. "He is teaching. Is secret. Until now."

"It would seem," the nurse said, "that Frankenstein over here has some medical training. It would also seem that we would have to shackle him to keep him out of this hospital. So we've come to an agreement. I'm the nurse. He's in charge." She chuckled softly under her breath, but then her face hardened. "And you, young lady, are sorely in need of rest. And some respect for rules."

"Come with me, Jo," Daddy said, prying her hand off the bedrail and gently pulling her away. "He's in good hands."

"Good hands," Bruno repeated, holding up his recently scrubbed paws.

"Wait," Jo said, and took something out of her pocket. She showed it to the nurse. "I think it will make him feel better. When he wakes up, I mean."

The nurse frowned. "He can't eat it."

"He won't want to," Jo said. She looked up at Bruno. "From Buster."

Bruno took the *pfeffernuss*. He inspected it with a little frown, raised it to his nose, sniffed, and then understanding lighted his eyes. Smiling, he tucked it in his shirt pocket. "He will know," he said, nodding toward Dieter.

"I hope so," Jo replied.

As they walked the length of the hospital ward and through the door, Jo swiped at her tears again. "If they can have a female nurse, why can't they have visitors?" she grumbled.

"I suspect things will continue to relax as time goes on," Daddy said. "But it's still a prison camp. And she was right. You must respect the rules."

"Do you really think he's in good hands?" Jo asked. "That nurse wasn't all that friendly, even if she did seem to like Bruno."

"I'm not talking about earthly hands," Daddy said.

Jo shook her head. "I don't know that I trust the heavenly ones, either," she said. "God could have turned the flames. He could have—"

"But He didn't," Daddy said gently.

"*Why?*"

"Sometimes, instead of calming the sea, He calms us."

"That's not an answer," Jo protested.

"It's the Lord's job to rule. It's mine to let Him. We can trust Him to do all things well, Jo—in light of eternity, not in light of our selfish desires."

Jo shook her head. "I can't see it."

"If you could see it, sweetheart, it wouldn't be faith."

As they approached the truck, Uncle Will sat up. Daddy gave a quick report, and with a nod, Uncle Will started the truck. Jo was asleep before the pickup topped the first rise on the way home.

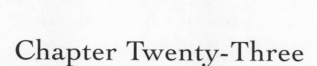

Chapter Twenty-Three

But love ye your enemies, and do good, and lend,
hoping for nothing again; and your reward shall be great,
and ye shall be children of the Highest: for he is kind
unto the unthankful and to the evil.

LUKE 6:35

UNTEROFFIZIER DIETER BROCK tried to fight his way out of the nightmare. Voices swirled around him, yammering nonsense. Just when he thought he might swim through the murk around him, agonizing pain took his breath. He would gasp, and descend once again into an abyss. He visited the desert . . . wandered bombed cities . . . fought battles . . . was part of a throng crowded into a square . . . heard a familiar and yet hated voice screaming slogans. There were gentler dreams, too. His mother smiling over him. A giant looming large in the night, offering him water . . . begging him to eat . . . wiping his brow . . . drying the tears he could not hold back when shrouded figures said they were helping but caused him such agony he screamed and fainted.

Gradually, the periods of consciousness lengthened. Memory returned. And then, one blistering hot August morning, Dieter opened his eyes and asked Bruno about Mia Frey.

Bruno reassured him. "The little *fraulein* is all fine."

Good. That was good. Now he wanted to see his foot. To know what was going to happen. When they would send him home.

"You are in such hurry," Bruno scolded. He claimed he didn't know anything.

Dieter asked the ward nurse, a middle-aged woman built like a battleship, with hair the color of steel and gray eyes that met his without blinking. "You'll have to speak to the doctor about that," was all she would say. Dieter suspected she knew more than she would say, but at that moment in his recovery, her resolve was stronger than his will to argue.

Pastor Hale visited. So did Miss Jackson. Even Will Bishop stopped in, to tell him Buster was settling back down. He reported that Jo had spent some time in town right after the fire, but she was back at the ranch now, working with Buster every day until she left for school. And they planned to build a new barn on the old site.

He dared not ask more. *She is going to school.* That would have to suffice.

So. What had never existed was over. It was time to go home. If only the foot would heal. If only he would be able to walk again.

———

Hank hadn't counted on all these feelings coming back. He thought he'd gotten past the worst of the memories, but the smells in the hospital room, the tent over Brock's foot . . . and what he knew must lay beneath the clean white sheet . . . brought it all back—longing for morphine . . . dreading the saline baths . . . trying not to scream . . . screaming . . . skin grafting. Hank barely managed not to shudder as he stood looking at a sleeping Dieter Brock.

When Brock opened his eyes and saw Hank, he asked a question in German, then switched to English. "Where is Bruno?"

"Just outside," Hank said. "Making sure I don't do anything wrong."

Brock sighed. "Having Bruno for a friend is not unlike having a faithful shepherd dog at one's feet." He winced. "Are you the new chaplain?"

The flawless English threw Hank. The guy didn't even have an accent. At least not one you would recognize as German. "No . . . I . . . ." Hank swallowed. "I'm Mia's father. I wanted to thank you." He looked down at the bed. "But I don't really know how."

"You just did," Brock said.

"It's not enough," Hank said. He motioned toward the foot. "Is it bad?"

Brock shrugged. "It is . . . inconvenient. It keeps me here, while my friends make their way home."

"Are they taking good care of you?"

Dieter shrugged. "As good as they know how. Unlike you," he said, "they have little knowledge of burns."

Hank nodded. He pointed at his own face. "Hash-browned climbing out of a wrecked B-17," he said.

"They did much damage to our cities," Dieter said. "Sometimes the guards taunted us with pictures."

The two men stared at each other for a minute. Dieter broke the silence. "But that is past now. The duty has been done. One side has lost, the other has won. Probably one will be a lot better off than the other. And the other will have to pay its dues." He paused before forcing a smile. "I am truly happy the little one is all right. When the roof began to fall in . . . all I could do was say a prayer and throw as far as I could. Toward the light."

Hank looked away. "She didn't even have a smudge on her beautiful little face."

"God is good," Dieter said.

Hank had warred with himself for many nights over this meeting. It was not at all as he had expected. In spite of what Helen had told him about the PWs, he had expected to see the enemy incarnate—a sober-faced, hard-jawed German with hatred in his eyes. Dieter Brock was a wounded young man with nothing in his eyes but pain and what Hank thought might be kindness.

The medic named Bruno came in. "He must have this," he said, wielding a syringe. Brock protested; Bruno insisted. Brock drifted off. His mouth fell open. He began to snore. "He must sleep now," the medic said, and shuttled Hank toward the door.

Hank turned around and pointed to Dieter's leg. "Is it . . . all right?"

Bruno shrugged. "What is 'all right.' I don't know. The doctor does not seem to know, as well."

"What do you mean—the doctor doesn't know?"

" 'I don't know so much about burns, but I will do what I can.' That is what he said." Bruno shrugged. "You Americans have been good to us. It will be what it will be."

———

"Too old," Jo said, and laid her pink sweater aside.

"Too frumpy," she said, and discarded the straight gray skirt.

"Too plain . . . too baggy . . . too short. . . ." One by one, as Delores watched, Jo deposited most of her clothing on her bed, rejecting each item as being unfit to wear to the V-J Day celebration. There would be a parade, followed by a dance, and in honor of her best friend's visit home, Jo had been given permission to attend both.

Yesterday, after asking permission and hearing the response, she had stared at her mother in disbelief. "You do know it's a dance, right?"

Her mother had nodded and said, "And you do know your father and

I expect you to behave appropriately, right? Which, in this case, means no slow dancing with strangers."

"Define stranger," Jo teased. At her mother's look, she laughed nervously. "Just kidding, Mother. And . . . thanks."

"I'll be working in the kitchen at the Servicemen's Club. And Helen and Stella will be there, too. So—"

"All *right*," Jo said. "I get it. You'd think I was about to elope or something."

It had been a truly momentous occasion for Clarissa Hale to give her daughter permission to socialize with the soldiers from Fort Robinson. But now that she had permission, Jo didn't know if she even wanted to go. She said as much to Delores.

"What's the *matter* with you?" Delores sat on Jo's bed, alternately approving or disapproving as Jo took inventory of her wardrobe. "For the first time in our lives, both our mothers are agreeing to let us go to the Servicemen's Club . . . and it's not just any old party, it's the *end of the war* celebration. Come on, girl, get with it! The Bobby *Mills* Band is playing! They're great!"

Delores leaned down and looked up at Jo's face. She patted her knee. "I know what it is. You're at loose ends. Johnny's coming home, but he isn't here yet, so you're waiting. You can't decide about school or—anything—until he's home."

Jo frowned. "I can decide anything I want. I don't need Johnny telling me what to do. 'Johnny this and Johnny that'—everyone keepings talking about it. It's like we're already married." She ran her fingers through her blond curls. "I wish people would just *shut up* and stop planning my life for me."

"Hey, kiddo, are you having second thoughts?"

"*Second* thoughts? I never really had *first* thoughts. It's always just been assumed. By everyone. Including Johnny."

"Wow." Delores leaned back against the headboard and crossed her arms. "Have you told him?"

Jo shook her head. "I wasn't about to write a 'Dear John' letter to a guy who's off defending motherhood and apple pie." She grimaced. "Sorry. That wasn't very respectful. But I don't know, Delores. I just don't know."

"Have you met someone else since I enlisted? Down at the Servicemen's Club? Or at those chapel services your daddy started? One of the guards, maybe?"

Jo jumped up and began returning clothes to her closet at a furious pace. "Why is it that everyone always assumes a woman is just naturally planning her life around a *man*? Why can't I just go to school and study and come home and run the ranch or join the Red Cross or be a WAAC or move to Germany or do whatever I want?! Aunt CJ never got married, and she seems happy enough!"

"Hey," Delores said, holding up both hands. "Don't yell at me. I'm on your side, remember? Come on, Josephine. . . . What is it? To look at you, you'd think we're going to a funeral instead of the V-J Day celebration."

Jo sighed. "Sometimes I wish I'd gone with you to Des Moines. Maybe things would be less confusing."

Delores studied her friend. "Okay, Josephine Hale. I'm just going to throw out a wild guess here, but I'm thinking this blue mood of yours doesn't have much to do with Johnny. But I'm also guessing—since you are protesting so *very* loudly—that it is about a man." She waited. When Jo said nothing, Delores tilted her head. "It's about him—the guy you didn't want to talk about before I left. Isn't it?"

Jo looked out her bedroom window toward the garden. So much had happened since she planted the rows of snow peas. They were long gone, replaced with hills of pole beans. By the time the pole beans were harvested, Jo would be in Lincoln attending classes at the university, and Dieter Brock would be . . . gone. How quickly a person's life could change. Sometimes she almost felt old.

"Is he *still* him-who-you-can't-talk-about?" Delores asked.

"I probably shouldn't," Jo sighed. "I don't know. I just can't seem to take it all in. Ever since the fire . . ." She shook her head. "I'm confused."

"About what?"

"Everything," Jo said.

"Try to be more specific, honey," Delores said.

"You sound like your mother, *honey*."

"Some people think I *am* my mother," Delores quipped. "Down at the Servicemen's Club last night Mrs. Fosdick called me Stella more than once. She's a hoot. All sweetness now that I'm wearing this," Delores spread her hands out like a fashion model.

"You look great in that uniform, by the way," Jo said.

"Thanks. You want to hear something funny? I *love* the army. I'm not kidding. I love it. They are going to have to drag me out of the service kicking and screaming."

"I'm glad you're happy," Jo said.

"So . . . is this an attempt to get me off the subject of your true confession?"

"For now," Jo laughed.

"Touché," Delores said. "But it's time to decide. Are you going to the parade with me or not?"

"I thought you'd be *in* the parade," Jo said.

Delores shook her head. "Nope. I'll be at the club all morning making coffee and serving up your mom's cinnamon rolls—how many hundreds has she made, anyway?—and then I'm solo for the parade. So, I repeat—are you going with me or not?"

Jo nodded. "Sure." She pulled on her pink cashmere sweater and turned around so Delores could button it up the back.

"Do try to smile, honey," Delores said. "We did win the war, you know."

———

Hank Frey donned his full dress uniform. He had yet to make peace with mirrors, so Helen straightened his tie.

"Calm down, sweetheart," she said. "The parade is to celebrate the victory, and you are the best trophy of victory this town has." She kissed him on the cheek. "You've won over all kinds of enemies—foreign and personal."

"I'm a trophy, all right," Hank muttered, "a trophy of fear." He put his hat on. "There. Not that it helps any."

"What's a fee-a-fear?"

Hank wheeled around to face Mia. "What'd you say, Spridget?"

"What's a fee-a-fear?"

"Fear," Hank said. "I'm nervous about the parade."

"You're scared people will stare. Like you said in your book."

Hank nodded.

"I'll hold your hand," Mia said. "I'll walk with you. Then you don't have to be afraid." She slipped her hand into his. "All right?"

"You can't be in the parade, sweetheart," Helen said.

"Why not?"

———

On September 2, 1945, Crawford, Nebraska, joined the nation in celebrating the victory over Japan. Flags flew all over town. Helen Frey draped their entire front porch with red, white, and blue bunting. Stella Black wrapped her porch railing with patriotic streamers. Together, Helen, Stella, Delores, and Jo made their way downtown.

They viewed the parade from in front of Hank's Garage, alongside

Mrs. Koch, ensconced in a chair brought for her by Reverend Hale just for that purpose.

Mrs. Koch rose to her feet as the last surviving Civil War veteran passed by, waving from the rear seat of Virgil Harper's Model T Ford.

Egged on by her friend Stella, Mrs. Reverend Hale forgot herself and blew a kiss as Ben passed by, head and shoulders above most of the other veterans of the War to End All Wars.

And Helen stood on the curb with tears streaming down her cheeks, as the town hero, Hank Frey, strode along, with his daughter in his arms and a smile lighting up his scarred face.

Chapter Twenty-Four

Trust in the Lord, and do good. . . .
PSALM 37:3

IT WAS THE APATHY underlying her daughter's compliance that worried Clarissa Hale more than anything. "She just isn't herself," Clarissa said to Ben one evening.

"I know," Ben teased, "she's been far too easygoing."

"Don't joke," Clarissa said. "Something's wrong. But I can't tell what. She *seemed* to enjoy our visit to Lincoln. She *seemed* to be happy about the plan for her to stay out at the ranch through the fall to help CJ and Will recover from the fire. She helps me bake cinnamon rolls for the Servicemen's Club every week. She spends time with Mia. I know she hears from Delores because she tells me her news. But it's all so . . . completely without enthusiasm."

"Honey," Ben replied, "for most of Jo's life the two of you have been in a constant state of turmoil. So I can't help but wonder about the fact that it's *now*—when Jo is doing exactly what you ask, including cooking and sewing—that you're worried?" When his wife didn't reply but only sat on the porch looking at him, Ben frowned. "All right. You may have a point." He filled his pipe. "You want me to talk to her?"

"Well, she's not going to confide in me," Clarissa said.

"Now, honey—"

"I'm not whining. That's just the way it is. And you know it." When her husband didn't respond, Clarissa said, "She got a letter from Johnny today."

Ben puffed on his pipe before asking, "So what's the news from John?"

"I don't know," Clarissa said. "She hasn't opened it yet. It's still in there on the buffet."

Ben frowned. "I'll talk to her tonight."

"Thank you, dear," Clarissa said.

Ben stood up and stretched. "Need to run a little errand out at the fort." He bent over and kissed his wife on the cheek. "Won't be late."

———

Gone to have coffee with Stella. Pineapple upside-down cake in the oven. Share a piece with your father when he gets home.

Mother had paper-clipped the note to Johnny's letter.

"All right," Jo muttered, plopping down at the kitchen table. "I can take a hint." She ripped the letter open.

"You don't seem overly eager to get John's news."

She looked up at her father, who was standing in the doorway, car keys in hand, watching her manhandle Johnny's letter. Jo sighed. She pointed to her mother's note. "It says here I'm to share some pineapple upside-down cake with you." She stood up, went to the oven, and pulled out the cake—which Clarissa had already inverted onto a plate.

"Makes my mouth water," Daddy said. "Just look at that caramel."

"I'll cut you a piece," Jo said. "But . . . could you get it over with?"

"Get what over with?"

"Whatever the trouble is I'm in," Jo said.

"What makes you think you're in trouble?" Daddy sat down at the table.

Jo shrugged. "Mother's been like a detective looking for clues to a murder mystery for the past few days."

"We're both concerned about you. You haven't been yourself." He took a bite of cake. "Only difference between your mother and me is, I think I know what's wrong."

"I don't know what you mean."

"I think you do," Daddy insisted.

"I'm just . . . tired. I spent most of the summer entertaining Mia. Then the fire. Now I can't start school right away."

Daddy nodded. "I know. It's a confusing time to be alive for everyone." He rattled the car keys. "Let's go for a ride."

"Now?"

"Nice night for a ride. Beautiful evening. Full moon. Fall air." He stood up. "Come on."

———

"It's all right, Jo," Daddy said. "It took some convincing, but Captain Donovan approved it. One time only. And we don't make it a topic of conversation in town."

Jo slid out of the front seat of the Nash and followed her father. Just inside the hospital front door, they were met by the same nurse Jo remembered from weeks ago. The woman had nearly chased her out of the hospital ward then. Now she met them with a grim smile and a nod.

"What happened to her?" Jo whispered as they followed the woman down a corridor and up a flight of stairs.

At the top of the stairs, the nurse turned around and faced them. "What happened to me," she said, "is watching your father with these men. Knowing he has a good heart. And trusting that he's not a complete fool."

Jo pressed her lips together. She could feel herself blushing. "I'm sorry. I didn't mean for you to hear that."

"It's all right," the nurse said. She led them down another hallway and outside a door. "Ten minutes," she said, looking intently at Daddy.

"We understand," Daddy said. "Thank you."

With a nod, the nurse was gone, and Jo was following Daddy into Dieter Brock's room.

He looked better than she expected. Almost better than she remembered. He was tired, but the blue eyes were smiling.

Jo smiled back. She had daydreamed about what she would say if she ever saw him again. But now those things seemed silly. Trivial.

Daddy stayed by the door. She could feel him watching her. He cleared his throat. "You two can talk, you know."

Dieter nodded. He smiled at Jo. "Buster is all right?"

Jo nodded. "I-I'm going out to the ranch on Sunday. To stay for a few weeks. Until I go away. To the university." She bit her lip. "We're building a new barn. Where the old one was. The men—Rolf and the others—they helped clear the site."

"Rolf told me," Dieter said.

Quiet again.

"Miss Jackson and Mr. Bishop are well? And John? He comes home soon?"

"Everyone's fine," Jo said. She didn't want to talk about Johnny. Not with him.

"They are taking me to the East," Dieter said. "To another hospital. Then home."

Jo nodded. "That's good." *That's awful. I don't want you to go.* She swallowed. "It's healing, then."

"Thanks to your friend."

"My friend?"

"Mr. Frey. He made the doctors call all the way to England. He paid for the calls."

Daddy spoke up. "Hank came out to visit. Thought Dieter would benefit from a second opinion. He arranged to have the doctors here consult with a Dr. McIndoe—the doctor in England who treated Hank."

"I-I didn't know that," Jo said. *God bless Hank Frey.* "So everything will be all right. You'll be able to ride again. When you get home."

He nodded. "And finally I have heard from my mother."

"That's good."

This was awful. She thought it would be wonderful. It wasn't. It was too hard to look at him and think she'd never see him again. Too hard. Tears were pressing against her eyelids. She reached up and swiped at the corner of her eyes. She cleared her throat. "I . . . I hope—" She broke off. What could she possibly say, when all she wanted was to feel those arms around her. Just once.

"We'd better be going, Jo," Daddy said.

"Thank you," Dieter said to Daddy. "For this."

Daddy put his hand on her shoulder. "Say good-bye now, Jo."

"Good-bye." It was a whisper—all she could manage without bursting into tears.

"God be with you," Dieter said, "blessing you and keeping you always." He faltered, swallowed, then grinned at her. "Give Buster the *pfefferneusse* from Dieter."

Jo nodded. She turned to follow her father out of the room, but at the door, she turned back. Rushing to Dieter's bedside she took his hand. Leaning down, she kissed his cheek. "Come back to me," she whispered, and fled the room.

———

Clara Joy

"What do you mean you are going to send a Christmas package?" Will scolded. "You don't even know if Dieter is home yet. For all you know, he's still in that hospital back east. For all you know, his mother has moved. For all you know—"

"Just hush up and find me a box," I said. So Will grumbled and complained and went and got a box. I filled it with soap and combs and all the kinds of things Tom Hanson said the men had been buying up to get ready to go home. There were only a few hundred PWs left over at Fort Robinson by Thanksgiving, which is when I got the idea to send a little Christmas spirit overseas.

I sent the package to the address Dieter had left with Ben. And even though I didn't get an answer, I sent another one a few weeks later.

Johnny came home at Christmas. With a war bride from Japan! Now how is that for a surprise? Will and I were both just plain flabbergasted, but it didn't seem to bother Jo one bit. I have finally realized that everyone's expecting that they would get married was just that—everyone else's plan, not theirs.

Johnny and Kim Su moved to Omaha so Johnny could go to engineering school.

Jo began her studies in Lincoln at the beginning of the new year.

And in the early months of 1946 we finally heard from Dieter Brock.

My dear American friends,

Your wonderful and generous packages have arrived and with each one my mother claps her hands with joy and blesses the Americans who were so good to her son. I wish to thank you for everything you did for me that gives me a hope-filled future. Even though I have left the land that is the most free under all the sun, still I carry with me the memory of your kindness. I think that if more of my comrades had come into contact with persons like you, it would be better for all the world. You showed a high measure of tolerance for us, and you did many things to lighten our burden.

Please greet the beautiful Josephine for me. I hope that her studies are going well and that she is still making friends with Buster. I have many regrets, not the least of which is the reason I was in America, but there is also the regret that I will not see Buster through all of his training. You asked my advice, and I say yes, he has the heart to be a fine jumper. Josephine also has the heart. She only lacks the skill, which can be learned.

Your friend,
Dieter Brock

———

Will and I were drinking coffee on the front porch one spring morning, listening to a meadowlark make a racket. I was feeling mighty satisfied with having the new barn up and three mares in foal to Buster when, out of the blue, Will set his coffee cup down and started talking about the fire.

"I don't think I will ever be able to get the picture out of my mind of you riding that tractor and it dying on you." He shook his head. "I've had nightmares about what might have happened if the wind would have blown a different way."

I have never heard Will Bishop talk so fast. I think maybe he'd been practicing. Anyway, all of a sudden he took his hat off and said, "Just how'd you like to prove what an old fool I really am? Marry me. I love you, old gal. I should'a asked you every day for the last twenty years until you said yes. And that's the truth."

For a minute I thought of saying something snappy, like maybe he was touched in the head with spring fever. But for once in my life I zipped my lips long enough to use my head, and I realized that you do not turn a man like Will Bishop down twice in one lifetime. Not unless you are a complete fool. And I am not that. Although, I guess I do fool around now and then—when it's just Will and me.

Chapter Twenty-Five

Wait on the Lord: be of good courage,
and he shall strengthen thine heart.
PSALM 27:14

Summer 1947

"I JUST DON'T WANT to be a teacher," Jo said. She looked across the kitchen table at her mother. "I tried it your way for almost two years, Mother. Can't I *please* transfer over to the Ag College for my junior year?" She paused. When her mother said nothing, Jo added, "You can't change a zebra's spots."

"Zebras do not have spots, Josephine," Mother said.

"And I don't have what it takes to be a teacher."

Daddy spoke up from behind his newspaper. "You played right into her hands, Mrs. Hale."

Mother sighed. Finally she said, "Reverend Hale, there are monumental decisions being made in this kitchen, and I would appreciate your putting that newspaper down."

As Daddy lowered the paper, he winked at Jo. Mother spoke up, pretending to be upset. "You two have already talked about this, haven't you?" She looked from husband to daughter. "Sometimes I wonder what other secrets you've kept from me over the years." She sighed. "All right, all right. I give up. I never could do anything with either of you."

Jo jumped off her chair and did a little dance in the kitchen before bending over to kiss her mother on the cheek. She headed for the back door.

"Where are you going?"

"To tell Aunt CJ!" she said.

"You could call, you know," Mother said.

"Huh-uh," Jo shook her head. "This is too good to be shared on the phone."

Jo climbed the ladder to Aunt CJ's dormer, a fabric-covered box that had once held John Bishop's letters tucked under one arm. The box still held letters—nearly two dozen signed *Your friend, Dieter Brock*—letters Aunt CJ kept for Jo to read whenever she was at the ranch. Not once had Dieter complained, but between the lines of what he said, Jo read the truth. It was a struggle to get enough to eat. He talked of learning to eat new things and deciding that rich foods were not good for him. New clothing was almost impossible to find. He made it a joke . . . thanking God for providing through his mother's ability to remake the old and mend and make things last. He called Fort Robinson his "golden cage," because of the abundance of food and the warm barracks.

They laugh at me, but I tell them I have seen one of the finest places in the world to raise horses, with excellent grass and water, and terrain that develops great strength and substance and wind in the horses that live there. . . .

His foot had required grafting and surgeries. Some of them had been less than perfect, but he said he walked without a cane and only limped a little. He was going to church. He was doing office work again. His knowledge of other languages kept him in demand. He was managing for himself and for his mother. He was philosophical, talking about how things that men had meant for evil, he could now see God using for good. Even things like his injury, which he said ended up giving him the friendship of a wonderful American family and hope for the future.

Jo's heart thumped. Was he talking about her? Was he sending a message about the future . . . and what she had whispered to him that night in the Fort Robinson hospital?

Summer 1948

The horse beneath her lowered its head and planted its front feet, watching every move the jittery cow made. Whether they won or lost the event, it would be mostly up to Bruno—the heavy-boned quarter horse who had earned his name when Uncle Will called him a hulk, and they all ended up reminiscing about the PW named Bruno Bauer and wondering where—and how—he was. Jo held the reins, but the horse was really in charge, and they both knew it.

After a long summer of hard work with Jo in the saddle, Bruno was proving his mettle. As the cow bawled and took off in a desperate attempt to rejoin the herd, Bruno whipped around and prevented the reunion. The crowd roared its approval. Jo took off her hat and waved it toward the place where Mother and Daddy, Uncle Will and Aunt CJ, and the Freys stood applauding and cheering. *Miss Josephine Hale,* the paper would say, *astonished the judges at the fortieth annual Fort Robinson Gymkhana today, by winning the cutting contest astride her registered quarter horse, Bruno. Miss Hale's victory was made more impressive by the reputation of the assembled contestants, among them some of the best known riders in this part of the state.*

January 1949

It was funny, Jo thought, how a person could work and work toward a goal and finally reach it and then . . . still feel like something was missing. She wondered if it would always be this way. She had a tendency to take on things just to prove a point, and even when the point was proven, it didn't satisfy. In her head she knew that she was supposed to trust God's plan for her future, but lately the sense that she might never be happy was beginning to haunt her.

Johnny and Kim Su Bishop were expecting their second child. Hank and Helen Frey, their third—after giving Mia a baby brother three years ago. Even Aunt CJ had a man to love her. Now that they were married, Uncle Will seemed to be trying to make up for all the years they'd been too stubborn to admit they loved each other. Mother had written that he bought Aunt CJ a gift every time they came to town. He'd bought himself a new suit and seemed to honestly enjoy squiring her to church.

Delores's mom was engaged to Tom Hanson—and had become such a radical Baptist she had alienated half her old friends by asking them if they were saved. Jo could just hear her, "Listen, honey, I thought I was all right with Jesus, too. But you know how it is. Sometimes a girl just has to wake up and think for herself. And I've gotta say, if you're trusting anything but Jesus to get you in, you're out. And out, honey, is a hot, hot place." It would be just like Stella to single-handedly start a revival in Crawford. But while Delores's letters had expressed disdain for her mother's newfound devotion to God, Jo's mother wrote about how happy Stella was, and how devoted Tom Hanson was to his bride-to-be. Everyone, it seemed, was doing great.

Sometimes Jo caught herself thinking "what if." It was a bad sign to be twenty-three years old and be wondering "what if"—as if your life was over. When she felt that way, she gave herself a pep talk. She told herself to work harder at school. It was going to take her an extra year to get the degree she wanted, thanks to Mother's insistence that she start as an education major. But that was all right. Jo had never been afraid of hard work. She would graduate summa cum laude. She would, once and for all, throw away the letters and put the past behind her, where it belonged.

She had no one to blame but herself. She had sent him her address in Lincoln. And Dieter had written. Seven letters just for her. Seven letters—and then no more. To her. He had continued writing to Aunt CJ, who talked about him sometimes when Jo visited home. But Aunt CJ didn't offer to let Jo read the letters anymore, and Jo didn't ask. It would hurt too much. Aunt CJ seemed to understand.

And so Jo kept her worries to herself and her goals before her: Train Bruno to be a champion cutting horse. Graduate summa cum laude. Throw away Dieter's letters.

By the summer of 1949, she had accomplished two of the three.

———

June 1949

When the train slowed at the Crawford station, Jo already had her cosmetic case in her hand and was waiting to jump down onto the platform.

"Where's Mom? Is everything all right?" She hugged her dad with a little frown of concern.

"You know your mother," Daddy said. "Always looking for an excuse to show off. She's arranged a little graduation party for you."

"I told her she didn't have to," Jo said.

"And she didn't *have* to. She *wanted* to. Let her show you—in her own way—that she's proud of you."

"No matter *what* my degree is in?"

"No matter, honey," Daddy said, smiling. "We're just glad you aren't marrying a rancher from Wyoming and taking off for the mountains."

"Not a chance," Jo said. "He told me learning dressage was a waste of time and steeplechasing wasn't a real sport." After retrieving Jo's luggage, they made their way toward the street. Daddy stopped beside a tan Chevrolet and opened the door. "Don't tell me—"

"Yep." Daddy nodded. "The Nash finally gave up the ghost." He closed the door and walked around the car. "This was Mrs. Koch's car."

"Then it's a good one," Jo said. "I bet you got a good deal."

"Very good," Daddy said. "She gave it me." He winked at her. "The Lord provides." He patted her hand. "Welcome home, honey. Aunt CJ and Uncle Will can't wait for you to come out."

"I'm ready to get to work," Jo said. "I told Aunt CJ I'd be out after church on Sunday. If you can take me?"

"I can take you," Daddy said. "But I think we'll just go on out there tonight if it's all right with you. Your aunt CJ is very excited about you coming home."

"She isn't coming to my party?"

Daddy shook his head. "No. Something came up."

Jo tried not to be hurt. After all, Uncle Will and Aunt CJ weren't getting any younger. Soon she was surrounded by the Frey family, Stella and Tom Hanson, and what seemed like half of Crawford. Home again. Life was good.

———

"What do you *mean* she's hired a new foreman?!" Jo spun in the seat and looked at her father in disbelief. She sat back. "No wonder she didn't want to come to my party."

"Now, Jo," Daddy said. "Before you jump to conclusions—"

"I'm not jumping to conclusions," Jo muttered. "I completely understand Uncle Will's wanting to slow down. But they don't need anyone else. They've got me." She tried to keep the tears from falling and failed. "What do they think I've been studying my brains out for?"

"It'll be all right, honey," Daddy said. "You'll see."

When they drove into the Four Pines, it was nearly dark. As always, when they came up over the last hill and looked down into the low spot where the ranch nestled between two spring-fed ponds, Jo felt something give way inside her. Finally, she could breathe. The moon was full. Jo sighed.

" 'Trust in the Lord with all your heart,' Josephine," Daddy said. " 'And lean not unto your own understanding.' "

If Daddy was quoting Scripture at her, Jo figured things were going to be challenging. As soon as he pulled up to the ranch house, she grabbed her suitcase from the car and went inside, where the scent of Uncle Will's aftershave and the joy in Aunt CJ's eyes mitigated her disappointment.

"So," Jo said, setting her suitcase down, "Daddy tells me you've hired a foreman."

CJ nodded.

"Before he starts, can I at least make a case for my—"

"He's already started, honey," Aunt CJ said. "Last week."

The tears welled up again.

"Now, before you get all upset with us," Aunt CJ intervened, "we all think you should meet him." She looked at Uncle Will. "Didn't he say he'd be checking on Buster's leg this evening?"

"Buster's leg? What happened to Buster? You didn't tell me anything about—"

"Why don't you just go on over there and see for yourself," Uncle Will said.

————

"Hello?" Jo called out as she entered the new barn.

Buster nickered.

"Is anyone here? Aunt CJ sent me out here to meet—"

But they had met. And she had been haunted by those blue eyes ever since.

"H-how?" Jo asked.

"An American sponsor," Dieter said. "And forms, and applications, and appeals. And a thousand prayers answered yes, to reunite Mama with her brother in Chicago and to bring me here."

"Who?" Jo answered her own question. "Aunt CJ."

Dieter shook his head. "*Nein*. In truth, it was Mr. Bishop who signed my documents. He assured the authorities I would be a good citizen."

"You stopped writing."

"I was too much—" He stopped, put his hand on his heart. "Afraid. If everything ended with *no*."

"When you stopped writing . . . I thought about that night in the hospital . . . I thought you might be laughing at me . . . that maybe those letters were just . . ."

He stepped close. "Never." He reached up and touched the curl at her left temple. "A thousand times," he said, "my thoughts have rushed across the ocean, over the railroad tracks, and toward the prairie. A thousand times they have found their way to these hills of sand . . . and to a barn where there is the scent of fresh hay and a beautiful bay stallion with great dark eyes and an appetite for *pfefferneusse. . . .*"

"So that's it," Jo said with a nervous laugh. "It was the horse." As if on cue, Buster thrust his head over the top of his stall door and whickered. "He wants his treat," she said.

"He," Dieter whispered, "will have to wait."

———

Rise up, my love, my fair one, and come away.
For, lo, the winter is past,
The rain is over and gone.
Song of Songs 2:10-11